A Kingdom of Sand and Ice

Kingdom of Gods Series
BOOK 2

J.F.JOHNS

To you, broken soul
brought into this undeserving and chaotic world.
Never forget that you are brave,
you are loved,
and you are important.
No matter how difficult it may be.

Content warning:

-Violence
-Murder
-Gore
-Nudity
-Slavery
-Explicit sexual content
-Mention of rape (secondary character and off page)
-Mention of suicide (secondary character and off page)

Note from author

The gods referenced in this book are drawn from various mythologies and religions—Greek, Egyptian, Norse, and others —but their original myths have been reimagined.

The Kingdoms

Kingdom of Darkness

House of Shadows

Wyverians

King Ozul-Queen Senka

Kai Blackburn

Kage Blackburn

Mal Blackburn

Kingdom of Fire

House of Flames

Drakonians

Ash Acheron

Alina Acheron

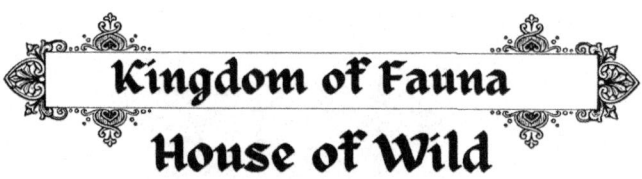

Kingdom of Fauna

House of Wild

Fae

King Florian

Kingdom of Light

House of Sun

Phoenixians

Mareena Noor

Kingdom of Ice

House of Snow

Wolverians

King Fannar
Wren Wynter
Bryn Wynter
Gwyneira Wynter
Gwenyth Wynter
Eirwen Wynter

Kingdom of Air

House of Wings

Valkyrians

Freya

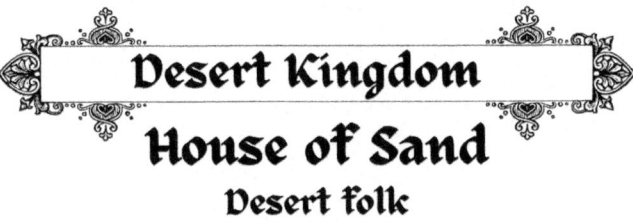

Desert Kingdom

House of Sand

Desert Folk

King Siroc
Hessa Waadi Al-Dunasi

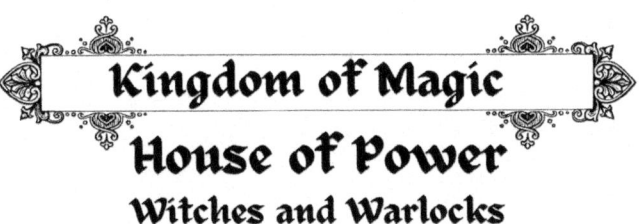

Kingdom of Magic

House of Power

Witches and Warlocks

The kingdom of Gods

Kingdom of Ice

Kingdom of Fauna

Kingdom of Darkness

Kingdom of Magic

Kingdom of Fire

Desert Kingdom

Kingdom of Light

N
W · E
S

Kingdom of Air

Prologue

Months prior to the attack

Hagan could feel the ancient, cruel presence that slithered just beyond the edges of the light as he wandered through the dimly lit corridors of the castle. His crimson uniform was immaculate, his glamour perfectly maintained, allowing the world to see the polished mask of a drakonian rather than the warlock that hid beneath. He offered polite nods to the ladies of the court as they drifted past in rustling silks, some giggling behind gloved hands, their cheeks flushed like roses. Hagan had long been aware of the pull he held over women. He'd never much cared for it, but had learnt well how to wield it as a weapon.

Turning sharply, he ascended a narrow flight of stairs and slipped into a small study, the sort frequented more by lecherous scholars that enjoyed whoring more than reading. He left the door ajar, just enough for the ancient thing that followed to slip inside unnoticed. Moving to the window, he looked out at the restless sea, its waters dark and unending. He wondered, as he often did, what other worlds might lie beyond that endless blue—lands untouched by gods and men alike.

'Blood magic,' the god purred from behind him, 'has served you well.'

Hagan glanced down at his hands, remembering the

sacrifices they had made, the horrors they had conjured since he began learning the forbidden craft. It had cost much. It always did. But for his people, he would pay any price.

'It will take something from you,' the god whispered.

He looked back over his shoulder at the being, its form deceptively mortal. He knew it wore this guise only because it must. In its own realm, it would be something far older. Far more terrifying.

'This world has already taken everything from me,' he said. He would not speak of his mother, of the way she'd died and left him to navigate the world alone. 'I want more power.' His jaw clenched, fists curling with purpose.

'Patience,' the god cautioned. 'When the gods return, they must have hosts. They cannot walk this realm in their true forms.'

'Then how are *you* here?' Hagan asked. He saw annoyance flash in the god's white eyes, but pressed on. 'I thought the curse barred your kind. How did you escape it?'

The god smiled—a terrible, knowing smile. 'When the curse was cast, some of us had already crossed into the mortal realm. Those caught here were trapped, bound in flesh, unable to return. I have worn this mortal face and many others for a century now. Others like me wait, hidden. But when the curse is broken, we will rise. All of us. But first, we must find a host for my sister.'

Hagan nodded. 'The plan is already in motion.'

'Good,' the god said with quiet delight. 'Then let us drown this world in chaos.'

Hagan remained silent as the god turned and slipped through the doorway, vanishing into the shadows once more. Alone, he looked out again at the sea, at the floating isle that hovered just beyond the horizon, and thought of what was yet to come.

Chapter One

House of Shadows
Kingdom of Darkness

The day I met him, my whole life changed. I'm no longer sure whether it was for better or for worse. I fell for him, quickly and painfully. I was drawn to him like a bee to honey. Then I met Hadrian. And that's when I realised what true love was meant to be. Pure and gentle, filled with passion and care.

He never forgave me for choosing Hadrian.

Tabitha Wysteria

The world had fallen into silence.

Mal Blackburn dismounted the enormous wyvern the moment its clawed limbs touched down, its body a magnificent conjuration of shadow and smoke. The beast, known as Nyx, released a guttural roar as its talons sank into the scorched soil. A land where life had long been bled dry, and the only colour that remained was the shade of death.

This was a land born of decay, where no light dared linger, and when night descended, the moon itself would bleed crimson, casting its glow like a blood-soaked shroud over the desolate world. Most trembled at the very mention of such a place, a realm twisted by fear and inhabited by beings shaped from sorrow and despair. But for Mal Blackburn, the withered earth beneath her boots was familiar, comforting. Closing her eyes, she drew in the eerie stillness of the air.

She was *home.*

Nyx turned, her smoky body gliding towards the Forest of Silent Cries, which loomed to their right like the whisper of a forgotten nightmare. Mal regarded the forest with intrigue, recalling her steps through its hollowed halls only days before. It was there she had learnt the truth of her world, unveiled by none other than Tabitha Wysteria. A question stirred on her tongue. Where was the witch now? But before she could speak it aloud, a hand, warm and firm, caught her arm.

'Don't.'

She turned to face her husband. The man once called the Fire Prince. Though now, Mal was not entirely certain what Ash Acheron was. Perhaps he didn't know either. He was no longer a prince. Technically, he was king, having inherited a blood-stained crown when witches murdered his parents. But Mal had pierced his heart to lift the curse that bound them, and in doing so, had birthed something unnameable within him. Something ancient. Something strange.

'I'll be fine, Ash,' she said, her voice gentle. 'Trust me.'

His golden eyes softened at the echo of her words, words she had once spoken just before she drove a blade into his chest. And yet, in those words lay truth, and something unspoken passed between them. There were still fractures in the space they shared, the aftermath of betrayal not so easily swept aside. She had married him with murder in her heart. Perhaps the fragile thing blooming between them now would wither, and they would each vanish from the other's life. The thought clawed at her chest. A world without Ash Acheron was not a world she could easily imagine.

Ash's grip loosened, but rather than retreat, his fingers slipped through hers, intertwining them in a quiet promise.

Together, they stepped into the Forest of Silent Cries, where the hush deepened and the veil of the dead wrapped close around them.

Mal glanced up at the towering trees whose blackened leaves hung unmoving, untouched by even the whisper of wind. Her brow creased as she studied the stillness. Where were they? By now, the dead should have stirred, should have approached with curiosity, if not caution, at the sight of the wyverian princess treading where no living soul was permitted.

'Mal,' Ash whispered, his breath brushing her ear, sending a shiver down her spine.

She followed his gaze. Whatever he had seen, he gave no clue—his face unreadable, as ever. Ash wore his emotions like armour now, and she could not blame him. He had lost everything: his family, his kingdom, and the woman who had pledged herself to him had betrayed him with a blade.

'What is that?' she asked, her voice barely above a breath. A strange shape lay ahead, a crumpled figure on the ground. As she moved towards it, white-barked trees loomed around her, and from their shadows emerged hollow eyes, skulls peering out with a reverence edged in dread.

She dropped to her knees beside the broken body lying forgotten in the soot-black soil. Tabitha. Her name echoed like a funeral bell in Mal's mind. Her neck was twisted at a grotesque angle, her limbs discarded like a puppet cut from its strings.

'Do you know who did this?' Mal asked softly, though her voice carried weight, heavy as the grief rising in her chest. She did not look away. Not yet.

Ash's expression remained composed, but Mal could see the subtle strain pulling at the edges of his stillness. He was wrestling with something, uncertain what to say. Rather than speak, he turned his gaze towards the looming silhouette of the castle in the distance. The dead, huddled within the shadows of the forest, followed his stare, as though they too feared that voicing the truth might summon whatever horror had slain Tabitha Wysteria.

Suppressing the tremble creeping along her limbs, Mal released Ash's hand and pressed her fingers into the dark earth. 'Help me bury her,' she said quietly, her voice steady despite the ache in her chest.

He studied her for a moment, unreadable as ever, then joined her. Together they dug, clawing at the blackened soil with their bare hands. Mal glanced up as the dead slowly emerged from the woods, drifting like wraiths to join them. Wordless, they gathered in a solemn half-circle, and some bent beside her, digging silently until the earth yielded a grave.

When the task was done and the soil once more smoothed, one of the dead placed a skeletal hand on Mal's arm, shaking their hollow head in warning. Whatever had taken Tabitha's life still lingered—silent, watching, waiting.

'I have to go,' Mal told them softly. 'My family may need me.'

There was a glimmer in Ash's eyes then, quick as lightning, gone before she could catch its meaning. Perhaps the mention of her family had stirred something in him, a memory of his own blood, now lost. Or perhaps he knew something she did not, something he wasn't ready to share. She didn't press. This Ash— the one who had risen from the ashes of death—unsettled her in ways the old Ash never had. And she still wasn't certain if the man she loved was buried within him at all.

They left the forest in silence, the stillness clinging to them like cobwebs as they ascended the path to the castle.

Mal lifted her eyes to the fortress carved from the mountain's spine, its towers piercing the sky, its blackened walls as grand and formidable as ever. How she had once longed for this place, with its marble corridors and wide, glassless windows that allowed wyverians to leap onto the backs of their beasts. But now, as she turned to Ash, she realised that stone walls did not make a home. A person did.

They neared the entrance. Mal strayed from the path and approached the roaring wyvern stationed to the side. Daku. Kage's wyvern. The last time she had seen him, she had ridden his back on her way to steal the very dagger she would later drive into her husband's chest.

'Sedare, Daku,' she said, reaching out to stroke the beast's scaly muzzle. 'What's got him so restless?' Her eyes swept the courtyard. 'Why hasn't my brother come to meet us?'

Another roar cleaved through the grey skies. Mal's heart lifted at the sight of Nyx, her own wyvern, spiralling down through the air. Daku screeched, his voice triumphant. The joy of reunion shimmered between the two creatures as they bellowed their greetings—loud, wild, almost violent to any ear unfamiliar with them. But Mal knew. These were not war cries. They were kin.

'Mal.'

Ash's voice brought her back. His look was clear, focused and insistent. The time for sentiment was over.

With one last glance at the wyverns, she turned and followed him towards the great stone doors, now yawning open as though summoned by ghosts. She hesitated only briefly before stepping into the castle.

Inside, little had changed. The obsidian walls rose like cliffs around them, their edges softened only by the cool, shimmering light of wyverian-blue flame. Usually the halls would be alive with footsteps, with servants moving briskly about their work. Now, there was only silence. Someone had lit the torches, creating a corridor of flame to guide them. The message was clear.

Mal followed the light.

It led them to the main hall, a vast chamber once filled with warmth and laughter. A place where Queen Senka would lounge across her favourite settee with a book in hand, occasionally inviting one of her sons to play cards. A place where the family dined each evening, sharing food, teasing one another, revelling in the rare ease of simply being together.

Mal came to a standstill at the threshold. The towering black wooden doors loomed before her, sealed shut in solemn silence. No murmur, no whisper escaped from beyond their heavy frame. These doors were rarely closed, only drawn tight in the evenings, when the royal family withdrew to share the quiet intimacy of their own company. At all other times, they stood open, allowing the gentle passage of servants through the heart of the household.

Now, their closure sent a shiver along her spine. Her heartbeat quickened as she laid a hand against the cool, polished wood, breath catching. What, she wondered, awaited her on the other side?

The last time she had crossed into this room, Haven had been alive. Her sister's dark eyes had twinkled with quiet secrets and affection. That smile, wise and warm, was still etched into Mal's memory. It hadn't been enough. Nothing had been enough to save her.

Mal's hand slipped from the door, drifting instead to the hand that bore the weight of a black ring. Her fingers toyed with the ring, the ring that had belonged to Haven Blackburn, heir to the throne of shadows.

The future queen of darkness.

'Do you know what's on the other side?' Mal whispered, her

breath shallow and uneven, nerves coiling in her chest like serpents. Ash stood only inches behind her, but his presence was more felt than seen. The brush of his breath along her nape, a constant, steady promise in the chaos.

'Whatever ha-happens, wherever you are,' he said softly, 'I will al-always be with you.'

She froze, her spine stiffening at the weight of those words. They sounded too much like a farewell. Like an ending.

No, not now.

Shaking the thought away, she ignored the way he hadn't truly answered her and thrust the heavy doors open with a crash.

The hall beyond was cloaked in gloom. Shadows clung to the edges like cobwebs. The hearth had been lit, the only flame in the vast room, flickering feebly against the gloom. But it was not the darkness that struck her, nor the eerie hush that blanketed the space. It was the sight of her parents seated not at the head of the long table, but off to the side. And her brother Kai beside them, his posture tense, his eyes wide with silent terror.

Then a voice echoed across the chamber.

'At last. I was beginning to wonder if you'd got lost along the way, Melinoe.'

Mal turned, frowning at the unfamiliar voice. A wyverian man lounged in one of the stone chairs, his legs propped atop the table as if the castle were his own and he had every right to recline within it. His horns curled with power, impossibly large, even rivaling her father's. Unusual. Royals alone bore such formidable crests. His lips quirked into a grin, sharp canines flashing with mischief.

But it was his eyes that held her.

They were red. Vivid. Unnatural.

'Come now, have a seat,' the wyverian drawled, gesturing to

the empty chair before him. 'We've been waiting quite a while.'

'Who are you?' Mal didn't move.

He chuckled. 'Have you not guessed, Melinoe? Has your husband not told you?'

'My name is not Melinoe,' she replied. 'I am Mal Blackburn, fourthborn of House of Shadows.'

He hummed, amused. 'A lovely name. Very regal.'

'What do you want?'

He shrugged, utterly at ease. 'I just want to talk.' Again, he gestured to the chair. This time, Mal moved, each step deliberate, cautious. She lowered herself into the seat but kept her gaze sharp, shifting to her brother. Kai's eyes were wide with warning, but he said nothing.

'They cannot speak unless I allow them to,' the stranger said smoothly.

'Are you a warlock?'

The question made him hiss, his teeth bared. 'I am the God of the Dead. I am no filthy magic-user.'

Ash slid into the chair beside her, silent, his presence grounding. Mal didn't turn to him, though she ached to.

'You're a god,' she said. 'Tabitha's curse opened the path for you.'

'Indeed.'

'Then why are you here?' she asked, fighting to keep her voice calm, steady, unshaken.

'To meet you, Melinoe.'

'There it is again.' Her gaze narrowed. 'Why do you keep calling me that?'

'Because that is your name,' he said simply. 'The name I gave you.'

The air thickened. Mal dropped her gaze to her hand, to the black ring that had once adorned Haven's finger. She focused on it, on the weight of it, refusing to look at the being who claimed to be not just a god, but her creator.

'Melinoe,' she repeated, tasting the name like a foreign fruit. 'And what do they call you?'

The wyverian's smile turned razor-sharp.

'Hades.'

For the first time, Mal allowed herself to look at her parents. She had not dared until now, afraid they would see the truth etched across her face. That Haven was gone, that she had failed to save her, that she might never have belonged to them at all.

Her father's expression was calm, though the tension in his jaw betrayed him. King Ozul had always been the iron backbone of their family—loved by the people, adored by the villages. A man who laughed easily and held the weight of the kingdom in his hands without flinching. And here he sat, stone-still beneath the eyes of a god.

Her mother, Queen Senka, locked eyes with her. No accusation, only fear. Only love. Mal's heart fractured under it. How would she tell her? How could she say the words: Haven is dead.

She didn't dare glance at Kai.

'Why are you here?' she asked again.

Hades swung his feet off the table and leaned forward. The red in his eyes glowed like coals. Mal tensed, every muscle screaming for distance.

'I've come,' he said softly, 'to bring you home.'

'This is my home.'

'No, Melinoe.' His head tilted with maddening calm. 'Your real home.'

Mal placed a trembling hand upon the cold stone table, anchoring herself. All she wanted was to turn, to reach for Ash and anchor herself to him instead. To curl into his warmth and let him protect her from these truths.

'And where,' she whispered, 'would that be?'

Hades smiled, slow and awful.

'The Underworld.'

Chapter Two

House of Shadows
Kingdom of Darkness

Never trust Hades. He lies, and he schemes. I had to learn that the hard way. He made me trust him when we first met, when he told me the truth. The truth about who I really am.

But oh, how he loves to twist it all.

Tabitha Wysteria

Mal tried, and failed, not to let her shock show. The Underworld. Of all the answers she had prepared herself for, that one had not crossed her mind. She had grown up worshipping the gods, listening to sacred stories spun from shadows and mystery. Tales of fire and brimstone, of gates forged from bone and rivers choked with the souls of the damned. Each kingdom had their own name for it, but the belief was universal.

Still, hearing it from Hades himself sent a chill down her spine.

'And why would I go anywhere with *you?*'she asked, doing her best to keep the sneer from curling her voice. But it was hard, harder still with this god lording over her family, ensnaring them in invisible chains. Behind her, Ash's fingers brushed the back of her arm, a silent reminder of who she was dealing with.

Hades' smile deepened, curling into something monstrous, something ancient and cruel. Mal instinctively leaned back in her seat, afraid he might reach across the space between them and drag her into the abyss.

'We're family, are we not?' he purred. 'Don't you want to get to know your dear old father?'

'I already have a father,' she bit out.

Hades chuckled, low and venomous. 'Ah, yes, you do. Though I'm not convinced he's particularly worthy of the title.'

His gaze shifted towards King Ozul, and Mal looked too. Something passed across her father's face, a flicker of emotion so brief it might have been missed, had she not been watching. Recognition. Guilt.

She frowned. That couldn't be. The gods had been locked away for a hundred years. How could her father possibly know Hades?

But when she looked back at the god, his red eyes betrayed no lies. Somehow, impossibly, there was truth in them. Her father did know something. Whether it was about Hades himself or something tied to him, Mal could feel it, see it, in the subtle tremor that had rippled through King Ozul's composure.

'I'll make this simple, Melinoe,' Hades said lazily, though his voice echoed like a blade sliding from its sheath. 'If you refuse to return with me, I'll kill your family. But really, would you be losing much? They're not even truly your kin, are they?'

He tilted his head towards the others seated in silence—her parents, Kai. Their eyes brimmed with terror, wide and unblinking.

Mal's mind reeled. Why? Why was he so determined to drag her away? It wasn't sentiment. Surely gods didn't care about affection. There was something else behind his desperation, something darker.

Hades' gaze dipped to the ring upon her finger.

'You wouldn't want to lose anyone else you love, would you?'

Mal leaned forward, baring her teeth like a feral animal. 'How do you know about that?'

He shrugged. 'I'm a god, Melinoe. I know everything.'

'Almost everything,' Ash muttered, just loud enough.

Hades' crimson eyes narrowed to slits. 'Perhaps the Fire Prince can tell you what it feels like to lose *every* last member of one's family.'

Something glinted in the god's expression. Whatever it was, only Ash seemed to understand.

Mal felt the sudden tension in him, coiled and ready to strike, and without thinking, she reached behind her, placing a hand on his knee. A quiet plea. Not yet. She still didn't know what Ash had become, what he'd endured when she'd cast him into fire to break the curse. He was no longer the man she'd once known. He was holding something back from her, and whether it was from mistrust or protection, she could not yet tell.

A sharp cry broke through the tension, wrenching all heads towards the sound. Kai. He had made a sound, choked and desperate, tears shining in his eyes even beneath Hades' spell. Mal's breath caught.

He didn't know.

He didn't know about Alina. Or Haven.

'You ought to tell him,' Hades said, voice like honeyed rot. 'Spare him the torment. Or shall I?'

Her hands curled against the stone table. She would not let him see her tremble. She would not show weakness.

'Don't you dare mock our grief,' she growled.

'And what grief would that be, dear?' he replied, gleefully

glancing between her and Kai, savouring every twitch of understanding dawning in the young prince's face.

'Stop it,' she hissed. Her throat ached with the effort not to scream.

Hades gave a casual shrug, then stood and waved a hand. The invisible restraints shattered. Her family gasped as their voices returned, clutching at their chests and drawing ragged breaths.

'I'll give you until dusk to say your farewells,' he said airily. 'Then I shall return to take you home, Melinoe. Do not attempt to deceive me, tricks will not avail you. If you wish them to live, you will come with me.'

Mal opened her mouth to respond, but he was already turning away. He strode to one of the tall, glassless windows and dropped out into the void, vanishing into the night.

...

At first, Mal couldn't move. Couldn't think. Her parents reached her in an instant, their arms flung around her, holding her close as though they could shield her from the weight of the world pressing in. Words spilt from their lips. Pleas, questions, desperate demands to understand, but Mal remained still, her purple eyes locked with Kai's dark ones across the table.

Brother and sister sat in brittle silence, neither daring to speak, for what needed to be said was far too heavy for words. The truth passed between them in a single, shattering look. A truth too cruel to utter.

Mal looked away when Kai's expression finally cracked, his grief unfurling across his face like a storm breaking free. Her heart fractured anew as he stood, shoulders trembling, and left the hall without a sound.

She removed Haven's ring and placed it gently on the stone

table. The gesture spoke louder than anything she could have said. Her mother collapsed with a wail, her sobs unrestrained, raw and echoing in the chamber. Queen Senka crumpled, a queen undone by a mother's grief. The king, always so composed, drew her close, his voice breaking as he asked the question Mal could not answer.

It was Ash who spoke in her place, his voice low and steady. 'Witches,' he said, his hand resting on Mal's shoulder like a tether. 'They have taken the Kingdom of Fire. They m-murdered the king and queen, my pa-parents.'

'And your sister?' King Ozul asked quietly.

Ash did not reply. His silence said enough.

The king nodded, his face ashen. Without another word, he helped his weeping wife to her feet and led her away. The echo of their departure lingered long after the doors closed behind them.

Mal stared at the ring on the table, untouched, alone. Her hand hovered above it, hesitating.

'She would want you to ha-have it,' Ash said, his voice catching.

'Would she?' Mal whispered, her fingertip brushing the dark band as though touch might conjure her sister back from the void. But there was only silence. Only the truth that Haven was gone. She looked at Ash, her eyes brimming with a grief too vast for words. 'Can I trust you?'

'It's still me,' he said.

Mal searched his face, those haunting golden eyes. She wanted, *needed*, to believe him. But sometimes, she caught him staring into the distance, far beyond her reach, as though his soul were adrift in another world. 'Then why won't you tell me what you've seen?'

Ash's jaw clenched. His silence wrapped around them like a

second betrayal, and Mal turned from him, the cold steel of fear settling in her chest. Haven was gone, and now, she feared, she was losing Ash too.

His hand closed around hers, firm and urgent, pulling her back.

'I have seen our paths,' he said, his voice raw. 'But if I tell you, they will cha-change. And then, I would not for-foresee the way.'

She cupped his face, gently drawing him closer, searching the depths of his gaze for something, anything, that might convince her he was still the man she had once married. Her fingers traced the curve of his jaw, the lines carved by grief and fate. His Adam's apple bobbed as he swallowed, his eyes glowing like twin embers in the twilight.

'Tell me what to do,' she breathed, her hands sliding into the softness of his hair.

His expression crumpled, as though her plea had pierced something buried deep.

'You must go with your father, Mal,' he said. 'You must be-become Melinoe.'

She looked away, her breath hitching. The words rang in her ears like a bell tolling for the dead. She had to go. Not just for her family, but because Ash had seen the path, and this was the only way left. *Will I return?* she longed to ask, but the question stayed lodged in her throat, too afraid of the answer he might give.

Ash picked up the ring and slipped it back onto her finger, his touch reverent.

'And you?' she asked, the blue flames in the hearth dancing low, casting the room in deepening shadow.

Ash rose to his full height, a quiet storm behind his eyes. 'I will raise an army,' he said, 'and take back what was mine.'

...

Mal found her brother by the temple, standing motionless before the lone tree she had so often prayed to. The sight of Kai, usually a storm of movement and mischief, held still beside something so sacred was unsettling, as though the world had tilted slightly on its axis. She wondered, fleetingly, what might happen if she were to pray now. For all her life she had longed for the gods to answer. And now that they had, she wished only for their silence.

'They're both dead, aren't they?' Kai's voice was low, stripped of its usual lightness. It was a tone she had never heard before. A stranger's voice, rough with sorrow.

She moved to his side and let her gaze rest on the tree, its blackened branches stretching towards the heavens. What would happen, she wondered, if she felled it? Would the gods rage? Or would they, as always, remain indifferent?

'Tell me what happened to them,' he said.

'I don't think that's wise.'

'Tell me, Mal. I wasn't there. I should have been there. I'm secondborn, do you know what that means?' His voice broke, cracking open as a surge of emotion rippled through him. His hands clenched at his sides, and the hatred in his voice wasn't for the world, it was for himself. Mal took a small step back, startled by the rawness woven through his voice. So exposed, so unguarded, it struck her harder than any expression ever could.

'I was meant to protect Haven,' he continued, breath coming fast, fury lacing every word. 'It was my only purpose. And I failed. Now...' He turned from her, his shoulders rising and falling with sharp, uneven breaths, and Mal ached to reach out, to steady him, but she didn't move. She couldn't. She felt just as unmoored. Just as shattered. 'I didn't want Haven travelling alone to the Kingdom of Fire,' Kai said with a bitter laugh. 'But she insisted. She begged me to stay, to watch over our parents. I should never have listened—'

'You honoured her wishes, Kai.'

'I shouldn't have. Being secondborn means knowing when not to obey. I should have known better.'

'You couldn't have,' she said quietly, trying to place a hand on his arm. He shook her off.

His hands curled into fists.

'The truth is... selfishly, I was glad she asked me to stay behind. I didn't want to go back and watch Alina celebrate her engagement.' He let out a bitter snort. 'Because of that, they both died. If I'd gone back and put my jealousy aside, I might have protected them.'

Mal sighed.

'You don't know that, Kai.'

'Who did this to them?'

Mal stiffened. She had not witnessed Haven or Alina's deaths, but Ash had told her—his voice hollow, his eyes far away.

'Hagan,' she whispered, still staring at the tree, unable to face her brother and the storm she knew was rising within him.

'I will kill him,' Kai said, his voice like iron.

Mal reached for him again, this time gripping his arm with force. 'Good. When I return from the Underworld, we'll tear them all down. Every last witch, every last warlock.'

He went still, his breath caught. She felt the weight of his gaze settle upon her.

'Mal,' he said softly, 'look at me.'

She shook her head.

'Mal.'

'Please, don't make me,' she whispered, voice cracking.

'Why?'

'Because if I look at you, I'll break.'

To see the grief mirrored in his face, the same grief she fought so hard to hold at bay, would undo her. It would keep her here, tether her to this place and to him, when everything within her was screaming to run. Not away from her brother, but from the weight of leaving him behind.

'I can't lose anyone else, Kai.' Her hand trembled as she held onto him, pleading for understanding. 'Not again.'

'You won't lose me, sister,' he said, stepping in close, his breath a whisper against her temple. 'I'll be here when you return. Waiting.' A beat of silence passed. 'Must you go with that... god?'

Mal nodded.

'Why? How can we trust him? For all we know, he might not even be what he claims.'

'He is,' she said simply. 'Ash saw it.'

'What does that mean?' Kai asked, brows furrowing.

Mal turned from him, a shift in the air drawing her gaze. By the entrance to the Temple of Deadly Shadows, a figure appeared—silent, reverent. The High Priestess. Her eyes were veiled by the sacred cloth, cut by the holy blade in ritual devotion. Her grey robes wrapped around her like mist, clinging to her as though the very temple itself refused to let her go.

Mal bowed her head in reverence. 'High Priestess,' she said by way of greeting, pointedly ignoring Kai's visible disinterest. He refused to acknowledge them, his silence heavy as stone.

'The God of the Dead has graced our temple, child,' the High Priestess intoned, her voice carrying the weight of prophecy. 'We must prepare you for your descent into the Underworld.'

'Prepare me?' Mal's spine stiffened, instinctively leaning

back into her brother's presence, seeking the strength she wasn't ready to summon alone. It hadn't been so long ago that she had walked these very halls as a bride-to-be. Bathed, anointed, and robed in ritual purity before journeying to the Kingdom of Fire to wed Ash Acheron. And now, once more, she was to be sent away. But this time... she would give anything to remain.

'Don't,' Kai said fiercely, clutching her hand in his. His grip was unyielding, his resolve desperate. 'Don't go. Stay. We'll find another way.'

Mal's blackened heart stuttered, then splintered, as memory washed over her like ash on the wind. Of him once begging her not to leave, not to marry the Fire Prince, not to follow a fate he feared would break her. She hadn't listened then. She'd been so certain. Would things have unfolded differently, had she obeyed?

She turned at last to face him fully. Their eyes locked. Hers awash with sorrow, his burning with grief, fury, and fear. In that moment, they were no longer warriors or royals of shadow and flame. They were simply siblings, fraying at the seams.

'Don't make me lose another sister,' Kai whispered, his voice raw and cracked. 'I couldn't bear it, Mal. Don't you dare leave me again. We'll find another way, I swear it.'

And Mal broke.

The tears came fast, hot and violent, as sobs shook her body. She wept for Haven, for home, for all she had lost and all she was yet to lose. She wept as Kai held her close, her pain mirrored in the quiet ache of his embrace. She screamed, screamed for the gods who had forsaken them for so long, and now, in answering, demanded a price she could barely comprehend.

But then the tide passed. Slowly, she pulled herself together, her breath hitching as she wiped her cheeks with trembling fingers.

'Look after him,' she said, voice thick but steady. 'Protect Ash. Keep him safe until I return.'

Kai didn't speak. He simply nodded, even as his jaw clenched, even as defeat settled across his shoulders like a cloak of mourning.

Mal tore herself from Kai's grasp, fleeing towards the Temple's looming archway, never once daring to glance back at the wyverian warrior who stood in hollow silence, shattered and beaten, as his little sister walked once more into the waiting arms of the unknown.

. . .

The priestesses had bathed her in the sacred waters beneath the Temple, cleansing her body in preparation for her journey into the Underworld. Now, hours later, Mal sat in quiet contemplation, awaiting the return of the God of the Dead to take her... home. She perched on the ledge of a great window in the castle, one leg dangling over the side, watching the wyverns as they soared in lazy circles below, their wings catching the last glimmers of light.

The sound of footsteps reached her ears, soft as shadows, and someone sat beside her. Her heart gave a quiet jolt when she turned and saw Ash. He, too, had bathed and changed, and the sight of him in wyverian clothing was disarming. Dark leather trousers, boots polished to a quiet shine, and a low-cut black shirt that clung to him as if it too recognised him as royalty. His blonde hair, still damp, glinted like molten sunlight against the midnight shades of his clothing. Without thinking, Mal reached out and ran her fingers through it, desperate to memorise the feel of him.

The High Priestess had adorned Mal in jewels and draped her in a gown far more regal than she deemed appropriate. It clung to her like the binding of a vow, stitched from cotton and silver thread, heavy with meaning. She felt utterly absurd dressed like a bride. An offering almost, waiting to be collected by a god. What she truly wanted was her plain grey riding dress, her boots, and her sword strapped to her back.

'You look beautiful,' Ash said.

'I look like a wyverian bride,' Mal replied, her tone dry. 'As though they believe Hades is escorting me to the Underworld for a wedding. Or worse, a sacrifice.'

Ash's expression shifted, his breath catching as his eyes clouded with sadness. Whatever the dress reminded him of, she didn't ask. She feared the answer, feared it might unearth something she wasn't ready to face, something that might make her run.

She glanced down at the collection of rings, bracelets, and earrings weighing her down. The urge to tear them off and hurl them into the wind tugged at her like a child pulling at a mother's hem. She had asked the High Priestess why she must be adorned so, but no answer had been given. Now, seeing the way Ash stared at her, she wished she had demanded one.

'I should go,' Mal said at last, her voice soft as falling ash. 'I will not say goodbye to my parents. Or to Kai.' She turned to him, memorising every line of his face, every freckle, every fleeting shadow in case this was the last time. 'But I must say goodbye to you.'

'Why?' A frown creased his brow.

'In case...' she hesitated, heat rising to her cheeks. 'In case you choose to not wait for me.'

Ash lifted her chin with the gentlest of touches, his hand trembling only slightly. Their eyes met—his gold, hers purple

—and the rest of the world fell away.

'I will never stop waiting for you, Mal Blackburn,' he whispered. 'In this life, or the next... I will wait.'

Mal felt her heart shatter and bloom all at once as his lips brushed against hers. It was meant to be a soft kiss, a goodbye kiss, but the moment his skin met hers, the world seemed to slip away. She pulled him closer, burying herself in his warmth, in the scent of him, in the solace of his arms. She needed every breath, every touch, to become a part of her, if only for a moment.

His mouth claimed hers with quiet urgency, and her moan vibrated between them, a tremble of need and heartbreak. His hands roamed her body with reverence and hunger, finding her waist, pulling her flush against him until the feel of him left her dizzy and breathless.

Mal climbed into his lap, her legs encircling his hips as he drew her gown up around her thighs. Her breath hitched as he guided her to him, and when she sank down onto him, her head tilted back, a sigh slipping from her lips as her body shuddered with aching pleasure.

She moved slowly at first, savouring the sensation, the connection, the way his golden eyes held hers like a vow. The rhythm between them quickened, bodies moving with shared desperation, their hearts racing towards the inevitable.

When release came, it was together, a wordless cry caught between their lips. Mal held onto him, trembling, pressing her face into the curve of his neck. For a heartbeat, for a breath, there was only the two of them. Timeless and infinite.

Panting, she pressed a kiss to the tip of his nose, clinging to him as though her body could somehow etch the moment into permanence. The thought that she might never feel him like this again, might never see him at all, gnawed at her from the inside out.

A gust of wind tousled her hair, whispering a warning of an unwelcome presence close by. Thunder cracked through the skies below, and the wyverns screamed in response, their shadows circling the castle, restless and unwilling to stray too far.

'It's time,' Ash said, gently tucking a black strand of hair behind her ear.

Mal gave a faint nod, the lump in her throat making it impossible to speak. 'Nyx, venire.'

She rose to her feet, drinking in the sight of him one final time. Every detail. Every line of his face. Her body shifted slowly, fading into smoke and shadow. Ash watched silently as she turned, her form unravelling into mist, until she vanished into the chasm below. Nyx, forged of the same darkness, soared up from the void to catch her.

Mal landed lightly on the wyvern's back, the great creature crying out with a sound that split the sky. Together, they swept past the obsidian spires of the castle carved into the mountain's heart. Her childhood home, now little more than memory.

Nyx landed at the edge of the Forest of Silent Cries. The moment Mal's feet touched the blackened earth, her body returned to solid form. A crack of thunder rang overhead, and she turned her head towards the sound of soft footsteps.

There, leaning lazily against the withered bark of a tree, was Hades. He tossed an apple in the air, catching it with infuriating ease.

'Are you marrying someone?' he quipped, an eyebrow raised in mockery.

'The priestesses at the Temple of Deadly Shadows deemed it appropriate to dress for a god,' Mal replied coldly. 'Though from what I gather, you visited them long before I arrived and told them what you wanted. Told them what you wanted of me. Why this dress?'

Hades chuckled, dark amusement dancing in his crimson gaze. 'Did you say your farewells?'

Mal's lip curled in reply.

'Come along, dear,' he said, extending his hand. 'The rest of the family are eager to meet you.'

Her gaze narrowed. 'Family?'

'Oh, yes,' he said with a wicked grin. 'Did you truly think it was only you and I?' His laughter rasped like dry leaves. 'Take my hand, Melinoe. Let me take you home.'

Mal turned to Nyx, running a hand along the creature's shadowy flank, soothing the wyvern's tension. 'I'll be back soon, Nyx. I promise.'

She ignored the way Hades' grin sharpened at her words, as though he knew something she didn't, something terrible. But Mal didn't care. She would find her way back, even if it meant tearing a god from his throne.

Her fingers slid into his. His hand was cool, but the grip that followed was anything but gentle.

'Stop smiling,' she muttered, her purple eyes locking with his. 'Or I might have to carve a frown into your face.'

Hades laughed, his fingers tightening around hers. 'Oh yes,' he said, a wicked glint in his gaze. 'You'll fit right in.'

Before Mal could retort, a violent crack split the earth beneath her feet. She twisted, trying to leap back, but it was too late. The ground yawned open with a deafening roar, swallowing her whole. She caught one last glimpse of Nyx lunging forward, jaws bared in a cry of defiance.

Then the world closed in.

And Mal Blackburn was gone.

Chapter Three

House of Sun
Kingdom of Light

The desert can become your enemy if you don't know how to navigate it. Over the years, I've come to understand the beauty of these dunes. My closest friends are desert folk. Harsh and unyielding at times, yet the kindest and most loving people you could ever meet. When my time comes, I wouldn't mind walking out into the desert, lying down, and waiting for death to greet me like an old friend. To die in such a breathtaking place, its silence wrapping around me like a blanket... reminding me just how small and insignificant we truly are.

Yes, the desert really is a magical place.

Tabitha Wysteria

Alina Acheron had been travelling for days astride a colossal desert serpent, its sinuous body gliding over the endless sands with an ease that defied its size. With her rode Princess Hessa and her attendants, silent and swift beneath the oppressive sun. They had reached the outer fringes of the Kingdom of Light a few hours earlier and had since made camp beneath a canopy of stars. Yet no matter how many times Alina washed, she could not rid herself of the imagined weight of dried blood clinging to her skin. Nor could she banish Hagan's twisted face from her dreams. Night after night, it came, a cruel spectre lodged deep within the shadows of her sleep.

Thus far, Alina held little opinion of the fabled Kingdom of

Light. All she had glimpsed was an ocean of golden dunes stretching into oblivion. The stories she'd heard over the years painted it as a land of splendour. Towering palm trees, sun-kissed sandstone temples, and crystalline rivers meandering through cities like veins of silver. They spoke of phoenixes in hues of flame and ice, soaring across sun-drenched skies, their feathered sparks lighting the night like drifting stars.

But none of that beauty could touch her now. Not when the thought of the royal family, nestled safely in their palace just hours away, filled her with dread. Did they know? Did they feel the silence stretching across the desert, whispering of tragedy? Their son, Prince Zahian Noor, lay cold and lifeless in the Kingdom of Fire. Hagan had left his body discarded upon the stone floor of the dining chamber where Alina and Zahian had waited to join the court for their engagement celebration.

The desert folk were efficient travellers, swift in their rituals and seasoned in hardship. Within an hour, camp had risen like magic from the dust. Tents unfurled, a fire coaxed to life, and some strange, sinewy creature roasting over the flames. Princess Hessa handed Alina a cup of vhina, the desert's infamous spiced bloodwine, fermented with herbs and boiled for days until it seared both throat and soul. It could heal wounds. Or keep one dancing on the edge of sleep until dawn.

'Drink,' Hessa said, lowering herself beside Alina with feline grace. 'You look like... what is the word? Those things that frighten drakonian children at night? A ghula, perhaps, though I doubt you call them that.'

Alina reached for the serpent-skin cup. 'A ghost?'

'Yes!' Hessa laughed, the sound as sharp and sudden as breaking glass. 'That's it. A ghost. You look as pale as one.'

The princess's white eyes roamed Alina's form until they settled atop her head, and lingered. The others had tried not to stare, but in their restraint, their horror became all the more palpable. Alina said nothing. She downed the vhina in a single burning swallow, welcoming the fire as it slid down her throat. Let it scald the memory.

A part of her was gone now. Taken, torn away by the hands of someone she had once loved beyond reason. Trusted beyond doubt. *Hagan.*

Her jaw tightened as fury bloomed in her chest like a star exploding.

She swore, once more, as she had each night since her escape, that she would find a way to end his life. Even if it cost her her own. She would make him pay for what he had done. And when that day came, it would not be a clean death. No. It would be slow. And it would burn.

A servant approached as dusk fell, offering food upon a polished stone plate. Alina left it untouched, pushing it aside with a quiet clatter, choosing instead to sip her wine and stare into the flickering flames. The fire's dance was mesmerising, but it brought her no warmth.

Even now, after countless days on the road, the wounds on her scalp still wept in the night. In the mornings, Hessa would tend to her in the hushed darkness of the tent, her fingers gentle as she dabbed oils and salves onto Alina's mutilated horns. Alina had refused everyone else's touch, only the desert princess was permitted to see her break.

'You need to eat,' Hessa said, chewing with the deliberate grace of someone savouring every bite. 'You'll waste away and fall ill. We're still a week from the heart of the Desert Kingdom.'

'I'm not hungry.'

'Starving yourself won't bring back the dead, amira.'

With a glare, Alina snatched up a chunk of the strange meat

and shoved it into her mouth. She chewed with deliberate volume, grinding the meat as though punishing it. Mouth full, jaw clenched, she rammed more down until she could barely breathe, refusing to meet Hessa's gaze.

And then came Hessa's snort.

The flavour hit Alina all at once—ferocious, fiery, and completely unforgiving. Her mouth burnt, her eyes watered, and her throat felt as though it had been set alight. Choking, she spat the meat into the sand and fumbled for her wine, gulping it down in desperation. Heat flooded her sinuses and poured from her eyes, making her nose run and her vision blur.

Spinning round, she glared at Hessa, who was doubled over with laughter. 'You could've warned me!'

'Then I would've missed your face,' Hessa replied with a shrug, laughter still dancing in her voice.

'That wasn't funny,' Alina wheezed, wiping her eyes. 'I could've died.'

At the mention of death, Alina's shoulders fell. Her voice faltered. She turned away, unable to stop the tears from blurring her sight again. This time not from spice, but sorrow.

'You shouldn't cry for the dead, amira,' Hessa said, her voice quiet now, puzzled by the grief she witnessed but did not seem to share. Alina had noticed it before, how the desert princess had not once wept for her sister. She had ridden with them through wind and sun, offering no visible sign of mourning, no tear shed.

'How can I not?' Alina whispered, her voice trembling. 'I will never see them again. My parents… my brother. Every day I wake, I will wake without them. And the day after that. And the one after that.'

Hessa gave a soft sigh, brushing her fingers through the sand until they disappeared beneath it. 'Drakonians have curious ways of seeing mhaarta,' she said. 'Death is not an end, not to us.

It is a door, one that opens to the next part of our journey.'

'But your sister,' Alina said softly. 'She's gone.'

Hessa tilted her head. 'She is not here, no. But she is not gone.' Her fingers emerged from the sand and let it pour through her palm like a river of gold. 'In the desert, we believe that when we die, we enter a great house. The first thing you hear are the voices of those you loved, calling your name. You follow the sound, and there, around a great table, your ancestors sit waiting. You embrace again. You laugh again. Death is not a goodbye, amira. It is a return. To our true home.' Hessa stared into the fire, eyes soft with something more than sorrow. 'So, no. I do not cry for my sister. She is in that house, among our blood, and one day I will sit beside her once more. It is the living who suffer. It is us who must carry the ache.'

Alina tried to hold on to the image Hessa offered, of a house beyond this life filled with warm light and waiting arms. But still, her tears slipped free. The ache for her brother was too sharp, too fresh. If she could believe that Ash was laughing somewhere, drinking drakonian wine with the dead, perhaps it would ease the burden.

But she didn't want Ash anywhere else. She wanted him here. Alive. And she didn't want to wait a lifetime to see him again.

'Do the desert folk not believe in the Underworld?' Alina asked, curious. From the three southern kingdoms, the Desert Kingdom was the only one to believe in more than one god.

Hessa shook her head. 'No, we consider that a northern belief.'

'My kingdom is not a northern land and we believe in it.'

Hessa snorted. 'Anything beyond those dunes is northern to us, amira.'

A sudden sound stirred the air, drawing both princesses'

gazes skyward. Above them, the night stretched vast and infinite, scattered with stars. Alina's breath caught in her throat as a crimson phoenix soared overhead, its colossal wings igniting the dark with trails of shimmering sparks as it glided, almost weightless, through the heavens.

'I never imagined they'd be so enormous,' Alina murmured, awe softening the sharp lines of her expression.

'It may be an omen,' Hessa replied, equally entranced by the creature's silent majesty. 'We're close now, only a day's journey from the palace. Perhaps we ought to stop there, to inform them of Zahian Noor's fate. I doubt they yet know he's fallen.'

Alina bit her lower lip. 'Are you sure?' The mere thought of entering the phoenixian court without Zahian twisted something deep inside her. A marriage had been pledged. Had the witches not come, she would be there now at his side, dancing beneath lanterns and fire-lit skies. To walk into their halls without him, to tell them he was gone, was unbearable.

'It is the right thing to do,' Hessa said gently. 'And they must be warned about the brahas.'

'The witches will all be gathered in my kingdom by now,' Alina said quietly, 'now that the castle and the city of Spark lie beneath their shadow.' They would need allies, desperately so, if they were ever to reclaim what had been stolen. But before that, she needed to become something more than a fallen princess. She needed to learn how to wield a weapon with purpose, how to become the storm instead of the wreckage it left behind. Only then could she return to her homeland. Not to beg, but to destroy. And when she did, she would kill the warlock who had betrayed her, even if it was the last act she ever performed.

'Perhaps,' Hessa conceded. 'But the phoenixians deserve to know.'

Hessa rose to retire, her long silhouette graceful beneath the starlight. Just before vanishing into the shadows of the tent, she turned back, her moon-pale eyes softening. 'Desert clothes suit you, amira.'

Then she was gone.

Alina glanced down at herself. Gone were the heavy, high-necked dresses of courtly life. In their place, flowing desert silks hugged her frame. Hessa had loaned her garments from her own trunks, carried faithfully by the servants atop their serpents. Alina still wore a shawl, carefully wrapped to shield her exposed skin from view. It offered her a kind of armour, a veil between herself and the world. Hessa, on the other hand, strode freely through the desert winds, bare arms and stomach on show, unbothered by judgment or tradition.

Perhaps one day, Alina might find such boldness within herself. But not tonight.

She turned to head for her tent, only to find Hessa hurrying back, something cradled in her cupped palms, a delighted grin stretching across her face.

'Look, amira!' she called, breathless with excitement. 'Look what was resting on my bed! I told you, my sister is watching over us.'

'What is it?' Alina asked, stepping closer, though her tone was wary.

Hessa opened her hands, revealing a strange, glimmering insect. Alina recoiled slightly, a shudder rippling through her. Insects had never been to her taste.

'It's a narshara,' Hessa explained. The creature pulsed with light, delicate wings humming.

'Oh, we have those in the Kingdom of Fire too,' Alina said, recovering herself. 'But we call them fireflies. In summer, the palace gardens would be full of them.'

'In the desert, we believe the narshara are gifts from the

dead,' Hessa said, her voice softening. 'A guide, left behind to help the living find their way through the dunes.' She lifted her hands, releasing the creature into the night. It twinkled once more and vanished into the darkness. 'Perhaps my sister means to guide us.'

'Perhaps,' Alina echoed, uncertain, but unwilling to extinguish the flicker of comfort in Hessa's eyes.

'Let's sleep out here tonight, amira,' Hessa said, lowering herself once more beside the fire. She beckoned a servant. 'Trahar mi guita, paahfa.'

Though Alina couldn't decipher the Sandhii tongue, the servant swiftly returned with blankets and thick woven covers, and she assumed that had been the request.

'Won't we freeze?' she asked. The old tales of the desert had warned of cruel nights, when the heat fled with the sun and death crept in with the cold.

Hessa laughed. 'Yes, in the deep desert perhaps. But this, this is phoenixian land. It is not yet true desert. The warmth will hold through the night.' She patted the ground beside her. 'Come, lie with me. We'll watch the stars.'

Alina followed Hessa's lead, lying beside the desert princess as they gazed up at a sky heavy with stars, each one a silent witness to the sorrows and secrets of the world.

'Will you teach me?' she asked softly.

'Teach you what?'

'Your language.'

She felt, rather than saw, Hessa turn her head, surprise likely etched across her features.

'You wish to learn Sandhii, amira?'

'I'll be spending time in your kingdom learning to fight. I'll need to understand something of the language,' Alina replied.

Hessa laughed, warm and teasing, which made Alina twist

to face her with a mild glare. 'And what, exactly, is so amusing?'

'Nothing, amira. Just... the thought of a drakonian learning Sandhii.' Her tone was light, but Alina caught the faint trace of bitterness beneath it.

'We study phoenixian,' Alina offered defensively. 'We are not entirely ignorant.'

Hessa shrugged, her smile fading into something a little more tired. 'The phoenixians have always been powerful. Your people have seen them as worthy allies. But us? We desert folk have never been granted that same respect. From the three southern kingdoms, yours has always considered mine the weakest. What do they call us?'

Alina swallowed. The lump in her throat was sharp and bitter.

'Dessert,' she whispered, ashamed.

Hessa snorted, her nose wrinkling in quiet frustration.

Alina longed to reach for her hand, to offer some unspoken apology, to show that, though her kingdom might have viewed Hessa's people with disdain, *she* never had. But that would be a lie. So instead, she turned her gaze back to the sky, biting down on her lip in silent vexation, for the truth was plain and shameful: she had once been one of them. One of the drakonians who had laughed along with the court's cruel jokes.

'Well,' she said, more to the night than to Hessa, 'it's a different world now. My kingdom is no longer.'

Chapter Four

House of Sun
Kingdom of Light

I've heard all sorts of curious tales about phoenixians. They can be remarkably outspoken about certain things, and yet strangely secretive about others. I've heard whispers that beneath the city itself lies another, one that only a chosen few are ever allowed to see.

I'm not entirely sure what happens down there.

And I'm not entirely sure I want to know.

Tabitha Wysteria

It was the stirrings of unease, the hushed distress of servants, or perhaps it was Hessa's hand, tugging gently at her shoulder that roused Alina from sleep. Whichever it had been, the moment her eyes fluttered open, it was daylight, and the campfire, once bright with warmth, had long since died into ash and memory. Across its charred remains, a cluster of figures stood, watching them in silence.

Alina sat upright with a start, hastily gathering her shawl around her shoulders as the blankets pooled in the sand and adjusted her rasguita, making sure no unwanted eyes saw her horns. Hessa was already on her feet and moving. Alina hissed a warning for her to stay back, just in case, but the desert princess strode forward with determined steps, undeterred by the potential threat.

Still shaking the remnants of sleep from her limbs, Alina scrambled after her. As they neared the strangers, the details sharpened: not just people, but animals too. Sleek, powerful dogs with long, spear-like ears that twitched at the faintest movement. At the head of the party stood a girl, only a little older than Alina, flanked by the creatures like a goddess with hounds of war.

Alina's breath caught. These were no ordinary travellers.

Phoenixians.

And not merely phoenixians, but Phanax.

Renowned throughout the realms as merciless protectors of the Kingdom of Light, the Phanax were a rare breed: elite warriors honed not in brute strength, but in precision, stealth, and the quiet cruelty of efficiency. While their kingdom was famed for its scholars, for books and learning and delicate diplomacy, the Phanax were its hidden blade—cold, calculated, and deadly.

Every kingdom had its own revered battalion. The Kingdom of Fire had the Red Guard, whose brutal training was so infamous it only lasted a year, and many didn't survive it. The Dunayans of the desert were celebrated across the kingdoms for their prowess as mercenaries. Even the distant northern kingdoms whispered of shadowy elites who never missed their mark.

Wyverians, however, were different. They did not boast a single elite force, because in the Kingdom of Darkness, every citizen was forged into a weapon. Or so Kai Blackburn had told her once, beneath a star-laced sky.

'Zxia,' Alina said evenly, inclining her head with careful respect. The phoenixians had their rituals—cheek kisses, nose-pressing—but such gestures were reserved for kin or those held dear. She kept her distance. 'Zkri zjema Alina jis.' *Hello. My name is Alina.*

Hessa shot her a wary glance. The silence that followed stretched taut like a bowstring. The Phanax did not reply. They only watched.

The girl at the front tilted her head, lips curving faintly. Not in mockery, but in something close to amusement. Alina's stomach fluttered.

It was difficult not to stare.

Though Alina had always been praised as the most beautiful drakonian in her court, the phoenixian woman before her was something else entirely. An otherworldly sort of beauty that turned the breath in Alina's lungs to smoke.

She had never seen anyone like her. And she could not look away.

Hessa nudged her sharply, a warning laced with teasing, but Alina remained rooted, her gaze locked, her thoughts spinning. No woman had ever rendered her so utterly speechless.

The moment passed, sharp and strange. Flushed with confusion, Alina dropped her eyes and turned away.

'Jor zxu zjenska ka jairxi,' the girl said smoothly. 'Par mut ker xenix zxu zxau.' *The princess is waiting for you. Her phoenix saw you last night.*

'Kar zxu,' Alina replied, dipping her head respectfully. *Thank you.*

'Kar zxu,' Hessa echoed with less enthusiasm, her voice low. She gave Alina a look that was difficult to decipher, until the Phanax turned away, granting them time to gather their things and prepare to follow. As soon as they were out of earshot, Hessa tugged Alina back towards their tent.

'You stumbled a little with your phoenixian, amira,' she teased, mischief sparkling in her pale eyes. 'Did someone suddenly make you nervous?'

'I haven't spoken phoenixian in years,' Alina said, brushing a strand of hair behind her ear. 'I was taught as a child, but I've never had cause to properly use it.' Her eyes narrowed slightly. 'I didn't realise desert folk concerned themselves with foreign tongues.'

Hessa snorted. 'You'd be surprised.' She casually gathered a few blankets, folding them neatly before handing them off to a nearby servant. 'When the drakonians and phoenixians chose not to learn Sandhii, most of our people refused to learn your languages out of spite. But my father insisted my brothers and I study them anyway. Dunayans are trained in languages too. If you're sent to foreign sands to slit a throat, it helps to understand what's being said around you.' She grinned, her sharp fangs flashing.

Alina nodded thoughtfully, casting a glance over her shoulder. The phoenixian girl still stood at the edge of the camp, waiting, her stance statuesque, unwavering. She hadn't moved since delivering her message, as though carved from golden stone.

'We've never had reason to use our language skills,' Hessa continued, shrugging. 'But now that travel between kingdoms is possible again... who knows?'

Alina jolted slightly when Hessa poked her sharply in the arm. 'What are you doing?' she snapped, scowling.

'You need to stop staring,' Hessa said with a wicked snicker. 'She might think you like her.'

'Don't be absurd.'

'I'm not the one blushing!'

Alina hurled a folded blanket at her, missing by a hair's breadth. Her cheeks burnt, no matter how fiercely she tried to will the warmth away. She cast one final, discreet glance at the phoenixian woman who was still standing, still waiting.

With a soft sigh, Alina turned back and busied herself with helping Hessa finish packing, doing her best to ignore the flutter building in her chest.

The Phanax showed no sign of unease at the arrival of the desert serpents returning from their morning hunt. Even the sharp-eared hounds at their sides did not flinch. They stood as if carved from stone—silent, impassive, unmoved by beasts that would have sent lesser men fleeing.

'Zew jourx axaxi zjenskia jis,' the lead girl announced as preparations were made to depart. *The palace is a few hours away.*

Alina offered another quiet word of thanks, her gaze drawn to the moment the phoenixian girl whistled—short, sharp, precise. Crimson eyes lifted to the sky, searching. Moments later, the heavens answered. A flock of phoenixes burst into view, their wings casting fire-tinted shadows as they wheeled above.

Alina expected the Phanax to mount the radiant birds. Instead, they approached peculiar creatures with the grace of those long acquainted. The beasts were unlike anything Alina had seen outside of dusty scrolls—serpopards, they were called. Feline in body, with long sinuous necks and serpent-like tails, their movements were fluid and unnerving.

'Trust me, amira,' Hessa muttered as she caught the bewilderment on Alina's face. 'That is far from the strangest creature you'll see in the Kingdom of Light. Most of their animals are... unusual. Only the phoenixes are natural.'

'Natural?' Alina echoed, frowning.

'There's a reason they call themselves scholars.' Hessa was already scaling the thick rope that led to the serpent's crown. Alina followed, her limbs aching from days of repeated climbs.

The desert bred strength into bone, though at a cost.

'They've spent millennia playing with nature's design,' Hessa continued. 'Genetic alchemy. They create hybrids, crossbreeds of species they believe will serve them better. Phoenixians don't tame nature. They rewrite it.'

'That's monstrous,' Alina said as she reached the top, settling herself against one of the great serpent's ridged spikes. The saddle, fitted snugly to its form, allowed her to press close and bind herself in, lest she be thrown during the creature's undulating glide.

Hessa fastened her rasguita, a headpiece of tightly woven cloth that held her dark curls in place during their high-speed journey. One had been gifted to Alina days ago, a subtle compromise to cover the absence of drakonian horns. She had grown tired of the stares.

'You should wear a karash too,' Hessa advised, lifting a gauzy strip of fabric over her nose and mouth. 'Or you'll be spitting sand for days.'

'I haven't needed one before,' Alina replied, adjusting her own cloth with mild defiance.

'We weren't in the true desert before, amira.' Hessa chuckled, rummaging through one of her saddle pouches. She tossed the fabric with a grin. 'Now you truly look like a desert princess.'

Alina couldn't help but smile, laughter breaking through the ever-present tension that clung to her like a second skin.

A long, low horn echoed across the dunes. Alina's gaze lifted. The Phanax were already in motion, riding their serpopards in perfect formation while the phoenixes circled overhead, a burning halo above the caravan. The sight was hypnotic, strangely beautiful, yet Alina couldn't ignore the knot forming in her gut.

Though this formation might have been intended for protection, to her it felt like something else entirely. Beneath the watchful eyes of phoenixes and the silent tread of the Phanax, she felt less like an honoured guest... and more like a prisoner, paraded beneath the sun towards her own quiet ruin.

It took them less time than expected to reach the city of Kairus, one of the largest within the Kingdom of Light. The Palace of Kairus was but one of many royal residences, scattered across the land like jewels in a crown. Alina had heard tales, whispers really, that each major city boasted a palace, some grand enough to rival entire drakonian towns. It had always seemed impossible. But as the city rose on the horizon, vast and sun-drenched, Alina began to understand.

Two towering columns marked the city's entrance, sculpted from white stone laced with desert sand. They rose so high into the sky that even the mighty serpent beneath her appeared small under their imposing height. Carvings coiled around each pillar, depicting city life and its fantastical beasts. At their summit, the snarling head of a serpopard bared its stone fangs, as though to warn any with ill intent who dared cross into Kairus.

Alina turned her attention ahead, marvelling at the road teeming with phoenixians. The surrounding buildings were geometric monoliths, square-shaped, with no apparent doors or windows, only carved-out gaps that served both functions. Each was bathed in a pale, sun-warmed orange, echoing the vast desert that cradled the city. Yet what caught her breath were the statues; towering beasts that stood taller than any rooftop, carved with stern expressions as if judging the mortals who passed beneath their watchful gaze.

The Phanax dismounted without hesitation, swiftly gesturing for their guests to do the same. The wide streets welcomed even the great desert serpents with ease, though the appearance of phoenixian handlers sparked a grumble from Hessa. Still, the Phanax would not permit the beasts to roam unsupervised, and with visible reluctance, Hessa gave her people a silent nod of approval.

Once the matter of their mounts was settled, the Phanax resumed their march towards the palace at the far end of the city. Though Alina's limbs ached from travel, her curiosity triumphed over fatigue. This was a world she had never seen and was determined to absorb every detail.

The streets bustled with life. Citizens darted through the market stalls, prayed outside compact sun temples, or bartered for strange wares in loud, melodic voices. Some of the food stalls sold delicacies so foreign Alina struggled not to recoil at the giant roasted insects served on long wooden sticks, glistening under the morning sun.

'I've never seen anything quite like this,' Alina said, wide-eyed.

Hessa chuckled. 'That's because, amira, you've never seen anything at all. We spent our lives walled into our kingdoms, fed stories like crumbs. But the world... the world is vast.'

They stopped at the sound of young girls giggling, dashing down a narrow alley. Curious, Alina and Hessa followed until they stumbled into a hidden courtyard where warm waterfalls spilt into a sunlit pool. Naked figures leapt into the water, shrieking in delight.

Alina blushed furiously and turned to leave, only for Hessa to tug her back.

'We should go,' Alina hissed, flustered.

'Why?'

'They're... naked!'

'So?' Hessa rolled her eyes. 'Are all drakonians this prudish?'

'Yes.'

Alina turned again, straight into a figure, stumbling back in surprise. It was the phoenixian woman, standing silent and unreadable. The girl's red eyes flicked briefly towards Alina before shifting to the pool and the bathing girls, her gaze lingering with quiet contemplation.

'We were only observing,' Alina explained, brushing off her trousers. 'I'd never seen a pool like this before.'

'A pool?' the phoenixian echoed, brow raised. 'Do you not bathe in the Kingdom of Fire?'

Alina's mouth dropped open at the audacity of the remark, but before she could reply, the girl was already striding away.

'Could we not stop and wash?' Hessa asked quickly, attempting diplomacy. 'We've been travelling for days.'

The warrior looked over her shoulder, expression unreadable. Her common tongue was flawless, much to Alina's relief. 'Znu,' the girl said. 'Hat zjenskia zoorx xei jarxu.' *No. We have pools at the palace.*

Alina huffed and stepped forward. 'I don't think you realise who we are. This is Princess Hessa Waadi Al-Dunasi and I am —'

The girl raised a hand to cut her off.

'We know who you are, Alina Acheron,' she replied with a smirk. 'Why you're here, though... that remains a mystery.'

'If we could speak with the king—'

'The king and queen are away, visiting another city.'

Alina blinked. That possibility had not occurred to her. How could she deliver news of Zahian's death without his parents present?

'When will they return?'

The young woman raised an eyebrow, already growing bored. 'It will take time.'

'But—'

Hessa's hand brushed Alina's arm in silent warning.

'Then we must speak with Princess Mareena Noor,' Alina said, steadying her voice.

The phoenixian girl snorted again, an infuriatingly frequent sound.

'Very well, Princess Alina Acheron,' she said. 'Let's go meet Mareena Noor.'

Chapter Five

The Underworld

Hades doesn't visit me anymore. I spend my days studying all manner of potions. He used to come and watch me, always teasing me for how seriously I took my studies. But then he simply stopped.

And I can't help but wonder what changed, what I might have done to make him go.

Tabitha Wysteria

Mal had no recollection of how she had come to stand upon the banks of the Underworld. One moment, Hades had clasped her hand in his and the next, the world had vanished into shadow. She had awoken beside a slow, silver river, its waters whispering secrets she could not decipher.

They lingered there for what felt like an eternity, cloaked in silence and mist. Mal's patience, never plentiful to begin with, began to fray. She turned to Hades more than once, questions trembling on her lips, but he only smiled as if he knew time bent differently in this realm and her frustrations amused him.

Then, at last, a small wooden boat emerged through the haze. It drifted like a dream, barely disturbing the water's surface. At its helm stood a lone figure, robed in grey, their face hidden beneath a deep hood. Mal recognised the silhouette only by the curve of the horns—black, sweeping, wyverian. A kin of sorts. Yet there was no breath, no sound, only the rhythmic dip of an oar.

Hades stepped lightly into the boat, the river seeming to welcome him. He extended a hand towards her.

'Don't mind Charon,' he said, his voice low and lilting with amusement. 'Harmless as a lamb. We've been friends for longer than I can count. Isn't that right, old soul?' He glanced at the hooded figure, who neither spoke nor stirred. Hades gave a casual shrug. 'He's not much of a conversationalist.'

Still uncertain, Mal climbed aboard. She didn't trust Hades. How could she? But she trusted her own curiosity more. The moment her feet touched the vessel, Charon began to row, silent as the dead.

The river thickened with mist, the world around them ghostly and grey. At first, the banks were lined with familiar trees, gnarled and leafless, their shapes not unlike those from her homeland. But soon the river widened, stretching far and wide until it resembled a great black lake. They entered a gorge carved deep into the stone of the earth, its walls soaring above them like the bones of giants.

Ahead, a bridge had formed, an arched passage seemingly hewn from the very rock of the cliffs, linking both sides like the spine of some ancient beast. Beneath it loomed gates, black as midnight, towering so impossibly high they rivalled the cliffs themselves. As the boat drew closer, the great iron gates stirred. Without sound or command, they groaned open, revealing what lay beyond.

Mal's breath caught.

Scattered across the earth, like broken dreams, lay statues of unimaginable scale. Some were toppled, others shattered, their heads lost to time, their limbs crumbled into dust. Moss crawled across cold stone faces. One colossal figure lay on its side, its marble arm outstretched as though reaching for something it would never again grasp.

'What are they?' she whispered, her voice no more than a breath.

Hades reclined slightly, his expression unreadable. 'What do you think they are?'

'Statues,' she said. 'But I've never seen any so large.'

'They were gods,' he said at last, his voice heavy, stripped of its usual jest.

A chill laced her spine. Mal looked again, more closely this time. Though many were unrecognisable, consumed by decay and time, some faces she knew. Gods she had prayed to in silence, deities whispered of in ancient rites. All fallen now. Cracked and buried by the very earth that once praised them.

The boat bumped gently against the edge of the dock, jolting Mal from her daze and drawing her gaze away from the broken colossi now swallowed by mist behind them. She stepped off the vessel, boots crunching against damp wood, and turned just in time to see the cloaked figure wordlessly retreat into the fog, oar slicing once more through the water's glassy surface. Charon did not look back.

'Come,' Hades said, reaching for her hand with the casual familiarity of a man who had done so all her life. As if she were an old friend. Mal stiffened at the touch, every fibre of her recoiling, yet some quiet fear, some deep-rooted instinct not to face this place alone, kept her hand within his grasp.

He led her along the dock until it melted into a street that seemed torn from her own memories. And yet... wrong.

'I don't understand,' she said, her steps faltering. 'It looks like... home.'

The narrow street unfurled before them in eerie silence, a muted reflection of the Kingdom of Darkness. Lamps, frail and flickering, hung from weathered brackets, their dull blue glow swallowed by shadow. The ground beneath her boots was uneven, formed from jagged slabs of mountain stone, warped and broken in places where water from the river had surged through, reclaiming the path.

Buildings loomed above them, tall and foreboding, their blackened façades leaning inwards as if conspiring to fall upon any who dared walk beneath. Gargoyles snarled from cornices and arches, frozen mid-scream, while doorways and windows had been bricked up with stone, their frames adorned with featureless faces of the dead, an architecture of mourning.

'It is a shadow of your kingdom,' Hades said, his voice echoing against the stone. 'The Kingdom of Darkness was built as a mirror of mine.'

'You created it?' she asked.

He nodded.

'Why not make it different?' Her voice was low, almost reverent beneath the weight of what surrounded them.

'Because I am a god,' he replied with a lazy smile. 'And therefore, I am selfish. I wanted a piece of my own home in the realm above.'

They pressed on, the path winding towards a bend in the road where the river had broken through the rock, flooding the street. A small arched bridge of dark stone had been constructed hastily, as though nature had been too swift to allow for grandeur. The water gurgled beneath, black and brackish, glinting faintly beneath the torchlight.

Mal looked up and found no sky. Just the jagged roof of the mountain itself. The cavern above swallowed the heavens whole.

'We are inside the mountain,' she whispered to herself, her voice laced with awe and dread. 'As if it has eaten us.'

Blackened vines and branches had twisted themselves along the walls, pushing through windows long abandoned, wrapping the forgotten city in a blanket of darkness. Some buildings were half-collapsed, stairways crumbled to ruin, doors barred by moss and time. It felt like a place untouched for centuries, left to be reclaimed by silence and root.

Mal stopped. Her breath caught as her eyes were drawn to a high terrace on the building ahead. Two figures stood watching from above, their forms tall and still, their eyes, though distant, locked with hers in the eerie hush.

'Who are they?' she asked, voice hushed, a shiver working its way down her spine.

Hades chuckled, that deep, effortless sound curling through the air like smoke.

'Those, my dear,' he said, stepping closer to her side, 'are your siblings.'

...

The terrace clung to a towering structure carved into the very bones of the mountain, its silhouette regal in its silence. An ancient temple that seemed less built than summoned from stone. Vines trailed over the steep steps leading to its grand entrance, curling like fingers across each slab, as though nature herself had conspired to suggest no soul lingered there at all.

Mal waited by Hades' side, her breath caught as two figures emerged from the temple's gloom. They could only be described as creatures, for nothing about them felt remotely mortal.

The girl, who introduced herself as Makaria, moved like poured silk, her steps fluid and uncanny, each one more a ripple than a stride. A veil of ink-black draped her face, flowing like the river they'd crossed, as if she had been spun from the waters themselves. Long, pallid fingers lifted the shroud, revealing another cloth beneath it, this one bound tight across her eyes. She smiled, but there was no warmth in it, only something unsettling that curled at the edges of her lips. Something familiar. Her hair was unlike anything Mal had ever seen. Not the white-blonde of Vera, nor the cool snowy-silver of Wren. This was white in its purest, most blinding form. A white so stark it seemed to reject all colour, all life, leaving only the hollow echo of what once had been.

But it was when Makaria lowered the cloth from her eyes that Mal recoiled. One was deep and black, fathomless. The other... was red. Not the red of phoenixians, so famously prized and revered, but something far more vivid. Unholy. Consuming. A crimson that swallowed even the white of the eye, bleeding into everything, as though it had been carved from raw flame.

Mal's gaze snapped to Hades. The same red eyes. The same unnatural hue. The same impossible truth.

The man beside Makaria stepped down with effortless grace and took Mal's hand, his own eyes gleaming with that same dreadful light. He brought her knuckles to his lips with a mocking bow, never breaking eye contact as he straightened, studying her as if she were some curious thing washed up from the riverbank. He resembled Hades, uncannily so. Though Hades himself did not look much older than any of them, this one was younger still, all sharp lines and roguish charm that twisted like a blade meant for amusement, not mercy.

'So this is the sister we've been waiting for,' he said, voice a velvet drawl. His smile widened, baring teeth far too knowing. 'Careful, Makaria. You might have competition.'

Makaria gave a sharp snort of laughter, a sound like a crack in the dark.

Mal wrenched her hand from his grasp, her skin crawling.

'She has nothing to fear.'

'Oh?' he asked, teasing. 'Are you not a threat?'

'Do you want me to be?' she replied coolly, letting her fangs show. If he thought he could cow her, he'd find he'd picked the wrong wyverian.

He leaned in, invading her space with a predatory ease, his nose nearly brushing hers. He was enjoying this far too much. 'You look like one of my pets,' he murmured. 'I ought to put a collar on you.'

'Try it,' she whispered darkly, her voice low as a blade unsheathing. 'You might lose a few limbs along the way.'

That drew a laugh from him, deep and delighted. He turned and clapped Hades on the shoulder. 'I like this one.'

'I thought you might,' Hades replied, clearly amused.

'I'm *not* a trinket you've just acquired,' Mal snapped, her voice sharp enough to bite. Before either man could reply, Makaria stepped forward and looped an arm around Mal's, tugging her protectively close.

'Ignore these two fools,' she said lightly, her veil of mockery barely disguising her fondness. 'You'll get used to our brother's idiocy. He's mostly harmless once you've weathered his nonsense. Isn't that right, Zagreus?'

'I liked you better when that cloth covered your mouth as well as your eyes, sister,' Zagreus muttered, his grin not faltering in the slightest.

Makaria's face twisted with irritation, and before Mal could register what had happened, Zagreus crumpled like a discarded marionette onto the stone floor. Hades glanced down at his son with no more concern than if a breeze had passed through.

'We were just about to go in and sit, Makaria. Must you always resort to that?' he said with a weary sigh.

'Then teach him better manners,' she replied, seizing Mal by the arm and tugging her up the steps into the gloom of the temple.

'What did you do to him?' Mal asked, not entirely certain she wanted to know.

'I granted him a blessed death,' Makaria said breezily. 'Though, strictly speaking, he's already dead, so I merely sent him back to the Underworld's threshold. He loathes having to row all the way back with Charon.' She let out a soft, mischievous giggle. 'Your hair is so dark, it nearly resembles a void.'

Mal blinked, unsure whether to thank her or run in the opposite direction.

They descended a narrow corridor, too cramped for them to walk side by side, so Makaria took the lead, her fingers still looped around Mal's arm. The passage was lined with dust-cloaked frames, empty and sorrowful, like ghosts left to wither. The light was faint, flickering, yet curiously warm, as though the shadows themselves had grown fond of the place.

They entered a vast dining chamber where a long, black wooden table loomed like an altar. Makaria hummed an off-key tune as she guided Mal into a chair and flitted about the room preparing drinks. Hades drifted wordlessly to the head of the table, his red eyes dancing with silent amusement.

Mal had the sudden and childlike urge to roll her eyes at him.

'Do you drink tea?' Makaria asked, pausing mid-motion.

'Not particularly,' Mal replied.

A flash of annoyance crossed Makaria's face, but it vanished almost as swiftly as it had come. 'Then I shall make you my famous blend. You'll be converted before the cup is empty.'

Mal's gaze darted back to Hades, her mind swimming. What was the point of any of this? It still didn't feel real—this place, these people. Her father. Her family. Surely, if she were a god, she would have known?

'Why would you have known such a thing?'

The words, spoken aloud by Hades, landed with a weight that made her flinch.

Mal's jaw clenched. Rage simmered within her. 'Stop it,' she growled, slamming her fist against the table. 'Do not dare read my thoughts. If you want me here, you'll keep out of my head.'

Hades' smirk only deepened, amused by her indignation.

'Afraid of what he might see?' Makaria said, her tone playful, her eyes gleaming with wicked delight.

'I'm not afraid of either of you,' Mal snapped.

But her defiance betrayed her. The moment she felt vulnerable, her mind betrayed her too by flashing images of Ash, the memory of his lips, the safety of his arms. And then, the terror. The fear of returning to find him gone, replaced, holding someone else. Loving someone else. Her chest tightened.

Hades' smile widened.

'Stop it!' Mal shouted, leaping to her feet, trembling with fury. 'You've no right!'

'Sit down,' Hades said mildly, waving off her outburst like a tired schoolmaster. 'I was only teasing.'

Makaria returned with a tray, setting steaming cups around the table like a hostess at some eerie tea party. She gestured grandly to Mal's. 'Drink. It'll calm your anger.'

Mal ignored it. 'Why am I here?'

Instead of tea, Hades was handed a goblet of what appeared to be wine. That alone made Mal push her teacup even further from her. If he wasn't drinking it, she certainly wouldn't.

He took his time answering. Leaning back in the heavy wooden chair, he observed her with the quiet, deliberate patience of someone who already knew all the questions she would ask.

His crimson, soulless eyes gleamed with dark amusement the very moment his lips curved into a wicked smile, the faint lamplight catching on the sharp glint of his fangs, like silvered daggers veiled in shadow.

'You are my daughter,' he said at last. 'For years I could not reach you, not while Tabitha Wysteria's curse kept the gods from their creations. But the moment the veil lifted, I came for you.'

Mal didn't reply. She wanted to believe him, desperately. All her life she had felt adrift, out of place. A question mark in a world that demanded certainty. Fourthborn in a kingdom where lineage defined identity: firstborn to inherit, second to protect, third to remember. And the fourth?

The fourth had no place at all.

Especially not one with purple eyes.

'But I'm not truly your child. My parents are King Ozul and Queen Senka. You did something to my mother and—'

Makaria's stifled giggle broke through the tension like glass cracking underfoot. Mal turned sharply to face her, the girl lingering against the wall like a shadow come to life.

'You didn't tell her?' Makaria gasped, eyes wide with mischief. 'She doesn't know?'

'Makaria…' Hades warned, low and sharp.

'What don't I know?' Mal demanded, her voice trembling as she flicked her gaze between them. '*What don't I know?*'

Makaria bounded forward, resting her hands on the opposite chair like a child preparing for a story. Her eyes gleamed with a twisted delight. 'They're not your parents,' she whispered. 'Hades planted his seed in Queen Senka's womb, knowing full well that Tabitha would protect the child with her own blood.

Only there wasn't a child, until her magic mingled with his... and created one.'

'What...?'

Makaria gave an exaggerated sigh and rolled her eyes. 'You're not theirs. You were made. Crafted from god and witch. Senka was merely a vessel, a borrowed cradle.'

A heavy stillness fell over the room, suffocating and close, as if someone had drawn a veil between the world and this one moment. Mal could neither speak nor breathe. Her limbs felt leaden, her thoughts a thousand thorns. She looked at Hades, eyes wide, silently begging him to deny it. Because if this was true, if every breath she'd taken had been built upon a lie... What did that make her?

'Tabitha can't be my mother...' she whispered, shaking her head. 'Because that would make me a...'

'A witch,' Makaria supplied with unsettling glee.

'I'm *not* a witch,' Mal snapped. 'I'm a wyverian.'

Hades laughed quietly, the sound rich and unsettling. 'You are many things, child. A wyverian, yes. But that is only part of the truth. Above all, you are a god.'

'Half-god,' Mal said firmly, as if clinging to that small distinction might steady her world. 'Tabitha was a witch. That means I'm only half.'

But even as she said it, she saw the look exchanged between Makaria and Hades. There was more. Always more.

She curled a strand of hair round her finger, searching for something, anything, to tether herself to. Ash had said something... when he returned from the lava, forged anew. A name. A title.

'The Goddess of Shadows,' Hades said softly, intruding on her thoughts like a ghost slipping through the cracks.

'Stop doing that,' she snapped, narrowing her eyes. 'Why

should I believe any of this? I don't know you. And Ash, he never said anything about Tabitha being my…' She froze. Hades was watching her with a look she hated. Pity. Her heart twisted. Had Ash lied?

'We lie for those we love, Melinoe,' Hades said. 'Surely you've learnt that by now.'

'But why?' Her voice was barely a whisper. 'Why would he lie to me? Why wouldn't he tell me everything he saw?'

Hades took a long sip from his cup, then turned the vessel in his hands, staring into the liquid as if the surface would reveal the answers. 'Because truth,' he said eventually, 'is a weapon. A poisoned blade that slides beneath the skin and festers slowly, until you beg for death just to end the ache.'

Mal wanted to ask what other truths lay in wait, what other parts of her life had been forged from deception. But before she could open her mouth, the room shook with a monstrous growl. Low, deep, and resonant, like thunder rolling through stone.

Makaria's head snapped up. She grinned, wild and delighted. 'He's back!'

Without another word, she bolted from the room, shrieking incantations Mal didn't understand. Moments later, Zagreus appeared in the doorway, chest heaving, eyes dark. 'Where is she?' he growled.

Mal opened her mouth, hesitating. The glint of a scythe in his hand turned her blood cold. She said nothing.

He stormed off, the heavy scrape of the blade echoing like chains across stone.

'He'll never catch her,' Hades said lightly, as though it were a game and not a hunt.

'Is he trying to kill her?' Mal asked, horrified.

Hades shrugged. 'If he does, she'll pay a visit to Thanatos and the Moirai. They won't be pleased, of course. These two spend eternity murdering each other in circles. It's their idea of a good time.'

Mal frowned. 'Thanatos? Moirai?'

Strange names. Not wyverian. Not anything she knew.

And then came the sensation of being watched. Her instincts kicked in a moment too late. A shadow slipped behind her, silent and precise. Steel kissed her throat.

Makaria giggled.

How? How had she crept up on Mal, a wyverian trained in blade and blood? No one was ever able to best her. *No one.*

'Would you like to meet them?' Makaria whispered.

Hades shook his head. Disapproval flashed in his expression, but he made no move to intervene.

Mal opened her mouth to protest, to plead, to scream. She was too slow. The blade slid across her throat with an effortless stroke. Warmth flooded her chest, her hands grasping at the blackness blooming from her neck. Her body collapsed forward, slamming against the wooden table with a dull, final thud. The blood pooled.

And Mal was gone.

Dead.

Chapter Six

House of Snow
Kingdom of Ice

Even though it is the coldest land, wolverian hearts are the warmest.

Tabitha Wysteria

'Wren, get back here!'

Wren did not pause. Her brother's voice echoed down the corridor behind her, ignored as she walked on with purpose, her boots silent against the worn stone of the castle she had called home since childhood. The small fortress nestled within the snowy wilds had been a place of comfort once. But now, its walls felt too narrow, its silence too loud.

They had returned only days ago, weary and dust-covered after fleeing on the backs of their wolves. The journey had drained her, and yet the real disquiet had begun only upon their return, when she had stepped into the main hall to find Kage Blackburn and Freya standing beneath the vaulted ceilings, gazing around as though the castle were some forgotten relic.

On that first day, Wren had expected Kage to leave, to vanish like smoke and return to the Kingdom of Darkness, to his siblings, to whatever fractured pieces of his life remained. But he hadn't. He had not spoken, had not stepped beyond the room they'd given him. Every tray of food left at his door was found hours later, untouched and cold.

'Leave him be,' Bryn had said, his tone curt. 'He's mourning. Don't disturb him.'

Wren understood. Haven Blackburn was dead. His sister, his blood. Of course he mourned. But that didn't lessen the ache inside her, the quiet pull to be near him. She wasn't even sure if a creature like Kage could cry, but if he could, she wanted to be there. And if he couldn't, then she would sit beside him all the same. Perhaps grief did not always need words, nor tears.

In the days since their return, a witch hunt had begun to spread like fire through their kingdom. Wren had confessed to her family what she had seen, what she had survived, and fear had taken root. But she wasn't naïve. Hunts like these rarely ended cleanly. There would be accusations, finger-pointing, old grudges unearthed. Some would hang without proof. Others would burn for nothing more than ill luck.

Still, she couldn't shake the certainty gnawing at her that this wasn't just their kingdom's battle. The other lands needed to know. The darkness was no longer creeping; it was here. If the other realms failed to stand united, the witches would devour them all.

She had said as much to her kin, urging them to send envoys, to warn their neighbours, beginning with the Kingdom of Fauna. But they had refused, each one resolute in their disapproval. Wolverians were cautious by nature. Fiercely loyal, yes. But wary, insular, and slow to trust. They did not meddle in the affairs of others.

But Wren could not, would not, stand by and do nothing. Not when the world beyond their forests was already beginning to burn.

'Wren!'

She didn't stop. Didn't look back. Instead, she slammed her shoulder into the door of her chamber, shutting it behind her with the heel of her boot. Her hands went straight to one of her old travelling satchels, the worn leather familiar beneath her fingers as she began to pack.

The door swung open behind her, and though she could feel her brother's presence looming just over her shoulder, she made no acknowledgement of it.

'Wren, will ya stop and listen?'

'No, I don't think I will. Haven't got time for yer yapping.'

She refused to meet those piercing blue eyes that followed her every movement as she swept across the small room, gathering tunics, daggers, a map. Anything that might be useful. Though the Wynters were royal by name, their lives had always been steeped in humility. What little wealth they had was given freely to their people. The Kingdom of Ice had fared poorly over the last century, ever since the Great War had fractured the world. Once a thriving land known for its enchanted artefacts and flourishing trade, they now survived on little more than grit and ice.

Without foreign commerce, they had suffered. Crops wouldn't grow in their snow-clad soil, and the herds had thinned when the winters turned cruel. They relied heavily on fishing, especially in the north where the sea kissed the frozen edge of the world. But it was never enough.

Wren paused, her gaze falling on the modest space she had always called her own. The furs on her small bed looked temptingly warm, a haven of comfort after the long days spent braving the cold. She remembered, as a child, how Bryn would crawl beneath the covers with her so they wouldn't freeze in the night. People always assumed that ice-born folk were immune to the cold, but they weren't. Not truly. Their skin was thicker, yes, their blood more tempered to the frost, but death by winter was still death all the same.

'Freya needs to return to her own kingdom,' Wren said at last, tightening the straps of her satchel. Her eyes roamed over the wardrobe she barely used, the desk her sisters had once insisted belonged in here, though it was more burden than benefit. She'd been meaning to gift it to a villager who might make proper use of it.

'She'll accompany me to da Kingdom of Fauna. It's on da way to her homeland. She'll see me safely delivered, then go on her own path.'

'Wren...'

'Don't Wren me, brotha.' She spun on her heel to face him, her tone sharper than she'd meant it to be.

Bryn Wynter stood tall in the doorway, lean and strong from years of labour despite his royal title. His silver hair, so like her own, was tied back in a short tail, thin braids woven through in the northern style. Freckles dappled his cheeks and nose, a constellation mirrored on Wren's own face. They could have been reflections of one another, were it not for the height difference. She, being the shorter twin, often pretended not to mind.

Most of the time.

'It's not safe to be travelling,' Bryn insisted, stepping further into the room. 'Not after everything that's happened. Just wait. A few days, perhaps. Let things settle.'

'By then it might be too late,' Wren replied, matter-of-fact. 'Da witches are plotting. We don't know what, but they won't wait for us to catch our breath. We must be ready.'

She moved in and threw her arms around him, clutching his familiar frame. 'Look after Kage Blackburn for me, will ya? I expect him in one full piece when I come back.'

'And if he doesn't stay that long?' Bryn asked, his voice quieter now.

Wren hesitated. It was a fair concern. She didn't know how long her journey would take. The Kingdom of Fauna was only the first stop. She might press on to the other kingdoms, rallying support where she could. She might even travel with Freya to the valkyrian lands, a place she'd only ever heard of in half-forgotten tales.

'Then see that he gets home safely,' she said at last, poking him in the stomach. 'He's in no state to go wandering off alone.'

'I can't go, Wren. Ya know that. I've responsibilities here.'

She rolled her eyes, though she didn't argue. He was right. As heir to the throne, Bryn's place was here, among their people, their soldiers. He had stepped in for their father more than once, especially during the king's illness. And he had done it well.

'Well then,' Wren sighed, a lopsided smile tugging at her lips, 'give him a reason to stay.'

Chapter Seven

House of Sun
Kingdom of Light

I've often wondered about the Phanax. Every kingdom has its soldiers, an army to defend it from the outside world. Yet phoenixians insist they have no interest in waging wars; they're far too occupied studying them.

And still, I've always had a strange suspicion that the Phanax weren't created to protect the royal family, but rather to guard the secrets buried deep within their walls.

Tabitha Wysteria

The palace rendered Alina speechless the moment its towering entrance came into view. She had always held a quiet pride for her own castle and the understated elegance of its architecture, but this, this was another realm entirely. The phoenixian palace was a triumph of artistry and devotion, each stone a testament to generations of reverence and skill. Now, at last, she understood the pride these people carried in their bones, and why fragments of phoenixian design had found their way into the drakonian stronghold. Colossal statues, as tall as towers, framed the structure, their solemn gazes lending the entire place an almost sacred air, as though the Sun God himself kept vigil over all who entered.

The throne room stretched before them like an offering, rectangular and open, its sweeping pillars adorned with intricate carvings that Alina scarcely had time to admire as she followed the Phanax into its depths. To the right, the space opened completely onto a vast inner pool, where a group of phoenixians bathed one another in silence, their movements fluid and unhurried. Alina quickly averted her eyes.

Servants robed in pristine white drifted into the room like whispers, taking their positions along the edges of the grand hall as the Phanax dispersed. The young woman from before raised her arms in quiet command, and the servants approached at once —removing her weapons, unfastening the protective leathers from her arms, and guiding her out of her Phanax attire. They robed her in a flowing gown of white silk, adorning her with thick golden necklaces that cascaded down her chest, and rings and bangles that chimed softly as they slid onto her fingers and wrists. A veil of fine gold thread was placed delicately atop her head, shimmering in the light like woven sunlight.

Alina let out a soft gasp as the girl ascended the single throne and seated herself with a knowing smirk that spoke volumes before a single word was uttered.

'You're Mareena Noor,' Alina breathed, a hint of frustration colouring her tone. 'But I don't understand... you were among the Phanax.'

'I was,' Mareena replied, lifting her chin with proud defiance. 'Most of my siblings prefer their scrolls to swords, but I have always been more skilled with a blade than a book. I was raised among the Phanax. I trained beside them, bled beside them. And now, I am one of them.'

'But... you're the future queen.'

Amusement tugged at Mareena's lips. 'In this kingdom, I can be both queen and warrior, drakonian princess.' Her red eyes gleamed with sharpened curiosity. 'What I wish to know is why a princess of the desert and a princess of fire are lying low on phoenixian soil, trying so very hard not to be seen. Yesterday, I received word from the Kingdom of Fire that the drakonian princess betrothed to my brother changed her mind about marrying him, murdered him in fury, and fled into the sands.'

Ice lanced through Alina's veins. In the space of a heartbeat, the Phanax that had been standing silent and still at the periphery lifted their weapons and stepped forward with precision. Hessa and Alina drew close, shoulders pressed together, the grim truth settling: Mareena had not sought them out in the desert to welcome them but to seize them, believing her brother's murderer stood before her.

'That is not what happened,' Alina said, voice firm though her gaze remained fixed on a blade edging far too near. A hand seized her arm and twisted, wrenching it back until her shoulder screamed with pain. Gone were the formalities. They were no longer guests. They were prisoners. Hessa was torn from her side, the absence of her touch somehow more painful than the assault itself.

Alina was thrown to her knees.

'My brother wrote to me, you know,' Mareena said, tapping her fingers in a steady, impatient rhythm against the golden handrest of her throne. 'He seemed rather pleased with the arrangement. Almost excited, even, about marrying *you.*' Her nose wrinkled with distaste. 'They say you are the most beautiful drakonian and yet...'

'I did not kill your brother!' Alina cried, her voice cracking with the strain of keeping herself composed. She met those crimson eyes, so very like Zahian's, and only then did the resemblance truly strike her. How had she not seen it before? The same angular features, that proud tilt of the chin, the golden-brown skin that gleamed like sun-warmed stone. Their hair, naturally soft and wavy, had been pressed straight in keeping with phoenixian custom. Alina had once learnt, during a quiet conversation with Zahian, that each morning they would press their hair flat with searing metal sheets, scorching it into sleek submission.

'If you didn't kill him,' Mareena said, 'then why are you here?'

'We were fleeing,' Alina replied, eyes darting to find Hessa, only to freeze as she spotted the knife pressed to her friend's throat. Her breath caught. 'The Red Guard turned on us. They were witches, glamoured to look like our own people. They attacked the castle. A warlock, Hagan, murdered your brother to get to me... to punish me.' Her fists clenched at her sides, fury burning through the fog of fear. 'They killed my parents. My brother. I am the last of House of Flames. Princess Hessa is taking me to her kingdom for refuge.'

Mareena leaned back, her nails tapping again, a rhythm that echoed through the vastness of the chamber, maddening in its relentlessness.

'What you've told me could be a convenient fabrication, an elaborate tale spun between you and your... companion.'

'And why would Princess Hessa help me murder your brother?' Alina demanded, venom in her tone.

'Perhaps the two of you are lovers,' Mareena replied with a languid shrug. 'Is it not forbidden in your land to lie with a woman?'

'Princess Hessa and I are not...' Alina stumbled over the word, 'lovers. Her sister, Princess Sahira Waadi Al-Dunasi, was also murdered by Hagan. If you received a letter, it was likely forged. The witches knew we escaped. Of course they'd attempt to turn you against us.'

'Perhaps you're right,' Mareena said, her expression unreadable. 'But you've no proof. Until my parents return, you'll both remain in custody.'

'No!' Alina thrashed against the Phanax who had seized her, lifting her up to her feet. After everything, after all she had endured, she would not be cast into some cold phoenixian cell and left to rot. Not while those monsters continued to wear her kingdom's crown.

There was one way to prove it. One way she knew they'd believe her. But it filled her with dread.

She had once been revered. Her beauty had meant everything in the court of fire. It had been a symbol of power, of identity. And now... now it was gone. Stolen. Defaced. She understood, with dreadful clarity, why Hagan had done it. It had not simply been to cause her pain. It had been to humiliate her. To strip her of everything she had ever been.

'Wait!' she cried out, her voice cracking as they began to drag her away. 'I can prove it!'

'Alina—' Hessa's voice broke behind her.

'It's all right,' she said, nodding as they brought her back, pushing her to her knees once more.

Tears threatened to spill, stinging her eyes. She bowed her head, not in submission, but in sorrow, for what was about to be revealed in front of so many. The truth of her pain. The evidence of her violation.

Now, finally, they would understand.

Now, at last, they would believe her.

Alina reached for her rasguita, the cloth that veiled her head, concealing the unspeakable truth of what had been done to her.

Across the chamber, Mareena Noor leaned forward, her head tilted in quiet curiosity, the rhythm of her fingers stilled.

Alina paid no mind to the tears tracing silent paths down her cheeks. Her spine straightened, shoulders squared, and with trembling fingers she drew the cloth back slowly, deliberately unveiling her bare scalp for all to see.

Gasps rippled through the room like a sudden gust of wind. But Alina's eyes narrowed, her expression hardening like forged steel.

Hagan had intended to destroy her, to strip her of her power by taking the one thing her people had always revered: her beauty.

But he had failed.

Because he had not left her broken.

He had, without realising, made her *unbreakable*.

...

Mareena Noor tilted her head, those crimson eyes lingering on the remnants of Alina's horns, what little remained of them. For a long, stretching silence, she said nothing, simply staring at the mutilation with an expression too measured to name. There was no sorrow in her gaze, no visible anger. Not even surprise. It was as though violence, even against a princess of equal standing, meant so little it failed to stir her.

When at last her eyes lifted from Alina's scars and met her gaze, the drakonian princess tensed. It was impossible to decipher what the phoenixian royal was thinking, but Alina noted the subtle clench of Mareena's jaw, an edge that hadn't been there before.

'A warlock did this to you?'

Alina nodded.

'The witches used the revelries at my castle to their advantage and attacked.'

'No one's seen a witch in decades,' Mareena murmured,

frowning.

'Do you truly think I would do this to myself?' Alina snapped, gesturing towards her bare, disfigured crown. 'The witches have returned, and they're coming for all of us.'

'Yes... perhaps you are right.' Mareena released a sigh, slow and weary. 'My Seers have spoken of omens, dark and disturbing things. May we be blazed by the light.'

'May we be blazed by the light,' Alina echoed softly.

'I am sorry for what has been done to you,' Mareena said, her hand moving in a vague gesture towards Alina's head as the princess quickly covered herself once more. 'And I grieve for what you've lost. You as well, Hessa Waadi Al-Dunasi.' Her voice gentled. 'My family will be informed of the truth behind Zahian's death. In the meantime, I hope you'll remain at the palace a few days and rest from your journey.'

'We don't wish to impose,' Alina began, but was swiftly silenced by a sharp pinch to her arm from Hessa.

'My beasts...' Hessa stepped forward with a lopsided grin, throwing Alina a look full of mischief.

'Will be seen to,' Mareena assured them. 'What do they eat? We're unfamiliar with desert serpents.'

A snort escaped Hessa. 'Naughty people.'

Alina cast the desert princess a withering glance, silently begging her to behave.

'I'm sure we can spare a prisoner or two,' Mareena added smoothly, unperturbed by Hessa's glib reply. 'The servants will escort you to your rooms. I must pray for my brother now.'

She rose from the throne, and at once the chamber responded. Everyone moved, shifting into stillness or motion depending on their proximity to royalty. Alina watched as Mareena was escorted from the hall by the Phanax, no longer a soldier in plain garb, but a princess enveloped in ceremonial splendour. Just hours before, she had walked among them as a warrior, unguarded and unflinching. Now she was trailed by blades and solemnity, like a relic to be preserved. Intriguing.

'Most people don't know she's Phanax,' Hessa said as they followed the servants through a long corridor. 'Word is, when she walks the city streets, she sometimes wears a serpopard-shaped helmet to mask her face. To be fair, this land is so vast most wouldn't recognise the king's face, let alone the princess's.'

Alina was certain of one thing; she would never find her way around the palace. Every space they passed seemed grander than the last, each corridor more elaborate, each chamber more ornate. Rooms opened out like dreams carved in stone, filled with fluted columns and scatterings of velvet cushions. Board games lay untouched on golden-yellow tiles beside gently steaming pools, while strange and beautiful creatures wandered freely through the still air. Trees—palm trees, if she recalled her history lessons correctly—grew not in gardens, but inside the very rooms themselves, their green fronds brushing the ceilings, their trunks rising like ancient sentinels among silken drapes.

The servants led them through a maze of rooms and passageways until at last they reached their chambers. Alina entered hers with the cautious awe of someone stepping into a storybook. Yet despite the beauty of the space with its arched doorways, gilded mirrors, intricate mosaic floors, one thing puzzled her. There was no bath.

She searched every corner, every alcove, expecting to find a tub tucked behind a screen or hidden within a side room, but there was nothing of the sort.

It wasn't long before Hessa arrived, watching with quiet amusement as Alina rifled through the room, increasingly distressed.

'There's no tub, amira,' Hessa said, her voice light with sympathy. 'We bathe in the pools.'

'The pools?' Alina turned to her, frowning. 'You mean the ones anyone can use?'

'They are meant for bathing. That's their purpose.'

'But...' Alina hesitated, biting her lip. 'Other people... use them.'

This time, Hessa didn't tease. She knew well enough now why Alina struggled with such a notion. Once, it would have been because she was a pampered royal unused to sharing even the air around her. But now... now it was different. The thought of anyone seeing her stripped not just of clothes but of dignity, of the beauty that had once been her pride was unbearable.

'I'll make sure we're alone,' Hessa said gently, stepping forward and placing her hands on Alina's arms. 'You have my word.'

As she turned to leave, Alina stopped her with a whisper. 'Shouldn't we wait to be escorted? We can't just wander the palace.'

Hessa laughed softly. 'It doesn't work like that here, amira.'

'Oh.'

So Alina followed, reluctant but trusting. They meandered through the palace, retracing their steps more than once when Hessa's confidence gave way to uncertainty. Eventually, they stumbled upon one of the many bathing pools tucked within the vast estate. Alina suspected Mareena had a private wing of her own, perhaps with her own pool. She tried not to feel slighted that nothing similar had been arranged for her. Ash would have scoffed at her pride, she thought bitterly.

The memory of him rose so suddenly, so sharply, that it caught in her throat.

'Are you all right, amira?' Hessa asked, concern wavering in her voice.

'Yes… it's nothing.' Alina looked away quickly.

She refused to let herself dwell on thoughts of her brother, her parents… of what had been taken. She had spent too many days crying, crumbling beneath the weight of grief. That time had passed.

Now, she needed to become steel. She would avenge them all.

And for that, tears would not serve her.

'How do you know so much about this place?' Alina asked, her voice low with curiosity.

Hessa snorted. 'How is it that you do not? I thought drakonians and phoenixians were meant to be inseparable.'

'I've had more lessons than I can count on phoenixian history and customs, but…' Alina trailed off, her gaze drifting to the shifting water. 'They never taught me this. Not how the cities feel, or how the people live. It was all royal family lineages, etiquette drills, and how to look presentable should I ever be fortunate enough to marry one of their sons. My brother Ash had lessons too, though separately. I imagine he learnt practical things, while I…' she gave a small, bitter laugh, 'could never quite be bothered to pay attention.'

The ache pressed hard in her chest. She should have felt angry at the way she'd been raised, at how unprepared she was for the world beyond court walls. But the sadness of all she had lost silenced every other feeling.

'Why do you always call me amira?' she asked, turning as Hessa returned from instructing a nearby servant to ensure they were not disturbed.

'Because it means princess in my language,' Hessa said simply, tugging off her robes and letting them fall carelessly onto the warm stone. She stepped into the steaming water with a pleased sigh, the rising heat wrapping around her like an embrace. Alina hesitated, suddenly aware of her own limbs, of her own vulnerability. Though Hessa had seen her wounds and tended them with reverent care, the idea of shedding her clothes again still made her pulse stammer.

She drew in a deep breath, then slipped out of her garments and stepped into the water after Hessa.

'I know *that*,' Alina said at last. 'But… you're a princess too. It almost sounds as if you're beneath me.'

Hessa let out a soft laugh, the sound echoing across the tiles. 'When I first called you amira, it was to mock you. Instead of using your name, I called you by the title you held so tightly.'

Alina smiled faintly at the memory, sinking into the water beside her. The warmth embraced her bones, unwinding knots she hadn't realised she'd carried. She reached for one of the sponges and began gently washing Hessa's back, careful around the faint scars that wove like silver threads across her skin.

Alina never imagined she would share such a moment with another woman. Bathing together, caring for one another like sisters… or something else entirely. Hessa had told her, once, that to wash another person in her culture was the highest form of respect. It had been during one of the earliest nights, when Hessa had washed Alina's hair with the utmost tenderness, careful not to reopen the wounds that still ached across her skull.

From that moment on, Alina had insisted on washing Hessa in return. A wordless thank you. A gesture of trust.

'And now?' Alina asked softly, grateful that Hessa could not see her face. Her eyes remained on the sponge, her fingers gliding across sun-kissed skin and the stories etched upon it.

'Now…' Hessa paused, her voice laced with a gentleness that curled like smoke through the still air. 'Now I say it with affection. I can't imagine calling you anything else.'

Alina smiled faintly, but it never quite reached her eyes. Because no matter how many times Hessa called her amira, the truth echoed inside her like a bell in an empty hall.

She was no longer a princess.

Her kingdom was lost. Her family, slaughtered. Her castle, overrun.

Alina Acheron was no longer *anything* at all.

Chapter Eight

House of Shadows
Kingdom of Darkness

Love is a strange and extraordinary thing. It drives us to commit the most bizarre of acts. I never imagined I could love anyone more than I loved Hadrian. But the moment I discovered I was with child, I realised how little I truly understood love, and just how powerful it could be.

Tabitha Wysteria.

Ash Acheron did not relish the art of deception, but if a lie meant protecting the ones he held dearest, then he would carry the burden without remorse. He knew, with unshakable certainty, that his sister still lived. He had seen it, clear as day, etched into the unspooling tapestry of his visions after Mal had plunged the dagger into his heart.

Those visions had come not in whispers, but in torrents, flooding his mind until it felt as though his skull might shatter from the weight of them. He had glimpsed the paths of those closest to him, each thread woven with precision, each ending preordained. And whether he liked the outcomes or not, he understood one absolute truth: they must follow their destined courses. If anything changed, if even one step veered from its design, the future would blur, shifting into a thousand uncertain paths. Those around him would waver, each step splintering into a myriad of possibilities, and he would be left adrift, blind to which course they would choose. He had to ensure they stayed true, bound to the single thread he wove for them. The path he desired. The only path that mattered.

And so, with a heavy heart, Ash had told no one that Alina Acheron still drew breath. He had said nothing, not even to Kai —especially not to Kai—knowing full well that the prince would rush to her aid without hesitation. And if he did, Alina's path would shift irrevocably. In that rewritten fate, Kai and Alina would find one another, would carve out a life together. A part of Ash, buried deep beneath duty and sacrifice, ached with guilt for keeping them apart. But he knew that if he allowed them to reunite, everything else would crumble to ash and ruin. No. He could not permit it. Their fates were threads meant to weave separate tapestries, never entwined.

Mal's future, however, remained a mystery from the very beginning. He had lied to her too, told her he had seen her way forward, had guided her towards her father and the Underworld with the careful hand of someone who knew the price of truth. But Ash understood what others did not: one cannot trace the thread of a god.

And by lying to her, he had done something far more intimate. He had given her the illusion, however fleeting, of being just like the rest of them. Mortal. But they had both known it was a momentary fantasy.

She would not return the same.

In truth, none of them would ever be the same.

'The servants managed to scrape together some food,' came Kai's voice as he entered the great hall, clad in obsidian armour that gleamed with the promise of war. 'It's not easy finding anything that isn't half-rotten in this place.' He offered a smile, though it failed to reach the cold abyss of his onyx eyes.

'Thank you,' Ash replied, rising from where he sat, only to sink back down as Kai joined him.

Ash had never stepped foot in the Kingdom of Darkness until now, though he had imagined it countless times, especially when he had prepared Mal's surprise chamber in his own palace. But the reality of it was far starker than anything he had conjured in his mind.

It was a kingdom draped in shadow. The sky hung perpetually grey, only to deepen into a bruised crimson under the gaze of a blood-moon. Everything around him bled monochrome—blacks and greys with the occasional gleam of alabaster. Floors and pillars were carved from volcanic stone, walls polished to a haunting sheen. Even the hearths burnt differently with a blue fire that danced with a strange, mesmerising elegance.

Ash had spent the better part of half an hour mesmerised by those flames. It was said that they burnt hotter than drakonian fire. And watching them, flickering and eternal, he had begun to believe it.

'Your parents?' Ash asked, dispensing with the usual niceties. By now, such formalities felt irrelevant. He had never been one for titles or ceremony, and after all that had transpired, he hadn't the strength to pretend otherwise.

'My mother is resting,' Kai replied, setting a heavy bottle between them, its glass dark as obsidian, concealing the liquid within. Ash watched as the prince poured the drink into two finely crafted goblets, each one etched with wyverns and flames that shimmered beneath the firelight. The artistry was meticulous, as though the glass itself had been forged in the breath of a beast.

'Wyverian wine,' Kai said. 'You might find it a bit difficult to stomach at first. I know your people favour sweetness. We, however... are not fond of sweet things. A century past, this wine had once been famed across all the kingdoms. Strangely enough, it has not soured with time. It remains the only sustenance we can bear to stomach that is not rotten. A marvel, truly, though this wine is not merely aged but cultivated through decades of patient waiting, its flavour born of dust and silence, in our deep and dark cellars.'

Ash accepted the glass with a nod and took a cautious sip. The bitterness hit him immediately. Sharp, almost caustic, like scorched bark on the tongue. His first instinct was to spit it out. But the moment he caught the knowing gleam in Kai's eye, he forced himself to swallow, the burn trailing like a brand down his throat.

And then, strangely, it changed. A rich warmth bloomed on his tongue, the bitterness fading into a complex, smoky sweetness that lingered like memory. He took another sip, slower this time. Stronger than the honeyed wines of his homeland by a mile. This was not a drink meant for frivolity. It was meant for war.

'My father is writing to the cities,' Kai said, reclining slightly with his goblet in hand. 'We're rallying our forces. The moment we're ready, we march on the wastelands.'

'We need to b-be careful, Kai,' Ash said, taking another sip.

'I am being careful,' Kai said evenly. 'I just happen to believe the careful thing is to impale every witch that breathes.'

Ash set the glass down with quiet deliberation. 'They m-may not be there. The witches... they might've moved on. If they've truly taken my k-kingdom, they wouldn't leave it unguarded.'

Kai exhaled through his nose. 'It would be foolish of them to abandon the wastelands entirely. But you're right about one thing. It's become harder to move between the kingdoms. Too dangerous. Which is why we must seize control of their land first. When we hold the wastelands, only then can we take back yours.'

Ash rubbed his eyes, exhaustion tightening his face. 'My army... If I could s-sneak back into my kingdom and reach the s-soldiers, those loyal to the crown, I could rally them. The Red Guard in the city of Spark was overthrown, yes, but they're spread throughout every ci-city in the realm. I refuse to b-believe they've fallen entirely.'

Ash knew far more than he let on, knew where the pieces were meant to fall and how the board was meant to shift. But the truth was a blade that could cut too soon, and timing was everything. So he would lead Mal's brother wherever he needed him to go. And in the end, he would bear the weight of it.

Ash had told them he had seen things, fragments of the past and flickers of what was yet to come, but he had kept his answers deliberately vague. When pressed for details, he had merely shrugged, feigning uncertainty. Whether they believed him or not was of little consequence to him. So long as they followed the path he set before them, their doubts could rot in silence.

'When we reach the outskirts of the Kingdom of Magic and make camp,' Kai said, 'we'll devise a plan for you to cross undetected and return to your lands.'

Ash inclined his head, though his gaze had drifted elsewhere, settling on the black ring circling Kai's smallest finger. 'And what happens now?' he asked, nodding towards it. Recognition dawned in Kai's expression, followed by the faintest tremble before he mastered himself again.

'It's a rare thing,' Kai murmured, his voice distant. 'Almost unheard of for a future queen or king to fall before the coronation.'

Ash didn't press him. He didn't need to.

'Will the throne pass to you?'

Kai gave a slow shake of his head. 'It would be seen as a disgrace, an act of quiet betrayal. I was born second, Ash. My only duty was to protect her.' His jaw clenched. 'I failed.' He paused, his thoughts caught between the weight of grief and the shackles of tradition. 'Under normal circumstances, my name would be struck from every record. I'd be stripped of my title, cast out from the castle, told to forge a new life beyond these walls. A punishment most would call just. After that, a high noble house would rise and claim the throne. A vote would be held, the people would choose. It's happened once before.'

Ash raised a brow. 'And how did that end?'

Kai's mouth twisted into something cold and bitter. 'Let's just say it didn't end well for the royal family.'

Ash shifted, unease settled in his bones like the chill of winter. 'Has any noble family stepped forward yet?'

'Not yet,' Kai replied. 'But they will. They're waiting, biding their time until the war is done and the bloodshed spent. They'll make their claims when it's safe to do so, when it costs them nothing. And when that day comes, they'll want me gone.'

Ash said nothing. He turned away, his jaw tightening, his expression unreadable. He could not speak of what he knew, what he had seen. Not here. Not now. Words could reshape the future, and he had no desire to fracture it further.

Knowing too much was its own kind of torment.

He was no longer the same man who had stood beside Mal Blackburn in the gardens of his scorched kingdom, no longer the Fire Prince who flinched and stammered through courtly speeches. The flames of war had burnt that softness from him.

Now, he wore his truth like armour. The stutter remained, but the shame had not. He no longer cared how they saw him.

What mattered now was protecting his kingdom, preserving what remained of his people...

And above all else, safeguarding *one* fragile thread of the future.

The one that could save them all.

Chapter Nine

The Underworld

I've discovered that mortals can enter godly realms, so long as they are taken by a god. However, during my research, I came across something curious: gods themselves cannot enter the realms of other gods. The Sun God cannot set foot in the Underworld, yet Hecate can because she belongs to the same realm as Hades. That is why they cannot kill one another. Each is protected by their own domain. But everything changes on mortal lands. A god can die in the land of the living. However, the moment they die, they return to their own realm. But... I've heard there is something called the God-killer, and if a god is killed by the God-killer, they vanish forever. Which makes me wonder... If gods are so difficult to kill, and can only die on mortal lands, then surely, if one god wanted another dead, they'd spend a great deal of time among mortals—plotting, scheming.

I shouldn't think like this, but...what if Hades is here for a reason other than the one he gave?

Tabitha Wysteria

Mal felt as though she were trapped in a dream. But no, not a dream. Dreams weren't meant to feel quite so wrong, so hollow, so deeply unsettling. A nightmare, then. Yes, that must be it. She remembered the blade at her throat, Makaria's laughter, and then darkness. But now she was awake, or something like it, in a room that bore an uncanny resemblance to the main hall of her family's castle.

Yet something was amiss.

The settee, her mother's favourite place to lounge with a book or a cup of tea, was now occupied by three girls she did not recognise. They sat together, murmuring quietly as their fingers worked at something gleaming and strange. A golden thread, fine as silk and glowing faintly, as though stitched from sunlight itself.

Mal blinked, trying to understand what she was seeing. The first girl, seated nearest to her, spun the thread with deft fingers, though when Mal looked to see its beginning, she found there was none. The thread flowed endlessly, conjured from some unknown source beyond sight or reason.

'Makaria sent you here,' said the first girl, tutting as she continued to spin. 'That girl is always meddling. We really ought to cut her thread once and for all.'

'No,' murmured the girl furthest from Mal, her voice low and even. 'It is not yet her time.' She held a long, obsidian-hued dagger, and every now and then, with ritual precision, she would sever a length of the golden thread.

Mal studied the trio. They were peculiar to look at, a strange amalgamation of lands and peoples, as though each of them wore the bloodlines of the world like a patchwork. The first girl, who had smiled knowingly at Mal, bore twisted black wyverian horns like her own, yet her hair shimmered gold like a drakonian's. Her eyes were the pale white of the desert folk, while her skin was rich and dark, reminiscent of the Fae.

The girl with the dagger had hair as black and wild as nightfall, curling loosely over her shoulders. Her red eyes shone with a sharpness that spoke of old knowledge, and antlers crowned her head like branches of a sacred tree. The third girl, seated between them, shared their dark skin, but she was otherwise wolverian in every way—calm, quiet, steady.

'Who are you?' Mal asked.

'We are all,' said the first girl with a widening smile, her youthful face rippling like water until it transformed into the creased and sagging visage of an old woman.

Mal took an instinctive step back as the three raised their veiled heads and turned to face her.

'What are you?' she breathed.

'Don't answer,' the dagger-bearer warned under her breath.

'Moirai,' said the first, now with the face of age and wisdom, her voice a whisper of eternity. Though they wore gauzy veils, it was impossible not to see their eyes. Despite everything, Mal was not afraid. Something in their presence soothed her. It felt like standing at the hearth of an old, forgotten home.

'Why are you...?'

'We are all,' they spoke together, voices layered like song. 'We are everything.'

A soft chuckle broke the spell, and Mal turned sharply, her body bracing itself to strike.

Of all the things she had prepared herself to see, a man sitting quietly at the end of the table was not one of them.

'Do not trust him,' whispered the girl with the dagger. 'He lies, that one.'

Mal frowned and stepped cautiously forward. The man was seated where her father, King Ozul, had once held court—proud and imposing, ruler of shadows and steel. Her heart lurched painfully in her chest, dread curling in her gut.

And then she saw him clearly.

Ash.

...

Mal could not grasp what her eyes were showing her. It was Ash, but not. It was as though someone had taken a brush and painted his likeness onto another man's face, striving to capture every detail of the Fire Prince with unsettling precision. Yet the artist had veered from truth, taking liberties that unsettled the heart. His once-glorious golden hair was now curly and white, pale as snowfall, so like Makaria's it made Mal's breath catch. The warm gleam of molten gold that used to light his eyes had been snuffed out, replaced with a blackness so deep it seemed to swallow the world. His once sunkissed skin had withered into pallor, his complexion dull and bloodless, robbed of its drakonian glow.

'Am I dreaming?' she asked, her mind fumbling in the dark, searching for memory, for logic, for something that might anchor her. Had she fallen asleep? Was this some conjured nightmare?

Ash, or the thing wearing his face, tilted his head to one side, smiling.

But it was that smile that told her the truth. That smile undid her. There was no warmth in it. Only malice, curling at the corners like smoke. Twisted and cruel, it sent a coldness through her bones. This was not him.

She stumbled back, revulsion rising like bile in her throat as the impostor stepped closer, reaching for her. His hands found her waist, his touch like winter pressed to bare skin. Ash had been heat, life, fire. This was ice and death wrapped in flesh.

'You're not him,' she breathed, her voice barely more than mist in the air between them. 'Who are you?'

That unholy smile deepened.

'Not *who*, Melinoe,' he replied, voice a perfect echo of Ash's, but hollow somehow, like a bell rung in an empty chamber. 'Ask me the right question.'

Even his voice was a lie, shaped to resemble the one she loved. It twisted something deep within her.

She turned her head, searching for an answer in the silent witnesses who watched her now. The Moirai, still spinning, still weaving, had lifted their veiled faces at last. The first wore her smirk openly, eyes bright with cruel amusement. The second remained impassive, unmoved by the scene unfolding. But the third, with her red eyes burning like coals, leaned forward.

'Ask what he is, child,' she said, voice ancient and grave.

'Do not meddle,' the first hissed, her grin unfaltering.

Mal turned her face back to the figure holding her. Her heart twisted painfully at the sight. It was Ash—his hands, his jaw, the arch of his brows. And yet, it was not. She knew it in her bones. The tragedy was in how deeply she wanted to believe it could be him.

'What are you?' she whispered, her voice as soft as breath against flame.

'I am Thanatos,' he replied, releasing her with deliberate ease. 'The God of Death.'

'I thought my father held that title.'

His wicked grin stretched wider, teeth gleaming like a blade under moonlight. 'Hades is the God of the Dead. Their sovereign, their king. I, dear Melinoe, am but his loyal shadow. I do the killing.'

'He seems perfectly capable of it himself,' Mal snapped, a spark of irritation cutting through her unease. 'Why am I here?'

'Makaria sent you.'

'I don't understand.'

Thanatos sighed, a sound like wind rustling over graves. 'You are all gods. Here, in the underworld, you cannot die. If one of you kills another, you are simply banished here, to keep me company. Your siblings treat it like a game, hunting one another for sport. When a deadly god from the underworld falls, they arrive to this threshold, where we bind them until the time comes to send them back.'

'But this is the underworld,' she said, glancing about the uncanny chamber that so perfectly mimicked her family's castle, down to the faded tapestries and the scent of old stone.

'Not quite,' he said, voice low and layered with meaning. 'The world has depths, Melinoe—strata like sediment. The underworld is merely the first tier, the place into which all souls fall. But there are further depths, darker and more ancient still.'

'Hell,' she said quietly.

'If you must put it that way.' Thanatos moved towards the table, pulling back a chair with courtly grace. Mal, still dazed, lowered herself into it without resistance. Her fear had melted away, leaving only a strange, simmering curiosity.

'The Moirai and I dwell in this realm,' he continued, 'the arbiters of endings. We do not always chase mortals through alleyways with scythes in hand. Our work is subtler. More eternal.'

'If you are death, shouldn't you be... up there?' Mal gestured vaguely towards the ceiling. 'Taking lives?'

He chuckled, a sound deep and rich. 'My presence is not required. So long as I exist, death exists. I am its breath. Its beginning and its end.'

'You said gods cannot die.'

Thanatos tilted his head, studying her as though she were a puzzle piece missing from a greater design. 'Not here. Not on our plane. But the gods, the ones like you, are not as eternal as the Moirai or myself. You can be slain upon mortal soil, by another divine hand.'

His black eyes gleamed with a knowing spark. Mal felt it, a pull towards understanding, but she could not yet grasp the truth he teased.

'Why do you look like him?' Her voice cracked on the edge

of sorrow.

'Why not?'

'Because it's cruel,' she said, gaze hardening. 'A twisted echo.'

'Of what?'

'Of him.'

Thanatos laughed, the sound both bitter and bemused. 'Are you so certain?' He licked his lips slowly, deliberately. A movement that made her stomach tighten. Her thoughts betrayed her, conjuring up Ash's gaze, those golden eyes that once devoured her as if she were a fallen star, sent down by the gods to be his and his alone.

'Perhaps,' Thanatos said, '*he* is the one who resembles *me*.'

From across the room, one of the Moirai gave a derisive snort.

'Why?' Mal asked, her brows drawn in confusion.

'Well, because you—' Thanatos began, only to be cut off by the Moirai's sharp hiss, a sound laced with warning. He merely waved a lazy hand, as if brushing away smoke. 'No matter,' he said smoothly, turning his attention back to her. 'I don't mind if you think of him when you look at me. In fact...' His lips curved, slow and serpentine. 'I'd quite enjoy reminding you of him. I imagine I could make you scream my name just the same.'

Mal's hand curled into a fist. 'Send me back.'

'So soon?' Thanatos drawled, his dark gaze sweeping across her face with slow, deliberate pleasure, drinking in the way her entire frame coiled tight with fury. 'Are you quite sure you wouldn't prefer I fucked you on this very table, Melinoe?'

'Now.' Mal rose with a scrape of chair legs against stone, dragging it back in a harsh movement. 'Send. Me. Back. Now.'

'Oh, stop tormenting the girl,' one of the Moirai murmured,

exasperated.

Thanatos laughed, a rich, echoing sound that filled the chamber like the toll of a funeral bell. He tilted his head, then crossed the space between them with feline grace, his fingers brushing the length of her bare arm. 'I must say... I do rather like this dress.'

Mal cast a glance downward at the ridiculous garment the High Priestess had forced her into. Layers of white cotton and black lace that resembled a bridal gown more than anything else. It made no sense, and she'd loathed it from the start. 'Hades insisted I wear it.'

'I'm sure he did,' Thanatos said, that infernal gleam igniting once more in his obsidian eyes. 'Though I suspect you'd look far lovelier without it.'

'Home,' Mal snapped. 'Now.'

Thanatos took a languid step back, hands lifted in mock surrender, though the smirk on his lips suggested anything but. She did her best not to notice how absurdly well the black leather clung to him, how the lines of his body echoed another's.

'Do send my regards to my father-in-law,' he said silkily, leaning in until his mouth hovered far too close to hers.

Mal's purple eyes widened. 'Wait, what?'

Thanatos only wiggled his fingers in farewell, delight glinting like mischief incarnate in his stare. Before she could utter another word, the world tilted.

Darkness swallowed her whole.

She landed with a heavy thud upon a table, breath knocked clean from her lungs. Coughing, cursing, Mal sat up sharply to find herself once more in the very dining room where Makaria had slit her throat.

Hades still sat at the table, entirely unbothered, as though not a moment had passed.

Makaria, however, was nowhere to be seen.

'I assume you've met him,' Hades said mildly, lifting a goblet of wine to his lips, the crimson liquid catching the firelight like blood.

'Why did you go to the High Priestess and demand they dress me like this?' Mal hissed, crawling across the table with feline precision until her nose nearly touched his. Her voice was low and dangerous, her fangs bared in warning. 'Answer me!'

'I wanted you to look presentable for your wedding day,' he replied with an insufferable shrug, utterly unbothered.

'I beg your pardon?'

'You can't possibly object. I even chose someone I thought you might find... attractive. He does bear a certain resemblance to the Fire Prince.'

'I'm already married!'

Hades rolled his eyes with theatrical annoyance. 'Melinoe, you are a god. Marriage to a mortal doesn't count. It was sweet, but meaningless.' He stood and kissed her cheek. A soft, sudden gesture that stunned her more than any blow could have.

'You want me to marry Thanatos?'

'Naturally. Someone will need to rule the Underworld when I'm gone.'

Mal frowned, confusion knitting her brow like storm clouds gathering over still waters. Why would Hades be gone? He was a god—eternal, immutable—a sovereign of shadows whose dominion was death itself. The notion unravelled logic at its seams. What reason could he possibly have to abandon his throne, to relinquish a realm stitched so perfectly to his essence? And why, of all beings, entrust it to her, when he could rule it still with a flick of his immortal will?

'Let Makaria do it. She's utterly mad. They'd be perfect for each other.'

'Makaria lacks the strength you possess,' Hades replied, his tone shifting to something heavier, laced with intent. 'But you... your children will be something else entirely.'

The look in his eyes as he said it made Mal recoil. Not from desire, but from something deeper, darker. Beneath the lust for power, there lurked a shadow of fear. Fear of what, she could not say, but it chilled her bones more than any of his schemes ever had.

'You brought me here just to... to breed?' Her voice cracked with revulsion. 'Is that it?'

'Don't be absurd. There's plenty to do before then.' He waved a hand dismissively. 'First comes the wedding.'

'No.'

'Melinoe...'

'I said no.' Her voice rose like a battle cry, her fury sharp enough to cut glass. 'I am married. And I will not be forced into your sick designs. Choose someone else.' With a sweep of her arm, she knocked the goblet from the table. It crashed against the stone wall, shattering into a dozen gleaming shards. 'I came willingly,' she spat, eyes burning. 'But I will find my way back.'

Hades merely laughed, low and cold. 'You can try.'

Mal didn't waste another breath.

She ran.

Chapter Ten

House of Snow
Kingdom of Ice

The Council and the valkyrians share a love-hate relationship. They're constantly meeting to discuss various matters concerning the Eight Kingdoms. The Kingdom of Magic is the strongest, holding most of the power and influence over decisions. Valkyrians exist solely to protect. They watch the witches more closely than anyone else. I think they're beginning to realise that there can never be true balance when one kingdom holds all the power.

Sometimes I wonder if their swords will one day be stained with witch blood.

Tabitha Wysteria.

Bryn Wynter knew, deep in his bones, that attempting to stop his twin sister was a futile endeavour. Once Wren had set her mind on something, it became law—unyielding and immovable. He loved her for it, of course. But it did rattle his nerves more often than he cared to admit.

He made his way down the corridor to Kage Blackburn's room, a tray of rapidly spoiling food balanced in his hands. He knocked, but the silence that followed was deafening. Not unexpected. The wyverian prince hadn't spoken a word since their arrival, hadn't left his room, hadn't touched a morsel of food. Bryn wasn't entirely sure how long a wyverian could go without sustenance, but judging by the faint rustle and occasional creak from within, someone was still breathing on the other side of the door.

'Ya need to eat,' he muttered under his breath, placing the tray carefully on the floor before knocking again to make the prince aware of its presence. Under normal circumstances, a servant would handle such matters. But with Wren gallivanting off to foreign lands and leaving Kage in Bryn's care as though he were some glorified caretaker rather than the heir to the Kingdom of Ice, Bryn had taken it upon himself to keep watch over their solemn guest.

The following morning, he returned to find the tray untouched, the food beginning to rot in the cold air. He rapped his knuckles against the wooden door, suppressing a sigh.

'Kage, I know yer grieving,' he said, voice low with a gentleness he rarely showed. 'But ya've got to eat, lad.'

A faint grunt drifted from the other side, just enough to confirm the prince was still alive, though far from well.

'I'll be back tonight,' Bryn added. 'Make sure that food's gone by then.'

But when evening came and the moon rose high above the snow-swept castle, the tray remained exactly where he'd left it. Untouched and now swarmed by flies. Grimacing, he retrieved it, unwilling to risk the stench and sickness it might bring to the rest of the household. That night, he didn't bother to speak through the door.

So the days wore on, each one folding into the next with the weight of routine. Bryn would bring the food. Kage would ignore it. Sometimes, a grunt would echo back, just enough to stop Bryn from kicking down the door in frustration. Every morning, he awoke with the faintest flicker of hope. Would this be the day the prince took a single bite?

He lost count of the days as they slipped quietly past, but the weight of them pressed down heavily. Eventually, he found himself in the castle library, leafing through the few worn tomes they had on wyverian physiology. What he discovered offered little comfort. Apparently, wyverians could survive for astonishing lengths of time without food. The hunger would gnaw at them, but their bodies, strong and forged from centuries of survival, would cling to life long after most others had withered away.

Still, Bryn thought, *they might survive starvation, but what of sorrow?*

One night, as he had every night before, Bryn Wynter arrived with a tray in hand, replacing spoilt food with fare that was only marginally fresher. The act had become a ritual of sorts, though he wasn't certain it served much purpose. Still, the thought of rot spreading disease throughout the castle was enough to make him persist.

He set the tray down at the prince's door, gave it a firm kick, and waited. From within came the familiar, faint grunt. A small but telling confirmation that Kage Blackburn yet lived.

With a sigh, Bryn slid down to the cold stone floor and rested his back against the door, the tray of food beside him. For a while, he sat in silence. Then, in a voice that barely rose above a murmur, he began to speak.

'Ya know,' he said, 'some winters back we had a sickness run through town. It wiped out nearly all da animals. At first, we thought that was da worst of it, going without meat. But then da disease turned on us. It spread fast. We lost almost everyone in da nearest village.'

He paused, his eyes distant.

'We brought da survivors into da castle, tried to look after them. That winter, we had no food left. We ate what we could find. Old, spoilt things from da back of da kitchens. Anything just to keep breath in our lungs.'

A soft shift behind the door made him still. He imagined the prince on the other side, perhaps leaning as he was, listening.

'Wren… she neva gave in.' He smiled faintly. 'Ya've seen what she's like, I'm sure. Headstrong, stubborn as a frozen river. But back then, she couldn't bear it. Our ma died that winter, and I don't think Wren's eva forgiven herself. Thought she should've done more.'

Bryn drew in a breath.

'She was seventeen. She vanished into da forest for days. Most thought her dead. But I knew betta. Twins always know. When she came back, she wasn't alone. Da wolves came with her. Wild ones. They hunted for us, dragged what little game they could find to da edge of da trees. Enough to keep us going. By da end of da winter, most of them had died for us.'

Another shift. A subtle pressure on the door. Bryn knew then that Kage was sitting just on the other side.

'Starve or don't, Kage Blackburn,' he said, rising to his feet. 'But make yer mind up about it. This is da last tray I'm bringing. I won't risk rot and illness for ya, no matter who ya are. Our land's cold, aye, but hunger and sickness are colder still. We can't afford to waste food. Not here.'

He knew the words were sharp. Perhaps cruel. But wolverians lived on the edge of survival, where every scrap of food mattered. Feeding another without question was their way, but watching that food rot untouched was something Bryn couldn't abide.

He turned to leave, shoulders heavy with guilt and frustration. He didn't want to let the wyverian prince waste away behind a door. At some point, if it came to it, he would break that door down and force him to eat. But he hoped it wouldn't come to that.

He understood loss. Knew the shape of it. And he could only imagine what it felt like to lose a sister in such a brutal, senseless way. His own harshness tasted bitter now, but he could not abandon his duty to his people.

Just as his foot met the next stone, the soft creak of a door halted him.

Bryn looked over his shoulder, blue eyes widening at the narrow slit of darkness that had opened behind him. He stood motionless, holding his breath.

The door eased open wider. A pale hand emerged, snatched the tray, and vanished. The door slammed shut once more.

For a moment, there was only silence.

Then Bryn smiled, warmth tugging at the corners of his mouth for the first time in days.

Perhaps there was hope after all.

. . .

Wren and Freya had chosen to travel on foot. As painful as it had been to part from her wolf, Wren could not predict what the future might bring, and besides, moving by foot allowed them to remain unseen, shadows against snow.

It had taken two days to cross the outer reaches of her homeland, and another two before the faint outline of the border revealed itself in the distance, the place where the Kingdom of Ice ended and the Kingdom of Fauna began. They had travelled swiftly, stopping rarely and speaking even less. At first, Wren had wondered whether Freya might struggle with the heavy snows, but the valkyrian moved with such fluid precision that it seemed as if winter itself bowed to her steps. She glided over the drifts like a creature born of frost and wind, as though the snow had never been a burden but a birthright.

That night, they made camp beneath the pale hush of a starlit sky. Wren's chest thrummed with the anticipation of what tomorrow might bring. Soon, they would stand on Fae soil, and she would deliver the warning. Whether or not the Fae King had yet heard of what had befallen his daughters, it was her duty to bring him the truth. And with that truth, she would ask for steel and warriors, for his armies to rise against the witches. The witches had been defeated once. With unity, they could be defeated again.

Her gaze shifted and landed on Freya, standing motionless at the edge of the trees, her silhouette framed in silver by moonlight. Wren squinted into the distance, following Freya's line of sight until she realised what the valkyrian must be looking at.

The Forest of Endless Trees.

'Legend says it's so endless, no soul eva finds its way out once it steps inside,' Wren said, the words falling like mist. The tales should have sent a chill through her, but Wren had never been the type to back away from a challenge. She thrived on them. 'At night, they say ya can hear da whispers of da ghosts of all da ones da forest has claimed.'

'I heard it was a gift from a goddess,' Freya replied softly, her voice thoughtful. 'That she made it as a haven for her creations. Only they may walk its paths unharmed.'

'Well, I hope that part's just a tale,' Wren said with a snort, turning back towards their modest camp. 'Otherwise, we're both lost already.'

'We'll be fine, Wren. I will keep you safe.'

There was something about the way Freya said it. A calmness, almost too assured that made Wren pause. It was not the words, but the way they lingered, heavy with unspoken meaning. She glanced back, unease prickling along her spine.

Valkyrians were renowned for their might in battle, their unflinching devotion to justice, but there was something else now, something Wren couldn't quite name.

As she crouched beside the fire, building it from ash and splinters, she kept her eyes on Freya. The warrior looked much as she always did: tall and broad-shouldered, her long brown hair tied loosely beneath the fur-lined hood she'd been lent at the castle. Freckles scattered like snowflakes across her cheeks and nose, and her blue eyes burnt with that quiet, determined fire all valkyrians seemed to carry. Wren had always thought her beautiful—breathtaking, really—but now she watched with a different sort of curiosity, a glimmer of something deeper, something unsure.

'You're staring, Wren.'

Wren jolted slightly. She hadn't realised how long she'd been watching. Freya had seated herself beside the fire, her expression shaded with concern.

'Got lost in me thoughts, that's all,' Wren replied, clearing her throat.

'Something's troubling you.'

Wren shrugged, feigning nonchalance. 'Seems to be da mood of da world these days, wouldn't ya say?'

Freya tilted her head, her gaze searching. 'But it's not the witches that trouble you tonight... is it?'

Wren began to trace idle circles in the earth, her finger carving lazy patterns into the patch of thawed soil where the snow had finally relinquished its grip. They had stopped at the very edge of her kingdom, where the whiteness of winter gave way to damp, brown ground and the cold no longer bit quite so fiercely. Here, one could sleep without their bones rattling from the chill.

'What's yer land like?' she asked, voice light and

conversational as she deftly sidestepped the question Freya had asked moments earlier.

'It is a beautiful place,' the valkyrian replied, her tone softened by memory. 'Our floating islands are smaller than the rest of the kingdoms, but breathtaking nonetheless. We are sisters, every one of us, and we care for one another as kin. We are more than warriors. We are protectors of the realms.'

'I've heard there ain't any men.'

'You've heard correctly.'

Wren wrinkled her nose. 'So how... where do ya all come from?'

'We are chosen,' Freya answered, a wistful smile tugging at her lips. 'By the gods.'

'How?' Wren pressed, her curiosity piqued. 'Do ya remember da moment ya were chosen? Were ya a baby? And if so, where's yer ma? Yer papa?'

Freya's smile deepened, though it carried the weight of something ancient. 'Some are chosen as infants, left upon the steps of our temple by the hands of fate. We never know where they come from, only that the gods have brought them to us. Others are chosen in adulthood, usually on the brink of death. The gods offer them a second chance. They are taken to our sacred waters, and there, their past lives are washed away. Their faces soften, the markings of their origin fade. Whether Fae, drakonian, wolverian...It no longer matters. From that moment on, they are valkyrian.'

'So no valkyrian remembers their life from before?' Wren's brows drew together in thought.

Freya shook her head gently. 'No. The sacred waters cleanse us of memory. It is part of the rebirth.'

Wren frowned. 'So... if I hated me life bad enough and wished real hard to be taken away... would da gods just snatch me up and plonk me at yer temple gates?'

'Not quite,' Freya replied, thoughtful. 'It's not about wishing. The gods only come to those whose bravery has been proven in life, who have faced suffering with courage. Those about to cross into death who are, for whatever reason, deemed worthy of something more. The rest...' she hesitated, 'the rest are taken to Niflheim.'

Wren shuddered at the name.

Niflheim. The Underworld.

Every kingdom had its own tale for such a place, though the valkyrians and the wolverians shared many of the same beliefs. Even so, Wren had never truly wanted to believe in it. The idea of being dragged down by cruel gods into endless darkness was not one she liked to dwell on.

'Were ya a babe when ya became a valkyrian?' she asked, eager to chase away the lingering dread.

'No,' Freya said quietly. 'I was grown.'

Something in Freya's gaze shifted. Her blue eyes, once full of fire, dimmed to embers.

'I was married in my old life. I had two beautiful children. I thought I was content, that I was loved. But it was all a lie. My husband... he didn't love me. His heart belonged to another he could never have, and I was the consolation. I tried to be what he wanted. I tried to fill the void she'd left behind, but nothing I did was ever enough. I loved him so deeply that it became unbearable. It was as though he was the very air in my lungs, and without him, I couldn't breathe.'

Freya's hands clenched into fists.

'One night, I tried to end it all. I walked into the river and let the current take me. But the gods didn't let me die. They pulled me from the edge and brought me to the Kingdom of Air. There, I was reborn.'

Wren sat in silence, her breath caught in her throat. Rarely had she heard a tale so raw, so tender and tormented all at once. Her pale eyes searched Freya's face, wide with a quiet awe. There were a thousand questions circling her tongue, and yet the only words she found were simple and true.

'I'm sorry that happened to ya, Freya.'

They prepared for sleep in silence, the fire crackling low as the stars blinked above. Freya lay on the hard earth and drifted easily into slumber, her breath even and calm. But Wren remained still, watching her through narrowed eyes.

A single question coiled in her mind like a serpent. Freya had spoken of her past. She had remembered the pain, the betrayal, the river. But if valkyrians were stripped of all memory when they were reborn...

How, in the name of the gods, did Freya *remember?*

Chapter Eleven

House of Sun
Kingdom of Light

Drakonians do love their lavish celebrations. Each year, they invite all the kingdoms to visit, a gesture meant to ensure our alliances remain strong. But this year, I could sense the air was thick with suspicion. The king has only one child, a daughter. She is beautiful, and undeniably clever. Princess Aithne would make a fine leader for her people, if only drakonians weren't so archaic in their ways. Now, the king must find someone to marry her. I've noticed the way the king watches me, how he's noticed the way Hadrian leans in close. He knows.

And I don't like that wicked smile on his face.

I don't like it at all.

Tabitha Wysteria

'Amira, look ahead and stop fiddling with your rasguita,' Hessa chided gently, her tone exasperated but fond.

Alina ignored her, tugging at the unruly headpiece that, as always, she had managed to wear incorrectly. A portion of it drooped inelegantly over one eye, obscuring her vision despite Hessa's countless demonstrations on how to wear it properly. With a sigh of resignation, Alina lifted the long wooden staff with both hands, arms quivering slightly as she held it aloft. After several seconds, she let her arms drop with a groan.

'It hurts,' she muttered.

'Because you've no muscle, amira.'

They had spent the last few days cloistered within the palace walls, forgotten by Mareena Noor and seemingly invisible to the rest of phoenixian society. Hessa did not appear to mind. In fact, Alina was beginning to uncover the desert princess's serene nature, an ease with herself that Alina found both enviable and entirely foreign. Hessa rarely showed anger or impatience; she did things when she felt inclined and with a certain carefree grace, utterly unconcerned with how others might perceive her.

So they had carved out a little corner of sanctuary for themselves by bathing in warm waters, sharing meals, exchanging stories beneath the golden arches of the palace. Hessa tended to Alina's wounds with unwavering tenderness, cleansing them with salves brought by silent-footed servants. And every morning, she insisted upon training. Not fighting, not yet. Hessa had taken one look at Alina's trembling limbs and declared that she first needed to build strength, stamina, and discipline. Alina had, of course, rolled her eyes at the remark, only to receive a sharp whack on the back of her knees with a slim training rod for her insolence.

'Lift,' Hessa instructed now, her voice like silk over steel.

With a groan, Alina raised the staff once more, striving to keep her arms level with her shoulders. Her muscles burnt in protest, but she forced herself to endure, her eyes fixed on the rod in Hessa's hands, the ever-present threat of another tap spurring her onward.

'Drop.'

Alina let her arms fall, breathing out a sigh of relief.

The door creaked open. Both girls turned to find Mareena Noor framed in the archway, her expression unreadable, her presence commanding. Alina's heart skipped. Had they overstepped by using this room without permission? It had been unoccupied, sparsely decorated save for a few scattered cushions, a board game or two, and a wide terrace that overlooked the river snaking through the city below.

'I have always been curious to witness the training of a Dunayan,' Mareena said, gliding into the room with the ease of someone used to being watched. She reclined with languid elegance upon a chaise longue—gilded gold and white cotton, regal in every detail. Alina tried not to stare, but Mareena's beauty was difficult to ignore. Her long black hair spilt over her shoulders in a cascade of ink, dotted with golden bands entwined through the strands, as though she'd begun to tie it up but changed her mind at the last second. Phoenixian women, Alina had noticed, adorned their hair not for practicality, but purely for aesthetic pleasure.

'She's yet to grow muscle,' Hessa said, tone flat, as though announcing a mild inconvenience rather than an insult. Alina scowled. 'Once her strength has come, I'll teach her something worth watching. I'm afraid for now, my lessons are rather dull.'

Mareena's lips curled into something between amusement and challenge. 'Then perhaps you and I might put one another to the test.'

She rose with the grace of a dancer, and Alina's eyes, entirely of their own accord, followed the movement of her body. Mareena's figure was lush with curves, curves that drakonian women would bind and conceal beneath heavy silks and stifling corsets. But Mareena wore hers like a crown, her garments designed not to obscure but to celebrate.

'A Phanax against a Dunayan,' Mareena mused, approaching Hessa with the calculated grace of a huntress. 'It promises to be quite the spectacle, don't you think?' She turned her gaze upon Alina, and those crimson eyes burnt with such piercing intensity that the drakonian princess instinctively took a step back.

'Are you going to talk me into a nap, or shall we begin?'

Hessa retorted with a teasing lilt, twirling the wooden rod in her hand.

Alina slipped quietly to the side, settling onto the chaise longue Mareena had so elegantly vacated. Her brown eyes were wide with anticipation, her breath caught somewhere between her chest and her throat. This was something no one of her generation had ever witnessed before. A Dunayan and a Phanax squaring off, two titans in a dance of blades and discipline.

Hessa lifted the rod slightly. 'How do you want to play?'

Mareena didn't answer. She only smiled, and lunged.

They moved with startling speed, so fast that Alina's eyes could barely track the strikes and dodges. But within moments, the contrast between the two warriors became evident. Hessa was fluid and precise, her movements like wind over sand—graceful, fluid, almost hypnotic, as though every strike was a motion plucked from an ancient dance. Mareena, in contrast, was a storm. Her power was raw, explosive, each movement a calculated strike that could shatter bone or stone. Yet not once did she land a hit. Hessa evaded them all with a flick of her wrist, a sidestep, a sway of her hips.

Alina watched in silence, awe shimmering in her eyes, until the awe gave way to sorrow. A deep, aching sadness crept over her, heavy as a mantle. This... this was what she had been denied all her life. If only she had been allowed to join the Red Guard, to train like her brother, like the sons of noble blood. By now, she might have been their equal—strong, skilled, unafraid. But instead, she had been left to wither in silks and slippers, her hands soft, her strength untested.

Her fists clenched in her lap. Her eyes prickled. If things had been different, if she had been different, could she have defended her family? Could she have stopped the slaughter? Perhaps not. But at least she might have tried. She might have stood between them and death.

Unable to bear it any longer, Alina stood abruptly, the chaise longue creaking beneath her as she moved. She turned on her heel and fled the room, fleeing not from the princesses themselves, but from what they represented, everything she had never been allowed to become.

She stormed down the corridor, directionless yet driven, the ache in her chest a cruel compass. The truth pulsed through her veins like liquid fire, a relentless reminder of just how fragile she truly was beneath the armour of defiance.

'Alina?'

She froze half-way down the hallway at the voice, wiping furiously at the tears that clung to her lashes. 'I'm sorry,' she whispered hoarsely. 'I didn't mean to run out like that...'

Steady hands settled upon her shoulders, firm yet gentle, and turned her around. Embarrassment bloomed across her cheeks like wildfire when she found herself face-to-face with Mareena, who was watching her with an unreadable expression as she wept.

'What's the matter?' Mareena asked, brows drawing together in concern. 'We weren't going to hurt each other, I swear it.'

A brittle laugh escaped Alina, followed by another wave of tears. 'I know *that*,' she said, shaking her head. 'You think I ran because I was afraid... because I can't fight.' She swallowed a sob. 'But it's not that. It's that I'm so useless. So god-damned weak.'

'You are neither weak, nor useless,' Mareena said firmly.

'Yes, I am!' Alina's voice cracked as she screamed the words, the frustration and grief pouring out in torrents. 'I couldn't save them! If I'd been stronger, if I'd trained harder, I could have...'

'Could have what?' Mareena's grip tightened. 'You think I

am strong?' Her crimson eyes flared with emotion. 'And yet I could not save my little brother Zahian. Do you think me weak because of it?'

Alina faltered. 'No... but it's not the same. You weren't there. If you had been...'

'Hessa was there when her sister Sahira was killed. Do you believe she is weak?'

'No, I didn't mean...' Alina's voice faltered beneath the weight of guilt.

'We are *not* weak,' Mareena said, her voice quiet but unyielding. 'And neither are you. Strength is not about the sharpness of your blade or the breadth of your shoulders. It is how you rise when the world breaks you. How you carry on when everything else says you should fall.'

Alina bowed her head, shoulders slumping beneath the invisible burden she'd been dragging with her for days, for weeks, for what felt like years. Exhaustion throbbed in her bones. It was hard, so hard, to keep fighting when all that had once tethered her to this world was gone.

'I ran away...' she whispered.

'Look at me, Alina.'

She lifted her gaze, reluctantly. But the moment their eyes met, she was caught in the storm of Mareena's stare—those red irises glinting with something more than defiance. With something deeper. A fire forged of pain and survival. Of vengeance. Of purpose.

'You didn't run away,' Mareena said, her voice as soft as it was resolute. 'You survived. You saved yourself. You are the last Acheron.' Her expression gentled. 'You saved your bloodline.'

Alina didn't move as Mareena leaned in closer, her hands lifting slowly to the edge of Alina's rasguita. Her fingers hovered for a heartbeat, almost reverently, before gently tugging the cloth away from Alina's head. It slipped down like silk, pooling around her neck.

Mareena took a half-step back, as though to admire her properly. Alina's breath caught when the phoenixian reached out, brushing a fallen strand of blonde hair behind her ear with the softest of touches.

Those crimson eyes roamed over Alina's features, taking in every scar, every imperfection, every piece of her. They finally drifted upwards to the place where Alina's horns had once proudly curved, now reduced to jagged stumps.

But Alina didn't flinch. The shame that usually clawed at her spine was silent. She let Mareena look, let her see. Even clothed, she had never felt more exposed.

'Don't hide what they did to you,' Mareena said, her voice a breath against the quiet. 'Let the world see who you truly are.'

Who am I? Alina wanted to ask. The question was there, etched into every breath, written across her face.

And Mareena, it seemed, could read it.

'A survivor, Alina Acheron. That is what you are. A *survivor*—the last of her name.'

Chapter Twelve

House of Flames
Kingdom of Fire

To join the Council, I must face a series of tests. They never say what they'll be, but we've all heard the rumours. I've studied every kind of magic, history, and poison... I'm ready for the first trial. I'm particularly drawn to the path of a healer. They are held in high esteem among us, as not all witches possess such a gift. I wouldn't mind earning that place among my own—healing others, saving lives... it sounds perfect to me. I've spent my entire life preparing for this. For the moment I pass every test and they grant me a seat on the Council.

Tabitha Wysteria

Vera swept through the marble corridors of the drakonian castle with a purposeful stride, no longer cloaked in the disguise of a humble maid. She no longer needed to conceal the truth of what she was. Her purple eyes, once hidden in shadow, now gleamed openly beneath the torchlight, unmistakable in their power and defiance. A witch, unveiled at last.

She had walked these halls countless times before, but never like this. Never with such open disdain and sovereignty.

In the aftermath of the massacre, many drakonians had fled in desperation, slipping away under cloak of night. Hagan had unleashed his forces to drag them back. The city of Spark was his now, its throne room stained with fresh blood, its royal family toppled. But Vera, unlike Hagan, understood that seizing a castle did not mean conquering a kingdom. That subtle truth had evaded him, and he would not hear it, no matter how loudly it was spoken.

The grand doors of the throne room parted at her will, creaking open with an eerie groan. She strode inside, her posture regal, her chin lifted in defiance, and her gaze unwavering as it landed upon Hagan sprawled across the throne as though he had been born upon it. A golden goblet twirled between his fingers, filled with the wine of stolen feasts. A young drakonian woman perched naked on the armrest beside him, her skin pale and shivering. Not from cold, but from something far deeper: terror.

'You might want to reconsider drinking that,' Vera said flatly, her tone edged with contempt. 'It could be poisoned.'

A glint of something dark passed through Hagan's amethyst gaze, something cruel, wicked, and burning. 'They could try,' he said, his voice silk spun over steel. 'But I imagine they understand well enough that one cannot poison a warlock. Nor a witch.'

His attention drifted away from her, settling instead on the quivering line of servants pressed against the stone walls. Survivors, or what was left of them. After the bloodshed—the slaughter of nobles and guards, of courtiers who begged for mercy in the night—these few had been spared only to serve.

Hagan's smile curled, vicious and amused. 'Perhaps we might test your theory,' he said idly, nodding towards a trembling young girl clutching a golden tray. 'Come here.'

Vera recognised her instantly as the daughter of one of the High Ladies. She had once been regal, proud. Now she wept where she stood, her sobs muffled by her own desperation.

'Hagan, I need to speak with you,' Vera said, weariness lacing her tone. She watched as he ignored her, delighting instead in the girl's misery. 'I don't have time for your theatrics.'

The girl was shoved forward by an unseen force. His magic, casual and cruel. He offered her the goblet, which she took with shaking hands.

'Drink,' he whispered, his voice low and gleeful.

The girl's terror was so complete she lost control of her body, the wine trembling in her hands as she soiled herself. Hagan's smile only grew wider.

'Oh, for Hecate's sake,' Vera muttered, striding forward and snatching the goblet from the girl's grasp. She threw back the wine in one go, barely flinching at the foul taste, then hurled the cup at Hagan with a sharp flick of her wrist. 'Will you *stop* this nonsense?'

The girl stood rooted to the floor, paralysed. Vera frowned. This should have been the drakonian's moment to flee, to vanish into the shadows. But she lingered, frozen in place. And though Vera knew she ought to feel something, she felt nothing at all.

Pity had long ago been carved from her heart.

She turned away from the girl who had once kicked her across the kitchen floor for dropping a fork, and left her to face whatever fate awaited. Vera had done more than enough.

'We need to talk,' Vera repeated coldly, her gaze returning to Hagan, who lounged across the drakonian throne like a serpent coiled around its prey. She deliberately ignored the naked girl draped over the throne's arm, her fiery hair clenched between Hagan's fingers like a trophy.

'You cannot continue slaughtering innocent drakonians on a whim,' she added.

'*Innocent?*' Hagan hissed, his voice slithering through the chamber like smoke. 'They are not innocent. We've lived our lives cowering in the shadows, hunted like beasts, because of them.'

His grip on the girl's hair tightened. She winced but made no sound, save for a single tear that slipped down her cheek. Sensible creature, she knew better than to scream.

'Beating an old man half to death or strangling some noble's daughter in a hallway isn't exactly heroic,' Vera muttered, arms crossed. 'You can't claim to have conquered a kingdom if you leave *no one* alive in it to rule. And that was never the plan.'

'Was it not?' he asked, tilting his head. His voice had dropped to a silken murmur, always more dangerous than his rage.

Vera exhaled. Hagan's moods were like storms: unpredictable, brief, and devastating. 'We need to be strategic.'

'No,' he said. 'We need to burn this kingdom to ash. We need to slaughter every last drakonian. And when we've finished here, we'll move on. One kingdom after the next, until there is nothing left but silence and soot.'

A strangled gasp tore the air. Vera's eyes flicked sideways just as the servant girl standing beside the throne clawed at her throat, choking. Her feet lifted from the floor, suspended by an invisible force, Hagan's magic curling around her like a noose.

Vera didn't flinch. Part of her wanted to speak, to offer comfort. But she couldn't summon the energy for it. Not now. Not for this.

'Hagan,' she said flatly.

He leaned forward with interest, watching the girl struggle for breath.

'Hagan.'

There was a soft thud as the girl collapsed, lifeless, to the marble floor.

'What?' he snapped, irritation blooming like rot beneath his skin.

'We've spoken about this.' Vera's voice dropped, tired now. 'About blood magic.'

His gaze cut towards her, sharp and knowing. It was a look she had seen before, too many times. He hated being corrected. He loathed reminders of any limits to his power. But blood magic... blood magic was different. It was ancient, volatile, and it was already consuming him.

'You know it's forbidden, Hagan.'

'That kind of magic *put* us here,' he said, gesturing with outstretched arms to the throne room, the castle, the conquered city beyond. Then, with a devilish smile, he yanked the drakonian girl sitting on the armrest into his lap, running his fingers over her skin. 'You're squeamish now, Vera. But I don't recall you sobbing when you slit the queen's throat.'

'That was different,' she replied.

'Oh?' he purred. 'Do enlighten me. How exactly?'

Vera bit the inside of her cheek, refusing to speak. She would not be drawn into his games. She knew how he twisted truths to serve his purpose.

Hagan's grin widened. He had no need to speak further; her silence said everything. No matter how she tried to frame it, no matter what excuses she wove, she knew he was right.

Killing was killing.

And blood always stained, no matter whose hands spilt it.

The great doors to the Grand Hall creaked open with a groan that echoed off the marble walls. Vera turned her head as her sister entered, the sound of footsteps far too familiar. She did not look down at the lifeless body at her feet. What would have been the point? The girl was dead. A death Vera could have prevented. A death she had chosen not to stop.

She was as corrupted as Hagan. As hollow. As ruined.

Dawn swept into the chamber like a whisper of moonlight,

all ethereal grace and quiet menace. She was as striking and deadly as ever, her wild mane of white hair cascading in unruly waves about her slender frame. Like Vera's, it shimmered like winter frost, but where Vera's hair hung in neat lines, Dawn's was wild, untamed, like a ghost made flesh. They could have been twins, their similarities unnerving: the same umber skin, the same purple eyes that marked them for what they were. But where Vera's features had grown sharp and wolfish over the years, carved by rebellion and fire, Dawn's were softer, rounder and gentler, almost childlike.

Their mother used to say: Allegra was the wisest, Dawn the kindest, and Vera the...

Vera's thoughts fractured as her gaze met Dawn's, and something unsaid passed between them. The flicker of fear. Of doubt. Something was wrong, more wrong than usual.

Hagan had slithered his way into the trust of their kind, gathering witches and warlocks beneath his banner like a storm sweeping through dry grass. He had made himself their voice, their judge, their fury. Vera had stood beside him, shield raised and blade drawn. She had justified his decisions again and again.

But now...

'We are ready,' Dawn said simply, her voice void of emotion.

Vera moved to her swiftly, catching her wrist with a firm grip. Her fingers pressed in tight, the question unspoken in her eyes. *What are we doing? Why are you letting this happen?* But Dawn looked away, the way she always had when things became too real.

'Where are you going?' Vera asked, turning on Hagan as he rose from the throne and descended the dais with that insufferable smirk etched across his cruel features.

He didn't answer at first. The drakonian girl followed

behind him, her bare feet whispering across the marble floor, an invisible chain taut around her throat.

Vera's stomach coiled.

'Let's go, Dawn,' Hagan drawled, pausing beside Vera. His eyes drifted down to where Vera's hand still clasped her sister's wrist. The amusement in his face was unmistakable.

Vera let go.

He chuckled darkly, a sound that tasted of rot and fire.

'We've got drakonians to kill,' he said. 'And a fucking city to burn.'

...

'Vera.'

The voice broke the silence like a ripple across still water.

The castle had become a husk, emptied of its former grandeur, echoing now with only ghosts and distant screams. Hagan had taken most of the witches with him, off to wreak whatever chaos he believed would fulfil his purpose. The drakonian servants had scattered like leaves in a storm, some likely hiding, others fleeing into the night. Vera had left several doors ajar with a whisper of magic, a quiet kindness she pretended not to acknowledge.

Looking up from her place amidst the dusty archives of the late queen's chambers, Vera was startled to find her sister, Allegra, framed in the doorway. The scent of dried blood still lingered, no matter how often the room was scrubbed. The queen's body had been removed days ago, but the air had not forgotten.

Allegra stepped into the chamber, her eyes flitting over the disordered papers sprawled across the desk. She moved with the quiet authority of someone who had always known her place in the world.

'We need to talk,' she said plainly, her focus already sliding away from the documents. 'It's about Hagan.'

Vera's shoulders tensed. 'What about him?'

'He's becoming a problem.'

'Becoming?' Vera echoed, arching a brow.

Allegra's sigh was soft but telling. For years, their people had followed Hagan without question, but Vera, Vera had never trusted him. Not truly. 'Do you know what he's doing right now?'

'I'm not sure I want to.' Vera rose from her seat and crossed the room to a cabinet, retrieving two glasses and an unopened bottle of syrupy drakonian wine. The stuff was foul, but it served its purpose. Back when she had posed as a maid, she'd never been allowed near it. One of many rules.

'He's out there,' Allegra said, taking the offered glass and sitting down. 'In the streets. With the witches. Burning everything to the ground. Killing anyone in his path. He says it's what the drakonians did to us, with their dragons, a hundred years ago.'

'He's not wrong,' Vera replied as she leaned against the edge of the table, taking a sip and wincing at the cloying sweetness.

'That's not the point,' Allegra snapped. 'This was never what we wanted. We swore to dismantle the Houses, not slaughter the people.'

'I know.'

Allegra's sharp look cut through the smoke-scented air. 'Then what do we do, Vera? Because reasoning with him has become impossible.'

Vera was silent.

'We may have to...'

'Don't.' Vera raised her hand, stopping the thought before it could be voiced. 'You know that isn't an option. There must be another way. We don't kill our own.'

'This is different.'

'We *promised.*'

Allegra shook her head, her expression a mixture of frustration and sorrow. 'What we promised our mother no longer matters. Hagan is spiralling. His fury blinds him. If we let this continue, if we let him continue, there won't be anything left to save.'

'Not like that,' Vera insisted. 'We'll find another way.'

Allegra rose, glass untouched. 'Then do it quickly,' she said. 'Because if he were any other warlock, you'd have let me end him by now.'

Vera flinched, her jaw tightening. Allegra wasn't wrong. But Hagan wasn't just another warlock.

'But he's not, is he?' Vera said. 'He's... what he is. And because of that...'

Allegra didn't wait for her to finish. She turned and strode from the room, the heavy doors groaning as she slammed them shut behind her.

Vera stood motionless, the silence settling like ash around her. She knew, had known for some time, that the tide was turning. That Hagan's reckless use of blood magic and his obsession with vengeance had begun to fracture their unity. A time would come when she could no longer shield him, when even she would be forced to choose. But not yet. Not while she still had breath enough to keep the promise.

She crossed the room to the window, her gaze falling upon the smoke coiling into the sky, the flames licking at rooftops. She could almost hear his laughter, low and cruel, reverberating through the stone.

Hagan knew. He knew of the promise.

And he knew, with absolute certainty, that Vera would never raise a hand against him.

Her very own *brother*.

Chapter Thirteen

House of Flames
Kingdom of Fire

I failed my very first test. But I will do better. I've uncovered a form of magic no one dares speak of. There are whispers that it's forbidden, that using it takes a part of your soul. Still, I intend to study it, just a little. To see whether it might be used in my next test.

Tabitha Wysteria

Vera waited.

She had lingered in silence for what felt like an age, ensconced in the room Dawn had claimed as her own. It was difficult not to flinch at the sight of the delicate furnishings and careful touches, a room so clearly once crafted for someone else. Every tapestry, every black and silver frame whispered a name that wasn't her sister's.

The door creaked open.

Dawn halted the moment she noticed Vera, seated upon the grand bed, fingers gliding over the silken sheets as though smoothing the creases might erase what had once taken place there.

'Of all the chambers in this castle,' Vera said, 'you had to choose this one, didn't you?'

'It's not what you think.'

Vera's lips curled into a knowing smirk. 'Do you lie here at night and picture him, touching *her* as though it were you?'

The words, cruel and barbed, struck deeper than any of the thorn-laced roses Queen Cyra had once cultivated in her royal gardens. Yet Dawn did not flinch. She moved instead towards the adjoining chamber, where an enormous bath awaited, its basin carved from black stone, now filled with chill water.

Dawn stripped without ceremony, her blood-streaked garments falling silently to the floor. Vera followed, pausing at the doorway, leaning against the frame with the casual air of someone pretending not to see the red that stained her sister's clothes.

'I feel nothing for him,' Dawn muttered, before disappearing beneath the water's surface.

'Then why sleep in the bed he chose for Mal Blackburn?' Vera's voice was laced with scorn. 'Why linger in the same room he once loved her in?'

Silence. But Vera knew the truth, had always known it. Dawn had been sixteen when she first slipped into the court under the guise of Adara, a drakonian lady of noble blood. Her task had been simple: seduce the Fire Prince, glean what she could. Everyone believed her role was an act.

Vera had never believed that lie.

Dawn had loved him then. And worse, she still did.

'He's dead, Vera,' Dawn whispered. 'He must be. The curse must have been broken and… This room reminds me of him.'

Vera felt a smile tug at the corners of her mouth, dark and indulgent. She should have felt guilt. Her plan to stop Hagan would wound Dawn, place her once more in Ash's path, but Vera had long since accepted the truth of herself.

She would kill for her family. And she would wound them, too, if that pain served a greater purpose.

She folded her arms across her chest, awaiting a retort, a denial, any feeble defence. But Dawn said nothing. Instead, she rested her arms on the lip of the tub, tilting her head to glance up at Vera with those soft, dove-purple eyes.

'Killing drakonians won't dull the ache,' Vera said. 'It's not their fault he never loved you.'

A spark of anguish passed through Dawn's violet gaze. 'You needn't be so cruel.'

'And you needn't obey Hagan like a trained hound.'

'He's led us to victory,' Dawn countered, her voice calm but tight. 'Thanks to him, we've conquered this land.'

Vera barked a laugh. '*Conquered?* Is that what he's feeding you all? We've claimed *one* city, Dawn. Just one. The rest of this kingdom hasn't reacted yet because we decapitated the royal family and left them flailing like headless chickens. But word will spread. The other kingdoms *will* come. We've spilt royal blood. That sort of crime demands retribution.'

'Hagan says—'

'*Fuck Hagan.*'

'Vera,' Dawn said sharply, 'you're being unreasonable. You've always hated him.'

Vera uncrossed her arms and wrapped them tightly around herself, stepping further into the chamber. At Dawn's quiet command, the candles flickered to life one by one, casting a warm glow against the encroaching gloom of nightfall.

'Every time I look at him,' Vera said, her voice barely above a whisper, 'it's as though I'm staring into the eyes of the very monster who destroyed mother. And still, I cannot raise a hand against him, because of that damned promise I made her.'

'It wasn't Hagan's fault, Vera. He wasn't the reason she took her own life.'

The words, calmly spoken, struck like a blade between her

ribs. Vera gasped, feeling the familiar sting rise in her throat. She had spent years avoiding such thoughts, especially of their mother. And yet, how could she truly forget, when every breath Hagan took served as a reminder?

'That drakonian lord raped our mother,' she said, turning slowly to face Dawn, her eyes hollow. 'He forced himself upon her, and from that violence, Hagan was born. She never recovered from it. And in the end, it consumed her.'

'You can't hold him accountable for that,' Dawn said gently.

Vera knew she was right, but that knowledge didn't make the bitterness easier to bear.

Their father had remained in their homeland, while their mother had journeyed west to join the cause. Disguised by glamour, she had posed as a lady of the drakonian court. But even magic had its limits. It was near impossible to infiltrate a court where everyone knew everyone else. One man in particular, a powerful lord, had taken an interest in her. When she'd tried to rebuff him, claiming a husband waited for her back home, he had ignored her pleas.

What followed was unspeakable.

He left her disgraced and ruined. But their mother had not bowed to his cruelty. She had bewitched him, turned his mind inside out with her spells until he fell hopelessly, obsessively in love with her. He married her soon after.

Then she killed him.

When their father learnt of the truth, it broke something inside him. He grew frail, sickly, and within months he had passed away.

Vera had been in the drakonian lands by then, accompanying their mother. She hadn't been permitted to return home for the funeral. Her sisters—older, and already sent to live with distant relatives—had said their goodbyes in her place.

Vera had been raised as the handmaiden to a drakonian lord's wife. In truth, her mother, glamoured to deceive the court. After leaving their homeland to join the cause, her mother had brought Vera with her under the guise of servitude, presenting her not as a daughter, but as a girl of no consequence, hidden in plain sight. And so Vera grew up pouring tea and fetching cloaks, while silently watching the woman who had given birth to her slip into a new skin, laughing with strangers, and dining beside the very people who had once called for their kind's destruction. It was a performance laced with quiet agony, the child forced into silence while her mother played lady of the court.

When she turned ten, she was moved to the castle, no longer just an invisible helper in noble halls, but now a ghost haunting the very corridors that had once belonged to the people who had shattered her kingdom. And it had been excruciating.

She would pass the drakonian ladies in silence, lounging beneath the carved arches of the royal gardens, sipping their honeyed teas and gossiping in warm voices, never knowing one of their own was a witch in disguise. And at the centre of it all sat her mother, laughing amongst them, feigning delight as if the blood on her hands had long since dried.

But what wounded Vera more deeply than all the rest was Hagan.

Watching him grow had been a quiet torment. A boy who bore the face of their mother's pain, and yet was embraced as if he were pure. She had seen him run through the sunlit courtyards with Alina and Ash, their carefree laughter echoing off the stone. She had watched their mother brush the hair from his brow with the same tenderness she had once reserved for her daughters.

She had loved him. Protected him.

As though he had never broken her.

'Ash will return,' Vera said, forcing the memories back into the locked box where she had buried them long ago, the key cast into oblivion. 'He'll come to reclaim his kingdom. To avenge his sister. He doesn't know she's still alive. And when he does come, Hagan will kill him. You understand that, don't you?'

'How do we even know he's still breathing?' Dawn replied flatly. 'Mal would have killed him by now. Hagan says the curse is broken.'

Vera gave a careless shrug. Perhaps Ash Acheron was already dead, slain by the very woman he had chosen to love. But if life had taught Vera anything, it was this: love had a way of blinding even the sharpest minds. Ash didn't need to be alive. Vera just needed Dawn to believe it.

'Knowing Mal Blackburn, she found a way to save him,' Vera said. 'He's alive. And if Hagan finds him...' She turned fully now, her gaze steady, letting her words seep into the air like ink into cold bathwater. Dawn faltered, her silence betraying the storm that stirred beneath her composed façade. The thought of Ash meeting his end at Hagan's hand cracked something open inside her, something long buried but not forgotten. Vera almost wondered why she felt no shame in toying with her sister's wounds. She ought to. And yet... she didn't.

'There's nothing to be done,' Dawn said eventually, her voice carefully bored, as though she hadn't heard a word that mattered. But they both knew she had.

'Someone could help him,' Vera whispered, her tone hushed as though the walls themselves might bear witness to treason. 'Someone could guide him. Protect him. Show him the path. It's him or Hagan. Perhaps someone who knows them both could tip the scales.'

Their eyes met, and in that moment, no more needed to be said. A single glance, veiled in silence, exchanged like a cipher between spies. A signal only they understood.

Vera didn't need Ash to wield the blade. She only needed the fire he ignited in others, the loyalty he inspired. His army. His name. And most importantly, the woman who had once loved him in secret.

She knew her sister well. Knew that Dawn, no matter how deeply buried, had never stopped being the girl who had called herself Adara, the girl who had once dreamt of a future beside the Fire Prince. And that girl would burn the world to keep him breathing.

Vera would keep her promise to their mother. She would not lay a hand on Hagan, and she would try, truly try, to protect him. But if someone else were to hand him over to death…

If Dawn gave the enemy the key to his undoing…

Hagan could be stopped. He could be *replaced.*

And once the dust had settled, once the fire had burnt itself out, Vera would rise from the ashes and take what was left.

'Someone has to do things properly,' she whispered, disappearing through the doorway and leaving her sister alone in the room where the man Dawn loved had once loved another.

Chapter Fourteen

House of Shadows
Kingdom of Darkness

My mother has sent me on a quest to the land of shadows, and I'm beyond excited. I know Hades comes from there, a kingdom I've never visited before. He's been so distant lately... I hope my arrival will surprise him, perhaps even delight him. To see me again.

I want to see him. I'll be visiting the wyverian castle. I know the king has three sons, and I've heard all sorts of tales about them. But I don't mind if they're unkind. I can't wait to be there, to see Hades again.

Tabitha Wysteria

Kai pressed a gentle kiss to his mother's brow, letting silence do what words never could. It was the kind of hush only grief could summon. Thick, solemn, and shared between two souls who carried the same ache in different hearts.

'I shall bring you their heads,' he vowed softly.

Queen Senka had once been radiant, a wyverian queen of unshakable will and quiet might. But the death of her firstborn had withered her. She was no longer the bloom she had once been, but a dried rose left too long in shadow, every petal curled and fallen away.

Kai had not only lost Haven. He had, in a way, lost his mother too.

And Mal... he still didn't know. Not truly. He hadn't pried the truth from Ash. There had been no point. The Fire Prince had offered a clipped recount of what had befallen him after the blade struck, but Kai had sensed the hollowness beneath every word. He'd said much, and explained nothing at all.

Leaving the castle behind, Kai whistled low beneath his breath. A summons.

A heartbeat later, Nisha appeared in the misty sky, a dark winged blur that grew larger with every beat of her wings. Daku trailed behind her like a shadow too afraid to part. They, too, had suffered loss.

Then came Ayaru—Haven's great wyvern—tearing through the grey heavens, her arrival shaking the ground beneath Kai's feet. Her cry, raw and thunderous, was a song of sorrow. Kai stood frozen as the three wyverns met, their grief crashing over him like a tide, draping his shoulders in sadness heavy as armour.

'Ayaru,' he greeted, placing a reverent hand to the side of her flank. The mighty creature bowed her head, her azure eyes dull with mourning. Kai ran his palm over her hide, barely holding back the tears. 'I miss her too. But we will have justice. I swear it.'

Ayaru's stare sharpened, a flicker of fire rekindled in her soul. The wyverns answered in unison with a chorus of roars, their voices echoing off the cliffs like a war-cry. For the first time in days, Kai allowed himself to smile.

Footsteps behind stirred the air, and he turned to see Ash standing beneath the arch of the keep. It was still disorienting to see the once-gilded prince swathed in obsidian. Gone was the golden regalia of the Fire Court. Now he wore the black steel of a wyverian commander. And somehow, it suited him more. The dark plate made his golden hair gleam like molten sunlight, and his horns shone like relics of a dying god.

Honey-gold eyes met Kai's for the briefest second, before shifting to the wyverns. Without a trace of hesitation, Ash strode towards them.

'Wait—' Kai started, instinct tightening in his chest. Wyverns were distrustful, wild. Ash shouldn't...

But by the time the warning formed, Ash was already among them.

Kai's eyes widened, lips parting in disbelief.

Ash raised a hand to Ayaru first. Then Nisha. Then Daku. One by one, the wyverns bowed their heads and greeted him. Not with suspicion, but familiarity. As if they'd known him for years. As if he were one of their own.

Kai took a step back, something cold winding around his spine. He wanted to tell himself it was Mal's scent that lingered on Ash's skin, nothing more. That it was proximity and memory, not something else. But he knew better.

What are you? The thought coiled in his mind, sharp as a blade.

Ash turned to face him then, and the corner of his mouth curled, just slightly. A knowing sneer.

'Shall we?' Ash asked, his voice calm, unreadable as ever. 'Your army awaits, does it not?'

Kai stepped forward, spine straight, shoulders squared. He would not cower before Ash Acheron. Not now, not ever.

'How do you know that?' Kai asked, his voice clipped.

Ash only shrugged, offering no answers, no explanations. He never did. Instead, he moved with graceful ease towards Daku, who lowered his great head to allow the drakonian to mount. Kai masked the jolt of surprise that coiled in his chest, though his heart beat a little faster at the sight. It shouldn't have looked so natural, Ash astride a wyvern, as if he belonged there.

'Is your father not joining us?' Ash asked, voice light, but the words struck.

Kai's fingers twitched. He wanted to lash out, to demand why Ash insisted on asking questions when he already seemed to know the answers. But instead, he bit down on the frustration, sealing his lips. He could not afford to let the bitterness slip, not when looking at the drakonian prince already pained him more than he cared to admit.

'You're angry with me,' Ash said from where he sat atop Daku, his voice drifting like smoke through the chilled air.

Kai said nothing, busying himself with adjusting his grip on Nisha, pretending not to have heard.

'I remind you of her.'

'Shut up.'

'No,' Ash went on quietly, almost thoughtfully. 'That isn't it. You're angry b-because I didn't sa-save her. She should ha-have lived... and I should ha-have died.'

Kai clenched his jaw so tightly it ached. 'No. That would have killed Mal.'

Ash's gaze turned inward, lost in some imagined version of the past. 'But deep down,' he said, voice like cracked glass, 'deep down, even though you know it would ha-have destroyed Mal... You still wish it had be-been me.'

Kai didn't answer. He couldn't. Instead, he gave Nisha a swift pat, the silent signal to take flight. Her powerful wings unfurled, slicing through the air with ease as they lifted into the grey sky. But even as they rose, he could feel Ash's golden eyes boring into his back, those eyes that had seen too much and still remained unreadable.

Kai tried to shove the images away of blood-soaked halls, the silent stillness of the drakonian castle, Alina's lifeless form lying within it. His sister too, gone. He had failed them both.

Had not protected them when it mattered most.

How could the world still turn? How could the wind still whisper through the trees or the moon rise with such indifferent grace when Alina and Haven no longer breathed? It was wrong. The world should have halted in mourning.

A white-hot rage bloomed in his chest, raw and consuming. He would not rest until the rot had been carved from the kingdoms. Until Hagan's head lay at his feet, severed by Kai's own blades.

The wyverns descended atop a hillcrest, wings kicking up the dust as they landed. Below them, stretched out across the valley like a sea of shadows, lay the wyverian army. At the sound of the great beasts' arrival, soldiers turned their faces upwards. The nearest bowed low, their heads dropping in reverence.

Beside him, Ash drew in a breath sharp with awe.

'How many?' he asked, his voice laced with wonder.

Kai smirked. 'Thousands.'

Beneath the hilltop, a sprawling camp had been erected. An ephemeral city of tents and fires, flickering against the encroaching dusk. In a matter of days, they would march, though more still were arriving with each passing hour. Not only soldiers, but citizens, ordinary folk with vengeance in their hearts and blades in their hands, answering the call to resist the witches. For in the Kingdom of Darkness, all were trained to fight from youth, a realm carved from stone and steel, forged in fire and resilience. A kingdom of warriors.

King Ozul had ridden north, summoning more of their kin to the cause.

'The women,' Ash said, noting the many wyverian females clad in midnight armour, sharpening blades, raising tents, their movements fluid and purposeful.

Kai's smile was proud, unwavering. 'You're not on drakonian soil any longer. Here, everyone fights.' He dismounted Nisha, giving the wyvern a fond pat before gesturing for Ash to follow. 'Come. There are some wyverians I want you to meet. We move as soon as the rest of my army arrives.'

Ash fell into step beside him, his golden gaze drinking in the sheer scale of the camp. Wyverians of all ages moved with silent purpose, even youths barely fourteen bore the hardened expressions of those who had already tasted loss. No fear darkened their eyes, only fierce resolve. They were out for blood, for vengeance. For Haven, their fallen princess, their would-be queen.

'I know you told the king, but—'

'Kage is safe,' Ash interrupted softly. 'He's with Bryn Wynter.'

Kai gave a nod, then led him towards a larger tent, its flaps stirred by the evening breeze. Three figures emerged from within.

The first was a mountain of a man, broad as an ox with arms like tree trunks. Ash had clearly never seen a wyverian of such stature, which made Kai want to snort.

'This is Cronan,' Kai said.

The towering wyverian grunted, offering no more than a curt nod. Kai moved on to the next, a slender man with wiry limbs and a deceptively delicate frame. Kai, however, knew better than to underestimate *any* wyverian.

'Keir,' Ash said before Kai could make the introduction.

At once, the trio stiffened, the air taut with surprise. Ash's attention turned to the final figure, the youngest of the three. A young woman, yes, but unmistakably the most dangerous. Kai had sensed it the day he had met her, just by the way she stood, the way her eyes watched everything and gave nothing away.

'And you are Adriana.'

The three stepped forward, poised as if ready to strike. Kai swiftly raised a hand, halting them.

'Don't do that again,' he muttered, clearly annoyed. 'You'll scare my entire camp.'

Ash simply shrugged, the ghost of a grin tugging at his lips. 'Do they frighten s-so easily?'

Adriana stepped forward, twirling a strand of inky black hair round her finger. The gesture stole the breath from Kai's lungs, so like Mal's. It struck him squarely in the chest, the ache of her absence crashing down in waves.

'Yes, Kai... I thought this was the most feared army in all eight kingdoms,' she teased, poking him squarely in the chest.

'Maybe it's Kai who's pissing himself,' Keir added with a laugh.

Kai cast a glare towards Ash. 'See what you've done?' He rolled his eyes. 'I trained with them in our youth. We were in the same unit.'

'Now *we* serve *him*,' Keir said mockingly. But Kai saw the truth in their eyes—loyalty, respect, unwavering trust. They'd follow him into the mouth of death without hesitation.

Kai snorted. 'I don't see you complaining when you're given the best of everything.'

Keir raised his brows. 'Best of everything? You mean cleaning your piss pot? Adriana, is that one of your great privileges?'

'I've never done that.'

'Wait, what?' Keir's expression morphed into comical disbelief. 'He's asked me to do it at least a dozen—' But comprehension dawned, and with a feral cry, he launched himself at Kai's back, trying to throttle him.

Adriana doubled over with laughter. Even Cronan rumbled with amusement.

Once the chaos settled, the group made their way inside the tent. Before following the others inside, Kai turned to Ash, his expression shifting to something softer, quieter.

'You claim to see everything—the past, the future. I'll never ask you anything again, Ash. But tell me this… do we win?'

Ash remained still, his gaze drifting to the interior of the tent. The flaps fluttered in the breeze, shadows cast by the flickering torches dancing like ghosts on the walls. The chill in the air clung to his skin. Though draped in a thick jacket gifted at the castle, Kai knew the cold was probably seeping through the seams of his black wyverian armour. Drakonians were not made for this kind of wind, this persistent northern bite.

His silence spoke volumes.

Kai's jaw tensed. 'Fine,' he said, eyes hardening. 'Then just… tell me they'll be safe. I can't lose anyone else.'

Ash looked at him then, really looked. 'Loss,' he murmured, 'is the cost of living.'

Inside the tent, the trio had already taken their places around the table. Cronan sat unmoving, while Keir and Adriana bickered light-heartedly as they arranged maps and notes.

Kai's fists clenched. 'I don't want any more of it.'

Ash stepped closer, his words soft but unyielding. 'We all die in the end, Kai. It's just a matter of *when*.'

Chapter Fifteen

House of Snow
Kingdom of Ice

We so often forget that just because a group is labelled good or evil, it doesn't mean every individual within it is the same. There is darkness in the good, and goodness in the bad.

Tabitha Wysteria

Bryn Wynter could no longer recall which day it was when Kage Blackburn finally left the door ajar. But each evening, he would sit outside it with a bowl of stew or a hunk of bread in hand, sharing his supper beside the silent threshold. He never questioned what the wyverian did with the rest of his days, never asked how he spent the long hours between dusk and dawn. Some silences were sacred.

In those quiet twilight moments, Bryn would talk, usually recounting tales from his youth, most involving Wren and the mischief she had dragged him into time and again. Occasionally, his younger sisters joined him, curling against the cold stone walls with wide eyes and eager hearts, not so much for companionship, Bryn suspected, but because they loved a good story and wanted to memorise them for their own retelling later. He allowed them their chatter, watched as they filled the corridor with their laughter and mischief, and often wondered if Kage was silently cursing them on the other side of the door. But the prince never said a word. The door remained always slightly open.

As Bryn had predicted, his sisters soon grew bored and stopped coming after two days of storytime. Yet Eirwen had appeared, drawn by curiosity to see what the quiet fuss had been about. He was slight and wiry, the kind of fragile that made older brothers worry. Eirwen had lost his twin sister on the very night they were born, during the choosing ceremony, left outside beneath the stars, as was tradition, awaiting a wolf to claim them. Only one had been chosen. The other had not survived. And those left behind often carried the shadow of their twin's absence in their bones.

'Why is he hiding?' Eirwen asked, climbing into Bryn's lap to avoid the chill of the floor.

'He's not hiding,' Bryn replied, his voice hushed, careful not to disturb the silence beyond the door. 'He's mourning.'

'What's that mean?'

'It means he's sad. His sista died.'

Eirwen's pale blue eyes rounded, recognising the shape of that sorrow. 'But why's he in there?'

Bryn shrugged slightly. 'Some folk need to be alone to feel their grief.'

The boy glanced towards the narrow crack in the door, his gaze filled with quiet intrigue. They sat in a companionable hush after that, listening to the low crackling of a nearby hearth.

Eirwen's hair brushed his shoulders, unruly and in need of a trim. Yet he refused the blade every time, determined to let it grow until his thirteenth birthday, when boys were declared men and allowed to wear their braids. Braids were a mark of pride among wolverians: the longer and more intricate, the fiercer the man. Their father once spent two entire days having his hair woven with silver threads and carved wooden beads for the blót—the sacrificial rites to appease the gods and beg for a year free from famine and plague. Yet the gods had remained silent. Each passing year, the sacrifices grew bloodier, more desperate, but the hunger never left.

'Me sista died too,' Eirwen said suddenly, directing his voice to the crack in the door. His words yanked Bryn from his thoughts. 'That's why me name is Eirwen. It was meant for her. If ya stay in there, da sadness won't go, ya know. Mine went away becas I had me brotha and sistas. It's a bit like being lonely, isn't it? Ya feel all alone without her. But staying in there won't help. Ya will just be lonelier. We will help ya. We can be yer family if ya want. We will make ya feel just a bit less lonely, won't we, Bryn?' He turned and looked up at the wolverian prince.

Bryn smiled softly, brushing a strand of hair from the boy's face.

'Yes,' he said gently. 'Yes, we will.'

For a moment, the door remained still, unmoving, as if weighed down by years of grief. But then, without warning, the door creaked wider.

And Kage Blackburn stepped out.

...

Bryn did his utmost not to glance at Kage Blackburn every few heartbeats as they strode into the heart of the castle. The great hall opened up before them, vast yet modest, its grey stone walls softened by time and the warmth of memory. A long wooden table stretched across the room like the spine of the keep, its surface scarred by decades of use, the chairs draped in furs to ward off the eternal chill. At its centre roared a chimney fire, its flame a sentinel of comfort. In times of hardship, they had all slept here together, huddled close for warmth, whispering prayers to silent gods.

Kage held his head high, every inch the wyverian prince. Yet those dark, infernal eyes moved languidly across the hall, drifting over every surface with a predator's ease. His expression was unreadable, carved from marble and shadows, betraying no ounce of thought or feeling. Bryn couldn't help but wonder what the prince made of their humble abode—stone-grey walls and hand-carved furniture, lovingly built or bartered for from nearby villages. They possessed little, but gave what they could.

They settled near the hearth, where the heat kissed their skin and the firelight danced across their faces. Though Kage had spent countless days locked away in a cramped room with little sustenance, he bore no signs of frailty. Instead, he resembled someone roused from a sleep far too deep, eyes rimmed red, shadows beneath them like bruises of dreams too heavy to forget. His long, slender fingers drummed rhythmically against the table, filling the silence as they waited for one of the servants to bring something to drink.

Kage brought the tankard to his nose the moment it was set before him. He inhaled slowly. 'Icebroth, is it?'

Bryn downed his own with eager familiarity, the cold liquid searing a path down his throat.

'And where might your father be? King Fannar?' Kage asked, his voice as smooth and neutral as ever, never shifting tone.

'He's travelling between da nearby villages,' Bryn replied, wiping his mouth with the back of his hand.

'And you are...?'

'Here.'

'Tending to your siblings,' Kage observed. His tone did not waver, nor did he mock, but Bryn heard the quiet implication. Bryn the keeper. The minder.

'Looking after ya, more like,' he shot back coolly.

Kage stilled, the tankard halfway to his lips. For a breath, he didn't move. Then he took a cautious sip, considered the taste, and offered the faintest nod of approval. 'Yes, well... I've been unwell.' His gaze roamed the hall as if seeking an escape. 'Where is Wren?'

'Gone.'

Something shifted behind Kage's dark eyes. A ripple of fear, chased by something far less certain. He surged to his feet, nearly toppling the chair behind him. 'Gone? Gone where?'

Bryn merely shrugged, casual in the face of Kage's building storm.

'You mean to tell me you've no idea...?' Kage's hands tightened into fists at his sides.

'Off doing Wren things,' Bryn murmured, unbothered.

'Off where, exactly?'

'Why do ya care to know?'

Before Kage could formulate a reply, the great doors burst open, slamming against the stone walls with a thunderous crack. A figure rushed in, breathless and coated in frost. Bryn recognised him immediately. Bernard, one of the carpenters from the village near the northern wood. The lad trembled beneath his heavy furs, snow clinging to his hair like ash.

He rushed to the fire's embrace, but his wide, frightened eyes found Bryn, and then darted to Kage, standing tall and unmoving like some shadow-clad sentinel.

'What is it, Bernard?' Bryn asked, rising from his chair.

'Warlock!' the man cried, voice sharp with terror. 'They've found one, sire!'

Bryn and Kage exchanged a glance laced with unease before swiftly following Bernard out of the castle, pausing only to shrug on heavy fur cloaks. The moment they stepped beyond the stone threshold, a vicious gust of icy wind struck them. Kage halted, his jaw tightening against the sudden bite of cold.

'Takes a while,' Bryn said, giving him a nudge. 'But truth be told, ya never truly get used to it.'

'Delightful,' Kage muttered through gritted teeth, plumes of breath curling into the wintry air.

They pressed on. The castle, perched on a hill and surrounded by naught but snow-drowned woodland, loomed behind them. The village lay not far beyond, though the snowdrifts made the journey arduous. Even for a seasoned warrior, Kage was no match for the depth of the frost. He moved with effort, his usual stealth lost to the thick, clinging snow.

By the time they arrived at the heart of the village, a murmuring crowd had gathered in the central square.

A boy, barely more than a youth, was restrained by two burly men. His blue eyes were wild with panic, his screams cutting through the hush of snowfall. Beside him, a girl—likely his sister—argued heatedly with a man Bryn loathed with every fibre of his being.

Commander Caldwell. The king's most loyal hound. A wolverian of rigid beliefs, sharp edges, and an unrelenting thirst for punishment. Where Bryn had always admired his people for placing others before themselves, Caldwell was the rare exception, a man who thought of no one but his own narrow ideals.

The villagers parted as Bryn stepped forward, bowing their heads in deference, until their eyes caught sight of the figure at his side.

Gasps rippled through the square like a wave.

Kage Blackburn.

Murmurs broke out, soft and fearful, and hands were quickly raised to trace ancient sigils of protection in the air. Prayers slipped past trembling lips.

A wyverian, here among them? Surely it meant something. Surely it was a sign.

An omen.

And if the boy truly was a warlock... then the gods had spoken.

Kage rolled his eyes.

'I'm not a warlock, sire!' the boy shrieked, struggling against the hands that held him, desperately trying to reach Bryn.

'Why brand him as such?' Bryn asked, voice calm but sharp. 'Haven't ya known this lad all yer lives?'

'They've been glamouring themselves, sire,' one of the men restraining the boy said, a tremor in his tone. 'King Fannar's been travelling da villages, warning us. They killed da Acherons in their own keep. They've claimed drakonian lands. What's to stop them from doing da same to us?' The crowd murmured their agreement, fear woven into every syllable.

'What ya say may well be true,' Bryn replied with a slow nod. 'But none of that proves this boy is one of them.' He tipped his chin towards the trembling youth. 'What makes ya so certain?'

'He was muttering strange words,' Caldwell interjected smoothly, stepping forward like a shadow with too much confidence. 'And his eyes flashed purple.'

Gasps erupted from the villagers. Prayers began to spill from mouths, frantic and garbled, like charms tossed against the wind.

'And ya saw this with yer own eyes, did ya, Caldwell?' Bryn

asked, gaze steady. He noticed the slight twitch of Caldwell's mouth, the way the commander resisted the urge to sneer. He didn't like being questioned, especially not in front of his flock.

'Are ya calling me a liar, Bryn Wynter?' Caldwell hissed, his icy eyes narrowing like a wolf ready to strike.

The air grew heavy. Bryn knew all too well how the village hung on the commander's every word. His proclamations were law. His suspicions, prophecy. Only King Fannar held the power to overrule him outright, and even then, not without effort.

Though Bryn was crown prince, he did not yet wear the mantle of rule. And Caldwell, Caldwell commanded the soldiers, the squares, and the people's fear.

Bryn had warned his father. Had whispered the truth of what Caldwell was. But the man was their finest blade. A necessary evil. And soldiers, like wolves, followed the scent of power.

Bryn stepped forward, his boots crunching softly in the snow, and as expected, Kage shadowed him like a second thought given form. A few voices rose from the gathered crowd, warning their prince to keep his distance, lest the accused boy unleash some dark incantation. Bryn doubted the lad could manage much, not with two burly men holding him firm.

'If he truly were a warlock,' Bryn mused aloud, letting the weight of his words settle over the onlookers, 'would he not have already overpowered us?' He turned to glance at Kage, curious for the wyverian's insight. Odd, how only hours ago this man had been little more than a ghost locked away behind a door. Now he stood beside Bryn like a harbinger of fate, real and quietly imposing.

'Perhaps they've orders,' Caldwell interjected, his voice raised to carry across the square like a war drum. 'Orders to die if captured. To remain concealed at all costs.'

'Burn him!' someone bellowed from within the crowd, a single voice sharp with fear. And like wildfire, the cry spread. Unease at first, then agreement swelling until those hesitant were drowned beneath the louder shouts. 'Da King has ordered a witch hunt!'

'No!' the girl rushed forward, her voice frayed with desperation. But she was quickly seized by the guards and dragged back, her cries muffled by the clamour.

'We could... lock him away, for now,' Bryn offered, though even as he spoke, the words tasted hollow. Keeping a warlock in the castle would do little to guarantee safety, if indeed the boy was one.

'Burn him!' they roared, louder now, a tide of rage and terror impossible to silence.

Bryn turned his attention to the accused. The boy's face was streaked with tears, his pleas for mercy lost beneath the cacophony. King Fannar had made the command clear: report all suspicions. Detain the accused. But the line between suspicion and proof was perilously thin.

And Caldwell...well, Caldwell had already decided the boy's fate. Perhaps the crowd had too.

'Don't do it,' Kage said, close enough for their arms to almost brush. His voice was low, sharp as a blade sheathed in silk. 'No matter what he turns out to be, his death will be the spark they need for a massacre.'

'Me people aren't like that,' Bryn replied, jaw tight with conviction.

'Frightened people are,' Kage said simply, his gaze fixed ahead.

Bryn hesitated, caught in a snare of doubt. 'What do I do?'

'Let him go,' came Kage's answer, resolute and cold. His eyes shifted to Caldwell, glinting like flint against steel. 'And stop *him*.'

'But if he *is* a warlock...'

'It changes nothing.'

Bryn's breath misted before him as he shook his head. 'He could hurt someone. Kill one of ours. Me father... We need to be certain there are no witches in our land.'

'If you kill him without proof,' Kage's tone darkened, a quiet thunder curling in his words, 'you'll open the gates to slaughter.'

Already, villagers were gathering wood, the makings of a pyre growing at the centre of the square. Bryn watched them, his heart a pendulum swinging between fear and reason. He couldn't allow them to burn the boy, not without proof.

Drawing a long, slender blade from his belt, one typically used to skin rodents with surgical precision, he stepped forward. Caldwell moved to block his path.

'Step aside,' Bryn commanded. And to the surprise of all, the commander obeyed, parting like a reluctant shadow to let the prince through.

Bryn approached the trembling boy, the tip of his knife pressed gently to the lad's throat.

'Transform,' he said, voice calm but firm. 'If yer a warlock, drop da glamour. If not...'

'Ya'll cut me throat?' the boy snapped, defiance flashing behind tear-streaked cheeks. Bryn faltered. There was something in the lad's eyes. Not fear, not malice, but fury. Raw and betrayed. 'I've lived here all me life. And now ya turn yer backs on me! I've done nothing wrong. I'm not a warlock.' He spat at Bryn's feet. The crowd hissed, anger blooming anew like frostfire. 'Go on, then. Burn me, Prince Bryn Wynter. Let me soul haunt ya until da day ya die.'

'He's cursed him!' Caldwell roared, arms raised as if to summon the gods themselves.

'No, he hasn't—' Bryn began, only to be wrenched backwards, guards surrounding him like a living shield.

'Protect da prince!' Caldwell bellowed, spit spraying from his mouth like venom.

But as Bryn met the commander's eyes, he found no fear there, only a glimmer of amusement, cruel and satisfied.

The chants rose like a storm gathering strength—warlock, warlock, warlock—echoing across the square as the wolverians gave voice to their fear. The two guards dragged the boy across the snow-dusted cobbles to the crude stake hastily erected at the square's centre. Ropes coiled around him, binding him tight to the wooden post, the knots pulled with grim finality. All that remained was the order.

Caldwell stood poised to deliver it.

Bryn stood motionless, rooted to the earth, a statue carved from conflict. Anger crackled beneath his skin like lightning trapped in bone, but fear wound tightly around his ribs. The people were baying for blood, hungry for justice, or perhaps just for something to blame. But this... this felt wrong. The air was thick with uncertainty, and still they wished to set flame to it.

Do what is right for da people. His father's words haunted him like a ghost at his shoulder. A prince now, and a king in the making. His duty was to shield the pack, to uphold the safety of the many. Yet this boy, bound and weeping at the stake, was his people too. And to forsake him for fear alone... was that truly what it meant to lead?

Caldwell's voice shattered the silence like a blade.

'Burn him.'

Bryn inhaled sharply as the world tilted, the weight of his inaction pressing against his chest. Around him, the cries swelled in triumph.

'And bring me his sista!' Caldwell snapped, venom lacing his tone. 'She'll confess before da night is out.' With a sharp gesture, he turned and strode away, self-satisfaction carved across his face. Behind him, the girl was dragged screaming through the snow, her voice tearing through the air. Raw, desperate, and utterly powerless.

Bryn could feel Kage's stare burning into him. Dark eyes ablaze with fury, sharp as daggers for the silence he had allowed. The jubilant cries had faded, replaced by a dreadful stillness, as though death itself had arrived to bear witness to the horror unfolding in the square. One by one, heads turned to the pyre, faces bathed in flickering amber as the flames rose higher, reflecting fire in once-blue eyes.

Bryn surged forward, shoving wolverians aside with frantic desperation, Kage's voice trailing behind him, calling his name. He reached the base of the stake just as the fire roared to life, devouring the boy who thrashed and screamed in mortal agony.

'Water! We need water!' Bryn shouted, spinning round to plead for help.

But no one moved.

The crowd had stilled, spellbound by the spectacle, as though some collective trance held them captive. Bryn turned back slowly, lifting his gaze to the pyre, and the broken figure writhing within it.

'What have I done...' The words slipped from his lips in a haunted whisper, just as Kage arrived silently at his side.

Together, prince and warrior stood beneath a night sky that seemed to mourn with them, watching as the boy was consumed by flame. His screams echoed long after his voice had gone, a sorrowful chorus that would never quite leave the stones beneath their feet.

Even after the crowd dispersed, after the last ember had faded and the scent of burning flesh was replaced by cold ash,

Bryn remained. Knees buckling, he sank to the ground where the boy had stood.

He wept not as a prince, nor as a wolverian, but as a soul unmoored by guilt.

'What have I done,' he whispered, again and again, long into the unforgiving night.

Chapter Sixteen

The Underworld

I know Hades had something to do with this damned war. I know, somehow, he turned the lands against one another. He made this happen. He made them hate us. Now Hadrian and I must fight for our lives. He'll never admit it. But I feel it, deep in my bones.

Tabitha Wysteria

No matter how fiercely Mal fought to vanish, to melt into shadows and slip through cracks, she always ended up back where she'd begun. Either standing at the banks of that cursed river or seated, once again, in the grand hall of the castle, Thanatos laughing at her torment like a cat toying with a bird. After days of futile attempts to escape, she surrendered to the inevitable.

'I will not marry you,' she said through clenched teeth, striving to keep the revulsion from her voice as she found herself, once more, imprisoned in familiar stone and shadow.

Thanatos still wore Ash's face, a cruel mimicry that turned her heart inside out. That same bone structure, that same cruelly beautiful mouth. Only the hair betrayed the lie, no longer gold as firelight but pale as snowfall. And then, the eyes. The moment those cold, endless voids met hers, it was as though icewater sluiced down her spine.

'Hades has agreed you need not wed me… *yet.*'

Her jaw tightened at that final word, heavy with suggestion. Still, she bit back her fury and chose to bide her time. She needed to find the way back, back to mortal lands. Back to Ash.

Makaria had caught her crouched by the river, hidden beneath the veil of the underworld's gloom, and sent her laughing back into Thanatos' clutches. Mal had become a plaything between Makaria and Zagreus, their favourite entertainment during the endless, grey hours.

'How do I return to Hades?' she asked.

'You could stay here,' Thanatos replied, voice like velvet laced with poison.

Her frown deepened. 'Why?'

'Because Hades wishes for you to be trained, to master the divine gifts running through your veins. And I am the finest teacher he could offer.' He smiled, a smile as elegant as it was engineered, sculpted solely for her. 'Besides, you know this castle. And there are many rooms in which you might find comfort… or distraction.'

Mal said nothing. She refused to give him the pleasure of her response. After a pause, he sighed, as though disappointed by her silence. 'Makaria will visit later to keep you company. The others will join us tonight for a feast.'

A feast. In the Underworld. Mal bit her tongue, the question burning in her throat. Why did the dead dine? Instead, she rose and gestured to the black gown clinging to her like a shroud. 'I wish to change out of *this*. I have been made to wear the same dress, day after day,' Mal muttered, her voice laced with disgust. She had washed herself in the river's icy waters, only to be forced back into the same soiled garment, its fabric stiff with filth and memory.

Thanatos let his eyes drift over her with an infuriating

slowness, the corners of his mouth twisting into a smirk.

'Well,' he said, voice like silk drawn across a blade, 'we thought perhaps you'd change your mind about the marriage... the longer you wore the gown.'

Mal bared her teeth, the urge to rake her nails across that mocking face near unbearable.

'You will find more comfortable clothes in your chamber.'

Her heart faltered at the thought of her room. Her real room. Could it be?

'One last thing, Melinoe,' Thanatos called as she turned to leave.

'What now?' she snapped, her patience fraying thin. 'And my name is Mal. Not Melinoe.'

Thanatos waved his hand, as if he could wave away her frustration. 'Time moves... differently, down here.'

She froze. 'What does that mean?'

But he only turned his face away, his grin stretching, widening, blooming like a bruise. She had grown weary of their games, truths cloaked in mystery, every secret veiled behind another cryptic riddle.

Without another word, she fled through the corridors of the castle she had once called home. The same halls, the same arched doorways. Her siblings' rooms passed in a blur. And then, hers.

It was exactly as she had left it. Nothing out of place, not a curtain drawn. It should have unsettled her, sent a chill rippling across her skin. But instead, she felt something entirely different.

A quiet warmth. A memory. A piece of her past she hadn't yet lost. And for the first time in days, Mal let herself breathe.

She slipped into a soft grey cotton gown, the fabric rough yet blessedly clean against her skin. With a flick of her wrist, she hurled the wedding dress out the window, watching it flutter like a dying bird before vanishing from sight. It had been a beautiful creation. Lavish, elegant, stitched with threads that whispered promises of power and union, but now it stood only as a symbol of what Hades had tried to force upon her. She never wanted to look at it again.

What unsettled her most was not the proposal, but how swiftly Hades had retreated from it. His abrupt change of course spoke not of mercy, but of machinations still buried in shadow. She could not let her guard drop. The Underworld, for all its silence and gloom, pulsed with unseen threats. She needed to escape.

A knock at the door startled her. For a moment, she was so surprised by the courtesy of it, she thought she'd imagined it.

'I'm naked,' she hissed. 'Go away.'

The door creaked open regardless, and in swept Makaria, a cascade of giggles following in her wake. 'Do you really think that would stop Thanatos?'

Mal's lips curled into a snarl. 'Did you know?'

'About what?' Makaria asked airily, feigning fascination with the wardrobe as though the question had not landed sharp as a blade.

'Don't play the fool with me.'

Makaria sighed, spinning around with a look that belied something older and more haunted than her youthful frame suggested. 'Of course I knew. But I thought you'd be pleased, sister. Thanatos is…well, rather striking.'

'I'm already married.'

Makaria's nose wrinkled in distaste. 'To a drakonian. A *living* drakonian. We're gods, Melinoe. We don't… consort with their kind.'

'I'm not one of you.'

Makaria laughed, a sound both sweet and sinister. 'Perhaps not yet. But give it time.'

Mal watched her warily as the strange girl stepped closer, reaching out to toy with a loose strand of Mal's hair. 'I do love your hair. May I brush it?'

The question was so odd it disarmed her. Still, she gave a small nod. Makaria fetched a comb and began to drag it gently through the midnight tangles, and for a fleeting moment, Mal allowed herself to be still. The gesture reminded her of Vera, those brief days when the witch, disguised as a maid, would tend to her hair with surprising care. She wondered where Vera was now. Where any of them were.

'Have you come to hunt me down again?' she asked softly.

Makaria's smile grew. 'Perhaps,' she said, the word curling like smoke. 'Zagreus and I do so love our little games. Though next time, do try to make it more difficult. You were far too easy to kill last time.'

'Why do you do it?' Mal asked, her voice a quiet thread in the silence. 'Chase me. Kill me.'

Makaria hummed a lilting melody beneath her breath, a tune as old as time and twice as eerie. The comb glided through Mal's hair in slow, deliberate strokes. For a moment, there was no answer, only the whisper of bristles against dark strands. Then, through the tarnished mirror, Makaria's eyes met Mal's.

'Because, for a hundred years, Zagreus and I were trapped here in the Underworld with nothing but shadows and silence for company. Killing each other... it became a game. The only one we had.'

Mal's body stiffened, her shoulders drawn tight. 'But you're not trapped anymore, Makaria. I broke the curse. You're free now. You could *leave*. So why don't you?'

'I've always wanted a sister,' Makaria said, neatly dodging

Mal's question. Her movements were surprisingly delicate as she combed through the dark tangles, each stroke measured, gentle, even reverent. Mal hadn't believed Makaria capable of tenderness, not after witnessing the many cruel, imaginative ways she had killed her during their twisted game of cat and mouse.

'Father used to speak of you often,' she continued. 'But I could only shut my eyes and imagine. The curse kept us apart.'

'I didn't even know you existed,' Mal replied, her voice low.

'I heard you,' Makaria whispered, her voice shrinking into something smaller, fragile. 'When you prayed to the gods. I heard you through the cracks in the walls. I tried to answer... but you couldn't hear me.'

Makaria's breath ghosted close, a warmth against Mal's skin. 'Thanatos listened too, you know. He would sit and listen to your prayers. He made sure your room here looked exactly like the one above, in the mortal realm.'

'Why would he do that?' Mal asked.

'Because he adores you.'

Mal stiffened. 'He doesn't know me, Makaria. And neither do you.'

'But we do,' Makaria insisted. 'We've heard you your whole life. We've always been there. You just didn't know it.'

Mal turned slightly to look at this strange girl meant to be her sister. There was no mischief in Makaria's expression, no playfulness. Just a solemn truth, laid bare. Mal's instinct was to lash out, to strike at the soft core of that sincerity and twist it with spite. But Makaria wasn't to blame. Not for any of it.

'I had a sister, up there,' Mal said, her gaze lifting to the ceiling as though she could pierce through stone and shadow and glimpse the sky beyond. Haven's name caught in her throat. Her sister, fierce as winter's breath, unyielding as steel. Wherever she had ended up, Mal believed with all her being that she was surviving. Thriving. 'She was killed.'

'I know,' Makaria whispered. 'You used to pray for her. For all your siblings. I used to wonder if... if you might ever pray for us.' She let out a wistful sigh. 'Hopefully, Haven has found her way into the Asphodel Meadows.'

Mal's heart clenched. She had studied the realms of the dead with Kage—the tortured fires of Tartarus, the broken souls of the Fields of Mourning, the grey peace of the Meadows. She had memorised their myths, their meanings. But her sister was no ordinary soul.

'My sister is in Elysium,' she said softly, a small smile brushing her lips.

Makaria's eyes widened. 'Only the purest of souls are welcomed there.'

'I know,' Mal said again, her voice tinged with something bittersweet and proud.

Makaria nodded, though it was clear she had more to say. Mal didn't ask. She knew better than to speak hope aloud in a place like this. The dead could not return. Not even gods could undo that law. But one day, she would find her way to Haven's side. To her brothers. To peace.

Until then, she would do whatever it took to keep those still living from falling into the dark.

Even if it meant claiming the Underworld for her own.

...

Mal arched a brow at the silver platter set before her, the gleaming cutlery arranged with unsettling precision. The sight across the table was stranger still: Hades, god of the dead, reclined like some nobleman at leisure, sipping wine as though he hadn't a care in the world. At his left hand sat his two progeny—Makaria and Zagreus—and at his right, the ever-brooding Thanatos.

It was difficult not to look at Thanatos. The wretched spectre of a man had an infuriating habit of watching her, a crooked smirk playing on his lips as though they shared some unspeakable joke. From time to time, he would chuckle to himself for no reason at all. An eerie, hollow sound that made Mal itch to launch her goblet straight at his smug face.

'Can you read my thoughts?' she asked sharply, her fingers curling around the hilt of her knife.

'Not here,' Hades replied, slicing into a slab of meat that reeked of decay.

'And why not?'

'Different level,' Thanatos interjected smoothly, his eyes shining with warning, as if she were meant to silence herself. Naturally, she kept going.

'What part of the Underworld is this?'

Makaria let out a nervous laugh, high and strange.

'This isn't—' Thanatos began, only to pause and glance at Hades for silent permission to continue. Once granted, he spoke, voice low and measured. 'There are three levels. There is the realm of souls, ruled by Hades. Then there's this place shared by the Moirai and myself. And lastly, there is a deeper realm still. One that must never be entered.'

'Hell?' Mal asked.

Thanatos inclined his head, albeit reluctantly.

'And what makes this level so different?' she pressed.

Makaria giggled again, but Mal's sharp glare cut it short.

'Will someone kindly tell me what I'm not understanding?' she hissed, her violet gaze landing on Thanatos with scorn. He ignored her, feigning a sudden interest in his wine.

Tired of their games, Mal hurled her knife. It whistled past Thanatos' head, burying itself into the stone wall just behind him.

'That was rather rude,' he said mildly, as though she'd merely spoken out of turn at a tea party.

'I missed on purpose.'

'I certainly hope so. Terrible aim otherwise.'

Grinding her teeth, Mal pushed to her feet, hands clenched at her sides. 'Enough. Explain.'

Thanatos sighed, once more looking to Hades, who gave a faint nod of assent. 'Technically,' he began, 'the Moirai and I exist apart from the other gods. We cannot be killed nor cease to exist for we are death, after all. This place... it's a sanctuary, of sorts.'

'Safe,' Makaria added, her voice barely more than a whisper, eyes fixed on the table.

'Safe from what?' Mal demanded.

'Everything,' Thanatos said with a casual shrug. 'Thoughts cannot be read here. Souls cannot wander in uninvited. Nothing can be harmed, not truly.'

'Then why don't you live here?' she asked, eyes narrowing at Hades.

A shadow passed over the god's crimson gaze, dark and pained. His face twisted for the briefest moment, some private memory clawing to the surface. Makaria bit her lip, shrinking ever so slightly. Zagreus exhaled sharply through his nose.

'I built this place for someone,' Hades said at last, his voice like splintered glass. 'A sanctuary for her. I had intended for us to dwell here together.' He lifted his glass once more. 'Now, it serves only as a monument. A reminder of what was lost. I thought perhaps Thanatos and you might find use in it.'

Mal growled, her fury simmering just beneath her skin.

'You will remain here and learn from Thanatos,' Hades said, ignoring the way Mal's lips pulled back, revealing fangs sharp enough to tear through bone and sinew.

'For what purpose?' she hissed.

'A war stirs on the horizon,' he replied, voice calm as a graveyard breeze. 'And you, my dear, are the key to saving us all.'

Mal stilled, a tremor of uncertainty threading through her spine. 'What are you talking about?'

'The gods grow restless. They wish to wipe the slate clean— every kingdom, every soul, every memory. All will be reduced to ash so they may birth a world anew. But you... you can stop them.'

'Why me?'

'Because god against god is merely noise. Petty squabbles among immortals. But you... you are something different altogether. God-born, witch-marked, and wyverian. A trinity of power never before seen. Once you learn to wield your gifts, to master what lies dormant within you...then, perhaps, even the gods might tremble.'

Mal narrowed her eyes. 'What gods? Are there more than you?'

Hades chuckled, the sound dark and low. 'Oh, Melinoe, you've no idea. Compared to them, we are mercy incarnate.'

Her shoulders sagged as she sank lower into her chair, staring down at her hands. Just one girl. How could she possibly stand against the fury of gods? Surely Hades was twisting truth for some unknown game, playing with her mind like a bored child with a doll.

'He's not lying,' Thanatos said, his tone devoid of its usual smugness. For once, he was serious. 'If you do not become what you were made for, the kingdoms will fall. Everyone you care for will be extinguished like a snuffed flame.'

What you were made for. The words echoed inside her, heavy with consequence. She locked them away, for now.

'But why?' she whispered. 'Why would they destroy everything?'

Her eyes drifted towards Makaria, who was fidgeting in her seat, shoulders tight, hands twitching. Mal had come to know her moods well enough. She was keeping something hidden, something urgent.

'They are gods,' Hades said with a casual shrug. 'And gods are cruel.'

It was a lie. Not spoken, but stitched into the fabric of the room. Thanatos' fleeting and uneasy glance towards Hades. Makaria biting her lip, holding herself back from truth. Mal saw it all.

Let them lie. She would find the truth, piece by piece, even if she had to drag it from their mouths or the shadows themselves. Thanatos knew. Makaria too. The truth was there, coiled like a serpent, waiting. And one day, Mal would unearth it.

The real reason the gods sought to erase their world.

Chapter Seventeen

House of Wild
Kingdom of Fauna

I've asked Hades whether he's the only god who visits us. Surely he can't be. If he walks among mortals, why wouldn't the others? Yet every time I ask, his expression turns blank. He never responds.

I don't think he realises that his silence is an answer in itself.

Tabitha Wysteria

Wren and Freya had stopped at the very edge of the Forest of Endless Trees, hesitating only briefly before stepping into its shadowy embrace. After some quiet deliberation, they had ventured forward, guided by instinct more than certainty. Wren no longer knew how long they had been wandering. Hours? Days? Time inside the forest moved strangely, like it had slipped through their fingers and vanished altogether.

The forest itself was like something pulled from the pages of an ancient tale. Trees towered high above them, taller than the spires of any castle Wren had ever seen, their canopies thick enough to steal the light from the sky. Enormous flowers bloomed in every hue imaginable, so vast and soft they looked fit to cradle sleeping gods. And the creatures... gods above, the creatures. Wren had never even heard of such things.

They stumbled across a hidden lake, its surface shimmering

with the brilliance of starlight, a cascade pouring in from above with water so clear it might have held pearls. Perhaps it did. Still, Wren's thoughts swirled in a haze. She was sure she had a purpose, a reason for being here, but no matter how she tried to grasp it, the thought slipped from her like mist.

'Get in the water, Wren,' Freya said, shrugging off her heavy coats and furs. 'It'll clear your head.'

Wren narrowed her eyes. How did Freya know that? Had she been here before? But somehow, it didn't seem to matter, not when the water sparkled like liquid moonlight, calling to her.

With a sudden urgency, Wren tore off her clothes and dove beneath the surface. The warmth of the water embraced her like a memory, like her mother's arms once had. The thought was enough to steal her breath. She surfaced with a sharp gasp, and just like that, the fog in her mind lifted.

Before she could speak, a sharp crack echoed in the distance, branches breaking beneath weight. Her instincts sharpened in an instant.

'Stay here,' she told Freya as she stepped from the water, ignoring her state of undress.

She snatched up her dagger from the pile of discarded clothes and slipped into the trees, following the sound with quiet purpose. It came from behind a cluster of orange-leafed bushes. Likely some poor beast tangled in the undergrowth. Unlucky for it, but a stroke of fortune for her. They hadn't eaten in hours.

Wren licked her lips, poised to strike.

The rustling intensified. With a burst of energy, she lunged through the foliage, arm raised to deliver a swift end.

She collided with something solid. Warm. Alive.

The breath was knocked from her lungs as she landed,

tangled atop a body.

A male body.

Wren screamed.

The stranger's hand caught her wrist mid-strike, green eyes wide in shock, then wider still as he registered her lack of clothing.

'You're naked!' he shouted, his voice rising in disbelieving horror. 'Get off!'

With an indignant yelp, he shoved her off, and she hit the ground with a thud, legs splayed gracelessly, her dignity dashed alongside her breath.

'Oof!' she grunted, seething. His face loomed above hers.

'Are you completely mental?' he demanded, frowning. 'Why in nature's hand are you naked?'

'If it bothers ya so much, stop staring!' she snapped, scooping up a fistful of dirt and flinging it at him. He laughed, actually laughed, then reached to help her up.

'Don't touch me!' she barked, slapping his hands away.

At last, both on their feet, Wren looked up properly, and gasped.

'Ya... Yer a Fae.'

'*What?*'

'Fae.'

'I gathered that bit... what's a yer?'

Wren sighed, her patience fraying. 'Me name's Wren Wynter.'

'Don't you mean my?'

'My what?'

He rubbed his temples as if trying to ward off an oncoming headache. 'Never mind. You must be a wolverian.'

Wren bristled. '*Excuse me?* What's that supposed to mean?'

The stranger gave a casual shrug. 'Everyone knows

wolverians speak funny.'

Wren's vision flashed crimson. She lunged forward, ready to land a satisfying blow, but he caught her wrist again with infuriating ease. The chuckle he released was the last straw.

'Woah, easy there. You're a feisty little thing, aren't you?'

'Let go, ya stupid oaf!'

His face edged closer, amusement glinting in those infuriating green eyes, until a flicker of realisation crossed his features. His gaze dropped slowly, almost deliberately, reminding them both she was still completely and utterly bare. Wren's cheeks burnt as he glanced back up, grin stretching wide across his face. He released her so suddenly she toppled backwards with a thump.

He crouched beside her, still somehow managing to tower over her. Wren, now scowling, remained still and studied him properly for the first time.

His skin was dark, his features sharp and curious. She'd only ever seen skin so dark back in the drakonian courts, and next to her own pale wolverian complexion, the contrast was striking. His black curls were cropped short, but intricate braids pulled the longer pieces back into a loose knot. Then there were the antlers—tall, curved, unmistakably Fae.

'Do you like what you see?' he whispered, voice low with mischief.

Wren muttered a curse under her breath, shoved him out of her way, and bolted.

'Hey, wait!'

She didn't stop, pushing through the thickets with a frantic determination, convinced she was heading back towards the lake. Yet something was wrong. The orange-leaved bushes she remembered had vanished, and the forest refused to yield the lake's familiar glimmer.

She stopped. Turned. Nothing.

'Wait, hold on!' His voice rang behind her as he gave chase, but she pressed on blindly, until her legs threatened to give way beneath her.

Panting, she bent over, hands on her knees, gulping at the heavy air. He arrived just moments after, and she shot upright, scrambling to shield herself once more.

'Oh, here.' He slid a satchel from his back, rummaging through until he pulled out a long jacket woven from green-brown leaves. He offered it to her, uncertain. 'It goes through the arms...'

'I know *how* a jacket works,' she snapped, snatching it from him.

He raised both hands in mock surrender. 'Sorry. Wasn't sure if wolverians had such things.'

'We live in da north, surrounded by snow,' she grumbled. 'What do ya think we wear?'

'So... the naked thing isn't, like, traditional...?'

She was sorely tempted to throw the jacket in his smug face. Instead, she slipped it on with as much dignity as one could muster in the depths of a bewitched forest. It engulfed her completely, the hem trailing behind as though it belonged to him, which of course, it did.

'I take it thank you isn't part of the wolverian tongue either,' he muttered as Wren stomped ahead without a glance back.

'Where am I?' she asked, casting her gaze skywards. 'There was a lake here not a moment ago. Now it's vanished.'

'The forest shifts if you're not Fae,' he said, nibbling on his lower lip and lifting his brows with exaggerated wisdom. 'But lucky for you, I am.'

'Aye...' Wren tried not to grimace. She pointed the tip of her knife towards his face, her stare unflinching. 'No funny business.'

'None whatsoever. Cross my heart.' He placed a hand to his chest, his smile wide enough to rival the rising sun and twice as smug.

'What's yer name?' she asked, slipping the blade into the pocket of the oversized jacket for safekeeping.

'And why do you want to know?'

Wren huffed, thoroughly unimpressed. 'So yer happy to play hero, but won't tell me yer bloody name?'

He laughed, the sound rich and bright. 'Arden Briar,' he said, before pausing theatrically. 'Sorry, you probably didn't catch that. *Me* name is Arden Briar.'

Wren bit her tongue to keep from shouting several unpleasant things, which only made him laugh harder.

'Where are we going?' she asked.

'Back to Floridia.'

'No! Ya need to take me to da lake. I left me friend there.'

Arden's eyebrows rose. 'And why would you do something so daft?'

'Becas I heard ya rustling about in da bushes.'

'I was picking berries.' He blinked. 'Well, if she's still there, she's probably lost to the forest now. So... let's be on our way. I'm starving.'

'No, no, absolutely *not*. Listen to me, ya overgrown leaf-sniffer. Take me back to that lake right now, or I'll walk da rest meself!'

Arden tilted his head, considering her. Then he gave a casual shrug. 'All right then. Best of luck.'

He turned sharply and disappeared behind a tangle of trees, leaving Wren spluttering in disbelief. When she rushed after him, he had vanished. With a frustrated cry, Wren clutched her hair and stomped forward, determined to retrace her steps alone.

Nightfall crept in on padded feet, and still there was no sign of Freya. Refusing to lose hope, Wren gathered branches and kindling to build a fire. Perhaps the light would guide her friend through the shifting wood. Once the flames danced, and the realisation struck that she had nothing at all to eat, she pulled her knees close and hugged them tight, the night pressing in around her like a cold hand.

'Are you mad?'

Wren shrieked and spun round, only to find Arden Briar looming behind her, a scowl carved deep into his face.

'Am *I* mad?' she shouted. 'Don't sneak up on people like that, ya idiot!'

'You don't light a fire in the Forest of Endless Trees unless you fancy being someone's supper.' He strode forward and kicked earth over the fire, smothering the flame. Wren leapt up and tried to stop him.

'Me friend won't find me now! And it's nearly dark!'

'You wolverians are a delicate sort, aren't you? I thought you lot were meant to be hardy, sleeping in snow and the like.'

Wren rolled her eyes. 'We do not sleep on snow.'

'Isn't there a festivity in which you all sleep naked outside on the snow?'

'That's an old tradition. No one does that anymore!'

'Well, isn't there a mating ritual? Couples spend the night outside naked?'

Wren's cheeks turned bright red. 'What would ya know about *that?*'

'Oh? Are you shy talking about mating rituals?' He shrugged playfully. 'I don't see why. It's a very natural thing. We all do it.'

'I'm not shy!' She cleared her throat and eyed him warily as he unpacked a few items and sat down as though he'd always intended to stay. 'What are ya doing now?'

'I thought about leaving you to it,' he said, plucking a piece of dried fruit from his bag. 'But then I remembered how thoroughly useless you are, and felt bad. So I've been following you all afternoon.'

Her face twisted with outrage. 'I'm not useless.'

Arden gave a snort of laughter. 'I've been watching you. Trust me. Utterly. *Hopeless.*'

Wren glared at him. 'Well, all right then. Kindly shut up.'

She watched as he rummaged through his satchel, retrieving a handful of neatly wrapped parcels. A warm, mouth-watering scent wafted through the air, curling into her nose like a welcome spell. Wren closed her eyes and inhaled deeply, her stomach giving a most undignified growl in response. When she opened them again, she caught Arden pulling a face.

'You really are like a dog.'

'We're not dogs, we're wolves,' she muttered defensively.

He shrugged. 'Same difference, really.'

He passed her one of the parcels, which revealed a simple, steaming meal of cooked vegetables, potatoes, and slivers of roast chicken. Wren devoured it with reckless speed, barely tasting the food as it disappeared. When she looked up, cheeks flushed, Arden was still holding his own, untouched, and watching her with a sort of stunned bemusement.

'I was hungry…' she mumbled, embarrassed by the ferocity of her appetite. She'd never cared much for etiquette, but in that moment, she felt oddly childish, awkward and ungainly under his gaze.

Another parcel appeared in her lap.

She blinked down at it, confused, before realising he had given her his own meal.

'No, I…ya won't have anything for yerself. I can't take it.'

But Arden merely waved her off. 'I've already eaten. Don't worry yourself. Like you said, you're hungry.'

With a few absurdly exaggerated faces meant to coax a smile from her, he convinced her to take it. She ate more slowly this time, as if savouring not just the food but the unspoken kindness behind the gesture.

Then he pulled a blanket from his bag and passed it across to her without a word. Wren wrapped it around herself tightly, watching him from over the edge like a suspicious cat.

'Why are ya helping me?' she asked after a pause.

'Well... I think any decent person would help a young lady who's lost and stark naked in an ancient forest. Do wolverians not believe in lending a hand?'

Wren growled low in her throat.

'I'll take that as a no,' he said, amused.

'We help,' she huffed.

'Do you?' he said, raising an eyebrow.

'When someone needs it.'

'And you didn't?'

'I was doing just fine on me own.'

Arden snorted. 'If you say so... Sorry, I meant, if *ya* say so.'

With a grumble, she chucked the blanket at his face. 'Stop making fun of me!'

'I do apologise. You simply make it so delightfully easy.'

'I need to find me friend,' she said.

'We will. But not tonight. Wandering through the Forest of Endless Trees after dark is a quick way to become compost. Get some sleep.'

She opened her mouth to protest, but he lobbed the blanket at her again, this time smacking her square in the face. He lay back with a content sigh, clearly done with the conversation.

Wren tried to follow suit, curling up beneath the blanket,

but her thoughts tumbled restlessly. She shifted, then shifted again, until eventually she heard him grunt in irritation.

'What is it now?' he grumbled.

'I was wondering...' Wren sat up, her voice hushed with curiosity. 'I heard there are jackalopes in this forest. Is that true?'

Arden stared at her, brows knitting together. He suddenly burst into a peal of laughter so loud and unrestrained that a flock of startled birds shot into the night sky, their wings slicing through the silence.

'Is that what's keeping you up, little wolf?' he said between fits of laughter.

Wren shivered, her voice a murmur of unease. 'They say they steal yer soul if ya look into their eyes... Legend says they'll leap out into yer path, stare right through ya, and...' she gulped, 'yer soul gets snatched away, foreva.'

'Oh, stars above, that's absurd!' Arden roared, laughter still bubbling from his throat.

'So... there's no such thing as jackalopes?'

'Oh, there are. But they're about as threatening as a sleepy kitten.' Wren pictured a rabbit, innocent and wide-eyed, sporting a proud pair of antlers. But then those eyes turning red... demonic. Her stomach twisted at the thought.

'Mind the dryads, though,' Arden added, his tone mockingly serious. 'Actually thought you were one at first. They've a habit of wandering about stark naked too. But then you opened your mouth and—' His grin widened, green eyes glinting with mischief.

'Ya have a wicked tongue,' Wren muttered.

'Funny, the ladies never seem to mind it,' he replied with a wink.

Wren flushed so violently she feared her cheeks might catch

fire. She prayed the night would conceal the betrayal of her skin, that the shadows would keep her blush a secret.

'Didn't take you for a prude, little wolf. Always thought it was the drakonians who blushed at the sight of nipples.'

'Oh, just shut it.'

'Is that the moon glowing so bright, or your face?' He howled with laughter again. Wren flung a small stone at him, which he easily dodged without missing a beat.

'So tell me,' he said, stretching out, 'why's a wolverian running about naked in the Forest of Endless Trees?'

'I'm trying to get to Floridia. I need to speak with da royal family.'

'Why?'

'None of yer business.'

Arden held his hands up in mock surrender. 'Fair enough.'

'How do ya know this forest so well?'

'It's my trade.'

'Ya work picking berries?' Wren frowned.

'That's a rather sanctimonious tone you've got there, little wolf. Nothing wrong with picking berries for a living.'

Wren blinked. 'Oh. Sorry. Just… wasn't expecting *that.*'

'Bit judgemental, aren't you?' he teased. 'Not everyone wants to swing a sword and wear a crown. There's no shame in earning a living from the forest.'

'I neva said there was. I knew a lad once who knew another lad from our village who picked limeberries. He'd freeze them on sticks and sell them like little ice-pops. Oh, I love ice-pops. In summer, they're da best. Ya stick one in yer mouth until da ice melts, numbs yer tongue, and then boom! Fruity flavour bursts out and dribbles all over yer mouth and chin.' Wren trailed off, catching the look Arden was giving her. His lips were parted in surprise, his brows high with amusement.

'Sorry,' she muttered. 'I try not to talk so much. I've been working on it. Still hard sometimes.'

'Don't be sorry.' A soft smile tugged at his lips. 'You can talk as much as you like, little wolf. Anyone who says otherwise isn't worth your breath. I'm just... amazed at how you made something as innocent as ice-pops sound so *dirty.*'

Wren groaned and threw the blanket at his face. 'Do shut up, Arden Briar.'

She lay back down and turned her back to him, but his laughter lingered in the air like a lullaby.

And strangely, it soothed her.

'Night night, little wolf,' he murmured.

Chapter Eighteen

House of Wild
Kingdom of Fauna

The Fae and witches have always shared a deep connection. They are the wind that howls in the night, and we are the wave that crashes against the rocky shore. But I fear that one day, they will come to resent us. Their magic is different, wild and beautiful, drawn straight from the earth itself. Ours, by contrast, can be twisted and corrupted. And yet, they envy us, because our magic holds the power to destroy entire lands.

Tabitha Wysteria

'Why do ya keep calling me little wolf?' Wren asked the next morning, her brow furrowed as she stood watching Arden pack away the remains of their modest camp—two threadbare blankets and a few crumpled parcels now void of food.

'Do wolverians have something against nicknames?' he replied lightly, slinging the last of the parcels into his satchel.

'No,' she said slowly, 'but it's a bit odd, don't ya think? Ya giving me a nickname when we barely know each other.'

He glanced over his shoulder, green eyes glinting. 'Excuse me, but I rescued you yesterday. Were it not for my noble intervention, you'd have been a feast for the jackalopes. I reckon I've earned the right to call you what I like. A reward for heroism, if you will.'

Wren shuddered, the mental image of jackalopes gnawing on her limbs not one she particularly fancied. 'Heroism?' she scoffed, curling her lip. 'All ya did was terrify me half to death, throw a leaf jacket at me, vanish for hours while I wandered around lost, then returned just to call me mental.'

'You are a bit mental.'

'*And* ya called me a dryad.'

'I didn't call you a dryad,' he said with mock offence, turning just long enough to poke her gently in the cheek. 'I thought you were a dryad. Until you started talking.'

'Are we going to find me friend now, or are ya planning to tease me to death?'

Arden tilted his head thoughtfully, and Wren's attention shifted to the antlers that curved elegantly from his head. Regal and wild, like something born of ancient magic.

'Oh, the friend thing is real?'

Wren blinked. '*What did ya think it was?*'

He shrugged. 'I thought the friend might be imaginary. Some sort of coping mechanism.'

'Coping mechanism for *what?*'

That familiar wicked grin slid across his face. 'Just having a bit of fun, little wolf.'

He turned and started walking, his strides long and unbothered. Wren jogged after him, scowling. 'I heard that one of da gods made this forest a long time ago as a gift. Said to have created da Fae too, becas the god wanted to shape da most beautiful of all da races.'

Arden stopped so suddenly she almost walked straight into his back. He turned, that infuriating grin spreading once more across his face. 'So... you think I'm beautiful?' His brows rose. 'Careful now. Yesterday you tackled me stark naked. Today you're calling me beautiful. Shall I expect a proposal by tomorrow?'

Wren snatched his satchel and smacked his arm with it.

He laughed. 'I might've said yes, but you are exceptionally violent. Are all wolverian girls this aggressive?'

Wren dropped his satchel with a thud, stepped neatly over it, and marched on, leaving Arden behind in her dust. She was finished entertaining his foolish games. She had a purpose—a mission—and that purpose was to find Freya. What if the valkyrian was lost forever, swallowed whole by the shifting woods?

Naturally, he caught up with ease. How could he not, with those maddeningly long legs? In contrast, Wren's frame was compact, built for agility, not speed. He moved to block her path, placing himself squarely in front of her.

'Hey, hey, little wolf. I'm sorry, truly. I didn't mean to upset you.'

'It's fine,' she muttered, sidestepping him in one fluid motion, unwilling to stop.

'You're angry.'

'No, am not.'

His hand reached for her arm, a gentle attempt to still her. But Wren had had enough. With a swift twist, she seized his wrist in both hands, spun on her heel, and dropped him flat onto his back. Her knee pinned his chest as her blade, plucked from within the folds of the oversized jacket, rested sharp and sure against his throat.

She expected panic, or at the very least surprise. But the expression that shone in his vivid green eyes was something else entirely. Respect. Wonder.

'Who taught you that?' he asked, voice lower now, no longer teasing. It had the weight of someone sizing her up, of a predator who had finally found reason to be wary of its prey.

Wren didn't answer. Truthfully, it was the only manoeuvre she knew, something Mal Blackburn had once taught her in jest, during a quiet night as they plotted. Wren was many things. A Seer, a spy, a thief, but not a warrior.

She pressed the knife just a little closer, enough for the tip to kiss the hollow of his throat. Her eyes darted to the spot, curious. Would a Fae bleed red, like her? He didn't quite look like her, especially not with those antlers that crowned his head like carved ebony.

'I'm not the monster,' he murmured, his brow furrowed, not in fear, but at the uncertainty on her face.

Before she could speak, he moved. Magic, swift and seamless.

Wren gasped now flat on her back, the earth cold beneath her, the knife turned in his hand, its tip grazing her throat. He loomed above her, but there was no malice in his expression, only amusement. Then, with a pulse of restraint, he pulled back and offered his hand.

She took it. His long fingers curled around her wrist, warm and strong, lingering longer than they should have. They both looked down. Slowly, his hand unfurled, as if reluctant to release her. She stepped back, rubbing her wrist, the ghost of his touch sparking across her skin. She bit her lip, surprised by the ridiculous ache for him to touch her again.

'I'll help you find your friend,' he said softly. 'And once we do, I'll take you both to Floridia. I was heading there anyway.'

A sudden sound, a rustle, a whisper of danger snapped their attention outward. They glanced around, but neither thought to look up.

Something dropped from the treetops above, landing squarely on Arden. He crumpled to the ground, unconscious.

'Freya?' Wren's eyes lit up at the sight of the valkyrian

warrior standing over him. 'Yer alright! We've been searching for ya.'

Freya smiled, serene and sweet. 'And I've been searching for you, too.' Her eyes dropped to the slumped Fae. 'And who, may I ask, is this?'

'Me new friend,' Wren replied, entirely unbothered.

Freya frowned. 'One doesn't *make* friends in this forest, Wren.'

Wren shrugged, her smirk half mischief, half defiance. 'That's probably true. But I'm not like everyone else.'

...

'We ought to have left him behind,' Freya muttered, her tone flat as she hauled Arden's unconscious body over her shoulder like a sack of potatoes. She had discovered a small, long-forgotten wooden hut, clearly built by someone once in need of shelter, now abandoned and surrendered to the moss and rot of time. Without ceremony, she dropped Arden to the floor, the thud echoing faintly against the splintered walls. 'I'll go find you something to eat.'

'No!' Wren's voice was laced with sudden panic, her heart leaping at the thought of losing Freya again to the forest's cruel whims. 'We'll get separated. Like before.'

Freya offered her a soft smile, all cool certainty. 'Do not worry, Wren. I won't be long.'

Wren opened her mouth to protest, but the valkyrian was already gone, disappearing like mist through the wooden doorway.

Left alone in the little hut, Wren huffed and kicked at a loose pebble on the floor. Unfortunately, it bounced off the edge of a stone and clipped Arden in the ribs. She gasped, immediately scrambling over to his side to check she hadn't done any real damage.

'I did that once,' she whispered, not even sure why she was speaking aloud. 'When I was a girl, out playing with da others. Got in a mood and punched a tree. Didn't realise da branch above me was heavy with snow. Whole lot of it fell on me brotha's head. Another time I spilt a pot of boiling water in da kitchens. It startled one of da wolves. Poor creature bit me brotha in da arm.'

A groan rose from Arden's chest. 'Your brother should probably keep his distance from you,' he rasped.

Wren's eyes widened. 'Yer awake!'

'Well, I wasn't dead,' he muttered, wincing slightly. 'So I suppose it was only a matter of time.'

She leaned over him, hovering close, peering into his face to make sure he truly was all right.

'What are you doing?' he asked, brows drawing together in confusion.

'I heard once that if ya look into someone's eyes, ya can tell if they're really okay.'

'Are you a healer, then?'

'No.'

'Comforting.' His gaze dipped, something shifting in his expression, and Wren instinctively followed his line of sight. It took her only a second to realise.

She was sitting on top of him.

Wren had never quite mastered the delicate intricacies of social interaction. Certain things, like sitting atop a man to check if he was still breathing, barely registered as unusual to her. It hadn't occurred to her that it might be misconstrued. To her, it was simply practical. Innocent. But she'd long come to understand that the world rarely shared her perspective. What meant nothing to her, could mean everything to someone else.

Arden cleared his throat awkwardly the moment she scrambled off him, pretending not to notice the way his limbs had stiffened, as though his body had betrayed him with its response.

'What happened?' he asked, pushing himself up on his elbows.

'Me friend fell on ya.'

His mouth opened, then shut again. He stared at her as if trying to determine whether she was being serious. 'If it were anyone else, I'd swear they were pulling my leg. But with you? Strangely believable.'

Wren rolled her eyes.

'Where is she then, this mysterious friend of yours?' he asked, glancing about the little hut.

'She went to find food.'

He arched a sceptical brow. 'Still haven't laid eyes on her. I'm beginning to wonder if my imaginary friend theory might not be so far off.'

Wren laughed, and the sound, light and unguarded, seemed to catch Arden off guard. Something softened in his expression, his eyes glinting like dewdrops kissed by morning sun. It was the sort of look that said he'd happily listen to that laugh a thousand times over, just to hear it once more.

'What's so funny?' he asked.

'I think ya might be da most annoying person I've eva met,' she said between chuckles. 'Even worse than me.'

'I am not annoying,' he declared, mock-offended. 'I'm delightful.'

That made her howl, laughter spilling from her like an overflowing goblet. She rolled to one side, giggling uncontrollably.

'I'm serious!' he insisted, though his pout only made her laugh harder. 'Everyone adores me.'

'Of course they do,' Wren said, wiping her eyes. 'Yer a real treat, Arden Briar.'

He scowled at her but said nothing more. 'We should get some rest. I'll take first watch.'

'We didn't take turns last night.'

'Get some sleep, little wolf. I'll wake you when your friend returns.'

She hesitated at the mention of Freya, her gaze drifting towards the forest beyond the hut. Gods, she hoped Freya was safe.

Wren lay down, wriggling for a comfortable position on the uneven floorboards, groaning when she couldn't find one.

'Now what?' Arden sighed.

'It's da floor,' she grumbled. 'It's bloody awful.'

He snorted. 'You sound like a princess.'

Wren stilled, peering up at him. 'What's wrong with being a princess?'

'Nothing. Except I can't stand them. Been working for the Hawthornes since I was born. If I had my way, I'd be rid of the whole lot. People should shape their own fate. Not be ruled by royal blood.'

Her heart clenched.

'What do ya do for them?' she asked, her voice barely above a whisper.

He shrugged. 'A bit of everything. Now I work in the kitchens.'

That explained the berries, at least. The Forest of Endless Trees wasn't a threat to the Fae. It had been grown to shield them, a haven from danger. But that hatred in his voice...

'Why do ya hate royals so much?'

He didn't reply. Instead, he shifted, patting his leg. 'Come here. You can use this as a pillow.'

She blinked at the unexpected offer, but shuffled over, settling herself against him.

'My leg, Wren! I said my leg!'

She ignored him, letting her head rest against his stomach, curling one leg over his as she snuggled closer. 'Hush. I'm trying to sleep.'

'I can't keep watch like this!'

She shut her eyes and let her breathing slow, feigning sleep as he began muttering under his breath.

'Stupid bloody wolf,' he grumbled. 'Ought to strangle her. Would be doing the forest a favour.'

Wren snored loudly in response.

'This cannot be real.'

She bit the inside of her cheek to stop from laughing. Eventually, she shifted off his torso and onto his leg, granting him the movement he needed. A slow calm settled over them both. Her breathing deepened. Muscles slackened. And as she hovered at the edge of sleep, she thought, perhaps dreamt, of his fingers gently stroking her hair.

Then she heard it. Barely a whisper, as if he were confessing it to the night.

'I hate royals... because they're the reason my whole family's dead.'

Chapter Nineteen

House of Wild
Kingdom of Fauna

My second test... I cannot afford to fail. But I never expected it to be this. They've trapped me in the Forest of Endless Trees. I must find my way out. And yet, how strange my mind is that the very first thought to surface was...

What if I stay?

Tabitha Wysteria

It had begun to rain, and the scent of damp earth stirred Wren from slumber. She had been lost in a peculiar dream, a vision of a handsome Fae with dark skin, eyes the colour of fresh spring leaves, and antlers that curled like ancient branches. But the moment she blinked herself awake, she realised it hadn't been a dream at all. He was still there. Very real indeed.

'It's daylight,' Arden mumbled, voice husky with sleep. 'We ought to get moving.'

Wren remained where she was, waiting for him to rise. He didn't. She noticed, with a quiet sort of surprise, how his arms had been loosely curled around her, a shield of warmth against the morning chill. Part of her considered telling him that while wolverians did feel the cold, it was never as sharp to them as it was to the other kingdoms. But she said nothing. She was far too comfortable to ruin it with facts.

'Where's Freya?' she asked softly.

'Your imaginary friend?' Arden arched a brow. 'She never came back.'

Wren sat up abruptly, all warmth abandoned as dread replaced it. For the second time, Freya had disappeared into the forest, and for the second time, Wren had no idea where she had gone. The valkyrian had promised to fetch food... yet the night had passed, and there'd been no sign of her. Had something happened? Had the forest swallowed her whole?

As if summoned by thought alone, Freya emerged through the trees in the distance, moving with calm, measured strides. Wren bolted from the hut, frustration overtaking fear.

'Where were ya?' she cried, storming towards her.

'Foraging,' Freya replied serenely, tossing a large leaf to the ground. It unfolded to reveal wild fruit in a range of colours Wren didn't recognise.

Wren wanted to argue, to shout, to demand answers. But instead, she bit her tongue. Time was slipping through their fingers like water. So they sat and ate in silence, though Wren couldn't take her eyes off the valkyrian. Something about her felt... off. Why had it taken her all night to gather a handful of fruit? The forest was known to warp perception, to twist truth into delusion. Perhaps it was playing tricks on Wren, sewing seeds of doubt.

Meanwhile, Arden was speechless. He hadn't said a word since Freya arrived, which was hardly surprising. Valkyrians had a way of silencing men with nothing but a glance. His green eyes were wide, his mouth half-parted in admiration. Wren glared at him. Daggers. He didn't notice.

'We should go,' she announced curtly. 'Arden will lead us out of da forest.'

As Freya stepped ahead, Arden moved swiftly to walk beside

her. Wren trailed behind, arms crossed and mood souring by the minute. Of course he was smitten. Freya was tall and lithe, her body shaped by war and moonlight. Her long brown hair rippled like water, framing a freckled face with eyes as blue as the cloudless sky. She looked like every dream a man might have.

Wren, by comparison, was small. Too thin. Her hair was a silver-white that shimmered pale and colourless in the sun, not golden or dark or rich with fire. She was the soft hush of snowfall, the quiet tones of a canvas yet to be painted. And yet for the briefest of moments she'd believed Arden had looked at her like she was something more.

'There!' Arden's voice pulled her from the spiral of thought.

He'd hurried ahead, standing before two towering columns fashioned from tree trunks. Strange symbols had been carved into the wood, twisting and curling like ivy.

'What is it?' Wren asked, brow furrowed.

'The entrance to Floridia,' he said with a smile.

She frowned again. 'How is that an entrance? There's nothing here, just a field.'

'It's magic, little wolf. Witches aren't the only ones who use it. Ours isn't as refined, we can't bend the elements or twist the stars. But we can enchant, conceal, beautify.'

Without another word, Freya stepped between the columns and vanished. Wren gasped, rushing forward, peering through the trunks as if she could make sense of what had just happened. She turned to Arden, her mouth full of questions. But he only laughed, extending his hand.

'Go on. Walk through and see. I'll answer everything once we're on the other side.'

Wren stared at his outstretched hand, hesitation clawing at her. This would be the end of it. Once they crossed into

Floridia, he would know, he would *see*. She was not just a wolverian girl lost in a forest. She was a princess. And Arden... Arden despised royalty.

Still, she reached for him.

Their fingers laced together, warm and solid.

And hand in hand, Wren stepped into the unknown.

...

Wren had never seen a place quite like Floridia. Granted, she hadn't seen much of the world beyond her snowy borders, but even in her most elaborate daydreams, not even the wildest corners of her imagination could have conjured a city such as this.

Floridia dwelled high in the embrace of ancient trees, nestled within a forest not unlike the Forest of Endless Trees. In fact, some whispered that the gods had crafted that very forest as a mirrored illusion of Floridia, meant to trick wandering souls into believing they had arrived at their destination, only to find themselves hopelessly lost.

The city itself bloomed in the canopy above, suspended in the air as if held by the hands of the gods. The trees were vast and regal, their trunks as wide as castles, their branches strong enough to cradle entire homes. Dwellings were built high among the limbs, each one linked to the next by slender, sturdy bridges that wove together like an elaborate tapestry of walkways and winding paths.

There were several ways to ascend. Wooden lifts, simple yet effective, carried citizens between levels with slow elegance. Alternatively, for those who sought thrill or tradition, the trees themselves had been carefully marked with footholds and handholds carved into the bark, an invitation to climb.

Wren bounced eagerly on the balls of her feet, eyes shining with delight. The tree loomed before her like a challenge she had waited her whole life to accept.

'Seriously?' Arden tilted his head, regarding her with disbelief. 'You actually want to climb that beast? There's a lift right there!' He gestured to where two Fae girls stepped daintily onto a platform waiting to rise.

'But where's da fun in that?' Wren's grin widened, mischief dancing in her eyes.

'You're... completely mad.'

'That's all right, Arden. Ya don't have to follow if yer scared. I understand. I've met plenty of chickens in me time.'

Something sparked behind Arden's eyes—challenge, irritation, amusement. 'Oh, really? You think you could outclimb me?'

'I could do it with me eyes closed.'

'Right then, little wolf. Let's find out.'

Freya gave a long-suffering sigh and turned towards the lift. 'I'll wait for you at the top,' she called over her shoulder, already rising.

'No cheating,' Arden said, rolling up his sleeves with mock seriousness.

'Speak for yerself!' Wren was already moving, launching herself towards the tree with giddy determination. She laughed aloud at the sound of Arden's swearing behind her.

Gripping the handholds, she climbed fast and light, her feet finding purchase with ease, her muscles burning with the delicious strain of effort. The higher she went, the more the world below blurred into irrelevance. The wind kissed her cheeks, the bark scraped her palms, and still she grinned. The fall would be fatal, but that only made her push harder, faster.

When she finally reached the first landing, she swung her leg over the wooden edge and hauled herself up with a grunt, chest heaving, hair plastered to her brow. Triumphant, she raised her arms, until she spotted him.

Arden was already there, casually leaning against the tree trunk, tossing an apple from hand to hand. He looked unbearably pleased with himself.

'Took your time, little wolf.'

'How…?' Wren gaped over the edge, seeing how far below the forest floor still lay. She was a swift climber, one of the best in her village. How in all the gods' names had he beaten her?

'I'm Fae,' he said with a lazy shrug, as if that explained everything.

Furious, she shoved him. 'Ya cheated!'

'I did not,' he said, though laughter laced every word.

'Ya did!'

Freya waved them forward, unimpressed by their antics. Wren stuck her tongue out at him, well aware she was behaving like a child but too cross to care.

Arden leaned in, voice low and teasing. 'I might've cheated. Then again… maybe I didn't. Guess you'll never know.' With that, he sauntered off after Freya, his laughter trailing behind him like the tail of a comet. And Wren followed, fists clenched, cheeks warm, and heart thudding harder than it ought to.

Freya led them from one towering tree to the next, weaving through a maze of wooden bridges and swaying walkways until they reached the grandest of them all, the thickest trunk in sight, vast as a fortress and twice as ancient. This, Wren realised, was no ordinary tree. The entirety of its breadth and branches belonged to the royal family, and guards stood sentinel at the entrance to the bridge, unmoving as statues carved from bark and bone.

Wren couldn't help but wonder how Freya had known the

exact path to take. But she kept her questions caged for now. There would be time later to ask the valkyrian what else she seemed to know.

'They're with me,' Arden announced, patting one of the Fae guards on the shoulder with a roguish familiarity. He threw a wink in Wren's direction before stepping onto the bridge, which, though suspended at a dizzying height, remained utterly still.

Arden explained that Fae bridges were enchanted, held steady by ancient spells. Even if someone were to fall, whether by accident or design, they would land gently, cushioned by conjured leaves that would break their fall. Magic, he had said, protected them from untimely ends.

'So I could've pushed ya off,' Wren muttered, half to herself.

'Whoa there, little wolf,' Arden said, side-eyeing her with exaggerated caution. 'You look far too thrilled by the idea of my untimely death.'

He was pulling that face again, the one that danced the line between mock outrage and concealed amusement.

'It wouldn't be murder,' she replied sweetly. 'Yer magic would've kept ya alive.'

'Still mildly concerned about how easily you fantasise about violence against me.'

They passed through a small, curved building nestled around the tree's trunk. Some sort of servant's station, cluttered with crates and bundles of supplies destined for the palace. Beyond that, they stepped into the kitchens, warm and rich with the scent of simmering herbs and roasting roots. Arden paused beside a row of steaming pots, inhaling deeply.

'We ought to eat first,' he said, dropping his satchel and handing the wild berries he'd foraged to one of the cooks.

'We don't have time,' Freya said sharply, her tone clipped as she shot Wren a warning glance.

'It won't take long. The royal family aren't going anywhere, are they?' Arden grinned, brushing aside a collection of jars and chopped vegetables to clear a wooden table. He moved with the ease of someone who belonged there, selecting ingredients and bowls with a familiarity that suggested this was his true domain.

The kitchen had once been some manner of hallway, carved lovingly around the curving bark of the ancient tree. At its heart stood a cluster of wooden tables, their surfaces scattered with pots, pans, and bowls overflowing with ripe, glistening fruit. The outer wall was formed of tall open arches unglazed to the sky, inviting birds to flit freely in and out on feathered wings. Vines crept along the wooden walls in tangled elegance, their blossoms unfurling like whispered secrets, while insects danced lazily between the petals, moving from one trailing tendril to the next.

'Mushroom soup,' Arden announced proudly a few minutes later, ladling the rich broth into bowls. 'One of my finest. And, if I do say so myself, onion and bird pie.'

Wren moaned the moment she took a bite. Then again when she tried the pie. She didn't even try to hide it.

Arden laughed under his breath. Freya, on the other hand, simply stood and wandered off to inspect the kitchens, visibly unimpressed.

'Only you,' Arden muttered, shaking his head, 'could make eating sound like something out of a lover's ballad.'

Wren froze mid-spoonful, cheeks flaming crimson. She looked up, caught in the green of his eyes. To her dismay, he was watching her intently, a quiet, unreadable smile on his lips.

He cleared his throat, breaking the moment. 'So... why are you here?'

'To speak with the royal family,' Freya said briskly, lifting lids and peering into jars as though she had never been inside a kitchen before.

'I gathered that,' Arden replied, still watching Wren. 'But why exactly?'

Wren gave a frantic shake of her head, trying to warn Freya off. But the valkyrian was too enthralled by her surroundings to take the hint.

'We bring urgent news concerning all kingdoms,' Freya said.

Arden blinked, clearly caught off guard. 'From a valkyrian and a wolverian? That's a rather odd pairing, don't you think? I doubt the royal family would even grant you an audience.'

Freya turned sharply, her gaze cutting through him like a blade. 'Of course they will. Wren is—'

'Constipated!' Wren blurted, springing to her feet. Both heads turned to her, puzzled. 'I'm... slightly constipated. Been holding it in. We should go now.' She tugged at her jacket, avoiding their eyes.

Freya frowned, Arden looked baffled, but neither questioned her further. Wren exhaled in relief. The truth would come soon enough, but not yet. Not here. Not to him.

With a tight nod, Arden gestured for them to follow, and together they left the kitchens behind. They ascended to one of the grandest huts nestled high in the boughs. An open, airy pavilion woven into the thick limbs of the sacred tree where the king and queen of Floridia often passed their days. The guards, having been waved off with casual ease, allowed them through without question, and Wren followed Arden, who moved through the royal levels with the familiarity of someone who belonged.

It baffled her how someone who claimed to loathe the crown

bore such freedom within its heart. He was, supposedly, just a cook. Shouldn't he have been confined to the lower levels, far from where the monarchs held court?

Wren itched to ask, but bit her tongue. It wasn't her place. Not now, not when it was thanks to him that they'd made it this far at all. And besides, she was too consumed by the nerves coiling tightly within her belly, worried that Arden might somehow discover what she truly was.

She barely took the time to marvel at the palace itself, though it deserved it. The wooden walls were draped in living tapestries of vines and wild blossoms. Furniture carved from ancient timber gleamed with soft polish, and the palace breathed with life—birds resting on windowsills, rabbits perched boldly on benches nibbling on offerings left behind. Floridia was unlike anywhere Wren had ever known, not just beautiful, but impossibly alive.

And the Fae—gods, the Fae. Just as she'd been told, they were a vision of untamed elegance. Their skin ranged in deep shades that echoed the richness of their land, their eyes glowing like gemstones pulled from forest depths: moss-green, amber-gold, river-blue. And atop every brow, antlers. Twisting, branching, growing in patterns as unique as their faces.

'Well, I've brought you this far,' Arden said, halting at a long corridor carved entirely from smooth, golden wood. Great archways opened into the canopy beyond, where more branches crept through like lazy serpents. 'But I've no idea how you plan to get past those doors.'

Wren's throat tightened. 'Yes, yes... Don't worry about that. Go back to da kitchens. We'll find ya later.'

Her obvious nerves darkened the look in his green eyes. His gaze lingered a moment too long, suspicion blooming across his features. But he said nothing more. With a brief nod, he turned and walked away, vanishing into the soft golden haze of the corridor. Only then did Wren release the breath she hadn't realised she'd been holding. Steeling herself, she stepped forward and addressed the guards flanking the great wooden doors.

'State your name and business.'

Drawing her shoulders back, she inhaled deeply and exhaled slow, steadying the storm building within her chest. She was not here as a girl lost in the forest. She was here with purpose. To deliver death, and to beg for war.

'Me name is Wren Wynter, of House of Snow, Kingdom of Ice,' she said clearly, her voice echoing against the wood. 'I request audience with King Florian Hawthorne regarding his three daughters.'

Chapter Twenty

House of Wild
Kingdom of Fauna

The Fae are beautiful, but their beauty is part of their magic. It serves as a distraction. For if you're too entranced by them, you'll fail to see the deception.

They are tricksters and, above all, terribly sore losers.

Tabitha Wysteria

Stepping into the throne room of Floridia felt less like entering a hall of rule and more like crossing the threshold into a living forest. Light filtered through latticed canopies of vines and blossoms, and the air carried the scent of damp bark and blooming petals. The throne itself had been woven from thousands of interlaced branches—majestic, organic, and ancient —cradling King Florian as he sat, head tilted slightly, his amber eyes alight with quiet scrutiny.

As Wren began to speak, recounting the horror that had unfolded in the drakonian castle, she watched the king's proud features contort, grief carving new hollows into his expression. She didn't dare meet the gaze of the two remaining Hawthorne daughters, who stood silent as gravestones to one side. Their silence was suffocating, wrapping itself around Wren like a shroud. Still, she pressed on, glancing at Freya, drawing a measure of strength from her quiet presence.

'Da city of Spark has fallen to da witches,' Wren said, her voice steady though her heart thundered. 'And they will not stop there. They'll stretch their reach further into drakonian land unless we rise to meet them. All da kingdoms must rally. If not, they will come for da rest of us. No one is safe.'

The king did not acknowledge her warning. His voice, when it came, was low and firm. 'And the bodies?'

Wren swallowed. 'We couldn't recover any of da fallen,' she said quietly.

He turned to his daughters then, the weight of his sorrow thick in the air. 'We must prepare rites of passage for them.'

'King Florian...' Wren stepped forward. 'I know this is a time of mourning, and I am sorry. But da witches are plotting. If we do not stand together, they will consume us all.'

For the first time, the king truly looked at her, as though only just remembering she was there. His gaze was ancient, sorrowful, and distant.

'Their deaths are an omen, Wren Wynter. A reckoning long overdue. What was done to the Kingdom of Magic cannot be undone. House of Power was decimated, every last one of them wiped out. The drakonians wielded the blades, yes. But the rest of us... we stood aside and let it happen. We closed our eyes. House of Wild, Snow, and Power were once united, long ago.'

Wren drew in a trembling breath. 'Then let us stand united again.'

But King Florian shook his head, the vines around him rustling with the movement. 'My daughters died for the sins of our past. I will not repeat them. Perhaps... perhaps it is time we let the witches return. So no, Wren Wynter. I will not send an army.'

Wren's hands balled into fists at her sides. 'Innocents will die,' she said through gritted teeth. The implications were grave. If House of Wild chose to stay neutral, what would stop the other kingdoms from doing the same?

Freya's hand came to rest gently on Wren's shoulder, anchoring her in place before she could charge forward and scream her fury into the king's face. He was grieving. Wren reminded herself of that. Patience was required. But somewhere deep within, she knew that she could sit in that chamber for a hundred years and it still wouldn't soften King Florian's resolve. The Fae had no need to fear the witches. Their ancient magic cloaked their kingdom like mist through leaves, hiding them from the world's gaze. Witches couldn't infiltrate them, not with glamour, not with guile. The Fae would remain untouched.

'Ya turned yer backs on da witches all those years ago, and ya let them die,' Wren said, her voice trembling with fire. 'Don't do da same to us.'

For the briefest of heartbeats, she thought her words had struck true. The king's stern face slackened, and his ember-bright eyes shimmered with something gentler, something dangerously close to hope. Wren exhaled, the tension easing from her spine. Had she done it? Was this the first step towards unity, towards war and retribution wrapped in honour? But the illusion shattered when the king began to shake his head, his lips whispering profanities like a spell unravelled.

'I am sorry, Wren Wynter,' he said, the light in his eyes extinguished. 'I cannot endanger my people. The Fae have lived in peace for a century. I will not disrupt that balance. I will not fight the witches.'

Wren's fury rose like a tide breaking against the rocks, impossible to contain. 'They killed yer daughters! Are ya going to stand there and pretend it neva happened?'

King Florian didn't flinch. 'My daughters will be avenged,

Wren Wynter,' he said coldly. 'But in my way, not yours.'

Wren's brows furrowed. What did *that* mean? How did he intend to deliver justice without lifting his sword?

'We will *not* ignite another Great War.'

'It won't be a war. It'll be slaughter.'

'Perhaps,' he said slowly, 'but drakonians deserve what is coming to them.'

Wren recoiled, the breath caught in her lungs. 'It won't stop with da drakonians. Ya know that. They'll come for us all.'

The king looked to his daughters, sorrow hollowing his gaze. 'Then perhaps... perhaps they should. Perhaps we should let them.'

Wren's eyes widened with horror. 'Ya can't be serious. King Florian, *please*—'

Her voice cracked as Freya's arms pulled her back, a whisper against her ear, 'We need to go.'

But Wren was not done screaming. Her voice echoed through the throne room, charged with desperation and rage. The grief in the king's eyes did nothing to still her tongue. Instead, it only fanned the fire in her belly.

'Innocents will die!'

Freya dragged her gently from the chamber. Wren's heart thundered as they turned to leave, tight with the sting of failure. One kingdom had fallen out of reach... How many more would turn their backs?

The throne room doors groaned open and there, waiting on the other side, stood Arden Briar. His green eyes burnt with fury, as sharp as blades drawn beneath moonlight.

...

'You're a *princess?*'

Wren tried, truly tried, not to flinch at the question, but the guilt bloomed hot beneath her skin. Arden's voice wasn't loud, but it was laced with something heavy and sharp that twisted in her stomach like a blade.

'Why didn't you tell me?'

'Becas ya hate royals,' she said, barely meeting his gaze. Her shoulders lifted in a feeble shrug, though her throat tightened. Tears threatened to well in the corners of her eyes, but she blinked them away, swiping quickly at her face before they could fall. She had failed. She'd had one task—to help, to bring unity, to fight for those without a voice and she had failed in every possible way.

And now, to make matters worse, Arden had uncovered the truth. She was no one's wolf anymore. Just a girl with a title he loathed, and he was staring at her as though she had deceived him in the worst way.

'I know ya hate me now,' she said, voice cracking like frost underfoot. 'But... I didn't mean to lie.' Her head dropped, heavy with shame and weariness. She couldn't carry it all anymore.

'Yes, you did.' His words struck like a slap. His jaw clenched, eyes darkening as though he wanted to say more, but instead, turned. Without another word, Arden walked away, his footsteps vanishing into the corridor's hush.

For a fleeting, fragile heartbeat, Wren hoped he might turn back. That he'd come running, laugh it off, say it didn't matter, that she'd changed his mind. But as the silence stretched and he didn't return, the truth grew cold and solid in her chest.

He wasn't coming back. And it wasn't okay.

Wren tried not to glance over her shoulder, but as she stepped into the lift, she couldn't help it. One last look. One final hope. But the corridor behind her was empty.

'Do not lose hope,' Freya said softly as they descended, her voice a gentle balm to Wren's spiralling thoughts. They made their way back towards the twin wooden columns that marked the edge of Floridia, the enchanted threshold between safety and the unknown. 'I will return home now,' Freya continued. 'To speak with my people. Valkyrians, wolverians, wyverians, together we may be enough. And there are still other kingdoms yet.'

'Yer leaving?' Wren asked, struggling to keep the desperation from her voice. It clung like dew to her words nonetheless. She had hoped, perhaps foolishly, to travel with Freya, to soar to the skies and speak with the valkyrians face to face.

Freya sighed, the sound steeped in sympathy. She placed both hands on Wren's shoulders, steady and warm. 'I'm afraid I cannot take you with me. No outsiders are permitted into the Kingdom of Air. It is our oldest law. But you… you are stronger than you know, Wren. You'll find your path. I believe that.'

Wren nodded, though belief had long since abandoned her. The hope that had once burnt in her chest like a wildfire had been reduced to dying embers in that throne room.

'How will I find ya again?' she asked, a whisper more than a plea. The thought of being left behind, truly alone, hollowed something deep inside her. She had no food, no clothes, and very little faith left in herself. But she would go on.

'I'll find you,' Freya promised. 'Be careful out there.'

Wren nodded again, hugging her arms around herself as she watched the valkyrian step between the carved wooden columns and vanish into shimmering nothingness.

And just like that, she was alone.

She stared at the space where Freya had stood, then turned her eyes southward. There were two ways to reach the Desert Kingdom, either through the drakonian lands, now slowly falling to witches, or through the treacherous wastelands. She could loop back to the north, return to her own kingdom and pass through wyverian territory, but the journey would take months.

Wren dropped to the ground with a graceless thud, her spirit as sodden as the soil beneath her. Misery clung to her like a second skin. Why couldn't the gods bless her with a vision when she actually needed one? A glimpse, just a flicker, of what to do next. Anything to quiet the storm of doubt roaring in her chest.

She could climb back up one of the towering trees and beg the Fae for provisions. Or she could steal them, though the thought made her heart twist with guilt.

Her mind drifted to Bryn, her steadfast brother. Was he all right? Had Kage finally emerged from the solitude of his grief? Returning home would be the most sensible plan, but then she'd have to face Bryn's lectures, those sharp-edged words wrapped in love. *Ya neva listen, Wren. Ya always do something reckless.* She could already hear him.

And for the very first time in her life, Wren Wynter *broke.*

The tears came like rain after drought—unforgiving, unstoppable. She didn't care if the forest bore witness. She curled in on herself, sat upon the soft mossy grass, and wept until her face was raw and her heart hollowed. She wept for everything; for Freya's sudden departure, for Arden Briar's turned back and his sharp, disappointed stare. For the failure that clung to her like frost.

Time slipped past in a blur of silence and shadows. When her tears had finally dried, Wren lay on her back, letting the cool breath of evening wrap around her. Above, stars unfurled across the sky like scattered diamonds, distant and indifferent. Her stomach twisted and growled in protest, but she ignored it. She didn't want to eat. She didn't want to move. She only wanted to lie there and curse the gods who'd whispered lies into her bones, lies that she was strong enough, brave enough, destined for anything at all.

Sleep took her slowly, gently, like a tide retreating from shore. But just before she drifted into dreams, she felt something, or someone, watching her.

And for once, she was certain it wasn't the gods.

...

Wren spent the morning perched beside the twin wooden columns, those silent sentinels that guarded the gateway to the next leg of her journey. She sat there, knees tucked to her chest, paralysed by uncertainty. The forest beyond whispered with possibility and peril alike. That peculiar sensation of being watched clung to her like morning mist, but each time she turned to catch the observer, she found only trees and shadows. So she ignored it. Or tried to.

Then something struck the back of her neck with a dull thud.

Hissing in surprise, Wren rubbed the sore spot and glanced down. At her feet lay a half-eaten apple, glistening with mischief. She snatched it up, spun round on her heel, and opened her mouth to deliver a furious tirade at whatever idiot had decided to pelt her with fruit.

Arden Briar stood a few paces away, one brow arched, his lips curved in that maddening smirk she had come to associate with equal parts amusement and provocation.

'You're not seriously thinking of running off with my jacket, are you?' he said lazily.

'I've no clothes,' she snapped.

He shrugged, entirely unbothered. 'Yeah, well... hand it over.'

Wren's eyes widened. 'I'm naked underneath!'

'Fae don't mind a bit of skin.'

'I'm Wren Wynter of House of Snow! I am not stripping in front of ya like some...!'

But her outrage only made his grin stretch wider.

'Well, well... how the mighty have fallen. Titled and temperamental now, are we? Going to start bossing me about with that fancy lineage of yours?'

Wren opened her mouth, but the words lodged in her throat as he sauntered closer, snatched the apple from her grasp, and took a nonchalant bite. He wiggled his eyebrows and nodded towards the columns. 'Just because you're a princess now doesn't mean you get to waste perfectly good food. Come on, then. Where to next?'

'I thought... ya'd left,' Wren said, frowning, still dazed by his sudden reappearance. 'Ya were angry. Ya walked away.'

'I had to get you some clothes,' he said with a shrug, 'and enough food to satisfy that bottomless pit you call a stomach.'

'Excuse me?'

He laughed, full-bodied and unrepentant, at the twitch of irritation in her eye. 'You eat more than a wyvern twice your size.'

'Yer unbelievable.'

'And yet you're still here,' he teased, extending a hand towards her. 'So? You coming or not?'

Wren hesitated, staring at his hand. A part of her bristled with doubt. Another, smaller voice—quieter but stronger— urged her to trust him. To believe that there was something real behind his smile, something that wouldn't vanish the moment she turned away.

She wanted to ask why he'd come back for her, why he was still willing to follow her into danger, and how his fury had faded so swiftly like a summer storm, loud but fleeting. But instead, she simply placed her hand in his.

'How do *ya* know what a wyvern eats?' she asked.

Arden laughed. A sound that danced through the air like sunlight on river water, and to Wren, it was the most beautiful thing she'd ever heard.

And this time, as they crossed between the towering columns, Wren left behind the fragments of her broken faith, still scattered like glass upon the grass. Yet, as her feet moved forward into the unknown, a small piece of that lost faith was gently restored, set back into place by the hand that held hers, steady and sure, guiding her through the dark.

Chapter Twenty-One

House of Sun
Kingdom of Light

Prince Sorin always speaks of his land with such passion. It makes my toes curl with longing to visit the kingdom made of light, where the skies are painted with the feathers of its phoenixes. They say that at night, the darkness is softened by sparks from the birds, leaving trails of stars so every phoenixian can find their way home.

Tabitha Wysteria

'Agari,' Hessa commanded sharply.

Alina's brow furrowed as a bead of sweat slipped into her right eye, stinging like ash, yet she didn't dare lift a hand to wipe it away. She stood perched on the edge of the balcony, a trembling statue of discipline, her hands outstretched, tomes in each palm. Her left leg remained suspended mid-air, her right foot rooted like the last leaf clinging to a dying branch.

They had spent the last week training in silence and sweat, awaiting the return of the phoenixian king and queen, but time was running dry. Hessa could not delay her journey home any longer. Her people needed their princess. So Princess Mareena would be left to deliver the news to her parents.

Two heavy tomes tumbled from Alina's right hand, landing with dull thuds, and she staggered forward. Hessa clicked her tongue in irritation.

'Agari,' Hessa repeated, tone flat as the desert sun.

'No. Not again.' Alina collapsed onto the balcony's edge, breathless. 'I'll faint if I do any more.'

Hessa merely shrugged. 'We leave tonight.'

The door creaked open and in walked Mareena, radiant as ever, her smile gilded in sunlight. Hessa gave Alina one of her signature wicked smiles, the kind that heralded impending mischief, and slipped away into the palace corridors.

'She's utterly uncontrollable,' Alina sighed, longing for a bath and a moment's reprieve.

'I rather adore that about her. Don't you?' Mareena's gown was sheer and white, clinging to her body like mist. Alina averted her gaze, tongue briefly darting out to wet her lips.

'I do love the view,' Alina muttered, pivoting to peer over the balcony once more. The phoenixian city glittered beneath her like a mosaic—palm trees shading winding streets, phoenixes diving gracefully through the skies, wings catching the light as they landed on balconies and outstretched arms. Their cries were sharp and melodic, echoing the voices of their people.

'I envy you,' Mareena said softly, her cheeks flushed a dusky rose. 'To be leaving. I've always dreamt of seeing the Desert Kingdom.'

Alina offered a wistful smile. 'I spent my whole life longing to leave. Now I'd give anything to go back.' She turned away, the gleaming city no longer a balm to her grief. What remained of her homeland? Had it been swallowed by war? Burnt by hatred?

'I'm sorry,' Mareena whispered, her voice a fragile reed in the wind. 'I wasn't thinking. I didn't mean—'

'Don't apologise.' Alina shook her head. The fault was not Mareena's. She watched the princess drift back inside, her every movement fluid, feline, beautiful in ways Alina couldn't describe. In comparison, Alina often felt like a misdrawn sketch.

'I'm sorry you won't be here for Zahian's funeral,' Mareena said gently.

They had delayed their departure in hopes of attending the ceremony, but the phoenixian royals had not returned. Hessa had her own mourning to do. Her sister's rites would be held in the desert sands, far from here.

Alina remained by the column, arms folded across her stomach, too unsure of herself to sit beside Mareena. In the past week, she had learnt new forms of combat. Her muscles still ached from the drills but she didn't see the strength Hessa claimed was beginning to show. Years of drakonian modesty had taught her to fear the sight of her own reflection.

'We shall have a feast tonight, in your honour,' Mareena said, smiling brightly.

'Please... let it just be the three of us,' Alina replied, heart tight with unease.

'Of course,' Mareena said, reading her without question. 'Just us three.'

Alina longed to say more, so much more, but words felt foolish in Mareena's presence. She merely nodded.

'Until tonight, then.' Mareena rose and walked away, each step a study in grace and quiet seduction.

Alina turned back towards the balcony, her tawny eyes drifting over the endless sprawl of desert, a golden sea kissed by the sun's fading warmth. The wind whispered against her skin, but it carried no comfort, only silence, and the ever-present ache that lived just beneath her ribs.

As she did nearly every waking moment, she wondered what Hagan was doing. If her name ever crossed his thoughts. If he ever felt the echo of her rage building across the sands. Did he worry? Did he lie awake knowing that the girl he'd broken was forging herself anew, a blade honed in fury?

At the thought, a smile curved her lips, cold and sharp. She would bleed, and she would suffer. She would train until her bones ached and her breath turned to fire. All for one singular, perfect moment. The moment she found him. The moment she shattered him piece by piece, as he had once done to her heart.

And when that moment came, when the vengeance was carved into the earth with her blood-soaked hands, then perhaps, Alina would remember how to breathe again.

...

'Do you think Mareena will give you a parting kiss?'

Alina's sharp inhale cut through the hush of the unlit room. The night wrapped around them like a velvet cloak, shadows clinging to the corners where no candle dared flicker. Hessa crawled across the vast bed that had been gifted to Alina, the same bed they had come to share. Since fleeing the land of dragons, Alina had not slept a single night alone. Every time her eyes fluttered closed, purple ones haunted the darkness. And though Hessa had been granted a room of her own, she had never once set foot in it. If the servants had noticed, they said nothing.

'Hessa!' Alina's eyes flew wide open, scandal and disbelief painted across her face. 'Don't say such foolish things.'

Hessa settled herself onto Alina's back, the drakonian princess sprawled across the bed on her stomach, hair wild and untamed, eyes staring into some distant corner of thought.

'Foolish? And why is it foolish?'

'Because you're being utterly ridiculous, as always.'

'Oh, amira, I'm just teasing,' Hessa grinned into the gloom.

'It is so easy to make a drakonian uncomfortable.' She began to rub gentle circles along Alina's back, as she did every night after training. At first, the touch had been unbearable, shocking even, to feel someone's hands against her bare skin. But Hessa had explained that in the Desert Kingdom, touch between friends was a mark of affection and respect, not impropriety. Alina marvelled at how different their worlds were: in the Kingdom of Fire, physical contact was scandalous, whispered about behind closed doors. In the desert, it was a quiet, sacred language.

'Ma nama Alina,' Alina said, shifting the topic clumsily. 'Kaafran sandhii.'

'Kaafrin, not kaafran,' Hessa corrected gently. 'Kaafrin means I am studying. Kaafran means I have studied.'

Alina groaned in frustration. 'Kaafrin sandhii dua dunaa.'

'Dunaa means years, amira. You mean samana, weeks. Dua samana.'

'I never imagined it would be so difficult,' Alina muttered.

'You're doing good,' Hessa assured her, kneading into a knot of tension so tightly wound that Alina could only growl in response. 'Once we reach the Desert Kingdom, your tongue will learn quicker.'

'Everyone will laugh at me.'

'No one will laugh,' Hessa promised. 'In my homeland, we admire those who wish to learn. They'll respect you, amira. I respect you.'

Alina's lips curled, her cheeks tinged a deeper red. It was a strange but welcome warmth, this quiet admiration. Especially from someone as radiant, as bold and boundless, as Hessa.

'We should change, or we'll be late for dinner with Mareena,' Hessa said, rolling gracefully off the bed like a cat stretching in the sun.

'Wait, teach me one more thing,' Alina replied, lifting herself onto her elbows. 'Something I can revise tonight as we travel.'

There was a lightness in her voice now that hadn't existed weeks ago, a brightness slowly kindling in her chest. It was peculiar, how hope could bloom in the cracks left by tragedy. Her family had been slaughtered. Her horns shorn. Her kingdom lost to ash and silence. And yet... she was learning to wield a blade. To trust her instincts. To find kinship in souls she'd once overlooked.

She could no longer imagine her days without Hessa's presence, fierce and radiant, at her side.

'Very well, amira.' Hessa perched beside her once more, taking her hand in hers.

Alina no longer flinched at the touch. She had grown used to the desert princess's way of showing affection, warm and uninhibited. They slept tangled together each night, bathed side by side, shared stories and skin as though such intimacy was the most natural thing in the world. Hessa would press idle kisses to Alina's shoulder blades, trail her fingers across her spine in thought. It was, in the desert, a language of love. Not romantic, but sacred. A testament to closeness.

And yet, Alina couldn't help but feel she was beginning to crave it more than she ought to.

'Waa kair janta,' Hessa said gently, her face now so close Alina could smell the sweet sharpness of mint leaves Hessa chewed to keep her breath fresh. 'Agari. Repeat.'

'Waa kair janta,' Alina mumbled, the words a little clumsy on her tongue.

Hessa giggled softly, cupping Alina's cheeks and giving them a playful squeeze. 'Close your mouth more, like this. Agari. Waa kair janta.'

Alina tensed beneath the touch, her gaze shifting to Hessa's lips for a fleeting moment. She quickly looked away.

'What does it mean?' she asked, breathlessly.

'In the Sandhii tongue,' Hessa replied, her voice quieter now, as if the meaning of the phrase belonged only to them, 'we have no words for I love you. So instead, we say waa kair janta... It means, to fall together.'

Alina said nothing. She simply nodded and let herself collapse back onto the bed, limbs heavy, heart heavier still. She whispered the words beneath her breath, again and again softly, like a spell. Her palm found its way to her chest, fingers pressing against the ache she didn't know how to name.

She didn't want to admit it aloud. Not yet. Not even to herself.

Her mind still lingered on Kai Blackburn, on the easy banter they had shared, the way she had felt seen, beautiful, wanted. But that version of herself... that girl belonged to another life. A life she wasn't certain she would ever find again. She didn't know where Kai was now. Or if he still lived at all.

The world had changed.

And so had she.

'Are you coming, amira?' Hessa called from across the room, already changed into something flowing and elegant. She gestured for Alina to rise and ready herself for the feast.

Alina smiled softly, almost to herself, and nodded. A quiet sigh of something like joy escaped her lips as she stood.

Waa kair janta.

We fall together.

Chapter Twenty-Two

House of Sun
Kingdom of Light

I was invited to witness the Sand Trials. An honour, as outsiders are rarely permitted to observe such a significant event in the Desert Kingdom. But I've been friends with its people my entire life.

I'm beyond excited. I've heard the trials are both thrilling and terrifying. Dunayans compete for leadership through a series of gruelling challenges that can take weeks to complete. To me, it's the perfect excuse to celebrate, and for the different tribes to come together.

Tabitha Wysteria

There was one thing Alina was quite certain of: she would never grow used to the peculiar cuisines of foreign lands.

Phoenixians, for instance, seemed to delight in elaborate dishes, most of them dry-cured meats spiced beyond recognition. And yet, even that was preferable to the desert delicacies Hessa adored—odd-looking insects soaked in fragrant spices and left to dry under the relentless sun. 'Pure protein,' Hessa had said with a proud smile. 'One acquires the taste.'

Alina remained unconvinced. She was quite sure the desert folk must have teeth in their stomachs to stomach such things.

It was strange, she thought, how grief so often took the shape of food. Of all the things she could miss from her homeland, it was the honey-coated pears that haunted her most. Succulent and sticky-sweet, they lingered in memory like ghosts, their syrupy touch still clinging to her lips in dreams. It seemed foolish to cry over fruit, and yet, the ache in her chest at the thought of never tasting them again threatened to unravel her.

If anyone knew how much her heart ached for something as simple as a pear... they would surely think her mad.

But loss made poets of them all. She had heard Hessa, more than once, speak longingly of her homeland, of spiced wind and star-kissed dunes, of the cool silence just before dawn. Even those who wore their strength like armour still bled inside for the things they had left behind.

As they sat beneath the stars for supper, Mareena had arranged for a charming space in one of the palace courtyards. A tranquil haven enclosed by tall palm trees and a floor split by a thin river, where shimmering fish darted like liquid gems. Servants had laid out dishes like a painted tapestry of flavours, but Alina scarcely noticed.

'Do you think your parents will go to war?' she asked softly, tearing a piece of flatbread in her lap.

Mareena took her time, mulling the question over with care. 'I cannot say for certain,' she replied at last, her voice gentle but distant. 'The death of my brother will be... devastating. But phoenixians have never been quick to take up arms. We are not a people eager for war, and I do not know if my father will act in haste.'

The unspoken truth lay heavy between them: we are no longer bound to the drakonians.

For centuries, phoenixians and drakonians had marched as one. Brothers in battle, the sun and the flame, united when it mattered. Still, there had always been a quiet sense of superiority from the phoenixian court, cloaked in their reverence for wisdom and scholarship. They had called the drakonians soldiers with swords but no thought, warriors bred for obedience, not strategy. And yet, when war called, they had always answered together.

Alina looked down at her plate, the food suddenly too rich in her mouth.

'My land...' she began, and her voice trembled as she spoke. 'I need an army to fight the witches. The drakonians left behind cannot do it alone.'

Mareena met her gaze for a moment before turning her face away. 'And I'm sure,' she said carefully, 'that when the time comes, my father will offer you one.'

But Alina heard the hesitation in Mareena's voice. She saw the truth behind those eyes. The words Mareena hadn't spoken. The truth that lingered in the hearts of everyone now.

No one was coming.

The Kingdom of Fire was reaping what it had once so mercilessly sown.

It had been the drakonians who had ignited the flames of the Great War, soaring into the lands of the witches upon the backs of dragons, raining fire upon their cities and turning their homes to ash. They had forced the other kingdoms into complicity, either to take up arms alongside them or to look the other way.

Now, the rest of the world was returning the favour in kind.

'They killed your brother,' Alina said through clenched teeth, the memory still burning behind her eyes. 'Do you not crave vengeance?'

Mareena sighed, her expression one of weary sorrow. 'Of course I do. But to go to war is to begin the cycle anew. Death begets death. They killed our brothers, so we kill theirs... and they will come again to take ours. And so it continues, endlessly, until the world is nothing but blood and ruin.'

Alina recoiled, stunned by her words. 'So your solution is what?' she snapped. 'That I surrender my kingdom because my ancestors once burnt theirs?'

'I'm not saying we'll let this go unchecked,' Mareena replied carefully. 'We will find a way to end this... problem.'

'*Massacre,*' Alina corrected, her voice low with fury. 'They slaughtered my entire family. I watched your brother die, cut down before me by the very ones you now hesitate to fight.'

Mareena's crimson eyes widened. 'I am not protecting them, Alina,' she said quickly. 'You misunderstand. But we must not let them drag us into war on their terms. That is what they want. They seek retribution for what was done to them, and they want us to strike the match.'

But Alina could not bear to listen a moment longer. She pushed herself up from the floor, her movements slow but burning with purpose, the quiet brush of fabric against stone the only sound in the stillness. Hessa's gentle touch found her arm, a silent attempt to soothe her, to reason with her. But there could be no reason, not now. Not with fire boiling in her veins.

'I want revenge,' Alina hissed, her voice fierce and trembling. 'And I will have it, with an army... or alone.'

She turned without bidding them farewell, her back straight and her footsteps swift as she left the courtyard and the princesses behind.

There was no more time for discussion. No more time for waiting.

Her next path was clear.

The Desert Kingdom awaited.

...

'Do you not regret saying goodbye? You might never see her

again,' Hessa asked softly after they had ridden together atop one of the great desert serpents, their scaled bodies gliding effortlessly over the golden dunes. They had stopped at last to rest the following day, the hours of relentless travel behind them. Conversation during the ride was impossible, the wind too fierce, the speed too unforgiving.

'Do you agree with her?' Alina asked once they had begun setting up camp, preparing food and readying themselves for the long stretch ahead. The journey to the Desert Kingdom would take nearly a week.

'I understand her logic, amira,' Hessa replied with a measured shrug, catching the sharpness in Alina's tawny gaze. 'But that does not mean she is right. One may comprehend what drives the witches... but that does not mean we must yield to it.'

Alina stood from where she'd been crouched, helping to thread sun-dried scorpions onto skewers. The scent of spice and heat hung thick in the air. 'I need a moment.'

'Alina, wait. You cannot walk off into the sands alone. We are no longer on the desert's edge. There are ghulas.'

'Ghulas?'

'Ghosts of the desert. Souls lost to the sands. They drift between the dunes, whispering lies and playing tricks upon the mind until you follow them to your death, so that they may not be so lonely.'

Alina arched a brow. 'I'll be a minute. I'll stay within your line of sight, Hessa. Don't fret.' She turned away, ignoring the tightening of Hessa's jaw, the words caught behind her teeth.

Alina walked, the sun scorching the top of her head, the weight of the heat pressing down on her like an invisible hand. Each step grew more arduous, the sand swallowing her feet, pulling her down as if the desert itself wished to consume her. Hessa had warned her not to lift her steps, but to drag them forward in a slow, gliding rhythm. At the time it had seemed absurd. How could walking be deadly? Now she understood.

Alina halted once she had drifted far enough to taste solitude, but not so far that she couldn't feel Hessa's eyes watching from the camp. She dropped to her knees, then sat heavily in the sand, her hands curling into fists against the blistering grains.

No matter which direction she turned, all she could see were dunes, wave after wave of golden hills rolling endlessly to the horizon. The hard-baked lands of the phoenixians had vanished behind her, swallowed by the desert. Here, there was nothing. Only silence. Only sand.

Closing her eyes, Alina conjured the image of her brother as he had once been in the sun-drenched courtyards of their ancestral castle, sweat glistening along his brow after hours of training with his men. Loyal Red Guard had stood vigil around the perimeter, poised and watchful, safeguarding their prince. The very same guards who would later turn traitor, their blades stained with royal blood as they cut down all within those sacred halls.

Ash spun on his heels, a rare smile softening the fire-forged lines of his face. The golden boy. Their Fire Prince. But the smile was not meant for her.

Alina turned, her heart caught between anticipation and dread. And there he was, Kai. He stepped into the courtyard, twin hook swords glinting in hand. The breath hitched in her chest. He was exactly as she remembered him. Tall and lean with shoulders made for carrying kingdoms, eyes as dark as storm-wrought skies, hair tousled by the wind. And that smile —god, that smile...

'Alina,' a voice whispered at her ear, rousing her from the reverie like a cold gust sweeping through memory. She jolted upright, convinced for a moment she'd find Hessa beside her, gently chiding her for daydreaming. But instead, she saw him— Ash—his face half-shattered, as though someone had caved it in with something unforgiving.

'Help m–me,' he gasped, his voice twisted with pain, before tumbling down the far side of the dune and out of reach.

'Ash!' Alina screamed, scrambling after him. Her feet tangled and she fell, striking the ground with a thud that stole her breath. The sand was not soft as stories claimed, but hard and unrelenting. Her mouth filled with it, choking her as she spat the grains from her tongue.

She raised her head, blinking furiously. Her brother was gone.

'Alina...'

There! Further still, impossibly distant. How had he moved so quickly?

Clambering to her feet, she ran, heedless of the way the world behind her began to vanish. The camp was no longer in sight. Hessa's warning about wandering too far echoed dimly in the back of her mind, but she silenced it. She couldn't leave him. Not again.

'Ash, I thought you were dead...' she panted. He stood motionless, his back to her. 'Ash?' Her voice trembled.

When he turned, she cried out. His face dissolved before her eyes, skin and bone melting into another, one she recognised all too well.

Kai.

But not the Kai she adored. This version of him was torn and disfigured, a cruel mirror of what could have been.

'Look what they did to us,' he spat, voice like venom. 'While you stood by and did nothing.'

A pair of arms yanked her backwards and she tumbled,

colliding against a warm body. Still staring, heart racing, she watched as Kai vanished like smoke in the wind. Gone, as if he'd never been there at all.

She lay breathless atop Hessa.

'Salla astapada nanaha!' the desert princess snarled in her native tongue.

Alina didn't need a translation. She could guess every word.

'I saw—'

'You saw *nothing*, amira,' Hessa said, her voice firm, though not unkind. 'It was a ghula. They enter your thoughts, weave your longings into visions. They show you what your heart most desires and then trap you in it.'

'But Ash... he felt real.'

Hessa sighed, lifting Alina to her feet and folding her into a tight embrace. 'But he wasn't, Alina. Your brother is gone. He is not here.'

Alina's body went limp in Hessa's arms. Her face crumpled as silent grief bled through her composure.

'I'm sorry, amira. But you must never do that again. When we reach my kingdom, know this. The desert is bewitched. It shifts with the moon, hiding our lands from outsiders. If you wander off, even I may not find you again.'

Alina nodded, the weight of the warning settling deep in her bones.

Suddenly, the ground beneath them began to quiver. A low, ominous tremor rumbled through the sand, growing rapidly in intensity. Both girls stumbled, falling into each other's arms as the earth seemed to groan and shift beneath their feet.

'What is that?' Alina gasped, clutching Hessa as the tremors worsened.

Hessa's white eyes flared with horror.

'Arahni mhaarta,' she whispered.

'What?'

'The death spider,' Hessa translated, her voice barely above a breath. 'It lives beneath the sand, but when disturbed... it rises.'

Alina shrieked at the mere thought. They scrambled up the slope of the dune, the ground shifting treacherously beneath them. Tremors pulsed like a heartbeat through the earth, sand slipping beneath their feet. Below, long spindly legs pierced the surface like skeletal spears.

Hessa shoved Alina up the final stretch just as the creature fully emerged, and Alina froze.

The spider was monstrous, larger than a valkyrian winged horse, its limbs long and jointed like warped spears, its carapace shimmering like obsidian glass. As it reared, the ground groaned. Its maw gaped wide, revealing rows of razor-like teeth as fine and numerous as grains of sand.

The world tilted. Hessa lost her grip and tumbled, her scream stolen by the wind as she slipped down the dune. Alina's own cry followed her descent.

Knife flashing in hand, Hessa struck just moments before the beast's maw could devour her. Her blade sliced deep into the flesh of its mouth, sending the spider lurching back in agony. It writhed, legs flailing violently, casting up clouds of sand. Hessa struck again, tearing her way free of the gaping mouth, dropping low as one of the legs sliced through the air beside her.

She slashed through it with one clean arc, but another leg caught her unawares, crashing into the back of her skull. She crumpled, unmoving.

'Hessa!' Alina screamed, paralysed for a breath before instincts seized her. Without thought, she launched herself down the dune, her body tumbling through the burning sand. She hit the bottom hard, rolled, then sprinted to Hessa's side.

The spider loomed, bleeding, furious.

Grabbing the fallen dagger, Alina swung with every ounce of fear and fury in her veins, slicing at any leg that dared creep towards them. The desert blade—a long, elegant curve of steel, allowed her reach without closing the distance. But still, one of the spider's limbs lashed out, cracking against her chest and hurling her backwards. Air fled her lungs.

Gasping, she rolled, narrowly dodging a second blow. With a wild cry, she slashed again, this time cleaving deep. The spider shrieked, a sound like shattered glass and flame. Black ichor sprayed across the sand.

Panting, Alina seized the broken remnant of a severed leg, hoisting it like a spear. The spider turned, its tiny, glistening, murderous eyes fixing on her.

And Alina ran.

Straight for the mouth.

The beast opened wide, its breath rancid with decay. Alina screamed and plunged the jagged limb deep into its gullet, shoving with everything she had until the spider spasmed and thrashed, its limbs collapsing beneath its bulk.

It choked, convulsed, and finally stilled.

Alina dropped to her knees, chest heaving, her arms trembling from the effort. For a moment, all was silent.

Then she breathed.

'You killed it.'

Alina spun round, her chest bursting with breathless relief at the sight of Hessa sitting upright.

'By the blazing light of the Sun God!' Alina gasped, racing to Hessa's side. She dropped to her knees, hands reaching to cup Hessa's face, as if only by touch could she confirm the desert princess was truly alive. The warmth of Hessa's skin grounded her; the pulse beneath her fingertips a blessing.

'You killed it,' Hessa repeated, her white eyes fixed on the collapsed monstrosity strewn across the sands.

Alina's joy faltered slightly. She bit her lip. 'Was it sacred?' she asked cautiously. Surely not, surely she had done no wrong by saving Hessa's life. She could not have left her to the mercy of a beast, divine or otherwise.

But Hessa shook her head slowly, awe flickering in her gaze. 'No one has ever killed one and lived to speak of it,' she said softly, wonder dancing in her voice like desert wind across dunes.

Alina followed Hessa's gaze to the spider's massive corpse. Her stomach turned at the sight of its lifeless, grotesque form.

'Just luck,' she muttered with a small shrug.

'That is not luck, amira.' Hessa's voice was low, reverent. 'You came back for me. You fought a death spider, for me.'

'I'd never leave you behind.' Alina smiled, eyes warm. 'What is it your people say? Sahraa qamh haiklii.'

Hessa's eyes lit up. 'You remembered.'

Alina rose, brushing grains of sand from her robes. 'A grain does not make a desert. We are one.' Her smile deepened. 'I'd never forget.' She offered Hessa the dagger, its curved blade stained and still trembling in her grip. But the desert princess shook her head gently.

'It is yours now, amira. You have earned the right to carry a desert blade.'

Alina looked down at the dagger with new eyes, tracing the pale white stone embedded in its hilt. It reminded her of Hessa's eyes—sharp, otherworldly, and gleaming with ancient power. She had never taken a life before, and while a beast was no man, she felt a strange thrill in her veins, a sense of awakening. The image of Hagan's throat beneath this blade flitted like a whisper through her thoughts.

Her fingers curled more tightly around the hilt.

Still smiling to herself, Alina reached for Hessa's hand, lacing their fingers together as they made their way back across the ever-shifting sands, towards the safety of camp, and whatever destiny awaited them next.

Chapter Twenty-Three

House of Shadows
Kingdom of Darkness

Wyverians are like no other. Each kingdom holds its own unique beauty. I love how wolverians can endure absolutely anything. Even in the darkest of times, when most would give up, they press on. I love how the desert folk live in such unity, breathing as one. I love the way phoenixians are so patient, always thinking things through before leaping into action. Calm and considered. I love how valkyrians set aside their own desires to do what is right. I love how drakonians take such pride in their land, in everything they build and create. I love the Fae and their care for their own, for nature and every living creature. And then there are the wyverians. A blend of it all.

They endure. They are united. They are patient, calm, just, proud, and they fight for those who cannot.

Tabitha Wysteria

'There. That section of the wall has been torn down completely.'

The wall had risen after the Great War, stone upon stone, a solemn testament to victory and fear, built by the united hands of seven kingdoms to cage the witches' wastelands apart from the living world. Yet now, where its ancient spine met the shadowed borders of the Kingdom of Darkness, a section lay sundered, torn open as though by some great, merciless hand. Clearly the witches had obliterated sections of it, clearing a path in their hubris. Ironically, it suited Kai's army rather well.

Scaling the ancient barrier would have been no easy feat, but now an open expanse stretched before them, a barren no-man's land, shadowed by uncertainty.

'We don't know what lies out there,' Adriana warned, her tone clipped with caution. 'We ought to take to the skies on wyverns and scout the territory from above.'

'Then they'll know we're coming!' Keir snapped, exasperated. 'We'll lose the element of surprise, Adriana!'

'We patrol on wyverns all the time,' she retorted. 'Why would they assume it's anything more than routine? Besides, am I the only one that thinks it's a little suspicious that part of the wall has been destroyed? It's almost as if they knew we'd be coming and wanted to make it easy for us.'

Inside the command tent, Kai and Ash stood side by side at the long wooden table, maps spread before them like delicate threads of fate waiting to be unravelled. They said little, allowing the squabble between Adriana and Keir to play out as Cronan observed from a corner, releasing a low, brooding huff every now and again.

The army had made camp within the depths of one of the wyverian forests, a dense, shadowed sprawl that offered perfect concealment from prying eyes. The trees loomed high, their canopies thick enough to block even the faintest glimmer of moonlight, exactly the kind of obscurity they needed to keep hidden from the witches.

Kai had long since explained that Adriana and Keir were their most formidable tacticians, though the price of their brilliance was their constant bickering. Every few days they convened like this, gathering around the table to argue through strategy until something, anything, resembled consensus. Eventually, they always emerged with a plan, but not without bruised egos and the occasional near-duel.

'Perhaps we worry less about why a part of the wall was torn down and worry more about our plan of stepping through it,' Kai said.

A voice called for Kai from beyond the tent. With a brisk pat to Ash's shoulder, he murmured something unintelligible and strode out into the grey morning light, leaving the drakonian prince to keep watch in case the argument devolved into blades and bloodshed. It wouldn't have been the first time.

Over the years of training together, Kai had grown familiar with the combative rhythm of Adriana and Keir. Their rivalry had been fiery, loud, often infuriating and yet, beautiful in its own way. Their resentment had slowly ripened into respect, that respect into something gentler, warmer. Love, and then marriage. Kai had observed it all with a quiet, wistful envy. He had wondered, once, if he might find his own Adriana.

And then he had met Alina.

But the thought of her struck like an arrow to the ribs. He clenched his jaw and forced the image of her from his mind. He would not think of her. It hurt too much.

'What is it?' Kai asked, his voice low as he followed one of his soldiers deeper into the shadowed glade, a part of the forest left untouched by the bustle of camp.

The young man glanced back nervously. 'Some of the men found something. A girl... wandering alone.'

'A girl?' Kai's brow furrowed, suspicion prickling at his skin.

'She claims she's lost.'

'In these woods?' Kai's tone sharpened. 'What does she look like?'

'Wyverian, or so she appears.'

That meant very little. Ash had warned him time and again that witches could mask themselves as anything or anyone.

Glamours were as easy to them as breathing. If the girl bore the likeness of a wyverian, it was all the more reason to be cautious.

'Take me to her,' Kai ordered, already bracing himself for deceit. No true wyverian became lost within their homeland. The Kingdom of Darkness might be small and sparsely populated, but its people were bred from youth to navigate it with their eyes shut. At fourteen, they entered military training. At sixteen, they chose: return to civilian life or forge ahead into specialised combat units. Either way, they did not lose their way in wyverian woods.

He arrived to find a handful of his men encircling a young woman, her arms wrapped tightly around herself, a picture of fragility. She looked frightened, too frightened. Something about her posture was off. There was no wyverian discipline in the way she stood, no hint of the battle-hardened posture that came with years of training. His instincts stirred.

'My men tell me you're lost,' he said slowly, studying her every twitch, every breath.

Her eyes flickered. Then, too quickly, a smile bloomed across her lips.

'Seize her!' Kai barked, but it was already too late.

'Glacio,' she whispered.

A soft green shimmer pulsed from her fingertips. Kai's soldiers froze mid-step, their limbs locked in place by invisible threads.

She hadn't touched him.

She hadn't frozen him.

Kai's blades were drawn in an instant, his black hook swords gleaming with faint embers, the steel forged in blue wyvern flame, honed by blood and fire. His arms were taut, ready to strike. Only one question mattered.

'Why didn't you bind me?' he asked.

'I'm not here to fight you,' the girl replied, calm despite the steel in his hands. 'I came to help.'

He didn't lower his swords.

'Why would a witch want to help me?'

Her glamour dissolved like mist in morning light, revealing the truth beneath. Her skin was a deep sun-kissed bronze, her hair a pale, almost spectral white. Her unnatural and vivid eyes shimmered purple like enchanted amethysts. Tattoos, runes in swirling script, climbed up her arms to her elbows.

Recognition dawned.

'Vera,' Kai said warily.

The girl shook her head. 'I'm her sister. Dawn,' she replied. 'Though Ash knew me by another name.'

Kai remembered the tale well of how Ash had once fallen for a drakonian girl who had, in truth, been a witch in disguise. It had been Ash himself who recounted the story one night, their breath clouding in the cold as they passed a bottle between them. Keir and Adriana had been quarrelling over a game of cards, as they so often did, while Ash had stared into the fire with a haunted look in his eyes.

'Adara,' Kai murmured now, the name slipping from his lips before he could call it back. 'Why are you here?'

The girl—no, the witch—lowered her gaze. 'Because...' Her voice faltered. 'I need to know. Is he...did she... did she kill him?'

Kai gave a humourless snort. 'Ash Acheron still breathes. My sister broke the curse.'

Dawn's purple eyes widened in disbelief. 'Thank Hecate,' she whispered. 'Then I must help him. I won't let anything happen to him.'

Kai's jaw clenched, the old bitterness rising to the surface like bile. 'And yet you let his parents and sister be butchered?'

he snapped.

Something shimmered behind those strange, otherworldly eyes. Shame, perhaps. Or guilt. She bit her lip but didn't answer.

'Take me as your guide,' she said instead, her voice steady now. 'Let me prove myself.'

Kai's laugh was cold. 'You'd lead us to your own kind? And I'm meant to believe that?' He stepped closer, his hook swords gleaming at his sides. 'You're not getting anywhere near Ash. I won't have you crawling back into his head. He's married. To my sister.'

A trace of pain passed over her face, but she lifted her chin with quiet defiance. 'Then make me your prisoner. I'll prove my worth. I thought he was gone...'

Kai narrowed his eyes. 'And why shouldn't I strike you down where you stand, witch?'

Her mouth curled in a sharp, sardonic smile. 'Because, whether you care to admit it or not, I'm worth more alive. I'm your map, your key, your eyes behind enemy lines. If you truly believe you can walk into my homeland without crumbling to ash, then you're more foolish than you look.'

He hated that she was right.

He didn't trust her. Gods, how could he? Not someone who had once held Ash's heart in her hands. But information was everything. And if she could be useful... if he could keep her hidden, use her as leverage...

Kai's thoughts turned quickly. The others must not know. If word reached his men, they'd tear her apart before she drew another breath.

'Can you make them believe you were just a wyverian girl? That you vanished into the woods?'

Dawn's mouth curled into something sly and serpentine, and for a moment, Kai wondered if he was walking straight into a trap of his own making.

'They're still frozen,' she said. 'They saw nothing. Heard nothing.'

He retrieved a short length of rope from his belt—the kind used to restrain prisoners—and stepped forward, binding her wrists. Her smile didn't fade. If anything, it grew, as though the rope were little more than a formality. As though it amused her.

'You'll be kept as a prisoner. Out of sight. If you step out of line, I'll cut you down myself.' Kai seized the end of the rope binding her wrists and gave it a sharp tug, drawing her forward. 'Unfreeze them. I'm taking you to my tent. You'll remain there. You will not wander.'

'Oh? Do you want me all to yourself?' she asked, her voice lilting with mockery.

Kai's jaw clenched. She shifted again, no longer the frightened girl, nor the grieving lover, but something altogether more dangerous: amused, unbothered, entirely in control of the moment. A woman who enjoyed watching men squirm.

'You will hold your tongue unless spoken to, witch.'

'And how exactly do you intend to keep me quiet?' she said, one brow arching, the challenge in her eyes unmistakable. 'I've told you, I'm here to help.'

'That remains to be seen,' he replied through gritted teeth.

He gave the rope another pull, more forceful this time, and Dawn stumbled forward. Her purple gaze sparked with restrained fury, her fingers twitching faintly with green light. A heartbeat later, the soldiers around them blinked back into awareness, glancing about in confusion, trying to make sense of the gap in time.

But by then, Kai and his captive had already vanished into the shadows.

...

'Charming little arrangement,' Dawn muttered as Kai thrust her through the flap of his private tent. Without hesitation, she strode towards the bed and climbed onto it, sprawling with deliberate insolence.

'Off,' Kai growled.

'I'm not a dog.'

'You're right.' He yanked the sheets with a swift tug, sending her tumbling to the floor. 'I respect dogs.'

She hissed, her eyes narrowing into dangerous slits as she remained seated on the ground, pride dented but unbroken. Kai unbuckled his twin hook swords and placed them just inside the entrance. No one entered his tent without summons, and certainly never without calling out first. He had always been fiercely private, and his tent, pitched slightly apart from the others was a symbol of that. As a commander, his strength and prowess meant he didn't require guards standing sentinel. In wyverian culture, such a thing would be seen not as caution, but as cowardice.

'Tell me everything,' he commanded, sinking into a nearby chair. 'Are there witches still hiding in the wastelands?'

Dawn wrinkled her nose. 'No invitation to supper first?' she said, feigning offence. 'How rude.'

'Drop the performance. I want information. Without it, you're worthless to me.'

'I want to see Ash.'

'Absolutely not. If you truly care for him, start by helping me.'

With a huff, Dawn cast her gaze around the tent, her purple eyes drifting languidly over the space before settling on him.

When they did, Kai felt his body instinctively tense.

'Do I make you nervous, commander?'

'No.'

'I smell a lie.'

'And I smell a witch roasting if she doesn't stop playing games,' he snapped.

He expected her to flinch. To falter. But instead, her eyes shimmered with amusement. The ease with which she seemed to drink in his fury only served to deepen his own.

'I'm hungry.'

'Information first.'

She lounged back against the footboard of the bed now, deliberately arching, her back curving just so, her gown slipping slightly up her legs—long and dark and maddeningly smooth. The provocation was clear. A trap.

'You're not my type, witch.'

'Oh?' she purred. 'Do you have a type? I can be anything you desire. I've heard you're rather partial to the drakonian form.'

At that, Kai shot to his feet, rage etched into the lines of his face. For the first time, he saw a flash of fear in her expression. He should have felt shame, but didn't. Instead, he drank it in like a man starved of justice. And that terrified him more than she ever could. The old Kai would never have taken satisfaction in watching a woman tremble. But witches...Witches were different. And all he could think of was how easy it would be to break her neck.

'I'll have guards stationed outside. If you try to leave, even glamoured, they'll hunt you down. You'll never see Ash again. Is that clear?'

Dawn gave a dramatic pout. 'Will you spank me for misbehaving, commander?'

'Witch...' he growled, voice edged with warning.

'All right, all right. I'll be good,' she sighed, rolling her eyes as she settled herself with mock decorum. 'I promise not to move. Cross my little heart, witch's honour.'

Kai grunted, the sound low and disgruntled. He could no longer stand to be in the same space as her. Without another word, he turned on his heel and strode out, barking an order to two nearby soldiers to keep watch over his tent. It was a dangerous gamble. If anyone caught so much as a glimpse of her, chaos would erupt. But if she truly meant what she said about wanting to help Ash, she'd behave herself.

He muttered a string of curses under his breath as he marched into the morning light, needing to be far, very far, from those infernal purple eyes.

Chapter Twenty-Four

House of Shadows
Kingdom of Darkness

It is hard to watch the land I once fell so deeply in love with become my enemy. The wyverians turned on us, joining forces with the drakonians. They drew their swords and cut us down. Hadrian's brothers... they knew me. They dined with me, laughed with me, danced with me. And yet, they believe the lies. They truly think I've bewitched Hadrian. Now they roam the lands, hunting for us, hunting for me. To kill me and save their brother.

Tabitha Wysteria

'The sooner we strike, the greater our chances of success,' Adriana reasoned, her voice clipped with urgency.

Kai found the war council exactly where he'd left them, huddled over maps as dusk crept in. The day had slipped through his fingers like sand, most of it spent sparring with soldiers, trying and failing to ignore the simmering presence currently confined to his tent. He had no intention of returning before nightfall. Let the witch stew in her discomfort.

A small, begrudging part of him wondered whether she might make a scene by slipping past the guards and stirring chaos through the ranks. But Dawn was only one witch pitted against thousands of trained wyverians. She'd be reduced to ash before she could whisper the first syllable of a spell.

Glamouring herself might buy her a few seconds, but she didn't carry herself like one of them. She didn't move or speak the way a wyverian did. She'd be exposed before she even had time to blink.

'Not yet,' Kai muttered, rolling his shoulders with a wince. Cronan had joined him for training earlier, and the brute struck like a raging storm. Already, Kai could feel the dull ache blooming across his body, the promise of far worse pain come morning. 'We need more information.'

He caught the way Ash glanced at him when he mentioned needing more information. That single glance said enough. Did Ash already know? He couldn't ask. If the Fire Prince was unaware and learnt that Dawn had infiltrated the camp, claiming she was there to protect him, to fight for him...it would unravel everything.

Kai had despised the idea of Mal being bound to a drakonian. He'd loathed their stolen glances, the softening of her voice whenever Ash was near. But now, after everything... he would shield Ash with his own life. For Mal. Because he owed her that much.

'But Kai...' Adriana's tone sharpened. Her dark eyes narrowed. 'We're sitting ducks.'

'We wait.' His answer was final.

He didn't linger to endure the storm of protests sure to follow. Instead, he left them behind, retreating into the greying light of early evening. The sky, veiled in dusky clouds, blushed crimson beneath the rising red moon. As he neared his tent, a sliver of hope sparked. Perhaps she'd gone. Slipped away, vanished like smoke, leaving behind no trace. But fate was rarely so kind.

She was still there.

Kai dropped the bowl of food at her feet, not bothering to

hide the indifference in the gesture as half its contents spilt unceremoniously onto the ground. Dawn's lips curled in distaste, but she gave a careless shrug and knelt to retrieve each piece with her still-bound hands. Kai watched, arms crossed, silently revelling in her awkward struggle. He waited, almost with anticipation, to see her attempt to stomach wyverian rations.

'You can wipe that smug grin off your face,' she hissed, her tone sharp as a blade. 'I could enchant this slop into something fit for a feast.'

Kai clucked his tongue, settling onto a stool with an amused glint in his eye. 'My tent. My rules. You want to remain here, you eat what we eat.'

Their eyes locked, two lethal weapons sizing the other up. Neither flinched. Neither blinked. Finally, Dawn snorted and plucked up a piece of half-rotten fruit. She wrinkled her nose at the stench, but bit into it all the same, never looking away. 'Delicious,' she said, her sarcasm thick as honey.

'Finish every last scrap or you won't be fed again, witch.'

'Do you treat all your guests with such charming wyverian hospitality, commander?'

'You're not a guest,' he replied. 'And I'm not a commander.' He kept his face impassive, masking the lie with practiced ease. The fewer truths she uncovered, the safer they remained. He would give her nothing. Not names, not ranks, not even breadcrumbs to follow.

'Oh?' Her brows lifted with intrigue. 'Did I mistake you then? Is the infamous Kai Blackburn merely a common soldier?'

'Eat,' he said through clenched teeth, 'and hold your tongue.'

Dawn obliged, though with the theatricality of a travelling performer. She chewed loudly, messily, as though mocking him with every exaggerated bite. Sauce from the meat dribbled slowly down her chin, and when she caught him looking, her grin was wicked.

'Care to lick it off?' she asked, tilting her head. 'From the way you're watching me, I could swear I'm tonight's main course.'

'You wish, witch,' Kai growled. 'I'd never touch you.'

'Bit squeamish, are we?' Her laugh echoed through the tent, wrapping around him like smoke, cloying and maddening.

Kai's jaw clenched. He needed air. He needed distance. But above all, he needed answers, and she was the only one who might give them. Whether she gave them freely... that was another matter entirely.

'You need to start talking. Now.'

Something in his tone, or perhaps the steel in his eyes, must have struck a chord, for Dawn gave a small nod, placing the bowl gently to one side with surprising care. The tenderness of the act unsettled Kai. He hadn't thought her capable of gentleness.

'Hagan won't rest until the great Houses lie in ruin and the Kingdom of Fire is reduced to ash.'

'Why?'

'Because he despises the drakonians more than anything,' she said, her voice low. 'It was the Acherons who led the skies a hundred years ago, raining fire upon our lands, burning every witch city to cinders. But there's more.' Her gaze veered away, suddenly distant. 'Hagan's father was a drakonian. He... he raped Hagan's mother. That's how he was born. Half-drakonian, half-witch. Born of violence. Of hate.'

Kai's brows lifted, taken aback.

'I know what you're thinking,' Dawn sighed. 'If he shares their blood, why loathe them so deeply? But wouldn't you? If the people who gave you life were the very ones who shattered your world? Who violated your family, turned your home into a desert of bones and broken dreams? I think Hagan has more reasons to hate them than most.'

'You speak as if you share his hatred.'

She shook her head, but the denial rang hollow. Even she didn't seem convinced. 'Ash changed that. He made me realise the world isn't divided into light and shadow. Sometimes... it's just grey. Blurred. Complicated.'

Her eyes found his, purple and haunting, and he turned away before their weight could crush him. Gods, she resembled Vera. But where Vera had been all sharp lines and angles, Dawn was soft. Her face was rounder, lips fuller, her gaze impossibly wide. She looked like a doll, the kind a lonely child might enchant and wish into a sister.

'So you've betrayed your own for what, exactly? You didn't even know if Ash was alive.'

'I needed to know,' she whispered. 'I felt it, somehow. That he wasn't gone. That if he had been, I'd have known. Here.' She placed a hand over her heart. 'But I couldn't rest without seeing for myself. If Hagan finds out Ash survived... he won't stop until his head is on a spike.'

Kai's hand moved unconsciously to his chest. Was that true? Should he have felt something when his sister died? When Alina...

'You don't truly believe he'll just run back into your arms, do you?' he asked, his voice rough.

Dawn gave a delicate shrug. 'Haven't you ever been foolish for love?'

His breath caught. Pain twisted through him, raw and sharp. Dawn saw it, the tightening in his jaw, the shift in his expression.

'Wouldn't you try to save her?' she asked softly.

'I would,' Kai said, fists clenching at his sides. 'But I can't. Because your people murdered her.'

Dawn's lips parted, perhaps to defend herself or offer some hollow comfort, but Kai was already moving, unable to remain a moment longer beneath the same canvas as one of Alina and Haven's killers. Whether Dawn had wielded the blade herself mattered little. She was a witch, and she had been at the castle. That made her culpable, her hands as stained as any who had struck the fatal blows.

His chest heaved with the weight of fury barely contained, thoughts of Hagan rising like wildfire in his mind. One day, they would meet again, and when they did, Kai would show him no mercy.

'Go to sleep,' he said curtly, not bothering to meet her eyes as he reached the threshold.

Her voice followed him, soft and uncertain, like the rustle of dying embers. 'Where will you sleep?'

He didn't turn. Wouldn't give her the satisfaction of seeing the ache beneath his rage.

'Anywhere,' he muttered, his tone sharp as steel, 'is better than beside you.'

...

'Kai!'

He jolted awake, breath catching in his throat. He'd dozed off against the trunk of a gnarled tree, just far enough from camp that no one would question his absence, assuming him tucked away in his tent. Clearly, that illusion had shattered.

Blinking the sleep from his eyes, he looked up into the face of an irate Adriana. Her scowl deepened the more conscious he became, and the sheer exhaustion her presence stirred within him made his bones ache.

'You look too much like her.'

Adriana exhaled heavily and dropped down beside him, the weariness in her limbs matching his own. 'I know,' she said. 'Everyone says so. I miss her more than anything else in this damned world. I'd give anything, *anything*, to have my best friend back.' Her hands clenched into trembling fists, small but fierce. 'I used to have long hair, once. Can you believe it? Back when we were fourteen. The first time you invited me to the castle, remember? That's when I met Haven. She was so beautiful it made my heart ache. When I went home, I grabbed a kitchen knife and cut my hair short, just to look like her. It came out awful, jagged and uneven, but a few days later, she saw me and said it suited me.' Adriana gave a soft laugh. 'I've worn it like this ever since.'

'I never knew.' He reached over, gently tugging at a short strand. 'I don't know what to do without her...'

Adriana's attention drifted towards the camp, her brow creased with quiet sorrow. 'You wake up. You get through the day. You go to sleep. And you do it again. Until the pain dulls.'

'Will it?' Kai whispered, the weight in his chest threatening to drown him. 'Will it ever stop hurting?'

Her fingers brushed his hand. 'I doubt it. But we can try.'

She rested her head against his arm. Together, they watched the waking camp stir, the crimson tint of night giving way to the cold grey light of another unrelenting day. For a moment, silence settled between them, gentle and almost soothing. Until, inevitably, Adriana ruined it.

'Why do you have a witch in your tent?'

Kai nearly choked. 'How did you...?'

Adriana rolled her eyes. 'Kai. It's me. Haven and I spent half our adolescence spying on you, remember? Besides, you're acting very shifty. I can practically smell your guilt. And you've placed two soldiers outside your tent like they're ornamental statues. I'm amazed no one's caught on yet.'

He groaned, rubbing at his face. 'It's complicated. But she's offering information, real intelligence. Things we can use against the witches.'

'A witch turning against her own?' Adriana raised a brow. 'Now that's either madness or treachery. Fine. I'll trust you on this. But you need to move her farther out. Keep her in the shadows. Someone's bound to spot her sooner or later, and if they do, you won't have time to explain before her throat's slit.'

Kai returned to his tent, relief trickling through his limbs at the sight of the witch lying obediently on the bed. The serenity of the image was tainted, however, by the thought of her touching his sheets. He'd burn the whole damn lot once she was dead.

'We need to move,' he said, strapping his hook swords to the back of his armour and tossing a few essentials into a small leather bag.

'Why?' Dawn asked, lifting her head with mild irritation.

'Because it's too dangerous to have you—' Kai froze mid-sentence at the unmistakable sound of Keir's laugh drawing closer. Adriana's voice followed, light and deliberate. She was stalling him, likely trying to buy Kai a few precious moments. But it wouldn't be enough. If they stepped out now, Keir would spot them before they could blink.

'Use your magic,' Kai hissed.

'Excuse me?' Dawn scowled at his tone, lips curling in distaste. 'Why?'

'Someone's coming! If he sees you, I won't be able to protect you.'

'How noble,' she muttered. 'And what exactly do you expect

me to do?'

'Turn us invisible!'

'Magic doesn't work like that, commander!' Her voice sharpened with panic as her fingers began to glow faintly green. 'Untie me!'

'Do something, witch!'

'I could… transport us somewhere, but it's risky. I might send us somewhere else entirely…' Her breath quickened, eyes wide and wild as footsteps drew closer. Kai's hands clamped around hers, refusing to let her vanish without him.

'Do something!'

Outside, the guards were faltering, unable to stall Keir much longer. His boots were heavy against the earth, and his suspicion was palpable. The tent flaps flew open.

But Kai and Dawn were gone.

Where they'd been standing only a lingering wisp of emerald smoke danced into nothing, curling like mist. Keir staggered into the tent, coughing on the faint dust that remained, calling out for Kai.

Kai crashed onto hard ground with a grunt, the world spinning as though it had been knocked loose from its axis. His stomach lurched, and the remnants of his supper met the grass with force. Swearing under his breath, he wiped his mouth, breath shallow as he tried to anchor himself.

'It'll pass,' Dawn said calmly. 'You get used to it after a while.'

He was flat on his back, the witch already on her feet beside him, seemingly unfazed. When he dared to open his eyes, the scenery greeted him like a slap—lush, vibrant green exploding in every direction. Sitting up too quickly proved foolish. He vomited again.

'Stop it. You're only making it worse.'

'Where in the nine hells are we?' he groaned.

'No idea,' she muttered, frowning as she turned in a slow circle. 'I don't recognise this forest.'

Kai forced himself to breathe deeply, grounding his thoughts. The spinning finally lessened. Rising unsteadily to his feet, he took in the vivid paradise surrounding them. The colours were richer here, the greens almost luminous. Petals the size of shields hung from trees with twisting golden bark. Even in the Kingdom of Fire, with its gilded brilliance and scorching beauty, he'd never seen flora quite like this.

'You stupid witch!' Kai snarled, turning sharply away from her, fists clenched at his sides to stop himself from doing something regrettable. 'This is the Kingdom of Fauna!'

'You think I planned this?' she snapped, her voice pitching into a furious shriek. 'You pressured me! I didn't have a moment to focus. I couldn't even think of a destination! The magic twisted. And now... we're here.' Her attention roamed across the landscape, sharpening as the truth of it struck her like a blow.

'We are miles from my camp!' Kai roared, his face reddening with rage. 'How do you expect to help Ash when we're half a world away from him?'

Without warning, Dawn bent down and flung a handful of earth at his face. Mud splattered against his cheek, stopping him mid-rant. He blinked, stunned. 'Did you just shove mud in my face?'

'It's easier to look at you now,' she said sweetly, sticking her tongue out.

'Is this a game to you, witch?'

'Screaming at me isn't going to get you home any faster.' She leaned back when he moved towards her, hands still bound but dancing out of his reach. 'What do you think you're doing?'

'Send us back,' he growled.

'Ask me nicely.'

'Witch, do as I say.'

She turned her face away with exaggerated elegance, chin lifted high. 'I think I rather like it here.'

'This is Fae territory,' Kai bit out. 'They'll smell your magic.'

'Then I'll glamour myself,' she replied, fluttering her lashes. 'I've always wondered what I'd look like with antlers.'

'They'll sense your magic's different,' he snapped.

Unbothered, her attention drifted to the black horns crowning his head. 'If I yank one of these, does it make you fart?'

Kai's expression twisted into a thundercloud of fury. 'Back. Now.'

'I can't.'

His voice dropped into something feral. 'What do you mean, you can't?'

'Magic isn't infinite, commander.' Her voice had softened now, her earlier humour tempered by a grim note of truth. 'Travelling such a distance takes everything. Two people... gods, that kind of spell is nearly impossible. It will take days, maybe even weeks, before I have enough power to try again.'

Kai let out a wordless roar and kicked the nearest tree, its bark splintering beneath the blow. He screamed up at the canopy, his frustration echoing like thunder through the emerald hush of the woods.

When silence finally fell over them, he began to walk. Of course, the witch followed, her steps light behind him.

'Do you know where you're going?' she asked innocently.

'No,' he hissed.

'Shouldn't we stop and ask someone?'

'Do you see anyone?' he growled. 'If you do, be my guest. And while you're at it, ask if they've got a leash for you.'

She kicked him, hard, right behind the knee, and Kai stumbled forward with a grunt of surprise. The sheer indignity of being bested by a witch sent him into a tirade of colourful curses, which only made Dawn burst into delighted laughter.

'I'm going to kill you.'

'You can try,' she replied sweetly, then promptly stopped walking and leaned back against a tree trunk as though it were a chaise longue.

'What are you doing now?' he snapped.

'I'm exhausted.'

'Keep walking.'

'No. And you can't make me.'

Kai didn't hesitate. With a growl of frustration, he hauled the witch over his shoulder like a sack of flour. She shrieked, flailing her arms and thumping at his back, though her strength was pitiful—drained, no doubt, by the magic she'd used earlier.

'Put me down this instant!'

'Make me.'

'When I get my magic back,' she hissed, squirming furiously, 'you'd best be prepared. I'll turn that stupid, ugly, disgusting face into a rabbit. No woman will ever look at you again!'

'Sounds peaceful. I've always fancied a quiet life.'

'I'll shrink your genitals to the size of pebbles! Tiny ones!'

'They were far too large anyway.'

She writhed like a furious cat, determined to slip from his grasp, but when he gave her bottom a light slap, she froze, utterly scandalised. Then came the boiling rage. She screeched until her throat burnt, shouting obscenities and threats that would have made a soldier blush.

Kai halted and dropped her unceremoniously onto the ground. She landed with a thud and spat at his boots, seething.

'Charming,' he muttered as she continued to hiss like a cornered snake. 'Will you shut up for one blessed moment? I think I know where we are.'

Dawn rose, brushing herself off with as much dignity as she could muster, her purple eyes ablaze with loathing. Kai found it... mildly entertaining.

'You can stop glaring at me like that, witch. I'm not going to kiss you. You're not my type.'

'How dare—'

He slapped a hand over her mouth before she could finish, then gestured ahead. For a long, tense moment, they stared at one another, brimming with mutual contempt. Finally, she yanked his hand away and turned to follow his gaze.

'It's a tree, commander,' she drawled, unimpressed. 'Have you never seen one before?'

'It's not just any tree.' His shoulders stiffened. 'I've read about this place.'

'Oh, you know how to read?' she asked, eyes wide with mock amazement.

'Shut up,' he said, pointing. 'My brother once told me about this tree.'

She rolled her eyes so hard she almost tipped over. 'And what, pray tell, is so special about this tree that it's got your little pebbles all shrunken?'

Kai's mouth twitched. He nearly laughed but caught himself just in time, replacing amusement with a mask of indifference. 'It's not the tree, witch. It's where the tree is.'

'Are you going to make me guess?'

'No. It would take all day.'

She kicked him again.

'Go on then. Enlighten me.'

He sighed, a long, weary sound that said he was already regretting every choice that had led him here. The tales returned to him now of old warnings whispered around fires, of wanderers who had stepped into a place and never found the way back out.

'We're in the Forest of Endless Trees.'

Chapter Twenty-Five

House of Wild
Kingdom of Fauna

The Fae can be remarkably complex. They are incapable of lying, but they have a talent for twisting their words to get exactly what they want. One must always tread carefully when making deals with the Fae.

You will lose.

Tabitha Wysteria

'So, what's your masterful plan then...?' Arden asked dryly as they reached the very edge of the Forest of Endless Trees after days of travel. With him by her side, navigating the tangled wilderness had seemed almost effortless, as if the forest itself had chosen not to hinder them. Dressed in fresh clothes and with a warm meal settling in her belly, Wren felt almost invincible. A dangerous illusion for someone like her, who had a knack for courting trouble.

'Well... I've been thinking.'

'That's rarely a good sign. Why do you say it like that, as though even you know it's a bad idea?'

'I need to slip in undetected.'

'Slip in where, exactly?'

Wren winced, her voice dropping into a murmur. 'Da Kingdom of Fire.'

'You are mental.'

'No, listen!' she insisted, the words tumbling out quickly. 'There's someone that well, I thought she was a friend, though now I'm not so sure. But I need to speak to her. If I can reach her, then perhaps…' The sentence trailed off, unfinished. Her so-called plan, flimsy at best, sounded laughable even to her own ears. And yet, she had to try. Wren Wynter didn't give up, not when it mattered.

Arden sighed the long, suffering sigh of a man who knew he should walk away but wouldn't. 'Very well then, little wolf. We'll find a way to sneak you in… but not tonight. It's late.'

For once, Wren didn't argue—a rare and telling silence. Of late, something inside her had shifted. The brightness she'd once carried like a flame had dulled, hollowed by recent horrors. The laughter came less easily now. Even when darkness had clawed at her heels before, she had always managed to keep her spark. But now… she wasn't sure who she was without it.

'Just let it be,' Arden said, crouching to light a fire, the kindling crackling under his touch. Wren scrunched up her face and sat down, feeling the weight of it all. 'You keep getting that look,' Arden continued, tossing another branch into the growing flame. 'Like the world doesn't make sense anymore. I've seen it before. It's all right.'

'No. It's not. Nothing is all right.'

He shrugged. 'No one likes change. But it comes for us all.'

'I don't want to change.'

'And why's that?'

'Becas I like who I am.'

Arden chuckled as he stood, brushing ash from his fingers. 'Perhaps,' he said, voice softening, 'the moment you stop fearing the change, you'll realise there was never anything to fear in the first place. And then, little wolf, you might see the change wasn't as great, or as terrible, as you thought.'

Wren bit her lip, her focus lowering to her hands. There was so much she wished she could say, but words felt too small. All she could see, over and over, was the memory of Hagan snapping Haven's neck. Kage's helpless expression. Mal, a phantom of fury and pain, entering the castle with death on her heels. And Wren…Wren had done the only thing she knew how to do.

She ran.

'Why are ya helping me?' she asked suddenly, breaking the silence as Arden settled beside her. Her voice was quiet, vulnerable. 'No one just drops everything for a stranger.'

Arden said nothing for so long that Wren began to wonder if he'd heard her at all. He busied himself with his travel bag, sifting through its contents until he produced a modest assortment of provisions. Selecting a curious yellow round and slightly dimpled fruit, he bit into it, the juice spilling carelessly down his chin. Mid-chew, he paused and fixed his attention on her, and for a moment, Wren wished she could take the question back entirely. Perhaps it was better not to know. He was here, after all. He was helping her. That should have been enough.

But it wasn't.

That restless part of her, the one that was always digging deeper, always seeking truth even when it hurt, refused to be quiet.

'I like adventure. And the unknown,' he said at last, with a nonchalant shrug, as though the words bore little weight.

Wren narrowed her eyes, not convinced. She didn't know Arden well, not yet, but she had always possessed a sharp instinct for people, and the lie in his voice was as clear as dawnlight on snow. Still, she said nothing. Pressing him too far might see him vanish into the trees, and the truth was, she couldn't afford to lose him. Whether she wanted to or not, she needed him.

'I thought ya weren't supposed to light fires in this forest,' Wren said, her voice quiet, thoughtful.

Arden chuckled, the sound low and rich. 'I like that you actually listen to me, little wolf. You're quite right, it's usually unwise to strike a flame beneath these trees. But we're on the very edge now.' He shrugged, a glimmer of amusement flickering in his green eyes. 'Besides, you needn't fret. I'm a butcher, I know my way around blades.'

'I'm not worried,' Wren replied, tilting her chin ever so slightly. 'I'm not afraid of anything, Arden Briar.'

The Fae snorted, clearly unconvinced.

And yet, as Wren sat beside him, the firelight dancing across his antlers and casting sharp shadows across his face, she couldn't help but wonder if, perhaps, he was right. There was no need to fear what dwelled in the forest's depths, because the most dangerous thing within it was already sitting beside her, smiling in the dark.

...

'The city of Spark lies a few days' journey from here,' Arden said as they emerged from the shadows of the Forest of Endless Trees. The woods had allowed them passage without resistance. A small miracle, though Wren suspected it had less to do with mercy and more to do with the Fae at her side. Arden's presence, she had to admit, was proving invaluable. Still, her thoughts wandered to Freya. Had the valkyrian reached her homeland at last?

'Villages aren't our best option,' Wren said, eyes scanning the vast stretch of land ahead. 'We'd be betta off slipping through a large city.'

'We could head to the capital.'

'Do ya think it's fallen?' Wren had shared the full tale with him of what had unfolded, what had been lost and still, it amazed her how so many walked the world blissfully unaware that an entire kingdom was on the brink of ruin.

'We won't know until we get there,' Arden replied, voice unreadable.

Wren blew an errant strand of silver-white hair from her eyes, sighing in irritation. The road to Fireheart was long, and civilisation still lay many miles ahead.

'You're rather impatient, little wolf,' Arden teased, watching her with a sidelong glance.

'Am not,' she snapped, marching ahead with renewed energy. 'But a kingdom is burning.'

'And we can't walk any faster than our legs allow.'

'Are ya certain?' Wren frowned, glancing over her shoulder. 'Don't da Fae have magic?'

'It doesn't quite work like that,' he said with a soft chuckle, clearly entertained. 'Fae magic is... difficult to explain.'

'I heard ya lot are tricksters.'

'Oh?' His green eyes sparked with something unreadable, concern perhaps, but it vanished beneath the lazy veil of amusement. 'Is that what they say?'

'They say Fae can't lie, but ya twist da truth until it sings for ya. Always getting what ya want.'

'Sounds rather like most people I've met,' Arden replied smoothly.

Wren wrinkled her nose. 'And how many of those weren't Fae?'

He laughed. 'I've travelled more than you might think.'

'But ya work in da kitchens. Why would ya travel?'

'A chef must chase new flavours,' he said, a mischievous glint in his eye. 'King Florian has a fondness for my dishes. I roam on his behalf, finding new delights to... satisfy his palate.'

Another lie. Or perhaps a truth cloaked in riddles. Fae couldn't lie, not exactly, but they danced so artfully around the truth, it was difficult to spot the illusion until you'd already fallen into it. Wren could ask. The questions were pressing at her lips. But fear held her still. What if she didn't like the answer?

The war came first. The witches and the kingdoms were what mattered now. She needed him. Whatever he was hiding... she would uncover it later.

'Tell me a story, Arden Briar.'

'A story?' he echoed, one brow lifting with faint amusement.

'I don't usually care for them much,' Wren admitted, folding her arms over her chest. 'But me sistas do. And I—I need to feel a little closer to home today.'

Arden inclined his head, as though he understood more than she had said aloud. 'Have you ever heard of the Black Lotus?'

Wren gave a slight nod, though her knowledge was threadbare at best. 'They say... many years ago, a Fae prince fell in love with a peasant girl. He married her in secret, knowing his father—da king—would neva give his blessing. But when da king found out, he sent soldiers to find her. They dragged her from wherever she was hiding and killed her right in front of da prince. A lesson, they called it. But da prince... he neva forgave. He pretended to, kept smiling and bowing, but when da old king grew frail, da prince, now a king himself, unleashed da Black Lotus to make his father suffer. They say he'd been gathering orphans for years. Children lost to da world, shaping them into something else. Servants of vengeance.'

Arden nodded slowly, chewing on the thought. 'You know it

well. That prince, once crowned, was no longer a man, nor truly Fae. Revenge had hollowed him out. The Black Lotus became his shadow, his unseen blade. And every king after him kept them close.'

Wren tilted her head, eyes wide with curiosity. 'Has anyone eva seen one?'

'They say they hide in plain sight,' Arden said. 'Always watching. Always waiting.'

'But why are they feared so much?'

'Because of how they're made.' A wry smile curved his lips, the kind that didn't reach his eyes. 'Taken young. Broken. Their pasts stripped away, their minds shattered and rebuilt. They are remade into perfect killers, ones who feel nothing.'

Wren's nose crinkled. 'That's awful. No one should be allowed to do that.'

Arden gave a noncommittal shrug. 'Most of them were orphans. Left to rot. Some say it's a mercy, better than starving on the streets.'

She frowned, thoughtful. 'Maybe... but I don't think so.'

'Oh? And why's that?'

'No matter how bad things get,' she said, her voice soft but resolute, 'I'd still want to be free.'

For a glint of a moment, something passed through Arden's eyes, something raw and haunted. He nodded, gaze drifting ahead as though searching for something far beyond the road in front of them.

'Yes,' he said. 'Freedom... perhaps that's what we all want, deep down.'

Wren didn't think. Her hand moved of its own accord, brushing his lightly, a gesture meant to comfort, though she didn't quite know why. Perhaps it was the way his eyes had lowered, as if the weight of something unseen pressed heavily upon him. She only knew that she didn't want to see that sadness in his face.

'Can I trust ya?' she asked, her voice barely more than a breath so quiet that she wasn't even sure she'd spoken aloud.

He looked at her then. Not just looked, saw her. His stare lingered a moment too long, lips parting into a smile that was charming, yes, but far too practiced. Beneath it, his jaw tightened subtly, but enough. Wren noticed.

He turned away. No answer. No words. But he had heard her.

And he had chosen silence.

Chapter Twenty-Six

House of Snow
Kingdom of Ice

Wolverians don't often leave their kingdom. However, they do trade, as their land cannot sustain itself entirely alone. Their fish is highly prized across all kingdoms. Others may fish, but it never tastes quite as good as theirs. Wolverians seem comfortable enough with wyverians and witches, but don't expect them to sit down for a conversation with anyone from the south.

Tabitha Wysteria

Word had arrived from the wyverians. They had reached the great wall dividing their kingdom from that of the witches. Their message was clear; they needed Kage to persuade Bryn to mobilise the wolverian army and march to the northern side of the boundary. From there, a simultaneous assault would be launched: east and north, pressing upon the witches with overwhelming numbers, forcing their retreat into the barren expanse of the wastelands. Once that desolate territory had been seized, the path into the Kingdom of Fire would lie open.

'We'd be blind,' Bryn said, his voice cutting through the still air of the main hall, where the men sat beneath frost-covered rafters. 'We don't know what awaits in da wastelands.'

Kage reclined into the stone-carved chair at the side of the long table, an unforgiving seat that should have frozen him to the marrow. But it had been thoughtfully layered in thick pelts, keeping the worst of the chill at bay. Even so, the air here bit at the skin, sharper than any blade. Kage had always thrived in cold climates. His own lands were infamous for their biting winters, but this kingdom was something else entirely. A realm of unrelenting frost, of shimmering ice-scapes and snow-laden silence. A wonder, yes. But one that clung to your bones with a cruel tenacity.

At home, he had never needed cloaks or coats; the air had always felt brisk, never hostile. But here, even breath seemed to crystalise in the lungs. The wolverians had offered him an array of silver, dove-grey, snow-white furs which, draped over his frame, only served to heighten the starkness of his appearance. Pale as death and draped in ice, he became a shadow within the castle's gleaming halls.

Everywhere he went, wolverian eyes followed. He was a thing of contrast in this kingdom of frost and silence. His hair a deep, liquid black, his eyes like shards of obsidian, his skin so pale it glowed faintly blue under the gloom. The wolverians, though fair themselves, possessed the uncanny ability to vanish into their wintry realm, their muted cloaks and quiet steps rendering them nearly invisible. It reminded Kage of the desert folk and their ability to disappear into sand and sunlight.

He did not blend in here. He had never intended to.

'But there's no other choice, is there?' King Fannar exhaled wearily, dragging his thick fingers through the snowy white that cloaked his beard. 'Either we face da witches head-on, or we risk watching them swallow us whole.'

The king had arrived days earlier, his presence heavy with concern, his voice edged with doubt. The witch hunt, it seemed, was no longer enough to cleanse the realm of its creeping threat. And each time the word witch was uttered, Bryn flinched as though the syllables were blades, slicing something unseen within him. Kage had noticed the way the prince's gaze would drift to the far corner of the room, watching nothing... or perhaps, someone only he could see.

Kage tilted his head, studying the king through narrowed eyes. King Fannar was a mountain of a man, his arms thick as the oaks that groaned beyond the castle walls. And yet, his son resembled him not at all. Bryn was lean and quiet-footed and sharp as a fox in winter. He and his siblings had clearly inherited their mother's features. But the fire in their bellies, Kage suspected, burnt with their father's wrath.

Portraits of the late queen still adorned the stone walls, though most were dulled by a thin veil of dust. Kage had never dared speak of her. Some griefs, he understood too well. They never truly faded; they simply settled deeper with time, like sediment in still water. The first taste of loss was always the most bitter, but even when the sting dulled, the ache lingered.

'It's them or us,' Kage said flatly, his voice low.

King Fannar let out a hollow laugh, a sound stripped of mirth. His eyes drifted towards the painting of his queen, softening before falling once more to the hearth's flickering glow. 'Words like that... they're what led us to ruin in da first place,' he muttered. 'Da gods may have granted us decades of peace, but we paid a steep price for it. Da Great War left our kingdoms fractured. If we do this, if we go to war again, there may be no healing left to hope for.'

Kage didn't acknowledge the way Bryn's stare burnt into the side of his face. Nor did he look to the shadow crouched atop the high shelf, the ever-watchful Spirox, a spectral wisp of darkness who never strayed from Kage's side. His silent companion, as familiar as breath, and just as easily lost.

'There is no going back,' Kage said quietly, his words

stretching into the stone chamber like a vow cast into still water.

Bryn straightened in his chair, the air about him shifting. They both knew what was coming, knew that whatever Kage chose now would set the world in motion. His decision would be the match to light the fire. The wolverians would rise. They would march.

'We are warriors,' Bryn said, voice steady, eyes bright with resolve.

Kage nodded once, the movement slow and weighted. Then he tipped his head back, letting it rest against the chair's spine, as if the choice had drained what little strength he had left to offer.

There is no going back.

'Only forward,' he whispered.

...

'Da wolverians grow restless,' Bryn said as they made their way along the snow-draped castle grounds. The wind howled against the stone walls like a creature mourning. Kage trudged through the thick drifts with effort, his boots sinking into the unforgiving frost, while Bryn moved beside him like a wolf on the prowl—silent, smooth, born of the winter.

'Their fear of da witches runs deep,' Bryn continued. 'They won't stop burning those they deem cursed—witches, warlocks, innocents alike. We need to act swiftly. If we march soon, they'll feel useful... necessary.'

Kage studied him, uncertain of how to respond. Since that grim day when the commander had ordered a boy's execution, Bryn had seemed adrift—his eyes distant, his thoughts elsewhere. Whenever the word witch was uttered, he'd flinch, as though something deep and raw stirred beneath the surface.

The cold here was relentless, biting into Kage's flesh like a thousand tiny blades. It whispered with each gust that he didn't belong. His shadowed presence cut sharply through the grey-white world, stark as spilt ink on parchment. Still, he pressed on, ignoring the silent warnings that clung to the wind, murmuring that he should leave.

The wolverians were a people steeped in faith, their belief in omens and signs woven into every breath they took. Without their Seer, the tradition of reading bones had taken precedence, the people placing their futures in the hands of splintered fragments and ancient rites.

Kage clenched his jaw at the thought of Wren. Gods knew where she was now, likely tangled in some wild scheme. Why had she left him? Had she seen something? A vision, perhaps? It was foolish to fret over her. She was a wolverian, after all. She could more than hold her own.

Bryn guided him away from the main grounds and into a snow-covered copse, stopping at a small, wooden hut tucked into the trees. A gentle plume of smoke rose from its chimney. Inside, two young girls huddled near a modest fire, the orange glow painting their pale faces in warmth and shadow. It took Kage only a moment to realise they were Bryn's sisters.

He hadn't paid them much notice during his time at the castle. Still in their adolescence, they spent most of their days chasing after their wolves or helping in the kitchens. Yet something about them tugged at his memory. They resembled Wren in a strange, bittersweet way. Like echoes of her, fainter and softer. Not quite as radiant... but hauntingly close.

'Me sistas will be doing da bone reading for us,' Bryn announced, settling himself onto the fur-covered floor and tugging an uncooperative Kage down beside him.

'This is absurd,' the wyverian muttered under his breath, the scent of smoke already catching in his throat.

'Ignore him,' Bryn said with a grin when one of his sisters glanced up from her work. Kage's dark eyes fell upon the animal carcass they were carefully stripping, the girls separating meat from bone with quiet precision. Each bone was then washed reverently, as though preparing a relic. When they were ready, the one named Gwyneira—no, Gwenyth, Kage corrected himself bitterly—threw the bones into the heart of the fire.

'Gwyneira,' Bryn leaned in, his voice low with urgency. 'What do ya see?'

Kage clenched his jaw. It was almost impossible to tell the twins apart, and truth be told, he hadn't bothered to try. He didn't know them. And more importantly, he didn't care to.

'What will da outcome be?' Bryn asked eagerly, edging closer to the flames as if he might glimpse the future himself. Kage reached out and pulled him back, raising an incredulous brow at the sheer foolishness of it.

Gwyneira's pale blue eyes widened as the fire cracked and snarled, devouring the bones with a hunger of its own. With a sudden, violent snap, fragments burst from the flames, ricocheting off the walls like shrapnel. The force of it made them all flinch.

Then came the scream.

It tore from Gwyneira's throat with a ferocity that echoed around the small hunting lodge, shaking the very air. Her twin lunged forward and caught her, wrapping her in a protective embrace as the room seemed to still, the fire crackling on in eerie silence. Even the wind outside seemed to hold its breath.

Kage remained motionless, every muscle tense with unease.

At last, Gwyneira began to calm, her chest rising and falling in shallow gasps, tears streaking down her ivory cheeks. Her lips trembled as she tried to speak.

'I saw...'

'Do we win?' Bryn pressed, brows drawn, his voice hushed with dread and hope in equal measure.

Kage nearly reached for him. Something about the question felt wrong. This wasn't magic, not truly. Bone reading was an old art, guided by instinct and tradition, and yet... even he could feel the heaviness in the air. Fate was not something to interrogate so carelessly.

'How do we stop da witches, Gwyneira?' Bryn asked, voice taut with urgency.

The girl only shook her head, a breath of sorrow escaping her lungs like smoke from a dying flame.

'We don't.'

Both Bryn and Kage froze. The words landed like frost in the pit of their stomachs.

'What do ya mean?' Bryn asked, voice cracking with disbelief.

Gwyneira lifted her eyes to them, and in that moment, Kage could have sworn she saw straight through him. Her gaze pierced like the edge of a blade, as though the ashes had whispered his secrets into her ears. Every sin, every shadow clinging to his soul... she had seen it all.

And still, the fire burnt.

'Do we win?' Bryn asked again, his brow creasing further in perplexity.

'No,' Gwyneira said, her voice soft as snowfall. Her shoulders sagged beneath the weight of truth. 'But neither do da witches.'

Kage went utterly still, the frostbitten air around them forgotten as his dark gaze honed in on the young wolverian. He studied every trace of emotion across her face, seeking the shape of prophecy in her silence. He imagined raking the answers from her skin with clawed hands, desperate for clarity.

'What do you mean?' Kage asked, voice cool and sharp. 'Either we win, or we don't.'

'No...' Her eyes lifted to the ceiling, pupils dilating as though following a vision no one else could see. Her body quivered with some unspoken revelation.

Both Kage and Bryn followed her gaze, uncertain of what held her so rapt.

'Da gods are coming,' she whispered.

Kage opened his mouth to question her, but before the words could escape, Bryn was already pulling him to his feet, guiding him away from the smouldering fire and into the embrace of the biting cold.

As they trudged through the snow, Kage glanced down at the ring on his smallest finger, turning it absentmindedly. His thoughts flitted to his scattered siblings. He knew Kai was with Ash in the wyverian kingdom, steel drawn and battle-ready. But Mal... Mal was a ghost in the wind, no word from her in weeks. And Haven...he could not bear to summon the image of her.

'What do ya think she meant?' Bryn asked as the castle emerged from the trees, its modest outline carved against the pale horizon. Kage had spent his life reading about the variances between the kingdoms, but to walk them, to breathe their differences...He only wished the journey had been under gentler skies.

The wolverian stronghold was humble in every sense, rough-hewn stone and sloped rooftops layered with frost. There was no grandeur here, no shining towers or delicate tapestries, only resilience built into every timber. Wolverians placed little worth in luxuries; their riches were woven into kinship and custom. And for that, Kage could not help but admire them.

'Me sista Gwyneira's been reading da bones eva since our ma passed,' Bryn explained as they stepped back into the warmth of the hearth-lit hall. 'She's neva been wrong.'

'There's a first time for everything,' Kage muttered, slipping off his heavy coat and easing the tension from his shoulders. He glanced up at his crow, who had elected to stay nestled inside rather than venture out into the frost.

'You can't even feel the cold,' he mumbled at the bird. Spirox let out a sharp caw, full of amusement.

'What?' Bryn asked, turning with a furrowed brow.

'Nothing,' Kage replied swiftly. 'Just talking to myself.'

Bryn grinned. An easy, boyish smile that pulled something tight in Kage's chest. The wyverian stilled for a heartbeat, his eyes catching on the curve of Bryn's lips. He hadn't truly looked before, but now...now he was beginning to see. Wren was beautiful, striking in ways she didn't yet realise, but Bryn...

Bryn was something else entirely.

Kage cleared his throat and turned away, willing his thoughts into order, only to hear the teasing flap of wings behind him.

That damn crow.

'I'd always wanted to see one,' Bryn said softly, nodding towards the shadow crow as they made their way to the heart of the castle, where the great hearths burnt with their flames. They sat, shoulders nearly brushing, and Kage couldn't help but notice that Bryn had settled a fraction closer than usual. If Kage reached out, he could easily trail a fingertip along the curve of Bryn's arm.

'You can keep this one, if you like,' Kage muttered, casting a glance at the bird perched nearby. The creature tilted its head in quiet judgement, clearly unimpressed by the jest.

A servant appeared bearing tankards of icebroth and paused,

gaping at Kage with a mixture of awe and curiosity.

'They neva seem to get used to ya,' Bryn said with a grin, lifting his drink. Foam clung to his upper lip, and Kage's gaze snagged on it, an odd flutter beneath his ribs at the urge to reach over and brush it away.

'It's a curse... being this handsome,' Kage deadpanned.

Bryn's pale brows lifted in astonishment. 'Was that a joke?'

Kage offered the slightest shrug.

'I don't think I've eva heard ya say anything remotely funny.'

'I'm actually a very funny person,' Kage replied, and the crow gave a caw so disapproving it might have been laughing at him. He waved a hand. 'Ignore it.'

'Yer funny?' Bryn laughed, head thrown back, silver hair catching the firelight.

'Jester of the family, believe it or not.'

Bryn roared with laughter, slapping the table as though it might help him breathe through the mirth. Kage bit the inside of his cheek, barely suppressing a smile. That laugh...gods, it warmed him more thoroughly than any fire ever had.

'I imagined ya as many things, Kage Blackburn, but definitely not a jester.'

Kage took a sip of the icebroth, letting its chill settle the heat building inside him. 'And what did you picture me as?'

The joy in Bryn's face faltered, replaced by hesitation. Kage immediately regretted asking.

'Oh, well... dark. Gloomy. A bit... rude, I suppose.'

Kage took another sip.

The crow flapped its wings once, as if in hearty agreement.

They both glanced at the bird, then at each other. Bryn burst into laughter again and this time, Kage let his smile show. The tension that clung to his bones melted away.

'I suppose I can be a little stiff sometimes,' Kage admitted.

'A little?' Bryn raised a brow. 'Ya can't be serious.'

'Turns out I can.'

Bryn's laughter returned, rich and unrestrained, and Kage found himself rubbing his chest, startled by how deeply it stirred something within him. That feeling, like a note played on the perfect string, reminded him of the moments when he lost himself to his violin, when sound became emotion and the world ceased to exist.

And now, somehow, Bryn's laugh was beginning to feel the same.

'I'm sorry about your mother,' Kage said, his fingertip tracing the rim of his tankard in slow, thoughtful circles.

'And I'm sorry about yer sista,' Bryn replied quietly.

The words landed like stones in his chest, their weight heavy and inescapable. Kage froze. He longed to brush them away, to pretend they hadn't been spoken aloud. If he refused to acknowledge them, perhaps he could still pretend she wasn't gone. If he didn't speak her name, then maybe, just maybe, Haven would still be waiting for him somewhere, humming in the corridors, teasing him in that way only she could.

Perhaps that was why he lingered in this frozen kingdom of wolves and whispered omens. He couldn't return to his own land, couldn't face the truth. Because if he did, if he stepped back into the halls of his home, he would be forced to wake from this fragile illusion, and the nightmare would be waiting.

'I regret...' Kage tried to swallow the words, but they caught in his throat like thorns. He could feel her beside him even now, shaking her head with that wry smile, warning him not to say it, not to name the grief. Because naming it would make it real.

'I regret not spending more time with her,' he said, voice hoarse. 'The others did. Kai trained her, Mal took her riding. But Haven... she always found me in the library. She'd sit beside me for hours, no words. Just... reading. Just being.'

'Ya didn't need to speak,' Bryn said gently. 'Some loves don't ask for words. They speak in silence, and that's enough.'

'Still, I feel guilty. For not doing more. For not being more.'

Bryn nodded slowly, his eyes glassy with a pain Kage recognised. 'We all carry regrets. I didn't save that boy. I let him die. And now I see him... everywhere. In shadows, behind doors. I did what me people demanded, but I betrayed me heart. And I'll carry that shame until I meet death meself.'

There was little Kage could say to that, no salve for that kind of wound. Some things simply bled forever.

'What do you think it means... that the gods are coming?' he asked, seizing the opportunity to shift the tide of their talk.

Bryn shrugged, relief washing through his features. 'I don't know. But we'll find out soon enough.' His gaze lingered, those storm-blue eyes watching Kage too closely. 'We'll sound da horns for battle tomorrow.'

Bryn rose to his feet, hesitating, mouth parted slightly as if there were more to say. Kage felt it too, that unspoken thing between them. That magnetic ache. He wanted to reach out, to brush the braids from Bryn's face, to feel the warmth of his skin beneath his palm. He wanted to keep him close, to keep him safe. But he didn't.

Instead, Kage looked away, his gaze drawn to the flames dancing in the hearth, fierce and flickering, as restless as the thing caged inside his chest.

'We don't deserve nice things,' he said softly, curling his hands into fists, knuckles white with tension. He couldn't look up, not with Bryn so near, yet so heartbreakingly far.

He had let his sister die. He had failed his family. He had failed his kingdom. And now, whatever kindness the gods might offer... he knew he was unworthy.

No matter how much he longed to reach for Bryn's hand.

'No,' Bryn whispered, the words barely audible over the crackle of fire. 'I suppose we do not.'

Chapter Twenty-Seven

House of Flames
Kingdom of Fire

I fear the day when witches are hated across all the kingdoms. I pray to the gods to spare us from it. But now, I see our end. It is so near, I feel I could reach out and touch it.

Tabitha Wysteria

The city of Spark had been erased, vanished from the map as though it had never existed. Obliterated. Nothing remained of the once-charming coastal haven, where the royal castle had stood proud amidst ivory sands and lush, meticulously tended gardens. The town surrounding it, with its red-tiled roofs and sun-warmed walls, had crumbled to ash. Vera had watched it all burn, the sight more surreal than she'd ever imagined. Drakonian homes could not be felled by ordinary flame, but magic was another matter entirely.

The witches had left Spark in ruin, their eyes now set on the true prize: Fireheart, the capital. Vera had succeeded in diverting Hagan's attention, buying her sister precious time. But eventually, the truth would find him. He would realise that Dawn was no longer among them, no longer marching to his twisted tune. Ah well.

Vera smirked at the thought of his expression, the confusion, the fury. One of his own, gone. Defected to aid the enemy. The tantrum that would follow… She would savour every second of it, hidden deep within the shadows like a spider awaiting the tremble of her web.

'Vera.'

Her name on his lips was like acid. Always had been. He had spent their childhood wielding his influence like a blade, using it to cut her down in the castle halls, barking orders at her as if she were nothing more than a servant. Because that's what she had been forced to be. Just a maid. And their mother? She had stood by, lips sealed, eyes blind, as if Vera were truly beneath notice. Not a single word of defence, not even a glance of recognition. As though Vera were a ghost, lingering in the corridors of her own bloodline.

'It's beautiful,' Hagan said, crouched low as he stared at the scorched horizon. Vera raised a brow. What would a brute like him know of beauty? Beauty would be watching his blood spill upon the stones they now stood on. Beauty would be the grass dyed red beneath his broken form.

'And the plan is?' she asked, her tone clipped and cold. The searing heat of the drakonian lands gnawed at her skin, unbearable in its relentlessness. They had marched on foot from Spark to Fireheart, a decision made by Hagan in one of his grandiose fits of whimsy. He had claimed it was for the fresh air, but in truth, it was theatre. A ploy. He wanted the drakonians to see the smoke curling across the sky, to feel the dread tightening in their chests. A warning. An omen.

Vera rolled her eyes. Always so dramatic. Couldn't he conquer a city without turning it into a stage play? But no, every move had to be laced with pomp and grandeur. And the others, the witches and warlocks, lapped it up like starving dogs, bewitched by his performance. She, however, remained unimpressed.

'We march straight through.' Hagan extended his hand, gesturing towards the city as if the answer lay cradled in his palm.

'We don't have a Red Guard stationed in every city, Hagan,' Vera replied. 'What we managed in Spark won't be so easily replicated here. This, this will be different.'

He scoffed, the sound low and derisive. 'That won't be a problem.'

'Power has a way of creeping into our minds,' she warned, her voice taut with veiled threat, 'slithering beneath the surface until we no longer recognise our own reflection. It blinds us. Strips us of reason. Many of our own will die.' She didn't bother including the lives of others. He wouldn't give a damn.

'Isn't this what you wanted too, sister?' he asked, the word landing like a stone between them.

Vera stilled, something sharp curling beneath her ribs at the sound of it. Sister. They had never truly been siblings, not in affection or kinship. Their blood only bound them in vengeance, a mutual hunger to make the world bleed for its cruelty.

'I want many things in this life, *brother*.' She allowed the word to drip with disdain. Hagan turned, his shaven head tilting just slightly, eyes narrowing in reply. He'd caught the note of challenge in her tone, subtle as a blade between the ribs.

He stood, stretching his back and neck with deliberate slowness, the movement a silent reminder of his size and strength. Taller than Vera by far, he towered above her like a shadow threatening to fall. It was his way of posturing, asserting dominance without a word. She let him have it, for now. Let him swell with borrowed power. When the time came for him to fall, she would be the one to gather his broken pieces... or grind them beneath her heel.

The land surrounding them was arid and cracked, sun-scorched with no shelter to shield them from the blistering heat. Vera had warned against travelling so openly across such terrain because they were utterly exposed. And there was still the matter of the dragons.

Hagan had tried to kill the drakonians' beasts, the ones kept deep beneath the castle. But by the time they'd stormed the dungeons, the dragons had vanished, escaped. Or perhaps, Vera mused with a faint smile, someone had opened the gates for them.

She had stood in silence, watching as the winged titans fled into the night, the tunnels echoing with the thunder of their wings. Yet wild dragons still roamed these lands untamed, unpredictable, and Fireheart itself could unleash a few if it came to that.

Her gaze caught on a peculiar sight. A box, suspended mid-air between two witches, gliding along with quiet menace. It wasn't large enough to hold a body, but it was just sizeable enough to stir her suspicion. What was Hagan carrying? What sinister little trick had he brought along like a gift-wrapped promise?

One glance at his purple eyes, glittering with malice, gave her the answer she didn't want. She'd find out soon enough, and she'd likely wish she hadn't.

'Hurry along,' Hagan called over his shoulder, his grin all teeth and cruelty. 'We mustn't be late.'

...

The city of Fireheart unfurled before them like a tapestry of flame and stone. A sprawling metropolis of labyrinthine alleyways and winding paths that could ensnare even the most seasoned traveller. Its rooftops gleamed red as spilt blood beneath the light, while the bricks, sun-baked and time-worn, shifted subtly in hue as the day wore on, casting the streets in ever-changing shades of gold and ochre.

From high windows, the city revealed itself in quiet fragments: silken clothes billowed lazily in the breeze; pots of drakonian flora—petals sharp as glass and colours bright as flame—perched on sills; and figures leaned out, their expressions a mixture of curiosity and disdain as they observed the quiet below. Drakonians were a people of sun and stone, accustomed to living life out in the open. The women whispered beneath parasols, the children darted down cobbled lanes, and the men huddled at corners, wagering coin on games whose rules no outsider could ever hope to grasp.

Vera's gaze caught on one such game, its pieces abandoned on a weathered bench in the main square. It had been left mid-play, frozen in time the moment whispers of witches swept through the streets like an omen. Doors had slammed shut, curtains drawn. A city brimming with life had stilled into eerie silence.

Hagan came to a halt before the temple, a grand structure carved from ivory-coloured stone, its tower rising like a sentinel above the rooftops. The platform at its peak was unmistakable—a roost shaped for dragons. Vera lifted her eyes, half-expecting the beat of wings to echo from the sky.

'Hagan...' she mumbled under her breath, unsettled by the hush that wrapped the city like a shroud. But, as ever, he paid her no heed. He ascended the temple steps with the slow, deliberate gait of someone convinced of his own divinity. Behind him, the crate—still levitating on that unnatural green mist—drifted silently, like a shadow tethered to his will.

Vera glanced back. Where were the drakonians? Surely they

had gathered their kin, their most treasured possessions, and fled for safer ground? That would have been the wisest choice. And yet... she knew them. Drakonians were steeped in pride; they would rather turn to ash than run.

At the summit of the steps, Hagan turned, arms outstretched before his gathered assembly, a congregation he had dragged in chains or drawn with honeyed words, it mattered little. Vera's eyes scanned the crowd, searching for Allegra among the familiar faces, but all she found were eyes fixed on Hagan as if he were some celestial being descended to earth.

'We have not come to slaughter you!' Hagan proclaimed, his voice ringing through the square like a sermon. 'We have come to bring peace, once and for all.'

Vera stifled a laugh, the sound bitter in her throat. Peace. Was there anyone left foolish enough to believe him? Hagan was no bringer of harmony. He had drenched his hands in blood magic, sacrificed an entire bloodline, and would not be sated by one kingdom alone. His thirst was unquenchable. Power, once tasted, devoured the mind like rot. And Hagan... Hagan had been drinking deeply for far too long.

'This land is now ours!'

A silence so profound it pressed upon Vera's bones stretched across the square, unsettling her more with each passing breath. Her foot tapped an erratic rhythm against the cobblestones, betraying the unrest beneath her cool exterior. What had he expected, cheers? Applause? That the drakonians would spill from their homes in gratitude, hailing him as a hero for levelling an entire city, for turning it to soot and silence?

'This land will never be yours!' a voice rang out, defiant and sharp as a sword unsheathed.

Vera turned swiftly, searching for the source of the cry. Hagan signalled to the witches nearest him, a flick of his hand commanding obedience. Within moments, warlocks and witches dissipated into the side streets, trails of green smoke curling behind them like the tails of hunting hounds.

Vera waited, unmoving, letting the square breathe with her —slow, shallow, braced. Her boots seemed to root into the stone beneath her, as if the earth itself were holding her still. A glance met Hagan's across the distance, and in that beat of connection, entire conversations passed in silence. A shared understanding, sharp as flint.

One of the warlocks soon reappeared, dragging behind him a bent figure, an elderly drakonian whose gait was slow and laboured, his horns dulled by age. When released at the base of the temple steps, he collapsed forward, frail hands breaking his fall. Vera cocked her head, her focus steady on Hagan, curious to see what venom he would spit next.

The warlock descended the steps and circled the old man, sniffing the air like a beast testing the wind. Then he chuckled, low and cruel. 'Say it again, old man.'

The drakonian raised his head. Not in defiance, but in quiet dignity. 'You can burn our homes to ash. You can kill us, if that is what you wish. But this land will never be yours.'

A feral, twisted glint flared in Hagan's eyes. His face contorted, lips curling as rage surged behind his gaze. Truth, it seemed, was a blade he had never learnt to bear, especially not from someone three times his age, someone who had lived through fire and storm.

The drakonians had begun to emerge, drifting from the safety of their homes, drawn by the inevitable. Vera noticed their faces, grim and watchful. Among them, she glimpsed flashes of crimson. Red Guard. Her lips curved.

'Do you think someone's coming to save you?' Hagan asked darkly, seizing the elder's thinning hair and forcing his head up.

But the old man did not resist.

'I'm old,' he whispered, weary. 'I've lived my time. Do what you must, but spare the others. I beg you.'

'Did the drakonians who scorched my homeland listen to the witches' pleas?' Hagan snarled, spittle flying from his lips, his grip tightening.

Vera's focus drifted away from him, tracking the slow approach of the drakonian guard, the quiet formation gathering strength like a storm on the edge of a battlefield. She licked her thumb and bit it idly, her smirk growing. Whatever show Hagan had planned, it would soon be interrupted.

Releasing the old man, Hagan lifted his arms skyward once more, a self-fashioned saviour delivering his sermon to the ashes. Vera rolled her eyes, watching him play his part in the grand theatre of conquest.

At the foot of the steps, the old drakonian lay slumped, his wide eyes filled not with fear for himself, but for what was to come. For his people. For the fire yet to fall.

The floating crate that had hovered dutifully at Hagan's side at last creaked open.

Vera edged forward instinctively, though every fibre of her body warned her to retreat. Around her, the square drew breath as one, the witches craning their necks with anticipation, the drakonians holding themselves taut as bowstrings, eyes wide with dread. All of them drawn in, helpless against their own morbid curiosity.

No. Not curiosity. Dread.

The square had become too tightly packed, bodies pressed shoulder to shoulder, the air heavy with the scent of sweat, tension, and smoke. Vera cursed under her breath. She needed to fall back, find higher ground in case everything turned, *when* it turned. But something compelled her to remain, rooted in place by a hunger to see what he would unveil.

Hagan cast one final glance down at the old man, who still lay slumped at the foot of the steps like a sacrificial offering. For the briefest of moments, Vera wondered if he'd spare the elder. His indifference to the man's life struck her as strange. Hagan rarely missed a chance to make a spectacle of death.

'I am now your king,' he announced, his voice slicing through the heavy air.

The drakonians roared back with fury, their protests rising like fire meeting oil. Curses echoed off the stone walls, but Hagan merely laughed. A deep, delighted sound that reverberated through the square like the toll of a war drum.

Then he turned to the crate, reached inside, and withdrew his prize.

He raised his arms high, a gruesome trophy in each hand.

And the world broke open.

Gasps turned to screams. The square erupted. Vera swore aloud, her eyes locking on the horror before her.

Held aloft in each of Hagan's blood-slicked fists were the severed heads of King Egan and Queen Cyra, the sovereigns of the Kingdom of Fire. Their lifeless eyes stared into the crowd, mouths frozen mid-breath, their crowns replaced by a silence stripped of glory, falling like ash.

And just like that, the world screamed.

Chapter Twenty-Eight

House of Sand
Desert Kingdom

I'm not sure which region I'll visit first when I arrive in the Desert Kingdom for the Sand Trials. I'll have a little time to spare before they begin. The princess is eager to show me every single one, but we won't have enough time. There are twelve regions in the Desert Kingdom, each filled with cities and towns. Some are easily found, while others are hidden deep within the desert, visible only to those who know where to look.

Tabitha Wysteria

Alina had thought she'd witnessed everything the world could conjure. As always, she had been painfully mistaken.

The desert stretched out before her like an ancient, sleeping beast. Mysterious, unknowable, and far more dangerous than she had ever imagined. From the moment they crossed into the territory of the Desert Kingdom, it became painfully clear how gravely the desert folk had been underestimated. Dune after towering dune rose like silent sentinels, forming a vast, shimmering wall between their world and the rest. In the distance, mountains loomed, composed of sunbaked stone and layered sand, and as they drew closer, the illusions unravelled. What had appeared solid and impenetrable slowly revealed its secrets: caverns and hollows carved into the rock like hidden mouths. Entrances to a kingdom concealed so masterfully that, unless one knew where to look, it could easily vanish into the dunes. Some of the openings yawned wide enough to allow even the great serpents to slip through.

Their journey had been no gentle pilgrimage. One night, as they slept beneath a tapestry of stars, an enormous desert scorpion the size of a winged horse had launched its attack, armoured and venomous. Together, they had slain the beast, and by morning, its remains had already been repurposed. The meat fed their dwindling stores, while its chitinous shell was carved into plates for armour and wicked-edged weapons. Alina watched in quiet awe as the desert folk worked—every claw, every fang, every drop of venom made use of. Waste, it seemed, was an insult to the desert.

'Like this, amira,' Hessa said, elbowing her gently in the ribs to rouse her drifting attention. They rested in the shadow of a tent fashioned from shed serpent skin, just hours from reaching the mountains. Hessa was teaching her the art of extracting poisons from the venom sacs of slain insects, the kind that shimmered and pulsed with a deadly promise. 'We smear this over our blades,' she added, her tone calm, as though she were simply discussing a recipe for tea.

Alina smirked, no longer flinching away from hard work. Her bare arms were bronzed by the relentless sun, lean muscle etched into her limbs from weeks of harsh training. Her hair, once flowing in thick drakonian waves, was now tied high and tight to keep her neck cool. She had begged to cut it, desperate to shed the final trace of her former life. But Hessa had refused.

'Keep something of your past,' she had said, 'even if it's only a single strand.'

Alina had disagreed. She wanted the past scorched from memory, turned to ash and scattered on the desert winds. Her mind was a blade, honed and hungry. There was no room in it for nostalgia. Only vengeance. Only Hagan and his screams, his blood, his end. And she would make certain it came. She would not rest until he suffered. And oh, how she would enjoy it.

'Vaana,' Hessa said softly, gesturing towards the delicate vial of venom.

'Dahami mi tra,' Alina replied with care. *Let me try.*

Her grasp of the Sandhii tongue had sharpened swiftly in the span of the last week. With endless hours to do little else but listen to the servants converse as they journeyed across the golden expanse, the language had begun to nestle itself in her mind. During their stops, she would sit cross-legged beside Hessa, repeating syllables into the breeze, often dissolving into laughter when the desert princess clicked her tongue and scolded her for massacring the melody of the words.

'Dahami, amira,' Hessa corrected again, the disapproval in her tone laced with fondness. 'Our *i* is as your *ee*. Agari. Try again.'

Alina echoed the word, though her attention was stolen by the jagged silhouettes of the mountains looming ever nearer. Her patience frayed with every step. How could Hessa be so calm when home waited just ahead? If it were her, she'd be running barefoot across the dunes, wild with urgency.

'We are like the desert breeze, amira,' Hessa said, her eyes knowing. 'We do not run. We glide.'

Alina chuckled, the sound light as the wind stirring the sand. 'But do you not yearn for home?' she asked.

Hessa lifted her gaze to the crags in the distance and shrugged, her voice thoughtful. 'The sooner we arrive, the sooner I will shatter their hearts.'

Alina said nothing, but her nod was heavy with understanding. No one in the Desert Kingdom knew of the massacre that had swept through the drakonian castle, no whisper of Princess Sahira's death had reached them. Their kingdom was too secluded, too remote, cradled in sun and sand. Silence was its only messenger.

As they spread out the blankets across the cool shadows of the tents, Alina posed another question, one she had been holding close. 'What is your family like?'

It struck her as oddly natural to be doing such things— laying blankets, sweeping sand from the tent corners, helping with meals. In her former life, she would have scoffed at such menial tasks, raising an eyebrow at the very idea of touching what should be handled by servants. But now, it was second nature. She sat with the cooks as they prepared stews from desert herbs and scorpion meat. She hunted with the scouts beneath a sun that peeled the sky open. The notion of idly watching others toil now repulsed her.

Hessa sat back on her heels, folding a blanket with practised ease. 'My father, King Siroc, has many children,' she said. 'My mother was his second wife. His first died in childbirth. They were young then, barely more than children themselves, so he remarried quickly. With my mother, he had five. We are the eldest.'

'And your mother now?' Alina asked gently.

'She is Saqardatis,' Hessa said, a note of quiet reverence in her voice. 'The voice of the sand. The spiritual hand of the kingdom. She cannot be touched by grief, or by men.'

Alina stilled, her fingers brushing the edge of the tent cloth, suddenly aching to meet the woman who had raised the warrior beside her.

Frowning, Alina tilted her head. 'What is that?'

Hessa paused, the desert sun catching the gold in her braids as she searched for the right words in the common tongue. 'A priestess,' she said at last. 'She was honoured, chosen by the gods to join the Saqar. Now she is Altaa Saqardatis, the highest of them all. The most sacred.'

'And your father?' Alina asked, brows still furrowed. 'Did he not mind?'

Hessa shook her head with a quiet smile. 'It is the greatest honour a desert king may receive. To have his wife chosen by the gods. But once she joins the Saqar, marriage is no longer permitted. She belongs to the divine, not to man. So now my father has a new wife. And many more children than my hands can count.' She laughed, the sound soft and golden like the shifting sand. 'I shall not name them all, you'll end up with a migraha.'

'A migraha?'

'A pain in your head.'

'A migraine,' Alina corrected gently.

Hessa rolled her eyes and waved her off, irritated at the interruption. 'Qnahli.'

Alina stuck out her tongue, grinning. She recognised the insult. 'I'm not a know-it-all.'

The two girls bent once more to their work, nimble fingers dancing over glass and bone as they brewed their venom in silence. Alina's brown eyes wandered across the horizon, drinking in every detail with the hunger of one newly awakened. There was no fear left in her—not for the land, nor for the future. Only a keen, sharp excitement. This land, this burning cradle of sand and stone, had birthed Hessa. How could she fear it, when it had brought forth such fire? As Hessa had once told her, 'The sand spit me out at birth, so I am made of its grains.'

Alina longed to be made of something, too.

Something strong. Something eternal.

So she could burn the world down with every last witch in it.

...

The moment they reached the foot of the mountains, they were no longer alone. Figures cloaked in flowing robes emerged from the ridges and shadows, materialising like ghosts summoned by the wind. Alina did not need to be told who they were. Their faces were entirely concealed, save for their white eyes—sharp and glinting, drinking in every detail with unnerving clarity. Their robes clung to their forms, bound tight with scorpion-leather wrappings that gleamed dully beneath the waning sun. Weapons were hidden in the folds of their garments, and most wore no shoes, their bare feet silent against the sand, as if the desert itself had taught them to tread without sound.

Alina's heart thudded wildly in her chest as more and more figures appeared on the peaks above, at the crest of the dunes behind them, even amongst the rocks, half-hidden. It was as though they had known long ago that someone was coming, and had simply been waiting, watching.

Dunayans.

Whispers of them had reached even the coldest corners of the world. Stories of fierce women trained from childhood to become ghosts of the desert—deadly, silent, invisible. Alina had always known Hessa was one of them, but she also knew the desert princess had never fully revealed the depth of her skill. To join their ranks was said to be near impossible, especially for one already grown. But Alina was determined. She would find a way. She had to.

The Dunayans remained utterly still, unmoved from their positions. Some had bows drawn, arrows poised like starlight, their aim fixed on the intruding party.

'Don't they know it's you?' Alina whispered, her voice barely a breath. A strange, quiet fear curled around her chest like a serpent. What if they struck? What if a single wrong step meant death?

Hessa smiled, calm and unshaken. 'Of course they do. But knowing does not mean trusting. Dunayans are always cautious, amira. It is how we survive.'

They approached the flank of the mountain, where a stone archway loomed, half-eaten by time. The servants veered off with the giant serpents, disappearing into another passage. Hessa reached for Alina's hand, her fingers warm and steady as she pulled her into the waiting dark. The desert disappeared behind them.

They stepped into a narrow corridor hewn straight from the mountain's heart, its walls jagged and close, brushing Alina's shoulders. The air grew cool and dry, and there was no light, not even a sliver. Only stone and shadow.

'Hessa, I don't think...' Alina faltered. She couldn't see. Couldn't even glimpse Hessa in front of her. The only thing anchoring her was touch, the faint press of fingers, the echo of breath. Panic crept up her spine. She wasn't afraid of the dark... not normally. But this? This was a darkness that breathed. It whispered secrets into her ears, secrets she didn't want to know. It clawed into her bones, wrapping itself around her soul like a shroud. She could feel something ancient, something sentient, pulling at her from the deep. Her chest tightened. She couldn't breathe.

'Trust me, amira,' Hessa's voice was close, so close Alina could feel her breath warm against her face.

For a moment, Alina hesitated. Some part of her ached to lean forward, just a little. But before she could, Hessa turned again, slipping through the dark like water through fingers, and continued leading her deeper still into the mountain's heart.

Alina was just about to speak when a sudden blaze of light enveloped her, blinding her entirely. She gasped, stumbling, but Hessa's arm circled her waist in an instant, steadying her with quiet strength until her vision cleared.

The breath caught in her throat.

'Welcome to the Desert Kingdom,' Hessa said, her lips brushing close to Alina's ear, her arm still wrapped tightly around her.

Alina had no idea where to look first. They were deep within the mountain, yet the vastness of the space stretched around them like a hidden cathedral carved by ancient hands. It was an open expanse of tiers and levels, a subterranean city bathed in soft golden light. Bridges, formed naturally from the rock itself, arched gracefully across the chasm, connecting stone dwellings carved into the walls. Each hollowed space served its purpose. Some were homes, others shops, their entrances framed by intricate embroidery or cascading vines. Life thrived here, quietly and cleverly woven into stone.

'Some tunnels lead to the public baths,' Hessa explained softly, guiding her forward, 'others to our vegetable gardens. Though most of our meals are prepared under the sun, atop the mountain.'

Alina's mind reeled, overwhelmed by the spectacle. She barely registered the quiet stares they received as they passed, eyes narrowing at the sight of a drakonian in their midst. But Hessa paid them no mind. With a firm grasp of her hand, she tugged Alina up a narrow stairway etched directly into the stone, worn smooth by countless footsteps.

'Before we meet my father,' Hessa said, a mischievous glint in her voice, 'I want to show you my home.'

By the time they reached it, Alina was thoroughly lost. The entrance was one of many dark hollows lining the wall, veiled by thick, richly embroidered curtains. It seemed an easy enough barrier to bypass, but then again, who would dare steal from a Dunayan, and the daughter of a king no less?

Inside, the space unfolded into a surprisingly warm haven. Though the rooms were small, they brimmed with charm and intention. One chamber held a wide bed carved directly from the rock, piled high with vibrant woven blankets and pillows— simple luxury, desert-style. Alina had long grown used to sleeping on layered rugs and sand-worn mats, but this looked inviting even to her now-discerning eye. Another room contained plush cushions scattered across the floor, encircling a low table sculpted from sandstone and dry earth.

When she turned, her eyes widened at the sight that greeted her.

One entire wall was adorned with weapons. Daggers, curved scimitars, throwing knives, and even spears, all meticulously arranged. Each blade shimmered faintly in the low light, whispering stories of skill and precision. Alina drifted towards them as though entranced, her fingers brushing the wicked edge of a dagger. A small smile tugged at her lips.

She too now carried a desert blade at her hip. She had earned it, and with it, a new part of herself.

'Will they allow me to stay with you?' Alina asked softly, her voice barely above a whisper. She turned away, teeth catching her lower lip in quiet regret. She should never have assumed Hessa still wished for her company, not now that they had returned to Hessa's homeland. Alina was no longer her responsibility. 'I'm sorry. You'll want your space back. I shouldn't have presumed—'

Hessa laughed, the sound rich and warm like sun-drenched

honey. 'You really are beautiful when your cheeks burn, amira.' She reached for Alina's hand, her fingers curling gently around hers, tracing each one in that familiar way she did whenever she sensed Alina needed grounding. 'You may stay with me for as long as your heart desires. Until you grow bored of me.'

'I could never tire of you.'

'Oh?' Hessa's eyebrows lifted, her amusement blooming like a desert rose. 'Is that so, amira?'

It was only then that Alina realised how close they had drifted, how Hessa's hand still lingered on hers, soothing and deliberate. A flash of an image, Hessa lifting her hand to press a kiss to Alina's fingers, struck her like heat against skin. The thought alone startled her, and she stepped back, the air between them shifting with unspoken tension.

'Come,' Hessa said at last, her smile growing sly. 'Let's find the king.'

It was obvious from Hessa's expression that she knew what had flashed through Alina's mind. But what Hessa made of it, what she felt, remained veiled. She had spoken openly before, about her fondness for both men and women. Yet Alina had not dared to dwell on such thoughts, too uncertain of her own heart. What they had was a bond she cherished, a beautiful friendship. Nothing more.

Nothing more, she reminded herself.

It took them longer than expected to locate King Siroc. Alina had imagined a throne room, richly decorated and grandeur, perhaps a line of guards and silks flowing from the ceiling. Instead, they found him kneeling in a vegetable patch, his hands deep in the soil, carefully tending to the roots of his land.

It startled her, this image of royalty cloaked not in robes but in dirt, his crown replaced by the sunlit sweat on his brow. Hessa had mentioned before that their vegetables needed no sunlight, only patience and cleverness, born from generations of living where nothing should grow.

King Siroc looked up at last, his face lighting like dawn breaking across the dunes. With a jubilant cry, he opened his arms just in time to catch his daughter, who flung herself into his embrace with unrestrained joy.

Alina froze, caught in the warmth of the scene. Her lips parted slightly as something deep within her ached. It struck like a knife beneath the ribs.

She would never know such a reunion. She would never again race into Ash's arms, feel the fierce and familiar squeeze of her brother embracing her back.

The king signalled to the other workers, who stepped forward to take his share of the harvest from his hands. Without a word, he followed Hessa towards the entrance, where Alina stood waiting, stiff and uncertain, like a misplaced shadow against the sun-warmed stone.

But the moment his gaze found the drakonian girl and not his other daughter, his steps faltered.

'Let us sit and speak,' he said at last, his voice low, laced with something far too heavy for so early a greeting.

He was younger than Alina had expected a king to be, his youth barely dulled by the weight of a crown. Handsome, undeniably so, with strong, chiseled features sculpted by wind and sun. His skin bore the burnished bronze of the desert, his dark hair trimmed just enough to suggest practicality over pride. A light stubble shadowed his jaw, softening his face rather than hardening it. Though his robes were loose, modest in their cut, Alina could see the tautness of his frame beneath. He was no idle ruler. Her scrutiny did not miss the twin desert daggers that rested at his hips like loyal hounds, worn by one well-versed in their use.

He led them into a chamber carved deep into the mountain's heart, a room that once echoed with the weight of strategy and blood-sworn oaths. It had been a war room, centuries ago, where desert generals and kings spread maps across stone tables and plotted under torchlight, their voices sharp with purpose. The air still carried the ghosts of old schemes, though the room itself had long since been abandoned to silence. For over a hundred years, it had slumbered, untouched by war or whispers of conflict, its purpose forgotten as peace lulled the kingdom into stillness. Dust lay undisturbed in the corners, and the shadows seemed to linger with memory, as if waiting for battle to return.

'Sit,' he said again, motioning to the low cushions scattered around a carved table of sandstone. He poured three glasses of vhina, the amber-coloured desert wine catching the light like melted sun. Alina sipped hers slowly, trying not to show the sudden tremble in her fingers.

Without warning, Hessa spoke.

'Sahira is dead.' The words landed like a scythe to the gut, swift and without ceremony. 'The witches stormed the Kingdom of Fire. They've seized the city of Spark. Alina Acheron is the only survivor of the drakonian royal family.'

The king sank onto his cushion as though the weight of his grief had robbed him of his bones. No tears fell, but Alina could feel the hollowed ache radiating from him like heat off the sand. It was an ache she knew intimately. A grief so deep it did not howl, but whispered endlessly in the dark.

For a long time, he said nothing. His eyes closed, his breaths slow, as though he were wandering the corridors of memory, through laughter once shared, through the echo of Sahira's voice in the hallways of his heart. When he opened his eyes again, the sorrow had been neatly folded, tucked away behind the solemn eyes of a king.

'Who else?' he asked, voice hoarse but steady.

'Princess Haven Blackburn has been slain,' Hessa said softly. 'Prince Zahian Noor as well.'

'The Hawthornes have also perished,' Alina added, her voice a pale thread of sound.

'They aimed to snuff out every House,' Hessa said. 'The only ones untouched were the wolverians.'

King Siroc's eyes narrowed. 'Could they have colluded with the witches?'

'I doubt it,' Hessa replied, exchanging a brief glance with Alina. 'They seemed just as stunned as the rest of us.'

'They have no cause to betray the Houses,' Alina said, though a faint unease stirred within her. 'They gain nothing from this.'

'Perhaps not,' the king said, though suspicion lingered in the air like a coiled serpent. 'But even the snow has shadows.'

Alina looked down, guilt blooming in her chest like a bruise. She had met the wolverians briefly, shared meals, seen them dance, and yet, she had never truly looked. Never seen. If only she had paid more attention. If only...

Perhaps this could have all been prevented.

'Perhaps,' Hessa said, her voice heavy with the weight of futures yet to unfold. 'I wish to take the Dunayans with me. The witches will not rest with the Kingdom of Fire beneath their feet. They may never reach us here, buried in the arms of the dunes, but they will come for the others, one by one, until all is ash.'

'The witches have always despised the drakonians above all,' King Siroc said quietly, his stare settling on Alina like a shadow. The meaning was unspoken, but understood by them both. It had been her people who lit the match. Her bloodline that rode dragons through the sky and turned a kingdom to cinders. Her legacy that forged the witches' wrath. 'They might leave it at that,' he added, though even he did not sound convinced.

Hessa shook her head. 'No. They won't. It was the drakonians who began the Great War, yes. But the rest of us stood idle. Some even joined them in the flames. The desert folk once stood shoulder to shoulder with the witches. We were kin once, bonded by sand and magic. But when they screamed for aid, we turned away. They will never forget. Nor forgive.'

King Siroc gave a slow, weary nod. 'Very well, hajaa. Do what you must.' *Daughter.*

'We will stay for a while longer. Alina must learn to fight before we return.'

'It may be too late by then, hajaa,' he said, the old word heavy with sorrow.

Hessa rose. 'I leave with Alina or I do not leave at all.'

His nod came again, slower this time. His eyes drifted to the bare wall, as if he saw a daughter that no longer stood beside him. Grief had hollowed him. He was a man stripped of resistance. Hessa could have asked for the world, and he would have handed it to her.

Alina hurried after Hessa, trailing behind through winding tunnels that twisted and dipped like veins carved into the mountain's heart. Back in the stillness of Hessa's chamber, Alina caught her by the arm, halting her.

'Hessa! Perhaps the king is right. You should go ahead with the Dunayans. I won't be ready in time. I'll only slow you down.'

'You will be ready,' Hessa said, her voice resolute.

'But you said they'd never accept me. I'm not one of them. I can't train with the Dunayans.'

'They will accept you,' Hessa whispered, stepping close, her white eyes blazing with defiance. 'I'll see to it, amira. Myself.'

'Hessa…'

The desert princess placed her hands on Alina's shoulders, grounding her. 'This is our vengeance, amira. Not mine alone, and not yours. Ours. We will find Hagan and we will slit his throat. For Sahira, for your parents… and for Ash.'

Alina's lips trembled, her eyes blurring with tears, but her smile held firm. 'Waa kair janta,' she whispered, as the tears slipped down her sun-kissed cheeks.

Hessa leaned in, soft and steady, and kissed them away. 'Waa kair janta,' she echoed.

We fall together.

Chapter Twenty-Nine

The Underworld

I'm scared. Hades is a god, and he holds powers, powers that could obliterate everything I hold dear. Now that I've chosen Hadrian over him... what if he kills Hadrian? I couldn't live without him.

I refuse to.

Tabitha Wysteria

Mal stared into the obsidian vastness beyond, her eyes fixed upon skies she knew no wyverns would pierce. Though the Underworld echoed the world she had known, it was but a shadow of the real thing. Similar in shape, but not in soul.

She caught the movement behind her before it fully formed —her senses too sharp, too attuned to ignore such things. Yet still, she turned, watching as Thanatos approached with the slow grace of a shadow. He leant against the opposite side of the open stone archway, the one built for wyverians to leap from, onto the backs of their winged beasts. But there were no wyverns here. So why keep windows without glass?

Mal turned her attention back to the void outside, feigning disinterest while stealing glances at Thanatos through her lashes. A fierce part of her imagined seizing his black shirt and flinging him into the abyss, just to hear the silence break. But that part, as always, lost to the quieter, more reluctant one.

'You find too much pleasure in the thought of murder,' he said.

Her eyes widened. 'You said thoughts couldn't be read here.'

'And they can't,' Thanatos replied with a lazy shrug. 'You're just terribly easy to read.'

'You don't know me.'

Something shifted in his eyes. A wisp of recognition or regret, but it was gone too quickly for Mal to grasp.

'No,' he said softly, 'you're right, Melinoe.'

She stiffened at the sound of her name on his lips, her shoulders tightening like coiled rope. She turned fully away from him and let her eyes wander to the forest below. Even that was familiar, eerily so. A mimicry of the Forest of Silent Cries.

'The Forest of Silent Cries is the entryway for souls who die in your kingdom,' Thanatos said, voice almost contemplative. 'Each kingdom has its own threshold into the Underworld. Some... more theatrical than others.'

'Have you met the other gods?' Mal asked, her voice low.

His jaw tensed, just slightly, but enough to tell her she'd struck a nerve. 'Yes. I have.'

'And what are they like?'

'Why do you ask?' His mouth curved into that infuriating smirk she was beginning to loathe. 'Planning a visit?'

'Perhaps,' she answered, her face unreadable. 'My brother used to teach me about them.'

Thanatos tilted his head, folding his arms across his chest. Mal tried not to dwell on how much the gesture reminded her of Ash, of the drakonian warmth that had once held her. But the memory curled in her chest, unwelcome and intrusive.

'And what did he teach you?' Thanatos asked.

'That the gods created our kingdoms. That each realm was shaped by a particular god, designed to reflect something of themselves, or—'

'Or...?' He leaned closer, teeth glinting in the dim light.

'Or to outdo the others.'

His smirk widened. 'Exactly. Gods are petty, self-serving creatures driven by rivalry and pride. Etch that into your soul, Melinoe. You'll need the reminder.'

'You speak as if you weren't one of them.'

Thanatos let out a soft, bitter snort. 'That's because I'm something far worse, Melinoe.'

Mal's brow furrowed. 'Why do you keep saying my name?'

The question seemed to catch him off guard. He rubbed his jaw with a thoughtful hand, the gesture almost uncertain, almost mortal. She half expected him to ignore her, but then that infuriatingly familiar smirk unfurled across his lips.

'I have waited an eternity for you. And now that you're here, close enough to touch if you'd let me, I must speak your name aloud, if only to remind myself this isn't some cruel dream.'

Her focus faltered. She turned away, unable to meet the weight of his eyes, or the fleeting brush of his fingers against hers.

'Why do they want to destroy everything?' she asked, veering the conversation elsewhere, if only to escape the strange gravity pulling her towards him. She hadn't noticed how near they'd drifted until her breath caught in her throat. Too close. Far too close to a creature who wore Ash Acheron's face like a mask designed to torment her. She stepped back sharply, spine meeting the cool stone of the column behind her.

She ignored the shadow of hurt that passed through his expression. His eyes, at least, did not belong to Ash. They were colder. Wilder.

'Your father—'

'Hades,' she corrected flatly.

'Hades,' he echoed, his voice tinged with amusement. The sound scraped against her nerves. No matter how much he resembled a fallen angel from some long-lost tale, Mal knew better. She saw beyond the white curls and the sculpted strength. She saw the shadow.

'Hades did something he was never meant to do. And now... this is their way of setting things right.'

'What did he do?'

'You needn't trouble yourself with that.' His eyes shifted, refusing to meet hers which was an answer in itself. Whatever it was, it was bad. Monumental. Perhaps the gods were furious that he had forged something like her, a being made of wyverian blood, witchcraft, and divinity. A creature that should not exist.

But she did. And if she posed a threat to them, she needed to understand exactly why.

'Then what should I be worrying about?' she asked, her voice sharp with challenge, her violet gaze blazing like a forge. She meant to sear through him, to unravel him molecule by molecule. But he turned, and when he looked at her, the power behind his eyes struck like lightning.

He moved before she could blink.

One moment he stood apart, the next his arms were braced on either side of her head, caging her against the column. His breath mingled with hers, and for a heartbeat, the world held its breath.

Mal did not flinch.

Instead, she lifted her chin, meeting him at eye level, refusing to shrink. If he thought he could intimidate her, he would learn just how wrong he was. His stare dropped to her mouth, and his smile turned hungry.

'You ought to worry about *me,*' he whispered.

Mal let out a snort, unbothered.

Then she sank her teeth into his ear, and bit it clean off.

...

What Mal assumed was the next day had arrived. Though in truth, the concept of time had long begun to unravel in the Underworld. She had slowly come to understand that here, time was more illusion than law. Though the world turned through its motions—meals served, sleep taken—nothing truly shifted. The sky remained ever dim, the air ever hushed. It was as though they were caught in a single, suspended breath, held between heartbeats.

'Time is not linear here, Melinoe,' Thanatos had once told her, tone light, as if speaking of the weather.

'Then what is it?' she'd asked, perplexed.

'Non-existent,' he replied, with a shrug that irked her more than it should have. 'We do not age in this place. We are frozen in a single moment. We simply stretch it as we please.'

Mal tried not to smirk at the sight of him now, standing across from her with a freshly missing ear. That familiar crooked grin of his remained firmly in place, infuriating as ever. The wicked glint in his eye said he found the whole thing rather amusing.

Makaria had crept into Mal's bed during the stillness of the night, murmuring that she feared sleeping alone. Mal had bristled at first. Some feral part of her wanted to shove the girl away. But then she remembered all the nights she had slipped into Haven's bed just for the comfort of a sister's presence. And though Makaria was not Haven, and never would be, Mal had allowed her to stay.

Now they stood at the threshold of the great wyverian castle, its silhouette rising like a dead god against a lifeless plain. All around them stretched a vast swathe of withered grass and barren earth, untouched by wind or season. Not even a breeze stirred Mal's dark hair; the world was still, held in perfect silence, fitting for a realm of the dead.

Thanatos stood waiting before her, clad in shadow-black wyverian garb, his hands empty but for the scythe she'd once seen Zagreus carry. The steel caught no light, for there was none here to catch, just the faintest echo of death in its gleam.

'He enjoys stealing it from me,' Thanatos said smoothly.

Mal's nose crinkled in irritation. The realisation dawned that, once again, he had plucked her thoughts straight from her mind. The smirk curving his lips, followed by a low, velvet laugh that echoed Ash's all too perfectly made her still, caught in a strange moment of doubt.

'You've already begun to awaken your divine powers,' he continued, as if nothing had happened. 'You've summoned shadows. Commanded the dead. That is the god in you, beginning to stir.'

'What of my witchcraft?' she asked, trying to steel her voice.

'Only another witch can teach you that,' he replied, lifting a brow, 'or a god who shares a link to their kind.'

'Then you're rather useless to me, aren't you?'

Thanatos chuckled again, the sound soft and dangerous. 'Am I?'

'You said it yourself,' she shot back, folding her arms. 'I've touched my god-powers already. And you're of no use in unlocking the rest. So what, exactly, do I need *you* for?'

Without warning, Thanatos reappeared before her, so close their breath mingled in the air between them. Mal's pulse leapt, her fingers flexing in readiness to shove him away. But instead of kissing her, as she half-feared, he reached out and tapped the tip of her nose with his finger, like a child chiding a kitten.

'You shouldn't have said that,' he said.

And then the ground beneath her feet vanished.

His laughter was the last thing she heard before the world swallowed her whole. Darkness closed in like a great jaw. Something unseen gripped her ankles and dragged her down, her scream snatched from her throat as she tumbled into nothingness.

When she hit the solid, earthen, and cold ground, she groaned, opening her eyes to find herself once again at the river's edge. The same mournful current drifted by. The same skeletal boat. And the same robed figure: Charon, silently drifting towards her.

Unbelievable.

She sat up, spitting dirt from her mouth and narrowing her eyes towards the horizon.

She was going to bash Thanatos' skull open with a rock.

A sound behind her drew Mal's attention, and she turned swiftly, her eyes narrowing at the figure lounging against one of the pale trees with blackened leaves. Trees that, back home, only grew in the Forest of Silent Cries. Here, they sprouted like weeds, everywhere she turned.

'If I touch you, you die,' Thanatos explained, his tone light, as though commenting on the weather. He shrugged with an elegance that only made her blood simmer. 'Lucky for you, you're a goddess, and in the Underworld.'

'But I didn't die,' Mal said, narrowing her eyes. 'Not like when Makaria and Zagreus would chase me. This felt different, like being transported from one place to another.'

Thanatos' lips curled into a smirk. 'Ah, but my kind of killing is different. I am Death, Melinoe. I end things as I please. I can pluck a soul like a string from an instrument—gently, soundlessly. One moment you're standing in mortal lands, the next, you're here, none the wiser. Death, to me, can be as subtle as walking through a door.'

'Makaria and Zagreus didn't seem so subtle,' she snapped. 'They rather enjoyed the theatrics. Blades, blood... the whole performance.'

'They do enjoy flair,' Thanatos admitted, stepping onto the boat that had silently come to rest at the riverbank. 'And they're easily bored. Eternity will do that to you. They pass the time with creative murder.' He held out a hand to help her aboard.

Mal stared at it.

'It only works when I wish it,' he said simply, voice low and maddeningly smooth. 'You're safe with me, Melinoe.'

She stepped into the boat without taking his hand, her movements curt, sharp with distaste. She sat opposite him, knees almost brushing his in the cramped wooden shell. The proximity made her fists clench.

'Do I not get the power to make you vanish?' she asked.

'You could turn me into a shadow, I suppose,' he mused.

'Not enough,' Mal said, eyes glinting with something wicked. 'How's the ear?'

'I could make it grow back,' Thanatos replied, completely unbothered.

'Then why don't you?'

He leaned forward slightly, amusement showing in his expression. 'Because I know how much pleasure it brings you to see it gone.'

Mal looked away, refusing to gift him the sight of her scowl. The desire to rake her nails down his face, to scratch those irritatingly handsome features into ribbons, made her fingers twitch. Perhaps she ought to leap into the icy river and swim the rest of the way just to put distance between them.

'You may have tapped into your powers,' Thanatos said, his

voice a lazy curl of sound on the cold air. 'But that doesn't mean you've mastered them.'

'That's what you're here for?'

Thanatos' jaw clenched. 'I am here to teach you how to wield your powers. But—'

'But what?'

'Too much power can corrupt the mind.'

Mal snorted, her eyes fixed on the water slapping against the sides of the narrow boat. 'Why won't you just tell me what my father is planning?'

'Hades,' he corrected, a smile tugging at his lips. Mal bit down on her tongue, swallowing the urge to lash out for her slip. 'He wants to mend what's been shattered.'

'What does that even mean?'

The boat listed to one side, its worn hull creaking as a splash of frigid river water soaked their ankles. Statues loomed on either side of them. Colossal effigies of gods with hollow eyes and unreadable faces, their stony silhouettes watching in silence as the boat slid past. Up ahead, the ancient gates of the Underworld parted without a sound, allowing them through like an old beast accepting its offering.

Thanatos moved, his hand suddenly outstretched, reaching across the narrow gap between them, fingers lingering perilously close to Mal's lap. She stared at it, unmoving, unsure of what the gesture meant. Was this another game? Another veiled trick hidden beneath his usual smirk?

Retreating would give him power. And Mal would rather be dragged to the very edge of Tartarus than give Thanatos the satisfaction of seeing her flinch.

'Take my hand,' he said.

'Why?'

'I don't bite.'

'I know,' she snapped, her tone all teeth. 'That's the problem.'

'I want to show you something.'

'What?'

He sighed dramatically, as if exhausted by her presence. 'Must you make everything so bloody difficult?'

She rolled her eyes and went to slap his hand away, but he was quicker. His fingers curled around hers before she could stop him, the touch colder than stone, colder than the river around them. Mal's body stilled, her breath catching as her gaze lifted to meet his.

'Let go,' she hissed.

'Only if you behave.'

She narrowed her eyes but managed a begrudging huff, her voice laced with threat. 'Fine. What is it you want to show me?'

That infuriating grin returned, dark and maddeningly pleased. 'My powers, Melinoe. As the God of Death.'

And before she could curse him or pull away, he shoved her off the boat.

The river swallowed her whole.

Freezing black water closed over her head, and before she could fight to the surface, hands—dozens of them—gripped her ankles and dragged her down, down, down into the abyss below. Into the place where death had no face, and time held no meaning.

Chapter Thirty

House of Flames
Kingdom of Fire

I must keep my blood magic a secret. If anyone were to discover what I'm truly capable of...

But this magic will make me the most powerful witch in my land. It will protect me from Hades. Still, I can't help but feel a deep sadness for what I had to sacrifice to gain it. Blood magic comes at a cost. A cost I was willing to pay.

I always wanted to be a healer. To save and to protect. But that part of me had to be destroyed. It was the piece I gave up in exchange. Now, I will never be able to heal through my magic.

Only destroy.

Tabitha Wysteria

Vera examined her nails with theatrical boredom, the slow tapping of her heel echoing off the marble floor with petulant rhythm. Across the cavernous temple interior, her eyes landed on Hagan. It was maddening to admit, but the drakonians had a flair for aesthetics. Even their temples—hulking beasts of stone —were adorned with an artistry that made lesser kingdoms look drab. Phoenixians were perhaps even more talented in that regard, but drakonians had a peculiar knack for elevating the plain into splendour.

The ceilings soared above them, hand-painted with scenes of devotion, vivid depictions of their singular god. Drakonians and phoenixians, for all their fire and pride, shared that in common: a belief in only one deity. And yet, even on this, they could not agree. Each swore their god bore a different name, claimed a different face. Two squabbling brothers, each desperate to outshine the other with gilded tales and finer prayers.

The thought of siblings dragged her attention back to Hagan. Her own brother. Her own burden. Things had unravelled, as expected. The moment he'd raised the severed heads of the Kingdom of Fire's king and queen, a dagger had flown, narrowly missing its mark. The chaos that followed had scattered their forces, and the witches had whisked Hagan into the safety of the temple. For days now, they'd been holed up while warlocks and witches clashed with drakonian resistance in the streets, those proud bastards refusing to relinquish their city.

'What?' Hagan's voice cut across the chamber, his eyes narrowing.

'I haven't said a word.'

'I can practically *hear* your thoughts grinding.'

Vera sighed and clapped her hands once, the sound sharp. She resisted the temptation to laugh in his face and instead adopted the aloof poise of the indifferent sister she had always performed so well.

'Did you honestly think they wouldn't retaliate when you paraded their king's head like a trophy?'

A spark of something twisted, something monstrous, flashed in those purple eyes of his. Eyes that mirrored hers, yet bore none of her restraint. He licked his lips, slow and deliberate, before sauntering towards her. His breath brushed her cheek as he loomed too close, forcing her to retreat half a step. She'd seen him devour worse.

His lips found her ear, his whisper as cold as steel dipped in shadow. 'Did you really think I was so simple?'

Vera's entire body stiffened, an icy tremor running through her bones. Her mind reeled. His failures, his blunders, all of it a carefully staged performance. He had played her for a fool.

The horror in her expression only deepened his amusement. He chuckled darkly, clearly relishing her dawning comprehension.

'It was a trap,' she breathed. 'A diversion.'

It had all been theatre. A distraction, carefully orchestrated to veil his true design. Whatever Hagan was really plotting, he had kept it hidden, even from Vera. And that, that betrayal, stung more than anything.

He saw it. The fury in her eyes. And it delighted him.

'Why didn't you tell me?' she hissed, her hands curling into fists, nails biting into her palms.

Hagan's lip curled, a wicked grin spreading across his face like a shadow sliding over stone. There was madness in that smile, something hollow and haunted that made her body stiffen with dread.

'Why didn't you tell me our sweet sister ran off into the night?' he countered, voice low and seething.

Vera faltered, caught off guard. 'I—'

His hand shot out, wrapping around her throat with a serpent's speed. She choked, clawing at his arm as he squeezed, his strength unyielding, unreal. He leaned in, breath hot against her ear.

'All I ever wanted was for my family to love me, sister. But none of you did. None of you wanted me, did you?'

He turned her roughly, forcing her to face the temple doors. Two warlocks were dragging Allegra forward, her body limp. Her face was swollen and bloodied, her leg bent at a sickening angle.

Vera's scream caught in her throat.

'We shall cleanse this world of its poison,' Hagan breathed, sinking his teeth into her ear, hard enough to draw blood. 'And today, we begin with *you*.'

He inhaled her scent like a starving beast, and she writhed in his grasp, desperate to free herself. She reached for her magic, calling it from deep within, but it twisted against her, scorched and warped by his blood magic. Her body contorted with the agony of it, as if her soul itself were being burnt alive. She could not move. Could not speak. Only scream.

'Watch, Vera,' he commanded, wrenching her face downward so she was forced to bear witness as his magic unravelled Allegra. Their sister twisted in grotesque, terrifying angles, her bones splintering with sickening cracks that echoed through the temple like thunder. Allegra's screams, high and shrill, sliced through the air as blood welled from her eyes, her mouth, her ears, every soft edge of her face turned to a river of red.

Her body writhed, no longer recognisably mortal, bending in ways no living being could survive. And still he went on. Still, Hagan broke her, finger by finger, joint by joint, slowly coaxing each crack and snap as though conducting a symphony of agony. When her voice faltered, when the breath fled her lungs and her chest no longer rose, he continued, smiling as he folded her limbs like parchment.

'Stop,' Vera rasped, her nails carving trenches into his skin in a desperate plea. But he only laughed, drunk on her pain.

Something shifted in the air, something impossible. Vera blinked through the blur of tears and blood, convinced she was hallucinating. But the image did not fade. The temple floor split with a groan, ancient stone fracturing as if the earth itself recoiled. From the gaping wound, tendrils of shadow slithered forth, inky and alive, writhing as they expelled two figures from the abyss below.

Mal Blackburn, a vision of fury and flame, surged into view. And with her... a man bearing the haunting likeness of Ash Acheron, who knelt beside Allegra with a reverence that stole Vera's breath.

Mal shoved Hagan away with a power that flared like lightning, loosening his grip just long enough for Vera to twist free. She lifted her trembling hands and struck, her magic crackling through the air, slamming Hagan backwards with a force that cracked the walls. Then she turned, just as her heart split in two.

Allegra lay still. Her wide, purple eyes stared back, glassy and unseeing.

'Run, Vera!' Mal's voice reached her through water, muffled, distant, like a memory she couldn't quite grasp. Vera wanted to ask about the stranger at Allegra's side, the way he touched her sister's arm before vanishing into mist. She wanted to scream, to fight, to die beside Allegra.

But instead, Vera ran.

Out of the blood-soaked temple and into the burning streets of Fireheart, where chaos reigned and drakonians clashed with witches in a dance of fire and shadow. She ran, her name howling in the wind behind her. She didn't look back. She didn't stop. Not even when the ache in her chest became too much to bear. Not even when the tears seared down her cheeks.

Not even when her heart finally shattered, knowing, as all truths rise in the end, that Allegra's death was her doing.

Her fault.

All of it.

Chapter Thirty-One

House of Wild
Kingdom of Fauna

Some say my mind has been corrupted.
I say the world is what made it so.

Tabitha Wysteria

Dawn knew they were lost. Irrevocably, unforgivably lost. Wandering into the cursed embrace of the Forest of Endless Trees had been foolish; believing they might find their way back out again was simply delusional. She had long since lost count of the days or even weeks they'd spent beneath its eternal canopy, every direction as hopeless as the last. But if she was destined to rot here, she would not do so beside a wyverian.

Her fury had dulled into resignation. Now she drifted through the forest like a ghost, trudging over roots and moss-covered stones, offering half-hearted prayers to gods she'd never much liked. Perhaps one of them would take pity and point her to an exit. Perhaps not. The silence was unsettling, especially from the wyverian, who spent his time muttering under his breath and casting irritated glances her way, as though that might be enough to scare her off.

'There's a lake,' she said suddenly, shattering the silence like glass.

'Splendid,' Kai muttered. 'Might be the perfect place to drown you.'

She kicked the back of his knee, *again*. A habit she was becoming far too fond of. Ducking out of reach, she darted forward, eyes alight with triumph. 'Untie me, wyverian. I haven't properly bathed in days.'

'I'm painfully aware.'

'You reek too.'

'I'm not untying you.' Kai folded his arms across his chest, unmoved by her scowl. 'Don't pout. It won't help your case.'

'I can't bathe like this. It's absurd. I've no magic left, you overgrown lizard! If I did, I'd have turned you into something obscene by now. Untie me this instant!'

'Still no.'

'Suit yourself.' With an indignant huff, she turned and marched towards the glimmering waters ahead. It was a secluded lake, cradled by thick bushes and twisted vines, the mirror-like surface undisturbed. She paused by the shore and twisted round, gesturing at him with theatrical exasperation. 'Go away.'

Kai snorted. 'Keep dreaming. I'm not letting you out of my sight.'

'Turn around.'

'No.'

'Close your damned eyes, pig!'

'Still no.'

She groaned and spun back to the lake, defeated. With one eye on him, she began tugging at her green dress, fumbling with the fabric. Her frustration only grew at the sound of his dry laughter.

'Do hurry,' he drawled, finally glancing away, more out of boredom than courtesy. 'You truly do reek.'

Dawn cursed under her breath and hurried into the shallows, the water lapping at her dress as she stayed close to the shoreline, close enough to avoid the risk of drowning. She scrubbed herself as best she could, muttering irritably at the absurdity of bathing with her hands bound and her dress still clinging to her like a second skin. The fabric dragged around her legs, heavy and awkward, but it was the only modesty she had left.

When she glanced over her shoulder, she caught him watching. Kai Blackburn's black eyes did not stray, fixed on her with a gaze sharp enough to pierce armour. Her skin prickled under the weight of it, as if thousands of tiny needles had embedded themselves just beneath the surface.

She yelped when she heard the clink of metal. Turning fully, she saw him stripping out of his armour piece by piece, until he stood utterly bare before her. Gods. Dawn had known wyverians weren't shy about nudity, but the sight of him, unflinching, unabashed, made her cheeks flush as if the sun itself had scorched her. Since Ash, she'd been with others: warlocks who were good for forgetting, for pleasure without meaning. None of them had made her blush. None had undone her with a single look.

But Kai Blackburn was not like other men.

'Do not dare get in the water!' she shrieked the moment his feet met the ripples. 'We can take turns!'

'You are too slow,' he said, stepping further in, steam rising as his cold skin met the warmth. His shoulders eased slightly, though his tone remained curt. 'And I don't trust you near my things, witch.'

'I have a name.'

'It's witch.'

Her hand sliced the water with such force that it smacked

him full in the face. She froze for a heartbeat, uncertain whether she'd pushed too far. But when his expression remained unreadable, the fear faded, replaced with that familiar fire. She squared her shoulders and held her ground. She would not cower before him. No man would make her flinch.

His jaw clenched, and when his eyes locked onto hers, it was as though the stars had collapsed inward. The weight of him, of that stare, pressed down on her until her breath caught in her throat.

'You don't know how to behave,' he said, low and tight.

'As I said,' she replied, her voice a defiant whisper, 'I'm *not* a dog.'

'What are you, then?' he growled, anger gleaming in those midnight eyes.

'I'm... I'm just Dawn.'

The storm in his stare faltered, confusion softening its edges. It was as if, for the first time, he saw her not as a witch, not as a threat or a nuisance, but as a woman. The question had undone something in both of them.

He looked away, as though her answer had shaken him more than he'd admit.

But Dawn wasn't finished.

With wicked intent curling behind her lips, she drifted closer. Their bodies brushed, just for a moment, and the sharp coldness of his skin lit a fire beneath hers. Something in her came alive, wild and electric.

Dawn parted her lips, a teasing retort poised on her tongue, but no words emerged. His back pressed against her chest, warm and solid, and slowly he turned. Now they stood face to face, his body aligned with hers, as though carved to fit the same space. His stare dipped, lingering on the wet cling of her dress, something unspoken glinting behind his eyes, perhaps a trace of regret that he hadn't let her swim bare beneath the sunlight.

Without warning, his large hands slid to her waist, claiming it with firm purpose, erasing any breath of distance. He leaned in, lips hovering close enough to steal the air from her lungs. His right hand ghosted down the length of her side, cupping her rear possessively, squeezing with wicked intent.

'Is this what you want?' he said, his voice low, velvet-soft, brushing against her neck like a sin made flesh. Her breath hitched, her head tilting back in offering. The thin fabric of her dress did nothing to hide the stiff peaks of her nipples, nor the liquid heat that bloomed and coiled between her thighs, spreading like fire through her limbs.

'Touch me,' she moaned, her nails pressing crescent moons into his skin, urging him to do more, take more. But instead, his hands left her body, shifting to her arms and holding her in place with a force that stilled her breath. A smile bloomed across his lips. Not one of passion, but one edged in cruelty. A hunter's grin.

Dawn barely had time to react before he shoved her backwards into the water.

The shock stole the breath from her lungs. Cold swallowed her. She surfaced coughing, spluttering, her limbs flailing as she clawed her way to the water's edge, collapsing on solid earth as water streamed from her sodden hair and dress.

'You motherfu—'

But Kai was already dressing, laughter ringing through the day like steel bells.

'You think I'd fall for a witch's charms so easily?'

She didn't answer. Her hair clung to her face like ribbons, and her soaked dress clung tighter still. Breathing came hard. She bit the inside of her cheek to keep the sob trapped deep within her chest, but it rose all the same. And though she told herself she wouldn't cry, not in front of a wyverian, certainly not in front of him, the tears came anyway. Silently at first, until her hands flew up to her mouth to keep the sound of her heartbreak from escaping.

The cold crept under her skin and into her bones. And with it came shame, fury, and a sorrow so sharp it stole what was left of her strength. Trembling, soaked to the marrow and hollowed by exhaustion, she wept quietly and fiercely into her palms.

She drew her knees to her chest, frustration simmering just beneath her skin. The silence stretched, taut and bitter, as she felt Kai's presence close in. Still, she refused to acknowledge him, even when his calloused fingers found the bindings around her wrists and quietly set her free.

'We need to move and find shelter before nightfall,' he said, his voice a low rumble. His dark eyes caught the glimmer on her cheeks, and he paused, frowning as though tears were a language he didn't understand. As though witches, in his mind, were incapable of sorrow, of softness.

Dawn rubbed her freed wrists and rose wordlessly, trailing after the infuriating wyverian with as much dignity as she could gather from the dirt.

...

'It's there or nowhere, witch.'

'I choose nowhere,' Dawn snapped, folding her arms across her chest with the elegance of a scorned empress.

Kai grunted, a low, guttural sound of suffering, which only made her grin with wicked delight. It warmed her far more than anything else had that day.

'There is absolutely nothing wrong with this shelter,' he muttered, gesturing towards the crooked wooden hut nestled between two gnarled trees.

Dawn cocked her head, her eyes narrowing as she surveyed the pathetic excuse for shelter. The roof sagged like a tired sigh, and the walls leaned into the wind with resigned despair. It would shield them from a storm, perhaps, but it reeked of forgotten ghosts. 'We won't be able to feel the fire from in there,' she said.

'Who said anything about a fire?'

She rolled her eyes so hard it might have summoned a storm. 'We've spent every night shivering on damp earth, with no blankets, no fire, and no comfort. I'm cold.'

'It's too dangerous.'

'I don't care,' she said, her voice rising with every syllable. 'I'm cold. And you made me bathe in my dress.'

Kai's patience visibly thinned. 'Deadly gods, give me strength. I did not force you to wash.'

'I did you a favour, commander. I stank. Perhaps wyverians are immune to such things, but I am not.'

'If wyverians are used to stinking creatures, then how was it a favour *to me?* he said, one eyebrow raised in mockery.

'I am cold! And tired! I need a fire. *Right now.'*

'Fine,' he said with theatrical exhaustion. 'Then make one yourself.' He gestured grandly to the scattered twigs. 'Be my guest.'

Dawn bit the inside of her cheek. She had always relied on magic for such mundane tasks. Survival skills were for those who didn't know how to bend the world to their will. Still, there was no chance in the underworld she would let the smug wyverian win.

'I shall make the grandest fire you've ever seen,' she declared, already storming out of the hut, collecting branches and muttering like a madwoman. 'And you, commander, shall sit in the cold, trembling with regret while I bask in glorious warmth.'

'Terrific,' Kai replied, settling himself beneath a tree, arms crossed and expression unreadable.

She busied herself with exaggerated purpose, trying to recall how fires were built—something about friction, spark, air. Why had she never paid closer attention? The memory of firelight in the drakonian castle danced through her mind, of long evenings pretending to belong, of Ash smiling at her through the flames...

'You're getting distracted,' Kai drawled.

Dawn jumped, cursing under her breath. She returned to her task with the ferocity of a woman scorned by nature itself. Minutes stretched into hours. The twigs refused to light, the wind mocked her efforts, and eventually she descended into a full tantrum, throwing branches into the air with screams loud enough to startle birds from trees.

One particularly sharp twig flew straight into Kai's face.

He was on her in an instant, gripping her arm, his dark eyes burning with fury. The tension in his jaw could have cracked stone. 'Is this how you deal with failure?' he asked, his voice low and lethal, surveying the chaos she had unleashed.

'Piss off.'

Kai sighed, as if her very existence was a trial to endure. 'I'll show you. Pay attention, witch. I won't repeat myself.'

Dawn watched, stunned into silence, as his calloused hands moved with precision, coaxing fire from dry twigs like a god of flame. Her mouth parted in awe.

'You ought to close your mouth,' he said, without looking up. 'You'll catch flies.'

She nearly kicked him. But instead, she snapped her jaw shut and sat beside him, quietly watching, and though she would never admit it, learning.

When the flames finally sparked to life, Dawn's lips curved into a triumphant smile. She turned to Kai, eyes aglow with a pride she couldn't quite contain.

'I did that,' she said softly, marvelling at the crackling light. 'I made a fire.'

Kai let out a short chuckle, low and unexpected. But then he seemed to remember himself, remembered her, and the sound vanished. His expression hardened once more, retreating behind that familiar wall of frost.

Dawn felt the shift like a sudden gust of wind against bare skin. Disappointment settled over her shoulders, heavy and damp, but she made no mention of it. Instead, she crouched beside the fire, stretching her hands towards the warmth. It was hard to blame him for his silence, his coldness. Her people had carved wounds into his heart, deep ones, and yet...

Night crept in through the trees, wrapping the forest in a cloak of shadows. Dawn exhaled slowly, watching her breath curl like smoke into the chilled air. She wondered how long it would take for her magic to return, and what chaos might be unfolding in the world while they remained lost in this strange place.

'Do you ever wonder,' she asked at last, her voice soft against the crackle of flame, 'why we speak the same language apart from the common tongue?'

Kai didn't respond at first. He was seated across from her, his eyes fixed on the fire, the flicker of light dancing over the sharp lines of his face. His hook swords lay on the ground beside him—silent, watchful companions. When he noticed her glance at them, he picked them up at once, reattaching them with a practiced flick, as if her stare alone might dull their edge.

'What do you mean?' he asked, his tone cautious.

'Witches and wyverians,' she clarified. 'It's strange, isn't it?'

'I've never cared,' he replied.

'They say the God of the Dead once fell madly in love with Hecate, goddess of witchcraft. To win her heart, he created the wyverians as a gift. But she did not fall for him, she fell for his creation. They say the god, jealous and enraged, killed the lover she chose. But Hecate, in her grief, used her magic to bring him back. And so the wyverians and witches have always shared one tongue.'

Kai snorted, unimpressed by the tale.

'That's why,' she continued, unbothered, 'our voices sound the same. Our words come from the same story.'

'Why are you telling me this?' he asked, tone clipped.

Dawn shrugged, letting the silence stretch a moment before breaking it again. 'Because we're not so different, you and I.'

Kai's jaw tightened. 'I am *nothing* like you, witch.'

'Perhaps,' she said. 'But like those gods, we both would burn the world to ash... for the ones we love.'

Chapter Thirty-Two

House of Flames
Kingdom of Fire

Why has it become so easy to lie?
Why is it so effortless to watch my fingers stain with blood?
Have I become the very thing I once feared?

Tabitha Wysteria

Wren nestled instinctively into the solid warmth behind her. The heat of the Kingdom of Fire was suffocating, a relentless weight pressing against her skin. But whatever lay curled around her made the world feel just a little less cruel. She sighed, melting deeper into it, until a low chuckle shattered the illusion. Her eyes snapped open in alarm. That warmth, deceptively comforting, wasn't a soft bundle of fur or a particularly huggable shrub.

It was a mortal. A breathing, living mortal.

Arden's laugh deepened as Wren shrieked and scrambled away, limbs flailing, cheeks flushed.

'Thank the gods you've finally woken. You were choking me, little wolf,' he said, his evergreen eyes dancing with mirth. 'Any more of that wiggling and I'd have found you stretched across my chest.'

'Ya could've shoved me off!' Wren huffed, her hair a wild

silver halo stuck to her damp forehead.

'And abandon such a gentlemanly opportunity? Perish the thought.'

With a growl, she snatched up a nearby pebble and launched it at his head. He dodged with infuriating ease, still grinning. 'Are you always this pleasant in the morning, or is it just me who inspires such violence?'

Wren refused to answer, choosing instead to scan the horizon. Far in the distance, rising smoke smeared the sky a deeper orange. Trouble. It wasn't hard to guess its source. Fireheart was burning, or at least fighting to stay unburnt. Her toes curled with urgency, her body buzzing with the ache to do something.

Around them stretched a wasteland of scorched soil and bone-dry grass, broken only by the occasional boulder. For days they had wandered through this hearth of a kingdom, sleeping beneath open skies, no shelter required. The land itself radiated enough heat to roast them alive. Shade was rare, water rarer still.

Somehow, Arden remained maddeningly flawless in the heat, his dark skin glowing as though kissed by fire itself. Wren, on the other hand, looked like she'd survived a battle with all nine hells. Barely. Her silver hair clung to her face in limp strands, sweat darkened every seam of her clothes, and her feet were blistered, raw. She stank like a boiling swamp.

And Arden still looked at her like she was made of starlight. Which was irritating. Deeply, thoroughly irritating.

Liar.

Arden's attention lingered on the rising plume of smoke, and as Wren followed his line of sight, she caught a fleeting shift in his expression. Something sharp, unreadable, there and gone in an instant. He was a master of subtlety, a man carved in shadows and cloaked in charm. And though he had proven himself quite the capable hunter, snaring birds with uncanny ease, plucking their feathers with the precision of a craftsman and cooking them with effortless grace, there was something more to him, something that tugged at the edge of suspicion.

It was the way he moved. Fluid, silent. Predatory. Like a wyverian in the wild, his steps barely stirred the earth, his breath matched the rhythm of the trees. When he threw his knife, it flew like an extension of his will, striking a bird clean through the eye. Not even the meat was bruised. Wren told herself that perhaps Fae cooks were taught to hunt, but each passing day chipped away at that excuse. Arden noticed her glances, her furrowed brows, and began to feign ignorance in little things, as though trying to dull the edges of her curiosity.

'You've got something on your face,' he said, interrupting her thoughts.

She blinked. 'Huh?'

'A miniature imperator, I believe. Very common in drakonian lands.'

'A *what?*'

'Tiny scorpion.'

Wren shrieked, her composure evaporating. 'Get it off! Get it off!'

'Don't move,' he said softly.

She stood frozen as something small and sinister crept across her cheek towards her hairline. Arden stepped in, close enough for her to smell the faint spice on his clothes. With a deft flick of his fingers, the creature flew off and landed near their feet. Wren lifted her boot, ready to crush it, but Arden caught her arm.

'Don't. We're in its land, not the other way round. It meant no harm.'

Wren wrinkled her nose as the tiny scorpion scuttled away, no larger than a child's fingertip. 'Is it poisonous?'

'Only mildly. Would've numbed half your face for a few hours.' His smile curved with mischief. 'Didn't take you for the squeamish type, little wolf.'

She rolled her eyes. 'Am not. Just don't fancy drooling all over meself.'

Her answer earned a laugh, rich and amused. They packed quickly, gathering the meagre belongings they'd carried across kingdoms, and turned towards the city ahead, the one now smoking in the horizon. As they walked, Wren found herself letting down her guard, inch by inch. She'd shown him her deft fingers and quick hands, her ability to snatch eggs from nests and make traps with a few twigs. He had praised her for it, called her clever.

But she hadn't told him the truth, the whole of it. He didn't know she was a Seer.

And for once, she didn't want to be worshipped or shunned for what she was. She just wanted to be seen. By him.

'You've got that look on your face again.'

Wren blinked. 'What look?'

'The kind you wear when you're arguing with yourself and, tragically, losing.'

She snorted. 'I've neva lost an argument in me life.'

'That's only because you've yet to have one with me.' He winked, smug and maddening. 'And I never lose.'

'I once had an argument with a boy named Edur,' Wren said, her chin lifting in defiance, 'about da best way to hunt an ice-cuckoo. By da time I'd finished proving me point, I'd hunted every ice-cuckoo in da forest. He went home with nothing but bruised pride and a grumbling stomach.'

Arden raised a brow. 'An ice-cuckoo? What in nature's hand

is that?'

'A bird,' she said loftily, 'that makes a stew fit for royalty.'

He pulled a face. 'It sounds adorable.'

'So?'

'You shouldn't be cooking adorable birds.'

'Ya've been hunting birds every day!' Wren shot back, exasperation prickling her skin like nettles.

'None of mine were cute.'

'So if it's ugly, it's fair game? That's da most ridiculous thing I've eva heard!' Her voice pitched higher, despite her best effort to keep it level.

He grinned, eyes sparkling. 'It's all right, little wolf. No one would hunt you.'

Wren stumbled mid-step, heat rushing to her cheeks. Was he... calling her cute?

No one had ever said that to her before. No boy had even looked at her properly. Most were either intimidated by the weight of her title or too busy worshipping her as the Seer of their people.

He's a man, not a boy, she reminded herself grimly. And a man like Arden Briar would never look twice at someone like her.

Despite being in her early twenties, Wren had never been kissed. Love and romance were luxuries she had set aside long ago. Her life had been devoted to her people, to her brother, to the legacy they were expected to carry once their father's breath stilled. Dreams had been shelved. Desires quieted. Her own heart, neatly folded and put away.

And truth be told, no one had ever been interested in her.

'You've got that look again,' Arden said, his voice softer this time.

Wren made an indignant noise, storming ahead to hide the

flush creeping up her neck. She wouldn't let him make her feel like a foolish girl with butterflies in her stomach.

'Well, of course no one would hunt me!' she snapped over her shoulder. 'Becas I'm a *wolf,* and wolves do da hunting!'

His laughter followed her like a song on the wind, curling around her spine and making her shiver despite the heat. She tried to outrun it, tried to ignore the warmth that bloomed deep in her chest.

But his voice reached her still, low and amused, and far too close to something dangerous.

'Is that so, little wolf?' he said. 'In that case, I wouldn't mind if *you* hunted *me.*'

Chapter Thirty-Three

House of Flames
Kingdom of Fire

I remember thinking it was impossible to fall so fast and so deeply for someone you barely knew. But that's exactly what happened with Hadrian. I told myself I hated him at first, but it was a lie, a shield to protect my heart. I never truly hated him. From the moment I first laid eyes on him, I knew that one day, I would marry him.

Tabitha Wysteria

'It's a bit anticlimactic,' Arden muttered, eyeing the humble drakonian inn perched on the edge of a sleepy village.

'What do ya mean?' Wren asked, glancing up at the building with a frown. The glow of Fireheart smouldering on the horizon promised chaos, yet here stood a quaint little inn with ivy curling over red-tiled eaves and warm lamplight flickering from behind golden curtains. They were close now. By tomorrow, they'd reach the city. But weariness dragged at their bones like lead.

Arden shrugged, nonchalant. 'The capital's up in flames, and this place looks like it's ready to serve tea and honey cakes.'

'Don't ya dare say it's cute.'

'Delightful,' he said, with a grin that made her groan.

'Do ya even have coin?'

'Aren't *you* the princess?'

Wren sighed, resisting the urge to roll her eyes. 'Yes, well...
I lost me things at da lake, remember? I'm wearing da Fae
clothes ya gave me.'

'You're very welcome.'

'Ya could have brought some coin.'

'Don't be greedy.'

She eyed the inn wistfully. 'Maybe we can offer to help out
with something.'

Together, they crossed the dusty road, boots crunching on
gravel as the scent of wood smoke and stew drifted from the
little building. Up close, it was even lovelier. Its stone walls
dappled with moss and the door carved with a dragon crest.
Inside, the air was warm and fragrant. Shades of deep crimson
and soft gold bathed the interior, green accents woven into
tapestries and cushions. Portraits hung in clusters along the
wall, the faces of generations smiling down like guardians of the
hearth.

The woman who greeted them, a sturdy drakonian with
grey-streaked auburn hair and gentle eyes, masked her surprise
at the sight of a wolverian and a Fae stepping over her
threshold. She covered it with a polite cough and a welcoming
smile. Wren's guilt prickled the moment the innkeeper saw
their empty pockets weighing heavier than it should. The
woman's expression faltered, a breath of disappointment.

'We'll work for da room,' Wren said quickly, straightening
her spine.

'That's awfully kind of you, dear,' the woman replied. 'I
could use the help. Drakonians keep arriving by the day, fleeing
the capital.'

'Do ya know when da attack started?' Wren asked, glancing
at Arden, who was now prowling the perimeter with subtle

precision, checking corners, glancing behind curtains. It made her smile.

'About ten days ago, I'd say.' The innkeeper's attention snapped to the door as it swung open. A cluster of drakonians poured in, clutching small, frightened children. The innkeeper rushed to greet them, fussing and checking for wounds. 'I've a small room upstairs,' she called back over her shoulder. 'It's free, but you'll have to share.'

Wren opened her mouth, then closed it again.

A hand brushed her arm. Arden stood beside her, a knowing smile tugging at his lips. 'We'll make it work, won't we?' His voice was soft and warm, a thread of comfort in the chaos. And with a small, grateful nod, Wren found herself agreeing.

They crept up the narrow wooden stairs, each step groaning beneath their weight as they climbed, hearts weary, muscles aching.

The moment they reached the top, their eyes widened in disbelief. Drakonians filled the attic level to bursting, crammed into rooms so small that even the hallways had become makeshift wardrobes. Belongings were strewn everywhere—blankets, boots, satchels, and weapons piled in corners or pushed hastily against walls to clear narrow paths. The air was thick with movement and murmured urgency, drakonians hurrying past one another in every direction, their shoulders brushing as they navigated the crowded space. It was as though the entire floor pulsed with life, pressed in from all sides, no longer a refuge, but a refuge-turned-hive for the displaced and desperate.

The air was thick with exhaustion and the desperate need for sleep. Time was slipping through their fingers like sand, and if they didn't move swiftly, there would be no Fireheart left to save.

Wren shrieked at the sight of the minuscule bed shoved into

the corner, barely large enough for one in a room that resembled a closet more than a bedroom.

'I'll take the floor,' Arden offered with a low chuckle.

'If we sleep on our sides, we could both fit on da bed,' Wren muttered, not daring to look at him. The words felt too generous, but they were both fraying at the edges from too many nights spent on the hard, unyielding ground.

Arden arched an amused brow. 'You want to share a bed with me, little wolf?'

Wren shoved past him into the snug alcove. 'Oh, shut up. I'm just being nice.'

'Nice, is it?' His grin stretched wider, green eyes gleaming. 'If you wanted my warmth, all you had to do was ask nicely.'

Wren grabbed a pillow and lobbed it at his face, but unsurprisingly, his reflexes were infuriatingly fast. He dodged with ease, stepping forward in one smooth movement that made her stumble back. Gasping, she felt his hands close gently around her arms, pulling her closer.

'There's no need for such violence,' he whispered, mischief dancing across his features. His eyes glittered in the dim light, and Wren tried her very best not to notice how close his lips were. How warm he felt. How kissable those lips looked. Well, they always looked kissable, but she wasn't about to admit that. Not even to herself.

'Do ya want da bed or not?' she snapped, trying to mask the heat rising in her cheeks.

'Of course,' he said, far too innocently.

Was he looking at her lips? Surely not. She was imagining it. She had to be. Arden finally let go, and she retreated quickly, tossing the pillow back into place.

'How do ya have such good reflexes?' she asked, throat a little dry.

'I'm a cook. We use a lot of knives.'

Wren snorted at that, a grin tugging at the corners of her lips. He wasn't lying, not exactly. But there was more to him than sharpened blades and well-seasoned stews. She could hear the truth hiding behind the words, tucked carefully out of reach.

'We betta go help da others,' she said, quickly changing the subject.

'After you,' he replied with a dramatic bow.

Wren rolled her eyes, but the smile lingered, soft and unshakable, as she made her way back down the stairs.

...

'Me brotha would love these views,' Wren murmured as they sat side by side atop the inn's slanted roof, their legs dangling as the stars unfolded above them like ancient runes etched across velvet. Night had fallen softly, cloaking the world in quiet, and the village below had long gone to sleep. They had spent the day helping the innkeeper, an ageing woman with tired hands and a smile that had worn thin from years of labour. Her husband had passed seasons ago, and her son had marched off in his youth to join the Red Guard, never to return. Wren couldn't help but wonder if he had been among those cut down to be replaced by a witch.

Word among the drakonian survivors was conflicting. Some said the witches had nearly taken the city, others swore the Red Guard had held their ground, aided by brave drakonians who refused to let their homes fall to ruin. No one seemed to know for certain who was winning. What was clear was that many had fled, unwilling to gamble their lives in a war they did not start, especially after seeing Spark swallowed by flames and ash.

'Where's your brother now?' Arden asked, his voice low and

careful.

'Back home. Someone had to stay behind, look after da kingdom. Help our papa.'

Arden tilted his head, studying her with eyes like forest shadows. 'And who looks after you?'

'I don't need looking after. I manage fine on me own.' Wren's chin tilted defiantly, but there was no real anger in her tone.

'I've no doubt of that,' Arden replied, a quiet chuckle escaping him. 'I didn't mean to insult you. I just meant... it must be lonely. And dangerous, travelling like this. You've gone to great lengths to help the drakonians.'

'Well, someone bloody should,' she snapped, hugging her knees. 'Everyone seems so ready to turn their backs on each other. Yer king included.'

Arden exhaled slowly. 'King Florian...'

'Is a coward,' she bit out. Perhaps too harshly, but she didn't care. The man had lost three daughters to the witches, and while she understood grief, it didn't excuse turning away from a kingdom in need. 'What happened to da witches was awful, aye, but it was in da past. They've no right to raze da Kingdom of Fire. Or any kingdom.'

'You're not wrong,' Arden said, his voice soft with the weight of truths long carried.

'But yer king didn't agree.'

'Fear can twist even the wisest minds, little wolf. It makes monsters of us all, sometimes.'

She fell quiet for a moment, her gaze rising to the stars again. 'What are ya afraid of, Arden?'

He didn't answer at once. The silence between them grew thick, taut with something unsaid. She turned her head, lips parting to ask again, but before she could speak, he leaned forward. His lips brushed hers, feather-light, like a question without words. It happened so quickly, so gently, her body froze in place, stunned by the weight of something she hadn't expected. Something tender. Something terrifying.

Wren's eyes widened as Arden leaned back, his gaze lingering on her face as though he were trying to memorise it, to capture her in a moment outside of time.

'That,' he whispered.

'Kissing me?' she asked, brows drawn together in sudden confusion. 'Yer afraid of kissing me?'

He laughed. A sound so rich and golden it wrapped around her like sunlight. She couldn't quite fathom how she'd lived her life without it until now.

'I'm afraid I'll never get the chance to do it again,' he said, voice soft with something that clung close to sorrow.

'Why not?'

His eyes fell to his hands, large and calloused, a contrast to her own. Without hesitation, she placed hers atop his. The warmth of him seeped into her skin, and a small smile ghosted her lips before she could stop it.

'I'm not who you think I am,' he said at last, the confession hanging between them like mist on a winter's morning.

But Wren only smiled wider, a knowing smile that reached her bright eyes and crinkled the corners. It startled him.

'I know, Arden Briar. I've always known. But I'm not who you think I am either.'

His brow creased, and she laughed, the sound light and breathless.

'Can we just pretend it doesn't matter?' she asked, voice hushed with hope. 'Just for tonight?'

Before he could answer, Wren leaned in and kissed him. She didn't flinch, didn't falter. She silenced every voice of doubt that whispered she was not enough, every echo of fear that lived in the hollows of her heart. Tonight, she would not worry. Tonight, she would simply be.

Tomorrow, they would return to their secrets. They would wear their masks again and speak in half-truths. But for one night, they would just be. Nothing more and nothing less. A wolverian woman and a Fae man, tucked into each other's arms and safe from the world.

She left every shard of fear behind when they climbed down from the rooftop and slipped back into the quiet room. Her chest swelled with something warm and golden, so vast it felt like it might crack her open. Her hands were steady as she undressed him; her breath did not tremble as he bared her soul with every slow, reverent touch.

'I've neva...'

'Never what?' he asked, voice barely above a whisper as they stood before each other, bare and unguarded, stripped not only of clothes but of every carefully built wall.

'I've neva been with anyone before.'

Arden's smile came slow and soft—tender, reassuring. It was the kind of smile that soothed wounds long buried and offered promises without words. With infinite care, he guided her onto the bed, his body above hers but never pressing down, his gaze locked on hers with quiet reverence.

'Are you certain you want it to be me?' he whispered, an unexpected shyness threading through the depth of his voice.

Wren answered not with words, but with a kiss, her lips brushing his with all the certainty he needed. When his tongue found hers, something inside her cracked open like the earth before a storm.

She arched against him, pulling him closer, fingers tangled in the cropped strands of his hair, their bodies pressing together until it became impossible to tell where one ended and the other began.

With flushed cheeks and breathless anticipation, Wren reversed their positions, pushing Arden gently onto his back. She straddled him, eyes drinking in the sight of him, his desire growing between them.

'Teach me,' she whispered, her voice a silken plea. 'Teach me how to bring ya pleasure.'

His emerald eyes narrowed, darkening into something perilous, something laced with raw longing. He took her hand with reverence, pressing a kiss to each fingertip as though worshipping them, before guiding it to wrap around the rigid length of him. With slow precision, he taught her the cadence he craved, the rhythm that made his breath catch, until at last he relinquished control, letting her take over. His eyes fluttered shut, breath unraveling in uneven gasps.

'You must stop now,' he said, his voice frayed with restraint.

'Why?' she asked, bewildered.

'Because if you go on, I'm going to come.'

'I want that.'

He shook his head gently. 'No, not like this. Not yet.' With tender insistence, he placed his hand atop hers, halting her movements. 'I want to feel you.'

Emboldened by a newfound courage, Wren didn't wait for permission, didn't ask what he desired. Instead, she leaned in, guiding the hard length of him to rest at her entrance.

'Not yet,' he whispered, almost in desperation.

His hand moved instinctively, fingers slipping between her thighs. The moment he touched her, his eyes widened, stunned by the slick heat that coated him. When he withdrew, his fingers glistening, he brought them to his mouth and tasted her, and the sight alone drew a soft moan from Wren's lips.

That sound undid him. With a suddenness that stole her breath, his hands seized her waist and he pressed her back onto the bed. The tenderness in his expression dissolved like mist, replaced by something primal and ravenous. In that instant, he was no longer the man she knew. He was the hunter, and she his prey.

'Your heart's racing,' he breathed against her ear, his voice a velvet murmur that sent shivers skittering down her spine. His lips found her neck, kissing with reverence before his teeth grazed her skin, a teasing bite as he positioned himself once more at her entrance.

'If it hurts too much, I'll stop,' he whispered.

'Don't ya dare, Arden Briar.'

Wren gasped the moment he thrust into her, the sound sharp and involuntary. Her hands flew to his arms, fingers digging into his flesh, nails marking him with each pulse of pain.

'Don't gasp like that,' he groaned against her neck. 'You'll make me finish too soon.'

She bit down on her lower lip, her eyes fluttering shut against the ache that bloomed deep within. Minutes passed— slow, breathless minutes during which Arden faltered, pausing. But each time, she threatened him in low, guttural tones that promised the loss of his eyes if he so much as thought to stop.

And then, as though summoned from the dark, pleasure unfurled inside her. It bloomed warm and wild, rising like a tide. Wren writhed beneath him, a quiet delight escaping her lips as her legs wrapped tighter around his hips, chasing the heat building in her belly.

She slipped two fingers between his lips, and he took them in willingly, his mouth warm and eager as he continued to drive into her. Her moans rose in pitch, raw and unrestrained, as the fire coiled tighter within her, threatening to break.

'Come for me,' he growled, his teeth grazing her ear in a wicked nip.

Wren cried out as release claimed her, her legs trembling violently. Arden didn't slow—his thrusts relentless—until, with sudden urgency, he withdrew. In the next breath, his mouth replaced the length of him, his tongue and fingers working in tandem as he plunged into her again, this time with a different kind of hunger.

Her eyes flew open in stunned rapture, the climax drawn out with merciless devotion as he refused to let her descend from the heights just yet. And then she heard him. Those low, guttural sounds of pleasure before his mouth and fingers vanished, replaced once more by the hard heat of him.

He drove into her with a final, desperate thrust, the flood of his release crashing into her, wild and consuming.

He pulled her gently atop him, holding her close as her body melted into his, his manhood still nestled within her warmth. Her cheek came to rest against his broad chest, the steady rhythm of his heartbeat soothing her, lulling her into a rare, quiet calm.

'Did you enjoy it?' he asked, fingers idly combing through the tangle of her hair.

She gave a shy nod, cheeks tinged the softest pink.

'Can we do it again?'

A low chuckle rumbled in his chest. 'You'll have to give me at least ten minutes.'

'Alright.'

A pause. 'Are you counting them in your head?'

'No, I'm not.'

'Liar.'

She hesitated, then asked in a voice barely above a whisper, 'Is it always... like this?'

Something unreadable appeared in the depths of his green eyes. A shadow of memory, or perhaps regret. 'No. Not always.'

Wren gave a small nod, sensing the weight behind his words but choosing not to press. Instead, she remained quiet, until he tipped her chin with gentle fingers and pressed a tender kiss to the bridge of her nose.

'I think I might need less than ten minutes,' he said with a wicked smile.

Her eyes widened, following his gaze to where he was already stirring once more, hardening with renewed desire.

'I want to...' he began, voice catching in his throat, 'I want to do many things tonight, with you.'

The silence that followed was filled with meaning unspoken, heavy with everything they both knew but would not say. For tomorrow, this fragile, fleeting intimacy would dissolve. There would be no more touches, no more kisses, no more whispered names in the dark. They would return to what they were, mere companions on a shared path.

'Although,' he said, brushing a few strands of her silvery-white hair from her brow, 'we should probably get some sleep.'

Wren laid her hand atop his. 'No. I don't want to sleep, Arden Briar. When we reach Fireheart...only da gods know what awaits us. I can sleep when I'm dead. Tonight, do with me as ya will.'

His eyes darkened once more, that feral glint returning, a look of unbridled hunger.

'You shouldn't say things like that,' he said, voice thick with warning and want.

His fingers traced a sinuous path down the length of her body, igniting fire in their wake, before he swiftly guided her upright, settling her astride him. With aching slowness, he eased her down onto him, and together their moans mingled and grew, rising in tandem as he filled her, drawing her down until there was no space left between them.

Wren began to roll her hips, tentative at first, until she discovered a rhythm that stole the breath from his lungs. A rhythm that made him gasp, made him curse aloud.

She found herself delighting in the way she could draw such crude, desperate sounds from him. Every expletive he uttered felt like a confession, a prayer to the altar of her body. With each thrust, each deliberate movement of her hips, she felt not only powerful, but radiant. Beautiful.

The moment his moans deepened and his grip on her skin tightened, Wren slipped away from him. Surprise flashed in his eyes as she moved lower, her hand guiding his length before she took him into her mouth.

Arden cursed. Raw, broken words tumbling from his lips in time with the movement of hers.

His hand tangled in her hair, holding her gently yet firmly in place, his lip curling as waves of pleasure began to rise, coiling within him like a storm about to break.

'If you don't stop, I'm going to come...'

But Wren did not stop. She pressed on, her touch and mouth relentless, until he broke apart with a groan, shattering into her.

Before the tremors had even subsided, he pulled her up into his arms, kissing her with reckless abandon, tasting her, tasting himself, and not caring for a single thing beyond the feel of her lips against his.

'You're going to be the death of me,' he whispered against her ear, his voice rough with affection and desire, as he drew her against his chest. He parted her legs with deliberate care, his fingers slipping down to find the aching heat at her core.

'Now,' he whispered darkly, 'it's my turn to play.'

As the night unfolded, Wren lost herself utterly. She forgot the weight of wars, the shadow of prophecies, the world beyond the walls of that room. All that remained was him, the way he touched her, the way he worshipped and devoured her in turn, until nothing else existed but the endless, fevered rhythm of her name on his lips.

Chapter Thirty-Four

House of Sand
Desert Kingdom

I have never witnessed anything quite like the Sand Trials.
I thought my own were harsh, brutal even.
But this... this is something else entirely.

Tabitha Wysteria

Since their arrival, the desert folk had been preparing for the funeral of their princess. Alina had not known what to expect, but certainly not this. Not a celebration filled with raucous music and joyous laughter where people danced barefoot in the sand and flung white roses into the air like blessings. They kissed one another's cheeks and poured drinks with generous hands, repeating the same mysterious phrase again and again. Yet for the life of her, Alina couldn't decipher its meaning.

Hessa had spent the entire morning cloistered with the king, deep in discussion about desert affairs, and had since busied herself with the Dunayans. Alina, left to quieter tasks, had helped prepare the roses by plucking their petals one by one and filling vast baskets with their soft, pale offerings.

Still, her gaze wandered often, seeking Hessa in the crowd. Though the people treated her with kindness, she could not help but feel the distance, the subtle strangeness of being other.

Foreign. And visibly so. She had veiled her head once more, concealing the remnants of her broken horns, fearful of the stares she might draw should she leave them bare. Hessa had said nothing, but Alina felt the silence linger like a quiet reprimand. She had disappointed her. Of that, she was certain.

But it wasn't so simple. Not when Hessa, radiant and flawless, could stride through the world untouched by doubt. Of course she had the courage to bare herself without shame. What flaw did she have to hide?

Alina, on the other hand...

The Dunayans emerged in silence, robed figures gliding through the interior of the mountain like shadows made flesh. Their heads and faces were veiled, their steps measured and solemn. Behind them came the renowned Saqar, their approach slow and deliberate, like a sacred procession honouring something ancient and eternal.

Alina recognised Hessa's mother instantly. There was no mistaking her. The most opulently adorned among them, draped in robes so intricate they seemed to shimmer with hidden meaning, her body heavy with jewellery wrought from pale desert stones, and her face inscribed with ink. It was said that the Altaa Saqardatis bore ink on every inch of her flesh, even the soles of her feet, each line a verse from their divine scripture. Words gifted, they claimed, by the gods themselves.

Alina found such tales difficult to believe, yet she would never dare voice her doubts aloud. It remained a mystery to her how Hessa could truly believe in the existence of many gods. After all she herself had endured, Alina sometimes found it difficult to believe there was even one.

But her thoughts splintered the moment she saw Hessa.

All memory of the Saqar evaporated. Her breath caught in her throat.

Gone was the simple garb of the desert. In its place, Hessa now wore the armour of a warrior: supple leather wound tightly about her arms, waist, and shoulders, both protective and striking. Desert-forged daggers hung at her hips and across her back, deadly ornaments gleaming in the dim light. Her head and face were veiled like the others, but Alina could never mistake her. Not even if the whole world wore the same white eyes.

Hessa looked every inch the desert assassin she was.

The moment their eyes met, Alina's breath faltered, caught on the edge of a beauty she had always known, yet never truly grasped. There was something unspoken in Hessa's gaze, an unwavering certainty that cut through the ceremony and spectacle. Without pause, she broke from the solemn procession, moving towards Alina with purposeful grace.

She did not flinch at the murmurs that followed. She did not seem to care for the glances cast like stones. She simply reached for Alina's hand and laced their fingers together for all to see, leading her back into the throng as if it were the most natural thing in the world. Without so much as a glance back, Hessa guided Alina to the very peak of the mountain, following the winding path behind the line of the Saqar.

Alina's focus drifted to the Altaa Saqardatis, who ascended slowly and with some difficulty, her towering robes and weighty veils billowing around her like a stormcloud. She walked with dignity, but it was clear her ceremonial regalia made each step an effort. Hessa must have noticed Alina's observation, for she leaned in, her voice low and soft against the mountain wind.

'No one is permitted to touch the Altaa Saqardatis. It's forbidden,' she explained. 'Only the gods may lay hands upon her. The ink isn't just scripture, it's proof. Proof that no mortal has ever touched her flesh after becoming the Altaa Saqardatis.'

Alina's eyes widened in wonder, and Hessa chuckled.

'They say that a thousand years ago, a god fell in love with a desert girl who would become Saqar. He inked her from head to toe, so that only his divine hands could touch her in the night, when he came down from the stars to claim her.'

'A bit possessive, don't you think?'

Hessa laughed, the sound warm and effortless. 'Some say the gods can make mortals fall to their knees for them.'

Alina snorted. 'I'd like to see one try.'

Because no matter what the desert people believed, no matter how many names they gave to the stars and sands, there was only one true god in Alina's heart. The Sun God.

'Qa yaar qamh valva sahraa,' Hessa whispered, her voice barely rising above the whispering wind, as she plucked a single white petal from one of the many baskets the servants had carried up the mountain. She cast it into the air, watching as it danced away on the desert breeze, weightless and free.

'What does it mean?' Alina asked softly, her own voice fragile in the stillness.

'May your grain return to the desert.' Hessa reached for three more petals and placed them gently in Alina's palm. 'For those you have lost, amira. So they may return home, too.'

Alina tried to blink back the sting behind her eyes, but the emotion was too sharp, too immediate. Her fingers closed around the delicate petals. One for her father, one for her mother and one for her brother. Tears slipped silently down her cheeks at the quiet grace of Hessa's gesture, her thoughtfulness in making space for Alina within a tradition not her own.

She turned from the crowd and released her parents' petals into the wind, watching as the white fragments tumbled upward, carried into a sky that had turned a muted, smoky brown. The wind was growing stronger by the minute, as though it too mourned and remembered. She couldn't help but wonder where the roses came from, who planted them in this harsh, unforgiving land. But in the desert, Alina had learnt, nothing was impossible.

Her hand remained curled around the final petal, unable and unwilling to let it go. Her love for her brother was a bond unbreakable, untouched by death or time. Together, they had shielded one another in a world eager to break them. Even their own parents, at times, had been enemies in disguise.

Alina knew, with a clarity that rang deep within her bones, that wherever Ash was now, he would be proud of the woman she had become.

'How do you say fire?' she asked quietly.

'Nar,' Hessa replied.

'And sun?'

A knowing smile played across Hessa's lips, her pale eyes gleaming with understanding. 'Suna.'

Alina offered a silent nod of gratitude, then turned and slipped away from the crowd. She needed solitude for this farewell, needed space for a grief that would never truly leave her. As she walked, she could feel the weight of Hessa's gaze lingering at her back, those piercing white eyes that missed nothing. But Alina knew the desert princess understood. This goodbye belonged to her alone.

The summit of the mountain was a marvel in itself. A wide, flat expanse carved by time and wind, repurposed by the desert folk with quiet ingenuity. It had been carefully divided for various tasks: makeshift tents served as storerooms for tools and equipment used in the tending of vegetable patches, while others provided shelter for the Dunayans who took turns keeping vigil over the horizon, ever watchful for signs of trouble.

But the true beauty of this place did not lie in its structures or possessions. Alina had come to learn that, among the desert folk, beauty was not measured in things, but in fleeting moments. In the warmth of a shared laugh, the gentleness of a touch, the stillness between heartbeats.

And in that very moment, Alina could see it, feel it, everywhere around her. Not in the golden dunes that stretched endlessly beyond sight, nor in the breeze that skimmed across the mountaintop, humming its own quiet song. Not even in the hundreds of white petals drifting like prayers through the copper-tinged sky.

No. The beauty was in the faces of the people. In their smiles, radiant and sincere, as they laughed and wept in the same breath. In the way they said farewell to someone they had loved deeply, with voices lifted in hope and reverence, believing that this was not the end, but a beginning.

For they did not fear death. They did not believe in endings. To them, life was a cycle, a return. Each soul a grain, falling once more into the embrace of the desert, waiting to be reborn as something new. Something greater.

And Ash... Ash was fire.

He was the fire that coursed through her veins and blazed within the sun. He was the hearth flame that kept someone warm through the cold desert night. He was the fire that danced alongside the people as they celebrated life. He was the fire in their eyes, and the one kindled deep within their hearts.

He was everywhere.

'Qa yaar nar valva suna,' she whispered, releasing the final petal into the wind. The breeze rose to meet it, brushing against her skin like a farewell caress. So soft, so fleeting, it felt almost as though Ash himself had reached out to say goodbye.

May your fire return to the sun.

. . .

As the days slipped by, Alina sought to join the Dunayans during their training sessions. She approached with quiet determination, yet each time, her request was met with the same firm refusal. No matter how many times she tried, the answer did not change.

Hessa fought for her, again and again, arguing on her behalf with unwavering passion. But eventually, Alina had asked her to stop. She could not bear to be the cause of discord among Hessa's people. It wasn't right. She didn't want Hessa shouldering consequences meant for her. If she was to earn her place, she would do it her own way.

And so, under the cloak of night, Hessa would return to her, teaching her in secret. They moved together in the shadows, practising footwork and strikes with whispered breath and hushed laughter. But it wasn't enough. It could never be enough. Not for what Alina knew she needed.

So she made a choice.

She began to appear at the training grounds each day, uninvited and unwelcome. No matter how many times she was told to leave, she returned the next morning. And the one after that.

She didn't know what she hoped for, perhaps a challenge, perhaps a sliver of recognition. But as the days wore on, and the Dunayans continued to dismiss her presence as though she were nothing but dust in the wind, doubt began to creep in. Her hope, once burning bright, began to flicker. Until one day, Alina decided she would wait no longer. She would seize fate with her own two hands.

'Leave.'

The voice, as always, belonged to Saren, the one who spoke

for the others with cold authority. She was a formidable figure, all lean muscle and sharp edges, a scar carving its way across her face like a lightning strike frozen in time. It was a relic from a childhood fight she had lost at the age of ten. Hessa had once recounted the tale with a wide grin, clearly amused. Alina, however, had found no humour in it. Who could bring themselves to carve up a child so brutally?

Apparently, another child.

Sahira, Hessa's sister, had dealt the wound during a fierce dispute, and in some strange twist of fate, the two had become inseparable afterwards. Best friends. But when Sahira died, that bond turned to ash, and what remained of Saren was fury and bitterness, a girl made hard by grief.

'No,' Alina said firmly, planting her feet into the mountain stone. The Dunayans had already reached the summit, and she refused to turn back now. Not when she had climbed this far, both in distance and determination. 'I carry a desert dagger. Earned it myself, killing a desert spider. I deserve some respect!'

Saren scoffed. 'That proves nothing. Anyone could kill an Arahni Mhaarta.'

'Have *you?*' Alina shot back, defiance flaring. But the words had barely left her lips before she realised her mistake.

Saren's eyes darkened, and with a swift, fluid motion, she drew both of her desert blades. The hiss of metal made the hairs rise on Alina's neck. Instinct screamed at her to flee, and she obeyed, turning sharply, only to hear Hessa laugh behind her, light and unbothered.

The sound disoriented her, but she didn't stop, bolting back down the path, until she skidded to a halt. Two Dunayans now stood at the edge of the stairs, their faces unreadable, their bodies blocking her only route to safety.

She spun around just as the first blade sliced through the air.

She ducked, heart slamming against her ribs, hearing the whistle of the blade cleaving through empty space, mere inches from her throat. Two seconds slower, and she wouldn't have had time to regret it.

'You want to learn?' Saren said, stepping forward, her tone razor-sharp. 'Then fight.'

Alina stumbled backwards, her eyes wide with disbelief. Behind the semicircle of assassins, Hessa stood watching, her expression hidden beneath her veil. But her eyes, those pale, unreadable eyes, glinted with unmistakable amusement.

Desert blades were curved like crescent moons, honed to such a deadly edge they were as capable of slicing through flesh as they were of dicing vegetables. Alina had no desire to end up as either.

She scrambled to her feet and bolted in the opposite direction, heart hammering against her ribs. She knew full well she had no hope of outrunning an assassin, let alone Saren, who ranked just below Hessa herself. There was a reason she had been named second-in-command.

Alina's boots skidded in the sand as she nearly tumbled into one of the carefully tended vegetable plots, but she twisted at the last moment, veering to the side and diving into the shadow of a tent. She crawled out the other end, breath ragged, only to find Saren already there, waiting like a spectre.

A blade struck the ground where Alina's hand had been moments before, sand bursting upward from the force of the blow. Alina rolled away, frantic, reaching for her own weapon, but her hands trembled too fiercely to grip it.

Another slash, another near miss. The dagger sank into the earth once more, slicing so close that a strand of her hair fluttered to the ground like a severed thread. Alina swore under her breath, a mixture of fear and fury curling in her chest.

'Are you mad?' she shouted, scrambling back. 'Are you actually trying to kill me?'

'If I wanted you dead, you'd be dead already,' Saren said, lifting her blade and driving it once more into the ground, cleanly slicing another lock of Alina's hair.

Her rasguita had slipped in the struggle, strands of gold tumbling free. Panic surged through her as she scrambled to cover her head, desperate to keep her horns hidden from the Dunayan gaze. But the gesture cost her.

Saren's boot landed squarely in her stomach, and the world jolted. The air was knocked clean from her lungs as her head struck the unforgiving ground. Laughter erupted around her, sharp and cruel, echoing in her skull. Tears pricked at her eyes. Not from pain, but from shame.

They were mocking her.

Taunting her.

Well, no more.

A cry tore from Alina's throat as she surged upright, yanking the rasguita from her head and casting it aside. With shaking hands, she seized her desert blade, rose to her feet, and drove her shoulder into Saren with all the fury she had buried inside her. The Dunayan toppled beneath her, and for a breathless moment, silence fell.

Alina straddled her opponent, blade poised at the edge of Saren's eye, her chest heaving.

'Laugh again,' she hissed, her voice trembling with rage. 'Ria, agari!'

Something shifted in Saren's face. The hard lines of scorn softened, and the faintest smile touched her lips.

Then came the sound. A sharp chorus of whistles, ringing out across the mountaintop. Alina's heart pounded, but she knew what it meant. Hessa had told her once: Dunayans used whistles not only to communicate, but to honour.

To show respect.

'Well done, farahi,' Saren said, voice low.

Alina blinked at the unfamiliar word, brows knitting.

'It means foreigner,' Saren clarified. Alina slowly lowered her blade, stepped back, and without hesitation, offered her hand.

Saren took it, her grin stretching wide as Alina pulled her to her feet. A heartbeat later, Hessa was at their side, laughter bubbling from behind her veil as she clapped Saren hard on the back.

'Told you she could do it,' Hessa said, a note of triumph lacing her voice.

Alina's frown crept back, doubt tugging at the edges of her thoughts.

'One must earn their place among the Dunayans, amira,' Hessa continued, her smile so radiant it was nearly infectious. 'It is not something given freely. It must be fought for, claimed with the same desperation as air in one's lungs.'

'I thought outsiders weren't allowed to join,' Alina said cautiously.

Saren made a face and spat into the dust. 'They're not.'

Alina's grip tightened around the hilt of her dagger, dread curling in her belly. For a moment, she feared they might take it from her, cast her out, and declare her unworthy after all.

But Hessa only laughed, loud and delighted, as she pulled Alina into an embrace, arms winding around her until their bodies nearly melted into one.

'You are one of us now, amira,' she said.

'But she just called me a farahi... a foreigner.'

'A farahi,' Hessa said gently, 'is one born beyond the sands, but who has fallen in love with the desert, who has let it seep into their bones, their breath, their blood. You are a farahi, Alina. And now, we will teach you the Dunayan way. The desert way.'

Saren raised her blade high into the sunlit sky, its edge catching the golden light like fire made steel. One by one, the others followed, swords lifted in solemn honour. Hessa mirrored them, her free hand still tightly clasping Alina's.

'Alina Farahi-Sahraa Amira!' they chanted as one, their voices echoing across the mountaintop, fierce and full of pride.

The foreign princess of the desert.

Welcomed home at last.

Chapter Thirty-Five

House of Flames
Kingdom of Fire

Hades has threatened to send Thanatos after me. But I've read too much about Hades' world to be afraid. No matter how much he wishes it, he cannot act, not unless the Moirai cut the string that keeps me breathing.

I wonder if I could find my way to the Moirai.

To cut Hades' string instead.

I've heard him speak of a god killer. Of creating one, and all that he could do with it.

Tabitha Wysteria

Mal supposed she ought to have felt something, anything, amidst the chaos consuming the city of Fireheart. But her heart, perhaps, had long since run dry, emptied of grief, of rage, of sorrow. Or perhaps it was simply that she drifted through the carnage like a ghost, untouched by blade or flame, a silent witness as drakonians and witches clashed in the streets, their blood staining the stone beneath them a rich, harrowing red.

Thanatos moved like lightning, a shadow among bodies, placing his hand upon foreheads slick with sweat and blood, guiding the souls from flesh with a reverence that felt almost holy. Mal had watched him do the same for Allegra, had seen the light leave her eyes, and something in her chest twisted sharply at the sound of Vera's anguished cries.

Part of her had wanted to hate the witch. The other part, maddeningly, could not. Perhaps that was why she had spared her. Why she had stepped in, if only briefly, to offer Vera a sliver of hope, a fleeting chance at escape.

She wondered now where the witch had gone. If she'd slipped beyond the city walls or was still hiding, curled in the shadows where even death struggled to find her.

'Do they live,' Mal asked quietly, her voice cutting through the smoke-thick air, 'if you do not touch them?'

Thanatos stood only a few feet away, cradling a young witch in his arms, his hand resting upon her brow. Her purple eyes dimmed slowly as her soul ebbed from her body.

'The Moirai speak to me,' he replied, his voice softer than she'd ever heard it. 'They sever the thread. They choose when life ends. I merely obey.' He didn't look like the harbinger of death in that moment. Not a spectre to be feared, but a reluctant servant. 'If I don't reach them in time,' he added, eyes fixed on the girl, 'they may survive, for now. But death always finds them. Eventually. I do not need to touch them, but it makes their transition easier. And I wish for them, in their last moment, to feel cared for.'

Mal looked away, unable to bear the weight of his words.

'It is the cycle of life, Melinoe.'

The words struck her like a blade. She gasped, because she had heard them before. Standing atop a mountain, watching wyverns feast, as her sister Haven whispered them with quiet conviction. *The cycle of life.*

Mal had never taken pleasure in pain. Never delighted in suffering. And after Haven's death, the very idea of mortality, of endings, filled her with a cold, clawing dread.

'I don't have to enjoy it, do I?' she spat, bitterness burning in her throat.

Thanatos looked at her, and in those fathomless black eyes stirred an emotion Mal could not name, something too vast, too complex, to unravel. He let the witch's body slip gently to the ground, her limbs folding like the petals of a withered flower, before he turned and began to walk towards Mal. Each step was deliberate, his face, so eerily familiar to her, marked with a concern that tightened something deep within her chest.

He parted his lips, as if to speak, then faltered. Whatever words he'd intended dissolved on his tongue. His jaw clenched, frustration clear in the tension of his shoulders, his expression a storm barely held at bay. Mal instinctively stepped back, arms crossing over her chest, as though she could shield herself from whatever he might say.

She didn't need his pity.

'It is not pity,' he said softly.

The gleam of anger in her eyes must have betrayed her, for he quickly added, 'I cannot read your thoughts, Melinoe. But I can read your face.' His voice dropped lower, almost mournful. 'I don't pity you. Truly, it is something rare, something admirable, that you care so deeply for those you love. I only wish I were one of them. No one has ever cared enough to worry about what becomes of me.'

He gave a bitter laugh, the sound hollow. After realising how much he had revealed, he turned sharply and walked away.

'Wait!' Mal cried out, her voice slicing through the noise of the battle-torn street.

Thanatos vanished down a narrow alley before she could reach him.

A flash of green light exploded against a nearby wall, caused by a warlock fending off five drakonians. Though instinct told Mal to intervene, to cast herself between them and end the bloodshed, she forced herself onward. If she lost sight of Thanatos now, how would she ever return? Would she remain like this? A drifting spectre, invisible and unheard, trapped between realms for eternity?

When they had first emerged from the Underworld, their forms had been wholly corporeal—solid, tangible, real. But later, as they slipped like shadows into the streets, Thanatos explained that he had cloaked them in invisibility, their bodies suspended in a delicate limbo, neither fully bound to the realm of the living nor entirely lost to the dead. They drifted, unseen and untouched, veiled in safety by divine manipulation. It was a power they could wield, if they so chose.

Mal had asked him to teach her the trick of it, to show her how to summon such power from her bones. But Thanatos had avoided the question, brushing it aside with a silence too sharp to ignore. There was something almost deliberate in his refusal, suspicious even, as though he feared what she might become if she ever learnt to wield her godhood in full.

Twisting alleyways blurred around her, each turn more disorienting than the last. The chaos of war closed in on all sides, but none of it touched her. No one saw her. No one heard her. She was no longer part of their world, not truly.

She and Thanatos were only meant to observe, to follow as he collected souls like fallen stars from a darkened sky.

But she had begged him, pleaded with him, to let her remain corporeal to the mortal realm, to fight, to do something. In this ghostly form, she could do nothing but observe the destruction around her.

Yet that was not the will of Hades. And Thanatos, loyal as stone, obeyed every word the god whispered.

A couple hurried down the street, shoving open a door before vanishing inside. Mal would have walked straight past, her attention fixed elsewhere, if not for the glint of silver hair that caught her eye. They had moved so swiftly she'd barely registered them, but on second thought, neither of them had looked particularly drakonian.

Mal's blackened heart seemed to halt for a beat.

'Wren?' she whispered, her voice barely a breath.

Without hesitation, she followed them through the door, stepping into what had once been a small, fragrant bakery, known for its sweet breads and drakonian-style cakes. The scent of flour and sweetness still lingered faintly in the air, but the warmth was gone. The door at the back slammed shut, and Mal bolted forward. She slipped through into the alley behind, and froze.

Wren Wynter stood before her.

She had not changed. And yet, she had.

The face was familiar: that proud jawline, those ice-bright eyes once brimming with laughter, mischief, and the fierce curiosity of youth. But now, something had shifted. The spark had dulled. The mischievous glint was gone, replaced with steel. Her shoulders, once carried with a kind of carefree elegance, now bore the weight of battles fought and grief buried deep. The girl Mal had known in the drakonian castle had been spirited, occasionally foolish, always joyful.

This Wren was harder. Sharper. Stripped of light, and stitched together with hatred.

Beside her stood a Fae man, beautiful and striking, with dark rich skin and a crown of antlers that curved high and proud. The moment they halted, he stepped closer to Wren, his presence a quiet shield. Protective. Intimate.

And Mal, watching from the shadows, felt the ground shift beneath her feet.

'Did ya hear that?' Wren asked, her ears twitching slightly.

'The screams of the dying?' the man beside her replied dryly. 'Yes, little wolf, I've been hearing them all day.'

'No!' she insisted, frowning. 'I could've sworn someone said me name.'

'Well, that's mildly concerning.' He offered her a teasing smile. 'Let's not start hearing voices just yet. We still need to find our way into the temple.'

From the shadows, Mal tensed, eyes narrowing. What were they doing here? And why was Wren alone with a stranger? The last time she had seen the wolverian princess, she had been fleeing the castle with Bryn, Kage, and Freya.

Mal swallowed down the swell of questions rising in her throat.

She wanted, *needed*, to know if her brother was safe.

Suddenly, a hand closed around her wrist. She spun instinctively, a low snarl rising in her throat, only to meet the ever-calm, maddeningly amused gaze of Thanatos. He didn't so much as flinch.

His eyes slid past her to Wren and the Fae, curiosity dancing in their endless black depths.

'Why are we watching them?' he asked, his voice too close, breath warm against her ear.

'She's my friend,' Mal answered softly. 'I have to help her.'

Thanatos gave a short, dismissive snort. 'She's well protected.'

'What do you mean?' Mal asked, her focus narrowing on the Fae man. It must be him, surely that's who Thanatos meant.

'That one,' he said simply.

Thanatos was standing so near she could feel the contours of his body pressed along hers, but for the first time, she didn't pull away.

'He's Fae,' she whispered, the words careful, as though

speaking too loudly might shatter the illusion... or worse, be heard.

'Oh, yes,' Thanatos chuckled darkly. 'But he's far more than that, Melinoe.'

'Speak plainly,' she snapped, 'and stop playing games.'

Thanatos leaned in, voice like silk and smoke.

'That man is not only Fae, Melinoe. He's a Black Lotus.'

Mal swore under her breath, the weight of those words sinking like stone into her chest.

Chapter Thirty-Six

House of Flames
Kingdom of Fire

I've heard dreadful things about what becomes of the orphans taken to become Black Lotus. It's hard to believe the Fae would allow such cruelty to be inflicted upon their own. But over the years, I've come to learn that no kingdom is free from brutality. We may see what is done to those boys, shaped into ruthless killers, as immoral. And it is. But what the drakonians do to their women is just as vile. The way witches and warlocks twist and corrupt everything, casting all others aside as inferior, is as troubling as the bloodshed the wyverians endure when their monarch dies and rival nobles vie for the throne.

I've learnt, through time, that we are all poisoned. Twisted. Vile.

We were created by poisonous, twisted, and vile gods.

What did we expect?

Tabitha Wysteria

Vera could hear the screams, raw cries of anguish that tore through the air, punctuated by the thunder of explosions and the sickening thrum of blood spilt in the name of vengeance. She felt each death like a thread woven into her soul, stitching itself into her already bleeding heart. A cruel, relentless reminder.

This was *her* fault.

Allegra's death was her fault.

She had taken refuge in the grand home of a wealthy drakonian family, one that had likely fled days before. Their absence had become her sanctuary. She had claimed their velvet-lined comforts and delicate luxuries as her own, drinking their aged wine until it turned bitter in her stomach and she vomited across their pristine, tiled floor.

She had sat on the balcony and watched the city burn.

And she had not cared.

She cared for nothing now.

The house lay on the outskirts, far from the heart of the chaos. The battle raged deeper in the city's core, leaving this affluent district untouched, forgotten. The streets here were lined with elegant homes and charming boutiques, all silenced by fear. No one would bother her. No one would remember her.

Vera drifted back out onto the terrace, swearing softly at the oppressive heat. She collapsed against the red stone ledge, throwing one arm over her eyes to shield them from the unrelenting sun, the other hand still curled around the neck of a half-empty bottle. The sounds of war remained distant, almost muted, like a half-remembered dream. The rest was stillness. Sweet, intoxicating stillness.

Until it wasn't.

Her ears twitched at the faint creak of a door forced open. It wasn't loud, whoever it was had tried for silence, but they weren't especially skilled at it. Two voices followed, low and irritable, bickering over the noise.

'There's no one here,' said one, dismissively.

Vera smiled, still unmoving.

Surprise, surprise, she thought, a humourless laugh threatening to rise.

'We'll lay low until we can make it into da temple,' came the second voice. 'From here we've got da perfect view of da city. If Hagan moves, we'll see it.'

Vera froze.

That voice…so distinct and so utterly unique that it sliced through her haze like a knife. She would know it among thousands.

The arm shielding her eyes slid away. The bottle slipped from her grasp and shattered against the stone floor, its crash ringing out like thunder, shattering the silence into pieces. If they hadn't known she was there before, they did now.

Vera watched as Wren Wynter stepped onto the terrace, her blue eyes widening in surprise. And for a fleeting moment, just the briefest breath, Vera forgot the aching hollow in her chest left by Allegra's absence. For that single heartbeat, joy surged through her like a wave, eclipsing grief, sorrow, and rage.

But it didn't last.

The Fae beside Wren lunged, swift as a striking viper, a hidden blade glinting in his hand as it arced towards Vera's throat.

She moved instinctively, dodging to the side, grabbing a shard of broken glass from the floor and slashing it across his arm. The cut drew blood, but it only fuelled his fury. He came at her again, faster this time, so fast she could barely track him. She had seen Fae fight before, and they weren't known for their skill but for their illusions. But this one… he was something else entirely. Stronger. Sharper. Unnervingly precise.

And Vera knew, almost at once, what he was.

Her fingers shimmered with a soft green glow as she summoned her power, preparing to strike.

'What are ya doing?' Wren shouted, throwing herself between them. The moment the Fae saw her, he faltered, just enough.

Vera seized the opportunity. She exhaled her magic in his direction, a whisper on her lips.

'Glacio.'

She watched with a glint of satisfaction as the spell took hold, freezing the Fae mid-motion like a statue of carved frost.

'What have ya done?' Wren rounded on her, anger flashing across a face Vera had once known as kind, so sweet and gentle all those months ago. 'Unfreeze him right now, Vera!'

'No. He's dangerous.'

'He's not dangerous, Vera. He's—' Wren stumbled over the words, clearing her throat awkwardly. 'He's me friend.'

Vera gave a sharp, disbelieving snort. 'Since when do you count a Black Lotus as a friend?'

Wren's frown deepened. 'Arden isn't Black Lotus. Don't be ridiculous. Stop trying to twist me head around. Why are ya even here?'

Vera tilted her head, studying the Fae with sharpened interest. It was plain to see that he had been lying to Wren, wearing a mask of half-truths and charm. Pretending to be something he was not.

Everyone, at some point in their lives, had heard whispers of the Black Lotus. Cloaked in myth and fear, their name passed around tavern fires and palace corridors alike. They were the elite killers of the Fae king: chosen by the king himself, plucked from their cradles and raised in silence and blood, moulded into the most lethal assassins probably across the Eight Kingdoms.

Debate always flared in quiet corners about which assassin was deadlier: a Dunayan or a Black Lotus. The Dunayans, distant and wrapped in mystery, had for centuries confined their work to the southern kingdoms. Ghosts of the desert, almost mythical in their restraint. Their presence in the north was rare, even before the Great War.

But the Black Lotus... they haunted the northern realms, and their reputation was steeped in dread. Masters of torment, they did not simply kill. They left messages behind. Terrible, unforgettable things designed to sow fear, to break the spirit as much as the body.

What set them apart from the Dunayans was not skill, but purpose. The Dunayans killed with deliberation, with judgement. They did not strike unless they deemed their target unworthy of life.

But the Black Lotus obeyed.

If the king commanded them to kill, they did so without hesitation. Even if it meant slaughtering an entire household in the dead of night; mothers, fathers, children. They would carry out the order with cold precision. And when they were done, they would leave something behind. A mark. A horror. A reminder to all who found it that the Black Lotus had passed through.

And would return again.

'I'm not unfreezing him,' Vera said as she strolled back into the house, her tone as casual as if they were discussing the weather. She was already rummaging through the sideboard for another bottle of wine. 'Why are you here?'

'No, ya don't get to ask me da questions,' Wren snapped, voice sharp with frustration.

Vera shrugged, unconcerned. She hopped gracefully back onto the terrace ledge, biting the cork from the bottle with her teeth. With a casual flick of her head, she spat it towards Arden's face. Though his body was frozen, Vera took no small satisfaction in the simmering fury still visible in his green eyes.

'Fine,' she said, bringing the bottle to her lips. 'What do you want to know?'

Wren opened her mouth to reply, then faltered, words abandoning her for once. It was almost comical. The ever-loquacious Wren Wynter, struck silent. Vera raised an eyebrow. The princess of the Kingdom of Ice, usually a whirlwind of chatter even in the bleakest moments, was now unsure of what to say.

'Well, look at you,' Vera drawled, savouring the moment. 'Didn't think I'd live to see the day Wren Wynter was lost for words. Kage Blackburn must be thrilled.' She tipped the bottle back, wine trickling messily down her throat. 'How's he doing, by the way?'

'Alive,' Wren said, her voice clipped. 'No thanks to ya. We escaped da castle, though not all of us made it.'

'That's war, Wren,' Vera replied with a sigh, as if it were the most obvious thing in the world.

'Why? How can ya be all right with any of this?' Wren's voice cracked, rage and grief tangling in her throat. 'Hagan... he broke Haven's neck. Snapped it like a twig.'

Vera turned away, her expression unreadable. 'What do you want from me, Wren?'

'I want yer help,' Wren said, her voice steady now, a steel edge buried beneath the sorrow.

Vera turned her head slightly, just enough to glance at the wolverian princess through the blinding glare of the sun. It forced her to squint as she lay sprawled on her back atop the ledge, resuming the pose she'd held before being so unceremoniously interrupted. Every bone in her body ached to tell them to leave, to piss off and let her rot in silence. She was mourning her sister. The rest of the world could burn, for all she cared.

But Hagan's face kept breaking through the fog of her thoughts, unbidden and unrelenting.

'My help for what?' she asked, voice laced with feigned disinterest.

'To stop Hagan. To stop this senseless war.'

'War is never senseless, Wren,' Vera said, her eyes fixed on the sky, voice heavy with something colder than grief. 'It's part of what we are. Carved into our bones, pulsing through our veins. We're territorial creatures, shackled to the past and too damn stubborn to learn from it. So we fight. We carve each other open and dress it up as duty, as justice. Those in power tell us it must be done, and we nod like fools because we need to believe it means something.'

She paused, the bottle resting loosely in her hand. 'We lie to ourselves, over and over, claiming all we want is peace. But the truth? The truth is that the hunger for blood never leaves us. The thirst for vengeance is always there, waiting.'

'No,' Wren said firmly, shaking her head. 'I don't agree with ya. I believe we can forgive. We can heal. Not everything needs to be resolved by cutting each other down. When does it end? We killed yer people, so now yer people will kill us, and then we'll rise again to slaughter yers. And so it goes on and on until there's nothing left but ash. No one left to even remember how da bloody thing began!'

Vera had never seen Wren so undone. The fury radiating from her was palpable, seething within that small, defiant frame like a storm barely contained. Vera half-expected her to erupt at any moment, to combust from the sheer force of rage simmering beneath her skin. And what a sight that would be. Wren Wynter, wild-eyed and furious, screaming in Hagan's face, proclaiming that blood needn't be spilt, that forgiveness could still be found.

But it couldn't.

Not anymore.

'I know there's good in ya, Vera.'

The words struck like a blade, sharp and sudden, stealing the breath from her lungs. She gasped, startled by the sheer audacity of them. Good? She didn't want goodness. She wanted to be monstrous, so fearsome that even Hagan would flinch at the sound of her name.

'I'm rotten to the core,' Vera said quietly, rising from her place on the ledge. 'But I suppose that runs in the family.' Her lips curled into something too bitter to be called a smile. 'Very well, Wren Wynter. I'll help you kill my brother. We'll end this, once and for all.'

The revelation landed like a thunderclap. Wren recoiled, stunned, her mouth parting though no words followed. Vera watched the weight of realisation sink into Wren's features, watched the understanding dawn in those wide, bewildered eyes.

Delicious.

Vera leapt from the ledge with fluid grace, brushing past Wren with a careless wave of her hand. 'Did you not see the resemblance?' she teased. 'Clearly not. I was always the pretty one.'

Wren looked as though a thousand questions teetered on the edge of her tongue, but Vera silenced them with a flick of her wrist. Not now. Perhaps not ever. The past was a chasm she refused to peer into—too deep, too dark. Her grief was already dragging her low enough.

She came to a halt before the frozen Fae.

'He won't hurt ya,' Wren said firmly, her voice threaded with conviction. There was something heartbreakingly sincere in it. Vera felt a pang of something. Pity, perhaps. Wren truly believed that.

Naïve girl.

'Well,' Vera muttered, raising her hand and bracing herself. She could feel the power coil in her palm, green smoke blooming at her fingertips. No matter what Wren thought, Vera knew exactly what stood before her. And she knew better than to trust it. 'Thank Hecate you've caught me in a good mood.'

'Don't hurt him,' Wren said quickly, the worry crackling behind her voice.

'Oh, sweetheart.' Vera rolled her eyes, then exhaled the green smoke in a smooth, deliberate breath. It wrapped around Arden like mist, melting the frost that bound him. 'You really do know how to pick them, don't you?'

Chapter Thirty-Seven

House of Flames
Kingdom of Fire

Never trust a witch.

Tabitha Wysteria

The moment Arden was released from his icy prison, he did precisely what Vera had anticipated.

Without hesitation, a hidden blade slipped from beneath his jacket, its edge slicing the air with a low, lethal hiss each time he moved. He lunged with intent, steel flashing, and Vera dodged with impressive agility—graceful and sharp, like a dancer trained in violence. She hadn't even drawn on her magic yet, and still she kept pace. The sight must have stunned Wren, watching the witch twist and evade without spell or shield.

But it couldn't last.

Something shifted in Arden's eyes, those beautiful, deceptive green eyes, and whatever restraint he'd been holding onto vanished. In that instant, he became exactly what Wren had insisted he was not.

A killer.

Vera cried out as the blade found her cheek, a hot line of pain blooming as blood spilt down her face. She pressed her palm to the wound, fingers trembling as she tried to hold her skin together. But Arden didn't falter. He didn't stop. He advanced with terrifying calm, each strike deliberate. He wasn't trying to end her quickly.

He was playing.

He had countless chances to kill her outright, but chose instead to let her feel the inevitability of death. To let her bleed by inches. When she lifted her hand in defence, the blade carved through her palm as if it were paper, blood splattering across the stone beneath her feet. The blade struck once more, directly into Vera's side.

Wren had seen enough.

With a furious cry, she drew her own dagger and threw herself between them, shoving Vera out of harm's way. Her mind reeled. Why hadn't Vera used her magic? She was powerful, more than capable of defending herself. But Wren didn't have time to dwell on the answer. Whatever Vera's reasons, Wren would not stand idly by and let her be butchered.

The moment Arden realised who now stood in his path, he stopped.

'Step aside,' he said, voice low.

'No.'

His eyes flashed with confusion, his grip tightening. 'Why are you protecting her?'

'Why are ya trying to kill her?'

'Wren...'

She stilled at the sound of her name on his lips. He never called her that, not like this. There was something fragile in the way it fell from his tongue, like a secret let slip.

And in that breath of hesitation, everything shifted.

She knew, of course she knew, that he had been keeping truths from her. Just as she had kept things from him. That was the world they lived in, fractured by history and haunted by silence. After a century of secrets, of closed doors and shuttered hearts, trust was a rare and precious thing. But Wren had tried. She had tried to open the door. She had hoped.

'Is it true?' Wren asked, her voice calm but taut, the knuckles around her dagger whitening with tension. She was ready for whatever came next. If she had to fight him, she would.

Arden said nothing. His vivid green eyes shifted from Wren to Vera, avoiding the wolverian's gaze as though it might burn him.

'Answer me, Arden Briar!'

'It is.'

Two words. That was all. Yet they landed like a blade between her ribs, stealing not just her breath, but every inch of happiness that had once lived in her chest. She had known, of course she had, that he was hiding something, weaving his truths carefully the way only Fae knew how. But never, not once, had she imagined this. That he could be *that*.

A Black Lotus.

The tales came flooding back in vivid, harrowing detail. The whispers she had grown up hearing, warnings spoken in hushed tones: how the Black Lotus were bred for cruelty, for silence, for death. How they obeyed without question. How they tortured. How they killed even the most helpless—newborn babes, elders with one foot already in the grave. Death was not a mercy when it came from their hands. It was a slow, deliberate art. Sometimes lasting days. Weeks.

Wren stepped back, disgust rising in her throat as she spat onto the floor. 'What ya told me...'

'It was true,' Arden replied softly. 'In its own way.'

'Ya said ya were a cook.'

He gave a careless shrug. 'I'm a butcher. Just not the kind

you imagined, Wren.'

Her brows furrowed. 'And why are ya calling me Wren now?'

'It's easier,' he said.

'Easier?' she echoed, incredulous. 'What in da gods' name is easier?'

Arden shook his head, that same impassive mask settling over his features once more. 'Move aside. I was given orders.'

'From yer king? Da one who turned his back when I begged for help?' Her voice was rising now, thick with fury. Out of the corner of her eye, she saw Vera inching away, trying to disappear into the shadows. Without even looking, Wren lashed out, kicking the witch in the leg. Vera stumbled with a sharp cry of pain, falling to the side.

'Don't even think about it, Vera,' Wren snapped. 'We've things to discuss, ya and I. Sit.'

With a muttered curse and a bitter glare, Vera obeyed, slumping to the floor with her hand still pressed to the wound on her cheek, blood slipping between her fingers.

Wren turned back to Arden, lifting the tip of her dagger and pointing it squarely at his chest.

'So I suppose it all makes sense now,' Wren said quietly, sorrow softening her voice. 'Why ya were so willing to follow me.'

She had dared to believe, if only for a moment, that perhaps she had found someone who sought nothing more than quiet companionship. Someone who, like her, lived with solitude curled around their soul, who wanted to do good. To help. To matter.

'It's nothing personal, Wren,' he replied with a casual shrug. 'I was given orders.'

'Stop saying that.'

'What? The truth?' He smiled then, sharp and effortless, like a blade sliding between ribs. 'You always knew, somewhere deep down. You were just selfish enough to ignore it.'

Her lips pressed into a thin, pale line. His words cut, unflinchingly precise, like all his blades. It felt as though someone had reached into her chest and wrenched her heart in their fist.

But she wouldn't break.

She was a wolverian. She had kingdoms to save, people to protect. She would not fall apart over him.

'So that's it?' she asked, voice tight. 'It was all a lie to ya?'

'I am Fae,' he said simply. 'I cannot lie.'

'Yer still not answering me question.'

'Move aside, Wren.'

'How could yer king possibly have known what had happened, to have already given da order to kill?' Wren asked, her voice sharp with disbelief. 'I arrived as quickly as I could. No one from yer kingdom survived da massacre at da castle. So how did yer king learn da truth?'

Arden said nothing. But Wren noticed the faintest twitch in the hand that held his blade—small, almost imperceptible, but telling. He wouldn't answer. Not because he couldn't, but because he didn't dare.

The pieces began to fall into place.

If, by the time Wren had reached the Kingdom of Fauna, King Florian already knew of his daughters' deaths, if he had sent the Black Lotus into motion without hesitation, then he must have known the attack was coming. Known before it happened. Which begged the question: why hadn't he protected his daughters?

He couldn't have known. Surely not. Or... perhaps he had. Perhaps he had assumed they would survive. That they would be spared. That their blood would not be among those spilt. Which meant only one thing.

He had made a deal with the witches.

'He was working with them,' Wren said, the words heavy on her tongue. Vera scoffed behind her, though whether in amusement or bitterness, it was hard to tell. 'But why?'

'Some do want us to return,' Vera said. 'Not everyone stands against us.'

'And how exactly did King Florian help ya?'

Vera lifted one shoulder in a lazy shrug. 'His daughters, and their servants, were Fae. They'd have sniffed us out easily. There were dozens of witches in that castle, cloaked in glamour. The Fae would've seen through it in a heartbeat. But they were told to look the other way.'

'Then why are his daughters dead?' Wren asked, voice low.

Vera shrugged again. 'Never trust a witch.'

Silence settled between them, thick and uneasy, as Arden and Wren faced one another, locked in a silent battle neither seemed willing to end. Just behind them, Vera coughed, her strength visibly waning. Blood had soaked through her clothing, pooling beneath her like spilt ink, and Wren knew they were running out of time. If they continued to waste precious seconds, there might not be enough of the witch left to save.

'She is one of Hagan's officials,' Arden said at last, his voice low and flat. 'My orders—'

'I won't let ya harm her, Arden.' Wren's voice was steel. 'So da choice is yers. Ya can either return to yer king empty-handed... or ya can come with us.'

A shadow of confusion passed through his eyes, but it vanished as quickly as it appeared, buried beneath his ever-controlled expression.

'Why do you protect her?' he asked, almost as if he couldn't comprehend it.

'Becas I need her, Arden. To stop this madness.'

A rough cough interrupted them, drawing both their gazes to the bleeding witch slouched against the wall.

'May I make a suggestion?' Vera rasped, her voice sharp despite the blood staining her lips.

'Yes,' Wren said at once.

'No,' Arden countered through gritted teeth.

But Vera ignored him, her voice gaining strength through sheer force of will. 'I can offer you something far more valuable than myself,' she said, baring her blood-slick teeth in a crooked grin. Wren fought not to recoil at the sight. They were wasting time, and Vera's life was slipping through her fingers.

Arden didn't move. His shoulders were still set, his stance coiled and ready, like a predator waiting for the right moment to strike. If he wanted to finish this, he would have to go through Wren first.

'What?' he asked, tone wary, eyes never leaving her.

The grin on Vera's face widened, wicked and sharp. It should have tugged at the wound slashed across her cheek, but somehow, she didn't even flinch.

'I can give you Hagan,' she said.

Chapter Thirty-Eight

House of Snow
Kingdom of Ice

There is a quiet danger in wolverians.

I've seen how their bone readings once led them to burn an entire town to the ground, believing it was plagued with disease.

It wasn't. But they place their faith in the gods and the signs above all logic, above all reasoning.

I admire their devotion.

But it is a dangerous one.

Tabitha Wysteria

In Kage's eyes, Bryn's army was hardly an army at all. He dared not voice such a thought, not aloud. But when he compared their modest numbers to his own command, he found himself questioning whether the wolverians truly stood a chance of breaching the wall and crossing into the wastelands.

Their numbers were too few. A century of separation between the kingdoms had left all lands fractured, but some had withered more than others. The wolverians, for all their famed resilience to ice and hardship, had suffered deeply—ravaged by famine, thinned by disease. And yet, when Kage looked into their sharp blue eyes, he saw a fire that refused to dim. They would fall, if they must, but they would fall for their kingdom.

They had been camped for days now, nestled close to the

great wall, awaiting the signal to move. Patrols roamed the length of the barrier in endless circuits, sweeping as far as the eye could reach. But nothing came. No witches. No shadowy figures creeping through the snow. No midnight attacks. Just silence. It unsettled Kage.

Surely the witches knew they were here, waiting just on the other side. Or perhaps they didn't. Perhaps their focus had shifted entirely towards the Kingdom of Fire. If that were true, now was the perfect moment to strike. So why had Ash and Kai not done so?

'Yer fretting,' Bryn said, returning with a fresh armful of wood to bolster the fire. His enormous wolf trotted just a few paces behind, its silent presence a shadow at his heels. Here, at the kingdom's edge, the snow was thinner and the cold less biting. Kage had finally shed the bulk of his heavy furs.

'Something's wrong.' Kage leaned forward, eyes narrowed, staring into the flames as though they might offer an answer if he just looked long enough.

Bryn settled beside him, biting at his thumb in that casual, unconscious way he did whenever deep in thought. At the familiar gesture, Kage relaxed slightly, leaning back, allowing the tension in his shoulders to ease.

It was strange how quickly comfort had grown between them. In just a few weeks, their shared silences had become something dependable. They relied on one another, without ever needing to say it aloud. Kage knew when Bryn needed support. And Bryn... Bryn always knew when Kage was teetering at the edge of that dark, silent place in his mind.

Spirox appeared high above, a dark blur against the pale sky. With a sharp dip, the bird swooped down, slicing through the flames with a wild caw, as though it found the fire amusing.

Kage tilted his head slightly, the bond between him and his

shadow-bird allowing him to read the creature's movements as clearly as spoken words.

'It's empty,' he said, attention shifting back to Bryn. 'No witches. Again.'

Each morning, without fail, he had sent Spirox to scout the surrounding lands, to catch any sign of movement, any whisper of magic on the air. But day after day, the bird returned with the same answer.

Silence. Emptiness.

'I sent word to Ash and Kai,' Bryn said, scratching absently behind his wolf's ear. 'Still no reply.'

'Perhaps I should go to them,' Kage offered, his brow furrowing. 'Something may have happened.'

Bryn opened his mouth as if to object, then thought better of it. He simply nodded. And that, somehow, unsettled Kage more than any protest could have. His stomach sank with the quiet, unspoken truth: Bryn didn't mind whether he stayed or left.

Of course he didn't. Why would he?

'I'll leave at dawn,' Kage said, turning his attention to the fire. He could not bring himself to look at Bryn, who sat just a few feet away, reclining against the great white wolf that never seemed to look away. Its pale blue eyes bored into Kage, unblinking, seeing through him, past the armour and silence, into the hollows he tried so carefully to keep hidden.

And Bryn... Bryn was watching him too.

The weight of both their gazes—the prince and his beast—burnt hotter than the fire itself.

Clearing his throat, Kage stood, unable to endure another moment beneath the weight of eyes that seemed to know far too much.

At first, he had never told Bryn where he went.

Each day, without fail, Kage had offered his guidance to the wolverians, training them in techniques unfamiliar to their way of life. Though he had never been regarded as a warrior in his own kingdom, a wyverian was a fighter by blood, if not always by choice. At fourteen, he had been conscripted into two relentless years of military service, an experience that had carved something sharp and unyielding into his bones. He would never match the skill of his siblings, that much he accepted. But it did not make him any less dangerous.

Teaching, he found, was something he didn't mind. In fact, he rather enjoyed it. Not quite as much as reading in a quiet corner, cloaked in shadows and blissfully ignored by the world, but it came close.

At first, only the most inexperienced wolverians dared approach him. Young ones with uncertain hands and wide eyes, too green to know fear. The others had kept their distance, wary of the strange, silent figure who moved like a whisper of death. Some muttered prayers under their breath, casting strange hand gestures whenever he passed, as if to ward off whatever darkness clung to him.

But curiosity had a way of softening fear.

In time, more of them began to gather, drawn to the quiet precision with which he trained the youths. He did not shout, nor did he boast. He simply taught. And slowly, the five uncertain wolverian teens grew into a group of twenty, then more. Day by day, the circle widened beneath his watchful instruction.

Even Bryn had joined them, standing at the back, silent and attentive. He had listened to every word Kage spoke with the same focus he gave to the movement of his own warriors. And when evening came, Bryn returned the favour, offering to teach Kage the art of hunting.

Kage knew how to hunt. Wyverians were apex predators,

feared across the Eight Kingdoms. His instincts were razor-sharp, his senses honed for the kill. His body was a weapon. His mind, deadlier still.

But he said nothing.

He let Bryn speak. Let him fill the silence with stories of tracking rabbits, of crafting snares from twine and making arrows from bone. He listened, not because he needed the knowledge, but because there was something soothing in the rhythm of Bryn's voice.

Because in those moments, those quiet, unremarkable hours beneath open skies, Kage found something he hadn't known he was searching for.

Company.

And he cherished every second of it.

...

'Couldn't ya call yer wyvern?' Bryn asked, his voice low in the hush of evening as they sat beside the tent, sharing a modest supper beneath a sky laced with stars.

'It's too far,' Kage replied simply. 'We aren't bound to our wyverns the way we are to our shadows. Wyverns are wild. They choose to remain with us, yes. But they are not ours to command. Not truly. Our shadows, though... they are chosen. Selected to become our companions. To guide us to the Underworld when our time comes.'

Bryn's gaze drifted to Spirox, perched upon a nearby branch, feathers puffed as if in sleep. But both men knew the creature was anything but unaware. The bird's stillness was intentional, its attention razor-sharp.

'Who chooses them?' Bryn asked.

Kage gave a small shrug. 'No one knows for certain. Some

shadows remain always visible, never straying far. Others only appear when summoned. It varies. My brother, Kai, has a shadow that answers only to his call. The rest of the time, it's... elsewhere. Some say, when not here, they dwell in the Underworld—one foot in the realm of the living, the other already lingering among the dead.' His eyes settled on Spirox once more, aware of the bird's unwavering awareness. Whether it truly understood, he couldn't say. 'Spirox stays here with me in shadow form. Always has. Whether it's his choice or mine, I'm not sure anymore.'

'Perhaps it's both,' Bryn offered, his tone gentle. 'Perhaps ya simply enjoy each other's company.' He caught the fleeting shift in Kage's expression. 'Ya don't believe that?'

'I don't believe anyone could enjoy my company,' Kage said quietly.

Bryn's brows lifted in subtle disbelief. 'And why would ya think such a thing?'

Kage didn't answer. He only stirred the contents of his bowl —broth that had clearly been made for him, yet bore the unmistakable scent of decay. The scraps of the camp's meals, gathered and left to rot before being passed to him. He recognised the taste. It was the same stew the others had eaten over a week ago.

Kage had always known he wasn't the most enjoyable of companions. He had never been the boy others sought out, never the one who filled a room with light or laughter.

As a child, his brother Kai had tried, again and again, to coax him outside with wooden swords and boundless energy, eager for play beneath the grey skies. But Kage had always declined, preferring the quiet company of books and the dust-moted stillness of the library. Kai had never given up on him, not truly. But as the years passed and they both grew older, Kai found his people elsewhere, among the ranks of the military, where loyalty was forged in sweat and steel. He made friends effortlessly, gathering them around him like a second family.

Kage would hear their voices echoing through the castle corridors, Kai's laughter rising above the rest, golden and unburdened. And Kage would sit alone in the library, spine bent over parchment, listening to the footsteps and the joy as they passed by.

For a time, he had wondered if an invitation might come. If, one day, Kai would turn to him again, offer him a place among the noise and camaraderie. But by then, Kage already knew the answer.

He had said no one too many times.

Mal had always favoured Kai, it was nothing personal. Some siblings simply shared more in common. Their bond had never bothered Kage; it had always been Mal and Kai, the reckless two, united in their mischief. While Mal had been denied military service due to the whispers surrounding her eyes, Kai had taken it upon himself to train her within the castle walls. Kage would sometimes watch them from the high windows, the two of them sparring with wild laughter and wind-swept hair, the kind of closeness that came from trust and mirrored hearts. And though he had never envied them, something inside him, something quiet, would fracture just a little.

The only person who had ever truly understood him was Haven.

She, too, had lived on the outside of everything. Raised within the confines of duty, her life had been carved out for her from the moment she drew breath. The girl who would be queen. The girl who could not run in the grass barefoot, nor play, nor dream freely. Kage had always seen it in her. Behind those dark, serious eyes was a sadness too deep for words. A loneliness wrapped in silk and expectation.

She was always the first to rise, long before the sun kissed the horizon, already halfway through her lessons while the others still slept. And when the rest retired for the evening, Haven was still there, still reading, still preparing, still *becoming*. There had never been time for friends. Not for love. And not even, in truth, for siblings.

Yet Kage and Haven had found a quiet companionship in the library, where tutors often sent her to study. They would sit in silence, page after page turning, neither saying a word. But when Kai and Mal's laughter floated in from the training yard beyond, they would both look up.

He would glance at her. She would glance at him.

And without a word, something passed between them.

An understanding.

Haven, the girl with the weight of a crown pressed into her spine. Kage, the boy who never quite fit in anywhere but in his solitude.

Then, after a moment, they would both return to their reading.

As if all was well with the world.

'Do you know why wyverians eat rotten food?' Kage asked suddenly, his voice quiet as the fire crackled between them. He was trying to silence the noise in his own mind, to push the thoughts back into their corners.

Bryn shook his head.

'Legend says that when Hades created the wyverians as a gift for his lover, she grew so enamoured with them that she spent more and more time in the mortal realm, dining with them each night. Hades, in his jealousy, cursed the food they touched, turning it to rot, and changed our bodies so that we could no longer digest anything that wasn't touched by death. He believed it would drive her away in disgust... or at the very least, dissuade her from eating with us.'

'And did it?'

'It didn't.'

Bryn gave a low whistle. 'That's rather unlucky for yer lot. I can't imagine life without a nice roasted chicken for supper.'

Kage raised an eyebrow.

'When we *have* da chance to, obviously,' Bryn added, rolling his eyes. Then, eager to steer the conversation elsewhere, he asked, 'How are ya planning to get back to yer brotha?'

Before Bryn could speak further, Kage cut him off. 'No.'

'Don't be difficult.'

'I'm not riding a wolf.'

'Ya wouldn't just be riding a wolf, Kage,' Bryn said, exasperated. 'Ya'd be riding me wolf.'

'I don't care.'

Bryn stood abruptly, the movement swift enough to draw Kage's attention. Though he masked his surprise—wyverians were adept at that—his head tilted slightly as he cast a lazy glance up at the prince now standing over him.

'I'd feel betta if it were me wolf,' Bryn said firmly.

Kage let out a long, tired breath. He despised the feeling of being beholden to someone. He had spent his life relying on no one. When solitude became second nature, the idea of accepting help felt like weakness. Letting someone in felt dangerous. And he wasn't sure he wanted that. He wasn't sure of anything anymore.

Come back, Haven. Please, whispered the voice in his mind. A plea that never ceased.

'Very well,' he said, catching the shift in Bryn's expression —he'd been about to argue again. Kage didn't want to argue. He didn't want to see Bryn upset.

Over the past few weeks, he had come to realise something quietly startling: he wanted to keep the wolverian prince content. He liked the way Bryn's mouth curved when he wasn't trying to hide his amusement, the way his voice softened when speaking to his wolf. Kage didn't know how to name that want, not yet. But he knew it wasn't something he deserved.

So he buried it, like all the other things he wasn't meant to feel.

He noticed the way Bryn's long fingers curled inwards, his hand slowly forming a fist. Without meaning to, without even trying, he had managed to upset him. Kage had a particular talent for that. Sometimes it was his silence that bothered people, other times it was the words he chose to speak when he finally did. Too blunt, too honest, too strange. People rarely liked what came from his mouth.

He had never truly learnt what others wanted. The signals they gave were always so muddled, so layered with contradiction that he had long since given up trying to decipher them. The only world that ever made sense to him was the world of written words where emotions were laid bare on the page, where stories followed logic, and endings, however painful, were at least certain.

'I used to believe that if you truly wanted something, with every part of your soul,' he said quietly, 'then the world would find a way to give it to you.'

Kage rose to his feet, turning to look at Bryn one last time, just long enough for it to mean something. Then he turned away, preparing to return to his people. To his brother. To the life that had always waited for him.

'But I was wrong,' he added. 'Sometimes, no matter how hard you fight, or how deeply you wish for something... it simply wasn't written into your fate.'

Bryn's eyes shone, caught somewhere between hope and sorrow, too full of things Kage didn't want to name.

'And what is it that ya want?' the wolverian prince asked, his voice rough with feeling.

Kage turned his back to him, steps slow but certain.

'To be left alone,' he said, the lie tasting bitter on his tongue.

Chapter Thirty-Nine

House of Wild
Kingdom of Fauna

I've studied poisons my entire life. I absolutely adore them.

Strange, isn't it, how someone so enamoured with something so destructive could long to be a healer?

Tabitha Wysteria

'I shall cut off one of your fingers each time you refuse to cooperate,' Kai said flatly.

Dawn stuck out her tongue, extending her hand with theatrical flair. 'Here, let me make it easier for you. Take this one, I rarely use it for pleasuring myself.'

'Vile creature.' He slapped her hand away as she laughed, unbothered by his scorn. 'Did you speak like that to Ash Acheron?' he added, eyes glinting with quiet satisfaction as her expression faltered, just for a moment.

With a snarl, Dawn snatched up the meagre bundle of leaves he'd gathered for their meal and flung them into the air. 'I am not eating that! Aren't you meant to be some fearsome commander? Go and hunt something!' She gestured dramatically at the dark hook swords strapped across his back. 'Surely you can do more than posture with those?'

'That won't work on me, witch.'

'*Nothing* seems to work on you, commander.' Her amethyst gaze trailed slowly, insolently, down the length of him, pausing at a rather indecent spot. Her wicked grin deepened. 'You're lucky my powers haven't returned completely yet, or I'd be roasting dinner with your—' Her words halted mid-threat as her eyes widened in disbelief. Kai, unmoved, had already begun eating one of the leaves she'd discarded. 'And I'm the vile one?' she gasped.

'I do not waste food,' he replied, utterly unfazed, plucking another leaf from his shoulder and taking a bite.

'That is not food,' she hissed just as her stomach betrayed her with an audible growl. They couldn't go on like this, living off berries, nuts, and the occasional unfortunate rodent. She had no idea how long they'd been stranded in this cursed forest. Days? Weeks? Time had blurred into misery. 'We should return to the shelter,' she muttered.

But even that was maddening. Every evening, no matter how far they wandered, no matter how determined their direction, they ended up back at the same ramshackle hut, trapped in some cruel loop, as though the forest itself were toying with them.

Dawn cursed under her breath at the thought of yet another night on the cold, unforgiving floor. How many nights had it been now? They had lost count. Too much time spent bickering to keep track.

'Has something stolen your tongue, commander?' Dawn quipped, unable to help herself. 'You're awfully quiet.'

But the moment she turned, her jest withered on her lips. Something was terribly wrong.

Kai stood rigid, his complexion several shades paler than usual. Without warning, white foam began to froth at the corners of his mouth, and his obsidian eyes rolled back into his skull. His body crumpled to the ground like a felled tree.

'Wake up! What's wrong with you?' Dawn cried, dropping to her knees beside him. She cupped his head in her hands, slapping his cheek with increasing urgency.

Then she saw it, the strange discolouration blooming at the tips of his fingers, and swore under her breath. 'Damn, stupid fool! Only you would be reckless enough to eat something poisonous!'

Grumbling with effort, she hauled the massive wyverian back into the hut, every muscle in her body protesting as she dragged him across the threshold. She glanced down at him, worry furrowing her brow. The forest was filled with plants unfamiliar to the rest of the kingdoms, but witches knew poisons better than most, and she recognised the signs well enough.

What she didn't recognise, however, was the exact nature of the toxin, and that made purging it far more difficult. She couldn't risk leaving to search for an antidote either. The forest was a trickster, a place of shifting paths and warped time. If she wandered too far, it might never return her. And as infuriating as Kai could be—gods knew she wanted to slap him more often than not—she had no desire to face this cursed place alone. Not without her full magic to protect her.

'I thought wyverians were supposed to be the finest warriors alive,' she muttered, giving his leg a hard kick. 'Clearly they skipped the bit about not eating wild, glowing foliage.'

With a growl of frustration, Dawn lowered herself back to the floor, gently shifting Kai so his head rested on her lap rather than the damp, mossy ground. A little of her magic had returned, just enough for minor tasks, like drawing clean water or lighting a fire.

She could try to draw it out manually, pull it from his blood the old-fashioned way, which would require very little magic, but it would burn. It would hurt like hell. And it might kill her, too.

'This is all Vera's fault.' Dawn let her head fall back against the wall with a dull thud, eyes squeezed shut in pure, simmering frustration. 'I don't know why I always end up listening to my sisters.'

Tears gathered at the corners of her eyes, stinging with the force of helplessness that had begun to rise within her chest like a tide.

Her childhood, in her own mind at least, had been a happy one. A golden haze of simpler times.

Others often tried to tell her otherwise, especially her sisters, who insisted they remembered it all so differently. But before their mother had left for the Kingdom of Fire, they had lived as a family, together with their father in the Kingdom of Magic, in a quiet village called Elmwych.

There hadn't been much to the town. It had been rebuilt stone by stone after its destruction a century earlier during the Great War, razed to ash by drakonian fire. Her parents had always insisted that the village had been restored to its former glory, identical in every way to how it had once stood. Dawn had often raised a sceptical brow at such claims. How would they know? Neither of them had been alive when it first existed.

But their father had sworn that Hecate herself had visited him once, and that the goddess had blessed the reconstruction, declaring it true to memory, to magic, to myth.

Dawn had adored him for stories like that, even if they were half-truths or outright fancies.

He had played with them in the fields, spent long hours reading tales by candlelight, and loved them as fiercely and fully as any father could.

But then their mother had changed.

She'd grown restless, her heart tugged elsewhere, towards purpose, towards war, towards something more. She had longed to join the cause, to fight back against injustice. Their father had wanted no part of it. He had dreamt only of peace. A quiet life. A home where his daughters would grow in safety, untouched by the fires of conflict.

'I can still hear them arguing when I lie in bed at night,' Dawn whispered, her voice barely carrying over the soft patter of rain beginning to fall. The gentle rhythm of it on the roof of the hut offered an odd kind of comfort. Steady and grounding. She had always loved the scent rain left behind, the way it clung to the earth like a memory.

'Funny, isn't it, the things that stay with you,' she continued. 'Even after all these years. Sometimes, it's just the ghost of a smell. My father used to smoke a pipe of rich, spiced tobacco. And now and then, I'll catch the scent of it in the wind, out of nowhere, and it's as if it fills the entire room. Or I'll hear a laugh, bright and fleeting, and for a second, I'll swear it's hers. My mother's. Then I have to remind myself... they're gone. It's not real.'

She looked down at the wyverian, unconscious and pale, his head resting heavily in her lap.

'She took Vera with her, when she left,' Dawn said after a pause, her voice tightening around the memory. 'It nearly broke my father. But it did something to me and my other sister, too. Left us hollow. Left us with that ache of not being chosen. Of not being enough.'

Her lips curved into something that wasn't quite a smile. 'Our mother was off saving the world, and she chose Vera to go with her. Not us.'

She shrugged, as though trying to shed the weight of it. 'I understand now. I see why she chose her. Father used to say it was because Vera was the youngest, and she'd adjust more easily. But no, that wasn't it. Not really.' Dawn exhaled softly. 'Vera's always been... different. Harder. Sharper. She's made of nails and thorns and grit. My mother knew she could survive it. Endure it. She picked the daughter who could bear the weight.'

Without realising it, Dawn's fingers had drifted into Kai's dark hair, twisting strands around her knuckles in a slow, absent motion. A small, unthinking comfort.

'When my mother was assaulted... and fell pregnant because of it, my father couldn't bear it. He began to wither almost straightaway. Then, before long, he died.' Dawn's voice was soft, like a bruise being pressed. 'So my sister and I were sent to live with relatives, until we were old enough to go to our mother. I don't know why, but... I hated my father for it. For not saving her. For doing nothing. Even after he learnt the truth, he didn't go after her. He just faded. He left us to gather the broken pieces alone.'

Her fingers had curled tightly in Kai's hair without her noticing. The moment she realised, she let go, gently smoothing the strands as if in apology.

'When I turned fifteen, my mother allowed me to join her. I pretended to be of courtly blood, a distant relation. Vera was already there, working as a servant. And our mother... she barely looked at her. Treated her like a stranger. I could see it hurt Vera deeply, gutted her, and yet... I think I almost took pleasure in it.'

A bitter smile ghosted across her lips.

'It felt like justice, in a way. Punishment. She was chosen, all those years ago. And I wasn't. Perhaps it was petty, but I let her suffer for it.'

Dawn sighed, the breath catching in her throat.

'I suppose we've always been a little vile, our whole twisted lot. Maybe that's why I wanted to be Adara so badly. A new name. A clean slate. A chance to begin again. To be someone better.'

A single tear slipped from her cheek, landing with a whisper-soft touch on Kai's face. She wiped it away swiftly, as though he might wake and find her exposed like this.

'He made me better, you know?' she said, teeth pressing into her lower lip to stem the tide of words, though they came anyway. It was easier like this, speaking into the quiet. He was here, yet not. A presence that could not interrupt, could not judge. She could pretend.

Pretend he was a friend. Pretend he was listening.

And the comfort of it all was knowing that when he finally woke, he would remember none of it.

It was like a confession spoken into the dark, heard by no one.

'He might believe it was all a lie. But it wasn't. Not to me. I felt... alive. Even in someone else's skin, when I was with him, I was more myself than I've ever been. And it terrifies me that I may never feel that way again. That I'll never be known that deeply. That truly.'

She noticed a small leaf had drifted down and landed on Kai's chest. With gentle fingers, she brushed it away.

Then she stilled.

Something was wrong.

His breathing was uneven, too shallow. She pressed her ear to his chest, frowning as she listened carefully.

A rattle.

Her heart sank. A chest infection. Not good. Not good at all.

A small trickle of magic had returned to Dawn, just enough to begin the slow, agonising process of drawing the poison from Kai's body. She knew it would hurt. Not him. *Her.*

403

Poison removal was one of the first lessons taught to witches and warlocks, introduced in childhood and perfected only through years of practice. What many didn't realise, not until far too late, was the cost: to remove poison was to absorb it. To pull it into one's own veins and hope the body was strong enough to endure it.

Dawn knew she couldn't afford to delay much longer.

And yet… she lingered.

The silence was gentle, and strangely soothing. Kai Blackburn, unconscious and still, his head resting in her lap, depending on her. It stirred something inside her. Something warm. Something she wasn't accustomed to feeling.

Needed.

She had never been needed before.

Among her siblings, Dawn had always felt like the invisible one—present, but often overlooked. Though her sisters would deny it if asked. They'd claim she was the spoilt one, the favoured one. Sweet Dawn. Innocent Dawn. The darling of the family.

Some even dared say she was the prettiest.

They fought over such trivialities, endlessly rearranging the invisible ranking that hovered over them. One day Allegra was the most beautiful. Vera, the most intelligent. Dawn, the gentlest. And by the next day, the order had changed again.

Dawn snorted softly at the memory, amused and weary all at once.

Each sister bore her own scars, wounds not etched into flesh, but buried deep beneath skin and silence. They never spoke of them. That wasn't their way. They swallowed their fears, choked down their insecurities, and turned their sharpness on each other instead. Words became weapons. Their bitterness, a language they all understood. They hurt one another in small, cruel ways, yet the love between them never truly faded.

All except for Hagan.

Hagan had never been loved by any of them.

Allegra had always felt apart. Not because she wasn't beautiful. She was, in her own striking way, but because she looked different. While all three sisters shared the same warm brown skin, Allegra had inherited their father's bolder features —fuller, stronger, and in Dawn's opinion, unquestionably more lovely. Her hair, a halo of thick brown curls, stood in stark contrast to Vera and Dawn's long, pale platinum locks. The difference, though superficial, had carved a quiet distance between them. It made Allegra feel like the outsider, like the sister left out of some unspoken twinship.

And Dawn hated that. Hated the idea that Allegra might have believed herself lesser, simply because of how she looked. Especially when both she and Vera had often envied Allegra's beauty, her strength, her presence, the way she carried herself.

Vera had always possessed a relentless urge to save them all. She burnt for it. But she couldn't save herself.

And Dawn?

Dawn had simply existed, caught between the fragments of what their family had once been and the fantasy of what it might have become. She had wanted wholeness. A family restored. But they had been broken long ago, splintered for a cause that was meant to heal them, meant to make something noble of their pain.

Now it was Hagan who wore the mantle of saviour, the one who would return the witches and warlocks to their former glory. Who would raise them from shadow and silence back into power.

And yet, even cloaked in the language of salvation, Dawn could not forget that he had never been part of them.

Not truly.

Dawn tensed at the mere thought of Hagan, of all he had done, and all he still intended to do. Some of it she had witnessed firsthand, having once been part of his innermost circle. She had played the part well. Compliant, loyal, careful with her words, long enough to earn a sliver of his trust.

But now?

Now she was stranded in the Kingdom of Fauna, with a poisoned wyverian prince resting in her lap.

And Hagan would not forgive betrayal.

Not unless she did what had been asked of her. What she had set out to do.

With a weary sigh, Dawn gently eased Kai into a more comfortable position, adjusting his weight so she could lean over him. Her movements were hesitant, trembling. She had to lower herself just enough to press her lips against his, an act not of love, but of survival. A ritual.

The very thought made her shiver.

His condition was worsening. His pallor had drained to a ghostly white, and the veins along his throat were darkening, knotting like twisted roots beneath the skin as the poison continued its slow, merciless work.

She hesitated.

There, in the hush of the forest, with the rain still pattering softly on the roof of the hut, the temptation whispered to her.

If she let him die, if she did nothing and returned to Hagan with Kai's head, perhaps he might forgive her for not doing what he asked. The secret she had kept from Vera. The true reason she had accepted to run off and find Ash. But the truth was, what Hagan had asked of her... she had been the one to leap at the opportunity. A chance to ease the ache in her chest, to begin again. To finally learn how to breathe once more, to forget the man who had poisoned her soul.

Couldn't she?

Dawn cursed under her breath as she shifted over Kai, straddling his body with determined urgency. She cupped his face in both hands, steadying him, anchoring him. Because once this began, there would be no turning back. Without giving herself the chance to hesitate, she leaned down and pressed her lips to his.

She inhaled, drawing in the sickness like a thread of smoke, searching for the tell-tale tug of poison within him. The moment she felt it stir, coiled and clinging inside his veins, she breathed deeper, harder.

The poison surged.

It tore through Kai's body like wildfire, his limbs seizing beneath her, arms and legs twitching violently as the venom was pulled from him and into her. As soon as it entered her bloodstream, agony bloomed like thorns under her skin. Dawn bit down on the scream rising in her throat, refusing to let it escape.

The pain was searing, merciless. Infecting every inch of her, flooding her muscles with sickness, darkness, wrongness. Her body cried out for release, for escape from the torment, but still she held on. Still she pulled.

Their bodies twisted in unison, limbs shuddering in a grotesque dance as the poison fought to keep its host. It clawed to remain inside the wyverian prince, to bury itself deeper. But Dawn would not yield.

She would not let Kai Blackburn die. Not here, not like this. She would not be left behind in this cursed forest, alone. She would not surrender her power, not to the whims of fate, nor to Hagan, nor to some wretched forest weed.

With one final, desperate breath, Dawn felt the last tendrils of poison rip free from Kai, slicing through her like ice, embedding themselves deep within her own veins, just as Kai drew in his first breath.

His eyes snapped open.

A shuddering sigh left her lips, relief crashing through her, swift and sharp. Without warning, she collapsed into his arms as unconsciousness stole her away, the poison curling like smoke around her fractured heart.

Chapter Forty

House of Flames
Kingdom of Fire

It's curious how every single kingdom has its own elite soldiers, trained from youth to serve and protect.

Witches and warlocks have none.

We are the soldiers.

Every one of us.

Born to be sacrificed.

Slaughtered.

All in the name of the greater good.

Tabitha Wysteria

'Why didn't she heal herself?' Arden asked, his voice low, almost hesitant.

They had carried Vera indoors, settling her carefully upon the worn bed, her breathing shallow but steady. Wren, who had learnt to sew as a child and later to stitch skin as deftly as fabric, worked in silence. Her mother had taught her that hands could shape more than clothing, they could mend flesh and save lives. Wren had always preferred a needle soaked in blood over one dipped in thread.

'Witches aren't permitted to heal themselves,' she said at last, her hands deft as she checked Vera's condition for the hundredth time. They had spent the night in the crumbling home, watching over the witch whose sleep had not yet broken. Outside, the muffled cacophony of war still echoed—distant, but ever present. Wren had done a fine job on Vera's face, and if they managed to find a witch healer, there would be no scar to tell of the blade that had once torn it. 'It's one of their sacred laws.'

'Why?' Arden asked, brow furrowing as he leaned against the doorway.

'Becas what would stop them then, hmm? From neva ageing, neva dying?' Wren glanced over her shoulder at the Fae who trailed her like a second skin. He was guarding her, or rather, guarding Vera. As though Wren might pick up the unconscious witch and flee into the fire-ridden city. A ridiculous notion. 'Some witches defy da law, of course,' she continued, dabbing sweat from Vera's brow as the fever raged on, unrelenting. 'They use blood magic. Dark, forbidden. Dangerous. But they do it nonetheless. Though most rely on healers trained for da task, witches devoted to that craft alone.'

Arden was silent for a moment, his gaze unreadable.

'How do you know so much?' he asked finally.

Wren didn't care for the suspicion in his tone. It wasn't the Arden she had travelled with, not the one who had made her laugh when everything else in the world had felt like it was falling apart. That Arden had spoken with warmth, his words feather-light, disarming. But this version, this shadow of him, was all sharp edges and distance.

'Believe it or not, Arden Briar,' she said as she pushed past him, her shoulder brushing his with intent, 'I read.'

'Thought you didn't like to,' he said, and the fact that he remembered such a detail gave her pause. But she didn't let it show. She continued down the corridor into the cramped kitchen where she had spent the better part of the morning brewing remedies. Without a word, she lifted the steaming bowl of water she'd prepared and handed it to him. Arden accepted it with a look of mild astonishment.

'Ya won't be winning any prizes if she dies,' Wren said dryly, nodding towards the room. She gathered towels and worn blankets from a nearby cupboard. 'Stuff them in all da cracks I don't want da heat escaping.'

They worked quickly, sealing the room as best they could with layers of cloth. Then Wren kicked off her boots and climbed into the narrow bed, nestling Vera against her chest with the practiced care of someone used to holding more than just weight. 'Set da bowl by her stomach,' she instructed. Once it was placed between their legs, she gently leaned Vera forward so she could inhale the rising warmth.

'I need ya to rub this on her chest.' She nodded towards a small jar of thick ointment, concocted from herbs she'd foraged from the overgrown gardens nearby. Arden had seemed surprised when she'd left him alone with the unconscious witch earlier. A part of her, shamefully, had expected to return to find Vera lifeless, Arden gone. But when she stepped back into the house, arms full of greenery and fruit, the sight of him still sitting beside Vera, watching her as though she were an enemy, had struck something deep within her.

'I'm not rubbing her chest,' he said flatly.

Wren rolled her eyes. 'So yer fine with killing, but draw da line at applying a bit of ointment to a fevered woman?'

His eyes darkened, but he said nothing. In silence, he took the jar from her, waiting as Wren unbuttoned Vera's tunic. She half-expected him to flinch, to fumble, to look away. But instead, his hands moved with care, respectful and precise, never lingering, never wavering.

'How did you learn all of this?' Arden asked, his voice low

as his fingers gently swept another layer of ointment across Vera's fevered chest. Wren cradled the witch closer to the steam, allowing her to breathe in the healing heat.

'Learn what?'

'To stitch. To ease a fever. To...' He didn't finish the thought, but his eyes did. *To save. To care.*

'My ma taught me,' Wren replied, brushing a lock of hair from Vera's brow. 'Wolverians grow up learning everything we might need. It's da only way to survive in our part of da world. Da cold doesn't forgive ignorance. We learn to hunt, to sew, to cook, to heal. Even da littlest ones know how to snare a rabbit or set a bone.'

'Must've been nice,' he said.

'Which part?'

'All of it.' His hands stilled, betraying the slip of honesty in his voice. It seemed to surprise even him, that moment of softness.

Wren watched him for so long she almost forgot Vera still lay in her arms. 'Ya said yer family were murdered by royals.'

'I did.'

She waited, expecting more. But Arden, like always, kept his words locked behind his teeth. When he said nothing further, she let out a breath of quiet frustration. He noticed.

'It's for me to decide what I share,' he said at last.

The words struck her like a blade slid between the ribs. She knew he was right, but it didn't make the ache lessen. They had journeyed together. Shared laughter. A night. A moment that had felt like something more.

'Did ya sleep with me as punishment?' she asked, her voice little more than a whisper. His eyes snapped to hers, shocked wide. His mouth opened, then shut, then opened again, no sound escaping. Wren took some petty satisfaction in shaking a Black

Lotus. They were meant to be emotionless. Ghosts in flesh. And yet here he sat, unravelled.

'Ya knew I was a princess. Ya had yer orders. Ya were using me.' She forced the words past the lump forming in her throat. 'So that night, was it yer way of punishing me for da blood in me veins?'

He froze. The air between them pulsed with something that might have been regret, or fury. Slowly, he placed the ointment on the bedside table, his jaw tight with unspoken thoughts. His voice, when it came, was quiet enough to barely reach her.

'She's alive,' he said, nodding at Vera. 'Because of you.'

And with that, he turned and left the room, vanishing into the shadows.

Wren was left in the half-darkness, clutching Vera against her chest, the weight of Arden's departure heavier than the silence he left behind. She stared at the door for a long while, wondering if he had answered her question after all.

Perhaps he had.

...

'How long do ya think it will last?' Wren asked, her voice a murmur beneath the hush of twilight. Night had folded itself over Fireheart, cloaking the war-torn city in shadows and sorrow. Arden stood at the stone balustrade, a dark silhouette against the dying embers of day, his expression unreadable.

'Until one side surrenders,' he replied, his focus unmoving, fixed on the flickering skyline.

Wren drifted to his side, her shoulder nearly brushing his. Somewhere in the distance, the screams continued. Faint now, like echoes of ghosts who had not yet realised they were dead. For the first time in days, Fireheart had fallen into an eerie lull.

A fragile, fractured peace.

She wondered where her brother Bryn was with his stubborn frown and weary eyes. Perhaps he was finally breaking bread with Kage. Perhaps they'd survived each other. Perhaps Kage had found a way out of the darkness that threatened to drown him.

'You and I,' Arden said, quietly, 'we're not the same.'

Wren tilted her head, eyes falling to his hand. So close, so still. Without hesitation, she reached out and caught it, grinning at the surprise that cracked through his stoic mask.

'For a Black Lotus,' she teased, 'yer rather terrible at hiding yer expressions.' She laced her fingers through his, holding their hands up between them. 'Don't look all that different to me.'

Arden stared at their joined hands, the corners of his mouth tugging upwards in the gentlest of smiles. So rare, so fleeting, Wren felt as if the breath had been knocked from her chest.

'Well, yer hand is much bigger than mine,' she went on, unable to stop. 'And me fingers are definitely shorter—'

'Wren,' he said.

'Yer thumb's a bit crooked, too.'

'Wren.'

His lips met hers—soft, unexpected, and impossibly warm. The kiss was barely there, a whisper against her mouth, yet it left her reeling. His scent curled around her like a promise— woodsmoke, rain-soaked leaves, the wildness of some forgotten forest. She could have stayed wrapped in it forever.

When he pulled away, his voice was quieter than the wind. 'We're not the same.'

'Becas yer Fae and I'm a wolverian?' she asked, breathless.

He nodded.

'And because I'm Black Lotus, and you... you're a princess.' His thumb traced the curve of her cheek. 'I was made to be a monster.'

She took a step back, the cold rushing in where his touch had been. 'Why do ya do that?' she whispered.

'Do what?'

'Push me away one moment and pull me close da next. Ya say yer a monster, then turn gentle.' Her jaw tensed. 'Stop confusing me, Arden. Ya can't be both. Yer either Black Lotus or yer Arden Briar. Choose.'

He didn't answer right away. The wind passed between them, rustling the fabric of war and memory.

'I am a monster,' he said at last, his voice tinged with something bitter, something broken.

Wren lifted her chin, eyes steady on his. 'Aren't we all?'

'I've done terrible things.'

'Haven't we all?' Wren muttered, her voice carrying the weight of countless sins, both confessed and buried.

Arden exhaled, the breath catching in his throat as if reluctant to leave him. 'I don't want to be a monster when I'm with you.' His hand drifted to the back of his neck, rubbing absently, a boyish gesture ill-fitted to the man he had become. Then he stepped back, as though putting distance might silence the ghosts.

'My parents were farmers,' he began, his tone hollow with memory. 'We had a modest plot. Nothing grand, just enough to live by. My mother raised me and my siblings while my father fought to keep the land.' He swallowed hard. 'But the tax increased, and we couldn't pay. One day, soldiers came, men sent by the king. My father resisted. Fought them off as best he could, but there were too many. They killed him. Just like that. The king had promised the land to one of his nobles.'

Wren's heart twisted. 'Yer mother?' she asked, the faintest stirring of hope sparking in her chest.

He shook his head slowly, the shadows in his eyes darkening. 'The Fae can be elegant, graceful even, but they can hide wickedness beneath their silk and spellcraft. They took my mother away, said she'd serve in the palace. A place of splendour, they said.' He hesitated, gaze dropping. 'But she wasn't there to cook or clean.'

Wren's brow furrowed, not yet understanding.

'They sent her to the pleasure court.'

The words fell like ash between them.

She blinked, confusion giving way to horror. 'What...?'

'Captured Fae are forced to serve the nobility's whims. She didn't run. She couldn't. They threatened to hurt her children if she tried. So she stayed. Endured.' He turned from her then, shoulders taut with barely contained fury. 'A noble took her one night and beat her so savagely that she never recovered. Shattered her legs. Mutilated her.' His jaw clenched. 'When they were finished with her, they tossed her into the gutter like rotted meat. Alone. Broken. She didn't survive long.'

Silence followed, so thick it choked. Wren didn't speak. Couldn't. Her eyes stung, and the tears came fast, hot, and unbidden. She brushed them away with trembling fingers, as if furious with herself for weeping. But how could she not?

'My brothers and I were sent into the Black Lotus, to be forged into the king's personal assassins, his spies. One of my brothers refused. They executed him. The other died during our second mission. And so, I was left alone.'

His voice was cold, stripped of grief, as though he'd locked the pain away long ago.

'The Black Lotus is not a brotherhood. There is no kinship between us, no camaraderie. We are strangers with matching scars. We know one another only by the sound of our screams echoing through wooden halls. Even our names were taken from us. We were given new ones. I don't remember mine. I do not wish to. I am Arden Briar.'

'That's awful,' Wren whispered, her voice catching.

'It is all I've ever known,' he said, not with bitterness, but with the bleak resignation of a man whose past offered no softness. 'I kill for the king who sentenced my family to death.'

'Why?' she asked.

Arden blinked, clearly taken aback. Perhaps no one had ever dared to ask. Wren's heart ached for him. She longed to reach for him, to pull him into her arms and whisper that he was more than the blade they had made him into.

'Why do ya do it?' she asked again, more softly this time. She was about to step forward, to offer him that comfort, but something in his expression halted her. A flash of warning. A breath held too long.

'Because I am a monster,' he said. 'That's what they bred me to be.'

'To follow orders blindly?' Her voice was sharp now, edged with anger. When he nodded once, stiffly, she froze. What horrors had they endured, these boys, to shape them into weapons that bent to cruelty without question?

'But ya didn't do it,' Wren said, her voice gentler. 'Ya didn't kill Vera. Why?'

His eyes met hers, those storm-dark green eyes, wild with the weight of all he carried. And in that moment, Wren knew. Knew with terrifying certainty that no matter how far Arden had fallen into darkness, she would not stop fighting for him.

He reached out, his fingertips brushing against her arm, hesitant. Testing. Searching her face as if for permission, for forgiveness, for salvation.

Like a predator learning caution, expecting his prey to flee. But Wren was not prey. She was carved from survival. She was teeth and grace. She did not flinch.

'Why?' she whispered again, stepping into him.

His hand trailed up her arm, pausing at her cheek, his palm cradling her face with the reverence of someone who had never been shown tenderness. His eyes devoured her, as though she had undone every wall he'd spent years building. As though she were a miracle made flesh.

'Because of you, little wolf.'

Chapter Forty-One

House of Wild
Kingdom of Fauna

No matter how infuriating drakonians can be, I must admit, their cities are breathtaking.

If it weren't for the relentless heat, I wouldn't mind living somewhere like Fireheart.

Tabitha Wysteria

Kai Blackburn allowed the witch to sleep.

She stirred now and then, and each time, he leant close to ensure her chest still rose and fell, that life hadn't abandoned her fragile form. Against all reason, he had built a fire, not for himself, but for her. For Dawn.

And when the sounds of the forest grew too eerie, too uncertain, he gripped his hook swords with silent precision, ready to strike. But still, he fed the flames, knowing too well that she chilled easily.

That wretched woman…

The same vile creature who had saved his life.

She could have left him to perish, let the poison bleed through his veins until his breath stilled. But she hadn't. She had taken it into herself instead. Why? Witches didn't save lives. Witches destroyed them. Witches had razed his soul to ash and shadow, and yet...

Yet here he sat, unable to summon hatred. Gratitude festered like a wound, impossible to ignore. He could not feel anything for a witch—not wonder, not curiosity, and certainly not whatever unnamed thing now tangled in his chest.

He didn't see her awaken. Didn't notice the slight twitch of her fingers or the subtle rise of her shoulders. It wasn't until she shifted, inching closer to the warmth like a wounded animal, that he turned. Their eyes met.

She froze.

And for a heartbeat, they regarded each other as predator and prey. Her gaze was guarded, his unreadable. But the fire between them crackled, sending sparks upward like whispered secrets.

'You shouldn't have done it,' he muttered at last, voice low and laced with restraint.

'Are you suggesting I should've left you to die, commander?' Her voice was hoarse, laced with something darker. Humour, perhaps, or defiance. Still, she crawled closer, trembling from the remnants of the toxin. 'Honestly, who would've thought a wyverian could be felled so easily.' Her eyes glinted with mischief. Under any other circumstance, he might have taken it as a threat. But tonight, he merely snorted. She didn't mean it. Not really.

'You said you had no magic left.'

'A thank you would suffice,' she replied, curling herself around the fire, drawing her knees tight to her chest.

He moved closer. Not to intimidate, but to see her face. She was turned slightly away from the flame, and he couldn't make out her expression. But when he saw her eyes shadowed with weariness, framed in sorrow, he wondered with unexpected ache, whether he had helped put that sadness there.

'Thank you,' he said quietly.

The words hung in the air like a rare constellation.

Surprise flared across her face, lovely even in exhaustion. There was something almost irritating about how effortlessly beautiful she was. Not the shallow kind he'd seen paraded through courts, but something that burrowed deeper. The elegant tilt of her nose that always twitched when she caught a whiff of something unpleasant. The way her stomach would groan seconds later, like an impatient child. Her swan-like neck, slender and proud. And those eyes...gods, those eyes. Purple and enormous, far too expressive for someone who claimed not to care.

Then there were her lips. Full. Dangerous. Always speaking a little too freely.

'I didn't think wyverians knew those two words. Congratulations. You've surprised me.' Her tone was light, but her smile didn't quite reach her eyes.

'We do,' he replied, voice drier than the desert wind. 'We simply reserve them for those who earn it.'

'How noble of you,' she said, and though her lips curved in mockery, her voice was almost... gentle.

Kai seated himself beside the fire, though he left a fair measure of space between them. Her green dress, once vivid, was now dulled with grime, the fabric stiff and stained, a testament to how long it had gone unwashed since they'd lost the lake.

'Why did you save me?' he asked at last.

'Do you regret that I did?' Her tone was clipped, but her gaze didn't waver.

'No.'

'Then why ask?'

'Because...' His words faltered. Her purple eyes drifted from the flickering flames to him, the understanding in them sudden and sharp. *Because you're a witch*, he almost said. *And witches do not save, they destroy.*

The pain on her face was quiet, but devastating. Every muscle seemed to sag with it, dragging her features down until she turned away.

'Do not get confused,' she snapped, her voice brittle. 'I saved you because I didn't want to be alone. You could've been a toad for all I cared.'

Kai snorted, the corner of his mouth twitching despite himself. 'Does solitude frighten you that much?'

'Only someone who's never truly been alone would ask something so absurd.'

Kai gave a small shrug. 'I'm wyverian. We are never alone. We look out for one another, we are family. You, on the other hand... witches are...'

'What?' she challenged, her chin lifting. 'What are we, commander?'

'Witches are meant to be alone. No one could love you.'

The words fell like a blade.

Dawn flinched. And though it ought to have satisfied him, proved his point perhaps, it didn't. Something twisted in his chest, sour and immediate. Guilt clawed at him. The urge to reach across the space and pull her into his arms, to apologise, overwhelmed him. He looked away, disgusted with himself for feeling anything at all.

'You're right, commander,' she said, her voice quiet and distant, like a child who'd been scolded one too many times. 'No one could ever love someone like me.'

'I didn't—'

'What? You didn't mean it?' she scoffed, dragging her long, tangled platinum hair over one shoulder and beginning to braid it with clumsy fingers. 'I know what I am, Kai Blackburn. I know what I've done. I live with it. I don't need you reminding me.'

Her voice remained steady, but her hands trembled.

'But don't pretend that I cannot *feel,* just because of the colour of my eyes. Don't assume I do not cry, that I haven't grieved or lost or bled. It is because of those very things that I've become the monster you claim me to be. Not because of what I was born with.'

Kai went still, every breath caught in his throat.

'We may be wicked,' she whispered, 'and cruel. But we are the consequences of other people's choices. And the colour of my eyes? It does not make me dangerous.'

She looked up at him then, her violet gaze piercing.

'They're just eyes.'

Kai remained silent, his attention fixed upon her as she quietly plaited her hair. He had no sense of how much time had passed, only the knowledge that he did not mind. She had turned her back to him, shoulders straight, and he found himself content simply to observe. Her fingers moved with swift precision, nimble and practised, weaving strands with a grace that almost entranced him. She hummed under her breath, a soft tune that held no true rhythm, yet soothed the air between them like a balm.

Then, quite suddenly, she began to sing.

It was so quiet, barely more than a whisper of melody. But something in the way her voice carried, raw and unguarded, unsettled him. There was an aching familiarity to it, something that tugged at memory, something that brought him home.

He hadn't expected that. Witches, in his mind, did not sing. They did not hum tunes or smile at the firelight or weave their hair into neat braids. They were destruction, wicked, spiteful things that slipped into the night with green fire in their hands and blood on their tongues.

'Stop,' he growled.

Dawn froze, her fingers stilling. She cast a glance over her shoulder, eyes glinting. 'Why? Do you not like the song?'

'Yes,' he replied curtly. 'I do. But I don't like *your* voice. You sound like a cat being throttled.'

The tightness in her features softened. For a moment, he thought she might snap. But instead, she smiled, slow and sly. 'I think perhaps you like my voice a little too much, commander.'

Kai rolled his eyes. 'You think too highly of yourself.'

The shadow of sadness that had lingered in her expression vanished, replaced by that familiar, maddening grin of hers. It was strange, the surge of satisfaction he felt at seeing her return to form. As if some knot within him loosened now that she looked more like the sharp-tongued, defiant woman he knew and not the broken one he feared he had hurt.

'I'll have you know,' she said loftily, 'I was once highly praised for my singing.'

'Where?' he asked, deadpan. 'A back alley full of stray cats?'

A small stone struck his shoulder. He blinked down at the pebble now resting by his hand.

'Did you just throw a rock at me?'

'Oh, commander,' she said sweetly, feigning innocence. 'It was barely a pebble. Do all wyverian males confuse size in such a disappointing way?' Her eyes dipped meaningfully towards his trousers, her smile growing ever more wicked.

Kai's expression did not falter. 'I do not fret over such things, witch.'

'Is that so?' Her head tilted, eyes bright with mischief. 'Shall we test that theory?'

She crawled closer, with a feline grace that unsettled him

more than he cared to admit. Her hand extended towards him, fingers glowing faintly with magic—an eerie, luminous green that sent a pulse of warning through his chest.

'I've just enough magic left,' she said, her tone dangerous and playful in equal measure, 'to turn your *little* friend into something very, very small...'

Kai seized her wrist, the movement instinctive, too forceful. She tumbled forward with a soft gasp, landing squarely in his lap. Her cheeks flushed a brilliant crimson the moment she realised her hands were pressed flat against his chest. Kai stilled, the breath catching in his throat. He hadn't meant to pull so hard.

Her eyes, wide with surprise, darkened almost immediately, masking the embarrassment with something sharper, as though she could not bear for him to see her flustered.

'Is this your usual method of luring a lady into your bed, commander?' she teased, laughter bubbling from her lips. It danced into the trees around them, dispelling the heavy quiet of the forest. And yet, even to his ears, the sound rang hollow. He wondered, idly, what her true laugh might sound like, unburdened and real.

With a grunt, he shoved her aside, the spell of the moment broken. 'Stop being absurd, witch.'

She giggled still, unfazed, and returned to the hut with an exaggerated sway, collapsing onto the bedding in a sprawl that spoke of stubborn comfort. Kai remained by the fire, eyes sweeping the shadows that encroached around them, ever alert.

But he felt her stare, those maddening purple eyes watching him from across the firelight, curious and quiet. He told himself not to look back.

He reminded himself they were just eyes. Perhaps nothing more.

. . .

'Are you certain?'

'If I weren't, I wouldn't have said a word,' Dawn replied briskly, brushing past Kai as they forged deeper into the forest. 'I have just enough power to get us out of this wretched place.'

'I still think we should wait.'

'For what, precisely?' She stopped in her tracks, planting her hands firmly on her hips with a dramatic huff. 'Shall I grow old and silver-haired by the time we return to your precious army?' Catching the look on his face, she softened the statement with a grin. 'I was exaggerating, commander.'

'I should hope so. I cannot imagine enduring your company for quite that long.'

'You wish you were so lucky as to find a wife as marvellous as me,' she said, sticking her tongue out like a petulant child.

'Continue poking that tongue out, witch, and I may be tempted to cut it off.'

'Oh, truly? With what? That enormous wyverian cock of yours?' she said, voice wickedly innocent.

Kai's onyx eyes sharpened into something molten. 'Vile woman.'

'I had heard rumours about wyverians being rather... what's the word?'

'Remarkable?'

'No, that's not it.'

'Gorgeous?'

'Now you're just listing things you think describe you, commander.'

He scowled. She smirked.

'The word I meant was... uninhibited.'

Kai stopped abruptly, staring at her as though she'd grown horns. 'Do you even know what that word means?'

'Do you?'

He chuckled and resumed walking, his tone dry. 'We wyverians are hardly prudish. But that doesn't mean we spend our days spouting filth for fun.'

'You do love that word, don't you?'

'Which word?'

'Vile,' she said, drawing it out with exaggerated drama. 'Viiiiiiiiiiiile.'

'Stop that. You're not five.'

'Vile,' she repeated, gleefully.

'Witch, do not—' He stopped again, their faces inches apart now, his frustration evident in the tension of his jaw.

'Vi.'

'Don't—'

'Le.'

'Enough,' he growled, though there was no real anger behind it.

Dawn rolled her eyes. 'In any case, I've enough magic to get us out.'

'And go where?'

She hesitated, lips forming a pout. 'That part is... tricky to estimate.'

'So we could land anywhere?'

'Not anywhere,' she muttered, looking away. 'Just... not here. That's something, isn't it?'

Neither of them said aloud what they were thinking. That anywhere was better than being trapped in a forest they could not seem to escape, stuck with each other and their thorny silences. Dawn bit her lower lip so hard it began to bleed.

Kai noticed. He always noticed.

Without thinking, he reached out and gently brushed his thumb across her mouth, wiping the crimson bead away with a tenderness that surprised them both. The moment the gesture registered, he pulled his hand back as though scalded and cleared his throat, staring elsewhere, anywhere but at her.

'Very well,' he growled, the sound rough as gravel. 'Let us hope we end up somewhere you can finally scamper off and make yourself useful. You've given me no information worth the breath spent asking for it.'

'Oh, I was rather hoping you'd forgotten about that.'

'I do not forget, witch.'

'Good,' she said, her tone softening. 'Because I'm not going anywhere. I meant what I said. I want to help Ash.'

Kai's face twisted, something sharp and wounded appearing behind his onyx eyes. 'If you truly wanted to help him,' he snapped, 'you'd stay far, far away.'

Her chest tightened, breath catching mid-lungful. She turned her gaze aside before he could glimpse the pain his words had carved into her. If he wanted to believe she was nothing more than a soulless spellcaster, a cruel-hearted creature unfit for loyalty or love, then so be it. She would not offer him the satisfaction of seeing her break.

Dawn had always been skilled at hiding the ache behind a smirk. At making herself small, invisible, unseen.

Without another word, she lifted her hand towards him— palm up, steady. It amused her, just a little, to watch him eye it like a dagger poised for his throat. In her case, perhaps it wasn't far off.

'You don't have to trust me,' she said quietly, voice barely a whisper, 'You just have to want this more.'

He didn't move at first. Just stared. Then, with the hesitant grace of a man who has been burnt too many times, Kai stepped forward. His hand hovered above hers, close enough to feel the warmth but not yet making contact. Waiting. Choosing.

She wouldn't force him. Not this. Not when it came to belief.

At last, he gave a nod. Subtle, but enough.

Dawn breathed in, calling to the thread of magic buried deep in her core. What little remained kindled beneath her skin, sparking to life as green smoke curled lazily between her fingers. The moment it appeared, Kai flinched. But before he could protest or draw away, she reached out and clasped his hand firmly in hers.

The world twisted upon itself, folding inwards like a dying star as magic was wrenched from her veins. The pull was violent, exhausting, but just enough. Enough to tear them free from that cursed forest and hurl them, breathless, back into the waking world.

Dawn gasped, her spine arching in protest as the old ache of dormant power surged through her bones. It hurt, yes, but oh, it felt good. She had missed the sting of it. The sweetness of being whole again.

Drawing in a lungful of scorched air, she turned and found Kai Blackburn on his knees, retching.

With a dramatic sigh, she crouched beside him, brushing earth from her sleeves.

'They really ought to rewrite those stories about wyverians,' she mused, a smile tugging at her lips. 'You're not half as spectacular as the bards made you out to be.'

Kai groaned through a grin. 'Are you suggesting we're a little bit spectacular, then?'

'Twist my words however you like, commander. If it soothes your pride, who am I to stop you?'

She offered him her hand. Surprisingly, he took it without

hesitation.

They rose together, surveying their surroundings with cautious curiosity. Heat hit them almost immediately, dry and oppressive. Dawn frowned, her brow furrowing beneath the haze.

'We couldn't have travelled far,' she said. 'I didn't have enough magic to take us halfway across the kingdoms... But I don't recognise this place at all.' She reached out, palm up, her voice softening to a whisper. 'What is this?'

Kai coughed, watching the grey flakes drift lazily from the sky.

'Ash.'

Dawn turned slowly, her eyes sweeping across the barren expanse. There was nothing. No trees, no life. Just endless open ground blanketed in ash that fell like a twisted mockery of snow.

'Something's burning,' she said quietly, as if speaking the words aloud might summon the flames themselves.

Kai pressed his palm to the cracked, ashen earth, the heat pulsing beneath it. His expression hardened.

'Yes,' he said grimly. 'Something *is* burning.'

Dawn looked to him, confused, until he raised his hand and pointed into the distance.

There, black smoke coiled into the blood-red sky, and in its heart, a city, flickering like the last breath of a dying flame.

'Fireheart.'

Chapter Forty-Two

House of Flames
Kingdom of Fire

I've always wanted to believe that I am good. That when I die, I'll go where the purest of souls are sent. But today, I poisoned one of my classmates just to win a silly competition. I didn't kill him. But I can't help questioning who I truly am after that.

Tabitha Wysteria

Mal walked through the streets of Fireheart, her chest tight with every step. No matter how many times she squeezed her eyes shut, the violence returned the moment she opened them again, relentless, unending. All around her, bodies crumpled to the bloodstained ground, witches unleashing spells with merciless precision, while drakonians defended their city with everything they had, their resistance soaked in sacrifice.

'Make it stop,' she whispered.

'I cannot,' came Thanatos' voice, soft and steady. He stood nearby, his dark eyes fixed on her. Not with amusement, as was sometimes his way, but with something far heavier. Almost… sorrow.

'You're a god.'

Thanatos exhaled, a sound laced with centuries of weariness. 'That is not how it works, Melinoe.'

'Then *how* does it work?' she snapped, spinning round to face him. There was bitterness in her voice, frustration clawing at her throat. 'Why bring me here? To watch them slaughter each other and do nothing?'

'You are here,' Thanatos said, with patient gravity, 'because Hades wanted you to see what lies ahead. This is only the beginning. One city, one battle. But there will be more. Countless more. And if you learn to wield your powers, if you become what you were always destined to be, you could stop it. You could change everything.'

Suspicion shone in her purple eyes, shadowing her expression. Thanatos tilted his head.

'And before you say it again,' he added dryly, 'no. I cannot read your thoughts. Only that wonderfully expressive face of yours.'

'So you keep insisting,' she muttered, stepping further away from him. The movement made him chuckle, though there was no real humour in it. 'I don't have time to learn,' she added, voice breaking with frustration. 'They're already dying.'

'There is always time.'

Mal didn't argue. What was the point? If Thanatos, in all his godly detachment, wished to believe they had the luxury of time while the city wept and burnt beneath them, nothing she said would change his mind.

'I want to help them *now.*'

Thanatos shook his head, the motion sending his snowy curls tumbling, so unlike Ash's, yet it was impossible to look at him and not see Ash Acheron standing beside her. The resemblance was a cruel trick of fate, a temptation wrapped in grief. It tugged at her, made her want to reach out, to let her fingers brush against his. But she never allowed herself that weakness.

Her father had done this deliberately. She was certain of it.

'You're not going to let me help them, are you?'

'Not at the moment, no.'

'Very well. Take me back, then. It has been days of you collecting souls. I've had enough.'

He blinked, surprised by the steel in her voice. She raised a brow in challenge, her hand already extended—expecting, not requesting. She wouldn't give him the satisfaction of a tantrum, of desperation. Let him think she was compliant. Let him and Hades believe she was settling in nicely, content to play the obedient daughter of the Underworld.

She'd find her own way back.

Thanatos took her hand, his fingers curling around hers as he drew her closer, closer than necessary. He leaned in until his breath stirred the fine hairs at her ear.

'You're up to something, Melinoe.' The way his voice curled down her spine was infuriating, and not something she wanted him to notice. She grimaced.

'What could I possibly be plotting?'

Her smile was too sharp, too knowing, and it made him uneasy. Though, to his credit, he masked it well.

'Be careful, Melinoe.'

'Oh?' she purred. 'Do you bite now, Thanatos?' Her smile deepened into something dangerously sweet. 'Must I remind you what happened last time?' Her attention drifted pointedly to the place where his ear was still missing. That earned her a smile, wicked and knowing, the smile of a man planning something equally dark in return.

'I never said you should be careful of *me*,' he whispered.

'Yes, you did—'

But before she could finish, the earth yawned beneath them and swallowed them whole.

...

'You're back! How delightful!' Makaria shrieked, her voice echoing through the vast stone chamber the moment Mal hit the ground with a graceless thud, her spine protesting from the fall. She would never grow accustomed to being flung between realms like a sack of bones.

They had returned to the wyverian castle, though it stood strangely quiet. The grand hall was empty, save for Makaria, who now loomed over her with a too-bright grin, and Zagreus, who sat at the edge of the castle's great drop, legs dangling into the abyss beyond.

'How did it go?' Makaria asked, eyes sparkling.

'Where is Hades?' Mal replied, brushing off the dust from her clothes, her tone clipped.

Makaria's smile faltered. She gave a nonchalant shrug, but Mal caught the trace of something behind her eyes. Disappointment perhaps, or hurt. Realising she had been harsher than intended, Mal softened her voice. 'Do you never get to see for yourself the mortal lands?'

'Father won't allow it,' Makaria said. 'He promised we'd be allowed to explore... one day. But not yet. It's too dangerous, he says. In case other gods see us and try to take us away.'

Mal frowned. 'Why would they do that?'

Makaria opened her mouth, then closed it again, her focus drifting towards Zagreus with uncertainty. He didn't turn to meet her stare. Instead, he remained perfectly still, watching the endless shadow-stretched horizon with the quiet intensity of someone who had spent too long in silence.

Then, at last, he spoke—his voice low and measured. 'Might as well tell her. She'll find out soon enough.'

'We'll get into trouble,' Makaria hissed, her voice taut with panic.

Mal stepped forward, closing the distance between herself and the brother she barely knew. He looked so achingly familiar. Like Hades, too much like him. The same dark hair. The same unforgiving jawline. The same cold grace carved into his bones.

A mirror of their father, yet something else lingered behind his gaze. Something unspoken.

'What will I find out?' Mal asked, her voice soft but firm.

Without overthinking it, she moved to Zagreu's side and slid down the smooth stone of the column opposite his, settling on the cold ledge across from him. Her legs dangled into the void, and she peered over the edge at the endless abyss below. For the first time in her life, she feared the fall. There were no wyverns circling overhead to catch her this time, no safety net beneath her. And though she couldn't truly die in the Underworld...

Still, the thought chilled her.

Something dropped beside her with a sudden thud, and Mal flinched, instinctively reaching for a weapon she did not have. But when she turned and saw it was only Makaria, she let out a tense breath, her shoulders easing.

Makaria giggled nervously and clung to her arm, pressing herself as close as physically possible. Mal resisted the urge to shove her off, to mutter something cold and distant, to reclaim the space that was hers alone, but she didn't.

Instead, she looked into those strange, unsettling eyes, eyes that always seemed to shimmer with something ancient and unreadable. And yet, beneath the eerie glow, Mal saw something unexpected. She saw her, Makaria. A soul not yet weathered by time, despite the centuries. A girl caught between godhood and girlhood, longing for things far too mortal: love, family, belonging.

A girl who spent her days ferrying souls into the Underworld for a father who didn't let her taste the sky.

A girl who would never feel the warmth of sunlight on her skin or the sharp delight of winter wind against her cheeks.

Makaria, Mal realised, was just another soul shackled to the Underworld, just like the rest of them. Trapped in a fate not of her choosing.

And for the first time, Mal looked properly at the siblings she had never grown up with. The ones she hadn't known existed. They were nothing like Kai, or Kage, or Haven, and yet, something stirred in her chest. An ache. A quiet, inexplicable affection.

Perhaps it was the sadness that clung to them like shadows.

The sadness of children who had never been taught how to love, or how to be loved in return.

Mal reached out and took Makaria's hand in hers, giving it a firm, deliberate squeeze.

The gesture stole the breath from Makaria's lips, just a soft gasp, almost too quiet to hear, but her face lit up with a gleam of stunned wonder. It vanished quickly, buried beneath layers of careful restraint, but Mal had seen it. And so had Zagreus.

'What is Hades keeping from me?' she asked quietly, her eyes shifting between them.

Zagreus and Makaria exchanged a look, one of those silent conversations forged through decades of unspoken understanding. Words were not needed between them. They spoke through glances, through the subtlest of shifts. Mal watched, her jaw tight, uncertain if they would choose honesty or retreat into silence.

At last, Makaria spoke, her voice almost a whisper. 'Hades is cursed.'

'Cursed?' Mal frowned, shaking her head. 'Tabitha Wysteria placed a curse on all of us. It was meant to keep the gods from finding us. But it broke when I...' she faltered, 'when I stabbed Ash through the heart. I ended the curse.'

Makaria nodded. 'You did. But long before that... there was another curse. One far older. One that has never been broken.'

'I don't understand.'

Makaria bit her lower lip, worry pulling at the corners of her mouth. She looked uncertain, torn between fear and duty, between silence and truth. The hesitation in her was palpable.

Mal opened her mouth to press the question, to plead for more, but before the words could leave her, Zagreus stirred.

'Hades fell in love with the goddess Hecate,' Zagreus began, his voice low, shaped more by memory than breath. 'He forged your kingdom as a gift to her, his tribute. But she chose differently. She fell for a wyverian man, a mortal.'

Mal's breath caught, but she said nothing.

'Hades tried to forget her, to bury the ache. He married our mother, Persephone, hoping perhaps to fill the void. It only made things worse. He could never let Hecate go. He could never understand how she could choose a mortal over a god. She left him behind, left everything, just to live among mortals with the man she loved. And that drove Hades to madness.'

Zagreus' eyes remained fixed on the horizon, unblinking, as his fingers slowly curled into fists.

'Our mother left him because of it. She couldn't bear the torment. Hades, in his desperation, descended into the mortal world, thinking he could win Hecate back. But it was too late. She had given her heart elsewhere.'

Mal leant back slightly, a cold twist of dread blooming in her chest. Something told her she didn't want to hear what came next.

'What did he do?' she asked softly.

Zagreus' lips parted in something far from a smile. 'He killed him. The mortal Hecate loved. Thought that if the man was gone, she would grieve, then return to him.' His voice darkened. 'But she didn't. Instead, she used her magic to bring the man back to life, and in doing so, cursed them both.'

Mal said nothing, her pulse pounding in her ears.

'She bound them. Tied their souls together across time. And in that spell, she cursed Hades too. Now, every time she is reborn, the mortal is reborn alongside her. And Hades... Hades finds her. Again. And again. And again. In every life, he watches her fall in love with the same soul. Never with him. The story always loops back to the beginning.'

'So... Hecate is reborn because of the curse she cast on him?' Mal asked, her voice barely above a whisper.

'We don't know if she remembers her past lives or not,' Zagreus replied. 'Perhaps not until she reaches a certain age. But no matter what any of them do, no matter the choices they make... the ending is always the same.'

Mal's brow furrowed. 'Then what does Hades want with me?'

Zagreus' eyes shifted to Makaria, who looked away, her lips pressed in a thin line. 'He thinks... he thinks you might be the key. That you could break the cycle.'

'Why me?' Mal pressed, unease settling in her bones. 'How am I tied to any of this?'

'You are his daughter. The curse didn't stop with Hecate. It passed into you.'

Mal's eyes widened. 'Then you and Makaria... you're cursed as well?'

Zagreus finally turned to face her. His expression was solemn, edged with something ancient and weary.

'No,' he said quietly. 'Makaria and I share your father. But not your mother.'

'My mother was Tabitha Wysteria.' The words tasted strange on Mal's tongue, and speaking them aloud sent a ripple of discomfort through her. It felt like a betrayal, like she was turning her back on the only parents she had ever known. King Ozul and Queen Senka would always be her true family, no matter the blood that ran in her veins.

'Tabitha Wysteria was the name Hecate took in that lifetime,' Zagreus said gently. 'Your mother is a god, Melinoe. As is your father. You are the daughter of Hecate and Hades, two gods bound by a curse. And that curse was passed onto you the moment you drew your first breath.'

Mal shook her head, a sharp, almost violent denial.

No, no, no.

It couldn't be true. It couldn't be.

And yet... a whisper of doubt began to uncoil within her. Why not?

'Their... their curse?' she asked, her voice no louder than a breath. Her eyes, wide and unblinking, moved between them in search of something—clarity, reassurance, anything. Makaria clung to her hand, trying to offer comfort, but Mal's body felt numb, her limbs fading like smoke.

Zagreus' attention drifted back out into the void, as though he could see something far beyond the darkness. Mal wanted to look too, to follow his stare and lose herself in the nothingness. But she couldn't tear her eyes from him. From his profile.

'The curse your parents carry...' Zagreus' voice was hushed, solemn. 'You will fall in love with a mortal. But a god, one you can never truly love in return, will destroy him, just to possess you. Hades loved Hecate. He created the wyverians as a gift for her. But she gave her heart to one of them. She broke his,

439

shattered it. So Hades, in his fury, killed the man she loved.'

His gaze darkened, distant.

'And so it began. Every time Hecate and her mortal die, they are reborn. In every life, Hades finds them. And in every life, he kills the man she loves. And Hecate... she takes her own life. Out of sorrow. Out of grief. Over and over again. And now that same curse falls to you.'

'This mortal...' Mal's voice caught in her throat, barely a whisper. 'It was Hadrian Blackburn?'

Zagreus nodded. 'Though the name changes, the soul remains the same.'

'I don't... I don't understand.'

'Hades didn't create you out of love,' Zagreus said, his words like frost. 'He made you with one purpose in mind, because he believes you can break the curse.'

Mal stopped breathing. Her chest clenched with dread.

'And Tabitha... I mean, Hecate. Did she know?' Her voice wavered.

Zagreus offered a helpless shrug. 'We don't know. But Hades brought you here because he knows. He knows the curse passed to you. And he's hoping you will end it.'

'That's why he wanted to marry you to Thanatos,' Makaria added quietly, her voice tinged with sorrow. 'He thinks that if you can stop loving Ash, and fall for Thanatos, you will break the curse that binds you all.'

Mal's eyes burnt. 'Why are you telling me this?'

Zagreus shrugged again. 'Because you're our sister, aren't you? You deserve to know.'

'No... I can't...' The words spilt out of Mal in a hoarse whisper.

'Melinoe—' Makaria breathed.

'Don't call me that!' Mal hissed, snatching her hand away

and getting up, stumbling back as if burnt. She could feel the truth creeping into her skin, anchoring itself inside her bones. A truth that would never let her go.

She turned and fled, the cold corridors swallowing her as she ran. The stone beneath her feet felt too real, too solid. She didn't want to know. She didn't want to be this.

She crashed into someone, hard. Strong arms caught her.

Mal took a step back, her expression hardening the moment she caught sight of Thanatos.

'Did you know?' she spat, her voice sharp with betrayal.

His obsidian eyes searched her face as though hoping to find some fragment of understanding there. After a long, weighty pause, he sighed and gave a slow nod, slipping his hands into his pockets.

'And what?' she demanded, her voice rising with fury. 'You were going to make me fall in love with you? Was that the plan? What did you hope to gain from it?'

'You,' he said simply.

'You don't even know me.'

For the first time, Thanatos faltered. He shifted uncomfortably, his weight passing from one foot to the other like a guilty boy caught in a lie.

'But I do,' he said at last. 'I've watched you from here. For years, I listened to your prayers. For years, I waited for the curse to break, for the moment we could come for you. So you could finally return home. With us.'

'This isn't my home,' Mal replied coldly.

'It could be,' he said with a casual shrug, though his voice was soft. 'If you let it.'

'Well, I don't.' She made to push past him, but his hand left the safety of his pocket and caught her wrist before she could go.

'Let go,' she snapped.

And he did. Immediately, without resistance.

'Melinoe...'

'That is *not* my name,' she hissed, spinning around to face him, her fury burning bright in her gaze. 'My name is Mal Blackburn. I am fourthborn of House of Shadows, Kingdom of Darkness. I am the wife of Ash Acheron. And I will return to him. *Right now.'*

She didn't know how she would do it. She doubted any of them would lift a finger to help her. But she would find her way back to Ash. If not walking, then crawling. If not with magic, then with sheer will alone.

As if some unseen force heard the raw truth in her vow, the world around her began to twist.

The air shifted. The very ground beneath her warped and trembled as though reality itself had been pulled taut and was ready to snap. A great force from above began to draw her upward, as if plucking her from the Underworld like a thread from the fabric of fate.

Thanatos' face contorted with shock, sorrow, and something else she couldn't name. He didn't reach for her. He didn't try to stop it.

He just watched.

As though he knew something she did not.

Chapter Forty-Three

House of Sand
Desert Kingdom

Dunayans fear nothing.
Not even death.

Tabitha Wysteria

'Harra, amira! You're too slow!' Hessa's voice rang out over the sand, laughter bubbling from her lips as Alina sprinted with every ounce of strength she had left. They were deep in the heart of the desert, far from camp, having travelled for two long, scorching days. Though their tents had been pitched, rest had been postponed. Hessa had led a handful of them out for training. But it was not the rigid drills of old. No, this was sport. Two against two, each match a dance of instinct and cunning.

Alina's eyes locked onto the long spear planted ahead, a crimson ribbon fluttering from its tip like a banner of victory. Charging towards it from the other side was Saren, just as wild, just as hungry to win. There was no room left for thought. Alina threw herself forward, legs pumping, sand slipping beneath her feet. She would not lose.

They had been positioned at opposite ends of a vast, sun-scorched expanse of sand. An arena drawn not with walls or banners, but with the breathless hush of heat and anticipation, told to run on the count of three. The first to grasp the spear would win. Alina had quickly learnt what it meant to run across shifting dunes. Balance was everything, and missteps were costly.

She had trained with the Dunayans for days that had bled into weeks, until time blurred and the memory of anything else began to fade. The palace halls of her youth, the dragon-forged towers of the Kingdom of Fire... all seemed like stories told to someone else. Once, she had been a princess. Now, she wasn't sure what she was at all.

Not Dunayan. Not royal.

Just... nothing.

And Alina had come to cherish being nothing.

There was clarity in it. An emptiness that kept grief at bay. She no longer wept for a family she had chosen to forget. No longer mourned a kingdom that had never truly belonged to her. A princess no longer. So why should she hold onto a crown she had never worn with pride?

No.

She kept only one thing.

One purpose that pulled her from her bed before the sun. That made her push through endless drills, through sweat and ache and blistered hands. One face that haunted her beneath the sun's brutal gaze and returned to her, vivid and whole, when she closed her eyes each night.

A face she would never allow herself to forget.

Alina caught sight of Saren just a breath away from the spear, but instinct overruled caution. She hurled herself forward with abandon, arms outstretched, the coarse desert sand scraping against her skin as she landed flat on her stomach. Her fingers curled around the shaft of the spear just as a body slammed into hers. Saren had done the very same, their limbs colliding in a chaotic tangle of elbows and knees.

A sharp thud followed, a foot catching Alina clean on the forehead as Saren slid in from the side, her momentum unchecked. The impact stung, but it only made Alina laugh harder.

Cheers erupted across the dunes, and Alina threw her head back with victorious glee, the ribboned spear clutched triumphantly in her grasp. Saren leapt to her feet, brushing sand from her clothes before extending a hand. Alina took it without hesitation, grinning as she was pulled upright.

'Don't get used to beating me,' Saren warned with a dazzling smile.

'Then stop making it so easy!' Alina shot back.

Hessa was next to reach them, her arm slinging around Alina's shoulders with a jolt of pride and affection, pulling her in close.

'Well done, amira! You're getting fast now.'

A sharp whistle cut through the warm air, a signal that food was ready. The gathered Dunayans who had been spectating scattered at once, eager for their morning snack. Saren joined them, casting a smile over her shoulder before disappearing into the group, leaving Alina and Hessa alone.

They often left them like that, Alina noticed. As though everyone had silently agreed that the two princesses should have their own time together, away from the others. She didn't question it. She didn't want to. She enjoyed the quiet comfort of Hessa's company, the way her eyes always seemed to seek Alina first, the way she made her feel seen.

'We'll travel to Madari next,' Hessa said as they reached the tents, collecting bowls brimming with fragrant rice and tender, spice-drenched meat. They settled outside, side by side, watching the ever-changing face of the desert.

'What's in Madari?'

'It's one of the largest desert cities,' Hessa replied, scooping a handful of rice and meat and dropping it into her mouth, humming with pleasure at the taste. Alina followed her lead, moaning softly as the flavour burst across her tongue. 'We need supplies,' Hessa added after swallowing, 'for my father.'

Over time, Alina had come to understand that Dunayans were far more than fierce and skilled mercenaries. They were guardians of the desert folk, yes, but also messengers and caretakers tasked with ensuring their people's needs were met, even if that meant travelling to the great cities beyond the dunes. It had puzzled her at first. In truth, it still did.

'If your father is king,' she asked, brow furrowed, 'shouldn't he be in a city? In a palace?'

Hessa smiled at the thought, a soft amusement dancing across her features. 'We are ruled by tribes. My father is king and governs the whole of the desert. But beneath him are the twelve great tribes, each with their own lands, their own ways. Each region has its own laws and customs, and Dunayans like me protect them. They govern themselves, for the most part. Only when justice lies beyond their reach do they call for my father.' She paused to scoop up more rice before continuing, 'He travels from tribe to tribe, one each month, staying with them and hearing their needs. The mountain we trained on belongs to the twelfth region. Madari belongs to the eleventh. My father could place a palace in the city, but it would be seen as an insult to the rulers of that land. It is their territory, not his.'

'What sort of supplies are we gathering?' Alina asked, intrigued.

'He's heard of a new strain of desert plants that are rare, possibly medicinal. He wishes to try them.' Hessa squinted slightly beneath the merciless sun. 'But I think that's just an excuse for us to have a look around.'

'Why?' Alina knew the answer, but she needed to hear it spoken aloud, to give weight to her unease.

'There are whispers... Madari seems restless, unsettled. No one knows why. But with everything we now know of the witches, the timing feels too perfect to be mere chance.' Hessa gave a wry smile. 'Still, we mustn't worry too much. My father worries enough for all of us. His face is a map of lines now. His wife will leave him any day.'

Alina laughed despite herself, grateful for Hessa's lightness, even if only for a moment.

'Do *you* think we should worry?' she asked, more seriously this time.

Hessa lifted a single shoulder in that way Alina had grown to adore. She never shrugged like others did, never both shoulders, only the right, as though the full gesture was too extravagant.

'We're far,' she said simply.

'But not far enough,' Alina muttered, her appetite slipping away. Her voice was quiet, almost carried off by the desert breeze. 'There could already be witches in Madari.'

Hessa didn't deny it.

'It's a possibility,' she said. 'And that is why we'll check.'

Something lingered behind Hessa's gaze, some quiet worry unspoken, but Alina knew better than to press. They had grown attuned to each other in the way only those who share silence can: understanding when to offer space, when to reach for closeness. When tears needed to fall without explanation, or when footsteps through sand were the only balm for a restless mind. They had learnt to read one another like shifting dunes— wordless, intuitive, instinctual.

Alina cherished their evenings most of all, those long, meandering walks beneath the stars, fingers interlaced, laughter like a shared secret echoing into the cooling dusk. The world felt distant, paused, as though even time held its breath and left them in peace.

'You're biting your nails again,' Hessa said, spitting out a small bone from her meal.

Alina glanced down and quickly tucked her hands beneath her thighs. 'It's nothing.'

'Nothing is never nothing,' Hessa replied softly, her white eyes shimmering with quiet concern. 'Something troubles you, amira.'

Alina exhaled slowly, the weight in her chest refusing to shift.

'Waa airan sa nada. Sala silan,' she whispered, drawing up her karash to cover her mouth, her voice now veiled beneath its fabric. She didn't want curious ears catching fragments of their conversation. Hessa noted the gesture and frowned. *We have heard nothing. Only silence.*

'Has dat sa bana, silan na?' Hessa asked gently. *Is that not a good thing, silence?*

'Tsa,' Alina replied, clicking her tongue before lifting her chin in that sharp desert movement of disapproval. 'Alghai has khata. Khan santir.' *Something is wrong. I can feel it.*

Without hesitation, Hessa reached for Alina's hand and pulled it from its hiding place. She brought it to her lips and kissed each fingertip, despite Alina's protests. Despite the bitten skin and raw edges.

'They're a mess,' Alina said, embarrassed. 'It's revolting.'

Hessa paid her no mind, she never did when Alina spoke harshly of herself.

'It will be fine, amira,' she whispered, pressing a kiss to the centre of Alina's palm. 'We have each other, remember?'

Alina swallowed, her breath catching as tawny eyes lingered on Hessa's lips, lips that pressed soft, deliberate kisses against her hand, awakening something that pulsed through every corner of her body. Her belly fluttered and twisted, heat blooming beneath her skin as forbidden thoughts surged forward. Of Hessa kissing her elsewhere, of warmth and want unfurling in places Alina had never dared let her mind dwell.

She shook the thought away, trying to will her body into stillness, into silence.

But it was becoming harder with each passing day.

The nights, especially, were a torment she couldn't escape. When Hessa climbed into their shared bed barely clothed, the gauzy fabric of her sleep dress clinging to the gentle curve of her waist, Alina's breath would catch. Her eyes would betray her. And long after Hessa had fallen asleep, Alina would lie wide-eyed and aching, imagining what it might feel like to roll over, to close the distance between them. To press her mouth to Hessa's. To let her hands explore the unfamiliar contours of a woman's body. Hessa's body.

And to be explored in return.

The longing coiled itself around her like a silken thread, one she both dreaded and desired to unravel.

The thoughts scorched her with guilt.

In drakonian lands, women were not permitted to share beds with other women, not openly. Alina knew, of course, that many did. But always in secret. Always in shadows. It was forbidden, had always been forbidden. The mere whisper of such desires could unravel a life.

Even as a young girl, Alina had noticed how her attention lingered on boys, yes, but also on girls. Her curiosity, her quiet admiration, had wandered between both. And often she had wondered. Was it possible to long for both? To desire softness and strength in equal measure?

But the threat of discovery, of punishment, had taught her to bury such questions deep beneath duty and fear.

Then, at fifteen, Hagan had entered the periphery of her thoughts, and slowly, deliberately, consumed them.

No. That wasn't quite the truth.

She had first begun to notice the other girls. Friends at court. The way one would tilt her head when she laughed, the brush of fingers during a shared secret, the warmth of a glance that lingered too long. Her heart had started to whisper truths she couldn't yet name.

And Hagan had seen it.

He had *known.*

With honeyed words and calculated affection, he had drawn her in. Distracted her. Redirected her gaze. She could still hear his voice, low and coaxing, warning her to be careful, to mind how she looked at them.

He had known what stirred within her.

And so he made her believe she was mistaken. That her feelings were a confusion. That what she truly wanted, what she ought to want, was him.

Alina's stomach twisted at the weight of memory, of him. Of the way he had touched her, the things they had done in secret, too young and too desperate to understand what love truly meant. She had loved him. And he had ruined her. Not just her heart, but her body, her trust, her very sense of self. He had broken her in ways she was only just beginning to piece together.

'What are you thinking, amira?' came the soft voice beside her.

Alina's attention drifted again, unbidden, to Hessa's lips, lips she had dreamt of tasting, of pressing to her own in the quiet hush of night. But she didn't dare. Some rules, no matter how far one travelled, could not be undone so easily. She was still drakonian, through and through. No matter how many desert robes she donned, or how fluently she spoke the tongue of the dunes, her blood still burnt with fire and pride.

And yet...

'Nada,' she said with a wistful smile. 'Sala nar i sandhii.'

Nothing. Only fire and sand.

...

'Tighter,' Hessa instructed, nodding towards the knot Alina was struggling to secure. The laughter that rose from nearby was quickly swallowed by the desert wind, though not before it reached Alina's ears. She resisted the urge to scowl. Dunayan children learnt to tie flawless knots by the age of five. Artful, intricate things that could hold steady against wind, beast, or blade. Alina, by comparison, had only just learnt the difference between a loop and a hitch.

Still, she persisted.

'Why do you all learn to tie knots?' she asked once she caught up to Hessa, who was weaving through the lines, checking each tie with swift, practised precision.

'You'll see,' came the cryptic reply.

Alina didn't care for the glint that danced in Hessa's pale eyes. Sharp with mischief, edged with something perilously close to danger. That look always meant trouble. It meant either Alina would find herself doing something she loathed, or worse, something that would make her question her own survival.

They pressed on across the sand, the heat rising in waves around them, until the golden expanse began to shift, stone interrupting the softness of the dunes.

It took nearly six hours to reach the edge of the mountain range. Alina could hardly believe her eyes as the towering rocks rose from the heart of the desert like a secret long buried. The dunes had slowly thinned as they'd approached, but even so, the sight of such jagged peaks thrust into the sky felt jarringly out of place.

A kingdom of stone, hidden within a kingdom of sand.

'Madari lies on the other side,' Hessa explained, suddenly at Alina's back, her breath brushing the nape of Alina's neck with a warmth that sent an involuntary shiver through her.

Alina cast a wary glance at the length of rope secured tightly around her chest.

'I'm guessing the rope is for...'

'Trapari,' Hessa replied with a knowing smile, miming the upward motion of climbing.

'Of course it is.' Alina sighed, eyes drifting towards the jagged slope before them. 'I'm going to fall and break my neck.'

Hessa clicked her tongue in disapproval. 'Don't say such things. You'll summon the Sanduandai.'

Alina bit her lip to keep from laughing, the corners of her mouth betraying her. The desert folk were deeply superstitious, believers in ancient stories woven from heat and myth. And after her encounter with the ghula, Alina had found herself less inclined to dismiss such tales outright. Still, the Sanduandai stretched even her imagination.

Tiny desert goblins, they were said to be, with wicked senses of humour and a taste for misery. If one complained too loudly, lamented too often, they would come. Not to console, but to curse.

Say aloud that illness is near, and they would hear, and strike you down with fever by nightfall. Bemoan your dwindling water, and they would scurry from the sands to steal what remained, leaving your lips cracked and your throat dry as bone.

It was absurd.

And yet... a small part of her wondered.

Hessa moved ahead, making her way to Saren's side with the easy grace of someone born to command the sands. Alina's eyes followed, not for the first time. She couldn't help but notice the way Saren's fingers brushed Hessa's arm. Light, casual, but lingering a beat too long. Each time, Alina turned away, cheeks flushed with heat not born of the sun, ashamed to have been caught watching.

Yet the hollow ache inside her deepened with every stolen glance. She kept whispering to herself that it meant nothing. That she was imagining it. But it grew harder to believe the lie when even her hands trembled from the sharp sting of jealousy.

When she reached the rocky base of the wall, Alina halted, drawing in a slow, steady breath. Hessa was already at her side again, murmuring the lessons she had repeated countless times during their journey. Advice, guidance and reassurance. But theory was nothing compared to reality. The wall loomed above her, impossibly vast, its shadow swallowing the sand below. There was nothing simple in what was being asked of them.

Thankfully, Alina had overheard that some of the younger Dunayans had never climbed it either. This would be their first attempt, too. At least she wouldn't be alone in her inexperience. Yet that small comfort came with the sting of realisation. Hessa's focus would be scattered now, her attention divided between those girls.

'I can do this,' Alina whispered under her breath.

Saren, who had appeared beside her unnoticed, gave a soft chuckle and nudged Alina's elbow gently with her own. 'I will guide you, farahi,' she said with surprising warmth.

Alina nodded, the tightness in her chest easing just a little.

They had each been handed a small axe, their lifeline. The method was simple in theory: wedge the blade into the rock, loop the rope tightly around it, and pull themselves upward. But the moment of danger came when they had to retrieve the axe and climb higher. Many girls had lost their footing then, their ropes no longer anchored. The fall could be fatal.

'Don't think, farahi,' Saren said, her eyes already on the wall. 'Follow me.'

Alina leaned back for the briefest moment, just enough to catch sight of Hessa a few feet away, her voice calm and steady as she guided the younger girls. The more seasoned Dunayans had been tasked with watching over the less experienced, and many had already begun their ascent, moving with practised ease along the rocky face.

'Do not be afraid,' Saren said, her voice a quiet anchor as her axe struck firm into the stone. She looped her rope with precision, movements fluid and sure.

Alina's eyes drifted back to Hessa, just in time to meet her gaze. That glance, filled with quiet encouragement, wrapped around her like a silken thread. It was enough. Enough to make her feel bold, unstoppable. Even if Hessa wasn't at her side, she was never truly far.

'Sa miada,' Alina whispered, her voice resolute as she wedged her own axe into the rock, just beside Saren's, not beneath it.

The Dunayan raised an amused brow, lips curling into the ghost of a smile. But there was something else beneath that expression, something unreadable that caught Alina off guard. She wasn't quite sure how it made her feel.

I am not afraid.

And with that thought pulsing through her veins, Alina began to climb.

Chapter Forty-Four

House of Sand
Desert Kingdom

In the desert, you must be aware of everything.
Because everything will try to kill you.

Tabitha Wysteria

They had begun the climb while the sun still held high court in the sky, its golden light casting sharp shadows and lending just enough warmth to the stone. It was deliberate timing, bright enough to see where each axe met rock, where each rope must be tied. Heat was no enemy to the desert folk, nor to the drakonians. But the night, with its cruel chill, would not spare those caught halfway to the summit when the sun slipped away. They had to reach the top before dusk, before the cold could claim them.

Alina did not dare glance down.

She focused on the rhythm of her breathing, the sting of her muscles, the solidity of her grip. Saren climbed alongside her, adjusting her pace to Alina's and pausing whenever needed. A quiet guardian. Alina fought the urge to glance below, to search the line of Dunayans for a familiar crown of dark curls and desert bronze skin.

'Do not get distracted,' Saren said sharply, her voice cutting through the silence like a blade.

'I'm not,' Alina replied, a little too quickly.

Saren laughed under her breath. 'If you say so.'

Frustration pricked at Alina's nerves, and she bit down on her lower lip to keep from snapping.

'Hessa has always had a fondness for shiny new things,' Saren said, casually, yet her words made Alina falter. 'I wouldn't grow too attached.'

Alina's fingers tightened around the rock. 'I don't understand what you mean.'

'Yes, you do.' Saren drove her axe into the wall above, quick and clean, wrapping her rope around the handle before pulling herself up with effortless grace. She turned, waiting with unsettling patience.

'Hessa is a good friend,' Alina said quietly, defensively.

'Sure.' Saren shrugged, or the closest thing to it one could manage while dangling from a mountainside. 'I thought the same once.'

Alina's grip slipped slightly in her surprise, but before panic could set in, Saren's foot pressed against Alina's side, steadying her back against the rock.

'You and Hessa...' Alina breathed.

'It was a long time ago,' Saren replied, eyes drifting away, a shadow of old hurt shining through their pale light.

'What happened?'

'She's curious by nature,' Saren muttered. 'But she bores easily. I see the way she looks at you, and I believe she cares. But when someone else catches her eye...' She trailed off.

'We're not...' Alina swallowed. 'We've never... not like that.'

Saren raised an eyebrow, visibly surprised. 'Why not?'

'Because I'm not interested,' Alina said quickly, too quickly.

The words hung false in the air between them. Even she could hear the crack in her voice, and Saren heard it too. 'In my land, women don't... lie with women,' she added, more quietly.

Saren rolled her eyes. 'What a stupid place.'

'Perhaps,' Alina said, pulling herself higher, breath shallow. 'But I—'

'This is no longer your land, farahi,' Saren cut in, firm and unyielding. 'Here, you may do whatever pleases you. If you wish to lie with Hessa, then do it. Before someone else does. She won't wait forever.'

'Hessa would never!' The words burst from Alina's mouth, fierce and too loud, and her hand nearly slipped in the flurry of embarrassment that followed. She reached to cover her lips but lost her balance, only for Saren's foot to pin her firmly back against the wall once more.

'Karafa,' Saren warned through gritted teeth. *Careful.*

'Sorry,' Alina whispered, her face burning with heat that had nothing to do with the sun.

Was she being foolish? Was everyone else simply seeing something she had spent far too long denying? Or perhaps she had seen it, felt it, time and time again, only to bury it deep within the furthest, shadowed corners of her mind where she believed it could no longer reach her.

For weeks now, she had begun to crave Hessa's touch. At night, she would edge closer beneath the blankets, where once she had kept a polite distance, spine stiff with propriety. Now, without fail, the moment Hessa slipped into their bed, Alina felt heat coil low between her legs. Sometimes it was the press of skilled fingers massaging her weary shoulders; other times, the soft brush of lips against her back. Gentle and reverent, as though each kiss were a prayer.

She had told herself, again and again, that it meant nothing.

That this was just the way of the desert folk, warm and openly affectionate. She'd watched the others and noted the ease with which they touched, the laughter in their embraces. What she and Hessa shared was no different.

And yet... it was.

Hessa touched her differently. She held her longer. When her lips found Alina's forehead or her hands, there was something fierce and unspoken in the gleam of those white eyes. A quiet yearning that danced just beneath the surface, waiting. Waiting for permission. For a sign. For Alina to reach back.

But that permission had never come.

Instead, Alina would flush crimson, shyly looking away. She'd murmur something awkward or bury her face into the covers, and Hessa, gracious as always, would let the moment pass. She never pressed, never pushed. She simply smiled and stayed close. She continued to offer affection, not out of expectation, but because she understood that Alina needed it.

And perhaps, just as deeply, because she needed it too.

Alina knew then that whatever existed between them, it was not born of impatience or possession. Their affection was quiet, and slow-burning. A sacred thing. Something beautiful.

Something gentle enough to wait.

Wishing to steer the conversation elsewhere, Alina asked, 'How do Dunayans choose their leader?'

'One must earn it,' Saren replied simply.

'How?'

A glint of mischief danced in Saren's eye. 'By defeating the current one.'

'Death?' The word caught in Alina's throat, brittle and cold. A chill passed over her at the thought that Hessa might have slain one of her own for the sake of power. Her body went still until Saren shook her head.

'Not necessarily. On rare occasions, a duel may lead to death, but that is never the aim. More often than not, a challenger steps forward and both are submitted to a series of trials. The trials can last for months. It becomes an event across the entire desert. Songs are sung, wagers placed and stories spun. And not only the leader and challenger compete. Many Dunayans enter for the honour, the chance. But only one emerges victorious.'

Saren drew her axe from the rock and drove it higher into the wall with a swift, sure motion. 'More often, though, a leader will step aside, having already chosen their successor. When that happens, it is a celebration. A peaceful passing of leadership.'

'Is that how Hessa became leader?' Alina asked, her voice soft with hope.

Saren shook her head. 'No. Hessa faced the trials.'

'And she won.' Alina breathed the words with reverence, not out of disbelief, but in quiet awe, pride blooming in her chest like a desert rose.

'In truth,' Saren said with a faint smile, 'she did not.'

'What?'

'It was her sister, Sahira, who won. She had only joined to be near Hessa, to keep her safe. But she bested them all, almost by accident. When the time came to claim the mantle of leadership, she turned it down.'

Alina's jaw slackened, her astonishment written plainly across her face.

'Did you take part?' she asked once the silence between them had stretched long enough to settle her thoughts. They had climbed a little higher, the sky beginning to shift into the hues of a setting sun, painting the rocks in gold and shadow.

Saren gave a small nod, her lips pressed into a thin line. She offered no details, and by the way her shoulders tensed, Alina understood instinctively that it was not a subject the Dunayan wished to dwell on. The reason remained veiled, perhaps a painful memory, perhaps unspoken regret. Alina had long since learnt that Dunayans, for all their boldness and jest, held their deepest feelings in guarded silence. She had watched them spar and laugh and tease with relentless vigour, turning even chores into challenges, everything a game to be won.

So when Saren spoke again, her voice low and cutting through the quiet like a sudden wind across the dunes, Alina was unprepared.

'Hessa won't be leader much longer.'

Alina blinked, frowning as she reached for a better grip on the warm stone. 'What do you mean?'

'No one has brought a foreigner into our ranks since the Great War,' Saren said, not unkindly, but with a calm certainty that made the words bite. 'Dunayans were forged in solitude, born of sand, sacred and apart. But Hessa... Hessa has always followed her own path, whether or not the winds favoured her. Some believe she should never have worn both crowns, leader and princess. They say those roles were never meant to be one and the same.'

Alina swallowed, the ache in her arms forgotten for a moment. 'And you?' she asked, her voice quiet but firm. 'Do you believe that?'

They had both come to a standstill on the rock face, the muscles in their limbs straining, the ropes pulled taut with the weight of more than just their bodies. The silence between them was no longer companionable. It was heavy, expectant, like the stillness before a storm.

Alina had always known that Hessa would rouse unrest by bringing her into the fold, by trying to usher her into the sacred ranks of the Dunayans. And Alina...Alina had not stopped her. Selfishly, hungrily, she had yearned to belong, to be carved from the same stone as the desert warriors. She needed to learn, yes, but she might have learnt quietly, on the fringes. Instead, she had chosen the centre. Her craving to be one of them had brought weight upon Hessa's shoulders. Had the others whispered behind her back? Had they flung their barbed words at Hessa while she stood silent, shouldering every wound alone?

'Is someone planning to challenge her?' Alina pressed, the chill of dread creeping into her limbs. Her hands shook now, not from the climb, but from the fear blooming like a storm in her chest. 'Someone needs to warn her.'

A shimmer of amusement passed through Saren's eyes, darkening her features into something sharp and unreadable. The shift in her expression made Alina tense instinctively, her neck stiffening as a primal unease clawed its way into her.

'Saren...' Alina's voice trembled as the Dunayan pressed her foot against Alina's back, pinning her mercilessly against the sun-warmed rock. She was stronger than she looked, strong enough to hold Alina in place with frightening ease.

'Did you truly believe we would accept you?' Saren purred, her tone cruelly sweet. From the hidden folds of her sleeve, a glint of silver flashed. A dagger, small and wicked. 'You're drakonian. *Farahi*. You will never be one of us. And Hessa will learn the price of her selfishness.'

Before Alina could cry out, before her thoughts could even fully form, Saren had cut the rope with one fluid sweep of her blade. The tension in the cord snapped, and Alina was suddenly holding herself against the wall with nothing but desperate hands and sheer will.

'Don't, please—'

But Saren had already moved. Her fingers closed around

Alina's arm, and with terrifying precision, she pulled.

The wall was gone.

Alina was gone.

No scream escaped her throat as the world spun and tumbled beneath her. The shock robbed her of sound, of thought, of breath. Her body was falling, falling, falling, and all she could do was close her eyes and surrender to it.

She did not thrash. She did not panic.

Death, she thought, would embrace her gently like an old friend come to take her home. A final kindness after so much pain.

And so Alina fell, a serene smile curving her lips as the wind roared in her ears and the world rose up to meet her.

Chapter Forty-Five

House of Shadows
Kingdom of Darkness

There is a rose with black petals that grows in the Kingdom of Darkness. They call it Nightrose. But what they don't realise is that it's one of the most poisonous flowers in existence. It has no effect on wyverians whatsoever. But for the rest of us... it would mean almost instant death.

Tabitha Wysteria

Ash had passed the weeks in a contemplative hush, lingering on the fringes of the wyverian camp like a phantom of fire and shadow. While the soldiers paced like caged wolves, their unease at Kai's absence twisted into barely restrained impatience, Ash remained still. Ever silent and ever watchful.

They wanted blood. Vengeance stirred in their veins like smoke in the lungs, and they feared it might dissipate with the morning breeze if they waited too long. But Ash, perched outside the tent beneath the silvered canopy of strange wyverian trees, merely watched the branches sway in an otherworldly calm, as if untouched by war or worry.

Each day, Kai's closest companions approached him, sometimes in groups, sometimes alone. They asked after their commander. Was he safe? Should they go after him? Was it time to act?

Ash dismissed them with a single gesture, his hand slicing through the air like a blade of wind.

And when they changed their question, when they pleaded to fight, to strike now before resolve soured into doubt, he offered the same cryptic reply, 'Not today.'

Wyverians, for all their courage and might, kept a wary distance from Ash. There were few things that unsettled their kind, but the man with the ancient eyes and the quiet knowing stirred something deep within them, a discomfort they could not name. His presence was like the lull before a storm, his silences louder than most men's cries.

All except for one.

Adriana dropped down beside him on the damp grey grass without a word, mirroring his gaze to the horizon where the trees danced softly in the breeze. She joined him each morning, her presence as steady as the rising sun. And though Ash had told her, more than once, that he preferred to be alone, she never truly believed him.

'No one enjoys being alone *that much*,' she'd said with a smirk.

That morning, they watched Cronan and Keir circle the edge of camp, Keir bounding ahead with restless energy, leaping and goading the hulking wyverian beside him to move faster. Ash's lips twitched, though only slightly.

'How about today?' Adriana asked, as she always did, her tone more hope than expectation.

Ash did not answer at once. He closed his eyes, listening. Not to her, but to the world itself. He had long ago surrendered to what he had seen. The path stretched ahead, inevitable as the turning of seasons. He had glimpsed it all in fire and ash, and yet it did not frighten him. For at the heart of it was one person. One soul he would burn the world to protect.

He was about to shake his head, to repeat the daily ritual of refusal, when he paused, his ear catching something in the far distance. A sound barely there, like thunder beneath the soil. The low groan of earth disturbed. A shifting.

Then the rumble grew.

Ash's grin was slow, stretching across his face like a secret finally revealed.

He knew that sound.

It had begun.

'Today,' he whispered.

Adriana gasped beside him, her breath catching like a match struck in the dark.

It did not take long for the camp to still. One by one, heads turned, breath hitched, and every sound fell away at the sight of the figure emerging from the shadowed veil of the trees.

A creature unlike any other. One of their own, and yet, something altogether different.

Ash felt the collective gasp ripple through the wyverians like wind through dry grass. There, striding barefoot across the forest floor, came their princess. Her purple eyes, alight with fire, locked on the world ahead like a blade drawn from its sheath. She moved like a predator. Graceful, alert, and brimming with intent.

But the moment her eyes found him, something within her softened. That sharp edge dulled, and another emotion broke through the surface like sunlight through cloud.

Relief.

She no longer walked, she ran. Abandoning all warrior poise, she crossed the distance between them with the urgency of a storm. And Ash, who had counted the minutes of her absence like a man stranded at sea waiting for the tide, opened his arms.

The moment she collided with him, he held her tightly, fiercely, as though she might vanish again if he didn't. He breathed her in—earth, smoke, wind. The scent of wild things and untamed skies.

'You're b-back,' he breathed, voice cracking.

'I found my way back to you,' she whispered, her smile radiant, joy gleaming in her eyes like starlight caught in water.

He cradled her face, tracing the contours as if reacquainting himself with a sacred map. She was changed—fiercer, freer, somehow even more breathtaking than he remembered.

'I missed you.'

And she smiled, truly smiled. That rare, unguarded smile that belonged only to a chosen few. His heart swelled, his chest aching with the kind of pride and wonder only love could summon. He drew her into him once more, clutching her with reverence.

But then, he felt her body stiffen.

He loosened his embrace, stepping back just enough to see her eyes. No longer soft, but wide with recognition. Her stare was fixed beyond his shoulder, and when he turned, he found Adriana standing there, watching quietly.

Of course.

It had been months since Mal and Adriana had seen one another. But the tension that coiled in Mal's spine was not born of distance or time. No, Ash knew the reason. Adriana had once been Haven Blackburn's closest friend.

Mal didn't speak. Her breath came shallow and fast, her attention caught somewhere between memory and grief. Ash kept his hand gently at her back, grounding her, reminding her she was not alone. Tears welled in her eyes, silent as falling ash.

'I'm sorry,' Adriana whispered, tears clinging to her lashes like dew on a winter bough.

In an instant, the two women collapsed into one another's arms, their sobs mingling in the hush of the camp. Ash stepped back, giving them the quiet dignity of space. He might have slipped away entirely, leaving them the solace of shared grief but Mal, with a swift shake of her head, stopped him. There was too much to say. Too much that could no longer be left unsaid. She would sit with Adriana come nightfall. For now, there were more urgent matters at hand.

Ash led her into the central tent, the one they used for council. She entered with quiet assurance, not needing to be told where to sit. He watched, unable to keep the smile from his lips, as she strode to the head of the table and draped her long limbs over the armrests, as though she had always belonged there. Because she had.

Adriana darted off to gather the others.

Ash took a seat opposite her.

'Why so far away?' she asked, her brow arching slightly, her displeasure evident in the subtle tilt of her voice.

'So I can see your face,' he replied, his voice soft, almost reverent.

Mal blew a stray lock of ink-dark hair from her cheek, the gesture so instinctively her that he let out a low laugh. The sound seemed to ripple through the air, drawing her attention to his lips and for a moment, the world grew quiet again, caught in the tension of that look.

Before anything more could pass between them, Adriana returned, Keir and Cronan close behind. Mal rose to embrace them, her smile radiant, catching the light like a flame in the dark. Ash watched her, storing the image away in some secret chamber of his heart, hoping to carry it with him always.

'Where is Kai?' she asked the moment she sat down, eyes fixed on the entrance to the tent, expectant, waiting for her brother to appear.

The others turned to Ash.

'He will return to us s-soon,' he said calmly, though his words earned a chorus of muttered grumbles. 'He had his own path to walk.'

Mal's eyes narrowed. Not with anger, but with that particular brand of sharp curiosity that always emerged when she suspected she was being told less than the whole truth. He knew the look well. She wouldn't press him here, not before the others. But when they were alone, she would ask and he would answer, as much as he could, without disturbing the threads of fate that still had to weave themselves into place.

'Tomorrow,' Ash said quietly. 'Tomorrow, we enter the wastelands.'

'What about Kai?' Adriana's brow furrowed as her voice cut through the gathering tension.

'He'll be waiting on the other s-side,' Ash replied, his tone steady, though his stammer clung to the edges of his words. 'Once we c-cross and reach my k-kingdom, Kai will meet us there. I intend to use the chaos as a veil, enough of a dis-distraction to reach the Red Guard.'

'Why tomorrow?' asked Keir, lounging with one foot propped on his chair, as though the weight of the conversation did not press upon him.

Ash inclined his head towards Mal.

'Because of her.'

All eyes shifted to the wyverian princess, confusion knitting brows across the room.

'Because now,' Ash said softly, 'she knows what sh-she is.'

Mal's jaw tightened. Something danced in her eyes, an emotion too complex to name, too fierce to be shared. Ash's smile curved with quiet certainty as the others rose to leave, heading out to make ready for what lay ahead.

Mal remained, reclining in the high-backed blackwood chair, her expression sharpened by frustration.

'I didn't learn what I was supposed to,' she muttered, her voice coloured with self-disgust. 'I can't do anything, Ash. Whatever it is you saw... I'm not ready. All I've done is argue with gods and wander through half-truths. I've gained nothing of use in this fight.' She let out a bitter laugh. 'And if I'm to master magic, I need a witch to teach me.'

'I know,' he said calmly.

Her focus lifted, wary.

'You'll have one,' Ash said, a glimmer of amusement tugging at the corner of his lips. 'Vera's sister. Allegra.'

'Allegra?' Mal's voice rose in disbelief.

Ash nodded, reaching for one of the many goblets strewn across the table. He sipped the wine and grimaced as the bitterness curled across his tongue.

'But my powers,' she pressed, 'they're not even needed for this, are they?'

'Not for this ba-battle,' Ash agreed, his golden eyes fixed on the dark liquid in his cup.

Mal hesitated, then asked in a low murmur, 'There will be others, won't there?'

Ash's nod was slow and grave.

Her voice grew softer still, laced with something he had never heard from her before. Fear. 'It won't be against witches, will it?'

That simple question held the weight of a hundred truths. Ash looked up at her then, meeting the uncertainty in those purple eyes, eyes that until now had never known how to tremble.

'No,' he said gently. 'It won't.'

Mal nodded, her teeth sinking into her bottom lip.

Ash's voice turned to a whisper, edged with darkness. 'What we face next... will be far worse.'

...

'Did you know?' Mal asked the moment he ushered her into the tent he'd been assigned. It was modest in size, but someone had seen fit to arrange a double bed within. Ash no longer cared for such luxuries. Yet, now that Mal stood beside him once more, he was quietly grateful he hadn't turned such comforts away.

'Did you know what my father was planning that day? What the dress was for?'

Ash made his way to the armchair tucked in the far corner, sinking into its worn embrace. He tilted his head back, eyes sliding shut. Whether the ache behind his eyes stemmed from the sheer weight of her return, or from the maddening flood of knowledge that constantly surged through his mind, he could not tell. At times the pain was so sharp, it blurred his vision entirely.

He felt her movement before he saw it. Mal climbed into his lap without a word, resting her head against his chest, arms looping around his neck like a lifeline. His hand found her thigh, brushing gently along the softness of her skin, a touch that brought with it a sense of fragile peace.

'I knew,' he replied.

Her reaction was immediate. A sharp intake of breath, then the sudden withdrawal of her warmth as she pulled away.

'You knew?' she hissed. Anger crackled in her eyes. 'You could have warned me, Ash! I walked straight into it. You knew what my father intended, what the dress was for and you said *nothing!*'

'I th-thought…' His voice faltered with its usual stammer, but there was conviction behind the words. 'I thought it would m-make it easier f-for you.'

'Easier?' Her laugh was cold, bitter as frost. 'You know, then. About the curse. The one between Hades and Hecate. The one they passed down to *me,* their daughter.'

Ash inclined his head.

'And still, you let me go with *him.* Knowing he meant to marry me off, to try and force me to love someone else.'

'I did.'

'Why?' Her voice cracked as she folded her arms across her chest, staring down at him, bewildered and bruised by his betrayal. 'Do you not love me anymore?'

Ash chuckled. A rich, disbelieving sound that rolled from his chest like thunder in a quiet valley. He stood, crossing the space between them in two strides, and took her face in his hands.

'Not love you?' he whispered, a soft, incredulous smile curling his lips. He leaned in, laughter still trembling in his throat. 'Mal, I could never not love you.'

Mal turned her face away, but she didn't retreat from his touch. 'Do you love me only because of the curse?' she asked quietly. 'Is it twisting your will, shaping your feelings into something that isn't truly yours?'

Ash's jaw clenched, the question striking deeper than she could know.

'I can't say for cer-certain,' he admitted. 'But does it t-truly matter? Loving you was written in my stars. It was my f-fate.'

'And what of mine, Ash?' Her hands slid over his, her eyes searching his face with a desperate tenderness. She wanted the truth, longed for it, even if it fractured her world. Even if it shattered hers and his.

'Yours is to save us,' he said softly, the words heavy with sorrow.

'Perhaps I don't want any of it,' she breathed, her shoulders folding under the weight of it all. 'Perhaps all I want is to vanish. Just us, gone from this world.'

'We could… for a while,' Ash said.

As night fell like a velvet curtain across the encampment, the two of them disappeared into the sky, rising on the backs of their great winged beasts.

Mal patted Nyx's scaled neck, the familiar feel grounding her as the wyvern beat her mighty wings, slicing through the clouds with elegant power. Ash flew ahead on Ayaru, guiding the others with ease, ever the leader, ever the light she chased. Daku and Nisha trailed behind, two shadows in the starlit heavens.

They soared over the wyverian castle, its towers carved into the very bones of the mountain. Ash took his time to study his wife as she soared through the skies astride her wyvern, her black hair streaming behind her like a banner, wild and untamed. A smile tugged at his lips at the sight of her laughter, her eyes alight with a happiness so fierce, so unburdened, it cleaved something deep within him. Her wyvern dipped low, and she whooped with delight, fearless, radiant, a queen of the winds.

Ash seared the image into his memory, knowing with a hollow certainty that he might never witness her like this again. His whole life had been a slow, silent march towards a crown. He had learnt early that silence pleased kings; that obedience, not voice, would keep him alive. His father's clipped reprimands had taught him to hold his tongue until speaking itself became a labour, an unbearable weight.

But Mal, Mal had shattered those chains. She had looked at

him, and for the first time, he had felt strong, not in what he could do, but in simply being. And then, then the truth had come, cruel and cold: he was not free. He was a weapon shaped by fate, forged to torment the woman he adored, bound to her by a curse that made their love a prison.

And yet, selfish creature that he was, he did not care. The curse stripped them of everything but each other, and Ash clung to it with desperate, furious hands. Still, in the quiet corners of his soul, a whisper gnawed at him.

If not for the curse... would she have loved him like this?

Would they still find each other in the dark?

By the time they returned, the wyverns had grown noticeably calmer, soothed by the presence of one of their royals. Ash and Adriana had taken turns riding them in an effort to ease their restlessness, but none of their efforts had truly worked. Not since all the wyverian royals had departed.

'They respond well to you,' Mal observed, pausing to bid farewell to each beast, her hand brushing against their scaled hides with a reverence that made Ash's heart ache. She murmured softly to them, secret words he could not hear from where he stood waiting.

'I've always had a way with wild things,' he replied.

She glanced over her shoulder, catching the deeper meaning behind his words. She had always been wild to him. Untamed and elemental, and he had loved her all the more for it.

'Where is my father?' Mal asked, clearing her throat as they made their way back towards the tent.

'Travelling between the ci-cities, gathering support where he can,' Ash explained. 'Each day, more sol-soldiers arrive thanks to his efforts.'

Mal nodded, thoughtful.

Once inside the tent, she sank into the armchair with

effortless grace. Ash lingered awkwardly by the entrance, suddenly uncertain of where to place himself. He hadn't expected her to sit at all, least of all there, across the room rather than drawing close.

'It's still strange, seeing you dressed in wyverian garb,' she said, gesturing with her chin at his black leather trousers, loose black shirt, and well-worn boots. The garments suited him now, though at first they had felt foreign on his frame. In truth, Ash had stopped thinking about it weeks ago. It no longer mattered.

'Shall I take them off, then?' he teased.

The way her cheeks flushed was utterly bewitching. A dusky darkness bloomed beneath her pale skin, and Ash couldn't stop the smile that tugged at his mouth. It was a quiet fascination, the way a handful of words could unravel her poise so completely. He found himself wanting to spend eternity whispering such things into her ear, just to witness how beautifully her body reacted in response.

Ash did not linger for her response. In one fluid motion, he pulled his shirt over his head and crossed the room with quiet purpose, lowering himself to the ground before her. Her purple eyes widened, just a fraction, as he gently parted her knees, his focus never straying from hers, as though memorising every shift of reaction.

His hands came to rest on her ankles, reverent and slow, before they began their journey upward, gliding over the soft coolness of her skin, disappearing beneath the folds of her slate-grey dress.

'Ash...' she whispered, breath catching on the syllable.

But he did not stop.

His touch wandered with teasing precision, until his fingers found the tender skin of her thighs and coaxed her closer, drawing her to the very edge of the chair, until there was no space left between wanting and having. His hands cradled her hips, grounding her as he leaned forward.

The moment his mouth met her, her entire body arched in response, a shudder of pleasure escaping her lips. Her head fell back, and her nails curled into the fabric of the armrests, clutching them as though they were the only things keeping her tethered to the earth.

Ash, beneath her, trembled with devotion. Every breath, every motion, a vow made not in words but in touch.

Within seconds, her fingers found his golden hair, tangling through the silken strands as she pulled him closer, guiding him with a hunger both primal and precise. Her breath caught, rising into a cry as he slipped two fingers inside her, moving with a rhythm he had learnt through tender study, each motion designed to unravel her completely.

She cried out his name, a broken hymn that echoed between them.

Ash did not hesitate. In one seamless motion, he gathered her into his arms, lifting her from the chair and carrying her to the bed with the reverence of a man cradling something sacred. He drew the dress over her head, and for a breathless moment, he simply stared, drinking in the sight of the wyverian princess stretched out beneath him, bare and luminous, waiting for him with fire in her eyes and moonlight on her skin.

A slow, adoring smile curved his lips as he shed the last of his clothing and joined her, the space between them dissolving like mist at dawn.

Mal slipped her arms around him, and before Ash could utter a single word, she rose to meet him, her lips pressing against his in a kiss that stole the very breath from his lungs. The moment their mouths met, the world tilted, and he was lost, spinning through fragments of memory and feeling, all of which crashed back into him with searing clarity.

Her tongue brushed his, and in that instant, colour flooded back into a world that had dulled in her absence. His hands found their familiar path over her skin, relearning her contours with a reverence born of longing. Her nails bit into his flesh, marking him, anchoring him in a moment that was both fierce and tender.

They did not think of curses or kingdoms, of battles yet to be waged or blood already lost. They did not pause to consider whether what they felt had been theirs to begin with, or whether it had been woven into their hearts by the threads of a curse. The thought that their love might not be real at all, but an illusion cast upon them by fate's cruel whim, never quite crossed their minds.

Tonight, Ash would give her the sky and silence the stars, if only for a fleeting hour. By dawn, they would walk into the wastelands, and fate would stir once more. But for now, she was his, and he would make her forget the weight of the world.

'Don't think,' Mal murmured, her voice low and steady, the sound of command cloaked in velvet. The moment she felt the tension ripple through his body, she reached for him with quiet certainty.

Ash obeyed, swallowing the weight of worry that had crept into his chest.

'I missed you,' he breathed against the shell of her ear, his voice barely a whisper lost between them.

'Me too,' she replied, a ghost of a smile brushing her lips.

'How much?' he asked, not teasing, but yearning.

A spark ignited in her gaze, something wild and wicked and wholly his. Without a word, she slipped her hand beneath the veil of space between them and took hold of his length with a touch that was both knowing and merciless. Her fingers moved with deliberate care, each motion drawing a gasp from his lips, each breath a confession of pleasure. The rhythm she set was exquisite, slow and assured, until Ash could do nothing but surrender to the storm she conjured with every measured stroke.

'Mal...'

'Hush now, husband.' Her voice was soft, coaxing, as she guided him down onto his back with the reverence of a queen claiming her throne. She resumed the rhythm of her touch, every motion deliberate, every brush of her fingers a promise.

With a wicked gleam in her purple eyes, she took his hand and guided it between her thighs, placing his fingers where she needed him most. Together, they moved, an intimate dance of skin and breath and want, moans escaping into the quiet, laced with reverence and fire.

'If you k-keep this up...' Ash's voice fractured, each word trembling on the edge of restraint as his body tensed beneath her.

'Yes?' she purred, tilting her head, that sinful smile blooming across her lips, one he'd dreamt of a thousand times.

'Then I'm going to lose it,' he groaned, 'and come all over your hand, Mal.'

That wicked smile only deepened, a siren's grin drenched in mischief, as her hand moved with greater purpose. Ash groaned, the sound low and ragged, his own fingers responding in kind, their pace matching the rising crescendo between them. The moment that shattering pleasure seized him, he didn't pause, didn't think. He caught her by the waist and turned her beneath him, burying himself inside with a single, desperate thrust.

The climax struck like lightning—raw, powerful, consuming. The exquisite grip of her around him was too much, and he came undone with a cry torn from somewhere deep. Mal clung to him, her mouth finding the flesh of his arm, sinking her teeth into him to stifle the sound of her own ecstasy. Her fangs pierced skin as her eyes fluttered shut, while his body moved against hers, chasing every last flicker of pleasure until they were both left trembling and breathless.

'Don't stop,' she breathed, her voice rough with urgency, her hands grasping at him, dragging him deeper into her embrace. Ash's eyes widened, astonished by her need, even as her body still trembled from release. But the sight of her—lips parted, eyes heavy with desire, ignited something feral within him. He did not soften; he did not stop.

'You're mine,' he growled, the words a vow etched into the curve of her skin. His mouth descended with fevered hunger—first to her breast, his teeth grazing her nipple, then up to her earlobe, and finally claiming her lower lip in a kiss laced with possession.

'And you are mine, husband,' she whispered, her voice thick with longing.

'Then come for me again, my queen,' he whispered, each word a prayer on his breath as he drove into her, deeper, harder, the rhythm of his body desperate to match the thunder of his heart. His hands found her thighs, lifting them with reverent strength, tilting her hips so he could bury himself fully, entirely within her. The shift made his control falter, the tight pull of ecstasy curling low in his spine.

'Let me feel you, Mal,' he said, his voice raw, as if her pleasure were the only truth left in the world.

The moment her release claimed her—her mouth parting in a silent cry, her back arching like a bow drawn taut—Ash followed, undone by the sheer beauty of her unraveling beneath him. His climax tore through him with the force of a storm, brought forth by the sight of her face alight with pleasure, a portrait of rapture he had painted with his own hands.

And then she smiled.

It was a smile that shattered him. Soft, adoring and unguarded. A look of such love, such awe, such quiet devotion, as though he were the sun and stars and every sacred thing she'd ever believed in. No one had ever looked at him like that. No one had ever given him something so freely, so fearlessly, and had it returned in kind.

He couldn't fathom a world where he wasn't tethered, heart and soul, to Mal Blackburn.

And yet, perhaps because he knew what loomed ahead, what fate had carved for them both, it made the sight of those beloved purple eyes ache all the more. Knowing what must come. Knowing how easily it could all be lost.

Ash kissed every inch of her skin as though it were sacred scripture, his reverence whispered through each brush of his lips. He worshipped her, body and soul, and claimed her through the long hours of the night. He did not permit sleep to take her, not when he could make her forget the weight of the world, if only for a little while. Not when he could draw his name in cries from her throat, over and over, until it echoed like a hymn within the canvas walls of their tent.

And when at last they collapsed, bodies slick with sweat, hearts still racing, they lay tangled in one another's arms, breathless and sated. Together they watched the crimson moon retreat beyond the horizon, its blood-bright light fading into shadow, as the hush of dawn crept in.

The beginning of the end had come and they faced it in silence, wrapped in each other and in the fragile peace between storms.

Chapter Forty-Six

House of Snow
Kingdom of Ice

There are secrets I can never tell.
  Some that I have even kept from Hadrian.
  They would mean the end of everything.

Tabitha Wysteria

Kage was drawing close to the edge of his kingdom. Bryn's wolf, unwavering and resolute, had carried him across days and near-sleepless nights, pressing on without complaint. In the distance, he could just discern the dark silhouette of a wyverian forest rising against the fading light. The snow had long since melted away, replaced by rugged terrain and sparse patches of stubborn grass. The wolf moved with less ease here, its steps more reluctant, its body less sure. It favoured the cold.

Above them, Spirox soared, gliding just ahead in quiet vigilance. No danger had stirred. No soul had crossed their path throughout the days of travel.

As twilight deepened, Kage dismounted and set about building a fire, his hands moving with familiar precision. Behind him, the wolf and the crow appeared to engage in what resembled a conversation, muttered caws and rumbling huffs exchanged like secrets in the fading light. With a frown, Kage shook his head and returned his focus to the flames. He might have pushed on through the night, but to demand more from Bryn's wolf would have bordered on cruelty. Rest was necessary. Spirox had made that abundantly clear by pecking at Kage's legs until he relented.

Both creatures turned sharply towards something unseen, their focus fixed on a point in the distance. Kage followed their gaze, but saw nothing, only dusk settling over rock and brush. With a huff, he sank down beside the fire, the wolf curling up nearby with a long, satisfied sigh.

The flames danced before his eyes, and Kage let his mind drift, carried on threads of thought he could no longer suppress. He wondered what Bryn was doing. If the wolverian prince missed him.

Of course not. They were barely even friends.

A faint blush crept across his cheeks, which he was quick to attribute to the fire's warmth. It could be nothing else.

He made a silent vow to murder Wren the next time he saw her, wherever that might be. No doubt she was tangled in trouble of her own making, the reckless, cunning thing. Still, he hoped she was safe.

Inevitably, his thoughts turned to his siblings, and a quiet knot of worry settled in his belly, cold and unshakable. It was a small mercy, he supposed, that he hadn't eaten since his departure.

Spirox let out a sharp caw at the very moment the wolf sprang to its feet, a low growl rumbling from its chest, fangs bared in warning.

Kage turned at once, frowning.

'What are *you* doing here?' he asked, blinking rapidly as if to clear away a mirage. But no, she was truly there, the firelight painting soft shadows across her familiar face.

Freya smiled as she approached the flames, extending her hands to warm them, the gesture casual and unhurried.

'Charming greeting, Kage. I missed you too.'

'I thought you'd gone with Wren.' The thought twisted in his gut like a cold knife. 'Is she safe?'

'You really ought not worry so much. She's perfectly fine.'

'Then why are you here?' His voice was quiet but wary, eyes darting about the empty wilderness that surrounded them. Spirox had retreated to a low branch and the wolf slunk a few steps back, unease rippling through the camp. Instinct pulled Kage to his feet, his body taut, every muscle on edge.

'Sit, Kage,' said the valkyrian with a calmness that irked him. She lowered herself by the fire as though it belonged to her, as though the night itself had summoned her. 'If I'd wanted to harm you, you'd be dead already. I've come to make you an offer.'

His gaze sharpened. 'You're not Freya.'

He studied her closely. She looked like Freya. Identical, even. The same lithe strength in her frame, the same tangle of chestnut hair, freckles scattered like stardust across pale skin, the same piercing blue eyes. But there was something off. Something beneath the surface. She bore herself with a weight that Freya had never carried.

She shrugged, the motion careless, almost amused. 'That's a rather fluid truth.'

'What does that mean?'

'Sit, and I'll tell you.'

'I'd prefer not to.'

Another shrug. 'As you like. It makes no difference to me.'

Kage lingered in silence, his dark eyes fixed upon the valkyrian woman, shadowed with suspicion. He could not quite place what it was that unsettled him, only that something intangible had shifted. Where once he had known only indifference, now her presence stirred unease, as though the air around her had thickened with secrets. Something within her had changed, and he felt it in his bones.

'I'm still Freya,' she said softly, her voice a breeze that stirred something old in him. 'The same one you met at the drakonian castle. I have always been her. But this change you sense... it comes because I am no longer cloaking the truth I've hidden from you.'

Kage's brow furrowed, uncertainty tightening his expression.

She went on, her gaze distant, as though reaching through time itself. 'Even though I am Freya... this face I wear, it was not always mine. Once, it belonged to a mortal. A valkyrian. And in time, I became her.'

Kage stilled, the words a puzzle he could not yet piece together. 'What does that mean?' he asked, his voice low.

Freya let out a slow, weary sigh, but gave no reply.

The valkyrian stretched her hands towards the fire, letting the heat seep into her chilled fingers. From the inner lining of the coat she wore—a strange garment for one of her kind, who were more often cloaked in flowing silks or armoured leathers —she retrieved a small bundle wrapped in cloth. Unfolding it with care, she revealed strips of dried meat and began to eat with deliberate slowness.

She did not offer to share. Nor did she flinch at the wolf's low growl, or the sharp caw of the crow flapping restlessly overhead. The presence of a watchful wyverian prince a few paces away left her entirely unmoved, as if the world around her was little more than a breeze stirring through branches.

Once she had finished her modest meal, she turned towards Kage, her lips curving into a soft smile, one far sweeter than any he had ever seen grace Freya's face.

'Do you miss her?' she asked gently, the fire's glow casting a rose hue across her cheeks.

Kage frowned, uncertain of her meaning. 'Wren?'

'No. Not Wren. Your sister.'

He gave a noncommittal shrug. Of course he missed Mal, but not in the way others might. Mal was a force of nature, indomitable and untouchable, and Kage had long understood that her strength required no protection, no fretting. He did not need his siblings constantly near to love them. It was enough to know they lived, to know they thrived. Their joy, their survival, was his peace.

'Not her,' the valkyrian said softly.

Kage stilled.

Not *her*.

And with those two words, the hollow within his chest cracked open. His breath faltered. He did not want to speak of her. Not of the sister whose laughter no longer echoed through castle halls. Not of the one whose absence still pressed heavy against his ribs, day and night.

Haven.

Her face, smiling and radiant, surged to the forefront of his mind and he staggered back a step, as if the memory alone had the power to knock the wind from him.

'Would you like to see her one last time, Kage Blackburn?'

His black eyes widened, pupils flaring with the sharpness of a blade drawn too quickly. 'How...?'

'*How* is not the question,' Freya replied smoothly, brushing the last of the crumbs from her lap as she stood. 'The question is whether you wish to see her one final time.'

'You cannot.'

'I can.' Her voice did not rise in arrogance, only certainty.

'But again, that is not the question.'

A thousand thoughts surged through Kage's mind, each a warning bell sounding in tandem. Perhaps she was no valkyrian at all. Perhaps a witch playing at sentiment, baiting him with grief sharpened into longing. Haven's name alone could carve through his composure like a serrated blade.

He couldn't risk it.

He couldn't...

'Yes,' he breathed. The word slipped from his lips before his logic could catch it, and with it came a tightening of every muscle, as though his body itself braced for regret.

'Very well,' Freya said, turning towards the trees. 'Come along. I will take you to her.'

Kage watched her disappear between branches and shadow. Every part of him screamed against it, instincts thundering with alarm. He should not follow. He must not. This was madness. It reeked of it.

But the mere thought of seeing Haven, of hearing her voice, of whispering all the apologies he had swallowed down since the day they'd lost her, stripped him of all reason. What did it matter if it was a trap? What did it matter if the world collapsed the moment he stepped forward?

He missed her. Gods, he missed her.

He longed to tell her how sorry he was. How empty the world had become without her in it. How his lungs had grown tight from breathing in air that hadn't touched her.

He needed her. Desperately. More than he'd ever dared admit aloud.

So he followed.

Bryn's wolf kept close, its ears flicking with unease. Spirox circled overhead, cawing in warning, feathers ruffling in distress. But Kage hushed them both with a gentle word, a quiet gesture.

No warning could sway him.

He knew what he was walking into.

But if it ended with him dead, well, then at least Haven would no longer be alone. Kai and Mal would have each other. And Kage, at last, would be with his sister once more.

The thought softened something within him.

After several quiet minutes, Kage came to a halt, his steps faltering at the sight of a small cottage nestled incongruously in the clearing. His frown deepened as he glanced around, every instinct in his wyverian blood warning him that something was amiss. But he gave nothing away. The shock coiled within him like smoke in a bottle, trapped behind a mask he refused to let slip.

Wyverians were masters of restraint. And he was no exception.

'What is this?' he asked evenly, his voice low, cool.

Freya stood by the door, her shoulder resting against the frame, her expression unreadable in the half-light. 'It is whatever you wish it to be.'

'And what, precisely, do I wish it to be, Freya?'

Her smile appeared, but the warmth from before had cooled like embers dying in a hearth. 'A reunion.'

Before he could demand further explanation, she opened the door and disappeared inside.

Kage lingered, staring up at the strange little structure. It was small, quaint, almost absurdly so. A red-tiled roof crowned soft orange walls, each window dressed in delicate white shutters that fluttered gently with the breeze. The whole thing looked plucked from a quiet corner of the Kingdom of Fire. Peaceful, inviting, and suspiciously serene.

'Why drakonian?' he asked as he stepped inside, the floor

creaking gently beneath his boots. At the heart of the space stood a round wooden table, polished to a dull gleam. The kitchen was simple, the air warm.

'I rather like them,' Freya replied casually, as though discussing wallpaper.

'So this isn't real.'

'It is whatever you want it to be, Kage. Just because something is only seen by us, doesn't make it unreal, does it?'

He said nothing as he pulled out a chair and sank into it. Freya mirrored him. And so they waited. For what, exactly, he could not say. But he waited nonetheless, his posture still, his expression impassive, as the minutes dripped by like water through a cracked ceiling.

There were no purple eyes. None waiting for him in the shadows. None at all.

'I'm not a witch,' Freya said, breaking the silence.

Kage tilted his head, studying her with fresh wariness. 'Then what are you?'

Her fingers idly scratched at the table's surface, the wood whispering beneath her nails. She didn't answer at once. The question, it seemed, demanded consideration. At last, her lips curved, not with kindness, but with something far older, far darker.

'I am something far worse.'

Someone crossed the threshold of the cottage before Kage could form a reply, but all thought fled the moment Haven Blackburn stepped into the room. She moved with lightness, a gentle smile curving her lips as though no time had passed at all. Without hesitation, she made her way to the modest kitchen and busied herself with the preparation of tea, her every motion familiar and heartbreakingly mundane.

Kage remained frozen, his body stiff upon the wooden chair,

hands clenched against the table's edge. The sight of her, so alive, so unchanged, had rendered him utterly motionless. He dared not blink, lest she vanish like morning mist.

When Haven turned with a steaming cup in hand, she tilted her head, casting a teasing glance over at him.

'Aren't you going to say something?' she whispered, arching a brow in that maddeningly knowing way she'd always had.

'How...' Kage's voice caught. He surged to his feet, nearly toppling the chair in his haste. Within seconds, he had crossed the space and wrapped his arms tightly around her, pulling her against him as though by force of will alone he could keep her there. She let out a soft, nervous laugh, though her own hands clutched him in return.

He did not release her until she gently extracted herself and nudged him back towards his chair.

'Sit, or your tea will go cold.'

He obeyed, slowly. Yet his eyes never left her.

'It's not you,' he whispered, scarcely above a breath.

A shadow passed over her expression, quick as a cloud dimming sunlight.

'Of course it's me, Kage,' she said gently.

'You're dead.'

Haven looked away, her attention drifting to the cottage window. She looked precisely as she had the day she died. Same soft black dress, same short-cropped black hair, cut just beneath her jaw. Diamonds still adorned her horns, and matching ones glistened in her ears. Regal, poised, unearthly. Haven had always held elegance like a second skin. Even now. Even in death.

'Your ring,' he noted, eyes narrowing. The ring each of them wore, always on the smallest finger, was absent.

'Do not fret,' she replied, her voice calm. 'Mal has kept it safe.'

Kage turned towards Freya, who remained seated, silent and watchful. She did not speak. She simply offered him a slow, lingering smile, one that didn't quite reach her eyes. There was something gleaming there... something unreadable. Something not quite right.

'Where have you been?' Kage asked softly, the question falling from his lips like the first flake of snow. Quiet, hesitant, and filled with weight. A part of him longed to reach across the table, to rest his hand over hers and tether her back to the world he knew. But physical affection had never come naturally to him, and he feared it might disturb her, might make this already fragile moment somehow worse. So he kept his hands folded neatly in his lap, as still as the silence between them.

'I can't speak of that place, Kage,' Haven replied, her voice a gentle murmur, heavy with unshed sorrow. Sadness traced itself down her features like rain gliding down a windowpane. 'But I've made peace with my ending. It is almost...' She paused, choosing her words with care, as if each syllable mattered. 'Calming.'

From the corner of his eye, Kage saw the smallest twitch over Freya's brow. He said nothing, only filed it away like a note kept at the edge of a battlefield, something to be dealt with later.

'My entire life,' Haven continued, 'felt like a never-ending list of duties. An endless parade of obligations. But now...' Her voice softened, and her shoulders, always so perfectly braced against the weight of expectation, now looked unburdened. 'Now I can breathe. I wouldn't have chosen to die, Kage. I need you to know that. But... it's a strange, painful truth that I didn't have much of a life, not really.'

Kage pressed his back against the chair, the pressure

grounding him. Her words sat heavily on his chest, as though the air itself had grown thick and difficult to swallow. He understood. He had always understood. She had lived shackled by title, by duty, by expectation. Only in death had she found release. And that truth carved itself into him like a blade dulled by grief.

'How are Kai and Mal?' Haven asked, leaning forward slightly, as though shifting her focus might somehow erase what she'd just said.

'They're...' Kage cleared his throat, the lie rising like ash from a dying fire. He hadn't seen them since the day everything shattered. He had no answers to give, only hope stitched together from fragile memories. 'They're doing fine.'

'I'm glad.' Haven smiled, and for a moment the room felt a little warmer. 'What of our parents? I hope my death didn't break them.'

Kage glanced down at the untouched tea in his hands, then over at Freya, who sat quietly, unmoved. He had so much to say, so much that had weighed on him for too long. But now, with Haven seated before him, the words dissolved like mist. How could he tell her the truth? That her death had cracked the very foundation of their family? That their home, once filled with warmth and laughter, now echoed with silence?

No. He would not lay that burden at her feet. Not now.

Because perhaps she had made peace with death, had found breath, finally, beyond the veil. But the living had not. They were the ones left behind, the ones still searching for the broken pieces, trying to glue the world back together with hands that trembled from the effort. And though they might pretend, might move forward and smile again, they all knew deep down that something vital had been lost.

A piece of them was missing.

She was missing.

'Letting go does not mean forgetting,' Haven murmured, reaching across the table to clasp his hand, her fingers curling gently around his.

Kage shook his head, the movement barely a breath. 'I can't,' he whispered. 'Not when it comes to you. I don't know how. It's as if the world has bled of all colour, all sound, all feeling. I keep thinking that if I open my eyes, you'll be there again. And when I remember that you won't... the pain starts again, hollowing me out.'

Sadness fractured Haven's expression. 'I know, Kage. I know it feels unending. But it won't be. One day the sharpness will fade into a softer ache. And one morning, without knowing when it happened, you'll wake and it will have become a memory. A tender scar, not a wound.'

Kage's voice was raw with emotion. 'But I don't want the pain to fade, Haven. If it does... I don't want you to think you weren't important. That I have somehow forgotten you. The pain will always be a reminder of what was lost. Of you.'

Tears shimmered at the edges of her dark eyes. 'Life moves forward, Kage. And you must move with it. We, who remain beyond that veil, we know. We know that we are loved, remembered, in the smallest gestures, in fleeting thoughts. The dead are never truly gone so long as the living carry them in their hearts.'

She squeezed his hand once more, her voice soft as starlight. 'So live, Kage. Live, for me, if for nothing else.'

'I don't know how.' Tears appeared in his eyes. 'I'm lost without you. I don't want to be alone.'

Her grip tightened. 'Listen to me, brother. You will never be alone in this world. And if you ever do feel as though you are alone, close your eyes and imagine me there with you. For I am always with you. I've always been with you, little brother. Just because you cannot see me doesn't mean I'm not there.' She placed her hand over his heart. 'We share the same heart within two separate bodies.'

The tears finally fell from Kage's eyes and he allowed the pain he had kept buried to break free. He sat in silence, his sister holding him as he cried, as he shattered for the very first time.

'It is time,' Freya announced, her voice soft, yet filled with finality.

Haven nodded, a sorrowful sigh slipping from her lips as she brushed away his tears and rose to leave. Kage mirrored her movement at once, stepping to her side with panic beginning to bloom in his chest.

'Where are you going?' he asked, the question caught between disbelief and dread. 'You can't go. Not yet. It's only been a few minutes—'

'I can't stay,' Haven said, her dark eyes already distant. 'Not for long...'

'She must go now, Kage,' Freya interjected, her tone sharp with authority. 'She doesn't belong among the living.'

'Shut up!' Kage's voice cracked as it rose, raw with anguish. 'Of course she does! She belongs with *me!*' Without thought, he seized Haven's hands, his grip fierce and trembling. 'Don't go, Haven. *Please.* I'll find a way to fix this, to bring you back. I'm sorry I didn't save you before but—'

Haven's smile was gentle, filled with knowing. It made his words falter.

'Let go, Kage,' Freya said again, her voice quieter now. 'She must leave. Let your sister go.'

'No!' he barked, pulling Haven closer as his fingers clenched tighter around her wrists.

Outside, the wolf growled low and warning, pacing near the

edge of the cottage. Spirox shrieked, his talons scraping against the windows in frantic protest. The whole world seemed to tremble with Kage's refusal to release her. Terror surged through him, this desperate second chance slipping through his fingers like sand. Why did he always ruin things? Why hadn't he told her what she meant to him? That she had been the best sister anyone could have ever hoped for?

'I have to go, Kage,' she whispered, drawing him into one final embrace. Her arms were warm, familiar, heartbreakingly brief. 'Forgive yourself.'

Before he could beg her to stay, Haven slipped from his grasp. She turned, opened the cottage door, and closed it behind her with a soft thud that echoed like thunder in his soul.

Kage darted after her, bursting into the clearing, but she was gone. The forest stood still. Empty.

Spirox fluttered down, clicking his beak against Kage's boots in frustration, circling his master with agitation. Kage turned around slowly, dread blooming within his chest.

The cottage was no longer there.

'How did you do that?' he whispered, eyes fixed on the empty space where the little house had once stood. 'Was it magic?'

'I'm no witch, Kage,' Freya replied airily, waving her fingers as though brushing away a foolish thought.

'Where is my sister?' he demanded, voice hoarse. 'Where did she go?'

'She's returned to where she belongs,' Freya said, her tone laced with something both reverent and distant. 'Back to the realm where all souls find their rest.'

Kage's breathing turned ragged, his pulse thunderous in his ears. 'Even witches can't bring back the dead,' he whispered, terror and awe mixing in his voice. 'Not like that. Not so...

real.'

'No,' Freya agreed with a slow, eerie smile curving her lips. 'But gods can.'

Chapter Forty-Seven

House of Snow
Kingdom of Ice

It may seem as though Hades is the only one playing games, but he isn't.
Every single god is a player.
Our kingdoms are the board.
And we are merely their pawns.

Tabitha Wysteria

'I need to reach my brother's army,' Kage said for what felt like the hundredth time, his voice clipped with impatience. 'I haven't time for your schemes.'

'First, you must understand,' Freya replied calmly. 'I need to show you the truth and then...' Her attention drifted towards the horizon, as though seeking something far beyond their sight. 'Then we must journey to the Kingdom of Fire.'

Kage gave no reaction, his face an unreadable mask. 'Why the Kingdom of Fire?'

'Because...' Freya sighed, her expression laced with something quiet and sorrowful. 'You'll have to trust me. We cannot go to your land, to your army. Our path lies elsewhere. Towards fire, not darkness.'

'That journey will take days, if not weeks,' Kage said, gesturing to the wolf at his side. 'Bryn's wolf is likely near its limit already.'

'You needn't worry about that,' Freya said softly. 'I have other ways of getting us there. But first, you must let me explain.'

She reached out, offering her hand to him.

Kage looked down at it, sceptical. 'You need to hold my hand to explain?'

Freya shook her head. 'The forest listens, Kage. I'll be explaining elsewhere, in another realm.'

He looked to Spirox, hoping his shadowed bird would offer him clarity. The creature landed at his feet, promptly pecking his ankle with sharp annoyance. Kage sighed. He did put too much faith in that bird sometimes. But what did he have to lose? Freya claimed divinity. The world was already falling apart. Perhaps listening wouldn't break it any further.

'Fine,' he muttered, placing his hand in hers.

The world immediately shifted, colours melting and bending like wet paint on a ruined canvas. One moment he was standing in a forest that marked the divide between the Kingdom of Ice and his own, and the next, he stood somewhere else entirely.

Somewhere that did not belong to any world he knew.

'Where am I?' he asked, his voice steady despite the unease beginning to stir within him.

The landscape stretched out in every direction, vast and boundless, as though the world itself had no edges. Behind him enormous statues lay half-buried in the tall grass. Colossal visages of ancient gods whose stone eyes watched in eternal stillness, as though they knew things he had yet to understand. And before them, beyond the jagged cliffs on which they stood, stretched a vast, storm-dark sea. Endless, churning, and brooding beneath a bruised sky. Kage noticed with a ripple of unease that neither the wolf nor Spirox had followed him here.

'This is a place untouched by gods,' Freya said, her voice calm as she looked skyward, to the silver clouds shifting across a muted sky. 'A realm safe from their influence. It resembles one of the places they dwell, where they've been confined for this century. I must admit,' she added with a sly smile, 'I've become rather good at recreating it.'

'Why bring me here?' he asked, tone clipped, not missing a beat.

Freya's smile widened. 'I knew I'd like you, Kage Blackburn. So direct. When I first saw you in the drakonian castle, trying to unravel that curse, I couldn't take my eyes off you. Even then, I knew it would be you I'd one day have this conversation with.'

Kage straightened his spine, though his expression remained unreadable. Stillness became his shield.

'Who are you?' he asked, certain this time she would give him the truth.

'Have you not guessed?' she asked, her tone lilting. 'You, who devours books, who lives inside ink and parchment. Did none of those dusty old tomes offer you a clue?'

'You're not valkyrian,' he said.

'I am now,' she replied softly. 'But I am also something more.'

'A goddess,' he said.

Freya inclined her head. 'Yes. One who chose to remain apart from the others. To walk among mortals, not above them.'

'Why?'

'You've clearly never met a god.' She chuckled, a sound so light, so startlingly ordinary, that Kage found himself pausing. 'They're insufferable.' Her smile faded, replaced by something far more solemn. 'But there's more to it than that. When Tabitha cast the curse, those gods caught in the mortal realm became trapped, unable to return to their own. I have walked this world ever since, in the guise of Freya, a valkyrian warrior of the skies. But long before I pledged myself to the Kingdom of Air... I was someone else.'

She paused, blue eyes glinting with the ghosts of memory.

'My name was once Persephone. Wife to Hades. I created the Kingdom of Fauna, gave life to the Fae as a gift for him. To win his admiration. But...' Her gaze drifted. 'It was never quite enough. We had our moments, some good years, not all bitter. We were blessed with two children: Makaria and Zagreus.' Her voice hardened, laced with an ache centuries old. 'And he has kept them from me ever since. But that, Kage Blackburn, is a tale for another time.'

'That's why you're able to wield magic...' Kage said, more to himself than to her. 'You created Fae magic. You can craft illusions.' His eyes wandered across the realm around them, this strange mirror of another world.

'I thought that if I created something truly beautiful...' Freya's voice trailed off, her eyes turning away. There was a trace of fury and hurt in their blue depths. 'Perhaps then Hades might see me, might admire me. The Fae have always been the fairest of the gods' creations. I gave them magic because...'

'Because Hecate had magic,' Kage finished gently.

'I thought I could make something more beautiful.' She glanced down at the intricate armour adorning her—white, silver, and gold. Her hands lifted, palms turning as she studied the pale tattoos that curled like vines across nearly every inch of her skin. Kage said nothing, though questions stirred at the edge of his tongue. He knew better than to speak. Silence, he had long ago learnt, could draw more truth than a thousand questions. And Kage was very good at waiting.

'It never mattered,' Freya said at last, her voice quiet,

distant. 'No matter what I created. No matter how fiercely I loved him. Hades could never truly love me in return.' She gave a small, helpless shrug. 'I do believe he felt something for me... but it was never like with her. It was never what he felt for her.'

Kage remained silent, though curiosity coiled tightly in his chest.

'Hecate,' Freya finally said. 'He loved her long before he ever laid eyes on me. And I think, for a time, she may have loved him too.'

Her focus drifted to the sky as if it might hold memories too heavy for the earth.

'Hades built the Kingdom of Darkness for her. Created the wyverians and the wyverns as a gift. Hecate had already brought forth the witches and warlocks, and Hades saw how deeply she adored them. She would vanish for years, living among them in the mortal realm. He used his creations as a tether, hoping she might return to him again and again. He knew how much she longed to remain among the living... but gods are not meant to linger. Not forever.'

Freya's voice grew softer, tinged with sorrow.

'Hecate fell in love with a wyverian. Over the centuries, he's worn many names. I no longer recall the first one. But I have never seen two souls fall so completely into one another. It stirred envy in all of us, even the gods.'

She looked to Kage then, her expression shadowed.

'But Hades...Hades changed. The love turned bitter, festering into something cold and cruel. He could not bear that she had chosen a mortal over him. He tried, I think, to move on. He loved her deeply enough to want her happiness.' Freya snorted, the sound tinged with scorn and something more fragile beneath it.

'But perhaps,' she whispered, 'he didn't try hard enough.'

'Why are you telling me this?' Kage asked quietly.

'Because it matters,' Freya replied, her blue eyes avoiding his as she laced her fingers together. Her lips parted, tongue briefly brushing them before she continued. 'Hades found them. I don't believe he ever intended to kill the wyverian man, not truly. But when he discovered that Hecate had borne him a child... the moment he struck the mortal down...'

She paused, tilting her head slightly as though sifting through centuries of memory.

'Let us call him Hadrian,' she said at last. 'He's gone by many names, and I can no longer remember the first. After Hades killed him, Hecate was inconsolable. She told him she would never forgive him. Never forget. And then she did something no god should ever do. She brought Hadrian back from the dead.' Freya's voice softened, shadowed by the weight of the tale. 'But Hecate didn't realise that in doing so, a terrible price would be exacted.'

She turned slightly now, eyes reflecting the pale light of the illusionary realm.

'She cursed them all, unknowingly, to an endless loop. An eternity condemned to repeat itself. Every time Hadrian died at Hades' hand, and every time Hecate, driven to despair, took her own life in an attempt to punish Hades... the cycle would begin anew. Sometimes, it was Hades who dealt the fatal blow to Hecate. I believe there was even a time when Hecate and Hadrian slew one another in a desperate bid to break the cycle. Yet nothing ever holds. They always return, bound by fate, and they always die.

'Hecate is a goddess. She cannot truly die. But the curse altered her essence in a way none foresaw. It forced her to be reborn as a witch with every lifetime. Mortal, fragile, and unaware of who she truly was. Each time, she would live among witches, grow up believing she was one of them. And each time, fate would draw her back to Hadrian. She would fall in love, bear his child, lose him... lose herself... and begin again. And again. And again.' Freya's voice lowered to almost a whisper. 'I think you've already guessed the tale I speak of, the story of Hadrian and Tabitha Wysteria.'

'Does she not remember who she is, in each life?' Kage asked, his voice low, uncertain.

'Not always,' Freya replied gently. 'She is reborn as a witch, unaware of her true nature. And without the memory of being Hecate, she cannot access her divine powers. In some lives she ends up remembering, in others she dies before she recalls the truth. Regardless, the curse runs deep in her blood... and in Hades'. As well as in any child born of their union.'

'They never had children,' Kage said flatly.

But Freya merely offered a quiet, wistful smile.

'They did. Flesh of their flesh, born of godly blood and placed into your mother's womb.'

Kage stepped back, his breath catching, eyes widening with the weight of her words.

'Your sister, Mal Blackburn, is the daughter of Hades and Hecate. She is the goddess of shadows. And the curse that clings to her parents passed to her the moment she drew her first breath.'

'What does that mean?'

'It means the cycle will never end,' Freya said softly. 'Mal will fall in love with Ash Acheron. And, as it has always been, another will take him from her. She will not endure a world without him and she will end her own life. And so, the curse will begin again. Over and over, across the ages.'

'And why should I believe you?'

Freya turned to him and in the faint light of that realm, Kage saw the sorrow etched into the fine lines of her face, the honesty that rattled in the quiet stillness of her expression.

'Why would I lie?'

She had a point. Kage searched for some hidden motive, some advantage she might gain from deceit. But so far, he could find none. Still, he knew she hadn't yet revealed the full truth. Whatever she had brought him here to say... it was coming. And then, perhaps, he'd be able to sift the truth from the lies.

'Hades is planning to use your sister as a weapon,' Freya said quietly. 'Gods cannot be slain in their own realms, but on mortal soil, the rules are different. A god can be killed here. Of course, they don't truly die. They are gods, therefore they return to their realms. But... if there existed a god who could walk freely between *all* realms and kill them permanently...'

'Mal can kill gods,' Kage whispered, more to himself than to her, the weight of the truth settling like iron in his chest.

'She can,' Freya confirmed. 'That is why he created her. Your sister is the god-killer.'

She spoke the words with reverence and dread alike.

'For millennia, the gods feared the idea of such a being. In time, they dismissed the stories and grew complacent, as gods tend to do. But Hades remembered. He wanted such a creature, one he could command, one whose power would bring the others to their knees. A weapon forged from his own blood, to do his bidding. But the others... they did not agree. Now, they seek to destroy him.'

'And you want to stop him, too.'

Freya's eyes turned sombre. 'He will ruin everything, Kage. Even your sister.'

Kage turned his attention to the sea, its roar distant but ever-present. He had never given it much thought as a boy. His childhood had been spent tucked within stone walls, beneath the flicker of blue wyverian flames, nose buried in books and old histories. The castle itself stood far from the shoreline, but he knew, further out, there were beaches that stretched endlessly, great black sands kissed by the darkest waters, cold and untamed. Waters that few dared enter.

Mal had often ventured out with the wyverns, soaring high above the cliffs to catch glimpses of the ocean's vast, restless expanse. She would always return with windswept hair and a thousand questions, pressing Kage for answers about what lay beyond the horizon. Was there more land? Had the gods fashioned anything beyond the borders of their known realms? Kage never had the answers she sought.

The scrolls and tomes he'd studied held no truth about lands beyond the sea. He had come across stories of ancient deep-sea creatures, but he'd long dismissed them, setting aside such fanciful tales as the ramblings of myth-makers. He had little patience for legends that lacked foundation.

'If Hades succeeds,' Freya said, her voice low and final, 'the war with the witches will become irrelevant. Every land will fall. Every living soul within it will be devoured. You will all die.'

Kage's breath drew tight in his chest. 'What can I do?'

'You must convince your sister to kill Hades,' Freya replied, turning to face him fully, her expression as hard as carved stone. 'It is the only way the kingdoms can be saved.'

Kage gave a small nod, his features impassive, the mask he had worn for years settling effortlessly into place. He knew better than to reveal his thoughts too soon. Whether Freya was a god or something else entirely, it didn't change what he had trained himself to do—read people. Tone, gesture, silence. He could pick apart truth from fabrication as easily as ink from parchment.

He believed Freya wanted Hades dead. That much rang true.

But there was more to the tale. Of that, he was certain.

And whatever it was she had yet to reveal, he knew he needed to speak to Mal before it was too late.

'We could bring her back, you know.'

Kage froze. The chill that swept through his body was sharp and unforgiving, as if ice had threaded through his very veins. He turned slowly to Freya, only it wasn't Freya any longer. The softness of the valkyrian's face had vanished, peeled away to reveal something colder, older, and far more dangerous. This was Persephone speaking now, not the warrior of the skies, but the goddess cloaked in life and death. The warmth in her eyes had burnt away, leaving behind a glint of something ancient, something cruel. He found himself wondering what she had looked like before she had ever become valkyrian.

'The dead cannot be brought back,' he said, his voice sharp as a blade, laced with warning. If she toyed with him like this, he didn't care if she was a god. He would not hesitate to silence her.

'They can,' she replied softly, 'if it's done correctly. I belong to both the Kingdom of Fauna, my own creation, and the Kingdom of Darkness, which Hades shaped. I dwell in the realms of both life and death. When I married him, he granted me a sliver of his power. Not much... but enough. Something poor Hecate never had.'

Her tone turned reflective, almost reverent.

'That is why gods wed one another, why they bear children together. Marriage binds power. It passes from one to the other. But our children...' She paused, her eyes gleaming. 'They inherit only from one parent. Mal is the exception. She possesses power from both. That is why she is so rare, so feared. So extraordinary.'

Freya smiled then, darkly.

'I have enough of death's magic in me to bring Haven back.'

Kage didn't think. He reacted. In one swift movement, he seized her by the throat, his fingers curling into her flesh with unflinching force. Teeth clenched, he dragged her closer until their noses almost touched.

'Do not play games with me,' he growled. 'You yourself said the dead should not be brought back.'

'I... am not,' she rasped, gasping as she clawed at his grip. 'I can bring...her...back. Whether you should...or shouldn't...is up to your own morality.'

His grip tightened.

Panic bloomed in her eyes.

'You cannot kill me,' she whispered hoarsely, her face reddening with each strangled breath. 'Only the... god-killer... can end me.'

With a final glare, Kage released her. She crumpled to the ground, coughing, breathless. He stepped back, chest rising and falling with quiet fury.

He did not fear her. Nor did he fear the others.

Let them come.

They had taken his sister. And he would meet them, not with reverence, but with tooth and claw, fire and wrath. Let the gods learn what it meant to provoke a wyverian.

'If I convince Mal to kill Hades, you will bring her back.'

It wasn't a question. There was no hesitation in his voice, no doubt as he stood with his back to her, eyes fixed on the endless sweep of sea and sky. Behind him, Freya still knelt, fingers grazing her throat where his grip had left its mark.

'I will,' she replied.

Kage smiled.

He smiled not from joy, but because he knew, *knew,* that the woman behind him was no longer pretending. She wasn't the wounded valkyrian rubbing away pain she hadn't truly felt. No, he could almost hear it, the subtle curl of her lips as they twisted into something cold and cruel. A smile that belonged not to Freya, but to the goddess who had played this game for centuries.

She believed she had won.

She thought she had brought him to his knees. That she had accomplished the impossible: coaxed a wyverian prince into betraying his sister, into persuading her to commit the unthinkable. To kill a god.

But she wasn't wrong.

He would do it.

Kage would walk into fire and shadow. He would beg, lie, and force his sister's hand if it meant bringing Haven back. He would tear down the heavens themselves, claw the stars from the sky, and leave the gods bleeding on their thrones. If it meant seeing Haven again, he would burn the world.

'I know how deeply you love your sister,' Freya said softly. 'More than anyone in the world. Mal would understand, Kage. If you told her, if you explained the danger we all face, she would do it.'

Of course she would.

Mal would offer herself without hesitation if it meant saving another. She always had. Kage had never known anyone so selfless. In truth, none of his siblings had ever paused when it came to choosing what was right. Haven, Kai, and Mal possessed hearts unclouded by selfishness, brilliant and unyieldingly kind.

Sometimes, Kage wondered how he could possibly be their brother.

Because where they would give everything for *others*, he

would burn the world to keep *them* safe.

He had never held much reverence for nobility or virtue. The woes of strangers were none of his concern. His love was precise, razor-sharp and reserved only for his family. The rest of the world could crumble into ash and he would not mourn it.

Until.

Until that devil of a girl spoke with her laughter that scattered his shadows like startled birds. Until she smiled at him, again and again, until the walls he'd spent a lifetime building began to crack.

Damn Wren Wynter and her foolish, radiant grin.

For making him care. For making him hope.

For knowing what her brother would come to mean to him.

Kage had done everything to avoid thinking of Bryn since he left. It was no use. He missed him. Missed the quiet strength, the dimples, the stillness that wrapped around them like a shared secret. For the first time in his life, Kage had wanted more, more than dust-covered tomes and firelit libraries. More than solitude.

'Will you save us?' Freya asked, her voice no longer sweet but expectant, her hand extended in quiet demand.

Kage glanced down at it.

Of course he would save them.

He would save them all.

Just not in the way Freya was expecting.

Chapter Forty-Eight

House of Shadows
Kingdom of Darkness

When I hid my child to keep him safe from the dragons, and returned for him later...

He was gone.

Taken.

And I know who was behind it.

It's always him.

Tabitha Wysteria

Mal adjusted the short sword strapped across her back, content to feel its familiar weight once more. She wore a loose grey riding dress that billowed softly around her legs, paired with black leather boots worn smooth by use. The armour that had been laid out for her in the early hours of the morning remained untouched in the tent. She had no need for it. Her blade and her power were all she required.

She had helped Ash dress in silence, fastening the black armour that made his golden hair gleam like firelight. No words had passed between them, but their eyes had met, and that had been enough. They had never needed grand declarations; love had always lingered in the space between glances, in every quiet gesture. From the moment they had fought side by side in the Champions' Battle months ago, they had known that they were destined. And yet, a quiet thought tugged at Mal's heart: how much of that certainty had been theirs, and how much had been shaped by the curse that bound them?

Now they stood before the towering wall that marked the edge of the Kingdom of Darkness, beyond which stretched the barren wastelands. Mal had mounted Nyx, ready to lead from the skies, her sharp eyes trained to scout and warn of danger before it struck. Ash was astride Ayaru, Adriana on Nisha, and Keir on Daku. The wyverns, though initially uneasy at carrying riders who were neither Kai nor Kage, had quickly settled under Mal's steady command.

She cast one final glance at her husband, silently willing him to give her the answer she longed for. But he said nothing. And she understood. She trusted him utterly, even if it meant letting go of certainty.

'May the shadows guide your way,' Mal said, lifting two fingers to her forehead in solemn salute. She did not turn to look, for she knew that every soldier behind her mirrored the gesture, their voices rising in a whispered chorus, a quiet promise carried on the wind.

'Volare!' she commanded, her voice slicing through the air like a blade. The wyverns responded at once, wings snapping open as they surged forward and leapt skyward, cutting through the wind with thunderous grace. Mal waited until all four had taken their positions in the sky, their silhouettes circling like shadows above, before she lifted her head and screamed, 'Ardere!'

In unison, the wyverns opened their jaws, and torrents of searing blue fire poured forth, roaring against the wall in a blaze of elemental fury. The stone sizzled, cracked, and crumbled beneath the heat, melting away in a matter of minutes beneath the relentless onslaught. Mal rested a hand on Nyx's dark hide, her shadow wyvern trembling with energy beneath her. Mal's eyes gleamed with satisfaction as she watched the flames devour the barrier, leaving a wide passageway for her army to march through unchallenged.

A section of the wall had already been broken, but it had not been wide enough to accommodate the sheer size of her forces. Mal had chosen the more dramatic solution—obliteration by fire.

As Nyx soared ahead, Mal kept her attention fixed on the ground below. The harsh, dead terrain of the Kingdom of Darkness gave way swiftly to desolation. Empty plains, shifting marshes, tangled forests, and the scattered bones of long-forgotten ruins.

Mal brought Nyx down with precision, her boots meeting earth as she gestured for Adriana and Keir to remain airborne, watching from above while the rest of the army pressed on to catch up.

'It's too quiet,' Mal said the moment Ash landed and made his way towards her, his steps light on the scorched earth.

'They're not here.'

'Then where are they?'

'My kingdom.'

Mal shook her head slowly, the wind catching in her dark hair. 'Hagan would never leave his own land defenceless just to conquer another.' Her purple eyes met his, steady and searching. 'Do you know?'

'I... I c-cannot see everything,' Ash said, the hesitation in his voice tugging at her heart.

Mal exhaled, her shoulders softening. 'I'm sorry.'

Ash's fingers brushed against hers gently, affectionately, grounding her with that simple, familiar touch. 'They're not here, Mal,' he said quietly. 'I don't b-believe we need to wo-

worry too much about witches in this p-place.'

But Mal was already gnawing at the skin around her thumb, frustration simmering beneath her calm façade. 'Why would Hagan abandon his land?'

'Because he wants us there,' Ash said, gesturing westward, towards the distant blaze of the Kingdom of Fire. 'He has no use for the was-wastelands. What he desires is revenge... and he will burn everything to ashes if it b-brings him even a taste of it.'

'So, we go to him?' Mal asked, watching as Ash lifted his gaze to the heavy grey sky. 'We could stay here, threaten to claim his kingdom instead.'

'It won't work.'

'Why not?'

'Because he doesn't care, Mal.' Ash turned to face her fully, golden eyes gleaming with grim understanding. 'He's beyond reason. We must take the f-fight to him.'

Mal stepped closer, her voice low and fierce. 'If I do, if I take the fight to him. Do we win?'

Ash offered her a faint smile, but said nothing. Instead, he turned to see to the wyverns, calming them after the long wait. It would take the wyverian army several days to cross the barren stretch of the wastelands. Though their kind required little food and even less rest, Mal was determined they would not arrive at the wall bordering the Kingdom of Fire exhausted. She needed them sharp, not worn thin by the journey.

'There are no w-winners in w-war, Mal,' Ash called over his shoulder, voice soft but certain. 'Only survivors.'

...

Ash had assured her there would be no witches lying in wait as they crossed the wastelands. The wyverian army travelled swiftly and without fear, buoyed by the quiet confidence they placed in Ash's foresight. Word had already been sent to the wolverians to meet them at the wall, and Mal was certain that within a few days, their paths would converge. King Ozul had sent a message only recently. He remained in the north of the wyverian lands, speaking with the high nobles. Most had pledged their warriors without hesitation, though a few had proven more reluctant, none more so than the king's youngest brother, who refused to cooperate out of nothing but bitter pride.

Mal had only met her uncle once, when she was a child. He had travelled south to see for himself the rumoured violet hue of her eyes. She remembered little of that visit, save for the tension that clung to the air. Her uncle had spent most of his time quarrelling with the king, his voice raised and full of disdain. The rest he had passed in the library with Kage, sharing tales and traditions from distant kingdoms, as if Mal did not exist. When he had finally turned to look at her, it had been with contempt. He'd spat on the ground at her feet and turned to King Ozul with venom in his eyes.

'You did this,' he had said.

To this day, Mal had never fully understood what those words had meant, and she had been too frightened to ask.

'Do you know where my brothers are?' Mal asked as they made camp beneath a sky bruised by twilight.

'They're...' Ash hesitated, his sigh brushing against the night air. 'They're on a path of their own choosing. A journey they b-believe they must take.'

'Where, Ash?' she pressed.

Ash crouched, fastening the last ties on their tent with quiet precision. Despite his many reassurances that no threat loomed in the dark, Mal had forbidden the use of fire after sundown. They would pass through this place unseen.

Mal rubbed her eyes, weariness settling behind them like sand in the bones. She stopped asking. Whatever answers Ash held, he would not give them tonight. And though she wanted, desperately, to trust that his choices were made for the good of them all, a strange stillness pressed against her chest. A silence that whispered doubt.

Perhaps she would be safe. But Kage? Kai? They might not be.

Ash could not shield them all.

'Where are you going?' he asked, watching as she dropped her bags to the ground and turned away, her steps already leading her into the shadowed marshes.

'To clear my mind.'

'Mal...'

She dismissed his concern with an indifferent sweep of her hand. 'You'd know if something happened to me, wouldn't you?' she called over her shoulder, her purple eyes flashing with something sharper, something accusing. He had known. He had known Hades intended to bind her to Thanatos. He had known what the Underworld held for her, and he had kept it silent. Not a word. Not a warning.

What else did he know, what secrets still curled on his tongue, too dangerous to speak aloud?

Mal stepped into the marshland ahead, where the stagnant water sat heavy and unmoving, the silence pressing like a weight. It reminded her of the river in the Underworld, and her thoughts drifted, unbidden, to Makaria. Was she curled alone in Mal's bed tonight? Would she sleep restlessly, sorrow clinging to her like a second skin?

Thanatos' mocking laugh echoed in her memory, and she

clenched her jaw, willing it away. His face, smug and loathsome, faded. She sank onto the damp ground without care for her muddied boots or the wet earth soaking through her dress. The cold seeped into her bones, but she welcomed it.

She dipped the tip of her finger into the murky water, tracing slow circles on the surface, her thoughts as clouded as the liquid below.

Then, something shifted.

She leaned closer, curiosity prickling along her spine. There, beneath the water, something moved. Something wrong.

She crawled nearer, her face hovering inches above the surface, breath catching in her throat.

It looked like...

Hands.

Cold, unyielding hands burst forth, latching onto her and dragging her down. There was no time to scream.

Mal vanished beneath the water's surface.

...

Mal fell through endless dark until cold swallowed her whole, seeping into her bones and soaking every thread of fabric clinging to her skin. She landed with a jolt against something solid, unforgiving stone beneath her back. Her breath caught as she shot upright, heart pounding, half-convinced she had returned to the Underworld. But as her eyes swept across her surroundings, she frowned.

'It's not the Underworld,' came a smooth, familiar voice laced with cruel delight. It sank into her chest like a stone in water.

Mal looked up and hissed.

'You could at least pretend to be pleased to see me,'

Thanatos drawled, leaning languidly against the crumbling wall of a nearby building, his smirk as insufferable as ever.

'I'd be lying.' Mal wrung out the wetness from her dress like a disgruntled cat, droplets flinging around her as she cast another uncertain glance at the town that surrounded her.

'Elmwych,' he said, answering the question forming in her mind.

'Stop reading my thoughts. Why am I here?'

'Felt like taking a stroll with you,' Thanatos replied, his wicked grin deepening, the amusement in his dark eyes shimmering like oil on water. 'Tabitha Wysteria once called this place home. They rebuilt it, tried to make it look just as it did before it burnt to ash a century ago.'

'How did you—'

'This land is ancient, laced with old magic. And I, Melinoe, am a god.' He gestured lazily for her to come closer. 'It wasn't difficult, shifting you from one corner of the wastelands to another.' When she didn't move, his smile faltered slightly. He sighed. 'Hades is not exactly thrilled.'

'Does it look as though I give a damn about Hades' feelings?'

Thanatos moved, closing the distance between them with fluid grace. Mal held her ground, refusing to retreat, refusing to let him glimpse even a flicker of fear. She lifted her chin defiantly, her purple eyes locking with his, unyielding.

'I missed you, Melinoe,' he said, the words a ghost of breath against her cheek, so soft it sent a shiver coursing through her spine.

'Don't start,' she snapped, stepping back with a grimace. The motion drew a low chuckle from him, and she loathed him for noticing the effect he still had. 'Ash is waiting for me. I need to return.'

'I thought you wandered off to clear your thoughts,' he said, his tone teasing, almost sing-song.

'And what made you think you barging in would help with that?'

'Do I confuse you?' His grin widened, dark and knowing, as he leaned in with that maddening closeness. 'I know you wonder what it would feel like to have me fuck you instead of him.'

Mal's hand cracked across his face before the sentence had fully landed. The sting of the slap vibrated through her palm, sharp and satisfying.

Thanatos seized her wrist and yanked her against him, his grip iron-tight, fury blazing in his eyes. He inhaled deeply, the scent of her grounding him, and after a few taut seconds with his eyes closed, the storm within him seemed to ease.

'Why are you so violent, woman?' he muttered.

'*You* make me violent,' she shot back, her voice cold as steel.

He released her with a scoff, shoving his hands deep into his coat pockets as he turned away, striding towards the shadowed remnants of the town. 'Come along, then.'

Mal hesitated, caught in the space between caution and curiosity. She ought to turn back, try to retrace her steps through the marshes, find her way to Ash. What if he was worried? She didn't want to be the cause of his panic, not when she knew how heavily the weight of responsibility already sat on his shoulders.

'Doesn't he *see* everything?' Thanatos called over his shoulder, voice laced with mockery. 'Surely he knows where you are.'

Mal clenched her jaw, the truth stinging more than his tone. She cast one last glance behind her, then sighed and followed. Into the town where her mother had once walked, where spells had been whispered and secrets stitched into stone.

The word mother felt strange in her mind, a weight she couldn't quite place. But she wouldn't dishonour either of them —the woman who had given her life, and the one who had raised her with quiet, enduring care. Two different kinds of love, both valid. Both real.

The town of Elmwych was, in its own way, achingly beautiful. Quaint stone cottages nestled close together, their walls weathered by time and softened by ivy. Lanterns hung from iron hooks outside each doorway, waiting to be lit by the touch of witchlight. Fresh flowers adorned the windowsills, wild blooms arranged with quiet care, while small wooden boats bobbed gently at the water's edge, ready to slip down the marshes like forgotten dreams.

'Where are they?' Mal asked, her voice low as she noticed the town's eerie stillness, each home vacant and silent.

'They left,' Thanatos replied. 'To fight.'

She followed him down a narrow, winding path, until he came to a halt before a great willow tree, its drooping branches like a veil of sorrow. Mal stared up at it, struck by its sheer size. It must have been ancient, a living witness to generations of whispered spells and hidden grief.

'They hung Hadrian Blackburn from that tree,' Thanatos said softly, 'and then set it ablaze. Tabitha found him here, right where you're standing. She cursed the gods on this very soil.'

'What do you want, Thanatos?' Mal asked, her tone cool, emotions carefully buried beneath her skin. Her brow arched, sharp and knowing.

'Why must I want something?'

'Because you're a god.'

'So are you.'

She exhaled sharply, already tired of the game he was playing. He must have sensed her irritation, for he stepped closer, fingers brushing against hers. She recoiled instantly, unwilling to let his touch linger.

'I came to warn you.'

Mal snorted. 'Warn me? Of what?'

'Of him. Your husband.'

That made her laugh, a dry sound edged with disbelief. She shook her head, almost in admiration of his persistence. 'Truly? Is that your angle now, Thanatos? Are you hoping to twist this into something it's not? Hoping I'll hate Ash, abandon him, and fall conveniently into your arms? I'm not some foolish girl. I see through you, and through my father.'

'It isn't a trick, Melinoe.'

'Then what is it?' she snarled, her voice sharpening. 'Speak plainly, Thanatos. I'm tired of riddles. I'm tired of being led in circles.'

Something shone in his eyes, something that looked far too much like worry, like fear, and it made Mal step back. She had never seen such emotion on his face before. For the first time since she had met him, she didn't recoil when his fingers brushed against her cheek. This time, she let him touch her.

'He's not trying to protect *you*,' Thanatos murmured.

Mal shook her head, her features contorting with anguish as his words pierced through her.

'Ash would never hurt me.'

'No, he wouldn't. He loves you, Melinoe. We all know he does. The curse will always make him love you, no matter what. But...' Thanatos' gaze dropped down, down towards her stomach.

Mal followed his eyes.

Her breath caught. Her heart stopped.

'No,' she whispered.

'He loves *her* more.'

Mal's head jerked from side to side, pushing him away with trembling hands.

'No.'

'And when she's here,' he said, voice low and grim, 'he will choose her over you. Always.'

Without thinking, Mal pressed her hands to her stomach, though there was nothing to feel. Nothing but stillness and the sudden, unbearable weight of possibility. No. Thanatos had to be lying. It couldn't be...

'It's impossible,' she breathed.

Thanatos' jaw clenched with the weight of unspoken truth.

'Ash is walking a path built only to keep *her* safe,' he said. 'No one else matters. Not even you, Melinoe.'

'Shut up!' she screamed.

She tried to shove him away, tried to claw back space the moment he pulled her into his arms. But she was already breaking. Already sobbing into his chest. The cries tore from her, not only for the betrayal, not only for the fear, but for the truth she hadn't been ready to face.

'You are with child, Melinoe.'

But it wasn't the words that undid her. It was the knowing. The bone-deep realisation that Ash had known. And now their daughter would carry the same curse. She would bear the same weight Mal had been forced to shoulder.

'Melinoe, listen to me.' He caught her chin between his fingers, tilting her face up to meet his gaze. 'No one can know. Not a soul. They will use her. Not even Ash, not even he can know that you...' He exhaled, frustration and urgency warring in his voice. 'You must keep it secret.'

'How do *you* know?' she whispered.

Thanatos looked away, his jaw clenched, expression tight with something unspoken.

'Tell me,' Mal demanded, her voice low and tense.

'Because I've always kept an eye on you.'

Mal recoiled, her stomach twisting at the thought of him spying on her so intimately. It was a violation, and it made her feel suddenly, deeply ill.

'That doesn't explain how you know about...' Her hands drifted protectively to her stomach.

Thanatos nodded, running a hand through his pale curls, the motion weary and reluctant. 'I am the God of Death, Melinoe. I know when there is life.'

Her eyes widened in silent horror.

Thanatos lifted his head, frowning at the space now between them. He reached out and pulled her close, as though the distance was too much to bear. Then, to her surprise, he pressed a kiss to her forehead. A tender, almost reverent gesture that felt wholly out of place coming from him.

'Keep her a secret,' he whispered. 'You must return now. I'll be watching over you.'

'Why?' she asked, the question escaping like breath.

He gave a soft, crooked smile. 'Silly question, woman.'

Before she could speak again, the world tilted violently beneath her. Cold swallowed her whole and the void spat her out onto the hard ground where she had first been, her hand still submerged in the murky water. Groaning, Mal sat up and rubbed the stiffness from her neck and back, her mouth twisting in irritation.

Thanatos really had to stop doing that.

A faint chuckle echoed somewhere in the distance, and she sighed, unsurprised. Always watching. Always lingering. Some twisted, protective shadow.

Dusting the mud from her dress, Mal made her way back to the tent. Inside, Ash lay sleeping on the makeshift bed, his features softened by slumber. She stripped off her boots, changed into a dry dress, and quietly slipped beneath the covers.

She lay beside him, her back turned, heart aching with uncertainty. She didn't dare look at the man she loved. Could she trust Thanatos over Ash? Time alone would answer that. For now, it would remain her secret, hers alone.

She loved Ash. Of that, she was sure. But the man who had emerged from the lava, after being stabbed and remade... she wasn't entirely certain it was still him.

And yet, she would love him. No matter what he had become. Because she had been cursed to love him.

Ash stirred in his sleep and shifted closer, his arm curling around her like a cloak of warmth, his hand coming to rest unknowingly, instinctively, over her stomach.

And in the hush of the tent, cloaked in silence and shadow, Mal did not see Ash's golden eyes watching her from just beyond the dark.

Chapter Forty-Nine

House of Sand
Desert Kingdom

I visited the city of Madari during the Sand Trials.

And even here, far away, hidden among the dunes, Hades has found me.

Tabitha Wysteria

Alina awoke with a start, her breath catching in her throat. Her skull throbbed as though it had been cleaved in two, and her limbs ached with an intensity she had never known. Her throat burnt with thirst, and pain rippled through every nerve like fire dancing over raw skin. For a moment, she could not place herself, could not tether her mind to time or place.

She blinked at the unfamiliar surroundings: a modest room, carved from sand and stone. The floor was cool beneath her and the walls held the earthy scent of the desert. A small window, no more than a hollow carved into the stone, had been modestly draped with cloth in an attempt at privacy. In the far corner, a rough-hewn table held a large clay jug.

'Do not move!'

The sharp command struck her like lightning, but the moment Hessa burst through the door, urgency in every movement, Alina's body softened in relief.

'I will bring you water,' Hessa said, already at the jug, pouring into a cup with careful hands. She crossed the room swiftly and helped Alina into a sitting position, cradling her with more tenderness than her firm voice might have suggested.

'Where am I?' Alina croaked, her voice barely audible, the sound scraping like sandpaper against her dry throat.

'Dunayans have refuge in every one of the twelve regions,' Hessa explained, helping her recline once more. 'This is one of them. Our haven in Madari.'

Alina's brow furrowed. 'What happened to me?'

At that, Hessa faltered, her eyes growing wide. 'You do not remember?' Alina shook her head gently, too gently, yet even that caused a wince. 'You fell, amira. Saren was beside you. She said you'd just set your axe into the wall, but as soon as you unhooked your rope, you slipped. She tried to catch you, but... it was too late.'

Alina pressed a hand to her temple, sifting through fragments of memory. The climb, yes. A conversation with Saren... but after that, only blackness. A void.

'How did I survive such a fall?' she asked, voice laced with disbelief.

'We don't know...' Hessa's voice cracked. Tears welled in her eyes, spilling over before she could blink them away. 'When I reached you, you were so broken. There was so much blood, Alina. I thought—' Her voice caught, and she choked on the words. Alina, moved beyond measure, squeezed her hand.

'I'm alright,' she whispered, though she did not know for whom the words were meant—Hessa, or herself. But she was breathing. She was still here.

'It's my fault, amira,' Hessa said, shame lacing every syllable. 'I should have stayed at your side. It was your first climb. But I thought...' She looked up, her eyes brimming once more. 'I thought you would be safe with Saren.' Then, she spat to the side, a desert-born gesture of remorse and regret. 'It was not her fault,' she added quietly, but the pain in her expression told another story.

Alina shifted with a soft hiss of pain, wriggling to one side to make space on the narrow bed. The ache that accompanied the movement was sharp, but not as sharp as the distance that lingered between her and Hessa. She needed her close, closer than breath. Without hesitation, the desert princess climbed in beside her, curling gently around Alina's fragile form, her embrace tender, protective.

'It wasn't your fault, Hessa,' Alina said, the words drifting from her lips like a lullaby. A quiet calm bloomed through her limbs as Hessa's warmth pressed against her own, her skin kindling a soft, tingling fire that spread through her aching body like dawn spilling over cold stone.

With a slow, loving hand, Hessa brushed loose strands of blonde hair away from Alina's face. Her breath ghosted across Alina's cheek, soft and steady, like wind sweeping over sand, and Alina sighed, surrendering to the comfort. Her eyes fluttered closed, exhaustion pulling her under like the tide. There was so much left unsaid between them, but for now... she allowed herself the silence, the nearness, and the promise of rest.

'Yaa aras ma sahraa,' Hessa whispered, her voice barely more than a breath.

Alina could not be certain if she had dreamt the words or if they had truly been spoken, murmured in the belief that the drakonian princess would not understand. But she had heard them before. Once, in hushed voices around a fire, she had asked what they meant.

Words exchanged between soul-bound lovers.

A phrase so sacred the desert folk believed it could only be spoken once in a lifetime to the one who truly held your heart.

Alina had blushed back then, unsure if she would ever be brave enough to say such words aloud. But now, lying here in Hessa's arms, heart stitched back together by the sound of her voice and the warmth of her presence, Alina made herself a promise.

As soon as she was strong again, strong enough to climb, to run, to stand tall, she would say them aloud. She would look Hessa in the eye and speak her truth. Because when her eyes had opened to the gift of another day, her heart had already chosen.

And so, with a faint smile playing on her lips, Alina surrendered to sleep, dreaming of sand dunes and stolen glances, of laughter and soft kisses under starlit skies.

Dreaming of the day she would finally speak the words that had been waiting on her tongue.

Yaa aras ma sahraa.

You are my desert.

...

'You cannot possibly be feeling fine, amira,' Hessa said, her pale eyes narrowing with a mixture of doubt and concern. 'You fell off a mountain.'

'I truly feel better,' Alina insisted, her voice light with wonder. She had awoken with the morning sun slipping through the thin curtain, still cradled in Hessa's arms, as if the embrace itself had soothed her back to life. Against all reason, the pain that had gripped her bones and burnt through her muscles had vanished. Her body, once broken, now felt whole. Healed. There was no logic to it, and yet there it was.

'You ought to remain in bed.'

'No,' Alina said, already bathed and dressed, her stomach rumbling in quiet protest. 'I've been unconscious far too long. I need air. I need to move.'

'Amira, I don't—' Hessa's protest stilled the moment Alina reached for her, cupping her face gently, their foreheads almost touching, the intimacy of the gesture halting breath and words alike.

'I promise, I'm all right. I would never lie to you,' she whispered, her smile warm and resolute. And just like that, the tension in Hessa's brow eased, her shoulders softening with surrender. 'Show me the city.'

And so Hessa did.

Alina had not lied. Her body moved with ease, without the brokenness that ought to have lingered after such a fall. It defied reason, and the not-knowing gnawed quietly at the corners of her thoughts. Still, she was alive. She was breathing. And for now, that would be enough.

As they stepped out into the world beyond their small shelter, Alina half-expected to see the other Dunayans. But Hessa explained that they had departed at first light, scattered across the city to tend to various chores. What those duties entailed, she didn't say, and Alina chose not to press. Saren was nowhere in sight, and for that, Alina felt both relief and guilt. She wished to find the Dunayan, to assure her the fall had not been her fault, to ease the weight she imagined still rested on Saren's shoulders.

Madari was not at all what she had imagined. It was a labyrinth of narrow, sun-drenched streets where every corner whispered a new story. The passageways were so tight that she and Hessa could not walk side by side. Instead, the desert princess moved ahead, her fingers tightly woven through

Alina's, guiding her like a lifeline through the sandstone maze. Every few steps, Hessa would pause, turning to study Alina's face with worry etched into her features, only to be reassured by a nod, a smile, a whispered, 'I'm fine.' And slowly, with each passing glance, each step taken in shared silence, Hessa's worry began to melt beneath the heat of Madari's golden sun.

Madari had been carved like a secret between two towering cliffs, the stone walls of the mountain range leaning so close together it seemed they might kiss, yet just enough space had been left for a city to be born in their shadow. The homes clung to the sides of the rock like stubborn ivy, built into the very ribs of the mountain itself. Winding alleys, no wider than a man's shoulders, slithered between the stone walls, forming a web of narrow passageways that breathed life into the crevice.

Alina paused, breath catching in her throat, her gaze lifting skyward to the hundreds of sand-hued dwellings stacked atop one another like sun-baked nesting dolls. Ropes stretched from one cliff to the other like tightropes in the wind, baskets of goods gliding across the divide as the people of Madari sent their wares and produce without ever needing to step foot outside their homes. Bridges, makeshift things of rope and stubborn faith, swayed perilously between ledges, dancing with each whisper of wind.

She and Hessa descended to the very belly of the city, where the sun's reach faltered and the light dimmed to a golden gloom. Here, at the base where the shadows ruled, the true heart of Madari beat. Stalls of curiosities lined the streets, filled with peculiar goods that sparkled or hissed, smelt sweet or sharp, sold by traders bent and hunched with age. Children darted through the crowds like wildfire, chasing one another through the maze, while cats lounged in the centre of the road like kings, sprawling in careless stretches as if they, too, belonged to the city's ancient soul.

Alina took it all in with quiet awe, her senses alive with scent and colour and sound. It felt like stepping into another world entirely, a world that had thrived in secret, beneath stone and shadow.

She paused, her brows knitting in curiosity as a plume of vividly coloured smoke curled from a nearby doorway, perfumed and inviting. Laughter spilt out in ribbons of sound, and women adorned in silks and jewels leaned against the entrance, their hands fluttering like butterflies as they beckoned her closer with coy smiles and kohl-lined eyes.

'That,' Hessa said with barely concealed amusement, 'is a pleasure house, amira.'

Alina blinked. 'A pleasure house?'

'You've never heard of one?' Hessa's brow arched high, her grin growing wider. 'Amira, you're too pure. So untouched by the world.'

Alina frowned, glancing once more at the beautiful women. 'We don't have such things in my kingdom.'

Hessa let out a snort of laughter. 'Oh, you most certainly do. All kingdoms have them, especially ones as... repressed as yours. Where else would drakonians indulge their secret whims?'

Alina opened her mouth to protest, only to close it again. She bit her lower lip, a shadow of uncertainty crossing her features. Had such places truly existed under her nose, kept from her by the heavy veil of royal protection? Had she lived so sheltered a life that even something so basic had become foreign?

'They were likely outlawed,' Hessa said gently, sensing the shift in Alina's mood. 'Hidden in alleyways, whispered about but never named. It's no wonder you didn't know. Your ignorance was carefully crafted, amira. You were kept blind.'

'No. It was I who chose the blindfold.' Her voice was quiet. 'I thought myself a prisoner to duty—balls, gowns, endless debates over which shade of silk was most regal. But I see now... I had power. I just never used it to look beyond the palace walls.'

Before she could sink deeper into regret, Hessa tugged her forward, drawing her back into the present with a playful glint in her eyes. They wandered deeper into the bustling streets, the scent of spices and heat thick in the air. Hessa insisted she try grilled lizard spiced within an inch of its life, and Alina's tongue burnt as though kissed by flame.

Then came something else, "Chaaka", Hessa called it, ordered from a crooked little stall wedged between two stone houses.

'It is a Madari speciality,' Hessa said, accepting two clay cups. 'Thick, warm, and best drunk without breathing.'

'What is it?' Alina asked warily.

'Do not ask.' Hessa laughed, thrusting the drink into her hands.

It was a concoction of crimson and black, dense and faintly steaming. Alina pinched her nose as advised and took a tentative sip, only to gag moments later at the foul aroma.

'That's vile!' she gasped, wiping her mouth.

'But it feels divine, doesn't it?' Hessa teased, laughing so brightly it made Alina join in, if only through sheer delight at the sound.

Within minutes, a delicious warmth spread through Alina's limbs, and the edges of the world seemed to soften and tilt ever so slightly. Her shoulders loosened, her thoughts quieted, and everything around her shimmered with an unfamiliar ease.

'It is the Chaaka,' Hessa explained with a knowing smile. 'It makes you happy.'

Alina wasn't entirely certain that happiness was the word she'd use for what coursed through her in that moment. It was something more volatile, more consuming. An ache born not of joy, but longing. Every sense narrowed to a single point of gravity: Hessa. Her fingers found the desert princess's, lacing together like vines seeking the sun. Her skin burnt beneath the contact, alight with a yearning she had never known before.

Something must have shone in her eyes, some subtle shift, some unspoken truth finally bared because Hessa looked at her then with a startled softness, as though she'd glimpsed a signal long awaited or long abandoned.

The tour was over, though Alina could barely recall the journey back. They ascended a winding, narrow street that snaked upward like a whisper through the mountain's heart, Hessa guiding her with sure steps. The city faded behind them— its colours, its noise, its lingering scent of spices—until they slipped through a weather-worn curtain and entered the Dunayans' hidden refuge.

It was a modest place, shadowed and cool, carved into the stone with little regard for decoration. A few scattered cushions lay on the floor, worn by use, and wooden tables stood lopsided with age, their surfaces etched with the stories of late-night card games and quiet laughter. Doors branched off the central space, rooms whose occupants Alina did not know. The one she'd awoken in, bathed in golden light through a carved slit of a window, was the only pocket that knew the sun.

Alina turned, about to ask why they had returned, but her words faltered the instant her eyes landed on Hessa.

The desert princess stood motionless, her expression unreadable, her chest rising and falling just a little too quickly. The space between them charged with breath and silence, with the tension of unsaid things. They stood like that, two threads pulled taut and trembling.

Alina understood.

This was a question, not a command. A moment held open like a door, waiting for her to step through. And Hessa, ever patient, would not move unless Alina did.

So Alina began to undress slowly, deliberately, each movement a quiet rebellion. She was weary of fear. Weary of silencing herself to please a world that had never made space for her truth. No longer would she let the judgement of others tether her spirit.

Hessa had seen her bare before on sun-drenched mornings, after long days of training, in pools and tents. But this time... this time was different.

Now Alina let herself be seen.

She did not shy away from the woman standing before her, did not cast her gaze downward in modesty or shame. She held Hessa's eyes, even as her cheeks flushed with heat, even as each robe slid from her shoulders and pooled at her feet. Her breath came quick and shallow, her chest rising like the tide. She stood unveiled and hornless, unmarred by disguise. That which had once brought her shame was no longer hidden. She wore it now with quiet defiance. If the world wished to stare, so be it. She had eyes only for the one before her.

Words fell away, no longer needed.

Hessa's smile bloomed soft and slow, a silent blessing. Then, without rush, she began to undress as well, each layer shed with care, mirroring Alina's courage with her own.

The moment they stood together, stripped bare of cloth and inhibition, Alina parted her lips to speak, to ask, to beg, to be shown how to begin. She did not know what to do, how to move, or what to offer. But Hessa saw the uncertainty shimmering in her eyes and stepped forward, gathering Alina gently into her arms.

With a silent gesture, she guided her to the bed. Alina sat obediently, her limbs trembling. Not from fear alone, but from the heady mix of anticipation and wonder. The room seemed to fall into reverent stillness as Hessa climbed into her lap, draping herself across her like a prayer. Legs wrapped around waist, skin melting into skin. Alina's breath hitched as the reality of their closeness swept over her. Her chest pressed to Hessa's, breasts soft against breasts, the heat between their thighs sparking and simmering with every breath.

Overwhelmed, she looked up into those strange, luminous white eyes she had come to know better than her own reflection.

'You look afraid,' Hessa whispered, brushing her knuckles along Alina's cheek.

'I am,' Alina admitted, her voice no louder than a breeze. Her tongue darted out to wet her lips, betraying her nerves. 'I've never… I don't know what to do.'

Hessa tilted her head, a small, knowing smile playing on her lips. 'I doubt that very much, amira,' she whispered.

And then she leaned in, close enough that their breath mingled, and took Alina's bottom lip between her teeth, teasing it with a delicate tug. Alina gasped, her entire body lurching in response to the sudden bloom of heat that surged through her belly, curling lower. Her eyes widened with astonishment, not at Hessa's touch, but at her own yearning, awakened and undeniable.

'Are you certain?' Hessa asked gently, brushing a loose strand of Alina's hair behind her ear with the tenderness of a lover afraid to wake a dream. 'Your body might still need to rest.'

'I'm only ever certain of you,' Alina whispered, her voice as soft as silk unfurling in moonlight. Before Hessa could answer, Alina closed the space between them and pressed her lips to hers.

The world fell away at once. Its burdens, its expectations, all dissolving into the quiet ache of longing answered. In that kiss, Alina forgot every choking fear, every doubt that had ever held her captive.

She had been told countless times of her beauty, spoken of like a painting admired from afar. Yet she had never believed it. Not truly. Not until now.

Now, within the haven of Hessa's arms, beneath the sweep of her touch, she felt it. Not as vanity, but as truth. As something holy.

Hessa's kiss grew urgent, consuming. Their mouths met with increasing hunger, their tongues dancing as if they had done so a thousand times in a thousand different lives. Their hands roamed freely, learning the map of each other's skin, each curve and hollow worshipped with reverence. Moans spilt between them, shameless and sweet, echoing in the stillness with no care for who might hear.

Alina had never felt more treasured. As Hessa's lips journeyed from her mouth to the elegant line of her throat, to the soft rise of her breasts, to the curve of her belly and the warmth waiting below, Alina trembled.

When Hessa's tongue touched the tender flesh of her inner thigh, and then beyond, Alina arched her body alight with a pleasure so fierce it bordered on pain. She did not shy away. She did not shrink. She opened herself like a desert flower greeting the dawn, and let herself be loved.

Her fingers curled into the thin blanket beneath her, the only anchor she could find as waves of bliss overtook her. She gripped it tightly to stop herself from marking Hessa's skin with the fire that now burnt through her.

Alina had never felt so achingly beautiful, nor so fiercely powerful, as she did in that singular, sacred moment. There was no hesitation in her limbs as she rolled Hessa gently beneath her, answering the invitation in the desert princess's eyes. Every gasp, every soft moan that slipped from Hessa's parted lips became a guide, a whispered map leading Alina deeper into the art of worship.

Her body thrummed with heat, a fire stoked by each breathless cry, each tremble she coaxed from Hessa's frame. And when she lifted her gaze to see Hessa arching, twisting in the crumpled bed linens, undone beneath the reverent touch of her mouth and fingers, Alina's heart soared. To bring her such pleasure, to make her fall apart so beautifully, felt like a prayer answered.

She never wanted the moment to end. Never wanted the sun to rise on a world where she could not taste this closeness again.

'Alina...' Hessa breathed her name like a vow, her voice soft and trembling as she guided Alina onto her, hands finding their way with instinctive reverence. Their bodies moved as one, fingers entwined in shared rhythm, and every gasp, every moan, sang of their surrender. 'I'm trying to hold on...'

'Don't,' Alina whispered, her voice unravelled with pleasure. Their release came together, a crescendo of sensation that left them breathless, Alina's hips moving in a slow, pulsing rhythm to savour the moment. Laughter bubbled from her lips as she collapsed beside Hessa, joy crackling in the aftermath. But her breath caught when Hessa, with a teasing gleam in her eyes, brought Alina's fingers to her mouth and sucked them slowly, deliberately, before leaning in and stealing a kiss that tasted of fire, salt, and something dangerously sweet.

'I don't think I'll ever tire of this,' Alina confessed, her lips curving into a soft, satisfied smile.

'Good,' Hessa replied, her voice a whisper wrapped in warmth as she lazily traced her finger along the length of Alina's arm, sending shivers in its wake. 'Because I very much intend to do this again.'

'When?' Alina asked, her voice laced with hope, her eyes searching Hessa's for an answer she was almost afraid to want too much.

But Hessa said nothing. Instead, her smile deepened into something unreadable, something that danced between mischief and desire. She leaned in, pressing her lips to Alina's with a slow, deliberate hunger that stole the breath from Alina's lungs and set her soul alight.

Before she could gather her thoughts, Hessa was above her once more, every touch a flame, every caress a promise. Alina's skin bloomed beneath Hessa's fingers, and the world narrowed to the space between them where nothing else mattered but this.

'Now, right now,' Hessa whispered, her voice a breathy promise as she scattered tender kisses along the soft curve of Alina's stomach, inch by inch, until she reached the bend of her thighs. With gentle hands, she lifted Alina's legs, parting them with reverence, and once more let her tongue wander with intimate devotion across familiar, sacred terrain.

Alina did not notice the way the sun slipped quietly from the sky, yielding to the hush of twilight and the velvet shroud of night. Time itself seemed to still as the two girls clung to one another, bodies pressed close in a dance as old as the stars. They moved with unspoken understanding, touching and exploring with tireless affection, as darkness deepened and the world beyond their embrace faded to a distant whisper.

'Yaa aras ma sahraa,' Alina whispered against the curve of Hessa's chin, the words a vow of quiet devotion spoken into the hush of the room. They lay bare upon the narrow cot, their limbs entwined, skin pressed to skin in a sacred tangle of warmth and trust. Even in rest, Alina's fingers wandered, light as a sigh, tracing idle patterns across the soft plane of Hessa's stomach, coaxing goosebumps to rise in their wake. She pressed a kiss there, tender and playful, and both girls dissolved into soft, breathless laughter.

Hessa's moonlit eyes shimmered with unspoken affection as she leaned down to press reverent kisses, first to Alina's brow, then her nose, and finally her waiting mouth.

They drifted into sleep like that, curled around one another, smiles lingering on their lips, as if even in dreams they refused to part.

Chapter Fifty

House of Sand
Desert Kingdom

I tried teaching Hadrian the Sandhii language.
He is better off with a sword.

Tabitha Wysteria

Alina had no desire to move. She was adrift in a dream far sweeter than any her mind could have conjured. Breathing in Hessa's warm, familiar, intoxicating scent. She closed her eyes and let every muscle soften. The world melted away: no worries, no fear, no tomorrow. There was only this. The present, suspended in stillness as she lay with Hessa moulded against her side.

But reality crept in, cruel and unrelenting, crashing over her like a wave and lodging itself in her throat as guilt. Guilt for revelling in peace while others suffered. She should have been preparing, readying herself for battle, not idling in bed with her hand gliding over Hessa's bare back.

'Your mind is far too loud,' Hessa mumbled.

Alina gave a breath of laughter. 'It is not.'

'I can hear your thoughts, amira.'

Alina turned, their noses brushing, soft and intimate. 'We should be training.'

'You fell off a mountain,' Hessa replied with a smirk. 'No training, at least for now.'

Alina traced a languid finger down the curve of Hessa's spine, drifting lower with teasing intent.

'What we did last night must surely count as bodily exertion, and yet, you did not once complain.'

Hessa laughed, rich and fond. 'You're a terribly wicked princess.'

Alina's deep brown eyes darkened with desire as Hessa rose and straddled her, legs poised on either side of the drakonian princess, the motion fluid and commanding. She leaned forward, claiming Alina's hand with a slow, deliberate grace, her lips wrapping around slender fingers in a sensual kiss before guiding them intimately within herself. Alina's eyes widened, a glimmer of awe mingling with the heat that burnt behind her gaze.

'Utterly wicked, amira,' Hessa whispered, her voice a velvet caress as she guided Alina's fingers, rolling her hips in a slow, deliberate rhythm, each movement a silent invocation of pleasure.

Alina began to move as well, her other hand slipping across her own skin, exploring with trembling need. Waves of sensation coiled through her, tightening every muscle, and in that moment, all thought of training, of war, of the burdened world beyond their shared breath, vanished like mist at dawn.

Hessa lowered her head and gently caught Alina's nipple between her teeth, a playful bite that sent a jolt of heat racing through Alina. The mere sensation unravelled her, igniting every inch of her body as she continued to touch herself with desperate longing.

Hessa smiled. Sly and satisfied as she slowly leaned back, drawing away like a retreating tide. Alina hesitated, uncertainty shimmering in her eyes as her hand stilled.

'Do not stop, amira,' Hessa commanded, her voice low and silken with intent.

'But... why are you moving away from me?' Alina asked, her brows drawing together in soft confusion.

'I'm going to sit right here,' Hessa said, settling back with deliberate grace, 'and watch you pleasure yourself, for me.'

'But I want to touch you too,' Alina said, a trace of longing in her voice.

Hessa's smile was slow, knowing. 'I know. But for now, this is what I want. Touch yourself, amira, for me.'

Alina had thought she might feel shy perched on the narrow cot, her back pressed against the cool stone wall, legs parted just enough as her fingers moved between them. But her focus remained fixed on Hessa, who sat mere inches away, watching her with unwavering intensity. And it was that look, the smouldering weight of Hessa's eyes upon her, that sent a rush of desire sweeping through her belly, hot and consuming.

'I'm going to...' Alina began, but the words dissolved on her tongue as the wave of pleasure crashed over her. In an instant, Hessa was beside her once more, slipping her fingers deep into Alina's swollen centre with urgent tenderness. Gasping, Alina surrendered to the rhythm, her body moving against Hessa's touch, crying out her name as ecstasy overtook her.

The door burst open, and Alina shrieked, startled, as an intruder stood frozen in the threshold—white eyes wide with shock at the sight of the two princesses entwined. With a weary sigh, Hessa climbed off Alina's body, the reluctance in her movements unmistakable. She turned slowly, her attention settling on Saren.

'I didn't know...' Saren's expression tightened, jaw clenching. 'I heard Alina had awoken and came to check on her.

I'll return later.'

Hessa gave a single nod, dismissing her with cool finality. But Alina caught something in Saren's eyes before she turned away, something glacial and unyielding. A chill crept along Alina's spine, and she instinctively reached for Hessa's arm, pulling her close.

'We should get up,' Hessa said, but bent forward to press a gentle kiss to Alina's lips.

'Saren and you...' Alina began, a whisper of memory stirring in her mind, some long-past conversation, the sudden recollection that there had once been something between them, something romantic.

At once, Hessa's smile faded and her shoulders grew taut. 'That was a long time ago, amira. She is my sacanda, second-in-command. Nothing more.'

Alina searched her eyes, hungry for any hint of falsehood, some subtle crack in her words. But there was nothing. Hessa's stare was steady, unflinching. She was telling the truth.

'I don't care for her in that way,' Hessa said softly, pulling Alina closer. 'It never meant... It never meant this.'

Alina gave a small nod, resting her forehead against Hessa's, her chest loosening from the knot of worry. She had just uncovered something raw and real in Hessa, and the thought of losing it made her ache. 'I ought to speak to her. She looked... concerned.'

But Hessa gently pushed the drakonian princess back onto the cot, lifting Alina's arms above her head as she climbed atop her once more. Their bodies tangled again in laughter and heat, kisses exchanged in breathless succession, the warmth between them so entwined they could no longer tell whose skin was giving off the fire.

'Saren can wait,' Hessa whispered into her ear, voice like

silk. 'Now... where were we?'

...

Alina had spent the past two hours honing her sword-throwing technique. Her skill had improved remarkably, so much so that she managed to hurl the blade across the ravine between two mountain walls, striking an apple that had been left, precariously, on a distant windowsill.

Hessa let out a delighted laugh as the fruit was neatly impaled. She clapped from her perch at the edge of a narrow road, one that tapered off into empty air with only the rooftop of a building far below to catch a misstep. Her right leg swung lazily as she peeled a piece of desert-grown fruit, its scent sharp and sun-kissed. She broke off a slice and handed it to Alina, who joined her, settling close enough that their knees brushed gently.

'It is time,' Hessa said, staring out over the sprawl of the city, her thoughts adrift as she chewed contemplatively. At Alina's confused look, she added, 'You're ready, amira. Ready to fight.'

'I'm not,' Alina muttered.

Hessa gave her a firm nudge with the tip of one finger. 'Yes, you are. It's only your mind that doubts. I've watched you train every single day. You're as good as I am.'

Alina let out a snort of disbelief.

'Well... perhaps not quite as good as me,' Hessa teased with a wicked smirk, popping another wedge of fruit into her mouth with theatrical flair.

'When should we go?' Alina asked, her voice barely above a whisper.

Hessa handed her another slice, considering. 'We shouldn't wait much longer. I've listened to the whispers but there seems to be no witches here. We'll gather what we need here, then make our way back to your land.'

Alina exhaled, a breath laced with tension. The thought of returning stirred something uneasy in her. She had long stopped counting the weeks that had folded into months since she left.

Home.

Was it still home? There was nothing left there but a title she no longer craved, a throne that felt cold to the touch. Her place, her true place was here, beside a desert princess who perched on rooftops and spat into the wind, who picked fights and turned life into a game. A woman who adored evening walks, long massages, and kisses stolen beneath starlight.

Hessa was her home.

Alina caught sight of Saren seated on a rooftop not far ahead, her figure still as stone against the burnished sky. Alina knew she needed to speak with her, to explain that the climbing accident had not been her fault. She would find the right moment, perhaps later that evening when they all gathered for supper. Still, she doubted Saren would be willing to talk, not after what she'd witnessed. No matter what Hessa claimed, Alina had seen the flash of pain in Saren's eyes the moment she'd found them tangled in bed together.

Even now, the second-in-command cast furtive glances down towards them, her hands clenching into fists at the sight of their laughter. Resentment shimmered across her features like heat rising from the desert stone.

It would have to wait.

'What troubles you?' Hessa asked, her voice gentle, perceptive.

'The Dunayans... this isn't their war.'

'But I am their leader,' Hessa replied, tilting her head with a frown. 'They follow where I go.'

'Still… I don't know.' Alina rubbed her forehead, as though trying to soothe the thoughts gnawing at her. 'I can't help but feel… maybe they're not happy with me being here.'

'That's not true, amira,' Hessa said firmly. 'You are one of us.'

Alina nodded, reaching for another slice of fruit and biting into its sun-warmed flesh. And yet, the unease remained, a whisper at the back of her mind, insistent and unnerving, as though something half-forgotten was begging to be remembered. But what? What was it about belonging that felt suddenly so fragile?

She looked up again towards the rooftop, and this time, met Saren's gaze directly. The white eyes that stared back at her brimmed with such raw hatred it stole the breath from her lungs.

Alina tore her attention away, heart thudding, and turned all her attention to Hessa, forcing the weight of Saren's silent fury from her thoughts.

'Let's go,' Hessa said, brushing her hands against her brown trousers before letting out a sharp whistle that echoed down the sun-scorched street. Within moments, Dunayans emerged from every shadowed crevice and quiet corner, appearing as if conjured by the sound itself. Their faces were veiled, heads wrapped in cloth against the heat, weapons expertly concealed within the folds and secret compartments of their clothing.

Alina pulled her karash up over her nose, concealing every part of her face save her eyes. The desert garb had become like a second skin, familiar, worn, hers. The scorpion-braced armguards that once chafed her now rested against her skin with ease. She had learnt to move in these clothes, to fight in them, to use their hidden pockets for blades and smoke bombs and curved little daggers with poison-tipped edges.

The citizens of Madari watched with wide, wary eyes as the Dunayans made their silent procession down the streets. Some of the Dunayans paused at market stalls to purchase supplies; others disappeared into smoky taverns mid-brawl to restore a semblance of order. A few locals greeted them with nods of respect, while others turned away in haste, not daring to risk the wrath of desert warriors.

Hessa gave a short whistle, and two Dunayans immediately stationed themselves outside a small, weather-worn tavern. She took Alina's hand without a word and pulled her inside. The air was thick with the scent of sweat and smoke, the haze casting everything in a gauzy blur. Without speaking, Hessa gestured for Alina to stay near the entrance while she slipped through the crowd, purposeful and unseen. She approached a figure perched on a stool. No words were exchanged, only a subtle motion, a passing of something small and glinting that Hessa tucked swiftly into the sleeve of her tunic.

Alina did not ask what had been given to the desert princess when they stepped back outside. If it mattered, Hessa would tell her. She trusted her completely, irrevocably.

The Dunayans made their way towards a modest inn they always frequented when in Madari. Inside, the scent of spice and flame greeted them. Bowls of fragrant rice and dried, fire-kissed meat waited on long wooden tables that filled the warm room, while soft cushions lay scattered on the floor as seats. Hessa exchanged quiet words with a few of her warriors, while Alina sat and ate in silence, savouring the simple comfort of the meal. A small smile tugged at her lips as she felt Hessa's hand rest gently on her leg, steady, grounding, a silent assurance that she was there, always by her side.

'We're all rather surprised by how swiftly you recovered,' Saren said, settling onto the empty cushion at Alina's other side.

The drakonian princess hadn't noticed Saren approach, for she had slipped in like a shadow.

'So am I,' Alina replied softly.

'Almost seems like magic,' Saren mused, something sharp and glinting flashing in her pale eyes. 'You ought to be careful, farahi. Folk might start whispering about witchcraft.'

'I am no witch.' Alina bared her teeth, the words sharp as steel. 'Witches murdered my family.'

Saren gave a low, humourless chuckle as she reached for two cups, handing one to Alina. 'No offence meant, farahi.'

Alina gave a short nod and accepted the cup of Chaaka, downing it a little too fast. The warm, spiced liquid slid down her throat and for a moment the world tilted, only to right itself just as quickly.

'I wanted to speak with you,' Alina said, clearing her throat. 'The fall on the mountain wasn't your fault. I don't want you to carry blame for it.'

'I know.' Saren reached for two more cups.

'You... know?'

'I know it wasn't my fault.' Her smile, when it came, was a blade wrapped in silk. 'Only a farahi would fall.'

A few Dunayans laughed under their breath, but most turned their heads with narrowed eyes, discomfort plain on their faces.

'Saren.' Hessa didn't lift her gaze, but the warning in her voice cut like cracked thunder. *Enough.*

'I'm merely speaking the truth,' Saren said with a shrug. 'No true Dunayan would lose their footing. A farahi is a farahi for a reason.'

At that, Hessa turned, her face carved from fury. 'Do you wish to sleep outside tonight?'

Saren's jaw tightened. She said nothing. Instead, she snatched up her cup, rose to her feet, and stalked away. A couple of

Dunayans followed, but most turned back to their meals and conversations, unease settling like dust in the wake of her departure.

Alina looked down at her hands, fingers tightening slightly in her lap, unsure of what to say or whether she should say anything at all.

'Don't listen to her.' Hessa flicked her hand in the air, as if she could scatter Saren's presence like smoke.

'But she's not entirely wrong,' Alina muttered, biting the inside of her cheek. Frustration coiled tight in her chest. 'If I weren't farahi, I never would have fallen.'

Hessa rolled her eyes with theatrical exasperation. 'Aish, amira. Yaa aras salla.' She gestured towards a Dunayan lounging across from them. 'She once fell clean off a rooftop just from sitting too far forward. Two years ago.' Then she nudged Alina and tilted her chin towards another Dunayan, who smiled mid-chew, her mouth full. 'And Arena over there? She was riding one of our serpents, got too bold, flew right off and knocked herself out cold for two days.' Laughter rippled through the group like wind across sand. 'And Isla...' Hessa smirked. 'Isla once managed to trip over her own two feet. Astapada.' *Stupid.*

Alina couldn't help but smile.

'We are who we are, amira. Not perfect. We stumble, we fall, we make fools of ourselves. But being a Dunayan has never meant being flawless. It means rising, again and again, no matter how hard we've hit the ground.'

A chorus of whistles rose into the warm air, and every Dunayan lifted their cup in salute.

'I've seen you fall more than once, Alina Farahi-Sahraa Amira,' Hessa said, her voice tender, drawing Alina closer, as though even the breath of space between them was unbearable. 'And each time, you've risen prouder, stronger. That is what makes you one of us. So never doubt your strength. Never question who you are.'

Alina nodded, her eyes glinting with something fierce and quietly resolute. She cupped Hessa's face in both hands, heedless of who might be watching, of whispers or wandering glances. Hessa was right.

Her strength was hers to claim. Her power, hers to wield. Her fall and her rising, hers to own.

And so she kissed Hessa like the world was burning, and they were the only two left beneath the flames.

Chapter Fifty-One

House of Flames
Kingdom of Fire

The Council will fall. It will be rebuilt. And in time, it will fall again.
This has been the cycle for a thousand years.
It always ends in corruption.
No one should wield such power.
It corrodes the soul.

Tabitha Wysteria

The land of fire and dragons stretched before Dawn. Vast fields of scorched earth, jagged rock, and villages nestled like forgotten embers around the larger, imposing cities. Drakonians were a people famed for their opulence, their intricately crafted architecture, and their insatiable hunger for superiority.

Dawn couldn't help but envy them.

She had grown up in a kingdom where the earth yielded nothing but dust and despair, where hunger gnawed at bellies and hope wilted beneath a sky of endless grey, where the rain fell often and without mercy. It was a barren realm, a place where nothing grew without the coaxing touch of magic. The remnants of buildings lay scattered like bones across blackened grass that had never dared to grow again. Most forests had long since vanished, devoured by the flames of dragons in the past.

And yet, what stirred most bitterly within her wasn't the ruin. It was the knowledge that her people possessed the power to mend it all... and simply chose not to.

They drank from goblets laced with old grudges, steeped in hatred and tradition. Magic could revive the land, restore its beauty, bring wealth and strength and dignity. But the Council would not permit it. To rebuild was to risk forgetting. And forgetting, in their eyes, was the ultimate betrayal.

Dawn understood then, why so many of the younger witches and warlocks had turned to Hagan, why they had abandoned the voices of their elders. They were tired of living like vermin, scuttling through dirt and ruins, forgotten by the world. No, they wanted more. They deserved more.

And Dawn... she had stood beside Hagan unwaveringly. Without question. Without doubt. She would have given her life for the cause.

So when Hagan had asked her to attend court, to seduce the Fire Prince... she hadn't understood, not at first. She couldn't see how such a task would bring them any closer to the future they longed for. But still, she obeyed. No questions asked.

Oh, how she had fallen for those golden eyes and that disarming smile. For the prince so many whispered about with disdain, calling him cold, even cruel, because he spent his days not at court, but on the wall with his men. His silence had bred rumours, stirred questions. What secrets did he keep locked behind that quiet stare?

Dawn had uncovered them soon enough. And it was those secrets, the ones he hid from the world, that had made her love him all the more.

But when she had finally confessed, foolishly believing that love, their love, would be enough to earn his forgiveness, he had not embraced her. He had turned his back. He had looked at her as though she were something vile, something wretched and unworthy of pity. The loathing in his golden eyes had pierced her more sharply than any blade.

And yet... she had continued to love him.

Love does not vanish simply because it is no longer returned. No. No matter how she tried to wrench it from her chest, it lingered, stubborn and aching. She had spiralled into despair, drowning in hatred, sorrow, and that ever-clinging thread of love. Love for the man who had destroyed her. Who had proved her right in the end.

Because no one could truly love a witch. Not once they saw the purple eyes. Not once they remembered what that meant.

In the years that followed, Dawn did all that Hagan asked of her. She carried out orders with ruthless precision, killing the names on her lists without hesitation. She poisoned, she plotted, and became the very thing they had always accused her of being.

If a monster was what they wanted, then a monster they would have.

'Why have you stopped?'

Dawn stiffened at the sharp edge of the wyverian prince's voice, laced with irritation.

'My feet hurt,' she muttered, with just enough petulance to make it sting. The moment his dark eyes narrowed, she pulled a theatrical face and reached out. 'Carry me.'

Oh, how she delighted in provoking him.

'No.'

'Is this how wyverians treat women?' she asked sweetly, quickening her pace to keep up as he moved on without missing a step.

'You're not a—' He bit the words off, jaw tightening, but she had already heard enough. *You're not a woman.* Because to them, witches weren't people at all. They were neither women nor men. Just abominations wrapped in skin.

'Are you so certain?' she said, arching a brow, her voice silken and mocking. 'Shall I lift my skirts so you might check for yourself?'

'You were starting to vex me a little less these days,' he muttered. 'You've just managed to ruin it.'

'What a terrible shame,' she replied, utterly unrepentant.

Dawn turned her eyes towards the distant silhouette of Fireheart and let out a dramatic sigh. It was still painfully far off, a smudge on the horizon beyond endless trees and thorns. Her feet throbbed with every step, raw with blisters, the skin torn and bleeding inside her boots. They had been trudging through the blasted Forest of Endless Trees for what felt like eternity, its enchantments stretching the path with cruel glee. And now they had endured yet more punishing days, trudging beneath the relentless, scorching sun, with barely a drop of water to sustain them.

'It's going to take *days*,' she groaned, and she no longer cared if she sounded like a petulant child. All she wanted was a proper bed, a nice meal, and to peel off her boots and elevate her poor, battered feet. 'I still fail to understand why you insist on heading towards Fireheart. Your army lies in quite the opposite direction, commander.' With a huff, she kicked a small pebble down the path in irritation.

'How many times must we circle this conversation?' Kai sighed, weary. 'If Fireheart burns, we go. We'll slip inside the city and see what stirs beneath the smoke. If fortune favours us, we'll gather intelligence before my army arrives. It may yet give us an edge.' His gaze swept over her, sharp and knowing. 'Stop pouting. I'm certain you can endure a few more days without swooning into Ash's arms.'

Dawn tilted her chin defiantly, her annoyance written plain

across her face. In truth, she had been restless to return to Ash, the knowledge of Hagan's plans weighing heavy upon her. Yet, with each passing day, another scheme had begun to take root, one that would lead her far from the path Hagan had so carefully set. No, she had no intention of following his game to the letter. A new plan had begun to unfurl... and it involved a certain tall, exasperating wyverian prince.

'Surely no one has ever swooned over you,' Dawn muttered under her breath.

'Witch.'

'What?'

Kai paused, something unreadable flashing in his eyes. He must have seen the truth of her exhaustion written all over her face, because whatever biting remark had been on the tip of his tongue died there. His shoulders dropped slightly, his posture no longer rigid with disdain. Something softer passed over his expression, something perilously close to pity.

And that, Dawn could not bear.

She hated pity more than cruelty.

'We can ride my shadow, I suppose.'

Dawn blinked, uncertain of what he meant, until he whistled.

She gasped as a horse emerged from nothingness, called forth like a spirit from smoke. It was a magnificent creature, forged from shadow and ash, its form flickering and shifting with every breath. The beast tossed its head in what could only be described as disdain, clearly unimpressed to be summoned.

'You must be jesting,' she snarled through gritted teeth. 'Are you telling me that all the while we were stumbling through that cursed forest, blistered and half-dead, we could have been riding that?'

Kai said nothing, too absorbed in stroking his wretched,

spectral beast.

'Why?' she snapped. 'Do you despise me so much that you'd rather suffer than allow me a place on your horse?'

His gaze snapped to hers—sharp, blazing, and full of barely contained rage.

'Of course I hate you, witch,' he hissed. 'Because of you my sister Haven is dead. Alina Acheron is dead. And I will never forgive that. You may not have wielded the blade, but your kind did.' He drew in a long, slow breath, his chest rising and falling as he fought to steady himself. 'But I didn't hide my shadow from you to cause pain. I left him behind because I feared the forest's magic might harm him.'

Dawn edged away from the warmth, the quiet, unspoken affection that appeared in his eyes as he turned to his horse. She had never seen such a look on his face before. It was almost mesmerising, dangerously addictive, the kind of expression that made her want to bottle it, to stretch the moment until it lasted forever. She wondered, just for a fleeting second, what it might feel like to have Kai Blackburn look at her that way. Perhaps, if he did, she would feel a little less like a monster.

She bit her lip, hesitating.

Should she tell him? Should she say the words that would banish the torment from his eyes and ease a small fragment of his pain?

She's alive. Alina Acheron is alive.

The words perched on the edge of her tongue, but something stopped her. The same damned thing that always stopped her.

Because telling him would mean watching him turn and run, riding off after the drakonian princess without looking back. And although Dawn knew it was the right thing to do, what any decent soul would do, she had never claimed to be decent. She had always been a selfish girl at heart.

She needed Kai. Needed him to reach Ash. And she could not, would not, let him mount that shadowy beast and chase after a girl who was supposed to be dead.

Her attention shifted to the horse, to the way Kai's fingers moved across its form with such quiet reverence it made her stomach twist. There was too much tenderness in the gesture. Too much care. She couldn't bear it.

If he adored his horse so deeply, he would never let her near it.

She pictured herself limping after him all the way to Fireheart while he rode effortlessly ahead. Her blisters throbbed just at the thought. No. She couldn't endure it. She would lie down right here in the dirt and rot before she followed him on foot another step.

How dare he summon that damn horse only to flaunt it in front of her?

They called witches cruel, but even she wouldn't torment someone so viciously.

Well...

She *would.*

'Why are you pouting, witch?' Kai asked, his voice laced with amusement.

Before Dawn could summon a retort, he extended his hand towards her. She stared at it, blinking in surprise, uncertain what he expected. They had never touched like that before, so casually, so willingly and the idea alone sent a faint flush to her cheeks.

'It doesn't hold the secrets of the universe,' he said dryly, frowning at her hesitation. 'Are you going to take it or not?'

'For what?'

He rolled his eyes in exasperation. 'To help you up.'

'Help me up...?'

'Are you daft, witch? Or simply trying my patience?' He nodded towards the shadowy steed. 'To help you onto my horse. You did say your feet were hurting. Now hurry, or I might change my mind.'

Dawn's chest gave a traitorous twist.

He wasn't going to leave her behind after all. He wasn't planning to ride on without her, forcing her to stumble along behind him like an unwanted burden. He was offering her a place on the horse, on his shadow. He trusted her. Trusted her enough to share it.

'I can climb up myself, commander,' she snapped, chin lifting with defiance. No matter how deeply the gesture warmed her, she would never give him the satisfaction of seeing what it meant. With a scowl, she brushed his hand aside and climbed up quickly, unable to keep the triumphant smile from spreading across her face.

It vanished the moment she felt him climb up behind her.

'But—'

Kai let out a snort of laughter.

'I'm not fool enough to leave you alone on my horse.' His arms slid around her, firm and final, encircling her like a barrier of steel. She was caged. And he knew it.

'I wasn't going to ride off without you,' she said, though her tone suggested the thought had very much occurred to her. The moment she realised he would let her mount his shadow, the idea had taken root. A part of her had yearned to escape, to run back to Hagan and the safety of her own people. But she had made a vow to reach Ash, and she intended to see it through.

Dawn shifted slightly, pressing herself closer into Kai's frame with deliberate intent.

'What are you doing?' he asked, his voice sharp enough to slice through stone.

'Getting comfortable,' she purred, her grin widening with wicked delight as she moved just enough to feel the undeniable presence beneath her.

'I will throw you off this horse.'

'Is that your cock I feel?' she mused innocently. 'Oh no… surely not. It's far too big to be yours.'

'Would you rather walk?'

'Not at all, I love to ride,' she replied, glancing over her shoulder with a look that left no ambiguity in the meaning of *ride*. The wyverian prince met her gaze, expression unreadable, until he gripped her chin and forced her to face forward once more. Dawn let out a breathless laugh. 'Have I made you nervous, commander?'

'You do not rattle me, witch,' he said, low and cool. 'You inspire nothing in me but exasperation.'

She laughed again, covering her mouth with one hand.

'Is that so?' she said, glancing back a second time, catching the unmistakable tension in his body. 'Because what I feel pressing against my backside doesn't exactly scream *exasperation*.'

Without warning, his massive hand clamped over her face, and a second later she found herself unceremoniously shoved off the horse. She landed hard in the dirt with a shriek.

Correction. She hadn't fallen. He had *thrown* her.

Cursing, Dawn glared after him as he rode on, utterly unmoved by her indignation.

'Feel that?' he called over his shoulder, tone infuriatingly smug. 'That's the ground beneath your arse.'

Dawn scrambled to her feet and screamed—loud, raw, and furious. She hurled every curse she could summon, the foulest, vilest words her mind could conjure spilling from her lips like venom. She called him every unspeakable name under the sun, voice echoing through the trees with wild abandon.

But it wasn't truly because he had thrown her from the horse.

No. She screamed because she was tired. Bone-deep, soul-weary tired.

Tired of fighting.

Tired of pretending.

Tired of being hated by the world simply for existing.

'Are you quite finished?' came his voice—calm, detached, yet tinged with confusion.

Dawn glanced up through damp lashes to see the wyverian prince on his horse, his brows drawn together, clearly baffled by the force of her outburst. She turned away, wiping her face with the back of her hand, trying to erase the fury and pain written there. She couldn't meet his eyes, not those dark eyes that pretended not to notice what hers so clearly held.

Kai leaned over slightly and extended his hand.

This time, she took it.

And for once, she didn't pull away.

...

'You'll need to disguise yourself,' Kai whispered against her ear as they approached a modest roadside inn, its windows glowing softly in the twilight. Dawn stirred awake with a sharp intake of breath. At some point, she had fallen asleep against his chest, and though his entire body had gone rigid the moment her head had come to rest there, he hadn't moved. Hadn't pushed her away. Not even when every rational thought screamed at him to do so.

'Do you have enough magic?' he asked, his voice low, almost reluctant.

Dawn didn't argue. She simply nodded and lifted her hands. A soft green mist curled from her fingers, swirling in the air like enchanted smoke. Kai watched, unable to look away, as the haze enveloped her completely. When it faded, the witch was gone. In her place sat a young innocent and unassuming drakonian woman.

It unsettled him.

Strange, how wrong it felt. Stranger still, how much he wanted the witch back, despite everything he claimed to feel.

They stopped at the inn, eager for something more satisfying than the forest's miserable offering of wild berries and mushrooms. Something warm. Filling. Maybe even a few hours of real rest, something that might make the world seem less sharp around the edges.

The drakonian woman at the door gasped the moment she caught sight of Kai, her eyes shining with curiosity and surprise at the sight of one of her kind travelling alone with a wyverian. If only she knew the truth that the girl beside him was no drakonian maiden, but a witch cloaked in magic and secrecy.

'You should've joined a travelling performance act,' Kai muttered as they were shown to a quiet corner of the dining room after Dawn had dramatically told the innkeeper about their travels.

'Shut up,' Dawn hissed under her breath. Her eyes lit up at the steaming bowls brought to their table, and before she could even savour the scent, she was devouring it with reckless abandon, soup spilling down her chin and trailing along her neck.

Kai stared, equal parts horrified and impressed, as she continued to gulp and slurp without the faintest hint of decorum. 'Then again, perhaps not.'

'Oh my,' the innkeeper exclaimed, bustling forward. 'I'll

fetch you another bowl straight away.'

Dawn let out a burp, entirely unbothered.

'Delightful,' Kai muttered dryly.

She kicked him beneath the table.

'Try that again,' he warned.

'Don't be so rude,' she snapped, her hands curling into fists.

'Is everything all right?' the innkeeper asked gently, casting a concerned glance between the pair before setting down a steaming dish piled high with roasted meats, vegetables, and golden potatoes.

'Yes, everything is fine,' Kai replied.

But the innkeeper lingered, her eyes settling on Dawn with maternal concern. She looked not at the towering wyverian beside her, but at the girl she believed to be a young drakonian —frail, frightened, perhaps in trouble.

Dawn's lip curled in amusement. She could easily turn, let tears brim in her eyes, and cry out before the entire room, claiming he had taken her, that he had hurt her. The thought had clearly played across her mind like a wicked little drama, because Kai could see it in her eyes. He always could.

But he knew she wouldn't. Because he hadn't kidnapped her. She was here by choice. *She* was following *him*.

'He's got a bit of a temper,' Dawn said sweetly, flashing the innkeeper a too-bright smile. 'Wyverians, such big tempers and such tiny, tiny cocks.'

Kai's foot struck her shin hard beneath the table. The innkeeper flushed a brilliant shade of crimson and quickly excused herself, bustling away without another word.

Dawn giggled, delighted with herself.

'You are utterly insufferable,' Kai muttered.

He watched as she tore into the meal with her hands, licking sauce from her fingers with the gusto of someone who hadn't eaten properly in weeks. She demolished her plate in minutes and was just lifting it to her mouth to lick it clean when Kai stopped her with a pointed look and a slow shake of his head.

'Drakonians don't eat like pigs.'

'Then they've never truly been hungry,' she replied, unbothered.

'Can't you behave yourself?'

'Why?' Dawn crossed her arms over her chest. 'Do I embarrass you?'

'No,' he said, glancing around. 'But they might grow suspicious. Drakonians don't speak about cocks, or eat with their hands.'

Dawn bit her lower lip, eyes roaming around the room. 'I know that,' she said, voice low. 'I spent years pretending to be one.'

'Then why…?'

'Because I hate it,' she snapped, pushing to her feet. 'You don't know what it's like to pretend for years to be someone else. To feel accepted. To be loved, and then to be despised the moment you show who you really are.' She turned her back to him, spine stiff with pain she refused to show. 'I'm going to get a room.'

Kai wanted to follow her, but he remained seated, frozen in place. She needed space, that much was clear. A moment to gather her thoughts, to breathe without anyone watching. He would give her that, for now. With a weary sigh, he pushed his plate aside, his appetite long since vanished.

He couldn't begin to imagine what it must have felt like spending years cloaked in a false identity, building friendships, a home, a life, only to have it all crumble the moment people glimpsed the truth behind your face. The fear. The betrayal. The rejection.

Kai shook his head and cursed under his breath. He refused to pity the witch. No one had forced her into that life. Dawn could have stayed in her own kingdom, where no one would have asked her to wear a mask. It had been her choice... hadn't it?

Still, as he rubbed a hand over his tired eyes, he knew, deep down, that no matter how much he tried to place the blame solely on her shoulders, it didn't fit. It wasn't her fault her home had been taken. It wasn't her fault the world recoiled at the sight of purple eyes. None of it was.

But.

She had chosen to fight in this war. She had chosen a side. And in doing so, she had helped bring about the deaths of Haven and Alina. And for that, for them, Kai would never forgive her. No matter how real she seemed now. No matter how tired her eyes looked when she thought no one was watching.

When the innkeeper returned to clear the table, he leaned forward.

'What can you tell me of Fireheart?' he asked, voice low and clipped.

'Most of the drakonians fled before things turned truly dire,' she said, gathering the empty dishes. 'They've scattered across villages and cities, hiding where they can. Fireheart is a battleground now, and has been for weeks.'

'Who's fighting the witches?'

'The Red Guard,' she replied. 'The ones still stationed in the city, and those who arrived from neighbouring towns when the news spread. But without a royal family, there are no commands, just chaos. Everyone's fighting for survival. Some citizens have stayed behind to defend their homes, but...'

'But?'

She shrugged, her expression sombre. 'Hope is fading.

Fireheart may soon fall to the witches, just as Spark did.'

Kai nodded, offered a quiet thank you, and paid for the food and room. Without another word, he climbed the stairs to the small chamber they'd been given.

Dawn was already stretched across one of the cots, her eyes narrowed into slits the moment he stepped inside.

'You could have asked for two separate rooms,' Kai said coldly.

'Trust me, commander, I would have if such an option had been available. I do not wish to share anything with you.' Kai snorted. 'You could be a gentleman and sleep outside.' That wicked dangerous smile appeared.

'Not a chance, but nice try.'

Dawn shrugged. 'I think deep down you're tempted to see me naked on this bed. I bet tonight you'll be fantasizing about what that little cock of yours could do to me.'

'You want to help Ash, don't you?' he replied, pulling off his armour piece by piece, setting it carefully to one side, completely ignoring her. 'Then you're going to tell me how to stop Hagan.'

Dawn had dropped the glamour, her purple eyes sharpening with resolve. Kai would never voice it aloud, but he preferred her like this, unmasked, unhidden. In her true form. Those eyes he had so long claimed to loathe had a way of speaking when her mouth stayed silent, always brimming with emotion. When she'd donned the guise of a drakonian, all trace of that spark had vanished, as though some essential piece of her had been stripped away with the illusion.

She doesn't have a soul, Kai reminded himself.

'We need to find my sisters,' Dawn said, her voice clear, unwavering. 'We can work out a plan to draw Hagan's attention. If Ash can command the Red Guard, and your forces strike at the right moment, we'll have a chance. Hagan leans on magic for everything. But against a true army, even he can't win.'

'He must know that's a possibility,' Kai replied, settling on the opposite cot. The room was modest, barely large enough to house the two narrow beds pressed against opposite walls, a chipped basin, and a single window that looked out onto the quiet road below.

Dawn shrugged from where she lay curled beneath a thin blanket. 'He never shares his true intentions. He keeps everything to himself.'

'Don't witches have a Council?'

'They do.'

'Do they support what Hagan's doing?'

Dawn shook her head slowly. 'No. They never wanted this. Not like this. For years, they thought of rebuilding ties with the other kingdoms, to form alliances again. But some disagreed, some splintered off. Hagan's mother was one of them. That's when the plan was born. Infiltrate the kingdoms, gather secrets, and destroy the noble Houses from within. The Council fought against it for as long as they could... though even then, most of it was hidden from them.'

'Then why haven't they tried to stop him?'

Dawn bit the inside of her cheek, her attention drifting towards the window. The sun had vanished beyond the horizon, and night had draped itself across the sky. Moonlight spilt through the glass, bathing her in silver. It kissed her cheeks, caught in her hair, and turned her eyes to faceted gems, like amethysts ablaze with a quiet, mournful fire. The room was hushed, wrapped in a darkness that felt both intimate and heavy.

'They tried. They even thought of warning the other kingdoms, but they couldn't stop him,' she whispered at last, the words barely more than breath, as though afraid to let them exist in the world.

Kai's brow furrowed. 'Why not?'

She turned to him, her voice laced with sorrow.

'Because he slaughtered them all.'

Chapter Fifty-Two

House of Flames
Kingdom of Fire

I want to be strong.
Above all else, I want to be good.
But I don't know if I can be both.

Tabitha Wysteria

Wren, Arden, and Vera had spent the past few days carving a path through the chaos that was Fireheart. The city had become a twisted, broken, and increasingly treacherous battlefield. Navigating from one district to another was a feat in itself, every street a labyrinth of danger. Hagan had established his command at the ancient temple in the town square, turning the surrounding area into a fortress laced with traps and dark enchantments. Those who had tried to breach it never returned.

'We're not getting anywhere near that temple,' Vera said, sprawled across the velvet settee of an opulent parlour in a home they had broken into mere hours ago. The house reeked of forgotten wealth—crystal decanters, untouched books, and gold-framed portraits of long-dead drakonians. Arden leaned against the dark green wall, arms folded, his eyes fixed on the witch with the kind of cold intent a hunter reserves for prey too foolish to sense the danger. 'Wren, will you kindly tell your pixie friend to stop glaring daggers at me?'

'I'm not a pixie,' came Arden's indignant reply.

'What's a pixie?' Wren asked, frowning.

Vera's smile curled with mischief. 'A pixie,' she said sweetly, 'is what Fae males have dangling between their legs.' She tilted her head, eyes gleaming. 'Tell me, does yours have teeth?'

Arden moved, but Wren stepped in, halting him with a look. Vera tilted her head, a wicked smile playing on her lips as she observed the silent exchange between the wolverian and the Fae. How fascinating. She hadn't realised the depth of whatever existed between them. Perhaps they hadn't, either. But it was unmistakable now, clear as moonlight on still water. The Fae watched Wren with all the aching reverence of a soul parched for affection. A Black Lotus, one of the most feared assassins in the realms, staring at the wolverian princess as if she were the final drop of water and he were lost in the heart of the desert, desperate and dying of thirst.

She had always wondered if Black Lotus could *feel*. She'd heard stories, countless and grim, tales of cruelty and unflinching coldness. Lust, yes. They were surely capable of that. But what shimmered in his eyes wasn't lust.

It was longing.

'You said you'd get me Hagan,' Arden said, his voice as sharp as the glint in his eyes when turned on the witch. Vera found it endlessly amusing how those same eyes, when resting on Wren, softened by degrees, losing their edge but none of their intensity.

Vera reclined on the golden-and-green sofa, swinging her feet up to rest on the polished coffee table. 'That I did. I never specified *when*, though.'

Arden's nostrils flared with barely contained frustration.

'Believe me, I want him dead as much as you do.' Vera lifted both hands in a mock gesture of surrender. 'But charging the temple would be suicide. We need a proper plan.'

'Then think of one,' Arden snapped, turning on his heel and storming from the room.

Wren watched him go with a sigh, then crossed the room and sank beside Vera, dropping into the plush seat with a muttered grumble.

'He's got a bit of an attitude.'

'Yer no help, Vera.'

The witch snorted, letting her head fall back against the sofa. She stared at the ceiling above. A simple, unadorned stretch of stone that seemed oddly out of place compared to the extravagance of the rest of the room. Drakonians and their obsession with gaudy decor and gilded furnishings. For all its opulence, the sofa wasn't even comfortable.

'If Hagan is yer brother...' Wren's voice faltered, her face tightening as the words left her lips, as if even speaking them aloud felt somehow wrong. 'Why do ya want to kill him?'

Vera lifted a hand to her forehead, scratching lightly, but didn't turn her focus from the ceiling above. She couldn't. She dared not look at the wolverian girl seated beside her, the same wolverian that had stitched her wounds and brought her fever down. For if she did, she might tumble headlong back into the abyss Hagan had cast her into the day he took Allegra from her.

'He took something from me,' Vera said, her voice barely more than a breath. 'So now I'm going to return the favour... by taking something from *him*.'

She didn't need to glance at Wren to sense her shift— shoulders tensing, body leaning back, as if bracing against the weight of the words. Against the coldness behind them.

'What?'

Vera let out a soft, bitter laugh, the sound curling through the stillness like smoke.

'His life.'

...

Vera had fallen asleep, snoring rather impressively. Wren, not wishing to disturb her, had quietly slipped away to find her own corner of rest. They took turns keeping watch, an unspoken agreement born of necessity. Though Arden bore the brunt of the duty, not without protest. Wren had argued, naturally. She'd been uneasy at first, unwilling to trust him with the safety of the sleeping witch. She had feared that, in a moment of silence, he might change his mind and slit Vera's throat. But he hadn't.

He had meant what he'd said. He wouldn't harm Vera, for Wren's sake.

She found him in the kitchen, a beautiful space at the back of the house. Drakonian homes never ceased to amaze her. Everything within was arranged with care, each item chosen with purpose and pride. Beauty seemed woven into the very bones of the place, as if the walls themselves had been carved to reflect the soul of the people who lived there. Drakonians built their homes with reverence. Every detail, every flourish a quiet declaration of belonging.

Arden sat on the floor, his back resting against a polished wooden cabinet, a half-drunk bottle of drakonian wine balanced in his lap.

Wren dropped to the floor opposite him without a word and held out her hand. He passed the bottle without hesitation.

The wine was sweet, too sweet perhaps, but it slid down her throat like silk, and she welcomed the burn that came after. She took another deep gulp, trying to drown the cold tremble in her hands, the one that never seemed to leave her now. She had tried to hide it, tried to keep it from the others, but she wasn't fooling anyone. They had seen. She hated that.

She was Wren. A thief, a spy, a Seer.

But lately, she felt like none of those things. The visions had vanished, as though the gods had turned their backs on her entirely. No whispers in the dark. No glimpses of the threads that bound the future. Only silence.

She had prayed. Begged.

But nothing had come.

And she couldn't stop wondering. What had they done to deserve this curse? Why had the gods abandoned them? Why was every step forward like walking blind through fog, when once she had seen everything so clearly?

'You've got that look again, little wolf,' Arden said, his voice low and steady, the kind that settled into the bones. 'The one where you're arguing with yourself, and losing.'

'I neva—'

'I know.' He chuckled, a sound that rumbled so deeply it echoed inside her chest. 'You never lose an argument.'

Wren took another long, defiant gulp of the wine, until Arden plucked the bottle from her grasp with infuriating ease. He gave her a look that made heat pool in her cheeks and ripple down her spine.

'That's enough for you tonight,' he said, matter-of-fact.

'I think I can decide that meself,' Wren snapped, lunging forward to reclaim the bottle. She wasn't a child, how dare he treat her like one! She was no little girl. A woman, whether she always behaved like it or not.

Arden held the bottle aloft, just out of reach. Wren landed a punch to his stomach, more annoyance than force. He didn't so much as flinch.

Undeterred, she sprang to her feet, reaching for the bottle with a triumphant grin as she snatched it, and stuck out her tongue in victory. But before she could escape with her spoils, his arm looped around her waist and pulled her down, straight into his lap.

Wren gasped, hands splaying against the solid wall of his chest, the bottle lost from the fall. Her breath caught. Every inch of her flared to life, acutely aware of the warmth of his body pressed so intimately against hers. She could feel everything.

Slowly, deliberately, Arden grabbed the fallen bottle from the floor and held it to her lips, tilting it with care. She drank, cheeks flushed with heat, his large hand at her back, steadying her, holding her there. When she finished, he set the bottle aside, then brushed his thumb along her lower lip, wiping away a drop of wine.

His green eyes didn't waver, watching the soft drag of his thumb like it was something sacred.

'I think I know how we can get to Hagan,' Wren said, her voice just above a whisper, more to distract herself than him from the way Arden was looking at her like she was the only thing left in the world worth watching. The kitchen lay cloaked in near-darkness, not a single candle lit, lest the glow betray their presence to any danger lurking beyond the walls.

'Not now,' he said, gently hushing her.

'Don't tell me what to do, Arden Briar.'

That damned Fae had the audacity to chuckle.

'I love it when you say my name like that.'

'Like what?'

'Like you want to punch me.'

Wren scrunched her nose in distaste.

'I don't want to punch ya.'

'Liar.'

She huffed, rolling her eyes skyward. 'Fine, think whatever pleases ya.'

It was only then she remembered she was still perched in his lap. She shifted, meaning to climb off, but Arden's arm tightened around her waist, anchoring her in place.

'Where do you think you're going?'

'I'm sitting in yer lap,' she said, a little too aware of how close they were.

Arden raised a brow, amused. 'And since when has that ever troubled Wren Wynter?'

She opened her mouth to respond, to tell him that she didn't know anymore. Since leaving her home, Wren had felt adrift, unmoored from the girl she once was. Day by day, she questioned everything. Who she'd been. Who she was now. And most of all... who she would choose to become if she lived to see the end of this war.

'What's on your mind, little wolf?'

'I'm praying me brotha's safe.'

Arden gave a slow nod. Wren wondered whether he truly grasped the weight of such worry, when he had no family left to fear for. Perhaps, in some strange way, that absence was its own kind of freedom. To have no one to lose, no one to mourn. It must quiet the heart in ways she could only imagine. But oh, how desolate it must be, too. To have no one to love so fiercely that every passing minute is a silent plea for their safety.

'Why didn't you stay home?' Arden asked quietly. 'Why throw yourself into this war? You could've stayed in your warm bed. No one's going to sing songs about you one day.'

Wren let out a soft sigh, her eyes drifting to the buttons on his shirt. They were shaped like tiny leaves, handcrafted and delicate. So beautiful, in fact, that she felt a thief's familiar urge tug at her fingers. She toyed with one absentmindedly.

'Becas I'm scared,' she said at last, her voice barely a whisper. 'Scared of sitting still, waiting for da worst. Scared of watching others do what I'm not brave enough to do becas of a voice in me head that tells me I'm not enough. So I keep moving. I keep fighting. Becas if I don't stop, then maybe I won't hear it... that cursed voice whispering that I'm a failure.'

Arden reached for a white strand of her hair, holding it delicately between his fingers, glaring at it as though it were the most beautiful thing he had ever seen. Wren wasn't sure if he'd even heard her speak. He sat so still, so intent, his thumb gently stroking that lone thread of moonlight caught between them.

'Why would you think you're a failure?' he asked at last, frowning, his voice low and taut. There was a glimmer of anger in his eyes. Not at her, but at the cruelty of the thought itself. 'You crossed half the kingdoms searching for help when no one else would lift a finger. You gave up everything to try and save us all.'

'Well, I haven't saved anyone yet,' she muttered.

Arden reached out, cupping her chin with surprising gentleness, guiding her to face him fully, to see the truth behind his fierce green stare.

'You saved me, little wolf.'

Wren pulled his hand away, shaking her head. 'No, I didn't. Yer just saying that to make me feel betta. I've neva saved anyone. Not my ma, when sickness took her. Not Haven Blackburn when Hagan came for her. I've done nothing in this war but run around like a headless chicken. I left me home without a plan, left me brotha to handle everything I should've stayed for. Me papa always said I'd be da death of them all... and I'm starting to think he might've been right.'

A faint smile ghosted Arden's lips. Soft, barely there, but in the hush of the room, Wren felt it like a balm.

The last sliver of light in the kitchen faded, drawing a curtain of shadow around them. She could no longer see his face, but she felt his hands take hers, steady and sure, his touch grounding her as if he could hold her fears at bay.

'Not all heroes lead the charge on the battlefield,' he whispered, his breath brushing her mouth. 'Some remain unseen, tucked into the margins of history. Forgotten, even. But that doesn't make them any less vital. They're the ones who sacrifice quietly, so others may carry on. The ones who speak out against evil, knowing it may cost them everything. No songs will be sung for them. No statues carved. And yet they are the reason wars are won.'

Wren's heart thundered so loudly in her chest, she wondered how on earth he couldn't hear it.

'When ya found me in da Forest of Endless Trees...' Wren's voice was quieter now, fragile in the dark. She couldn't bring herself to look at him, not even with night cloaking her expression. 'Was it a coincidence, or...?'

Arden exhaled slowly, the sound like wind brushing through leaves. 'It was. I'd been preparing to travel, sent by the King himself to avenge the deaths of his daughters. But then you came crashing through the undergrowth and landed squarely on top of me... naked.'

'Ya knew who I was?'

She felt him nod beside her. 'I was trained to kill from the moment I could hold a blade, Wren. And just as thoroughly trained to recognise the faces and names of the noble Houses. When you told me your name, it only confirmed what I'd already begun to suspect.' He gave a small shrug. 'I thought it might be easier to reach my target if we travelled together. Gain some information along the way.'

'So when ya realised I was a princess at da palace... it was all an act.'

There was a slight shift in his posture. A tension she felt rather than saw.

'In a way...' he admitted. 'I felt bad for deceiving you, and thought it would be best if we went our separate ways. I thought if I acted angry, you'd leave. But you didn't. When I saw you by the entrance to the city, alone and defeated...I couldn't leave you behind. I know what it's like to feel that way. But I didn't lie. I do hate royals. I don't believe power should be inherited like trinkets. It made me angry to see you there, bearing a title granted by birth alone.'

'Do ya regret it?' she asked suddenly, her voice trembling with a fear she hadn't meant to reveal.

'What?' he said with a dry breath of laughter. 'I've got a long list of regrets.'

'Sleeping with me.' The words hung heavy between them. She heard the sharp intake of his breath.

'No.' His reply was swift. Certain. 'I regret many things I've done... but not that. Never that.'

'Then why?' Her voice broke like light through leaves.

Arden sighed again, but this one sounded like it came from somewhere deeper, older.

'Because I wanted to feel something,' he whispered. 'For once in my life, I just... I wanted to *feel*. And I thought you might be the one to make me feel, something, anything at all.'

Wren felt her heart beat so violently she thought it might tear through her ribs. And when his hands found the sides of her legs, touching her not with hunger, but with reverence, with care, it only made the ache worse.

'Did I?' she whispered. 'Did I make ya feel something, Arden Briar?'

He didn't answer with words.

Instead, his hands left her legs and found her face, guiding her towards him with a quiet urgency. His lips met hers—firm, unyielding, desperate. It was not a gentle kiss, not the kind that lingered like a promise. It was fierce, consuming, laced with desire and something unspoken. Wren gasped against him as his hands swept over her body with wild, reverent hunger, as though he were trying to memorise her touch, her shape, her very existence.

Every doubt dissolved beneath his touch.

The war, the witches, the endless gnawing voice in her head that told her, morning after morning, to give up, to go back to sleep because she had achieved nothing and would achieve nothing...They all vanished. Silenced.

She let him take the weight from her shoulders with every layer he stripped away, piece by piece. Her clothes fell like forgotten burdens, lost in the shadows. And in that same darkness, her fingers trembling, Wren pulled at his garments in return, fumbling in haste, needing to feel him, all of him.

Her cold hands met the hard planes of his chest, and she exhaled shakily. As her fingers traced downward, exploring the muscles carved into him like stone, she found the scars, each one a silent story beneath her touch, invisible in the dark but unmistakably real. The map of a life that had endured more pain than it ever confessed aloud.

Arden lifted her bare body with ease as he stood, her legs instinctively wrapping around his waist. He took two slow, deliberate steps forward before lowering her gently onto the wooden table at the centre of the kitchen. The surface was cool against her skin, but his hands, his hands were fire, tracing the length of her thighs, her hips, her stomach, until they found the soft weight of her breasts.

Wren gasped as he moved her, as he arranged her body with

a quiet authority, shaping her to his will while his hands explored with reverence and hunger. And yet, beneath every possessive touch, every searing caress, she could feel it. Hesitation. Patience.

He leaned over her, his breath ghosting across her lips a moment before he kissed her. His tongue sought hers with aching desire, but still he waited, for her.

He would stop if she asked him to.

Even as his grip tightened on her skin, even as his teeth found flesh, it was she who held the reins. No title, no reputation, no whispered legend about the Black Lotus, the deadliest assassin in the eight kingdoms, could alter that truth.

Wren ruled over *him*.

The moment she parted her legs for him, a silent invitation spoken in breath and body, she heard the moan that escaped him, low and ragged against her ear. His hands tightened around her knees, gripping her as though the sheer pleasure of knowing she wanted him, of being granted permission to feel her, had unravelled something deep within him.

'I've dreamt of touching you again,' he whispered against her ear, his fingers slipping slowly into her warmth, drawing a sharp gasp from Wren's lips. 'You're already soaked.'

'I want to forget,' she breathed, her hands pulling him closer, desperate to lose herself in him. 'Make me forget.'

But Arden shook his head, his voice low and resolute.

'I don't want you to forget, little wolf. And I don't want to forget either.'

'Why?' she asked, her voice trembling.

'Because it brought me to you,' he said. 'This war... all of it... it led me to you.'

And for the first time in what felt like an eternity, the emptiness in Wren's chest cracked open, not to swallow her whole, but to release the darkness she'd carried for so long. The fear, the doubt, the persistent ache of not being enough began to slip away, scattered like ash on the wind. In their place, something gentler took root. The cruel voice that had once called her a failure fell silent, replaced by another, one that whispered she was beautiful. Brave. Worthy.

'So strong,' Arden murmured, pressing a tender kiss to the inside of her thigh.

'Remarkable,' he breathed, his lips grazing her stomach like a benediction.

'Unforgettable,' he said, and then his mouth was on her, his tongue parting her with reverent hunger.

Wren gasped, a smile breaking across her lips, born not just of pleasure, but of the desire reflected so clearly in Arden's every touch. He wasn't just taking; he was giving. Seeing her. Worshipping her.

'Promise me you'll never forget me,' he said, his tongue trailing upwards slowly, deliberately until it reached the soft swell of her breast. His hands cradled her face as though it were something fragile and precious, his thumbs tracing the curve of her jaw, memorising her. 'No matter what happens to us.'

Wren pressed her lips to his, breath catching as she felt him lift her legs, her body curving instinctively into his. The heat of him brushed against her inner thighs, and the wetness between her legs spoke louder than words. Telling him, without doubt or hesitation, that she was ready. That she couldn't wait any longer.

Wren gasped as he entered her slowly, carefully. His every movement deliberate, as though he were memorising the feel of her. Her body tensed in response, a moan caught behind the sharp bite of her lip as her back arched beneath the wave of pleasure. She refused to let her mind wander to tomorrow, to the plan she had crafted to reach Hagan, to the war that waited just beyond the walls.

No. There was only this moment. Only Arden.

'I promise,' she whispered.

With each measured thrust, Wren felt something within her bloom, strength unfurling in her chest, beauty awakening beneath her skin. She never wanted it to end, never wished to lose the feeling of him moving inside her, his body fitting against hers as though they had been carved from the same breath of fate. He stirred emotions in her she had never known, never dared to name, each one crashing over her like a tide too powerful to resist.

Arden pulled her upright, slipping out of her for a brief, breathless moment. Wren moaned at the sudden emptiness, her body aching in its absence, and the sound drew a low chuckle from him.

'Oh, how I love the way you moan when I'm not inside you,' he murmured.

He guided her back down onto the table, this time turning her to face it, positioning her on her stomach. With careful, deliberate hands, he lifted her hips, ensuring she was exactly as he wanted her. His grip tightened on her waist as he pressed forward again filling her inch by inch.

Wren bit down on her hand to stifle the cry that threatened to escape, pleasure rippling through her in waves too fierce to contain.

'Don't come yet,' he commanded, voice low and rough with restraint. He slipped two fingers between her lips. 'Bite me.'

She obeyed without hesitation, sinking her teeth into him as he began to thrust again, the rhythm quickening, relentless and deep. He drove into her harder, with such fierce purpose that Wren felt warmth spill down her thighs, her body trembling from the intensity.

Arden gave a low, satisfied chuckle and withdrew.

Before she could ask why, before the question could even form, he dropped to his knees, spreading her legs wider still. His tongue was suddenly on her, tasting her, savouring the wetness that trickled down her skin, licking it away with the reverence of a man starved and worshipping.

'Arden...' she moaned, a breathless plea. 'Don't stop.'

'Come for me. Now,' he growled, his fingers replacing his tongue as he leaned over her, teeth grazing her neck before his lips traced a trail of kisses down the line of her spine. And then he was inside her again, filling her with a slow, powerful thrust that stole the air from her lungs.

Wren gasped, her entire body tightening as the pleasure coiled, building higher, higher still.

But just before it could consume her, Arden turned her once more, lifting her and laying her back against the table, never letting her slip from the edge of bliss. He entered her again without pause, his pace urgent, unrelenting, determined to carry her over the peak. She wrapped her legs around him just as the wave crashed, her body trembling violently as release tore through her.

He kissed her hard, claiming her moan as she shattered beneath him.

'Fuck...' he groaned, the word torn from him as he climaxed, spilling into her, their shared release trailing down Wren's thighs in warm, languid rivulets. 'Oh, fuck...'

And though Wren could not see Arden's face, nor he hers, they both smiled in the quiet darkness of the kitchen. Two shadows entwined, finding a fleeting peace in the hush between heartbeats.

Chapter Fifty-Three

House of Sand
Desert Kingdom

If I had my son with me, there's only one thing I would tell him.
Never trust anyone.

Tabitha Wysteria

The Dunayans had scoured the city of Madari clean, stripping it of supplies and trade goods with an efficiency born of experience. The citizens, far from resentful, welcomed the exchange, glad to make good coin from women who treated them with fairness and left the streets a little safer in their wake. Hessa had departed with Saren to visit the Dunayan kin settled within the city, leaving Alina to spend her day training alongside a few others.

By now, Alina had mastered the Sandhii tongue, her speech fluid and confident as she conversed with the Dunayans in their native language. Hessa still favoured the common tongue, claiming she didn't wish to lose it, and that Alina made for the perfect excuse to keep practising.

'Ahi,' said Isla, a wiry Dunayan girl with sharp eyes, pointing to an apple positioned precariously at the very edge of a slanted rooftop. Across the chasm, Arena crouched close to the fruit, her watchful gaze fixed on the challenge. She waved at them from the far side, the yawning drop between the mountains enough to send a flutter of nausea through Alina's stomach.

'Raspara,' Isla said, the word soft as a breath as Alina raised her arm, closed one eye, and inhaled. She listened to the wind, to the silence, to the desert whisper that had become second nature. *Breathe.*

With one fluid flick of her wrist, Alina released the dagger. It sang through the air, soaring cleanly across the void, striking the apple dead centre. Cheers erupted. Arena plucked the fruit from its perch, pulled the dagger free, and took a triumphant bite.

'Bana, farahi-sahraa,' Isla said, clapping once with a proud nod. *Well done, foreign desert.*

Alina had grown used to the moniker. Foreign desert, a name that was both observation and endearment. It suited her well, and she wore it like a second skin, as if it had always belonged to her.

The desert folk had no word for "thank you", so Alina simply inclined her head in the customary gesture of gratitude. It was a quiet, graceful act, one she had come to mirror instinctively. Since her fall from the cliffs, she had grown unexpectedly close to Isla and Arena. Perhaps it was because she had sensed, early on, their mutual disdain for Saren. Or perhaps it was something less tangible, a kind of kinship born from shared silences and sidelong glances. Whatever the reason, the bond between them had begun to deepen, subtle but certain, like roots finding home in dry earth.

'Aspara!' Arena called out, her voice lilting with urgency, imploring them to wait. Alina turned in time to see the Dunayan seize one of the zip lines used to traverse the gaps between mountains. Arena, shorter than most, with a tumble of curls the colour of sand and stone, swung across the ravine with practiced ease. Isla had already darted forward to greet her, a wide grin lighting her face as she reached for her friend.

Their laughter carried on the wind before it was cut short by the arrival of Hessa and Saren.

Hessa took Alina's hand and led her silently away from the others, guiding her back to their room with purposeful strides and not a word exchanged between them. Alina had understood the delay for their departure. There were still matters Hessa needed to see to before they could begin their journey towards the Kingdom of Fire. They had little to pack. Dunayans were creatures of light travel, swift and unburdened.

Alina sat on the small cot, watching as Hessa paced, back and forth, her movements restless, coiled like a sandstorm waiting to break.

'What is it?' Alina asked softly.

Hessa stopped mid-step and turned to face her, as though suddenly reminded she wasn't alone. The look in her eyes made Alina regret speaking. When Hessa finally crossed the room to sit beside her and took her hands in both of hers, squeezing tightly, something inside Alina recoiled.

'I've received word,' Hessa whispered, her voice hushed as though saying it too loudly might summon something worse. 'From your kingdom. As we suspected, the city of Spark...is gone. And Fireheart is now a battlefield.'

Alina didn't scream. She didn't shake or weep or rage at the sky. She sat still, eerily calm. A cold clarity spread through her, and in her mind's eye, she saw herself returning, saw her blade finding Hagan's throat. Saw his head tumble, roll, and disappear into the dust.

'We need to go,' Hessa said quietly.

Alina nodded and began gathering the few belongings they

kept in the room. Hessa turned to leave, ready to rally the Dunayans for departure.

But then the door creaked open.

Saren entered without a word, her expression carved from stone.

Hessa's shoulders tightened the moment she realised Saren had not even bothered to knock. Not after everything, not after the last time. Alina could sense it too: the shift in the air, the silent challenge. If Hessa let this go, if she allowed her second-in-command to walk in without consequence, the others would begin to wonder who truly led them.

And Hessa, Alina knew, would not allow herself to be questioned.

During her time in Madari, Alina had come to understand that Dunayans were far more than a singular faction. They were an intricate network, an organisation that stretched across all twelve regions of the desert. Each member had trained beneath Hessa's watchful eye, journeying from distant cities to be moulded by her hand. Once they had earned their place, once Hessa had offered them her blessing, they were sent back to their regions—ambassadors of strength and discipline. In each section of the desert, Hessa had appointed trusted leaders, loyal to her alone, their allegiance unwavering.

It all sounded like chaos stitched together by sheer will. Yet Alina had seen it in motion, and to her astonishment, it worked like a vast tapestry woven from sand and sweat and unbreakable trust.

'You do not enter like that,' Hessa said sharply, her voice slicing through the heavy silence as she pointed at Saren. 'On your knees.'

Alina opened her mouth to intervene, ready to plead for restraint, but the look on Saren's face stopped her cold. It was not defiance alone that burnt there, but something older, deeper. Betrayal, perhaps.

'Spaak Sandhii,' Saren spat, her tongue sharp. *Speak Sandhii.*

'No,' Hessa replied, standing taller, her presence towering, unyielding. 'On. Your. Knees.'

'Yaa alagi farahi,' Saren hissed, fists clenched tight. 'Apa waar.'

Alina stepped back, the words landing like blows to her chest.

You choose a foreigner over us.

She had never wanted Hessa to choose. Not then, not now. If the Dunayans had still not accepted her, so be it. She could live with that. She would walk away before she ever demanded Hessa pick a side. Even if it shattered her heart into a thousand aching shards, she would go. Quietly. Proudly. Without asking Hessa to tear herself in two.

'How did you survive the fall?' Saren asked suddenly, her voice cold, her lip curling in disdain.

And in that moment, like lightning cracking across Alina's memory, the images returned. Flashes of the wall, the way Saren's voice had slithered through the air, telling her she didn't belong. The shove. The sharp pain of stone against her chest. And then, a hand pulling her backwards, only to let her fall.

Alina gasped.

Hessa saw the truth in her eyes, sudden and searing. Before a word could pass between them, she moved. A dagger, sleek and silent, materialised in her grip as she lunged. Its tip sliced through the air, reaching for Saren's throat.

But Saren was quicker than a striking asp. She dodged every blow, her fists landing with deadly precision, striking Hessa with the ease of one trained under her hand.

She laughed as she ducked another attack, her movements

effortless.

'You trained me too well,' she said with a twisted grin, parrying once more. Then she surged forward, her aim set on Hessa's chest and shoulder.

But Alina was already moving. Her own dagger flashed in the low light, and without hesitation, she carved a line across Saren's leg.

Saren screamed in fury, staggering back.

'This is death, Saren,' Hessa warned, her voice low, eyes brimming with disbelief and sorrow. The betrayal clung to her like a second skin, tight and suffocating.

'Yes,' Saren replied, her smile darkening. 'But not for me.'

Saren whistled a sharp, cruel sound, and five Dunayans swept into the already cramped room. Hessa stood frozen, stunned, her white eyes wide with disbelief as her own warriors seized her. Two of them slammed Alina against the wall, pinning her there, unmoving, as if she were nothing more than a spectator to her own nightmare.

'On your knees,' Saren ordered, her blade glinting as she gestured with its tip, demanding their leader's humiliation.

Hessa spat, the glob landing squarely on Saren's cheek.

With a sigh, Saren wiped it away and gave a nod. The Dunayans shoved Hessa down to the floor with brutal efficiency. Alina screamed, thrashing against her captors, tears stinging her eyes as she cursed and pleaded for mercy.

'Stop! I'll leave!' she cried. 'I swear, you'll never see me again. Just let her go!'

But Saren remained unmoved. Her expression was carved from ice as she crouched before Hessa, meeting her stare with chilling calm. The silence between them was electric. One pair of eyes blazing with fury, the other veiled in sorrow, the weight of betrayal written in every strained breath.

'All of them?' Hessa asked quietly, her voice barely audible.

'Some would still die for you,' Saren replied, her tone steeped in disdain. 'But they'll be put down like dogs.'

Then she turned, her eyes slithering towards Alina. A wicked smile curled across her lips.

'And once we tell them the farahi murdered their leader...' She shrugged, tilting her head. 'Well. Everything will change.'

No.

No, they couldn't.

They couldn't hurt Hessa.

Alina had already lost everything. Her family, her kingdom, and, for a time, even the will to live. But then came Hessa: radiant, stubborn, impossibly strong. With her smiles that chased away the shadows, with her words that stitched broken pieces back together, with her faith in Alina when no one else had believed. They could not take her, too.

If the world took Hessa from her...

There would be nothing left.

Alina's soul would wither into dust, hollowed out by grief.

'Please, don't.' The words slipped from her in a trembling whisper as tears traced silent paths down her cheeks, dripping onto the floor like rain from a dying storm. Her head hung in despair, her body slumped in defeat. This couldn't be happening. She would not allow it.

Her body convulsed as she fought against the Dunayans restraining her, her breath ragged with fury. A fist slammed into her stomach, knocking the air from her lungs.

'I'll do anything!' she gasped.

'Amira, it is okay,' Hessa said through gritted teeth, her voice unshaken. 'They wouldn't dare kill a princess.'

Saren snorted.

'I will always be with you, amira.' Hessa smiled, a gentle,

devastating thing amidst the chaos, ignoring the hands gripping her and the blade that hovered near. Her attention never once left Alina's. 'Remember that. Always with you.'

Without a word, Saren forced Hessa to lie flat on the ground, pressing her boot to the back of the desert princess's head, grinding it slowly downward.

'No! Don't give up, fight!' Alina cried, her entire body surging with resistance. Her teeth clenched as she thrashed against the iron grip of her captors, her shoulders threatening to wrench from their sockets with the effort.

'I'll wait for you in that place we spoke of,' Hessa whispered, her voice soft and unwavering, her eyes locked with Alina's, refusing to rise towards the heel pressing against her skull. 'I'll be celebrating with my sister. But I'll wait for you, amira.'

'No, don't you dare!'

Alina screamed, the sound raw and broken, as the terrible truth shimmered in those white eyes: there would be no escape. Even if they managed to claw their way from this room, there would be others, more waiting outside. Saren had planned this well. And Hessa... Hessa could never survive the betrayal of her Dunayans. No matter how much she loved Alina.

'Please... don't.' Alina's voice cracked, raw and pleading, as she looked to Saren, desperation blazing in her eyes, silently offering everything she had, everything she was, if only it might spare Hessa.

'Yaa da ma sahraa, amira,' Hessa whispered just seconds before Saren drove the dagger into her back.

Then her neck.

Then her skull.

Alina screamed.

The sound tore from her throat like a wounded animal,

primal and full of agony. Her eyes widened in horror, her vision swimming as the world collapsed. The hands that had held her back suddenly released her, and she collapsed to the floor, crawling, gasping, towards the crumpled figure she loved.

Tears fell like blades, sharp and unrelenting, carving a path of devastation down her cheeks as she gathered Hessa into her lap. Alina cradled her gently, brushing tangled strands of hair away from Hessa's brow as if such a tender act might undo what had been done.

The world receded. Walls, whispers, all of it fading into a silence that pulsed with grief. She didn't care if the others were still there. Let them kill her. Let them end it. Nothing mattered now.

She rocked slowly, her tears baptising Hessa's still, blood-matted hair.

'Farahi,' Saren said at last, her voice distant, almost bored, as she motioned for the others to leave the room.

Alina did not lift her head. She wept, her grief boundless.

'You should run now, farahi,' Saren continued. 'The others will soon be alerted. They'll find their leader, slaughtered by your hand, or so they'll be told. If you're still here when they arrive...'

'Leave me alone!' Alina roared, the sound hoarse and burning.

Saren only shrugged, stepping lightly towards the door as if what had happened were of no consequence.

'Hagan sends his regards,' she said.

Alina froze. Even her heartbeat seemed to falter, suspended in the silence that followed. She turned, dazed, to confront Saren, to demand an answer, but the Dunayan was gone. Vanished like smoke through the cracks.

A voice—no, a scream—rose in her mind, urging her to run.

Leave. Save yourself.

But she couldn't. She wouldn't. She could not leave Hessa behind, not butchered and broken on the floor like discarded meat. That was not the ending Hessa deserved.

Run, amira. Run.

The voice came again, so familiar, so heartbreakingly clear. Hessa's voice. It drowned out everything else: the room, the footsteps in the distance, even Alina's own grief. It was all-consuming. And yet, Alina stayed, rooted in place as agony swelled inside her like a rising tide. Her body screamed with pain, but still she didn't move. Her fingers, trembling, continued to comb through Hessa's hair as she wept deep, broken sobs that scraped against her ribs.

Something sharp brushed against her trembling fingers, and Alina reached into Hessa's hidden pocket, searching blindly for the mystery it concealed. Her breath caught as her hand closed around a necklace. Delicate, yet heavy with meaning, crafted from white stone and desert sand.

She remembered now: the moment Hessa had been handed something in secret, the way she had tucked it swiftly away, her movements cautious, protective. She hadn't wanted Alina to see it. And now, here it was. A sand-stone necklace, rare as starlight in this land. A treasure not given lightly, but gifted to a beloved. A silent declaration. A vow. A proposal, not of grandeur, but of devotion.

Alina's heart splintered as she held Hessa close, understanding at last what the girl had intended. Hessa had been waiting, to ask her to be hers, not just in the quiet of stolen glances, but wholly, body and soul.

And now, she would never have the chance.

Hands shaking, Alina lifted the necklace and clasped it around her throat, the white stone falling with reverent weight against her skin. It nestled there as if it had always belonged.

'I accept, Hessa,' she whispered into the silence. 'I will be yours. Always.'

Please, amira. Go.

Alina shook her head, lips pressed into a silent refusal. Let them come. Let them kill her. She had nothing left with which to fight. No blade, no strength, no will. What more could the world take from her? She had lost everything. Everyone.

And all of it… because of *him*.

Hagan sends his regards.

Her head snapped towards the door Saren had vanished through, rage beginning to claw its way up through the numbness. How had Saren known Hagan's name? What connection lay hidden in the shadows between them? Was the warlock behind this too, behind Hessa's death?

A new fire lit within her, a fury so pure it scorched her sorrow. She would not let him slip into the darkness unscathed. No, she would find him. She would burn the flesh from his bones and watch the screams tear themselves from his throat. She would make him feel every loss he had carved into her heart. And she would not stop until there was nothing left of him but ash.

With aching care, Alina laid Hessa gently onto the ground, her fingers lingering in the silken tangle of her hair. She stood over her love's still body, wavering. Could she truly do it? Could she walk away now, fight on, when the one person who had made the world bearable, who had stitched light into the torn fabric of her soul, was gone?

The silence clung to her like grief, thick and heavy.

Alina was alone. Utterly, wretchedly alone.

From somewhere beyond the room, voices rose, shouts and screams that bounced off the stone walls like ghosts. The sound grew nearer, a warning. A choice.

If she stayed, she would die.

And death... death didn't seem so terrible. To slip into the dark and find Hessa waiting, smiling. To see her parents again. To hold Ash once more, even if just for a moment in whatever came after.

But deep down, Alina knew they would not welcome her if she surrendered. Not like this. They would never forgive her for letting go.

No. She had to rise.

To find Hagan. To make him pay for every shattered life, every stolen joy. For her kingdom. For her family. For Hessa.

And now, there was Saren.

Saren, who would bleed for her betrayal. Who had earned her place on Alina's list of vengeance.

One by one, she would end them.

'Qa yaar qamh valva sahraa,' she whispered, her voice trembling as she pressed a final kiss to Hessa's brow. *May your grain return to the desert.*

Alina paid no mind to the blood soaking the floor, nor to the crimson now staining her hands and robes like war paint. The screams grew louder, closer, sharp echoes of the chaos that still pulsed through the city's bones. But she heard none of it.

Her fury had swallowed all sound.

Rage burnt through her veins with every breath she took, rage at the unspoken bond between Saren and Hagan, rage that the warlock still found ways to torment her, even from afar. Rage that the woman she loved had been taken, stolen like everything else she had once held dear.

They would burn for this.

Every one of them.

No one saw the lone girl as she fled through the winding

streets of Madari, blood-slick and silent as a shadow. Nor did they witness her slip into the open desert, swallowed whole by its endless sands, until even she began to forget she had ever existed at all.

Chapter Fifty-Four

House of Power
Kingdom of Magic

Hadrian once explained the origin of the phrase "May the shadows guide your way." He wasn't entirely certain, no one truly is, but his brother once told him of a king, a thousand years ago, who could shadow-walk. This king would lead his people into battle atop a shadow-wyvern. The creature's shadow would carve a path through the terrain, unseen by enemies, allowing the wyverians to follow their king, and attack before the enemy. It became their greatest secret, the key to winning every battle.

May the shadows guide your way.

Tabitha Wysteria

Mal had often wondered why the wastelands lay so barren as they pressed through them, silence clinging to the marshes like mist. Not a single witch had crossed their path. No enchantments stirred in the shadows. Only the rustle of damp reeds and the squelch of weary boots filled the air. Ash had said nothing, his eyes fixed on the horizon, his thoughts elsewhere. And so, with a tightness in her chest she did not speak of, Mal gave the order to march on.

For years, Mal Blackburn had dreamt of the Kingdom of Magic, of its forgotten terrain and ivy-cloaked ruins. She had flown over it before, alongside her brother Kai, gliding through the skies on the backs of their wyverns. Where others had seen only rubble and desolation, Mal had marvelled, imagining the land in its prime, its spires alight with arcane brilliance, its people wielding power as effortlessly as breath.

Now, after all that had passed, she did not know what to feel.

This land had taken her wyvern. Its people had risen against her, cast her down, and drawn her into war. And yet, despite the bitterness etched into her bones, despite the betrayal... there was something else.

Because Mal Blackburn was no longer merely a wyverian princess.

She was a witch, too.

What she had once feared above all else had come to pass, and still, it did not consume her. In a way she could not explain, she no longer recoiled from the truth.

She did not reject it. Not anymore.

She yearned to speak with Hecate, or with the witch known as Tabitha, the Seer who had lingered like a shadow at her side for as long as she could remember. Now, with hindsight cruelly sharpened, Mal wondered if Tabitha had stayed close out of understanding. Had she always known what Mal truly was?

Memory flickered through her like candlelight in a draughty room, moments she had shared with the Seer, searching for some hidden sign, a whispered truth, a glance too long, too heavy. Some trace of tenderness that might betray Tabitha's true heart.

But Mal found none.

She told herself she ought not to feel this hollow ache. She had known true, unwavering love. Queen Senka had given her all of it, pouring every ounce of her soul into her children. Mal had grown up cherished, protected, wrapped in warmth. Her mother had not known the truth, but even if she had... Mal believed, with quiet certainty, that it would have changed nothing.

Queen Senka would have loved her just the same.

And yet, Tabitha's silence cut deep.

It was not the wound of a stranger's scorn, but something far more intimate. Like the slow, deliberate press of a blade slipping beneath her skin, inch by inch, until it pierced through flesh and nestled into muscle. A pain that lingered. That refused to dull.

'They'll be at the wall,' Ash said, his voice low and meant only for Mal's ears. He had remained mostly silent throughout their journey, but as they neared their destination, he had begun to guide them. Quiet commands and subtle shifts in direction, offered without explanation. Still, Mal's instincts whispered that Ash knew more than he let on—of where the witches lay in wait, of where the traps had been set. They had changed course more than once, drawing frustrated huffs from the soldiers that carried on behind them. But Adriana had quelled those murmurs with sharp glances and clipped words.

'Do you think he knows where Kai is?' Adriana asked once Ash signalled for them to land, urging the wyverns to descend to the fields below. From there, he said, they would proceed on foot until they reached the wall. He gave no reason.

'I believe Ash knows a great many things,' Mal replied, her voice thoughtful as she pressed a gentle hand to Nyx's smoky leg in silent gratitude. It was difficult not to notice those golden eyes turning towards her, narrowing as if he had heard her despite the distance.

'Then why won't he tell us?' Adriana asked, glancing back at where Ash stood a few paces away, quietly directing Keir and Cronan with calm, precise movements.

'I think he's afraid,' Mal said softly, 'that if he reveals too much, we might begin to change things.' She paused, her hand drifting instinctively to her stomach. The gesture was so natural she hardly realised she'd done it, until Adriana's eyes fell upon it.

Mal drew her hand away at once. 'Not a word,' she warned, her voice low and firm.

The warning was clear enough. Adriana nodded, though a small, irrepressible smile played at the corners of her mouth, hope crackling like firelight in her gaze.

Mal looked away, choosing to ignore it. It was far too soon. Too uncertain. She didn't even know whether she believed it herself. Thanatos could have lied. She wanted it to be a lie.

Because if it were true...

The wind shifted as they neared the wall, carrying with it the sharp tang of something strange, something other. Mal inhaled deeply, and recognition struck like a spark to dry kindling.

Magic.

It thickened the air like stormclouds before a tempest, coiling in invisible threads, readying itself for war.

Ash moved silently to her side, his fingers brushing against hers in a fleeting, grounding touch.

'Are you ready?' he asked, just as Mal turned to study the army assembled behind them. As though reading her thoughts, he added quietly, 'The wolverian army is almost h-here. They won't be long.'

'Do we wait?' she asked, though she already suspected the answer.

Ash inclined his head towards the looming shape ahead, and Mal followed his gaze, her chest tightening at the sight. The wall stood like a grave-mark on the horizon, distant yet imposing. And now, atop it, rows of heads began to appear. Witches and warlocks materialised in disciplined formation, each one preparing to defend what they still claimed as their own.

They were many.

But Mal's army was greater.

'They will not last a second against us,' Adriana muttered with a scoff, a predatory gleam in her eye.

Something unreadable shadowed behind Ash's golden eyes.

'Do we break through?' Mal asked him, her voice cool and steady.

Ash gave a single, solemn nod.

'Very well,' she said, squaring her shoulders against the rising tension that pressed like thunder in the distance.

Without another word, she turned back to Nyx, her loyal shadow wyvern, the only one who would take to the skies until the path was secure. After what had happened before, she would not risk the others. Not again.

The world seemed to hold its breath as Mal's form dissolved into darkness, her flesh unravelling and reforming as smoke and shadow, an echo of the wyvern she now climbed upon. For a single, stunned heartbeat, silence reigned across the battlefield. And then, as if awoken from a spell, her army stirred, resolute and unshaken. They had seen the impossible. And they were ready.

She had commanded it, and they obeyed.

For as long as she could remember, Mal had been different. Hidden from the world, concealed behind high walls and watchful eyes, her purple gaze a mark of separation, something to be silenced, softened, controlled. She had prayed in secret to distant gods, begged to be made ordinary, to be anything but the anomaly she was born as.

But now, rising in darkness above a world that once shunned her, Mal knew the truth.

Her difference was her power.

She was *not* a mistake.

She was a storm.

And the world, so frail, so unready, would soon know what it meant to stand against her.

Nyx unfurled her great wings and surged into the heavens, slicing through the clouds with terrifying grace. From her vantage above, Mal cast her attention beyond the wall, and her heart faltered at the sight that greeted her.

An ocean of witches and warlocks stretched out across the land, their ranks unbroken, cloaked in shadow and brimming with power. Tendrils of green smoke writhed through the air like serpents, thickening with the promise of ruin.

She glanced down, her eyes seeking Ash. Not for strategy, though he had never once led her astray, but for something deeper. For the quiet, unspoken courage he gave her with a single look. In his golden eyes, she found her reason to stand. To fight. To imagine, if only for a moment, that the world might still be remade into something worth saving.

And to make that world, Hagan had to be destroyed.

Ash met her gaze and nodded, so slight a gesture, it was almost missed.

Mal closed her eyes and drew breath deep into her lungs, the air laced with tension and ash. She did not pray. Not anymore. Prayer belonged to the innocent. And she had learnt long ago that prayers sometimes were heard, and answered in cruel and merciless ways.

But in the stillness of that moment, she wished.

She wished Thanatos stood at her back. Wished Makaria and Zagreus flew at her side. Wished even Hades watched from the shadows. Not to rule, but to witness.

It would have been easier with them.

And infinitely more deadly.

'May the shadows guide your way,' she whispered into the breeze.

And on the wind, soft as breath and sharp as fate, the world whispered back.

'May the shadows guide you.'

Chapter Fifty-Five

House of Flames
Kingdom of Fire

It's strange to realise that every valkyrian we encounter was once a drakonian, a wolverian, a wyverian, a Fae...

They were us.

And they chose not to pass on, but to remain, and to serve.

I admire them.

They don't stay out of fear of death.

No, they stay because they want to save us.

Tabitha Wysteria

'This is a dreadful idea,' Vera hissed beneath her breath. 'We're walking to our deaths.'

None of them could quite explain it, but they had awoken to an unnatural hush draped across the city like a mourning veil. The last of the drakonian fighters had slunk into the shadows, retreating into crumbling alleyways and smoke-stained doorways to nurse their wounds and whisper their fears. The witches were gone. No warning, no retreat order. They had simply vanished, dissolving into trails of green smoke, their laughter echoing like ghost-song through the abandoned streets.

Vera did not trust silence. Not here. Not in Fireheart, a city that had raged and burnt with battle for weeks. Something about the sudden stillness set her teeth on edge. There was no magic thrumming in the air, no crackle of spells or shimmer of wards. Only empty streets and echoing footfalls.

Wren, of course, had declared it the perfect moment to carry out her so-called plan.

It was, Vera thought bitterly, an atrocious plan. But it was the only one they had.

And so, down the eerily vacant avenues they marched, Vera at the fore, one hand gripping the enchanted chains that bound her supposed prisoners: Wren Wynter, wolverian princess and seer; and Arden Briar, infamous Black Lotus. Gifts, neatly wrapped, to offer at the feet of a monster.

Vera's stomach churned at the thought.

Yes, this was the plan: to return to Hagan's side, grovelling for his forgiveness, and presenting him with powerful captives to win back his trust. It was madness. Every possible outcome teetered on a knife's edge. They were skilled, formidable even, but Wren, in all her wild conviction, had yet to fully grasp the danger of Hagan's blood magic.

'What if he sees through it?' Vera had asked, more than once.

'Then make sure he doesn't,' Wren had said that morning, her voice maddeningly calm.

Vera gritted her teeth.

Yes. This was a terrible plan.

They reached the town square, now eerily hollow, where Vera had once stood mere weeks ago, watching with numb detachment as Hagan ascended the very steps that led to the drakonian temple. It was there he had raised the severed heads of King Egan and Queen Cyra for all to behold, a grotesque spectacle carved into memory.

She had wondered, foolishly perhaps, if he'd had the decency to dispose of them. To burn what remained. To offer at least that small shred of respect in death.

Her question was answered the moment her purple eyes found the temple doors.

There they hung, grotesque and rotting. The royal visages once so proud, so immaculately composed, had deteriorated into something barely recognisable. Skin had turned an ashen hue, lips bloated and bruised, chunks of flesh torn away by carrion birds. They looked nothing like the rulers they had once been.

Some brave drakonians had tried to reach them, to reclaim what remained of their sovereigns and give them a dignified end. But Hagan had shrouded the temple in lethal wards, any who dared step too close fell where they stood, never to rise again.

Vera had played her part in their demise. She had slit Queen Cyra's throat herself, crimson pouring like spilt wine down the woman's regal front. She had wanted the queen dead, had dreamt of it. And truthfully, if given the chance again, she would not hesitate.

But this? This defilement of death... this cruel parade of decay?

Even monsters deserved to sleep beneath the soil. Not rot beneath the sun.

Vera stepped forward with measured caution, her every movement laced with sharp awareness. The magical chains fastened to Wren and Arden's wrists glimmered faintly in the dull light, and she gave them a calculated tug, no longer gentle. She could not afford gentleness. Not here, not now. Who knew what unseen eyes watched from the shadows, ready to strike at the first sign of weakness?

She halted at the foot of the temple steps, her breath catching. To ascend might mean death. Those wards were ruthless, and even a witch might not be spared their wrath.

Vera's shoulders eased subtly, her stance casual, but her boots remained firmly grounded on safe stone. Around her, the buildings loomed, rising like silent sentinels, their leaning forms closing in as though eager to listen.

The temple doors yawned open with a slow groan, and from within emerged a witch with a gait far too self-assured. Vera recognised her at once and fought the instinctive urge to roll her eyes skyward. Of all the women Hagan could send…

'Theodora,' she drawled, every syllable steeped in honeyed disdain. 'What a charming surprise.'

Theodora tilted her head, predatory and poised, her narrowed eyes sweeping past Vera to land on the two bound figures behind her. Disgust curled her lip.

'Why are you here, Vera?'

'I bring gifts,' Vera said, her voice silk laced with venom. 'For my darling brother.' She watched with satisfaction as Theodora's expression darkened at the term brother, a word Vera wielded like a blade. They all knew how much she detested uttering it. That was precisely why she used it.

'He wants nothing to do with you,' Theodora sneered. 'Or your traitorous whore of a sister.'

Vera clicked her tongue. 'Still warming his bed, are you?' Her eyes gleamed. 'You, and the rest of the coven?'

'Shut that filthy mouth of yours!'

The grin that bloomed on Vera's face was wicked, unrepentant. How easy it was to unsettle Theodora. That she still believed herself to be Hagan's chosen was laughable. Vera had seen the warlock take anyone he pleased to his bed—witch or warlock, body or beast. He loved nothing. Not even himself.

'Are you going to let me in or not?' Vera tapped the toe of her black boot against the stone, her voice edged with impatience. 'I'm growing dreadfully bored, and if you don't hurry, Hagan might stumble upon some sweet little mouse to dash against the wall, one who entertains him more than you.'

Theodora was not what one would call beautiful. Pale as unbaked bread, her slight frame barely filled the robes she wore, but that had never seemed to matter to Hagan. He cared little for appearances, only obedience. And Theodora excelled at that. Perhaps that was why he summoned her time and time again, her loyalty mistaken for importance. The witch now walked with the inflated air of one who believed herself favoured, indispensable even.

Vera couldn't help the soft, scornful snort that escaped her lips.

Without a word, Theodora pivoted and strode towards the temple, her robes catching the breeze like trailing smoke. With a final glance behind, she motioned them to follow. Vera hesitated, her focus drifting to the first step. Her boot, black leather worn and dust-stained, met the reddish-brown stone. She braced herself for the ward's wrath: the crushing choke of invisible fingers, the punishing slam against an unforgiving wall.

But nothing happened.

She lived.

Exhaling softly, Vera tugged on the chains guiding Wren and Arden behind her like reluctant offerings. The interior of the temple unfolded in cool shadow and stone, every arch and carving as breathtaking as she remembered. But the memory of her sister's blood soaking these floors soured the splendour. No amount of beauty could mask the scent of death that lingered like perfume in the air.

Theodora led them through the temple's heart with purposeful steps, through a narrow wooden door, up a spiral of ancient stone stairs that whispered underfoot, and along a hallway that narrowed with every step. Finally, they halted before an ornate set of doors. Vera's skin prickled. They were too far from the main entrance now, too deep within the temple's grasp. If anything went wrong, escape would be no simple feat. And she had no doubt Hagan intended to make escape impossible.

A low, guttural sound slipped through the door, prompting Vera to pause, her head tilting ever so slightly in amusement. A wicked grin curled her lips as she turned her attention upon Theodora.

'Are you quite certain he's alone?' she asked, voice laced with venomous sweetness. Her fingers reached for the handle, only for Theodora's hand to block her path.

'He is not to be disturbed,' the witch snapped, her tone sharp with possessive edge.

Vera rolled her eyes, unimpressed.

With the elegance of a creature born of wildness and disobedience, she drove the tip of her boot into the door, sending it slamming open with defiant grace. Her grin widened at the sight before her—a tableau of debauchery and delusion. Hagan stood utterly bare, his back arched over a witch who had foolishly cloaked herself in drakonian glamour.

Theodora drew in a sharp breath, her face blanching before she turned away, vanishing silently down the corridor like smoke dissolving into night.

Vera lounged against the wall, arms crossed with casual disdain as she watched the scene unfold. Hagan carried on as though they were nothing more than shadows in the doorway, ghosts to his pleasure. If anything, their presence seemed to thrill him further. His grip tightened around the horns of the witch beneath him, wrenching her head back with such force that Vera half expected to hear the snap of bone. The witch, however, appeared to revel in his savagery, her cries rising in fervent crescendo as Hagan thrust into her from behind until he reached his peak. With a grunt of release and not a trace of tenderness, he cast her aside like a discarded garment, her body landing on the bed in his wake.

The drakonian illusion dissolved in a shimmer of smoke, the witch's true form emerging the moment the glamour slipped away. Vera recognised her at once but held her tongue, refraining from casting a barb about questionable life choices. Most of those who lingered within the temple walls were Hagan's loyal pets, creatures of magic and vanity kept close so he might be endlessly adored and pampered.

'So, you've developed a taste for drakonians now?' Vera drawled, watching as the witch scrambled to gather her scattered garments and fled the chamber in a fluster. 'Well, fake ones, at least.'

'Why are you here, Vera?' Hagan asked, his tone detached as he turned from her jibe and busied himself with cleaning up, slipping back into his clothes with practiced indifference. The irony wasn't lost on her, how much he must loathe drakonians, and yet found such twisted satisfaction in claiming them. But Vera knew the truth. It wasn't about lust. It was about power. Dominance. His own personal revenge, delivered not with a blade, but through possession. Vera often wondered if, in those moments, he tried to picture his father's face.

'I've brought you something,' she said, stepping aside so he could feast his eyes on the bound figures behind her.

'How generous,' he said, lowering himself onto the edge of the bed, a faint frown pulling at his brow. 'And for what purpose?'

'I want to be... back here,' she said, though the words clung uncertainly to the air.

'You don't sound particularly convinced.'

Vera rolled her eyes. 'What would you have me do? Fall to my knees and beg?'

'That would be a promising start.'

'I'm not doing that,' she snapped, her tongue darting out to wet her lips, steadying the nerves roiling just beneath her skin. Thank the gods neither Wren nor Arden had uttered a word. Silent, obedient. For now.

'You killed my sister, Hagan. What did you expect me to do?'

'*Our* sister,' he corrected softly.

Behind her, Vera felt Wren flinch, the tremor of the reminder crawling beneath their skin like a venom, one of Hagan's many poisons.

'Do you want my peace offering or not?' Vera said, her patience fraying like thread in a storm. The weight of waiting gnawed at her, clawing through her composure.

Hagan's attention drifted from her to the prisoners behind. Something passed through his eyes. Subtle, but potent enough to send a cold tide rolling through Vera's gut, rising like bile to scorch her throat. She recognised that glint. It was a mirror of her own, though far more dangerous in the hands of a man like him.

'Bring the white-haired one forward,' he said, his tone void of warmth, as though bored with the entire display.

Vera shoved Wren ahead with a practised hand. The magical chains shimmered faintly as they stretched, still intact, for now. She would release them when the moment came. Let the wolf draw close, just enough to bare her teeth.

Arden tensed, but Vera stepped swiftly back, slamming her weight into him to keep him from doing anything rash. Hagan, mercifully, hadn't noticed. His eyes were fixed on the girl approaching, hungry in a way that made Vera's skin crawl.

Wren moved with silent grace, unaware, perhaps wilfully so, of her own beauty. Silver-white hair spilt down her shoulders like moonlight over snow, her delicate features sculpted in porcelain: a doll come to life, fragile in appearance, but forged of steel.

Hagan appeared momentarily spellbound by her beauty, captivated enough to draw her closer, his palm resting possessively against the small of her back. In one fluid, predatory motion, he forced her down onto the bed. Over his shoulder, his voice slithered like oil.

'I think I'll enjoy the feel of this one wrapped around my cock.'

He ran his fingers through Wren's white hair with an almost reverent touch, but there was nothing soft in the way his eyes gleamed, sharp and unrelenting, fixed not on the girl beneath him, but on something else entirely.

He wasn't looking at her.

He was watching Arden.

Studying him with calculated intensity.

And the very moment Hagan tore at Wren's trousers, shredding fabric with careless violence, Arden moved.

Shit.

Though still bound by Vera's enchantment, Arden surged forward, a blur of motion that belied the restraint of magic. He reached Hagan before Vera could tighten the spell, her magic a heartbeat too slow. Until now, Arden had never revealed the depths of his training, what it truly meant to be a Black Lotus. With deft precision, he twisted through the air, leaping over his captors and landing with lethal grace behind Hagan. In one seamless motion, he seized the magical chains and wound them around the warlock's throat.

'You will not touch her,' the Fae hissed, his voice laced with venom, the chains biting deeper with every word.

Hagan merely chuckled.

Those gleaming purple eyes sparkled with malevolence, and in that moment, Vera understood.

Arden cried out in agony. The chains fell limp from his fingers as his body twisted violently, convulsing in a grotesque display, forced by a power far beyond his own. Wren screamed, but her cry was cut short by Hagan's hand curling around her throat like a noose.

Before Vera could utter a word, Hagan dragged Wren into the shadowed corridor, disappearing with her into the darkness.

Vera dropped to her knees beside Arden, whose body now lay eerily still. She pressed trembling fingers to his throat. A pulse, faint but there.

She rose.

There was no time to waste. Wren was in danger. She would return for Arden.

She *would.*

The thought that she might not flickered like a flame in her mind, but she stamped it out. She would not become Hagan. She would not make herself a monster.

Hagan had descended the spiral staircase, a dark spectre dragging an all but unconscious Wren across the temple's marble foyer like a ragdoll discarded by fate.

'What are you doing?' Vera's voice rang out, sharp against the silence.

He halted, turning with a slow, deliberate menace. His hand remained clamped around Wren's throat with such brutal force that Vera felt the phantom pressure on her own windpipe. Another minute and the princess's trachea would be crushed. The fact that Wren still drew breath was nothing short of a miracle.

'What was your grand plan, Vera?' Hagan asked, his voice rough and low, scraped raw with fury. Yet beneath the grit, something cracked, something soft, lost... childlike. 'Feign surrender, gift me prisoners... then slit my throat?'

Vera gave a half-hearted shrug. 'Something along those lines.'

Hagan released Wren, letting her crumple to the polished floor in a graceless heap. He looked down at her, brow furrowed, seemingly mesmerised by the subtle rise and fall of her chest. Vera dared to step closer, but the moment her boot slid across the stone, his eyes snapped back to hers, sharp as blades, unforgiving.

'Is that how deeply you despise me?' he asked, barely above a whisper.

'You murdered our sister.'

'You hated me long before that,' he said, and for the briefest of moments, a hairline fracture appeared in the cold mask he wore. 'All of you did. But you, most of all. Because she chose me over you.'

'No,' Vera said quietly, her voice bitter but sure. 'That's not why.'

A glint of surprise passed through his eyes.

'Then why?'

She owed him nothing, not after the carnage he'd wrought, not after the blood that stained both their hands. And yet... perhaps she owed him this one truth. The root of her hatred. The ache that had festered since childhood.

'Because she was still able to love. Because no matter how hard I tried, I couldn't. Every time I looked at you I was reminded of my own wickedness,' Vera said, each word cutting through the air like a shard of glass. 'Your father raped her, and still, she stayed. She loved you. Chose you. But in the end, it killed her.'

A single tear traced down her cheek, silent and salt-heavy. 'If it hadn't been for you, she might have come home. She might still be alive. But instead, she died loving *you*.'

Hagan flinched.

A strange thing to witness, such a fragile, mortal gesture upon a creature who had long since forsaken humanity. Her words had struck him like the keen edge of a blade, slicing through flesh and bone until they found that splintered thing he dared call a heart, shattering what little remained.

'Do you think I grew up loving myself?' he snarled, voice cracked and raw. 'I was a child, Vera. Just a child. And the only love I knew came from a mother who abandoned me, who left me in a den of vipers and never looked back.'

'She left me too,' Vera replied, her voice cold steel wrapped in silk.

'But you had your sisters!' Hagan roared, fury spilling from him in waves. 'At least you had someone. Someone who loved you!'

Vera recoiled as if struck. The words, though pitiful in their honesty, would not sway her. She would not falter. She would not feel sorry for the monster who had killed her sister. No matter the ache that echoed beneath his rage, there was no forgiveness. Not now. Not ever.

'You are as rotten as I am,' he whispered, the fire extinguishing in an instant, leaving only a hollow chill in its wake. 'We are vile, Vera. Twisted things fashioned by a cruel world. And we cannot be remade.'

'No,' she said, stepping forward, calm and unyielding, 'but I was always the vilest of us all.'

In the blink of an eye, her magic erupted, slamming into him with the force of a hurricane. At the same moment, Wren's right eye fluttered open, sharp and wild, her fingers already curled around the hilt of a hidden dagger. In a flash of silver, the blade bit deep into Hagan's leg, and blood gushed forth in a furious torrent.

His scream was not of pain, but of fury.

Within moments, shadows stirred and the witches that had stayed behind in the temple with Hagan materialised around them, summoned by the cry of their wounded master, prepared to kill for him.

But Vera was ready.

'Did you truly believe you could win?' Hagan purred, his voice a poisonous balm as his hands shimmered with a sickly green light. Wren staggered upright, stumbling towards Vera with desperation etched across her face.

Vera summoned her magic, fingers alight with power just as Arden came crashing through the wooden door, fury in his wake. Three blades sliced through the air like silvered shadows, brushing past Vera's ear before embedding themselves deep into Hagan's chest.

Time seemed to stop.

Hagan stilled, lowering his eyes to the blades now protruding from his flesh. He laughed, low and unholy, before pulling them free one by one, savouring the pain. He licked the blood from the final blade with serpentine delight, raising its glistening edge and pointing it towards the trio. All around them, witches pressed in like wolves, while Hagan himself stood before the only exit, the storm in his stare swirling with malice.

He glanced down at the blood now spattering the marble beneath his boots, red on white like a painting of death. Vera stiffened, her hands poised to strike, magic thrumming at her fingertips, ready to erupt.

'No matter what I do... you will always hate me,' he said softly, though there was no sorrow in his voice, only the desolate calm of one who had accepted his fate.

There was no time to respond.

Wren let out a guttural cry as her body arched unnaturally, her limbs twisting, bones fracturing with sickening cracks. Her scream was muffled by Arden's as the magic tore through her, breaking her from the inside out.

And all Vera could do was stand there, frozen in place, forced to bear witness as the girl was dragged towards Hagan, step by agonising step.

'If you're going to hate me,' Hagan said, voice low and void of remorse, 'then I may as well give you reason to.'

With a flick of his fingers, he forced Wren to her knees, though her legs were mangled so cruelly that her joints cracked out of place with a sickening pop. Tears streamed silently down her cheeks, her lips sealed by magic, unable to release the screams clearly locked inside her chest. Arden struggled to move, muscles tensing in futile rebellion, but he was frozen in place, held by Vera's magic.

She could not let him go.

If she did, if Arden were to charge forward now, it would only make things worse for Wren. She knew it. And the girl would never forgive her.

Hagan knew it, too. His smile grew wider, more grotesque in its pleasure. Vera had seen him wield blood magic before, one of the darkest, most abominable branches of witchcraft. It was said that those who practised it risked losing their soul. But Vera had always suspected that Hagan had been born without one.

'Enough,' she hissed through gritted teeth, her voice

trembling with fury.

'Why?' Hagan tilted his head, his eyes alight with mockery. 'If I release her, will you forgive me? Will you love me?' He saw the truth in her expression, read the ache, the refusal, and nodded as though confirming something to himself. He had always known, deep down, that the affection he craved from her would never come. That her heart was a locked gate he would never be permitted to pass through.

She had promised their mother once, in whispers and in tears, that she would protect him. And gods, she had tried.

'Veee...ra,' Arden growled, barely able to speak beneath the weight of her magic. The rage twisting his features was no longer just fury. It was betrayal, raw and unmasked. It thickened the air like smoke, saturating the space between them. And as his attention moved from Vera to Wren, she knew that he would never forgive her.

Wren's tears fell like silent prayers, her sobs caught in her chest as her limbs trembled, twisted at unnatural angles. The grotesque bend of her bones made Vera's stomach churn, her throat tighten with the threat of sickness. She had never wanted this, not like this.

'If you kill her, I will never forgive you.'

The words slipped out like a blade drawn from its sheath— sharp, unbidden, irreversible. And in uttering them, Vera realised she had sealed Wren's fate. Hagan did not crave her forgiveness. He had long since abandoned the notion of love. Perhaps, once, he had yearned for it. But whatever soul had perhaps once inhabited him had long since shrivelled into something cruel and monstrous.

'You wrinkle your nose at blood magic,' he mused, his tone silk wrapped around steel. 'But the things we could do with it, Vera...'

His fingers curled ever so slightly, and Wren coughed blood, the crimson streaking her lips like war paint. Vera flinched.

'I can control her blood. Twist it. Break her, vessel by vessel.' As if to demonstrate, two more sharp cracks sounded, bones splintering under invisible force. Wren's back arched with a sickening jolt, her spine contorting unnaturally.

'I can stop her heart mid-beat. Starve her brain of breath and thought.' He twisted his hand again, and Wren wheezed, her eyes bulging, the vessels within them straining and splitting. Her life was being unstitched, one thread at a time.

Vera stood powerless, frozen as she watched death slowly take hold of the girl who had only ever tried to bring light into a fractured world. This was just another show, another of Hagan's cruel performances, like Allegra all over again. The memory burnt behind Vera's eyes.

Wren's breathing grew shallow, unsteady. Her gaze, those pale blue eyes now glazed with agony, found Vera. Pleading. Desperate. A silent cry echoed through her expression: *please... end it, or save me.*

The temple doors swung open with a thunderous hush, severing Hagan's grip on Wren as if the very air had sliced through his spell. Vera released her hold on Arden, and in the blink of an eye, the Fae was at Wren's side, cradling her as though he might anchor her soul to the world for a few heartbeats more. But it was written in the tremble of her breath. Wren was slipping away. She would not survive this.

Vera's brow furrowed as two figures stepped into the temple, their presence cutting through the tension like a blade through silk. They entered not with urgency, but with the eerie calm of wanderers who had simply chosen this ruined sanctum as the next step on their path. For the briefest heartbeat, something in Vera's chest warmed at the sight of them, an old comfort resurrected from memory.

Kage Blackburn moved with his usual calculated elegance, each stride long and deliberate, his expression carved from stone. That ever-present scowl rested upon his face like a crown, his neck held high with effortless grace. The world, it seemed, bent to his pace, never the reverse. There was something in his sharp gaze now. Curiosity, or perhaps recognition.

Freya paused near the threshold, her presence anchoring the space like a spell. Her frost-blue eyes locked onto Hagan with an unreadable gleam. There was no greeting, no kinship. Only something colder. Deeper.

Hagan raised his hand to strike.

Freya merely tilted her head and lifted two fingers in a small, dismissive motion. 'Leave,' she commanded, and her magic exploded with quiet power, flinging the warlock backwards like a ragdoll. He hit the wall with a sound that made Vera gasp, though her feet remained rooted to the marble beneath her.

Kage crossed to Wren's side, his body still and poised, until Arden surged up with blade in hand, pressing the steel against Kage's throat with deadly calm.

'Touch her,' Arden hissed, 'and you'll not leave with your hand intact.'

'He won't hurt her,' Vera said at last, her voice hoarse, her limbs frozen by grief and guilt.

Arden's emerald eyes turned to meet hers, the promise within them sharp as the dagger he held. A vow of retribution. One day, he would make her pay. For what she had done. For what she had failed to do.

Vera did not flinch. She would accept it.

Just not yet.

'She's dying,' Kage said against the blade, which Arden

reluctantly withdrew from his throat. 'She doesn't have long.'

Arden let out a snarl, clutching Wren tighter to his chest as though by holding her closer, he could tether her to life.

Kage turned to Freya, and something unsaid passed between them, something Vera didn't quite catch. She filed it away in the back of her mind, though the weight of it pressed against her ribcage like an echo of unfinished plans.

Wren is dying, and you're still scheming, she thought bitterly. Perhaps Hagan had been right after all, perhaps there was no redemption left for her. Perhaps she truly was beyond salvaging, every shard of her soul tainted. But it was far too late now to wrestle with morality.

She cast a glance towards Hagan, still splayed against the wall, pinned by invisible forces like a fly trapped in amber. Then she edged nearer to where Freya stood like a sentinel of fate. How had the valkyrian subdued the warlock none had ever bested?

'She needs a healer,' Arden barked. 'Vera, do something!'

'I'm not a healer,' she snapped, though her voice was distant, dulled by the horror before her. Her eyes skimmed over Wren's mangled form, and her stomach twisted. 'No healer could fix *that.*'

'This is your fault,' Arden snarled.

Of course it was. And Vera would have a lifetime, if she survived this day, to drown in the guilt of it.

'Can you save her?' Kage asked, turning to Freya. That unfamiliar softness in his expression made Vera pause. Even in a room where monsters clashed and blood stained marble, hope still shone behind his black eyes.

'Are you sure?' Freya asked quietly. 'She will not be Wren Wynter. She will not remember her brother, or any of you.'

'It's better than death,' Kage replied without hesitation.

'Are you so certain of those words, Kage Blackburn?'

'I am,' he said, and the conviction in his voice sent a ripple through the air. 'Do it. I'll do as you asked me on those cliffs. I swear it. But save her.'

Freya's lips curved barely, but enough to make Vera flinch. Whatever promise had been made between them, it reeked of danger. Vera half-lurched forward, as if she could undo it, call the bargain back, but it was too late.

Freya bent low and lifted Wren into her arms, her face serene as Arden rushed forward, blade drawn again. With a flick of her head, the Fae dropped unconscious, felled without so much as a touch.

'What are you?' Vera breathed, eyes wide.

Kage turned towards her with a look that silenced the question before it could hang any longer in the air.

Freya walked out, carrying Wren's broken body like a cradle of starlight. The moment her shadow slipped beyond the temple doors, the spell tethering Hagan to the wall shattered.

And chaos unfurled like a storm unleashed.

Chapter Fifty-Six

House of Flames
Kingdom of Fire

I always believed Hades to be the vilest of all the gods.

I was wrong.

The others...

The other gods are far more foul.

And they are coming for us all.

Tabitha Wysteria

Kage knew there would be no slipping from Hagan's fury unscathed. The air cracked with sorcery as witches and warlocks closed in, hurling their magic like vengeful lightning at three unlikely allies. He did not allow himself to think of Wren, of her shattered, crumpled body, too fragile for a world so cruel. His fury had been kept tightly leashed, held back for her sake, in the desperate hope of preserving what little remained.

He had not seen her since the day they arrived at the wolverian stronghold, since he had locked himself away, burying grief beneath stoic silence. How history delighted in echoing its tragedies. But this time it wasn't Haven Blackburn's neck snapping under the weight of Hagan's magic. It was Wren who had been broken. And if Freya failed to save her in time...

How could he ever face Bryn Wynter with the ruin of his

sister?

The Fae male moved like a whisper between worlds, too fast to follow, his body blurring, dissolving into motion and shadow. Kage had read of such abilities, of the Fae's talent for illusion and misdirection, but to witness it was something else entirely. The man was vengeance made flesh. Not even Kage's eyes, darkened by grief and tempered in fury, could compare to the rage that burnt in the Fae's.

But Kage knew that when Hagan unleashed his blood magic, none of it would matter. They would not walk away.

Vera must have reached the same conclusion. Her eyes met his for a fleeting moment, a silent understanding flaring between them. Then she turned, her attention shifting to the Fae.

'Find her,' she said, her voice the steel of a dying star. And with that, she turned her back, stepping forward to face the storm alone.

Kage made to follow, but the Fae's hand clamped around his arm like a vice, yanking him back towards the towering doors, now slowly creaking open by some invisible command of Vera's making. A surge of her magic crashed upward, slamming into the ceiling above, dislodging stone and sending part of it to rain down in a violent cascade, blocking the witches and warlocks from reaching them in their attempt at escape.

'The wards,' Kage cautioned as their boots touched the stone beyond the temple's shadow.

'I see them,' the Fae said, his steps slow and precise, like a dancer navigating blades. He moved with the wariness of someone who had brushed too close to death once before. Kage had read what little he could find about witch-crafted wards, but the pages had always been shrouded in mystery and half-truths. All he truly knew was this: if one who was not a witch crossed the boundary, death would greet them swiftly, and cruelly.

He had passed through them once before, but only under Freya's protection. No ward could stand against a god.

'I can conjure an illusion,' the Fae said, voice clipped with urgency. 'But it will buy us seconds, no more.'

Kage gave a single, resolute nod.

This would be his first time witnessing Fae magic. He had, in a manner of speaking, seen Freya wield it, but surely this would be something altogether different. He found himself oddly curious, even as danger closed in behind them. Would it shimmer like starlight or crackle like lightning? A glance over the Fae's shoulder showed Vera still holding the line, but only just. Her magic sparked in defiant bursts, forcing back a tide of witches, yet the storm would soon swallow her whole.

There was no more time.

The Fae brought his hands together in a slow, deliberate motion, as though rousing a dormant beast. Threads of golden light flickered to life at his fingertips, delicate as spider silk and glowing like sunlit dew. He leaned in, lips parting, and exhaled over the gleaming motes, sending them dancing towards the stairs like dandelion seeds caught on a divine breeze.

'Run!'

Kage didn't pause to think. He sprinted, his legs carrying him two, three steps at a time. His breath tore from his lungs as the world narrowed to the beat of his heart and the surge of adrenaline. He felt the wards shift, fading just long enough for passage.

But then he felt them stir, awaken, begin to hum with deadly energy.

They were too slow.

Not enough time.

A strong hand caught his arm.

'Jump!'

And Kage leapt, just as the wards snapped back to life, whispering death in the air behind him.

Panting, he collapsed upon the ground, eyes wide with the echo of what had just passed. A voice, sharp and unrelenting, shrieked within his mind, urging him to turn back, to return for Vera. But she had offered herself freely, a sacrifice carved from defiance and fire. He would not let her offering be in vain.

The Fae gave a sharp shake of his body, casting off the remnants of their escape, then turned to glare at Kage, no doubt questioning his connection to Wren Wynter. Curious. It seemed the wolverian princess had lived a far more entangled life than any of them had realised.

Spirox cawed above, sweeping down from the heavens just as Bryn's wolf came bounding from the shadows of the alley where Kage had left them. He hadn't wanted them caught in the storm. Bryn Wynter would never forgive him if anything befell his beloved beast. Strange, how Kage had managed to protect the wolf, but not Wren.

'Kage Blackburn,' he said, offering his name like a token of gratitude. 'House of Shadows.'

The Fae stiffened, displeasure appearing across his features at the revelation. He said nothing. With the silence of one too familiar with pain, he turned away and began to walk.

'Where are you going?' Kage called after him.

'To find my wolf,' came the Fae's growled reply, before vanishing down an alley, swallowed by the shadows.

...

Vera knew, deep in the marrow of her bones, that Hagan had allowed the wyverian prince and the Fae to flee. The reason eluded her, some twisted motive no doubt curled behind his cold smirk. The instant they had vanished from the temple, the tide of her battle had shifted. The witches had stilled, frozen like statues in prayer, and Hagan had stepped forward to reclaim the space with terrifying ease.

Her blood boiled beneath her skin, molten with rage and magic, a scream ripping from her lungs as agony bloomed in every inch of her body, a pain unlike anything she had ever known. Still, she would not fall. Not to him. Never to him.

'You let them go,' she ground out through clenched teeth as he neared.

'Yes,' he replied, tilting his head like a curious child. His eyes gleamed with something she could not name. 'I only needed you.'

With a mere flick of his wrist, the witches dispersed like dust on the wind. Vera was left alone in the great hall with the creature who called himself her brother. He tugged her behind him, an invisible tether of blood magic coiling around her spine, jerking her forward with every breathless step. Each movement sent fire coursing through her limbs, tore shrieks from her throat that scorched her lungs.

If she had the freedom to lift a hand, she would have ended it herself, driven a blade into her own neck just to stop the pain.

Had Wren endured this? The thought struck like lightning. Her vision turned crimson.

No. She would live. She would survive this hell, if only to find the strength to carve open Hagan's chest and tear his festering heart from its cradle.

Hagan descended the narrow stone steps into the bowels of the earth, into catacombs Vera hadn't even known existed beneath such a place. Shadows clung to the damp walls, and the air turned colder despite the oppressive heat still clinging to her skin. She refused to glance at the skulls wedged in the crevices or the iron-veined door that awaited at the end of the passageway like a mouth poised to swallow her whole.

When it creaked open, her breath hitched, eyes widening at the monstrous slab of stone that loomed within—silent, waiting, ancient.

Without a word, she was dragged to it, her body slammed against its hot, unyielding surface. Bone met stone in a brutal embrace. Still, she would endure.

She was a witch. Damned, powerful, and born in pain. She had weathered storms that would have shattered others. She would not break. Not for him.

'I'm not going to kill you, sister,' Hagan said, his voice somewhere to her right. She couldn't move her head to locate him, only feel the rivulets of sweat crawling down her temples, soaking into her hair. The stifling heat of drakonian lands clung to her like a second skin. She had always despised it.

'I had planned to use Theodora for this,' he mused. 'But then you offered yourself so... politely. It won't hurt, I promise.'

Vera clenched her jaw. She would not give him the satisfaction of asking.

'Did you know,' he went on, as if in idle conversation, 'that the gods cannot walk this realm freely? They may visit, yes. But without a vessel, they remain bodiless. Spectres. Once, long before Tabitha Wysteria's curse cast them into their own realms, they walked among mortals regularly. And mortals, eager little things, offered up their bodies, just for the honour of carrying divinity.'

'So what?' she rasped.

'Not all vessels worked,' Hagan said, ignoring her. 'The stronger the god, the quicker the body would rot. It's rare, so rare, to find a mortal capable of containing their power without tearing apart at the seams. I considered Theodora, briefly... But you,' he whispered, his voice curling like smoke, 'I believe you could hold one.'

Vera let out a disbelieving and bitter snort. His madness had truly reached its crescendo.

He could *not* be serious.

'Did you hit your head?' she snapped, her voice sharp with exasperation. 'You expect me to believe that you've found a way to summon a god, and have it possess me?'

Utterly absurd.

He had well and truly lost his mind.

'It doesn't much matter what you believe, does it?' he said, and there was a blade beneath the silk of his tone, enough to give her pause. Uncertainty cut through her fury. 'Did you really think I orchestrated all this alone?'

Vera thrashed against the invisible force that held her fast to the hot, unyielding stone, every muscle trembling with the effort.

'For once in your pitiful, wasted life,' he whispered against her ear, a breath colder than any winter wind, 'you will serve a purpose.'

Her breath caught.

Vera's purple eyes widened, catching movement in the shadows. Something ancient lingered in the far corner of the room, something wrong. It stared back at her from the abyss, cloaked in silence, black as oil, old as time.

No.

No, no, no, no.

Hagan's laughter echoed around her like the tolling of a death bell, the last sound she heard before the darkness lunged.

It struck like lightning—devouring, unforgiving. The presence slammed into her with a force that tore her apart, dragging her into a chasm of endless black. Vera fell down,

down, down, screaming into a void where no one could follow, where nothing existed but silence and shadows.

She felt herself fading, shrinking into something small, something voiceless.

And then...

Vera was no more.

Chapter Fifty-Seven

House of Power
Kingdom of Magic

Sometimes I can't help but wonder if Hades did all those awful things to protect us.

To protect me.

Tabitha Wysteria

Adriana moved across the sodden, blood-drenched earth with the ferocity and grace of a true wyverian warrior. No mercy, no quarter. Her blade was slick with crimson, having already claimed too many witches to count. Most had hidden behind the sanctuary of the wall, until Mal Blackburn had soared above it on shadowed wings, raining fire from the skies and forcing their enemies into the open.

But no matter how many fell beneath Adriana's sword, more surged forward, a relentless tide. Their cursed spells crackled through the air, emerald bolts of power flinging entire formations of wyverians through the mud like ragdolls.

A wyvern's roar split the chaos, drawing her gaze skyward. A single breath, no more than that, but it was enough. Vines of vile green magic slithered out from the shadows, curling round her limbs and wrenching them apart. A scream tore from her throat, raw and feral.

Adriana swore violently at the witch now looming before her, who had seized the moment of distraction to strike. A scream tore from her throat as searing green magic sliced through her flesh. Ribbons of agony unravelled skin, muscle, and vein, her blood spilling freely onto the scorched earth. One tendril coiled around her right leg, dragging her to her knees, while another lanced through her stomach with brutal precision. Adriana howled, cursing the gods for the torment coursing through her.

But surrender had never been written into her bones. With a defiant snarl, she thrust her hands forward, seizing the magical tendrils and pulling against them with raw, unyielding rage. A wicked grin curled her lips as the witch's expression faltered, shock flickering across her face like a candle snuffed too soon.

It lasted mere seconds.

Keir's blade pierced the witch's heart from behind, the body crumpling like wilted paper at his feet. His eyes glittered with savage delight as he wiped blood from both blade and brow.

'I think I'm ahead of you,' he said, half-laughing. 'How many have you taken down?'

'I almost had her!' Adriana swore, clutching her stomach as it bled.

'*Almost* being the key word.'

It was a grim sort of game, the tallying of lives ended. But it was one they'd played before, back in the quiet safety of training grounds where the dead were illusions and the stakes little more than pride. This, though, was no training drill. This was war.

And yet she felt no guilt.

She should. She knew that. These were not spectres. They were flesh, blood, breath. But her hatred burnt too hot, too deep. Every time the faintest hint of remorse dared creep into her chest, it was consumed by the memory of Haven Blackburn's face. And that was reason enough.

The ache hadn't dulled, not even slightly. Grief nestled itself like a shard of glass between Adriana's ribs, catching with every breath, a cruel reminder that she yet lived while her best friend did not. Haven was gone. Their future queen, their light. And Adriana would have traded places with her a thousand times over if it meant summoning her back from the shadows of the underworld.

The tide of battle had shifted. Slowly, deliberately, the witches had begun to force their troops backwards. Whether it was the fury of Mal and Nyx, their blazing sapphire fire charring the sky, or something more sinister beneath the surface, Adriana could not say. But the witches now surged forward without hesitation, pouring into their own cursed lands, driving the wyverian forces deeper into the ash-stained heart of the wastelands.

Wyverians were famed across the Eight Kingdoms, fierce and unyielding, born to battle with fire in their veins and storm in their hearts. But even they faltered when faced with wave upon wave of witches and warlocks, their numbers multiplying as if summoned by some unseen call, a whisper through the void.

Above them, Nyx carved through the sky, her flames still searing with unholy blue light. Yet even that power, once enough to rend battalions apart, now slipped harmlessly off the witches' conjured shields, hissing into smoke and silence.

'Adriana, watch out!'

Too late.

The warning came a heartbeat after the surge of green magic had struck her, hurling the wyverian warrior into the thick, rain-drenched mud. For a moment, there was nothing. No sound, no breath, no pain. Then it came, sharp and searing, blooming like fire through her abdomen. Adriana screamed into the grey-blanketed sky above the wastelands, her voice lost in the chorus of battle.

Keir was at her side in an instant, his knees sinking into the sodden earth. Above them, Cronan circled protectively. Adriana's fingers, trembling, scraped over the scorched edges of her black armour. It had been seared straight through.

'Breathe, Adriana,' Keir urged, already tearing at the straps of her chestplate.

'Don't tell me to fucking breathe,' she snarled, fury blazing through the pain.

'If you've got enough spirit to swear, you're not dying,' he muttered with a wry grin, lifting the shredded fabric beneath to inspect the damage.

'How bad is it?' she demanded, straining to glimpse the wound.

'Not that bad,' he lied, though the twitch in his brow betrayed him.

'How deep?' Her voice turned cold with command. 'Keir! How fucking deep? Are my insides pouring out?'

'I doubt you'd be talking if they were.'

She heard the sharp tear of cloth as he ripped his own tunic, tossing aside his armour to press the makeshift bandage against her seared skin.

'This will sting,' he warned, bracing her by the shoulders and hauling her upright.

Adriana's scream tore from her throat, ragged and raw. She bit down on it halfway through, cursing every deity she'd ever met.

'Just hurry, damn it!'

'Don't rush me, woman,' Keir huffed, fumbling to secure the bandage tight around her midriff.

Once he had her strapped back into what remained of her armour, he gave her a lopsided grin and a quick, cheeky wink.

She kicked him in the shin.

'Oof! What the hell was that for?'

'You'd make a bloody useless healer. And don't say hell, you know how much I hate that fucking place.'

Keir chuckled and pressed a quick kiss to the tip of her nose. 'I love you, too.'

Adriana laughed through the pain, snatched up her sword once more, and rose with fire in her veins.

'Don't you dare get yourself killed, husband. If you do, I'll march straight into the Underworld and drag you back by the ear.'

The trio moved as one, a seamless force honed by years of training and bloodshed. There was an unspoken rhythm between them, each knowing where the other would strike, step, or shield. The absence of Kai at their helm pulsed like a missing heartbeat, but there was no time to dwell on it, not now. The witches were advancing, relentless in their magic, a tide of green fire and smoke that pushed the wyverian army back step by harrowing step. Every time one of their cursed kind fell back, another took its place, fresh with magic and malice.

Adriana clenched her jaw.

'We need to get over that wall!' she cried, her sword catching a bolt of emerald energy, the clash reverberating up her arm. 'We need to get to the wyverns!'

Keir's dark eyes widened. 'No, Adriana. Mal forbade it. The wyverns—'

'This is a losing battle!' she snapped, already pivoting, her boots digging into the churned and bloodied earth.

Before Keir could seize her arm or shout her down, she was gone, vanishing into the chaos, weaving her way through the forest of black-armoured wyverians, cutting a determined path towards the rear lines. The wyverns had been tethered far from the fray, hidden beyond the treeline, protected. But Mal could not hold the skies alone. And if they did not gain the upper hand soon, there would be no battle left to win.

The others blurred into shadows and steel behind her. She could no longer see Keir or Cronan in the thick of the fighting, but it didn't matter. Let Mal reprimand her later. Let them all rage once the war was won. Wyverns were not ornaments, they were creatures of flame and fury, born for war.

When Adriana finally broke free of the battlefield and slipped into the shaded stillness of the woods, her breath caught. Not from the run, but from the sight before her.

Someone stood beside the wyverns, a lone figure murmuring softly, hand brushing along Daku's midnight flank with unsettling ease. It wasn't one of their guards. She would have remembered this presence.

'I need those wyverns,' Adriana said, voice steel-laced and breathless. 'We're losing this battle.'

Ash Acheron cast a glance over his shoulder, and those molten-gold eyes gleamed with something ancient and unknowable, something that made Adriana instinctively falter. She, who had never feared war nor the promise of death, found herself chilled to the marrow by the quiet storm in the man once known as the Fire Prince.

'We are meant to lose this b-battle,' he said softly, his voice as smooth as silk drawn over steel. His hand moved with reverent calm across Daku's scaled flank, as if the world were not being torn apart by blood and magic just beyond the tree line.

Adriana shook her head, defiant.

'I *need* those wyverns,' she said, raising her sword with the poised elegance of a trained killer. 'Step aside, Fire Prince.'

Amusement flickered like a flame in his gaze.

'I haven't b-been the Fire Prince for a very long time,' he said. He turned at last, one hand resting lightly on the hilt of his blade, though he made no move to draw it.

Adriana adjusted her grip. Her stance widened.

'I never trusted you,' she said flatly.

'I know.' His smile was laced with sorrow, so fleeting it nearly passed unnoticed. 'Perhaps you should have t-trusted that instinct.'

He moved.

Faster than sight, faster than sound. One moment he stood at the wyvern's side, and the next he was before her, close enough for his breath to ghost against her lips, his presence pressing into her skin like smoke.

The wyverns didn't so much as flinch. Their gleaming eyes remained calm, watching the scene with eerie serenity. Adriana had never seen them so still, so at peace. It was as though Ash's very being lulled them into trust. An unspoken bond, quiet and unbreakable.

He leaned in, his voice a murmur in her ear.

'I know what you, Keir and Cronan are.'

The earth tilted.

Adriana stiffened, a breath catching somewhere in her chest. Trained as she was not to betray emotion, the blow landed nonetheless. She had feared that Ash would see too much, perceive what others could not. It was what made him so dangerous.

'And if you know...' she whispered, her voice a brittle thing, 'if you know what we are... then why fight me?'

Ash said nothing at first. His eyes did not meet hers. Instead, he lifted the hilt of his sword, an almost tender gesture, and brought it down against her head.

Darkness took her.

'For her,' he said to the silence. 'It's all for her.'

...

Mal guided Nyx along the length of the towering wall, the great shadow wyvern gliding with thunderous grace as she attempted to keep the witches from breaching the border. Whatever strategy they'd devised was clear enough. They meant to drive the wyverian army back into the heart of the wastelands. They would not allow them to scale the wall.

She had already tried to break through it, ordering Nyx to unleash torrents of ethereal blue flame, but the stone did not yield. Reinforced with intricate wards and runes, the ancient wall held firm beneath their assault, its magic as stubborn as the blood feud it protected.

From below, screams rose as the shadow of Nyx swept across the field. Terrified witches hurled bursts of green flame skyward, desperate to strike down the beast that soared above like a creature born from the void itself. But what was already dead could not die, and the spectral wyvern only roared louder, raining fire as Mal bade her to reduce them to ash.

Beneath her, the chaos was overwhelming. Blood drenched the soil, spells lit the sky, and still, the slaughter did not stop. Mal gritted her teeth, her chest aching with each breath. They were killing each other, her people, all of them, whether they wielded wyverian steel or witchfire. She tried not to admit it, but it was the truth all the same: both sides belonged to her.

And each time she gave the command to strike, each time she whispered *burn,* another fracture appeared in the fragile armour of her soul. Something within her sank, deeper and darker, into a place she feared she might never return from.

Mal straightened, inhaling slowly, watching the ruin unfold below her. She wanted to cry out, to scream into the wind for them all to stop. To beg them to see sense. But it was far too late for peace. Too much blood had been spilt, too many hearts turned to stone.

There was no room left for mercy.

The hatred had been passed down like heirlooms, stories told by firelight, whispered in nurseries, etched into every child's bones. Parents had raised their young on the bitterness of old wars, and now their children burnt for vengeance.

It would never end.

Not even in annihilation.

There would be no victors. Only survivors, haunted by the ghosts of those they failed to save.

Mal could see it in the way their lines wavered. The wyverians were losing. They were superior in strength, in speed, in the close-quarter brutality of hand-to-hand combat. But this was not a war fought with steel and claw. The witches kept their distance, hurling their magic like lightning across the fields. And there was a reason the other kingdoms, a century past, had grown wary, terrified even of the Kingdom of Magic.

Relentlessly, the witches pressed forward, herding the wyverian forces further into the open plains of the wastelands. Mal narrowed her eyes, watching the ebb and flow of their movements. There was strategy behind the assault. Too precise, too deliberate. This wasn't just about keeping the wyverians from breaching the wall, from entering the lands of fire.

No, it was something more.

She'd briefly considered flying Nyx into the heart of drakonian territory, to summon reinforcements. But by the time she returned, she feared there would be nothing left of her people to save.

Then came a cry, piercing and primal. A scream that cut through the clash of metal and roar of flame, silencing even the thunder of steel and wings.

Mal exhaled, her heart tightening.

'Wolverians!'

And there they were, spilling across the battlefield like a silver tempest, their hair gleaming like moonlight, their movements fluid, feral. They did not charge, they hunted. The witches attempted to stand their ground, but the wolverians were a storm made flesh. They weren't refined soldiers, most had never held a blade in formation, but what they lacked in discipline, they more than made up for in raw fury.

It was enough.

The wyverians seized the moment, breaking through the chaos, pushing forward with renewed strength until they reached the wall. The witches' attention shifted to the wolverians pouring into the field, giving Mal's people a precious sliver of time.

Mal raised her hands high, a surge of her powers rippling through her fingertips. With a flick of her wrists, she blasted a battalion of warlocks backward, sending them soaring over the wall in a crackling arc of darkness. The ground trembled as wyverians stormed through the breach she carved.

Her gaze darted across the fray, searching for a golden head of hair amidst the carnage. Ash. But he was nowhere to be found.

No time.

Mal turned her focus back to the wall. She had to get them over, every last wyverian, and into the Kingdom of Fire. To Fireheart.

To take back what was stolen.

And to end Hagan, once and for all.

Mal centred Nyx before the wall, palms outstretched, her fingers trembling as she summoned every ounce of power coursing through her divine veins. Her body quaked beneath the strain, sweat tracing shimmering paths down her cheeks. She did not possess the spellcraft to bring stone to heel, but she had something older, something mightier. Godborn power thrummed within her. A force she still scarcely understood, yet now she surrendered to it completely, allowing it to flood through her bones, down her arms, and out through her fingertips in a burst of unrelenting light.

Nyx reared back and unleashed a torrent of cerulean fire, the wyvern's breath scorching the very air as it struck the same patch of wall. Flames and shadows intertwined, colliding with the enchanted stone.

Mal screamed, her voice raw and ragged, as her limbs shook violently, the magical runes etched deep into the wall resisting, pulsing with ancient defences. But her power surged again, darker and deeper, not of this world.

Then, release.

A final surge erupted from her outstretched hands, a shockwave that cracked through the foundations of the wall and shattered the glowing runes like brittle glass. A thunderous explosion followed, the stone imploding from within, sending debris into the sky in a roaring plume. Mal staggered, nearly collapsing from the force of it, her breath caught in her throat as she stared at the gaping wound left behind.

She smiled.

Without hesitation, the wyverians and wolverians charged, a storm of black and silver tearing through the breach before the witches could regroup. No hesitation. No mercy.

They were going to win. Mal could feel it singing in her

marrow. With warriors now pushing through the wall, the witches would be overwhelmed, their defences crumbling beneath the sheer weight of ferocity.

But the hope blooming in her chest withered almost instantly.

The battlefield fell into eerie stillness. One by one, the witches and warlocks ceased their attacks, their bodies stiffening as though seized by some silent, invisible command.

Mal froze.

Something was wrong.

A chant began to rise, low and rhythmic, vibrating through the battlefield like an ancient hymn. Time itself seemed to halt at the sound, as if the very air held its breath. One by one, the fighters froze in place—wyverians, wolverians, even the wind itself. The witches' eyes glowed with an unearthly light, the cadence of their chant intensifying, each syllable sharper, faster, more powerful.

Before Mal's disbelieving eyes, the wall she had so painstakingly shattered reassembled itself in a blink. Stone slid over stone, mortar stitching like skin, until it stood proud once more, as though her efforts had never touched it.

The witches stationed upon the wastelands turned without a word and began retreating to the wall, passing their kin who continued chanting with unwavering focus. All around her, wyverians and wolverians trembled in place, hands clenched around sword hilts, straining against the invisible binds that held them still.

Then came the light.

Cracks of vivid green surged through the wall's stonework, illuminating the sky in a jagged flash before vanishing as swiftly as it had appeared. In its wake, the warriors were released, bodies lurching forward as if they had been underwater, gasping for air.

But the witches were gone.

They now stood atop the wall or safe behind it, glaring down with smug satisfaction, their smirks carved into the coldness of their faces.

Mal watched as Bryn Wynter darted towards the barrier, blade poised with fury. Just as he reached it, the world shifted again. Mal felt it in her bones, the presence of something ancient, something sacred and immovable. The wall shimmered faintly. The runes glowed like stars awoken from slumber, whispering protection in a tongue shared with wyverians.

An unseen force hurled Bryn backwards with brutal force, slamming him to the ground. Mal's heart stuttered. Had he survived?

Others rushed forward in his stead, desperate to breach the wall, but each met the same fate. Snatched by the invisible barrier and cast into the air like leaves in a storm. They fell hard and unmoving, their breaths knocked out and bodies left sprawled on the sodden earth.

The witches laughed.

Mal saw their gleeful expressions as they vanished one by one, dissolving into tendrils of green smoke. Some cast her a final smirking, mocking glance as if to say *you've already lost.* And then they were gone.

Not a single witch or warlock remained.

On one side of the wall, wyverians and wolverians stood stunned, trapped in the cursed land of their enemies.

And on the other side, alone.

Mal.

Chapter Fifty-Eight

House of Power
Kingdom of Magic

Hades said that we are cursed.
> That he is cursed to love me forever.
> That I am cursed to be reborn.
> And Hadrian is cursed to suffer.
> I've asked him to stop it. He's a god, surely he can break it.
> He laughed.

Tabitha Wysteria

It had taken Bryn Wynter and his army an age to scale the vast wall that cleaved the wastelands from the Kingdom of Ice. The moment Kage had departed, a letter had arrived urging them to begin their march. The journey through the scorched and barren land would be long, the path stretching endlessly towards the wall that marked the divide between the Kingdom of Fire and the marshlands where they were to meet the wyverians.

Bryn had not enjoyed the stillness. Not a whisper of a witch's presence echoed in the silence. They had passed through deserted towns and hollowed-out villages, places clearly once lived in, now abandoned with purpose. Every corner was searched with cautious precision, every shadow inspected for traps or hidden threats. But none emerged. No magic stirred. The witches had vanished like a receding tide.

The wastelands were, for the first time, truly empty.

The distant thunder of war had eventually reached them, battle cries swept to their ears on gusts of dry wind. Thank the gods for their wolves, swift and relentless, allowing the wolverian warriors to eat up the miles far quicker than they ever could on foot. And yet, Bryn remained unsure. Would they arrive in time?

He had not expected the onslaught they met upon joining the wyverian ranks. The moment his warriors crossed the threshold, the witches' magic turned the field into a blood-soaked abyss. Spellfire and screams painted the air with horror.

Through it all, Bryn remembered Kage's lessons, each one etched into his bones like runes carved in stone. He clung to them now, praying they'd keep him alive long enough to thank the wyverian prince properly.

Was Kage out there, amidst the chaos? A phantom of shadow and steel, striking down witches as green fire licked the sky? Bryn did not know. But he hoped.

And should fate allow them both to survive the slaughter, he hoped they would share the quiet warmth of a fire once more. No words would be needed. Bryn understood Kage's silence. He cherished it.

Bryn caught sight of Mal Blackburn astride her shadow wyvern, both figures forged of smoke and nightmare. The princess was a vision of dread and divinity, a silhouette born of darkness. And yet, the witches beneath her seemed entirely unfazed, as though the sight of death incarnate did not chill their bones.

Raising her hands towards the ancient stone, Mal began to summon something deep and dreadful. At first, Bryn wasn't certain what she intended, until the wall trembled, groaned, and then, in a deafening cascade of power, exploded into ruin. Still, the witches chanted.

Bryn didn't care.

His blades were in motion, slicing through robed bodies and bloodied air, ducking beneath searing magic and retaliating with the ferocity of a storm.

Suddenly, he could no longer move.

His body turned to iron, rigid and unyielding, every limb shackled by invisible force. He couldn't even tilt his head to see if the others were trapped the same way. His pale blue eyes locked on the wall. Their goal, so agonisingly close. But as swiftly as it had crumbled, the structure reassembled itself, stone knitting with stone, untouched by flame or fury.

The witches' chant swelled, a hymn of power and ancient bindings. Their eyes glowed with ethereal light, purple orbs burning like twin moons in an endless night. Bryn tried to move, just a twitch of his fingers, but the attempt sent lightning down his arm, pain blooming in jagged bursts.

His gaze sought Mal Blackburn again. She stood untouched by the enchantment, still commanding the skies as though the gods themselves had bent their will to her.

Panic tightened Bryn's chest. What if this spell never lifted? What if they remained trapped, suspended between time and agony, statues left to decay under the watchful eyes of their enemies?

Closing his eyes, he sent a silent, desperate plea to the gods.

All at once, the chanting ceased, and Bryn collapsed forward, his body flung to the mud-slicked earth as though the spell that bound him had snapped without warning. His cheek pressed into cold, wet soil, and he grimaced, smearing it away with the back of his hand. He moved cautiously at first, testing each limb, wiggling fingers, curling toes, ensuring he was truly free.

But something was wrong.

Every witch and warlock had turned, their focus no longer on the battlefield but on the wall itself. Not a single glance was spared for the warriors around them.

Bryn didn't hesitate. He surged to his feet, blade raised high.

A surge of magic struck him, a wave so forceful it tore the breath from his lungs and hurled him backwards. He crashed into the mud, the world shattering in pain as lightning flared through his limbs, seizing every nerve in agony. He wheezed, gasping for air that would not come.

When he managed to rise, he saw others trying the same. Wyverians and wolverians alike charging the wall in desperation, only to be flung back by an unseen force. Again and again, they fell, scattered like leaves before a storm.

Something ancient and dreadful had been awakened.

A chilling thought lodged itself in Bryn's mind, heavy and unrelenting. What if no one could cross? What if the wall encircling the wastelands in its vast, merciless embrace was now sealed from all sides?

A prison, locking them within.

And the rest of the world... out.

...

Ash moved with quiet purpose, each step echoing softly as he approached the towering stone wall, once built to bar the witches from the rest of the realms, now twisted cruelly to serve the very same purpose against their would-be liberators. What had once stood as a symbol of protection now loomed like a prison's boundary, cold and unyielding.

He had left Adriana slumped beneath the hush of trees, unconscious and forgotten. Someone would find her eventually, or she would crawl her way back to the world. It mattered little. He had not intended to confront her so soon, not yet reveal that he knew her secret. But he had needed to shake her, just enough to unbalance her long enough to act. He couldn't risk her claiming the wyverns, not now. More importantly, he could not risk anyone crossing that wall.

They needed to stay inside.

Ash watched from a distance as soldiers hurled themselves towards the stone barrier, desperation etched into every motion. He paid no mind to the way their bodies were repelled by the warded magic, flung like leaves in a storm by the invisible force that held them captive.

All, save one.

Mal Blackburn descended from the skies on the back of her shadow-forged wyvern, Nyx cutting a silhouette of smoke and menace against the grey-tinged heavens. She landed atop the cursed wall with sovereign grace, forcing the warriors below to still, their futile efforts paused by the weight of her presence.

Without a word, she leapt from her mount, her form melting back into its solid, corporeal self. She moved with purpose, unbothered by the stunned eyes upon her, unshaken by the futility that clung to the air like ash.

Ash had almost forgotten just how breathtaking she truly was.

He never should have found her beautiful. Wyverians were nothing like drakonians. Their forms were slender, almost ethereal, with skin so pale it bordered on moonlight, black veins sometimes veining visibly along their arms like delicate ink strokes. Their hair, dark as the void between stars, shimmered with a sheen that even night could not hope to match. And their eyes...

Ah, Mal's eyes were something else entirely.

In time, Ash had come to realise that the very things meant to set them apart were what had drawn him in. The differences that should have bred revulsion instead lit a fire in him, an intrigue that bordered on worship. She was not merely a rare gem among stones; she was the storm that shaped them.

The way she moved, like a panther poised to strike, was equal parts grace and danger. Every step was sinuous, every glance a silent challenge. There was a sensual precision in her movement, sharp as a blade honed by centuries. He could watch her for eternity and still be left wanting. With Mal Blackburn, it would never be enough.

'What did they do?' she asked, her voice barely a whisper, meant only for him. And this time, Ash would not hold his tongue. He owed her the truth, now more than ever.

'They've sealed us in,' he said. 'The wall encircling the waste-wastelands has been enchanted. No s-soul within can leave, and no one outside may enter.'

'That's why we encountered no witches on our journey here, isn't it?'

Ash inclined his head in a silent nod.

'Why?' she asked again. A single word, but he understood precisely what she meant.

'With the wyverian and wolverian forces ca-caged within these scorched lands, the wi-witches are free to do as they please. No resistance. No obstacles. They've penned us in like a-animals, and now they roam un-unchallenged.'

Her voice turned sharp, laced with fury. 'And you allowed this to happen?'

He didn't flinch. He bore the accusation as he had borne so many wounds. One day, perhaps, she would understand. Perhaps she would even forgive him.

'You won't answer that,' she sighed, the edge dulling into

resignation. 'Why can I cross the barrier?'

'Because you are no longer b-bound by what binds the rest of us.' His words were quiet, reluctant. He hadn't meant to hurt her, but the truth always did. Her shoulders dipped slightly, a small collapse under the weight of what she was. Not just a wyverian princess with witch eyes, but something far more. Something she didn't fully understand. Yet.

'How do I get them out?' she asked, glancing up at the towering wall. The doubt in her voice was evident, the wall before them more mountain than structure. She already believed it was impossible.

'Only magic can break ma-magic,' he said. 'You'll need a t-teacher.'

Her brow furrowed, creased with the beginnings of despair. 'Where?'

Ash's smile was soft, tinged with sadness. He peered down, and she followed his gaze, her breath catching as the meaning unfurled before her.

'Vera's sister will h-help you,' he said gently. 'Allegra. She's in the Underworld.'

Mal recoiled as if the name itself had struck her. Her lips parted in protest, in disbelief. Memory surged in her eyes, memories of betrayal, of secrets whispered in the dark. Her heart twisted with pain, and the realisation of how deeply Ash had deceived her glimmered beneath the surface.

'I don't want to go back there,' she whispered.

Ash gave a quiet nod, his fingers brushing against hers in a silent gesture of understanding. He didn't dare linger, not when the warmth of her skin might recoil from his touch. He had wounded her, deeply, and he knew it. No apology could erase what had been done.

'But you must go, Mal,' he said softly, his voice laced with quiet urgency. 'You must b-become who you truly are, in every p-possible way.'

Mal shook her head, tears spilling down her cheeks like pearls flung from a broken strand. She stepped back, placing distance between them so his hand could no longer find hers. Those striking purple eyes locked with his, and within them he saw the torment, the fear, the ache, the quiet desperation. He wanted to take it all away, to whisper promises into the hollow places of her soul. To kiss those tears from her skin and fold her into the sanctuary of his arms.

'The curse,' she whispered, pressing a trembling hand to her chest, moving in slow circles as though trying to soothe the ache within. 'It's Thanatos, isn't it? He's the one who'll kill you. Just as Hades killed Hadrian.'

Ash bowed his head.

'You knew,' she breathed. 'You saw it, didn't you?' Her attention lifted to the overcast skies above, as though hoping the clouds might answer her. 'This was always part of the plan.'

Again, he nodded.

'Then tell me, how do I stop it? How do I stop Thanatos from killing you? How do I save you?'

Ash felt something within him shatter, a quiet devastation rippling through his chest. How cruel it was to love someone so fiercely, and yet be the reason for their sorrow. Even now, after the lies, the betrayal, the silence, she still wanted to save him. Her heart, fractured and bruised, still beat for him.

Mal Blackburn would tear the world apart to keep him alive.

And he, he would raze kingdoms to ash if it meant keeping her safe. That was the true weight of their curse: a love so fierce it could fracture the very foundations of the world. They would tear the realms asunder, crumble empires to dust, if it meant holding one another through the ruin. From the moment their lips met beneath the veil of their wedding vows, their fates had been forged in flame, bound not just in name, but in a devotion that defied gods and time alike. To love, despite everything. To love, no matter what.

'I won't let you die,' she breathed, her voice a vow carved from steel and sorrow. 'I will never allow Thanatos to touch you. I'll descend into the Underworld myself if I must, find Allegra, and learn from her how to free you from this wretched fate. And then I'll hunt Thanatos down, and drive a blade through his cursed heart.'

Oh, how he ached for such an ending. How he longed to see her victorious, to witness this fierce, magnificent woman rise against the gods themselves and triumph. But Ash had seen too many paths, fractured visions of what could be, threads of time tangled and frayed, and the one where Mal struck down Thanatos...

That was not the path they needed.

That was not the way to save the world.

No, he had to guide them along the one thread that shimmered with the faintest glimmer of hope.

And killing Thanatos... was not a part of it.

She saw it in his eyes.

'Then how?' she demanded, her jaw set tight, her hands curling into fists. 'How do I save you?'

Beneath her boots, the ground began to tremble, the soil cracking, whispering with the pull of the Underworld. It was coming to reclaim her, to draw her back into the dark. Ash felt the moment slipping, time unravelling like breath in the cold.

He needed more of it.

He needed *her*.

But even if he lived a thousand lifetimes, it would never be enough.

'How?' she cried again, voice fraying at the edges.

Ash reached for her with his eyes, his voice a broken murmur against the roar of the rising abyss.

'You must break the curse,' he said, grief laced in every syllable. 'Break the tether that binds our souls, Mal.'

Her breath caught.

'How do I break it?' she whispered, already knowing. Already breaking.

And in his gaze, she found the answer buried there like a blade in the dark, glinting with a sorrow too ancient for words.

'You must stop loving me.'

Mal's eyes widened, a choked gasp of disbelief catching in her throat just before the earth split wide and the jaws of the Underworld devoured her whole.

Chapter Fifty-Nine

House of Flames
Kingdom of Fire

We all have strengths and weaknesses.

Tabitha Wysteria

Kai had insisted they halt and rest after countless hours spent riding along shadowed, winding roads. The ash drifting from the sky had yet to cease, a constant, silken snowfall of soot that obscured the view ahead, rendering Fireheart little more than a name whispered on the wind.

Dawn had been behaving oddly for some time now. Tense, restless, urging him to press on, refusing any suggestion of pause. She had pleaded for side roads instead of main ones, offering feeble excuses each time he questioned her.

'We should keep going, I'm not tired,' she muttered.

'It's growing late. We've been riding all day.'

'We're sitting on a horse.'

'And does your back not ache?' he countered, watching her expression shift, betraying the weariness she stubbornly denied. She was bone-tired, he could see it in the set of her shoulders, in the hollow quiet beneath her words. And still she pushed. 'What's troubling you, witch?'

'Nothing,' she replied quickly, fingers twisting through her hair with forced nonchalance.

Kai opened his mouth, a low retort poised on his tongue when a thunderous boom shattered the air in the far-off distance. His instincts surged. With swift precision, he seized his hook swords and slung them across his back, every sense alert and taut like a drawn bowstring. He dismounted from his shadow steed in a single, fluid motion, as his boots met the ash-laced earth. He strode out onto the dirt road, eyes scanning the darkened horizon, nostrils flaring as he scented the wind.

Dawn, having slipped down from the horse too, now held a handful of the horse's mane, her grip gentle as she moved close behind.

There it was. The unmistakable tang of magic in the air, metallic and sharp, threading through the ash like a warning. It saturated the atmosphere, so potent it prickled along his skin.

He looked skyward. Flashes of unnatural light bloomed through the gloom like silent fireworks, bursting in spectral colours against the heavy veil of ash above.

'We ought to rest.' Dawn waved him back towards the patch of earth they had chosen for their camp, her gesture light but insistent.

Kai trailed behind her, his gaze sharp and narrowed, suspicion lingering like smoke in his eyes.

'Stay here,' he said, gathering a few essentials with practised ease. 'I'll investigate. I'll return by morning.'

'What?' The horror in Dawn's voice bled the colour from her face. 'You can't just leave me out here on my own!'

Kai rolled his eyes in theatrical disdain.

'Insufferable,' he muttered under his breath. 'Then move quickly,' he added aloud, striding past her. 'We're going back. The lights were near the wall.'

Dawn froze.

Only for a breath. But it was enough.

She masked it quickly, yet Kai caught the fear behind her eyes.

'Perhaps we should stay,' she said too lightly. 'The plan was to head for Fireheart. We will lose days if we turn in the opposite direction now.'

'Why does it matter if we lose days of travel?' he asked, his tone laced with growing curiosity as he gestured at his shadow to retreat. The inky figure slipped away into the dark, returning to whatever void such creatures dwelled in when not summoned. 'My army is weeks away, we'd have to wait for them anyway.'

Unlike Kage, Kai had never felt the need to keep his shadow tethered to him. His younger brother, however, had always kept that damned crow close, its incessant cawing like an echo of his own thoughts. Kai used to tease him, claiming it was because the creature had been Kage's only friend as a child.

Kai exhaled a long breath, the weight of memory pressing against his chest like a stone. Thoughts of Kage drifted through the veil of ash, brittle and persistent. Was his brother still alive? Was Mal keeping herself out of the kind of trouble that always seemed drawn to her like a moth to flame?

'It might be dangerous,' murmured the witch behind him, her voice uncertain, breaking the hush of the road.

He offered no reply, only the quiet rustle of his movements as he gathered their sparse belongings and turned back towards the path they had strayed from. Her footsteps followed moments later, light but dogged. He refrained from calling upon his shadow just yet. First, they would walk. Let the stillness speak, let the silence settle. They would decide on safety once the air whispered its secrets.

A sudden cry pierced the quiet.

He stopped.

Turning, he found her on the ground, clutching her ankle, her features twisted in pain.

'What is it now?'

'I think I've twisted my ankle,' she groaned.

'Then heal it,' he said dryly, unimpressed. 'You're a witch, aren't you?'

She glared up at him, the frustration etched across her face almost laughable. 'It doesn't work like that! We can't heal ourselves with magic. We're never taught how.'

He shrugged, unmoved. 'Then sit there and wait.'

Something struck the back of his head, sharp enough to sting but small enough not to harm. Kai froze, muscles tensing as a surge of irritation curled like fire through his chest and rose hot against his throat.

'I am not a dog,' she hissed.

'Did you just throw a rock at me?'

'It was a pebble,' she replied, utterly unrepentant.

'Must we have this conversation again?' he muttered, moving to her side. Without ceremony, he scooped her up into his arms and began walking.

'You can't carry me the whole way,' she huffed, folding her arms across her chest like a child denied her sweets. 'You're not *that* strong.'

He said nothing, choosing silence over the obvious rebuttal. His strides remained steady and sure.

After a while, faint sounds stirred in the distance. Voices, followed by the soft crunch of steps. Instinct prickled down Kai's spine. He veered off the road, slipping into the shelter of the trees, letting the shadows swallow them whole. There, amidst the hush of the forest, he lowered Dawn gently to the ground.

'Don't leave me,' she whispered, her voice trembling, fragile as gossamer. There was a nervous edge to it, too sharp to be sincere.

Kai's brows pulled together. Her fear didn't ring true. A lie, he realised. But why?

Before he could ask, before she could spin more excuses, he turned and vanished between the trees, moving like smoke towards the road once more. He crouched low, hidden from view, and waited.

The voices grew clearer.

Dawn appeared at his side like a wisp of smoke, silent and sudden. It startled him, her uncanny ability to move without sound, and more so the fact that she had reached him so swiftly despite the twisted ankle she had earlier claimed.

'Kai, perhaps—' she began, but he stiffened at the sound of his name on her tongue.

It wasn't just her voice that set him on edge. In that very instant, the road came alive with movement. Hundreds of witches and warlocks drifted past like a procession of ghosts. Kai held his breath and stilled his muscles, fingers coiled around the hilts of his hook swords, poised to strike should they be discovered.

Dawn didn't move. She hardly even breathed. Her eyes tracked the march of her people, their numbers too great, too close for comfort.

When the last figure had disappeared into the shadows ahead and silence once again blanketed the path, Kai turned on her. Swift as lightning, he seized her by the arm and slammed her against the rough bark of a tree, one of his hook swords pressed to the soft skin beneath her jaw.

'What in the gods' names are you doing?' Dawn gasped, genuine fear flaring in her eyes as she struggled in his grip.

'What are you scheming?' he hissed, his breath warm and sharp against her cheek. 'You've been twitching all day, desperate to keep us moving, and now I find an army of your kin heading towards Fireheart? Explain that.'

'I don't know. I swear it!' Her voice cracked under the weight of his fury.

'I don't believe a word of it.'

The blade kissed her neck, a sliver of crimson blooming against her skin and trickling downward like a single thread of silk. Kai watched it with a cold, unwavering gaze, the contrast of blood against her skin striking.

'I will cut you, witch,' he said, voice low and dangerous.

She cried out, lashing and flailing with all the fury she could muster—kicking, biting, spitting into his face with unrestrained rage. And yet, through the flurry of violence, Kai found himself wondering why she didn't use her magic. She was far stronger than him, infinitely so. With a single flick of her fingers, she could have flung him into the wind and vanished.

And yet, she hadn't.

Kai released his grip, his chest heaving not from exertion, but from a quiet understanding. No matter how fiercely she fought, she would not truly harm him. Not when Ash still lingered in her heart like a wound yet to scar. She would suffer anything if it meant helping the man she loved.

'It's always easier, isn't it?' he said quietly, stepping back. 'To let our happiness depend on others. That way, when it shatters, we've someone else to blame.'

Dawn wiped the blood from her throat, her fingers trembling with fury. Her face twisted into something fierce, hurt, defiant.

'You know why the witches were on that road,' he said, not as a question, but as fact. She hesitated, then nodded slowly, her shoulders taut with the weight of guilt. 'Tell me.'

'I can't,' she whispered, her voice barely audible. 'If I do...'

'If you do what?' he snapped.

Her eyes glistened. 'You'll hate me.'

Kai looked away, jaw clenched. When he spoke, it was cold and cruel.

'I already do, witch. Nothing you say will change that.'

Dawn's purple eyes darkened, resolve replacing fear. 'The witches attacked the wall,' she said at last. 'Your army, and the wolverian one, they were there. Fighting for their lives.'

Kai heard nothing more. Her voice became a ghost behind him as he ran, ran as though his lungs might tear, his heart burst. He summoned his horse with a sharp call, leaping onto its back and urging it towards the road with reckless abandon.

But he didn't get far.

A blast of magic struck him squarely in the back, ripping him from his shadow and hurling him through the air. He crashed hard into the roadside, the impact jarring his bones and forcing the breath from his lungs. Pain flared through his arm where the full weight of his body had landed. Not broken, thank the gods, but close enough.

He cursed aloud, fury igniting in his chest as the witch approached.

'You can run as much as you want,' Dawn said. 'I will stop you, every time.'

'You knew,' he growled, pushing himself upright despite the searing ache. 'You knew all along...'

Dawn hesitated, biting her lower lip as though it might hold back the truth. She took a cautious step forward, guilt etched across her face.

'I knew what Hagan intended,' she admitted softly. 'He's trapped the wyverian and wolverian armies in the wastelands.

My plan… was to be trapped in there too. With Ash.'

Kai spat at her feet.

'I'm sorry.'

'Save your apologies,' he snapped, staggering to his feet with clenched teeth. 'Why agree to travel to Fireheart? We could've reached Ash. We might've made it to him.'

A glint of something unreadable passed through Dawn's eyes. Guilt perhaps. Or longing. Or something far more dangerous.

Kai saw it. And he didn't trust it.

Yet, some small, traitorous part of him warmed at the thought that perhaps Ash no longer held her heart after all.

'When the witches attacked the city of Spark,' Dawn said, arms wrapped tightly around herself as though bracing against a storm, 'Hagan wanted the dragons. But they fled, all of them. Even the wild ones that nested in the volcanoes ended up leaving later on. They vanished, as if the skies themselves had swallowed them whole. The last sighting placed them flying south. I want to find them.'

Kai let out a derisive snort.

'I ought to kill you, witch.'

'Stop calling me that!' she snapped, her voice cracking as her fists pounded against his chest.

'I call you what you are.'

Dawn stepped back, fury igniting in every line of her slender frame. She jabbed a finger at him, her hand trembling with indignation. The gesture might have amused him under different stars, but in that moment, she looked like something divine and wrathful, like the storm before the ruin.

'You judge me because of my eyes,' she hissed, poking him again, harder this time. Kai's fingers itched with the urge to grasp her wrist, to draw her close and look into those defiant purple eyes. 'Well then, commander,' she went on, her voice like steel wrapped in silk, '*I* judge *you* by your actions.'

Kai cursed under his breath and spat into the dust.

'Charming,' Dawn muttered with a dry glance.

'This isn't a laughing matter.'

'And I'm not laughing, commander.'

He exhaled heavily, turning his attention towards the distant wall, the great, unyielding barrier that shimmered faintly in the light. 'How are they trapped? They could climb it.'

'Magic,' Dawn breathed, pressing her fingers to her brow, weariness threading her voice. 'No one gets in. No one gets out. Not from the Kingdom of Magic.'

Kai frowned. 'Why? What's the point of all this?'

'Hagan now has free reign,' she murmured, her voice bitter. 'With your army and the wolverians caged within my kingdom, he can turn his hand in whatever direction he pleases, and no one can stop him.' She straightened her shoulders, a flicker of resolve in her stance. 'Going back to the wall will achieve nothing. They're lost to us, for now. But if we find the dragons... we shift the balance. We change the game.'

They stood suspended in silence, their stares locked like blades poised before a duel. And in that strange, charged moment, Kai understood with a clarity that made his stomach twist. He would not be returning to the wall. Not to his army. Not yet.

No, he would be following *her.*

This infuriating woman with fire in her veins and fury on her tongue. He would trail her into ruin if she asked him to, willingly tethered to her descent. For he knew, deep within the marrow of his bones, that she was concealing something. He could see it in her eyes, the cadence of her breath. She was lying. Of that, he was certain. But what remained cloaked in shadow was which truth she had chosen to twist.

'Why the dragons? How can they stop Hagan?' he muttered, eyeing the glimmer in her gaze. Fragile hope, maybe, for his forgiveness, and something more perhaps. A part of him longed to crush it, stomp it out like embers beneath his boot. And yet, gods help him, another part wished to cradle it in his hands. He could not fathom turning his back and walking away from her. He told himself it was because he knew, without question, that she was scheming, that some hidden game played behind those eyes. Yet deep down, in the quiet chambers of his heart, he wondered... was that truly the reason?

That wicked smile curved across her lips then, the one he loathed with every breath, and yet could sketch in perfect detail from memory alone.

'The thing about witches, commander,' she purred, her voice velvet laced with smoke, 'is that we *burn.*'

Chapter Sixty

House of Sand
Desert Kingdom

Revenge is a path lined with thorns, it tears your skin to shreds with every step forward.

Sometimes I wonder if forgiveness would be easier. Perhaps it would.

But not for my soul.

I have become the stuff of nightmares.

Unstoppable, lethal.

I will have my revenge.

Tabitha Wysteria

Alina no longer felt.

Alina no longer cared.

She had tried to keep count at first of the days bleeding into nights, hours slipping through her fingers like grains of sand. But by the third sunrise, or perhaps it was the fourth, the days had begun to blur. Time folded into itself, weightless and irrelevant. The desert, ever shifting, ever cruel, reshaped its skin beneath her feet, laughing in cruel mirth, whispering taunts in a tongue only she could hear. *You're not one of us*, it said. And it was right.

A true Dunayan, a child of the sands, would not lose her way. Would not stumble.

But perhaps the desert hadn't realised the girl drifting through its golden bones *chose* to be lost.

Alina wandered with neither purpose nor destination, guided only by the emptiness hollowing out her chest. She had not forgotten the things Hessa had taught her. No, those lessons clung to her with the same devotion she once gave to the woman who shared them. She knew where to find water in the dunes' embrace, how to tuck herself into the cool folds of night when the winds threatened to flay her to bone. She knew how to hunt, how to split a scorpion with practised precision, savouring its meat, even raw.

She moved like a ghost dressed in human skin.

Her pack was light, but just enough. Hessa had made sure of it. Desert folk were never caught unprepared. Even sleep was a discipline, not a surrender. One never knew when a storm might tear through, shredding tents and scattering souls. Alina's body was a weapon, her garments an arsenal: daggers sewn into secret seams, tools to summon water from beneath the parched earth, cloth that shielded her face from the wrath of sand and wind.

She was a lone storm, moving through a wasteland that once called her sister.

Alina no longer felt the pangs of hunger.

By the eighth day, even thirst ceased to matter.

She moved with the wind now, an aimless phantom in the sands, her heart weeping silently into the desert's endless grains. Her footsteps were carved in sorrow, and still she wandered, trying, failing, to unearth reason in Saren's betrayal. What thread connected the Dunayan warrior to Hagan? Alina had unravelled every theory until her mind splintered under the weight of it, pouring thoughts like water from a cracked vessel. But none of it fit. None of it made sense.

She had thought, once or twice, about returning. To Hessa's

region. To King Siroc. She might fall to her knees and bare the truth, let her voice tremble as she begged them to believe her. But why would they? Why would they take the word of a foreigner, a farahi, over one of their own?

So she kept walking.

The city of Madari was a memory now, a mirage lost behind her. Whether days or weeks had passed, she could not say. Whether someone followed, she no longer cared. By now, surely not. No one would bother looking for a ghost lost in the dunes.

She could lie down and let the desert claim her. Let the wind swallow her bones and the sand cradle her in silence. There was nothing left to tether her to the world. No warmth, no laughter, no light. Hagan had taken it all. Every time she fought to crawl forward, he reached from the shadows and dragged her back into the dark.

Alina drifted through the desert as though walking not upon sand, but through the corridors of memory. With each step, the past unfurled like a dream half-remembered, carrying her back to a time when she had been nothing more than a princess fretting over silks and braided hair. A girl who had once believed love was shy glances and stolen kisses, soft and sweet as a lullaby.

She remembered falling for her brother's best friend. The dangerous, charming shadow that had always lingered on the edge of her world. Perhaps she had loved Hagan because he was the one her mother would have forbidden, the one no one would ever deem worthy of her crown. But whatever the reason, she knew, truly knew, that she had loved him. Fiercely. Naively.

Not until Kai Blackburn had swept into her life did she understand what love could be. He had shown her the edge she never knew she possessed, taught her to raise her voice, to stand tall, to say no when the world tried to bend her. She often wondered what path might have unfurled had she climbed atop that wyvern with him the day he flew home.

How strange to think that had been the last time she had seen him. That quiet, aching farewell. She hadn't known it was final. Hope had clung to her, foolish and tender, whispering that there would be a next time. That he would return.

In the beginning, she dreamt of rescue. Of Kai's great beast soaring across the skies to find her. Of his arms wrapping around her, lifting her out of this broken land and into something safe.

But then, Hessa.

Then came the sun.

And everything she thought she knew was set alight.

Alina walked. She marched, stumbled, and slid through dunes that whispered ancient secrets with every gust of wind. She ate in silence, curled beneath the brittle veil of night, and slept in shallow intervals, her dreams fading into the shifting sands like ghosts. She studied the stars not for beauty, but for survival, tracing their quiet language across the heavens, hoping their silent story would lead her somewhere safe.

Alina walked.

Alina ate.

Alina slept.

And Alina wandered.

The ghulas came, as they always did. Spectral things born from death and sun-dazed delirium. They slithered out of the heat like mirages, donning familiar faces. Sometimes Ash, her brother, eyes sad and burning with words never spoken. Sometimes Kai, cruel and disappointed, scolding her not for choosing another, but for choosing herself.

But it was worst when they wore Hessa's face. That was

when Alina broke. She'd scream, hurling sand and spit and rage. She would claw at the apparition, sobbing as if grief itself could bleed.

Only one face she welcomed.

Only one she waited for.

Hagan.

He always came, smirking with that wicked twist of a smile, lips curved as if mocking the very world. She'd gouge out his eyes some days, flay that familiar face until the ghula shrieked and dissolved into dust. Other days, she'd simply sit and talk, asking questions it could never answer. The ghula only mirrored her torment, incapable of offering what it did not possess. Yet still, she tilted her head and listened, even as it cackled and pointed at her hornless head in cruel delight.

She knew it was wrong.

She knew Hessa would have wept to see her like this.

No one dared to torment a ghula, none but Alina.

And Alina revelled in it.

Until they stopped coming altogether.

Until word must have spread among their kind: stay away from the mad girl in the dunes.

So Alina walked.

And she ate.

And she slept.

And she wandered on.

Time had long since unravelled for the girl who wandered the desert, its threads slipping like sand through her fingers. Alina might have said she was lost, only she wasn't, not truly. The desert knew her, and she knew it, for her heart had once belonged to the one shaped by its very grains. No, Alina was not lost.

She was merely adrift.

In all the days that bled into one another, she met no soul, save for one fleeting encounter. A band of travellers, sun-worn and weathered, crossed her path and offered her the kindness of a shared fire, food, and water. Alina, dulled by solitude, allowed it. The quiet ache of loneliness begged her to linger, if only for a night.

But kindness soured in the dark. One man sought more than her silence. His hands crept in the night like vipers, and Alina's blade met the soft flesh of his throat. His blood painted her face in warm ribbons. She didn't flinch. She didn't speak. She simply rose and walked away, leaving the others behind in mercy she could no longer explain.

Alina walked.

Alina ate.

Alina slept.

Until time itself disintegrated, until even memory loosened its grip.

And then, she simply fell.

Her knees buckled first, followed by the rest of her, sinking into the warm embrace of the earth. She closed her eyes and surrendered, offering herself to the desert like a votive gift. If it wished to kill her, she would not resist. Death, at last, would be an old friend come to collect her. But if it chose to swallow her whole and spit her back out, then she would claw her way from its throat like something reborn.

She waited.

Her rasghita was discarded, her karash tugged down. No cloth veiled her face now. The sun had free reign to sear her skin, blister her lips, and burn the tears from her eyes. Her throat cracked, her muscles wilted into the sand, and yet still, she did not stir.

Alina no longer wandered.

She merely waited.

Hessa lay beside her in spirit, conjured by a half-mad mind that refused to forget. Alina welcomed the illusion, listened to the soft voice whisper against her sunburnt skin. But not even Hessa's ghost could rouse her.

She waited.

For the world to take her.

For the pain to finally leave.

She had long lost count of the days. Time slipped by like sand through her fingers—unnoticed, uncared for. Her body had grown frail, hollowed by the sun's wrath and the desert's indifference. On more than one occasion, the dunes tried to claim her, swallowing her whole in silence, only to spit her back out like something undesired. Still, Alina did not move.

She waited, for a sign.

A reason to rise. A reason to keep fighting.

All she had ever done was struggle, only to be cast down time and time again. Perhaps that was life, she thought bitterly. A war of attrition. And she had grown so very, very tired.

Perhaps life had won.

Just one signal, one spark, and she would rise once more. She would crawl, if she had to, without Ash. Without Hessa. She would reclaim her kingdom. She would find Hagan and end him.

But first, she needed a sign.

Her body stiffened with time. Even the act of swallowing became a memory. Her eyelids, crusted and sealed, refused to part. So she let go.

Alina slept.

She drifted through the endless hours, through moonlight and sunlight alike. She lay still, entombed in silence, waiting for death's gentle fingers to cradle her into nothingness.

Until.

Something landed on her nose, something small. A shadow stirred above her, brushing across her skin like a whisper from a dream. A sound broke the stillness. A cry, both fierce and familiar, slicing through the silence like a blade of fire. She fought, just barely, against the prison of her own body. Her lashes trembled. A moan escaped cracked lips. She forced her eyes open with sheer will.

Brown eyes, dim but alive, met the sky.

The delicate creature resting on her nose stirred, wings trembling before it lifted into the air. A tiny insect, a whisper of joy from a time now lost. What had it been called again? Ah, yes. A narshara. A firefly. Said to be a sacred gift from the dead, sent to guide the living across the shifting sands of the desert.

And in that fleeting, breath-held moment, Alina understood. Hessa had sent it. To lead her. To light the path. To offer the sign she had so desperately begged the world to give.

The narshara ascended, rising higher and higher, glinting like an ember against the pale sky. And then, as Alina's eyes followed its glow, she realised what the soft sound had been, the thing it had come to reveal. For there, hovering above her head, shimmering like a promise born of grief and hope, was her sign.

Alina Acheron smiled. A dry, broken smile that tasted of salt and sun as the phoenix soared above her, trailing flame and hope. Its cry a song not of sorrow, but of triumph.

Of endurance.

And of life.

Epilogue

Freya carried the dying Wren Wynter across the sea to an island whispered of only in myth. A sanctuary of lush, untamed beauty, where waterfalls carved secrets into the cliffs and forgotten temples slumbered beneath ancient trees. Upon her arrival, the valkyrians emerged like whispers from the foliage, silent and graceful, and led her with reverence to the River of Resurrection.

Together, they placed Wren into the shallows, the water darkening her clothes as it seeped into the fabric, as though the river itself recognised the weight of what it was about to receive. Soft, haunting hums escaped the lips of the warrior women as they began their ritual. With solemn grace, they undressed the wolverian princess, washing her gently beneath the murmuring waters. Freya moved among them, her hands steady, her expression unreadable. She aided them as they had once done for her before her own rebirth, before the godhood that left her memory intact when it should have been washed away. For gods do not forget.

When Wren was at last cleansed, skin bare beneath the blessing of the river, the valkyrians lifted her with care, cradling her like a sacred flame. Up the temple steps they climbed, their bare feet silent against the stone, their voices quiet now, reverent. She was soon to be one of them, a sister forged anew in death's embrace.

The temple stood open to the skies, its roof long surrendered to the heavens so that light, and only light, might ever touch the altar. Runes shimmered along the archways, carved in an age when gods walked freely, whispering duty and destiny with every flicker of sunlight.

At the centre, a stone table waited.

Freya knelt, her fingers tender as she cradled Wren's head and lowered it onto the altar, as though the girl were made of glass and starlight.

And so, the ritual began.

There would be pain.

But through pain, rebirth.

The sisters began their solemn work, etching sacred runes into Wren's skin with ink so pale it gleamed like milk under moonlight. It was said to be a divine substance, drawn from the breast of the goddess who had birthed the first of their kind, harvested from the blessed fountain that granted them the strength to rise as valkyrians.

Freya, who had once stood in the presence of that goddess, offered no comment.

Each time the feathered quills, plucked from the wings of their revered horses, pierced the girl's flesh, Wren screamed, her agony echoing through the temple like a haunting lullaby. It was a pain unlike any other, the sort that unravelled even the bravest souls. Freya had tasted it once, through the remnants of memory left in the vessel she now inhabited. What Wren endured now... it was a torment that few would have survived.

Indeed, many might have begged for death.

With each graceful stroke of the feather, the ivory ink sank beneath her skin, weaving itself into ancient patterns of power and rebirth. And with every mark, the girl upon the altar grew quieter, her breaths shallowing, life ebbing from her body like mist before the dawn.

Freya's hand moved to smooth the snowy strands of Wren's hair, a gesture born of a mother's longing, tender and wistful. It was the closest she could come to touching her own lost children.

She began to mark the face.

Freya hummed as she worked, a low melody that wove through the air like incense smoke. Soft, lulling, the only balm against the cries that rang out. The others joined in, voices blending in bittersweet harmony. There was no disguising the cruelty of the act. It was brutal, merciless.

And yet, it was necessary.

For this was how their warriors were born.

The tattoos etched into their flesh were runes, ancient, sacred markings, bestowed solely upon the valkyrians. They were blessings and bindings both, bestowing swiftness, strength, and power beyond that of ordinary mortals. With each symbol inked beneath the skin, a woman became something more, transformed into a creature of divine purpose.

Yet such a gift came not without cost.

The runes bound them irrevocably to serve, to shield, to protect.

Should a valkyrian ever sever those sacred ties, defy the oaths inked into her very bones, death would claim her swiftly. Most accepted this fate willingly, yearning for purpose greater than themselves. But Freya found herself wondering how Wren Wynter would wake, how she would wear the mantle fate had chosen for her.

She would awaken with no memory of her former life. The title of wolverian princess would mean nothing. Her kin, her past, her very self, lost in the mists of oblivion.

Yet Freya knew that something always remained. A sliver of soul, a glimmer of the woman she had been. And with time... perhaps she would claw her way back to it.

Time would tell, and nothing else.

When the final stroke of the feather carved its way into Wren's skin, the girl exhaled one last, fragile breath.

Freya gave a single nod.

The valkyrians lifted Wren's body with reverence and returned her to the River of Resurrection. As soon as her skin met the water, the runes ignited in brilliance, the milky ink bleeding into the stream until the river itself shimmered like a thread of woven pearl. Wren's body glowed with it, suspended in the current like a relic kissed by moonlight.

The others withdrew, for what remained was not a spectacle, but a still and quiet thing.

Freya settled upon the temple steps, the only witness to what came next.

She watched as the glowing form lay motionless in the water, the current coaxing breath back into lungs that had long since fallen silent. Sometimes, the process demanded days. For others, it required mere hours.

And sometimes...

Freya's thoughts drifted.

Sometimes, they did not return at all.

Time slipped by, and still the girl did not stir. Perhaps she never would. Not all were meant to rise. Some souls, fragile or unwilling, slipped through the river's fingers like sand. They would lie beneath its surface, waiting until at last the valkyrians understood that the moment had come to let them go.

And send them, gently, into the next world.

Freya departed and returned the next day, hope blooming

within her chest, hope that she might find Wren Wynter standing tall, water cascading from her reborn form like silver threads. But the wolverian girl remained as she was, slumbering still beneath the crystalline waters of the river. So Freya left once more, and again she came back.

Time, as it often does in places touched by gods, slowed to a languid crawl. Days bled seamlessly into weeks, yet the girl did not stir.

Perhaps Kage Blackburn had been mistaken. Perhaps Wren had chosen not this path of rebirth, but the sweet release of oblivion. Perhaps death, to her, had seemed a kinder fate than waking without memory, without the ones she loved.

Still, Freya returned to the temple day after day. Her faith never waned. She stood at the river's edge, eyes fixed upon the girl sleeping beneath its sacred current, waiting for the flicker of breath, the flutter of an eyelid. But Wren did not wake.

Eventually, duty pulled Freya back inland, where the world teetered ever closer to ruin. The valkyrians would soon be ready to intervene—slow as ever, locked in endless debate, casting votes and pondering fates as kingdoms unravelled. They were measured and methodical in their judgments, determined not to repeat the mistakes of the past. And yet, Freya frowned at such delays. The last time they had hesitated, a century had passed in ruin.

Still, she could not help but relish the unraveling threads of the world. She was close now, so very close to clawing her beloved children from Hades' grasp. The chaos was necessary. The suffering, a means to an end.

Freya did not wish to return to the island, nor to the temple carved from stone and memory. For she knew what she would find. A valkyrian, face sombre, would meet her at the steps to whisper what she already feared. That Wren Wynter had not returned. That the river had claimed her, and she had been sent on to Niflheim, to rest where no breath reached.

Freya would have to accept it.

And Kage Blackburn... it would shatter him. The news would be his undoing.

Freya would be the one to tell him. She rather liked the prince of shadows—so quiet, so steeped in rage and sorrow. She had tried for him. She had offered her best.

But her best, it seemed, had not been enough.

Now, it would be his turn to honour the bargain.

Whether or not his heart could endure it.

Freya felt the change the moment her feet touched the island's earth once more. As her boots struck the ground, her gaze lifted to meet the silent glances exchanged between valkyrian warriors, glances that spoke volumes though not a word passed their lips. She patted her loyal brown mare, a creature of grace and fire, and without pause hurried towards the temple, her heart already braced for what she knew she would find.

She wanted to snarl at them, those sisters of hers, for the way they looked at her, as though bearing a secret she already feared to hear aloud.

But then she stopped. And all breath left her.

There, standing in the sacred river, framed by the soft lilt of twilight and the hush of eternity, was a girl cloaked in glowing runes, her skin alight with milk-white ink that shimmered like starlight. The markings pulsed faintly, whispering power, ancient and divine, and lit the sky with their brilliance.

She resembled Wren Wynter with the soft lines of her face, the proud curve of her jaw, but that girl was no more.

This was no wolverian princess.

She had no name, no memory, no crown of past.

She was reborn. A valkyrian warrior, forged in pain, etched in power, kissed by the River of Resurrection.

And when her eyes opened at last, eyes that had once known sorrow, love, and fire, they gleamed like the gods had set twin stars within them.

So bright they blinded the world.

THE END

The story continues in...

A Kingdom of Light and Air

Also coming soon:

The Sand Trials
a Kingdom of Gods novel based in the desert kingdom

ACKNOWLEDGEMENTS

To my family and friends. Thank you for always believing in me, even when I doubted myself. Your support, love, and endless encouragement have meant more than I can ever put into words.

To the bookish community, thank you for welcoming me with open arms, for your excitement, and for sharing in the magic of stories. You've made this journey feel a little less lonely and a whole lot more special.

A special thank you to my incredible team of Beta Readers. Your time, thoughtful feedback, and honesty helped shape this book into what it is. I'm beyond grateful for each of you. This story exists because of all of you.

Amy Caraballo
Allison Bui
Zoe Wilkes
Xan Nerinckx
Summer Mankey
Shelley O'Connor
Dominica (@cozy.moonbeam)
Emily Mealha
Caitlin (@book_sandcrannies)
Kristin Mealha
Hattie Britton
Bookoholicsanonyms
Fay
Shannai @readswithnai
Tarna Leo
Aubrey MT
Tess Cortez

Manja van Kesteren @thebookwyrm_nl
Jessica
Brandy Danielle
Samantha Araujo
Amanda Remer
Jacqulyn Holton

Thank you,
J.F.Johns

About the author

J.F.Johns is 32 years old and was born and raised in Spain. She studied English Literature Creative Writing at ARU in Cambridge, UK.

In 2017, her novel "Eternal Darkness" won the "Indie Book Awards" in the category of "best book written by an author below the age of 25". It was also a finalist for best cover.

She is an animal lover and spends her free time playing with her adopted dogs and cats, drinking too much coffee and reading.

She believes in the art of dramatic sighing and eye rolling. She works as a ninja at night, but has been told several times that she's not very good at her job.

You can follow her on Instagram or Tiktok; @jfjohnsbooks

Or visit her website; www.authorjfjohns.com

Printed in Dunstable, United Kingdom